Advance Praise for
ONE MUST TELL THE BEES

"What do you get when you cross Abraham Lincoln with Sherlock Holmes? The alchemy of creative genius. Matthews brings us to the intersection of history and fiction in this beautifully written epic full of unfathomable twists and turns. This book is sensational."

— *Jim Campbell, syndicated radio host and author of*
Madoff Talks: Uncovering the Untold Story Behind the Most
Notorious Ponzi Scheme in History

"One Must Tell the Bees is an audacious, fascinating page turner that adds some unexpected twists to Arthur Conan Doyle's beloved character. It's also a timely reminder that we can't—and shouldn't—erase the past."

—*Bethany McLean, Co-Author of New York Times Bestseller*
The Smartest Guys in the Room

"Sherlock Holmes in America? An idea as immersive as it is plausible, in Matthews' skillful hands. This is a compelling, transporting feat of imagination."

—*Jonathan Stone, bestselling author of* Moving Day

"What a story! One Must Tell the Bees *charms you out of your world and into an irresistible adventure when Sherlock Holmes steps onto American soil, into the White House of Abraham Lincoln and, yes, joins the manhunt for John Wilkes Booth. Holmes's wit and Lincoln's genius shine through, and the colorful characters, plot surprises, and wonderful historical details so completely immerse you that by the last page you'll be happier and a whole lot wiser."*

—Layng Martine Jr., Nashville Songwriters
Hall of Famer-turned memoirist of Permission to Fly

"The historical figures loom large in this tale, and are portrayed in a realistic manner, but the thing that I find most impressive (and something I look for in every historical-fiction book I read) is that the fictional characters are crafted in such a way as to make them appear to be historical as well...and that, my fellow readers, is the mark of excellent storytelling where the line between history and fiction has vanished into the realm of believability."

—Hoover Book Reviews

"Bracing storytelling."
—Kirkus Reviews

ONE MUST TELL THE BEES

Abraham Lincoln and
The Final Education of
Sherlock Holmes

J. Lawrence Matthews

ISBN: 978-1-7366783-4-3 (Hardback)
ISBN: 978-1-7366783-3-6 (Paperback)
ISBN: 978-1-7366783-1-2 (eBook)
ISBN: 978-1-7366783-2-9 (Audiobook)

Library of Congress Control Number: 2021910065

Any references to historical events, real people, or real places are used fictitiously. Names, characters, and places are products of the author's imagination.

Cover and Book Design by Glen M. Edelstein
Cover and Interior Ilustrations by Robert Hunt
Cover photograph by Michelle Tricca

Books Fluent
3014 Dauphine Street
New Orleans, LA

DISCLAIMER

Again, for NJB
Love, JLM

CONTENTS

I.

THE ÉLEUTHÈRIAN MILLS

*"You don't know Sherlock Holmes yet...perhaps you would not care for him as
a constant companion."*

"Why, what is there against him?"

*"Oh, I didn't say there was anything against him. He is a little queer in
his ideas—an enthusiast in some branches of science. As far as I know he is a
decent fellow enough."*

"A medical student, I suppose?" said I.

*"No—I have no idea what he intends to go in for. I believe he is well up
in anatomy, and he is a first-class chemist; but, as far as I know, he has never
taken out any systematic medical classes. His studies are very desultory and
eccentric, but he has amassed a lot of out-of-the-way knowledge which would
astonish his professors."*

—John H. Watson, MD
A Study in Scarlet

FOREWORD

In preparing to set down for my readers this final and most remarkable adventure in a life of many such remarkable adventures with my friend, Mr. Sherlock Holmes, I thought it fitting to first reflect briefly upon my long association with the man, for I cannot imagine what a blank canvas my three-and-a-half-score years would have held but for the fact that this keenly inquisitive master of detection allowed me to share some small measure of his very full life.

In well over three hundred cases together (a fraction, admittedly, of the thousands of mysteries brought to Holmes's attention over the decades), I not only met and wooed my first wife[1] and made an astonishing variety of acquaintances, from reformed cutpurses to Bavarian kings and future Prime Ministers, but I was privileged to accompany Sherlock Holmes as he touched the lives of hundreds of troubled souls, from the humblest of origins to the most exalted in the land.

For that privilege, I shall remain forever in his debt.

Why such a remarkable individual offered to share his rooms with a wounded army surgeon just back from Afghanistan in the first place I

---

1 *Mary Morstan, who died in 1894 from an undisclosed illness. Watson later married her half-sister, Margaret —editor.*

never—until recently—understood, for Holmes was, as my readers well know, a most complex and secretive man.

On the surface, he was the most coldly incisive reasoner ever born—"a calculating machine," as I once described him—and yet his behaviour was always and forever governed, as my records of our cases together have shown, by the straightest moral compass I have ever encountered in a man.

Indeed, I have come to believe—without overstating the matter—that in forging his career as a consulting detective, Holmes was seeking to balance out the scales of justice in an unjust world, for he applied his unique skills in equal measure to all who sought his aid, from the richest of clients to the poorest of their class, with no consideration of the payment offered, but only the mental stimulation promised by the case.

And as my readers well know, his attentiveness to the outcasts of society—of which there were many, especially in his most active days during that period now known as the Industrial Revolution—was paid back many times over in ways large and small.

To cite just one example, the "Baker Street Irregulars"—as Holmes called his informal but highly effective network of street urchins—were able to gather information in ways no official police could do and would have walked over hot coals for the man. (Indeed, in one unpublished case involving a wayward collier and a hostage-taking, they literally did just that.)

Unfortunately, as my readers also well know, Holmes did not extend such good graces equally to all. He frequently put forth a most condescending demeanor towards the official police force—and anyone else in a position of authority, for that matter—who did not suitably appreciate his considerable gifts.

Worse, those gifts were frequently put at risk by his deep-seated need to be so constantly engaged in some form of mental stimulation that when no prospect of an *outré* mystery had reached our rooms at Baker Street after some few days of lassitude, such harmless recreations as pipe cleaning and violin playing inevitably gave way to the cocaine needle.

Time and again I watched in helpless dread as Sherlock Holmes removed that sleek, malignant instrument from its morocco case, ponderously drew into the glass tube a seven-per-cent solution from the blue bottle always at hand (secured by Holmes from a source whose identity was only made known to me during our last days together), hovered the needle over the pockmarked veins of his forearm in search of an unblemished locality, and then—to the detriment of both his mind and our relationship—drove its point home.

I did not rest easy until that appalling habit was conquered many years after my introduction to the man, and it is with no little pride that I can say I played a role in helping Holmes spurn that craving.

Why, you may ask, do I dwell on this singular and long-since-conquered blemish of my one true friend, here in this final reminiscence of our adventures together?

Because, dear reader, as you shall see, it was news of the revival of that habit which drew us together for Holmes's final case.

And while that adventure was as thrilling as any of our encounters with the most subtle and devious villains that England or the Continent produced in days gone by, it was as nothing compared to the story of Sherlock Holmes's very *first* case, the existence of which I learned only as our last adventure together was unfolding.

For it is in that first case of Sherlock Holmes—the recounting of which is to follow—that his loyal readers will finally be able to witness the spark which lit the great engine of his mind, and perhaps reconcile the many seemingly irreconcilable contradictions in the character of a man whose ceaseless craving for "mental exaltation" provided the adventures which have thrilled so many and given some little purpose to my own modest life upon earth.

Indeed, it is a case which, in the opinion of a man who respected Sherlock Holmes's unique abilities above all others, remains the greatest of his career.

And perhaps of *any* man's career.

—John H. Watson, M.D.
March 23, 1933

Chapter One

A PACKET FROM THE DIOGENES CLUB

It was in the early morning darkness of the second Tuesday in October of the year 1918—the last year of that terrible struggle we now call the Great War—that I was walking home from a long and weary vigil assisting at the unexpectedly difficult birth of the great-grandchild of one of my oldest and dearest friends. Pressing a handkerchief to my face against the thick, choking fog blanketing London, I kept my eyes alert to the shadows of horses and carriages that threatened to run me down at each crossing.

I had retired from my medical practice upon reaching my sixty-sixth year, the same year the Kaiser's armies stormed through Belgium, but the needs of His Majesty's Army had reduced the ranks of England's medical profession to such an alarming extent that I still kept busy assisting cases where my long years of experience might be needed.

The previous evening's case had taken a harrowing turn when the fetus demonstrated a malpresentation and the breech position could not be alleviated, severely testing my capacity and straining my nerves. Fortunately, Jackson[2] maintained his utter calmness and firmness of manner throughout, and he saw the patient through the birth of a healthy baby girl.

---

2 *Watson's medical associate who took over his practice when Watson retired.*

It was not until well past six in the morning, however, that both newborn and mother were out of danger and I had taken my leave. Cabs being dangerous in the thick, coal-black fog, I had set out on foot, making my way home through Kensington at a slow pace.

So tired and hungry was I that, upon reaching our doorstep, I had let myself in, set down my surgical case, removed my coat and hat, and exchanged my filthy boots for slippers without thinking to inquire of the girl[3] why a hansom was waiting at the curb outside our door.

Instead, I rang for breakfast and took my place at the dining room table, where the early edition of the *Times* awaited me. Coffee was soon poured, and the aroma of rashers and eggs rose from the kitchen as I turned my attention to a remarkable eyewitness account of the collapse of the German Army 5th Corps at the Saint-Mihiel salient, which told of a great panic sweeping the German troops as their ranks were thinned by the terrible influenza now general on the Continent. Soldiers seemingly healthy one minute were dropping dead the next.

I was about to turn the page to continue reading when a most interesting news item caught my eye near the bottom.

Headed "Death of a Wayward Soldier," it reported the demise of Colonel Sebastian Moran, age seventy-eight, under "mysterious circumstances" at Pentonville prison where he had been serving the twenty-third year of a life sentence for the murder of Ronald Adair, a young gentleman who had threatened to expose Moran for cheating in a game of whist at the Bagatelle card club unless Moran resigned his position and returned the ill-gotten winnings to the other club members.

It was the very case I had described in *The Empty House*!

Readers of that adventure will remember that it was Colonel Moran who assumed control of the vast criminal syndicate built by "the Napoleon of crime," as Sherlock Holmes had often described Professor James Moriarty, after the villainous Moriarty plunged to his death following a brief but savage struggle with Holmes above the falls of Reichenbach, in Switzerland, in 1894.

---

3 *A servant.*

I noted with satisfaction that the story made no mention of Holmes and his role in putting Moran behind bars for the shooting death of the unfortunate Adair, for my friend had never sought recognition in the cases he helped resolve where the official police had failed. (It was only my suggestion that the stories behind some of our cases together might bring his unique methods of observation and deduction to greater adoption which caused him to allow me to write them up in the first place and which eventually made his name famous to the public.)

I was recalling my own small role in the Adair case, which had prompted Holmes's dramatic return from three years of wandering the Continent incognito while I and my readers thought he had died along with Professor Moriarty in the deadly chasms of the Reichenbach Falls, when my reverie was interrupted by the arrival of my food.

I had turned my attention to the scrambled eggs when my eye next caught a most welcome report from Antwerp that the new German Chancellor had asked President Wilson for terms, and this I was reading when Margaret entered, assisted by her nurse. Although an asthmatic condition acquired during her youth in India left her confined to her room much of the day, Margaret always made the effort to eat her meals at table.

I helped her into her chair.

"Mother and child are well, John?" she asked anxiously. "You look exhausted."

"Yes. It was extremely difficult, but both are beyond danger. A healthy baby girl."

"Thank God."

"It was never in grave doubt, but there was a complication within the birth canal. Jackson is quite competent. I really offered very little in the way of assistance."

"It is well you were there in any event." She spooned honey into the tea that had been poured for her. "You are reading the papers?"

"Indeed! The German High Command has lost its faith in the Kaiser. This war may be over soon."

"I rather thought you would be reading the communication from Mr. Holmes. Yes, John, the packet there, at your elbow."

I set down the newspaper and picked up the bulky envelope which, in my tired and hungry condition, I had overlooked. It was addressed to my attention and marked *Urgent*. Turning it over, I saw that it carried the red wax seal with which I was very familiar: "D.C."

"The Diogenes Club," said I, breaking the seal. "I wonder what it can be?"

Letters from Sherlock Holmes were infrequent, for he preferred the brevity and immediacy of the telegraph to the post. Since his retirement to the South Downs in '05 to write his book and tend his bees, I had received perhaps a dozen such correspondences, all related to matters arising from the publications of our adventures; all by way of his brother, Mycroft Holmes; and all under the seal of the Diogenes Club.

But none had ever been stamped *Urgent*.

From the packet I removed a large envelope evidently containing a typewritten manuscript—not unusual in our correspondence, for Holmes always reviewed the stories of our cases before publication. Attached to the envelope, however, and by a rather distinctive triangular paperclip, were three slender items: a railway timetable, a map and a folded half-sheet of foolscap.

"Holmes hasn't sent me anything since he interrupted his retirement for that German affair we worked on just before this war broke out.[4] Perhaps these are his notes from that case."

"I think it is more than that, John. The cab outside has been awaiting your return. What, you did not notice him at the curb?"

"I saw," said I ruefully, recalling the hansom and its lathered horse outside our door. "But as Holmes would say, I did not *observe*. This may explain." I removed the foolscap and opened it. "Ah, a note, in Holmes's pen."

Printed in the familiar, precise penmanship of my friend were two concise sentences above his signature, as follows:

---

4 Described in His Last Bow, *which took place in August 1914.*

Watson—

That I have become addicted to a particularly malignant class of opiates is the inescapable conclusion to which I have arrived after a brief but intensive period of self-examination, and it is in this moment of lucidity I call upon you to come to my aid.

Bring your medical kit, and please, come at once.

—Sherlock Holmes

"What is it, John?"

I snorted and tossed the note across the table. "A schoolboy's prank. It's a wonder they still bother."

Almost from the very moment *A Scamdal in Bohemia* had appeared in the July '91 issue of *The Strand Magazine*, a steady stream of unsolicited correspondence had made its way to 221B Baker Street, where Holmes and I rented rooms from the good and loyal Mrs. Hudson in the years before my marriage. Some of it was legitimate, in the form of speech requests and the like, while others begged Holmes's aid in cases too ridiculous to mention here. Still others took more threatening forms, as in that business of the deadly ivory cigarette case.[5]

And then there were the pranks and practical jokes.

University lads invariably beseeched Holmes's help with some bodily function or other that bears no repeating here, always signing off under a vulgar pseudonym with the salutation, "*Elementary, My Dear Watson!*" even though, as has been pointed out elsewhere, that particular phrase never appeared in the public casebooks.

Thankfully, the volume of such chaff had declined after Holmes's retirement, but as neither Holmes nor I lived at Baker Street any longer, and his address in the South Downs had never been disclosed to the public, I remained the occasional recipient of correspondence intended for my old companion, sometimes several pieces a week.

But none had ever sunk so low.

I had resumed reading the *Times'* account of the German Chancellor's supplications to the American President when Margaret looked up from the foolscap in alarm.

---

5 As told in *The Dying Detective, published in 1913.*

"John, are you certain this is not from your friend?"

I nodded. "He is quite cured of that infirmity. I saw to it myself."

She held up the note for my closer inspection.

"But it looks like his hand, John, and it certainly carries his voice. And it is does appear to be what he was destined for—"

"He is cured!" said I, with some little annoyance, for I was proud of my role in rehabilitating Holmes from his dreadful habit, and Margaret's skepticism was all the more irksome because she was usually proven right in matters of human nature. "I kept a close eye on Holmes when we were together during that business with the German agent—he was hale and hearty."

"But he is an excellent actor, John. Isn't that what you always told me?"

This gave me pause, and for the first time I wondered if perhaps the note might be genuine.

"What else was in the packet?" said I, laying down the *Times* and retrieving the envelope and the other items that had been clipped to it.

The first was a timetable of the South Coast Railway with the 9:15 from Victoria Station to Eastbourne circled in the same ink as the note.

"Hum! I know very well the fastest train to reach Holmes's cottage—he would hardly need to indicate it for me!"

Setting aside the timetable, I picked up the second item. It was an Ordnance Survey map of the Eastbourne-Polegate-Birling Gap district, the very type Holmes had relied upon to triumphant effect in more than a few of our countryside cases together. When unfolded, it revealed a large-scale map of the very portion of the South Downs to which Holmes had retired. A neat circle, also in ink, had been drawn around the prominence labeled "Went Hill," just off the village green of East Dean, not a mile from the English Channel.

"What the devil? Holmes's cottage lies within that very circle!" said I, much puzzled. "But again, what of it?"

"I cannot think, John."

"Let us see what this holds." I slit open the envelope using a table knife and removed from within a slim manuscript, the pages of which were light-weight onionskin. On the title page was typed the following:

The Art and Science of Rational Deduction
By Mr. Sherlock Holmes
Went Hill
Sussex, England

"The manuscript!" I cried, glancing through the pages. "Holmes's manuscript!" The pages were neatly typed, the lines closely spaced, and the editing marks were in Holmes's neat hand. There were ninety-eight pages in all.

"Which manuscript, John?"

"On 'Rational Deduction.' The one Holmes has been promising to write his entire career!"

"Is it genuine?"

"It appears so. But there is one way to be certain." I studied the first page with exceeding care, running my eye down the text to the second paragraph. "There it is—the crippled 'Q!' This is indeed the genuine article!"

"Then this note is not a prank, John."

A cold hand gripped my soul. I sprang from my chair and snatched the foolscap from Margaret's outstretched hand. Holding the paper to the light of the wall lamp, I studied it carefully.

I could see no obvious signs of forgery, and the handwriting did indeed appear to be Holmes's own, although I had no samples with which to compare, for Holmes had long ago committed me to destroying all correspondence between us.

"The writing does possess his character, and the signature looks genuine, certainly," said I. "And this paper has no watermark." Holmes had always written his communications on such paper, for watermarks provided clues to prying minds.

I brought the paper to my nose and sniffed for perfume or other scents—my friend's favourite method of discerning the habits of his correspondents—and this likewise proved negative and entirely in keeping with Holmes's own secretive methods.

"I believe Holmes did write this, Margaret."

"Then you must go."

I had started for the door—a valise with my medical kit and a change of clothing would be all I would need for the journey—when I suddenly felt the ghostly hand of Sherlock Holmes upon my shoulder and saw, in my mind's eye, his face before me. He was puffing on his pipe and chuckling at his 'man of action,' as he had always called me when I moved too precipitately for his taste.

"Examine the data, Watson!" I could hear him say, urging upon me the kind of logical reflection which my haste typically did not allow. *"There are too many unanswered questions, don't you think?"*

Margaret had already rung the bell, and the girl stood at the door awaiting my instructions as I sat back down to collect my thoughts.

"What is it, John?" Margaret asked.

"One moment. How did this arrive?" I asked the girl, thinking through the questions Holmes might have put to her in my place.

"By messenger, sir. From Mr. Mycroft's club."

"What did he look like, this messenger?"

"A young man, sir—all out of breath, he was."

"Why did Mycroft Holmes not bring the packet himself?"

"Mr. Mycroft is ill and unable to travel. The boy said that, sir. Then he said, 'Mr. Mycroft wishes Dr. Watson to act upon this immediately.'"

The girl had been with us since our marriage and had always proved reliable and clear-witted, and I had no reason to doubt her veracity.

"Is the boy in the cab outside?"

"No sir. He was told to return to Mr. Mycroft's club once the message was delivered."

"Why, then, is the hansom there?"

The girl shook her head. "I don't know, sir."

"To take you to Victoria Station, I should imagine," said Margaret.

I glanced at the timetable again. The 9:15 departed in forty-five minutes—there was plenty of time. I studied the Ordnance map. "Why on earth would Holmes feel it necessary to indicate where his cottage lies?" I wondered aloud.

"That you should have the proper directions, I should think," said Margaret.

"But I have been there several times. He knows I need no reminder."

"He is out of his head. His note said as much."

I studied the handwritten note again. "Holmes knew I would be skeptical of such a note as this," I said, as much to myself as to Margaret. "After all, the package could have been intercepted and a false note inserted. *That* is why Holmes appended this map and this timetable! No mere university student would know the precise location of his cottage, or the fastest train to take."

"What say you then, John?"

"I say my friend is in grave trouble, and I must go to him."

I am, as I have said many times, an old campaigner from my days in Afghanistan, and it was not fifteen minutes before I had left the house with my lightweight valise packed with the few necessities I expected to need. The driver, a grim and taciturn man, said nothing, only tapped his watch with impatience as I climbed in. Then he gave the horse its head[6] and we were off, riding as swiftly as I had ever ridden through the now busy streets of London.

In my valise were my spare linens, Holmes's packet and my medical kit with a few essential medicines I expected his condition might require. Wrapped in my linens was my pistol. Although I had no inkling of danger, it seemed better to bring that peace of mind than to regret its absence later.

For good measure, before leaving the house I had dispatched a messenger to the telegraph office with a wire for the Eastbourne constabulary requesting medical assistance to be sent at once to the cottage of Sherlock Holmes, along with a constable escort in case foul play was at hand. Furthermore, I had determined that upon reaching Victoria I would send a second telegram with a comprehensive list of medicines and purgatives to bring to Holmes's bedside so that I would have every resource available upon my arrival.

---

6 *To loosen the reins and let the horse gallop.*

Having long been accustomed to the thorough methods of Mr. Sherlock Holmes, I must admit to some little pride at such forethought upon my part.

What I could not anticipate, however, was that the lines to Eastbourne were already down and my wires would reach no one but the elements.

Chapter Two

THE MANUSCRIPT OF
MR. SHERLOCK HOLMES

We arrived at Victoria with time enough for me to send the follow-up telegram to Eastbourne and to sit for a refreshing cup of tea and a biscuit at the buffet. Then I settled into a corner seat of the first-class railway carriage with the morning newspapers—a habit acquired during my travels with Holmes—while the engine built up steam.

I was anxious to read Holmes's manuscript, of course, but not in the company of strangers in a train. I therefore expected to use the journey to Eastbourne to catch up on the news and thus anticipate all eventualities before my arrival in the Downs. As the departure time approached, however, it became apparent I would have no company in my compartment, and so I gladly put the newspapers aside, removed the packet from my valise and extracted Holmes's manuscript from its envelope.

Just as I was about to begin reading, however, the corridor door was opened, and the ticket inspector entered. I hastily slid the document inside a copy of *The Standard* and glanced up at the man as if from reading the news. He was bespectacled, with bushy black side-whiskers and a thick handlebar moustache upon his face, and he brought with him the rich scent of tobacco smoke from a cigarette he had evidently stubbed out before entering.

Though young enough to be in Army service—I put his age at not older than thirty-five—his appearance in the train was explained by the war service pin on the lapel of his Southcoast Railway uniform.[7] To my chagrin, he began a running commentary on everything from the Kaiser's latest proclamation to whether it would rain in Eastbourne today.

As he punched my ticket, he glanced over his spectacles, eyed the newspapers warily and remarked that it would be very kind if I left the papers intact as opposed to balling them up and stuffing them in the overhead rack—the very habit of the friend I was on my way to aid and, evidently, more than a few of the train's regular passengers.

I assured him I would leave behind a tidy compartment so long as I could get back to my reading. At this he got a bit huffed, handed me my return ticket and took his leave as the whistle blew and the train lurched into motion.

Soon we were rattling across the great metal bridge over the Thames.

When the stop at Clapham Junction brought no new passengers into my compartment—and I was thus assured of solitude—I removed the manuscript from *The Standard*. Then, as we resumed our journey through the countryside towards the Sussex Downs, I slowly and carefully began reading the most remarkable document I have ever held in my hands.

---

7 *During the Great War, civilian Englishmen of age who were deemed unfit for Army service wore pins indicating they were engaged in 'military service' at home, so they would not be accused of shirking their duties.*

THE ART AND SCIENCE OF RATIONAL DEDUCTION

BY MR. SHERLOCK HOLMES
WENT HILL
SUSSEX, ENGLAND

A NOTE AT THE BEGINNING

I had rather anticipated that the existence of some sixty published accounts of my most salient cases—nearly all drafted by my friend and companion Dr. John H. Watson during and after our active years together—would have rendered the writing of this long-considered treatise on "The Art and Science of Rational Deduction" entirely unnecessary.

Unfortunately, in preparing those cases for serialization in the popular press, Dr. Watson too often veered from the path of logical reasoning to embrace the storyteller's art, creating drama by directing the reader's attention towards the emotional qualities of the individuals involved rather than the deductive capabilities I employed to untangle the mystery, and building suspense by means of that trick of withholding from the reader key facts of the case until the very end when all would be revealed.

Indeed, so indifferently was the methodology of rational deduction depicted by Dr. Watson the overall effect of the public record is, I am sorry to say, less to illuminate the process of rational deduction than to simply tell a good yarn.

Hence, this treatise.

Before delivering my discourse on rational deduction, however, I find myself compelled to comment upon certain biographical details of my life that found their way into Dr. Watson's often rather over-dramatic accounts of our adventures together.

In brief, those biographical details are not to be relied upon.

The reason is simple: certain facts about my upbringing, such as it was, were either withheld from Dr. Watson, or—to be frank—deliberately misrepresented by me in order that my trusted biographer would impart to his readers a false and misleading history of my early life.

This was not done to embarrass my friend, of course. It was done to confuse my enemies.

By removing from the public record certain intrusive facts that might have unintentionally aided any number of criminal adversaries in their never-ending quest to remove from the company of the official police Mr. Sherlock Holmes and his—if I may be allowed to say so—extraordinary powers of rational deduction, I was simply attempting to extend my own longevity.

Fortunately, friend Watson—being as guileless a man as ever lived—never thought to question the entirely faulty premise underlying my self-created personal history in anything other than a cursory and unscientific fashion, from the moment we met at Bart's chemical laboratory in late February, 1881, as I recall, to when last we parted ways in August of 1914 after resolving the little problem of the German legation.

I thank all that is irrational within the human mind that friend Watson took me at my word about my personal history—most particularly on the day we sat at our Baker Street lodgings some few years after that first meeting at Bart's, in the course of what Watson would later call "The Adventure of the Greek Interpreter," and discussed my supposed ancestral history as a descendant of "country squires."

Had Watson responded to my rather trite declaration that evening with a tightly reasoned line of inquiry, why, my fabricated clan of "country squires" would have been smashed to pieces on the hard rock of logical inquiry, and I would have been exposed then and there.

But he did not, nor did he ever express the slightest curiosity thereafter as to my family lineage, despite the logical inconsistencies that a more inquisitive mind would surely have deduced from a few simple observations during our life—and our many adventures—together.

Did it never occur to friend Watson, for example, that no engraving of the ancestral Holmes manor house adorned a wall of our rooms at Baker Street? That no tiepin from Father lay upon my dressing table? That no silhouette of Mother and her sisters stood framed upon the mantel?

Did it not strike him odd that none of the villages or country estates to which we travelled during our years together—tracking down phosphorescent hounds, milk-drinking serpents, camouflaged horses and other such manifestations of evil intentions—ever evoked some youthful memory of my days in that district as a descendant of its "country squires"?

That never once did a country innkeeper, parish vicar, publican or stationmaster recognize my family name and offer a reminiscence of an acquaintance from the Holmes line of old? That no old tutor of mine ever sought our aid with a mystery? That no aunt or uncle or distant cousin or long-lost great nephew ever appeared at the door of 221B Baker Street to declare a familial tie and while away the evening telling Holmes family stories on the expectation, perhaps, of receiving some percentage of the proceeds from Watson's books?

That neither baptismal notices nor wedding invitations from the Holmes line ever appeared in the post, and that I never once wore mourning costume for a relative or ancient friend?

Had my companion simply bothered to pick out the Burke's Peerage from our bookcase and scan its pages, he would have found only two possible bloodlines with the Holmes surname among the "country squire" set—one ending with the birth of five daughters and the other abruptly halted when the male heir was done to death during the Interregnum.

A second, though less obvious, method of unmasking my story would have been to inquire of my brother Mycroft the name of our baptismal parish, then catch the next train to that village and begin an examination of the parish records to confirm our family tree sprouting with country squires.

No such parish existed!

Looking back over my remarks thus far, they come across as being rather churlish towards my friend, but that is not my intent.

I seek not to criticize Dr. Watson, but to praise him.

After all, had the good doctor unmasked my lowly lineage for the world to see, it might have done irreparable damage to the mystique which that vague myth of my "country squire" upbringing gave to our efforts to rid the world of the criminal enterprise of Professor Moriarty and others of the criminal classes.

As it happened, my reputation was greatly enhanced by the legend of my having sprung fully formed out of the ether, with all my keen faculties owing themselves to a line of imaginary squires, and this gave me a not-inconsiderable advantage over others in my profession. Had my

enemies known the truth—that my brother and I were street urchins—
the scales would have fallen from their eyes, and, like a magician stripped
of his cloak and its hidden pockets, I would almost certainly have lost the
ability to dazzle my adversaries and bring them to justice.

And so, for the easy acceptance with which Dr. John H. Watson
greeted my contrived history, I offer my most sincere thanks.

In the main, I attribute Watson's unquestioning acceptance of my
autobiography not to any lack of native intelligence on his part but to our
years of working together and the complete trust we had developed in one
another through many a life-threatening adventure.

Simply put, he did not seek the truth because he did not believe such a
trusted friend could tell him a lie.

But, lie I did, and so it is that before taking on The Art and Science
of Rational Deduction, the autobiographical facts of my years prior to
Watson must, I believe, be presented, in order to correct the faulty history
transmitted by my good and loyal friend. "Rational Deduction" is, after
all, the pursuit of absolute truth through strict observation of the physical
world. Without spelling out the unvarnished facts of my own early years
to readers of this manuscript, all that follows in these pages could well be
challenged, rendering this text like the seed in the parable that is sown
upon rocky ground.

It would wither and die.

And, as I wish to sow my seed upon good soil in order that it may
yield a suitable harvest for the reader I must first remove the impurities
from it.

Now, before attempting to set down the true record of my formative
years, I confess to having had no little anxiety that my ability to recall
events from as many as sixty-odd years ago in a clear and accurate manner
would prove faulty, rendering a treatise on rational deduction of dubious
and questionable value.

Yet happily I find that, having long ago left behind London's teeming
streets and scheming criminal underclass for a peaceful acre of the Sussex
Downs, where only the gentlest species of nature—the honeybee—
demands my constant attention, the ability to recall the introductory facts

of my life has returned with surprising ease.

Indeed, with the attic of my mind now cleared of such dark and unpleasant furniture with which my years as Europe's premier agent of criminal detection had caused it to be stuffed, the capacity to recall more of the earliest years of my life—especially the long-buried memories of my very first case—grows every day. That great adventure, undertaken in just my sixteenth year upon earth and without friend Watson by my side (but with a companion equally brave and just as modest), proved to be the chance undertaking upon which I would consciously and conscientiously seek to build my career as the world's first consulting detective.

Such remembrances stir not unpleasant feelings as I recall them now—a welcome contrast to the melancholy I would come to know at the height of my powers, when all the world sought to glorify me—thanks in no small measure to Dr. Watson's rather fulsome accounts of our successes together; and yet I felt unable to measure up to the promise of that very first case.

Fortunately, the grim memory of that period fades as I return to my youth—or, more precisely, to the moment my brother lifted me up and out of the bleak house of our childhood and placed me upon a path that would lead, eventually, to a great enterprise built alongside the Brandywine Creek in Delaware, U.S.A., and thence to the forests and fields of Virginia for an adventure beyond my wildest imagination.

Of that adventure you shall shortly read.

But, first, one last word, patient reader. In the course of attempting to set down these, my earliest memories, I was reminded just how difficult it is to write in the engaging fashion mastered by the good Dr. Watson, who managed, somehow, to produce a voluminous and highly popular record of our cases together while also attending to his comfortable medical practice.

After several false starts at the task, I have discovered that the singular method to achieve an acceptable result was to seat myself in my comfortable armchair by the fire with a trustworthy typist nearby to take down my words as I spoke them out loud, but to an audience in my mind's eye, as it were, an audience that fully comprehended the inner workings of my mind and the savage contradictions within—the energy and the lethargy, the self-regard and the self-loathing, the self-denial and my own selfish addictions.

That audience, as it happens, is an audience of one.

His name, as readers will no doubt have anticipated, is John H. Watson, M.D., and it is to him these words are both spoken and dedicated.

—Sherlock Holmes

I Am Born

It is not being too dramatic to say that I was born twice: first, as a suckling on the floor of a rat-infested garret in Wapping, alongside a particularly sulphurous bend of the Thames in or about the year 1849[8]; and second, some few years later, as a young boy sheltered beneath the long table at which my older brother Mycroft manipulated his wondrous telegraph machine in a large, airy room of the Navy War Office in Whitehall, a brief stroll from Buckingham Palace.

As I have already confessed in my preamble, Watson, I was not descended from "country squires." My father was a costermonger, and a bad one at that—but a worse father, and as far removed from the ideal of the country squire as one might imagine.

By day he sold apples pilfered from the Queen's parks, rabbits pinched from warrens and whatever else he could purloin from the stalls about the Spitalfields market. By night he was a most excellent drunk. He drank to slake his thirst, he drank to steady his shaking hands, he drank himself asleep and he drank himself awake.

Indeed, my strongest memory of the man was not his face, which I cannot now conjure up before me, but the sharp stench of his breath when he pulled me up from my straw bed and sent me to fetch his breakfast beer. That foul reek—and the violent episodes in which his depravity took aim at our mother—are all that I remember of the man.

And good riddance to him. He took away my mother, Watson—in spirit, if not by the flesh. She died not many years after I had been born, during yet another childbirth (it was her sixth or her seventh; Mycroft was never certain), and so cruel were the circumstances of our upbringing that of those six or seven children, only Mycroft and I survived adolescence.

After our mother had disappeared from my young eyes—I did not understand life and its opposite condition just yet—our father's downfall was complete. Being no longer able to compel her to satisfy the debt collector in a most vulgar manner (the particulars of which I was shielded

---

8 _This would make Holmes five years younger than his biographers have placed him on the basis of a brief description by the narrator of_ His Last Bow, _and it only remains a question of whether that narrator deliberately chose to mislead Holmes's readers or was, in fact, misled by Holmes's disguise in that episode._

from at that time by my brother), he was thrown into debtor's prison and we never saw him again.

My brother and I were now out in the streets of Wapping, and I doubt a dirtier, more corrupting, disheartening and unimaginable way of life ever existed outside the pages of Dickens—although at the time, of course, I imagined no other way of life might exist.

So, live it I did, thanks, in the main, to the considerable advantage—I would not exaggerate to call it life-saving—of having an older brother to look after me.

But not just any older brother.

I Am, Once Again, Born

My brother was a most precocious and energetic individual, Watson, selling newspapers to keep us clothed and sheltered while teaching himself to read by studying the very newspapers he was hawking. My days were employed procuring food for the both of us. This meant fishing off the bridges over the Thames or, when the weather was fair and the eels were not biting, catching pigeons and other less savory creatures in the alleys of London.

Our ill-omened situation changed for all time, however, when my brother astutely spotted the opportunities afforded by the telegraph machine and so found steady employment for us both.

It came about in this way.

One afternoon along about 1854 or '55, while picking up the afternoon papers he was to sell, Mycroft witnessed a clerk dashing into the newspaper office waving a cable and shouting news of the victory of the Coldstream Guards at Alma, in the Crimea, the previous day.

The notion that electric impulses could transmit human knowledge instantaneously between continents had a most mesmeric effect upon Mycroft. He volunteered to assist the machine operator in any way required and was immediately taken in by the man, for in those days telegraphy was considered well beneath the lot of an educated gentleman, suitable only to compositors or typesetters.

Alone at a machine in which communication transpired via the creation and translation of electronic pulses rather than the human voice, my brother, who much preferred his own company to that of others, had found his métier. Indeed, it was as if telegraphy had been created to complement his peculiar makeup. (To this day he prefers it to the telephone, which he regards as a ghastly mistake.)

Mycroft so excelled at the task of swiftly translating dots and dashes into the written word that he was soon running the telegraph station in the newsroom. And when he suggested to his superiors that his younger brother's more primitive but equally useful attribute—swift feet—could help the newspaper stay ahead of its peers in gathering the criminal news from the local constabularies, they approved.

I had not yet developed a taste for tobacco and other bad habits that have long since slowed my pace, Watson, and I now spent my days dashing about Greater London, handing off and receiving messages and learning the fastest route between any two points of interest in the metropolis.

As Mycroft's reputation as a master of the telegraph grew—he particularly excelled at deciphering coded messages—he was eventually able to sell us as something of a package to the East India Company, which in those days ran its operations through a vast network of telegraph lines and overland riders connecting agents in far-flung corners of Her Majesty's empire to East India House in Leadenhall Street.

It was in this way my brother and I began to earn enough to provide for ourselves and to forever leave behind our life in the streets of Wapping.

Our ship fairly came in after the Mutiny of '57, however, when Her Majesty's War Department took over The Company's operations on the Indian subcontinent. Mycroft was moved to Whitehall, whence the laying of the first transatlantic cable to America—in '58 or '59, I believe—required operators willing to work late into the evening when the American operators were at their posts.[9]

Mycroft instantly volunteered.

The late evening shift provided him not only with extra pay but also <u>the opportunity</u> to spend his waking hours entirely alone at the machine.

9 *The first Atlantic undersea cable was laid in 1858 and functioned for several weeks before failing, but transatlantic messages continued to be carried by fast packet ships from Newfoundland to Ireland for transmittal to London.*

This suited him perfectly, for it enabled him to apply his considerable mental powers—which were, and still are, far greater than my own—to issues of great moment without actually having to speak to people, which he loathed to do.

The so-called "American shift" also suited me, Watson, for when I was not running to the office of Under Secretary Lord Such-and-Such in Whitehall or to the PM's secretary at Downing Street, I could rest snuggly beneath the table upon which Mycroft received and tapped out his codes. Safe from the elements and with no small amount of free time in between bursts of the most intense activity, it was beneath that telegraph table that my eyes were opened to a vast world beyond the telegraph room and to a means of living that I eventually determined to make my own.

For it was there I learned to read.

I DISCOVER A TRADE

My first choice of literature, of course, was crime—and the more gruesome the better. This owed itself to an offhand comment by my brother about the room in which I had been born being just a stone's throw from the infamous Ratcliff Highway Murder[10] house.

Every East End boy knew the Ratcliff Highway tale, and I pestered Mycroft for all the details he could provide until his knowledge had been exhausted, whence I set out to learn everything possible from other sources—which meant newspapers and periodicals.

The brutality of the murders, the telltale clue of the shipwright's hammer encrusted with human hair, the bloody footprints that had seeped into the floor (imagine what I could have done with those, Watson!), and the utter failure of the Bow Street Runners[11] to follow the chain of events to the culprit, all served to open my mind to "the thousand natural shocks that flesh is heir to," as Hamlet poetically spoke of the human condition, and to fire a young boy's conviction that I could have

---

10 One of the first sensational murder cases in England; never fully resolved.
11 The first organized police force in London.

solved the mystery on my own.

(Years later, after you had left our Baker Street lodgings for married life, Watson, I did attempt my own little investigation of the case, using my influence with our old friend at Scotland Yard, Inspector Lestrade, to review the files, but they proved utterly worthless.)

Of course, when one pursues a singular interest in a topic as gruesome as the Ratcliff murders, it swiftly leads down a rabbit hole to all manner of sensational tales, and soon enough I was devouring the penny papers (the "penny dreadfuls" we called them) and anything else I could find on every horror ever perpetrated in England.

In this way I acquired an encyclopedic knowledge of the depredations of Burke and Hare, the despicable Dr. Palmer, poor Eliza Fenning and many others. And when I had exhausted the famous English cases, why, I turned to the criminal news from the Continent and elsewhere.

It was while reading up on some of the more sensational American cases that I learned of a gentleman with an enchanting occupation, the allure of which would forever change my life.

His name was Allan J. Pinkerton, and his capture of the notorious Adams Express robbers had made headlines even in England.

And he was called a "detective."

Operating independently of the police, Pinkerton followed his nose wherever it led, bound by none of the strictures which compromised the typical flat-footed copper. He infiltrated counterfeiting rings for the Federal Reserve Bank of San Francisco, recovered diamonds stolen from the House of Saud and tracked a missing princess halfway around the world for the Maharajah of Jaipur.

But most thrilling to my young mind was the manner in which he had cracked the macabre grave-robbing scheme of the Febbraio Brothers of Cicero, outside Chicago. By impersonating one of that gang for months on end, the story went, Pinkerton had unmasked the entire sordid affair and sent the brothers to prison, along with Alphonso Marquette, the twisted doctor of medicine to whom the brothers had been selling the corpses.

I thought no better way to earn a living could be had and vowed that, one day, I would be a great detective like Allan J. Pinkerton.

But for now, my brother had the more urgent need of my swift feet and healthy lungs, for he had been appointed chief operator in Her Majesty's Telegraph Office.

In that capacity, he would become almost as well known among the notables of Washington City—as Washington D.C. was called in those days—as he was in Whitehall, and those connections would, a few years hence, allow him to send me on an adventure across the Atlantic that, quite literally, changed my life.

First, however, I think the question of how Mycroft and I acquired our names should be addressed.

I (ALMOST) GET MY NAME

My brother's duties on the American shift saw him working from eight o'clock in the evening to four o'clock the following morning, when the next day's communications from the Far East had begun to trickle in and a fresh operator took over.

This meant that I might be on my feet from supper to very nearly sunrise, dashing from office to office delivering envelopes to officious secretaries (sometimes after rousing them from their slumbers), then cooling my heels waiting for the replies to be thrust into my hand—frequently with threats of a boot ready to be applied to my backside if I lingered, which I never did, of course—and dashing to the next, and the next, and the next, until there were no more to be delivered.

It was after one such run—to Lord Palmerston's[12] office, as I recall—during a long night of unusually busy cable traffic from America involving the activities of a British citizen in America by the name of Hugh Forbes[13] that I returned to find my brother seated at his desk, fingering a telegraph flimsy—as the slim paper was called—with a beatific look upon his face.

It was in that dark, timeless hour when all the world is asleep and the mind opens up to those peculiar flights of fancy which, when later illuminated by the cold light of day, are revealed to be either gems of great worth or absolute coal dust—there is no middle ground at that hour—and

12 British Prime Minister during the years of the American Civil War.
13 A British mercenary who aided John Brown in planning the attack on the Harper's Ferry armory.

my brother was in the grips of one such flight.

"Now, Johnnie," said he—we had been the Barrow brothers, James and Johnnie, until that very moment—"read this cable and tell me, how does the name of the operator strike you?" He handed me the flimsy and sat back with a pleased expression as I looked it over.

The subject was innocuous enough—the season's tea leaf harvest in the Darjeeling district, as I recall—and the text, written out in my brother's precise hand, was similar to any number I had handled from the East India stations.

But in place of my brother's familiar sign-off—"Received By: James Barrow"—there was now written, "Received By: Mycroft Holmes."

"Who is this fellow 'Mycroft Holmes'?" I asked.

"Never mind that, Johnnie," said he, impatiently. "Just tell me: what kind of a man is this Mr. Mycroft Holmes? You enjoy speculating upon the people behind their names. Do your worst."

It was true, Watson. I had in those days made it a practice to conjure up the entire image of a man from his name on the telegram I was delivering, for it was a habit, I had read, of the great Allan Pinkerton, who bragged that he could describe the most salient attributes of criminals by their name alone.

"Very well," said I, repeating the name several times to myself while attempting to perceive by the gleam in his eye something of my brother's intention with this little exercise. "I should think Mycroft Holmes is, first of all, absolutely trustworthy; second, highly intelligent; and third, somewhat of a misanthrope. Altogether, precisely the type of individual who might be entrusted with the most sensitive of secrets of Her Majesty's Government."

My brother laughed his abrupt, harrumphing laugh. "Excellent, Johnnie! Excellent!"

"He is your friend?" said I.

"No, he is your brother."

"I beg your pardon?"

"From this moment on, my name is Mycroft Holmes."

I was thunderstruck. "You may do that? Simply change your name?"

"Why, I have done it!"

"And Mr. Farrington does not object?" Mr. Farrington was my brother's somewhat officious superior at the telegraph office.

"Not in the least. I explained that our father had died in a debtor's prison and I had no wish to carry any association with those burdens. Farrington gave me leave to do as I wished."

"Then what of my name?"

"You are Johnnie Holmes, if it pleases you."

I thought for some little time, repeating this curious moniker, first in my mind, and then aloud. I had long adopted various noms de guerre while playing at war with my fellow street urchins—we all did—but these had naturally run towards a more romantic cast: "Nelson," of course, and "Drake." But never "Holmes."

And "Johnnie Holmes" sounded less like a Hero of The Empire than some poor anonymous deck-hand on Nelson's Victory, lost overboard during the battle at Trafalgar.

"In no way does it please me," said I, finally.

"Then create a name that does," he replied in his abrupt manner.

I was about to respond when, at that moment, the telegraph machine began to click its familiar opening codes—"Turn up for Washington,"— and my brother swung back around to the receiver, murmuring to himself about the late hour.

Telegraphy in those days was a delicate business requiring interminable adjustments and tuning of the equipment, and the cable from America ran even more slowly and less reliably than those from the Continent, so all discussion of my new name came to a halt as my brother—now and forever more to be known by the exotic appellation of Mycroft Holmes—bent to the task before him while I listened carefully as the sequence came slowly across.

He wore a puzzled expression working out the first two words as they clicked through over the next few minutes. "Harper's Ferry," said he at last. "I am not familiar with that. Fetch me the atlas, Johnnie." But I had already taken it down from the shelf, for I had learned to translate the sound of dots and dashes even before I had learned to read.

"Why, it's a Federal armory," said he, glancing at the book as the machine came to life again. "'Situated at the junction of the Potomac and Shenandoah Rivers, fifty miles from Washington City.' This is a bad business, Johnnie."

His expression became grimmer by the hour as fresh reports arrived of the armory at Harper's Ferry being raided...of an abolitionist lunatic by the name of John Brown inciting insurrection among the slaves of the region...of Brown's capture by government forces under the command of an army colonel with the strong, upright name of Robert E. Lee.

The sky outside was not yet light when Mycroft—I was endeavouring to adapt to his new identity—pressed into my palm a half-dozen envelopes containing news of Brown's raid, reports of secessionist talk among the slaveholding American states and other dark business.

"To Palmerston's chambers with these," said he, adding firmly, "Be certain he is awakened and that he reads them at once—and wait for the replies."

I dashed down the stairs and out the door into the empty street, not knowing the course of my life would be forever altered by the reports from America which I held in my hand.

Consideration of a new name would have to wait for another day—and a different, more famous mentor.

MY BROTHER LIFTS ME UP

You may wonder, Watson, how, of the multitude of street urchins born to die unnoticed in the rookeries of London, two brothers were able to even perceive the potential to rise out of the gutter and establish a not inconsequential life for themselves, let alone to accomplish such a feat.

I attribute it all to Mycroft, for he possessed the intelligence and foresight to anticipate the new era ushered in by the revolution of telegraphy—something not even the highest and mightiest of the land had foreseen—and grasped the opportunity so surely that it vaulted him to equal standing with the University men of Her Majesty's Government and took me off the streets and into the warm, dry corridors of Whitehall.

Should it be any wonder, then, that when Mycroft one day suggested a new line of work for me—in the chemical laboratory at St. Bartholomew's Hospital where you and I would one day meet, Watson—I took it?

It came about in this way. Traffic on the transatlantic cable—though first intended for government and military functions—had quickly spread to commercial interests, and Mycroft suddenly found himself handling an unusual number of cables between chemists at Bart's in London and the Irénée du Pont de Nemours & Co. proprietorship in Wilmington, Delaware.

The DuPont Company, as it was more familiarly known (ignoring the French spelling of the family surname, for reasons obscure to me), was the largest industrial business in America in those days, manufacturing the most sought-after gunpowder in the world from a string of granite blockhouses along the Brandywine Creek—dubbed the Éleuthèrian Mills, after the company's founder, Éleuthère Irénée du Pont.

Irénée, as he was known, was a Frenchman who had worked at Bart's after studying chemistry under Lavoisier[14] in Paris and moved to America at the turn of the century to start his own gunpowder works. Owing to his early ties to Bart's, Irénée had enlisted the chemists there to conduct research for the DuPont Company, now run by his son, Henry du Pont.

Henry had earned the eternal gratitude of Abraham Lincoln—and half the U.S. Army's wartime requisitions of gunpowder—by stoutly refusing to sell DuPont powder to the secessionist states at the start of the American Civil War, and he was now pushing Bart's to develop a smokeless powder that could replace the existing, and ancient, "black powder" formulation of charcoal, saltpetre and sulphur.[15]

As you know from your adventures in Afghanistan, my dear Watson, black powder produces voluminous smoke that often interferes with a commander's grasp of the conditions on the battlefield—a veritable "fog of war," as it were.

And it was every chemist's dream to perfect a powder that burned

---

14 French nobleman considered the father of modern chemistry, beheaded during the French Terror.
15 Holmes uses British spellings throughout his manuscript, of course, and the editor has retained this custom.

without smoking.

But it was difficult work. Bart's chemists had settled on guncotton, a promising though volatile compound involving the treatment of cellulose with nitric and sulphuric acids, and so many cables had begun to fly back and forth between Wilmington and London that I soon became a familiar face in the chemical laboratory at Bart's.

One evening, upon my return to Mycroft's office in Whitehall—I had become fully accustomed to his new name by this time—I found him smiling with that visionary look once again upon his face.

There was, he informed me, an opportunity that might change my life. It seemed the laboratory chief at Bart's needed an assistant. It would be menial work—sweeping floors, washing beakers, trimming lamps—but it was work all the same and with a far better prospect than message-carrying.

"I have been considering this for some little time," said he, as if the matter were settled. "It would be well to get you off the streets and into a trade. One with a future."

Now, I had seen the Bart's men in their white smocks, toiling away at their Bunsen burners late into the night with little joy upon their faces, no gleam in their eyes—only a grim seriousness in their work—and I was rather skeptical of this new vision of my brother's.

"What kind of future could there be in a chemical laboratory?" I asked.

"A very bright one, my boy! A very bright future indeed!" Mycroft's eyes twinkled as his mind reveled in a future I could not then imagine. "It will take you all the way to America, if I am not mistaken."

"America! How is that possible?"

Mycroft looked in surprise at my wonderment. "Because there is war in America," said he, as if it were the most obvious thing in the world. "All great scientific progress comes out of war!" He nodded at the tin of condensed milk from which I was drinking. "Why, food canning sprang from the purse of Napoleon. Simple handwashing changed all primitive medical notions of contagion thanks to Miss Nightingale's efforts in the Crimea." He snatched a telegraph flimsy from the table and waved it above his head. "How would this report of yesterday's attempt on the

Governor of Bengal have reached Palmerston today without the undersea cables laid by Her Majesty's Navy?"

He turned back to his equipment. "Learn something of chemistry, my boy. It will take you far. Bart's has special relations with the DuPont works in America, and it is to America you must go."

I Debase Myself, and I Am Ashamed

I admit that I did not see it, Watson. I saw only men turning grey at their chemical benches. But I threw myself into the work at Bart's with the goal of becoming, I dare say, indispensable. I swept the floors and cleaned beakers, trimmed the lamps and measured batches, watched over simmering pots and monitored temperatures far into the night.

I even fetched food and tea for the chemists, when called upon.

Between such tasks I read Lavoisier's treatises on chemistry—they were there upon the shelves—and swiftly perceived the logical tidiness which the chemical elements brought to the physical world. I found the subject easy to grasp and soothing to the mind, presenting, as it did, a world in which, ultimately, all things appeared to be connected and might, therefore, be explained if one possessed the appropriate knowledge.

It was not long before I became as completely immersed in the field of chemistry as Mycroft had become in telegraphy, and I pursued my self-education with not merely diligence, but with purpose and pride.

There was, however, one incident during my time at Bart's of which I possess no pride—only great shame—yet so deeply had it been suppressed that it was not until sitting down to record these impressions of my youth that the memory returned.

I did, as I say, fetch food and drink for the men of Bart's. But it pains me to say that I once fetched a quite different subject, one I would rather not name, but must, if I am to make a clean breast of it in these pages.

Men have large appetites, Watson, and not restricted to food or drink. After some little time at Bart's I became aware that a number of the chemists carried on a shadowy intrigue in between their long hours at the benches.

Of an evening, perhaps once a week, I noticed these fellows chewing caraway seeds to sweeten their breath, then disappearing out of the courtyard door one at a time, faces flushed in anticipation of some pleasure I was too young to imagine. Upon returning to the benches some time later, they would appear altogether different—satisfied and mellow and grinning wolfishly as they whispered among themselves.

One day—I had been more than a year employed at Bart's—I was taken aside by one of this group and had it explained to me that, as I had demonstrated competence in the laboratory and "loyalty" to the men of "the club," I was being given a new assignment which I was to perform without question or remark to anyone.

The task was straightforward: I was to meet a certain cab outside the door at a certain hour, pay the driver with funds provided by these men and escort a young woman from the cab to a house across the courtyard from Bart's before returning to my regular tasks in the laboratory.

Next day, at the appointed hour, I met the cab, paid the driver...and sensed immediately that it was wrong of me.

She was still a girl, Watson, perhaps ten years of age—even younger than I—yet there was heavy makeup upon her face and the smell of beer upon her breath. But it was her eyes that alerted me to the sinister design of the occasion, for they were the eyes of my mother on those days in that garret when the debt collector banged upon our door.

I fled to Mycroft's office, but not, I am ashamed to say, before dutifully escorting the girl to the house where a sallow matron appeared, took the girl by the hand and slammed the door in my face.

I did not return to the lab that day (nor would I the next), for it was upon that evening, in the quiet of his telegraph room, that Brother Mycroft—gently and with the tenderness of an older brother upon whom the responsibilities of a family line have descended—explained to me the entire odious history of our father's behaviour towards our mother, a history which he had previously suppressed.

My brother held nothing back that night, including the true reason behind the dreaded visits from the debt collector—it was the only time

Mycroft ever saw our mother drink beer, which he supposed was to dull the apprehension—and why our father was nowhere to be seen when the fellow barged in, leering like a wolf, the scent of caraway seeds upon his breath.

I vowed then—well, I vowed quite a number of things in those days, Watson—but, as for women, I may say I have kept my vows, and in some small way repaid a measure of the hardships those men at Bart's inflicted upon that class.

I did not, however, change their behaviour.

"They'll find other boys with fewer scruples than you, Johnnie, and that business will continue," Mycroft had said, shaking his head before turning back to his machine—and he would be proven right. But my eyes were opened, Watson, and I had nothing to do with that sordid business ever again. In the words of the scripture writer, it was upon that evening that I put away childish things and became a man.

I could not save my mother, you see, but I could respect her memory.

I Escape

It was the 12th of April, 1864—I recall the date with ease, Watson, because it marked the third anniversary of the start of the Civil War in America—and very late in the evening. I had spent a full day at Bart's assisting with the investigation into smokeless powder, and Mycroft and I were sharing a cold beef sandwich at his table when the receiver came alive with a string of unusual messages.

They were from Henry du Pont of the DuPont gunpowder works, and they were unusual for two reasons. First, they were addressed not to the chemists at Bart's, but to Mycroft Holmes. Second, their content was marked "Highly Confidential."

They ran in this way: President Lincoln's Secretary of War, Edwin M. Stanton (a name to remember, Watson), had ordered the DuPont Company to build a laboratory in Delaware to perform the work on smokeless powder with more urgency than Bart's had demonstrated, and the building was nearly completed, but chemists with experience in that line were in limited supply in America. Might Mycroft Holmes have knowledge of an associate at Bart's who would relocate to the banks of the Brandywine, in America?

Mycroft did have knowledge of one such person, of course—his own brother.

Now, this notion was not as absurd as might appear on the face of it, Watson. I had made it my mission, through self-study and long hours of exertion, to earn a chemist's smock at Bart's, and although still young, I had acquired more experience in the smokeless powder investigations than any of the junior associates there.

My services were duly offered by Mycroft that very evening and, to my great delight, promptly accepted by Henry du Pont. I would become a junior chemist for the DuPont Company at the Éleuthèrian Mills in Wilmington, Delaware.

In America.

Now, it was not an easy thing in those days for an orphan lad of sixteen to find his way on board a sailing vessel across the Atlantic Ocean without ending up in the impress of the Royal Navy, but it happened that around that time Mycroft had been engaged in securing the return passage to America of a rather slow-witted youth by the name of Edwin Lamson Stanton, whose father, Edwin M. Stanton, was the above-mentioned Secretary of War for President Lincoln.

Young "Eddie" had been sent to London the previous spring under the pretense of getting an education in the law, when in fact it had been to keep him out of harm's way on American battlefields. But as the war dragged on and the Northern losses mounted, the elder Stanton had come under no little pressure to bring his son home and expose him to the same horrors he was calling upon all Northern men of age to endure.

Mycroft had earned the War Secretary's trust and confidence by handling the delicate correspondence between father and son during the boy's time in London—as well as by other, far more significant actions of which I was unaware at the time—and in that deliberate manner of his, my brother arranged not only the return of young Eddie Stanton to

America, but that I would accompany him.

Thus, in my sixteenth year upon this earth, my passage to America was secured.

We set sail, Eddie and I, the first week of May in the year 1864 out of Liverpool on the RMS Persia. She was a cross between a giant paddle-wheeler and a sailing ship, and quite large for the times, although a minnow compared to the class of leviathans that ply the Atlantic waters these days. She carried a crew of eighty-five and accommodations for one hundred or so well-heeled "cabin" passengers and double that number of immigrants in steerage.

She was also loaded with 80 tons of coal for the Atlantic crossing, half again that weight in provisions and a vast assortment of pigs, fowl, horses and more than a few pet dogs—not to mention rats, fleas and other vermin—and she would be my home for the next ten days.

The accommodations were tight but not unpleasant for a lad accustomed to sleeping under a noisy telegraph desk, and, in any case, I had little time for sleep, for Mycroft had arranged that I would work my way across in the galley serving the cabin passengers, as he had not yet accumulated the necessary capital to pay the cabin fare for such a voyage.

I scrubbed pots in boiling water until my hands were raw, swabbed floors, set out (and emptied) rat traps and performed much other unpleasant business to keep the cabin passengers—young Eddie Stanton included—comfortable.

Of Master Eddie, I saw little on the journey, for he remained in his quarters, blaming seasickness—although I suspected his constitution was less indisposed by the weather, which was mostly fair, than the prospect of a Union Army uniform awaiting him from his father's own War Department.

To make the hours of dull physical labour below decks go by, I honed the skills at mimicry I had cultivated during long hours delivering messages up and down Whitehall and refined a talent for voice-throwing that proved well suited to the confined spaces of that hot and cheerless galley. My most frequent target was the chief cook, an ill-tempered ruffian from Leith who maltreated the Irish boys on the crew and so frequently commandeered the cooking sherry for his own use that we were often forced to do his job as well as our own.

In this way I amused the crew and, after-hours, was given the run of the decks, where I soon learned a new skill that—like mimicry and voice-throwing—would stay with me the rest of my life.

I learned to play the violin.

My instructor was a most unlikely teacher—a broken, unkempt fiddle player—but he not only taught me how to play a most beautiful instrument, he fueled in me a not inconsiderable desire to make something of myself.

Even if he would never know it.

I Learn Something of a Craft and Much About Life

To his bandmates he was "Phil" or "Mister Harmonic"—most cruel appellations, I later learned—but his given name was Alexander Turner and he was billed as "Alexander the Great," the bandmaster of the Persia's eight-man orchestra.

I can picture him now, as flush-faced and dissolute a drunk as ever I had come across in the vilest alley in London.

To watch him attempt to light a cigarette, the match trembling in the grip of palsied fingers, one would think he could not even hold a bow, much less play an instrument. But when the fiddle was cradled in his neck and the bow settled in his hand, why he could produce as sweet an air as Paganini himself, so long as it was something his limbs and fingers had memorized down the years—"God Save The Queen," of course, as well as "La Marseillaise" and perhaps a dozen of the popular melodies of the day.

When something new or unfamiliar was called for, however, he was as far at sea as the Persia, but he had learned to disguise his handicap by following the other players for a time until he managed to guide them towards something he could play, yet always so slyly that only the band members who called him "Phil" or "Mister Harmonic" were aware of the chicanery.

I first heard him our second night out of Liverpool while clearing tables at a smoking concert for the cabin passengers. It was my first exposure to anything more tuneful than a marching band, Watson, and I was instantly taken—not only by the sounds of his playing, but by the pleasurable sensation of watching colours appear to emanate from the instrument.

At first, I thought this was a trick of stagecraft, but the colours were too vivid to my eyes and too quick to change as the tones moved from dark to light and back again. Later, of course, I learned this to be chromesthesia[16]—a condition not uncommon among musicians—but at that moment, I only knew that I wanted to learn how to play and to produce those colours myself.

The very next night, as "Alexander the Great" came offstage, I begged the maestro to teach me a note or two, which he was quite willing to do in return for a cup of the cook's sherry. (Shades of my father, Watson!)

I could not bring myself to add fuel to that debilitating fire and so offered to retrieve a shepherd's pie instead. This he gladly accepted, for a musician's life is a difficult one, and the moment he thrust the bow

---

16 *A type of synesthesia in which the hearing of sounds imparts colours in the vision of the afflicted. It was first empirically studied by Gustav Fechner in the 1870s.*

into my right hand and placed the neck in my left—even before he had turned his attention to the pie—I felt somehow at ease, not unlike my first exposure to the table of chemical elements.

I found my fingers were able to pick out the notes and find the tune—imperfectly and with no finesse, admittedly, but well enough to encourage another visit, and another, until, with the natural dexterity that youth possesses, I managed to acquire the ability to play a handful of tunes, much to the amusement of my fellow galley mates and to my own considerable delight.

In hindsight, the swiftness with which I took up the instrument must have been more than a little disheartening to my teacher, yet I realize now he came to rely too heavily on my handouts to end the lessons. In any case, so well did I advance that one evening when the fit came upon him mid-performance, "Alexander the Great" pulled me onstage to stand in his place while he dashed off for a nip. I sawed away enthusiastically until the song crashed to a halt, whence I was chased offstage by the trombonist, much to the audience's amusement.

But I pressed on with the lessons for the remainder of the voyage, determined to learn how to make those colours spring from that delicate wooden box at will—and learn to play I did, Watson, even as my instructor fell apart before my eyes, imparting a lesson I would carry with me the balance of my life.

It was the evening before our disembarkation in America. Passengers and crew were in a great bustle preparing their leave, and the band had found itself without an audience. When I had finished my galley chores for the last time, I found my teacher already waiting for me—and his pie—in our meeting place behind the paddle-box. He was well sauced and in a deathly melancholic mood.

He said nothing about his sentiments—he never had—but I divined he was dreading the end of the journey. Everyone around us had something to look forward to in America, of course, while all he could foresee, evidently, was a long and bleak voyage back to England.

I picked out an air while he ate in a sullen fashion and washed down his meal with the remains of a bottle of gin he had cadged, watching me with moist, bloodshot eyes without offering any comment upon my finger placement or the angle of my wrist, his face a picture of despair.

"D'you know how good I was, lad?" he suddenly asked, his eyes fixed upon mine, his fingers pulling a soiled and worn envelope from the inner pocket of his coat.

I stopped my playing and awaited the answer.

"When I was a young and able man, not much older than you, I'll wager, I was asked—I was requested—to audition for the greatest symphony orchestra in the world! See here!"

He handed me the dirty envelope, his red, watery eyes watching mine as I studied the engraved letters that identified the sender, Royal Liverpool Philharmonic, and the addressee: Mister Alexander Turner, care of the Parish of St. Anthony. Inside was a letter—the paper smudged, the ink faded—from the Orchestral Director, dated the 5th of April 1842, which began as follows:

The Royal Liverpool Philharmonic Society requests the pleasure of your attendance at auditions for the new season of the Royal Philharmonic Symphony Orchestra...

Now, I did not know what a "symphony orchestra" was, Watson, much less that in those days Liverpool's had indeed been considered the finest in the world. Indeed, I was struck not so much by the contents of the letter but its date, for a letter sent in 1842 to an eighteen-year-old would have put this depleted, ancient man at barely forty years of age, while I had taken him for sixty at the very least.

"That's good," said I, with forced enthusiasm. "Quite good indeed."

"It was very good!" he barked, snatching the letter from my hand. "The Liverpool Philharmonic Society requests the pleasure! Requests the pleasure. That's how good I was, lad!" He read the rest of the letter silently to himself before tucking it back in the envelope.

"And did you audition?"

"Oh, did I!" His face darkened. "Took the train to Liverpool all on my own, walked to the hall—couldn't afford cab fare, you know—and the first thing His Nibs there was on me about was my clothes. 'You won't be dressing like that at Covent Garden, will ye?' says His Nibs, looking me up and down. 'No,' says I, 'but I'll be playing like this,' and I start in on the Lieder.[17] Well,

---

17 *Short piano airs by Felix Mendelssohn, adapted for violin and very popular in their day.*

that shut him up good. Yes, it did. Shut him up good until the Spinnerlied…"

The maestro's face had become a mask of rage.

"And that's when it happened. His Nibs starts shouting, 'Adagio! Adagio!' Well, I didn't know what Adagio meant, did I? Never had a lesson in my life, did I?"

He put the bottle to his lips and tilted it back for the last drops. Then he smacked his lips and shook his head.

"So how was I to know the bugger wanted me to slow down?"

I thought the story was concluded and had tentatively begun to play again, quietly, when suddenly he sent the bottle crashing across the deck and lurched to his knees, grasping my collar and pulling my face to his and bathing me with his hot, sour breath.

"And that, my lad, is why the boys call me 'Phil Harmonic.' Cos I was turned down by the Royal Liverpool Philharmonic!"

He let go of my collar, and a wistful smile replaced the dark rage upon his face. "But by God, I was asked. None o' them scoundrels was ever asked so much as to sweep the floor, let alone audition. But I was!" He leaned back against the paddle-box and closed his eyes. "By God I was," he murmured. "By God…"

I played quietly, soothingly, until he had fallen asleep, whereupon I removed the letter from the clutches of his hand, slid the precious document inside his coat pocket and tucked the instrument and bow into the crook of his arm. Then I went below decks to my hammock for one last night's sleep on board the Persia.

It was light outside and the Persia was rocking gently when I was awakened by shouts that the quarantine officers were boarding and the crew was to turn out for inspection. We were anchored off the bar at Sandy Hook, New Jersey, and at rest for the first time in ten days. When I rolled over in my hammock to climb out, I felt an angular wooden object at my side.

It was the fiddle and bow.

There was no note, and their proprietor was nowhere to be found. Indeed, I never saw Alexander Turner again, Watson—but I never forgot him.

Nor did I forget his lost dreams.

AMERICA

After the quarantine inspection and a long wait for the tide to turn, the Persia cleared the sandbar and entered New York harbour, where she anchored off the Battery so that the ferries could remove the steerage passengers to Castle Garden[18] before she would tie up at the wharf on Manhattan Island.

It was the 15th of May of the year 1864. I had arrived in America.

The sun was high, the air warm, and when I climbed atop the paddle-wheel box to look out over the passengers crowded at the ship's railings, I found a scene of unimaginable colour and movement, of steam and smoke and life. All around us were tugboats and steamers, fast corsairs and sleek sailboats, oyster boats, packet ships, dredges, runners, barges and ferries carrying all manner of material and humanity across the crowded waters of the New York harbour.

Everywhere, too, were naval vessels—immense ironclads, smaller blockade ships and fast gunboats—all making for, or coming out of, the giant Navy Yard on the Brooklyn shore, where swarms of men hammered steel plates to wooden ships in the dry docks, producing a sound like thunder across the water.

As far as I could see, from Staten Island to Red Hook, wharves bristled with the masts of ships taking on or discharging their passengers and merchandise, and from every direction—north, south, east and west— there came the sounds of steam engines hissing, sails rippling, bells ringing, horns blasting...the full-throated roar of humanity filling my young ears.

This was America.

A prayer of gratitude for the foresight of my brother sprang to my lips as I jumped down from the paddle-wheel box and went below decks to retrieve my small sea chest. By noon, the Persia had docked at a Manhattan wharf, the cabin passengers had disembarked, and the crew were allowed to collect their pay and leave the ship.

I made my way to the baggage clerk and there found Eddie Stanton, with

18 Immigration station at the tip of the Battery, replaced by Ellis Island in 1892.

a porter bearing his several large trunks, in the company of a rather imposing man—a plainclothesman, as it turned out, sent by his father. The fellow took Eddie and me by our arms and steered us past the Union agents canvassing for recruits[19] to a waiting carriage and thence by ferry to Jersey City.

After a hasty luncheon at a tavern near the railway depot, and without time to let our stomachs settle, he saw us aboard the train bound for Washington City and waved a brusque goodbye.

I Find My Voice

Crowded into a rickety carriage with hard benches for seats and surrounded by a noisy company of soldiers headed for war, I found the train journey to Washington not quite so stirring as my first impressions of America from the paddle-box of the Persia had been, Watson!

Indeed, closing my eyes now, I can smell that carriage: a gritty odour of sweat and dirt and, above all, smoke. With no coal to spare for civilian railroads, the American engineers burned whatever wood they could find—green or wet, they didn't care—and it spit and crackled and spewed embers onto the roofs and cinder and ash into the windows, which nevertheless had to be kept open owing to the stifling heat in the cars.

It was unquestionably an uncomfortable ride. Young Eddie sat slumped in his seat, a handkerchief to his face against the smoke, his eyes alert for burning cinders. Yet I was entranced, for outside the carriage windows the buildings and factories of Newark had begun to pass us by, their chimneys belching black smoke from mighty furnaces fed by men blackened with the dust of the coal they were shoveling from mountains of the stuff piled to the sky.

It seemed the might and muscle of America were springing to life before my eyes.

When the factories and brick tenements gave way to farms and fields, my attention turned to our companions inside the carriage. They were a company of infantrymen from the area around Topsfield,

---

19 One in four Union soldiers were immigrants recruited by Army agents as they arrived in New York.

Massachusetts, on their way to join Grant's Army outside Richmond, and I can see those boys now in my mind's eye as clearly as I can smell the smoke of that train.

Though not much older than I, Watson, they appeared as warriors in their fine blue uniforms, all brass-buttoned and close-fitting, and they spoke a mile-a-minute in that strange, nasal accent of New England.

As we rattled along, however, their behaviour became something less than warrior-like, for it happened that their officers were seated in a first-class carriage, and soon enough several of the older fellows had broken out their flasks.

The coarse language grew in volume and creativity as the flasks were passed around, until, by the time we reached the Trenton station, our carriage had become the habitation of the rowdiest, vilest bunch of knaves this side of Wapping—so much so that Eddie Stanton (afraid, he later told me, that his father's name might be tarnished should he be identified among such "ruffians") switched to the first-class carriage.

But I stayed. Until that voyage, Watson, I had never heard that flat, practical American voice we would encounter years later in our very first adventure together.[20] Yet now it was all around me, bespeaking a new world to my young ears.

I delighted in the vitality of it, even as they turned their attention to me with a sudden volley of abrupt questions, for Americans are nothing if not disarmingly forward in their approach to new acquaintances.

Why was I in America? Where was I going? Was I a spy? A 'secesh'?[21]

My first attempts to answer them fell flat, however. Whether from their alcohol or my Cockney tongue, they could not make out my words! I might as well have been speaking German, one said.

And so, Watson, I switched to the Queen's English. This I could do as well as any country squire from my days prowling the corridors of Whitehall, of course, and it quite satisfied them. Indeed, our banter went on for some time—through Philadelphia and past Wilmington—until we

---

20 A Study in Scarlet, *1887.*
21 *Abbreviation of "secessionist." Pronounced "sa-SESH." Slang term for a Confederate sympathizer.*

halted at the Christiana River.

There, the drawbridge was up for a ship making its way to the Delaware River, "DuPont Company" painted upon the paddle-box.

Powder ship! the word went up, and the men—hunters, all— gathered at the windows and began to expound upon the quality of DuPont powder, fashioned at the very powder works where I would soon be employed as a chemist! As the realization set in that the ship was very likely bound for Grant's Army, however, the men around me fell silent as they watched this reminder of the true destination of their journey glide past.

And yet they did not appear alarmed by what they saw.

Rather, they seemed to take courage from it, Watson, and as the drawbridge came down and the train resumed its journey, the carriage was filled with talk about General Grant, his march on Richmond and the whipping they would help him deliver on Bobby Lee. This continued until the gentle swaying of the carriage and the aftereffects of the alcohol took hold and they all fell asleep.

So too did I, with dreams of what awaited me at the DuPont works, until the train lurched suddenly to a halt and shouts of "fire!" came through the windows. We were in thick woods somewhere outside Baltimore, and a seat had caught fire in the first-class carriage.

The men—who an hour before had been a rowdy mob of mischievous boys—swiftly roused one another, spilled out of the carriage and tramped down the embankment to a creek, where, under the direction of their officers, an improvised fire brigade was formed with the men of the other carriages.

Pails of water were passed along the line from the creek up to the train—the men singing "John Brown's Body" and filling the woods with a lusty cheer at the end of each verse—and almost as quickly as it had broken out, the fire was extinguished; the carriages were re-boarded and the train resumed its journey as if absolutely nothing out of the ordinary had occurred.

It seemed to me at that moment, Watson, that these men of the North must prevail in their dispute with those of the South. Not only did they have a vast machinery of war to supply them—the factories of Newark, the

Naval Yard at Brooklyn, the powder works of Wilmington—but they had brought such spirit to the task at hand that I did not see how they could fail to press those advantages to their ultimate benefit.

I did not yet understand how close a thing the struggle would be and that but for one man—the Great Man, as I will forever think of him—America might have remained torn asunder for all time.

My education in such matters would begin soon enough, as it happened, for when our train passed through the outskirts of Washington City and the platform of the Baltimore & Ohio Depot came into view, newsboys could be heard shouting of bloody battles fought in grim locations with names like "The Wilderness" and "Spotsylvania":

"Fierce fighting!...Grant's losses terrible!...Grant says: 'On to Richmond!'"

When the carriage finally halted at the station, the men from Topsfield gathered their haversacks and disembarked in silence, assembling on the platform in good order under the watchful eyes of their officers.

Soon the rat-tat-tat of the drummer boys sounded, and they began their march down Maryland Avenue towards the Long Bridge, which crossed the Potomac River into Arlington, Virginia. From there they would march south, past smoldering battlefields left behind by Grant's Army.

To Richmond.

We had said our goodbyes in the train—the men from Topsfield in their uniquely American voices, and I in my Pall Mall inflections, for I had decided to leave the voice of London's streets behind forever. Mycroft had done just that in his days at Whitehall, around the time he changed his name.

And so, I reasoned, could I.

I met Eddie Stanton on the platform, and a porter was found to carry his trunks to the Stanton carriage awaiting us. Young Eddie seemed none the wiser to my altered manner of speech, for he was a talker, not a listener, and I doubt he had heard me say five words since we had boarded the Persia in Liverpool. Soon, we were riding through the streets of the American capital city.

A greater contrast to London I could not imagine.

WASHINGTON CITY

Washington City seemed a half-built interruption of some very grand plan.

At the start of the government district rose the Capitol Building—try to imagine, Watson, a copy of St. Paul's among the shanties of Spitalfields!—while at the far western end, a mile or more away, the half-built Washington Monument stood like a giant, broken chimney not far from the more majestic White House [22] which itself had been erected next to a swamp.

Between the two ends ran a fetid, disused canal into which the residents threw their garbage!

Yet these strange sights and the pretense of grandeur did not disturb me, Watson, for the simple reason that there was optimism in everything I could see. To my young eyes, America was a country of great expectations—interrupted by war, yes, but no less shy about her ambitions.

Witness this capital city, which seemed an act of unbridled pluck.

Our carriage took us down Pennsylvania Avenue—the only cobblestoned street in Washington back then—past gleaming marble edifices alternating with cow pastures set apart by unpaved boulevards as wide as parade grounds. We saw scarecrow-looking Confederate soldiers being herded to prisons scattered around the city, dodged cabs and messengers in full flight, and passed slow-moving wagons loaded with wood, coal, hay and hogsheads of apples, pickles and beer.

As we approached the gated grounds of the White House—a grandly-columned and whitewashed edifice—the sulphurous stench from the nearby swamp that met our noses was appalling, although it did not seem to deter a swarm of office seekers awaiting entry at the gate!

President Lincoln, Eddie informed me, greeted all who made it inside and upstairs to his office. Some people, he said, waited outside two days or more for the chance.

---

22 *The Presidential mansion did not formally become 'The White House' until the 1900's, although it was indeed painted white in 1864 and commonly referred to by that nickname, as readers will see.*

After turning northward and leaving the swampy atmosphere of the White House behind, we reached Franklin Square in no more discomfort and halted in front of a fine, three-story brick house, the home of Mr. Edwin M. Stanton, American Secretary of War—and by all accounts the most powerful man in the country.

An aproned girl admitted us into a large entrance hall while the coachman retrieved the trunks, and it became immediately evident there was serious business being conducted in the house. Well-dressed, stone-faced gentlemen stood huddled in conversation in an anteroom lined with high bookcases off of the hallway, while a military guard stood at attention beside an inner door from behind which could be heard raised voices, apparently in some little heat.

"Father's study," Eddie said in a loud whisper as he led me down the hallway to the dining room. "He conducts business there on Sundays and days when the callers get too numerous at the War Department. Best to stay clear."

In the dining room Eddie rang the bell somewhat imperiously until the door from the kitchen opened and in stepped a tall, handsome, reserved woman in her forties. She introduced herself as Mrs. Ellen Stanton (she was Eddie's stepmother[23]), and her relief at Eddie's safe return was evident. He did not return the kindness, however. Instead, he addressed her in a rather stiff manner and inquired somewhat brusquely if there were any food to be had.

Soon enough the Stanton's cook bustled in with pickled oysters and biscuits, and we ate a hearty lunch while Eddie regaled his stepmother with tales of danger from our Atlantic crossing—made entirely out of whole cloth, Watson—while I said nothing.

Afterwards, Eddie visited his father while I was shown to my room on the upper floor of the house. My windows overlooked the carriage house and other outbuildings at the rear of the house—a view that would play some little role in the story to come, Watson—but I had no time to take it all in, for I had barely washed and changed my linens when an envelope was slipped beneath the door.

Inside was a note from the War Secretary—it was on his stationery,

---

23 Stanton's first wife, Mary, died of an undisclosed illness in 1844.

anyway—informing me that he would be pleased to see me in his study for a brief interview at the precisely stated time of five-fifty o'clock. The family dinner would be served at six o'clock, the note added, and it would please both him and Mrs. Stanton if I would join them.

I was not surprised at this summons—Mycroft had warned me that Mr. Stanton would want to take my measure before allowing me near the DuPont works. So, after a refreshing nap and with the self-confidence of a young man who does not yet know the things he should fear, I descended the stairs well before the stated time and took my seat in that small library outside the study alongside several nervous, grey-haired men.

And waited my turn.

The Most Powerful Man in America

Edwin McMasters Stanton was born and raised in Ohio, then the western frontier of a young, growing country. Thanks to a superior native intelligence and tireless work habits, he rose to the pinnacle of the legal profession, arguing cases before his country's Supreme Court—and winning more than a few of them.

His rise in politics was no less meteoric. Attorney General under the irresolute President James Buchanan, who dithered while southern states seceded, Stanton was called back to government service by President Lincoln in 1862 after Northern armies had suffered ignominious defeats at Manassas, Wilson's Creek, Ball's Bluff and elsewhere, to replace the corrupt and blundering Simon Cameron as War Secretary.

And in that all-powerful office, Stanton quickly proved his worth.

He cleaned out the "lunatic asylum," as the War Department under Cameron had become known; repaired frayed relations with the American Congress; and saw to a massive buildup in the means to feed, clothe and arm the Northern Army's half a million men—sometimes by the simple force of his very ample will.

Told, for example, that it would take three months to send twenty thousand troops under General Ulysses S. Grant to Chattanooga, Tennessee, to rescue a Union army trapped and starving under General William Rosecrans—who President Lincoln had been quoted in the papers saying appeared "stunned, like a duck hit on the head"—Stanton brought the chiefs of the Northern railroads to his War Department office and didn't let them leave until he had gotten the time down to two weeks by rail.

In the end, it took only eleven days. General Grant, with his customary resolve, saved Chattanooga—and it would not be an exaggeration, Watson, to say that Edwin M. Stanton had saved his country.

And it was outside this man's study door that I sat as, one by one, the nervous men awaiting their turn were admitted—the signal being a peremptory shout of "Guard!" from the War Secretary within as the previous guest was dismissed. This steady press of business suffered constant interruptions by messengers, however, who dashed into the house with urgent telegrams and left bearing equally important messages from the Secretary. It soon became apparent that my scheduled interview would be much delayed.

Sure enough, the appointed time came and went, and still I was seated. At six o'clock I saw Eddie and Mrs. Stanton retire to the dining room for dinner accompanied by several houseguests. Eddie gave me a sly wink as he passed. Clearly, I would not be joining them.

It would be another hour before I was summoned inside the office.

When my turn finally came, I found the War Secretary seated behind a large desk in a mahogany-paneled study, its walls covered with maps and so crowded with bookcases stuffed with rolled up maps and folios of maps that there was only room enough for two uncomfortable-looking armchairs between the desk and the fireplace.

The lone window was situated behind the desk, and I saw with a start that it looked out across Franklin Square, directly upon the White House.

My host remained bent to the task of signing papers for some few moments, his thinning hair the only quality of the man visible to me until he paused his work and glanced up, whereupon he examined me like a specimen placed upon a glass slide, with piercing eyes behind wire-framed spectacles.

"You're a good five years younger than I expected," he said finally in a not-unfriendly manner, putting down his pen and picking up an envelope from the desk. "You have experience in the chemistry of guncotton and other varieties of smokeless powders? Good. Your brother, I imagine, imparted upon you the vital importance of the DuPont Company to the Union war effort? Very good."

He held out the envelope and nodded for me to take and open it. Inside were two letters of introduction and a train ticket to Wilmington, Delaware. One of the letters was addressed to General Henry du Pont, proprietor of the DuPont Company; the other to the landlady who would let me a room.

"You shall report to General Henry—he prefers that appellation—at the DuPont powder works tomorrow morning, and you will do whatever he requests of you."

When I nodded my assent, but otherwise remained silent, Mr. Stanton regarded me with some little merriment in his eyes.

"Your brother Mycroft was right. He said you're a discreet one." Then he turned his attention back to the papers on his desk before adding, "And thank you for accompanying young Eddie to America. Mrs. Stanton thanks you, too."

Before I could reply, however, he glanced up at me with quite a ruthless gaze, then delivered a stern warning.

"Of course, the moment I receive word from General Henry that you have brought discredit to the Union cause in any way, you will be on the next ship back to England, steerage class. I hope that is clear."

I nodded.

"Guard!" he cried.

And with that I was dismissed.

THE ÉLEUTHÈRIAN MILLS

I alighted next morning at the Wilmington, Delaware, railway depot. It was Sunday and the streets were quiet. As my rooms were nearby on Shipley Avenue, I set out walking and quickly found the air a delightful change from the miasmic odours of Washington. Wilmington, you see, is bounded by rivers on three sides, and the presence of a nearby root beer factory considerably sweetened the atmosphere.

I soon reached my lodgings. The landlady was at church, so her girl showed me to my rooms. They were large and included a most excellent sleeping porch overlooking the alley, but it was evident my landlady was rather miserly, for there were not even matches to light the single lamp hanging upon the hook. (It was fortunate one always carried matches in those days before the electric light, Watson!) After finishing my toilet, I ate a simple breakfast of toast and coffee while inquiring of the girl the way to the DuPont works.

It was some two or three miles up the long hill above town, she said; a horse trolley ran there, but it would be idle, it being Sunday; yes, I could walk—the Kennett Turnpike led straight past the powder works, but the pike would cost me six cents.

As the day was fair and I wanted to see something of my new surroundings, I determined that the walk—and the six cents—would be no great hardship, and so I set out once more on streets largely empty of traffic and people. At the city limits I found the turnpike, paid my way at the tollgate and began the long walk uphill past farmhouses and fields, a fairground, a school, two churches and a Quaker meeting house.

When the gravel pike attained the crest of the hill, I could see something of my new surroundings. Behind me lay Wilmington and the Delaware River beyond. To my left, perhaps two miles down a long, cleared slope with cows and sheep grazing, glimmered the Christiana River where the day before we had watched the ship loaded with DuPont gunpowder making for the Delaware.

To my right lay the object of my visit: a great wood that descended into a valley—the valley of Brandywine Creek—where chimneys poked up through the trees and a sharp sulphurous scent wafted through the air. I now understood what the girl had meant, Watson, when she told me to "follow the rotten eggs to DuPont"!

From those woods, a cobblestone road emerged and crossed the turnpike directly ahead of me on its way down the long sloping hill to the Christiana wharves. At that crossroads, in the shade of a great clump of willow trees, a DuPont powder wagon was halted alongside a water pump. The teamster was moving among his horses, adjusting their harnesses, checking their buckles and soothing them with soft words.

I had approached to within perhaps fifty paces when the man stiffened and turned towards me. "Stop right there, son!" he shouted, the sharp tenor of his voice rooting me to the spot. "There's a ton and a half of powder in my wagon and you ain't coming anywhere near it 'til I look you over." Eyeing me expertly even from that distance, he pointed to my hobnail boots. "Those can spark, son. You'll get off cobblestones and walk in the mud, or we'll both regret it."

I did as the teamster said.

His name was George Bell, and he was taking his load from the DuPont powder magazine to the wharves on the Christiana. He had a schedule to keep, he said, handing me the dipper to refresh myself from the pump, for there was a shipment going out that day even though it was Sunday and the powder works were silent. More teams were on their way from the magazine and he would have to move on soon: the wagons kept a quarter-mile distance from each other—that was the rule, and nobody ever broke the rules. He was sorry he'd spoken sharply to me on first sight, but nobody with metal on them came near the wagons. Why, even the horses wore leather boots over their shoes!

Yes, Henry du Pont would be in his office, he said, in response to my question. General Henry worked seven days, everyone knew that. How to get there? Just follow the turnpike up past St. Joseph's church—the Catholic Church, "where the powder-monkeys go"—to the Barley Mill Road, which runs downhill through the woods, past the foreman's house to the main gate. The guard there would take me to General Henry's office.

He glanced at the woods where another DuPont wagon had materialized.

"There's Osterberg," said he. "He'll be resting his team for a bit. Quick, give my boys a treat while I grease the wheels. I always like to give 'em a little something when we get up here on the rise."

He handed me a fistful of hay. I offered it to the lead horse, which took it.

"You made a friend there, son. Here, take some more with you. Always keep hay in your pocket—you'll make friends wherever you go."

A shift in the wind brought back the sharp smell of sulphur to my nose, and the teamster laughed as he returned the small keg of grease to its place under the seat and climbed aboard.

"You'll never get that smell out o' your clothes so long as you work at DuPont!"

Truer words were never spoken, Watson.

I said goodbye and continued my walk. Soon I passed St. Joseph's church, where my ears were met with the pleasant strains of an organ being played and voices raised in song ringing from the open windows. The next turnoff was the Barley Mill Road, and this I followed down into the valley of the Brandywine, where grey granite buildings of various heights and lengths loomed up among the trees, and the sulphurous odour intensified as the sound of rushing water filled the air.

When I reached the gatehouse, an elderly watchman emerged to ask my business. I produced the letter of introduction from Mr. Stanton, and he read it and nodded. "All's in order. I'll take you to General Henry myself—he's expecting you. You won't mind if I ask you to turn out your pockets? Thank you—I'll take those matches. No, keep the straw. It's only the matches I care about. And you won't be wearing those shoes inside."

From the porch he retrieved a pair of leather moccasins, which he handed to me. "You'll put these on and leave your boots here. You can collect your boots on your way out."

And with that, my guide led me through the gates of the Éleuthèrian Mills. He walked slowly and with much huffing and puffing. Twenty years working in the sulphur refinery had made breathing difficult, he said, although he spoke of the powder works with evident pride. I found the moccasins, though somewhat ill-used and dirty, a delight to the feet, and I listened intently as my guide called out the name and use of each building as we passed them—somewhat in reverse order of their place in the production line, as it happened.

There was the magazine, where kegs of finished powder were held for the wagon ride to the docks; the packing house, where empty kegs were packed with finished powder before being taken to the magazine; the dust house, the composition house, the sulphur refinery—the many chimneys of which emitted the foul odour that suffused the valley air—and the charcoal house, where willow branches were burned to make the charcoal needed to produce gunpowder.

Finally, we reached the valley floor. There, across the millrace, a half-dozen grim, grey, granite buildings stood shoulder to shoulder alongside the rushing waters of Brandywine Creek.

"And this," said my guide, "is where the serious business of the Éleuthèrian Mills starts."

The blockhouses in which DuPont gunpowder was fashioned were curiously constructed. They possessed no chimneys or windows and were connected by a narrow-gauge train track (wooden, my guide told me, to avoid sparks!) upon which the quarry tubs full of charcoal, saltpetre and sulphur were moved from one mill to the next. And within their grim walls a mixture of those three elements was pressed and grained and glazed and corned into high-quality DuPont gunpowder.

As it was Sunday, the turbines were shut off and all was silent but for the chatter of swallows darting above the rushing waters of the creek. But come Monday morning, my guide assured me, the turbines would engage, and the machinery would begin to whir and grind in a most ominous commotion.

"Here," he said, "I'll show you the inside of a roll mill! Come on!"

A Most Serious Business, Indeed

We crossed the millrace—the waters of which drove the turbines that powered the machinery inside these mills—and entered through a narrow, granite-walled passageway, whence I found myself inside a close, dark room perhaps twenty feet long and the same again wide. The atmosphere reeked of sulphur, and the room was dominated by two steel wheels, each taller than a man, which stood in the center atop a large steel mortar bed like a pair of gigantic coins balanced upon their rims.

When the turbines were engaged, my guide said with awe, those eight-ton wheels would slowly rotate, crushing inexorably the three components of gunpowder beneath them into an ever-finer mixture. It was the most dangerous stage of making black powder, by far. An explosion could happen any time the wheels got too hot or a stray spark ignited the mixture.

He pointed out that we were surrounded by thick granite walls on three sides, but that the fourth side of the roll mill, which faced the creek, was made of thin planks of wood.

To my questioning glance, he chuckled grimly. "The genius of E. I. du Pont!" he said. "If it blows, it blows out there, across the creek!"

This was a most serious business indeed.

We left the roll mill and its companions behind and continued walking past a second set of blockhouses added to the Éleuthèrian Mills in several stages over the years. Then we struck off away from the creek, going uphill past the sweepings house (which is just exactly what it sounds

like, Watson—"No wasted here, sir!" said the guard) and made for steps
built into the valley hillside.

We climbed those steps—with some few pauses for the guard to catch
his breath—to the sounds of rushing water and chattering swallows
until those songs of nature were eclipsed by the strains of a waltz coming
through the trees.

"That would be the Éleuthèrian Players," the guard informed me.
"They entertain every Sunday at the picnic following mass at St. Joseph's.
If you play well enough, you might get asked to join!" He chuckled as
we resumed our climb. "General Henry likes his men God-fearing and
well-rested."

The steps ended atop a bluff, where we found ourselves upon a large,
stone-flagged balcony. Ahead of us rose a stately, three-story, granite-
walled house. It was the family home built by Irénée du Pont so as to
overlook the powder works in the valley behind us. Farther along the
bluff, we came to a small, one-story granite building.

"And this, sir, is the office." He knocked at the door, and after
some little time it was opened by a tall, red-whiskered man with a firm
handshake and a serious appearance befitting the proprietor of a very
serious business indeed.

"Excuse my delay," Mr. Henry du Pont said as two greyhounds sniffed
my trousers. "I am alone today. Thank you, Starkey."

And with that, I was admitted to the offices of Irénée du Pont de
Nemours & Co.—the DuPont Company.

The headquarters of the most important enterprise in America
held just two rooms. The first was for the secretary, with a tall
secretarial desk—its pigeonholes stuffed full of correspondence—and
walls lined with shelves groaning with account books. The second,
smaller room was the office of Henry du Pont. It held a modest desk
beneath a detailed map of the Éleuthèrian Mills, and a wood stove.

Many family portraits and framed documents hung upon the walls.

Henry du Pont studied the letter from Stanton by the light of
several candles upon his desk, then folded it up and handed it back
to me. "That will do. Secretary Stanton approves—as I had no doubt

he would. Your brother is as famous in Washington as he is at the Éleuthèrian Mills, you know."

I was puzzled at this last remark—I had never heard that adjective applied to my reclusive, if not misanthropic, brother—and my face must have proclaimed as much, for Mr. du Pont smiled.

"I gather Mycroft Holmes is as modest as he is competent. My nephew Lammot always said as much. Lammot is the chemist of the family. He met your brother some years ago. You might recall? No? Well then..."

He glanced among the framed documents adorning the walls, removed the very smallest and began a brief but remarkable story.

HOW MYCROFT SAVED THE UNION

"It was late in '61 and this war was no longer the trifling affair our politicians had expected. The DuPont Company needed three million pounds of saltpetre to keep the mills running for the Northern armies when word came to us that your Lord Palmerston had cut us off from our shipping agents because of that damned Trent affair.[24]

"As you well know, the best saltpetre in the world comes from Bengal, and we couldn't buy it! I was eight weeks from shutting down the powder works. It was a d--nable crisis.

"Lammot sailed all the way to England to see what he could do, but Palmerston refused to even meet him! So Lammot went to the telegraph office in Whitehall to cable me for instructions. Thank God your brother was transmitting that evening! He grasped the magnitude of the situation at once and took it upon himself—at enormous personal risk, mind you— to open the India lines for my nephew on the spot. Within two weeks, working under assumed names, Lammot had secured every cargo of saltpetre on the high seas and all the production from Madras to Bengal."

He handed me the framed document. It was a cable, faded but legible, dated November 3rd, 1861, and it read as follows:

---

24 *The British ship RMS Trent, carrying Confederate diplomats, was captured by a U.S. Navy vessel, triggering a diplomatic crisis that threatened to bring England into the Civil War on the side of the Confederacy.*

TO GEN'L H. DUPONT:
    PLEASED TO REPORT
    3MM LBS SECURED
    SHIPM'TS BEING ARR'GED
    LAMMOT IN AMSTERDAM
        —M. HOLMES

"My brother?" I said, with something of wonder in my voice.

He nodded. "Mycroft Holmes. Fortunately, President Lincoln settled that Trent business before Lammot's purchases could be traced to the DuPont Company and your brother's involvement was made known." He replaced the frame upon the wall. "It is no exaggeration to say that Mycroft Holmes saved the Éleuthèrian Mills. And if Mr. Stanton were here, he might well add that your brother saved not just the mills, but this country."

His smile broadened at my astonishment. "Now you understand why I so readily accepted your services—and why Mr. Stanton concurred?"

I did, indeed.

My host pinched out the three candles upon his desk, retrieved his hat and coat from the peg, then paused at the door, studying my feet. "Your moccasins are comfortable? Good. No matches on your person? Very good. No metal? That is excellent."

He held open a side door and the dogs charged out ahead of us. "Let me show you where it started—and all that your brother saved."

GOING ACROSS THE CREEK

"The Éleuthèrian Mills were conceived right here."

We stood upon the stone-flagged balcony, our backs to the house, looking out over the heavily wooded valley where the entire length of the Éleuthèrian Mills stretched before us, the dogs sitting patiently at Mr. du Pont's feet.

"Father had come to the Brandywine on a hunt. He sat on this very outcropping and saw at once the valley would make an excellent powder works. The Brandywine runs down from Chadds Ford and drops two hundred feet as it enters the valley there—" he gestured to our left "—which is more than enough to power the machinery. The granite bedrock all around us would be quarried for the buildings, the willow branches burned for charcoal. And there was a cooperage upriver to supply the kegs and wagon wheels.

"Thomas Jefferson encouraged the enterprise—he had befriended my grandfather in France[25]—so father bought the land and set to work. He built the first set of powder works right below us and put his house and office here on this bluff so he could track the machinery day and night. I remember him rushing from the table one day during lunch and thinking it very unfair our mother would not let me follow him. I did not understand he was placing himself in mortal danger. He very nearly died, more than once. Powder is a dangerous business."

My host leaned over the wrought iron fence and pointed to several blockhouses along the creek, singling out one that had evidently been reduced to rubble by an explosion which also left a charred clearing directly across the creek from it.

"Did Starkey show you how the mills are constructed to blow over the water? Well, you see that rubble and the clearing across the creek? That's what happens when something goes wrong with powder! We lost eight men in that blast, including my brother Alexis." He shook his head solemnly. "The men call it 'going across the creek.'"

As I gazed at the clearing, a boy, perhaps my own age, suddenly appeared there among the charred stumps, a fishing pole on his shoulder and a dog at his heels. He was glancing in pools—in search, it would seem, of a promising fishing spot. Suddenly his dog smelled the greyhounds sitting patiently at Mr. du Pont's side and began to bark. The greyhounds took up the chorus, and soon the boy spied us and waved. My host waved back.

"Billy Sumner," he said. "His family runs the cooperage. You'll see <u>Billy fishing the</u> different pools when the weather is fine. 'Sunshine Billy,'

25 Jefferson was Minister to France for the American Congress of Confederation from 1785 to 1789.

the men call him."

This struck me as a curious thing, Watson. My days spent fishing for eels in the Thames had taught me that fish are shy in the sun. Indeed, Mycroft used to jest that we always ate best when the weather was dreary—which is to say, most of the time! I vowed to meet this "Sunshine Billy" one day to learn his secrets.

But now it was time to meet Monsieur.

MONSIEUR VERNET

Turning our backs upon Billy, the creek and the powder works, we left the patio and walked past a very fine carriage barn, crossed a raked gravel drive and entered an ornate garden—"Irénée's garden," my host informed me—where neat rows of vegetables and rose bushes were framed by well-pruned fruit trees, grape arbors and several white boxes standing about chest high, a type of which I had never seen.

"Beehives," said my host, observing my curiousity. "Monsieur tends them. He is unique, as you will see. The laboratory where you will work is just there."

He pointed to a slender, one-story building on the edge of the woods, quite different from all the other buildings I had seen, for it was constructed of wood rather than granite and possessed large windows on all sides. Two chimneys and several metal exhaust pipes stuck up through the roof.

"That was Lammot's workshop, and we have made it our chemical laboratory. And after you spend your first week in the mills working with the powder men, it will be your home." He knocked at the door and waited. "I prefer our chemists to have a firsthand knowledge of the DuPont manufacturing method before they come up with new powder formulations. They waste less time on fanciful schemes when they understand the difficulties of manufacturing powder."

He knocked a second time, and when there was still no answer from within, he opened the door and I followed him into the most well-equipped chemical laboratory I could have imagined. Two long rows of tables held retorts, test tubes, microscopes, beakers and evaporation vessels of every size and shape. The familiar warm scent of Bunsen flames heating baths of chemical mixtures met my nose.

In an instant I felt at home.

"You will not meet Lammot today—he is away on company business—but you will work with his right-hand man, Monsieur Vernet." With that, General Henry nodded towards the only other occupant of the room.

He was a short, wiry man, evidently much older than my host, with an unruly mop of white hair, a bushy white mustache and a clean-shaven chin. Wearing a stained lab coat over a Sunday suit of clothing, he walked slowly between the tables, leaning over the countertops and eying the experiments, all the while holding to his lips a silver flute which he played in soft, sultry tones as he walked. Altogether, his appearance was that of a ghost weaving among the tables.

My host smiled. "Monsieur Vernet. He is, as I said, unique."

And indeed, Watson, as I would learn, Monsieur was entirely unique, although I fear you would find his habits distressingly familiar were you to fly back in time and spend an hour with him! All those little eccentricities of mine about which you complained to your readers—the emotional detachment, the secretive ways, the reticence to discuss a case—in some way derived from the days, weeks and months I would spend watching this man at work.

But at that moment I saw only a spry, white-haired eccentric playing a flute, his eyes fastening upon one experiment after another.

"Monsieur Vernet, this is Mr. Holmes! He will start work in the mills tomorrow before assisting you in the guncotton experiments!"

The notes of the flute paused briefly as the man gave a polite bow in my direction and then resumed as he continued his slow movement among the tabletops, eyes dancing about, flute at his lips.

"Monsieur is in one of his reveries. You will come to recognize them. When he is in this mood, he is unreachable. And yet, when the working fit is upon him, he will toil harder and longer than any man in these yards." My host glanced at his watch. "It should not be much longer, but I must take my leave now. Here—" he said, pressing a printed card of thick paper stock in my hand.

I still possess the card, Watson, though it is somewhat the worse for wear:

General Henry du Pont
Éleuthèrian Mills
Wilmington, Delaware

"Tomorrow you will take this card to Boyle, the head powderman. He will set you to work. The morning whistle blows at seven."

"I will do my best, sir."

"Aye, and you, sir," he said, "may call me 'General Henry'."

Now, I should explain, Watson, that Secretary Stanton had made mention of Mr. du Pont's preference for the appellation 'General Henry' during our brief interview the previous day, in this way: "The DuPont powder works lie within a slave state, and the DuPont Company came under no small pressure to supply the Confederacy with powder. But Henry du Pont refused to sell to Jefferson Davis a single keg. Thus, if he wants you to call him 'General Henry,' or 'Sir General Henry,' or 'Henry du Pont, King of Kings, Host of Hosts,' you will do so."

'General Henry' it would be.

But my mind, I confess, was far away from the question of how I would be addressing Henry du Pont and rather more occupied by the manner in which Henry du Pont had addressed me.

He had called me "sir."

In England, Watson, I had been a wraith—a faceless messenger with no past and most certainly no future, addressed only as "boy" or "scout" or "you, there." Yet now, here, in America, I had been called "sir."

As General Henry took his leave, the greyhounds flying out the door ahead of him, my mind was filled with the startling realization that I had become somebody.

A more powerful sensation has never gripped my consciousness to this day.

OBSERVATION AND DEDUCTION

His full name was Antoine Claude Jean-Horace Vernet, and, yes, my dear Watson, he was a descendent of Vernet, the French painter I led you to believe was a patriarch of the Holmes line when I dragged that red herring of the "country squires" across the trail of my family tree.

Unlike his famous grandfather, however, Monsieur Vernet of the Éleuthèrian Mills worked not in oils or watercolour, but in chemicals. A keen student of Lavoisier's treatises, he had travelled all the way from his native Montpelier, in France, in order that he might practice his art with the descendants of the great E. I. du Pont on the banks of the Brandywine—and had never left.

He stood barely five feet tall, spoke French when excited—which was most of the time he was awake—and a heavily accented English otherwise, and broke his fast each morning with cups of dark French coffee and a fresh baguette his wife baked for him.

And on Sundays he came to the laboratory after church services for what he called his *jour de pensée*, his day to simply think.

Wandering the floor in solitude while playing his flute in a most distracted manner—as he would later explain to me—allowed his mind to observe the patterns that lay buried within the jumble of data coming forth from the experiments. From these he could deduce how various chemicals worked together in ways that his conscious self might have missed.

Never once would he touch, adjust or recalibrate an experiment already underway, and never would he write anything down: the *pensée* was meant to allow his eyes to observe and his mind to deduce without hindrance.

And what observations, Watson! What deductions!

His *pensée* that Sunday had barely finished when he removed the flute from his lips and turned his attention to me, fixing me with a most penetrating gaze before speaking. "You came by train, I observe," said he, finally. "The state of your collar tells me as much. And yet you are native to London."

When I started, he wagged his flute at me. "Please, that is no mystery. I overheard your conversation with General Henry! You speak in the manner of the educated class of Britain, and yet I detect in your use of the definite article a hint of the Cockney pronunciation. Hence, London."

You can imagine my surprise, Watson! Never had I encountered a cross-examination where the answers were already known to the examiner. But before I could express my admiration, he asked a question that positively startled me.

"Would it be indiscreet if I asked why you came to Wilmington by way of Washington City?"

Seeing the incredulous look upon my face, he pointed his flute at my trouser cuffs. "That clay on the fabric is fresh, but not common to the Delaware basin. The pink colouration indicates the presence of arkosic sandstone of the Potomac region. Where else could such a clay have attached itself to your clothing but in Washington City? The war prevents you from travelling elsewhere on the Potomac."

I felt a thrill at this odd man's ability to deduce my journey from a few simple observations and to share them in such a precise, didactic manner. Before I could say as much, however, he glanced out the window, pursed his lips and motioned me to the door. "The sun is setting. I must say goodnight to the bees. Come." Setting aside his flute, he made certain all the gas burners were turned off and the main stopcock was shut, locked the door behind us with a thick wooden latchkey and led me into the garden.

The hives were busy and the air full of bees returning home in the twilight. Monsieur spoke softly and soothingly in their presence, his eyes and ears as alert as they had been inside the laboratory. Evidently satisfied by what he saw and heard, he beckoned me to a path alongside the laboratory that would, he said, lead us through the woods back to the gatehouse.

As we walked, I began to describe my journey and the reason for my visit. "I know a little something of why you are here," he said, cutting me off as we reached the guardhouse. "There is no need to explain. I will see you again in one week." Then he bowed his goodbye, turned on his heels and was gone.

I exchanged the moccasins for my boots and walked back to my rooms by the light of a rising moon, tired and yet elated, my heart racing, my mind turning.

From that slight, possessed man, I would learn to become a chemist of some little ability, acquire the facility to speak French and not a little Italian, learn much about the opera, develop a passable familiarity with most of the great painters of the world and some of its best poets (including the classic Persian works of which Monsieur was something of a recognized authority back in his home country), and cultivate an ascetic lifestyle which rather appealed to my young and impressionable mind.

Most important of all, however, I would learn the art—and science— of deduction.

Upon arriving at my lodgings that evening, however, I was quickly brought back from the world of future dreams to the world of everyday cares by the presence of my landlady. She was a large, heavy Swede, and before she showed me my seat at the dinner table she handed me a list of House Rules by which I was meant to abide.

I have kept that list, Watson—including her odd punctuation—and I reprint it here, for it recalls pleasant memories of my time in America:

<u>Rules of This House</u>
$3 a week for Bed
$5 with Supper
No more than three to sleep in one Bed
No Boots to be worn in Bed
No dogs in room.
Beer allowed in kitchen.
No Organ-Grinders taken in.

It was fortunate there was no provision against violin players, Watson! That very evening—as in the weeks and months to come—I relaxed my brain by practicing the tunes I had learned on board the Persia, scraping away softly on my sleeping porch while working through the events of a most busy, wearying and exciting day, until sweet Morpheus overwhelmed all thoughts but of sleep.

Next morning, I was ready to begin work.

GOLIATH OF THE ÉLEUTHÈRIAN MILLS

I caught the first horse trolley up the long hill to the Brandywine woods and made my way down the Barley Mill Road, where I found that the Éleuthèrian Mills presented an entirely different picture from the quiet, restful scene on Sunday. Powdermen emerged from hamlets tucked into wooded dens along the valley and streamed towards the gates alongside of me, ahead of me, all around me—talking and laughing, their lunch pails swinging.

At the gate I was fitted with a pair of wooden clogs in place of my boots, and when the whistle blew at seven o'clock sharp and its echoes had died away, the exertions of men at work filled the valley of the Brandywine with the sound of a giant enterprise coming to life.

And what a life it was.

From the gathering of willow branches for the charcoal house to the packing of wooden kegs with finished powder and every step in between, I would spend my first week learning with intimacy the DuPont method of manufacturing the finest gunpowder in the world, working alongside the "powder-monkeys," as they were called with unwarranted derision by those who could not appreciate the risks involved.

These were men who took a fierce pride in their work and who performed even the most mundane chores with care.

And it was well they did, Watson, for the business of making powder, as I was constantly reminded in my time there, was a most dangerous business indeed. Each of the three components of black powder—charcoal, sulphur and saltpetre—is poisonous to the lungs and noxious to the eyes, and when combined under pressure and at great heat, the chance of an explosion is ever present and the tolerance for error nonexistent.

It was labourious, gritty and not infrequently nauseating work. Even under the best conditions, disaster could strike at any time. A firm hand was needed to make the place run well and yet run safely.

And the hand General Henry had chosen to oversee the powdermen was a very firm one indeed.

His name—Denny Boyle—possessed the ring of a prizefighter, and he looked the part as well. Standing almost six feet and weighing no less than thirteen stone,[26] with a square, thick head set upon broad shoulders, his form filled the slender passageways of the granite blockhouses as he watched his men work, his narrow eyes hidden beneath a slouch hat.

With his arms folded and his fists bunched thick as sledgehammers, Boyle often appeared rather too willing to use those fists to get what he wanted from the men. And for reasons I could only speculate upon, Watson, he hated me from the moment I appeared at the sweepings house that Monday morning with General Henry's card in my hand.

"So, the General sent you, has he?" he said, gazing at the card, a sneering smile upon his lips. "I'm to be impressed by the General's card, is that it? Think I never seen it?" He let it flutter to the ground. "Now pick that up."

I already knew the very strict rules of the mill—nothing was allowed to litter the floors at any time for fear it might spark a light. So I picked up the card, pocketed it and stood at attention while he turned his attention to my hands.

"Let's see 'em, laddie. Hold 'em out. That's the boy." He made a show of inspection while others looked on. "No callouses!" he announced. "A good one for work, you'll be! Can you hold a broom, dearie? All right, then, start with that—" he stuck a broom in my hand "—you'll sweep today."

Thus, I began my first week at the Éleuthèrian Mills sweeping up the grains of powder left behind at each stage of the milling process and depositing those grains in the sweepings house, the contents of which would be emptied into the composition house for reuse the next day.

It was not a difficult task, Watson, but Boyle kept a sharp eye on me, prodding me to move faster or slower—there was no correct pace, it seemed—and showering me with slights and insults, except when General Henry or Mr. Gibbons, the foreman, appeared with a question for their chief powderman about some piece of business. On those occasions, Boyle masked his temper with a jolly exterior, only to resume his hectoring ways as soon as Mr. Gibbons or General Henry and his

26 180 pounds, in an era when an average male weighed only 140 pounds.

greyhounds had departed.

Something in Denny Boyle's manner told me there would be worse to come when the time served his purpose, but I ignored those premonitions and did everything demanded of me with alacrity.

At dusk I returned to my rooms as tired as I had ever been.

THE MAKING OF A GOLIATH

It has always struck me, Watson, how much people will tell you if you simply listen.

I was put to work next morning in the composition house, unloading hogsheads of raw sulphur and saltpetre brought from the Christiana docks by the teamsters. It was backbreaking work but not a particularly delicate business, as no gunpowder was involved. The men there were overseen not by the iron-fisted Denny Boyle, but rather by a pale, humourless bookkeeper who logged each wagonload as it arrived and weighed every quarry tub that rumbled away down the wooden railroad tracks to the roll mill.

Not a teaspoonful of sulphur or saltpetre went unaccounted for thanks to that studious man, and without Boyle looking over their shoulders the labourers performed their tasks in such an easy-going, but diligent, manner—all the while chattering nonstop—that by lunchtime I had been provided a history of the powder works and of the exceptional benevolence of the founder and his heirs.

Women who had been made widows by a powder explosion were allowed to live out their lives in their houses at the Éleuthèrian Mills rent free, they said, and General Henry was forever hiring back powdermen Boyle had fired for some perceived slight or other, on account of the men having to support their families. And there were the Christmas parties at the barley mill where all the mill children—more than one hundred, some years—were given a box of candy and a toy by General Henry.

I learned many other such agreeable stories of the du Pont men, and as the day wore on and our familiarity increased, I learned not a few far less agreeable things about Mr. Denny Boyle.

He owed his job, they said, to his grandfather, Mr. Jack Boyle, the very first powderman hired by Irénée in 1802, and the best and fairest chief powderman anyone at the Éleuthèrian Mills had ever known. Mr. Jack, as they called him, had "gone over the creek" in the terrible explosion of '18. Mr. Jack's son Tom had followed in the '57 blast that also killed General Henry's brother, Alexis.

Having one's forebears' blood spilled with the du Ponts' was seen as no small mark of devotion at the Éleuthèrian Mills, and so it was that young Denny Boyle stepped into the job of foreman at a tender age with General Henry's blessing, and he quickly demonstrated he could run the mills as efficiently as his father or his grandfather had done.

But he also proved as devious and underhanded as those men had been righteous and above board.

He "borrowed" cash from the powdermen on their payday with no intent to repay, stole tools from the maintenance shed and blamed it on village thieves and took bribes from tradesmen in exchange for business with the powder works. It was also said that he dealt in a far worse trade with certain of the powdermen's wives, but none of them dared speak of it—and I was never able to confirm it.

"But Holmes," I can hear my friend Watson asking, "why on earth would General Henry ever keep such a scoundrel?"

My answer would be this, Watson: "Because he made the mills hum, did Mr. Denny Boyle."

And as the war between North and South raged on and Secretary Stanton pressed for ever higher production from the Éleuthèrian Mills, Boyle and his men turned out ever more kegs. It was a source of great pride in Wilmington that the DuPont Company never once failed to complete and deliver an order of powder for the War Department when and where it was requested.

Such Herculean efforts came with a cost, of course, but the men under Denny Boyle spoke not a word about his transgressions to General Henry or foreman Gibbons, because their jobs were in Boyle's hands—and they were cowed by his fists.

But I was not cowed.

I had seen a few Denny Boyles in my early years, Watson—one did not inhabit the streets of Wapping in those days without encountering their type—and I believe Boyle saw it in my eyes. Why else would he mean to chase me out of the Brandywine Valley from the moment I appeared?

I wanted no trouble, of course—I felt the distant eyes of Brother Mycroft upon me—and I worked harder that first week than I had ever worked in my life to give the loutish Mr. Boyle no reason to find fault.

But my tireless industry only seemed to provoke the man's ire, and it was upon the last day of my week on the line that matters came to a head.

I Play at Matches

From the Monday to the Friday of that first week at the powder works I had assisted at every step save the most dangerous one: the roll mill, that grim granite chamber where those eight-ton steel wheels slowly compressed the three components of gunpowder together into ever smaller, more compact, more dangerous flecks of black powder for hours at a time.

So great was the danger that nobody remained inside the roll mill while the wheels were revolving. Instead, the powdermen watched through peepholes to monitor the conditions within and determine when to add water to the mix to keep the temperature down. Once the mixture (they called it "cake") had finally reached a proper size and consistency, the turbines were disconnected from the millrace, the wheels came to a halt and the hard work began—shoveling the "cake" into the quarry tubs that would carry it along the tracks to the corning and glazing mills for refinement.

It was the most difficult and most dangerous job in the Éleuthèrian Mills. The very shovels were made of wood so as not to provoke a spark.

On Saturday, Boyle placed me there, and my difficulties began almost as soon as the wheels had stopped moving and we entered that hot, close chamber to begin shoveling the cake. The intense sulphuric atmosphere in the confined space quickly sapped my lungs. Then too, being a good five stone lighter than the experienced men alongside me, I soon felt the shovel a heavy burden in my hands. It was readily apparent I could not keep up, and when the last of the cake had been shoveled out and rolled away, my Irish taskmaster entered from the passageway, a great smile upon his thick face.

"All right, Mr. Johnnie Holmes, all right, that's enough slowin' things down. Can't have that here. Me dad didn't go over the creek so mugs like you can gum up the works."

I was exhausted, Watson, exhausted from shoveling and sick from breathing those fumes. The only thought in my mind was of the cool waters rushing past the thin wooden wall just yards away and how delicious a thing it would be to burst out of that confined blockhouse and jump in the creek to cleanse my aching body and drink myself full.

But here was this ape strutting and cooing, sticking his finger into my chest and hopping from one foot to the other, while the men—tired enough themselves—leaned on their shovels, warily catching their breath as Denny Boyle circled me.

"What have we to do with Johnnie Holmes, men? Eh? What have we to do?"

I would not be provoked, Watson—I knew his game—and so I kept silent, but my silence only served to drive this blustering Goliath madder. When each poke of his finger brought no response, his face turned redder and his eyes bulged wider, until he fairly ripped off his cap from his head and waved the others away. "Stand down, boys. Get water."

I was alone with Goliath.

"Now, Mr. Johnnie Holmes, what say you? Nothin' to say? Hand in your pocket? Bit of a smirk on the face, is that?"

I had no smirk upon my face, Watson, I can assure you. I was doing everything in my power not to provoke the great Goliath, and I shook my head no.

"No? Then what's your problem? Can't shovel as fast as the poor Paddies on the line? Is that about the size of it?"

I nodded wearily. "Yes, that is about the size of it, Mr. Boyle." I said this without a hint of sarcasm in my voice—I was tired, Watson, not looking for a fight—but my words seemed to enrage him even more than my silence had.

"The size o' what? The size o' this?"

His fist crashed into my stomach so quickly I could not brace for it. I dropped in a heap, gasping for breath amid the poisonous fumes of the powder grains left behind on the unswept floor. Goliath stood over me now, prodding my legs with the tips of his wooden clogs. "Can't stand up, can ye? Come on Johnnie-boy, get up. Get UP!"

Breathing with difficulty, I managed to slowly push myself to my knees, then unsteadily to my feet.

"That's it. That's the boy. Let's see you now."

I had just turned to face him when the second blow came, as fast and hard as the first, and although I had braced for it this time, I went down sprawling, barely conscious.

The mind is a glorious thing, Watson.

Here was I, scarcely able to draw breath, pain radiating from every organ in my chest, and yet somehow my brain was active, working out how to find my way clear of this confrontation. The safest course, my mind quickly perceived, was to play dead. It was a ploy that had worked more than once in my younger days and was not difficult to perform—and I certainly felt closer to that state than any other.

But dull as the man may have been, he saw through my lifeless display at once.

"Play dead, will ye? That'll not do for a man. Only girls play dead, Johnnie-boy. Ah, there! Did I see a twitch?" His foot prodded, but I moved not a muscle. "No? Is Johnnie-boy dead? Or just playing dead?"

A sudden sharp kick to my ribs brought intense pain to my chest. "Still playing, he is. Still playing."

The turbines were stopped, the wheels were still and the powdermen had vanished. A silence had come over that gloomy granite space that was broken only by the soft rushing sound of the creek, the chatter of the swallows feeding on the insects above the waters and the panting breath of my tormentor, who appeared to be eyeing my most vulnerable position with a satisfaction that bespoke a murderous intent.

It was clear the dénouement would not be long in coming.

But in the quietude of that roll mill there now came—probably from a wagon team making a delivery at the composition house—the high, emphatic neighing of a horse. And thank God for that horse, Watson, because it put an idea in my head as I lay upon my side, pain in every bone.

Keeping my body as motionless as possible, I worked the hand hidden beneath my leg—unseen by Goliath—into the pocket of my trouser, fingers searching for what I had remembered was there. It took some little maneuvering to reach it without alerting my tormentor, but my fingers finally found what they sought just as Goliath was preparing his final act.

"What's to be done, Johnnie-boy? What...is...to...be...done?"

I opened my eyes as Boyle was bending his leg for a final ferocious kick, and before he could let fly I rolled away and brought myself to my feet, making a show of bringing the hand out of my trouser pocket and holding the slender item above my head, the tip of my thumb poised as if to flick it to life.

The smile vanished from Doyle's face and he froze in place.

"No, laddie." His voice was croaking, quiet. "You won't do that. You won't strike a match in here."

"Ah, but I will. And we'll go across the creek together."

"You don't want to do that, laddie." So vividly did the beads of sweat form upon Mr. Denny Boyle's forehead that even in the dim light of the roll mill, I could count each one as it appeared. "Why not? You're trying to kill me," I said flatly.

"No, son. Not I."

"You shake your head 'no,' but those fists say otherwise."

"No, laddie, it's just my way. The boys know. Tell him, boys." Boyle glanced about the room, but there were no powdermen in sight.

"They're gone, Goliath. You sent them away. And you'll be gone too, but forever. So say a prayer to Mother Mary, and when I count to three..."

"JESUS MARY AND JOSEPH!"

And with that, Denny Boyle bolted from the blockhouse as fast as his legs would take him.

Rejuvenescence

I had crumpled to the floor, gasping for breath.

After some little time, one of the powdermen looked through the peephole. "You have a match with you, son?"

"No," said I. "Straw." I held it up as best I could for his inspection, my fingers trembling. He stepped carefully into the blockhouse, his eyes fixed on the thin yellow stick. Then a smile came to his face.

"I'll be! You fooled old Denny Boyle with a piece of straw!"

He took it from my hand in wonderment, his smile as wide as his face. Soon his laughter brought the other men inside, and the straw was passed around while I was helped to my feet. The laughter grew when I pulled from my pocket the rest of the hay which I had kept for feeding the horses, and now it was handshakes and backslaps all around.

The men finished the work that day while I soothed my sore body in the creek. With no sign of Denny Boyle to trouble anyone, the laughter and the storytelling did not stop until every pound of powder had been rolled and nightfall had brought an end to the work. I reached my rooms that evening in a state of pain and exhaustion that could scarcely be overstated.

But very clever was Denny Boyle. There was no damage to my face, for his fists had landed where the wounds would not be seen. Pain enveloped me, but nothing was broken. It was a highly effective method of intimidation.

My landlady, who no doubt thought the working conditions at the powder works must be rather extreme, prepared a homemade poultice to apply to my sore muscles—which is to say my entire body—and served a large dinner of Swedish meatballs and potato soup that proved an excellent source of rejuvenescence.

So soundly did I sleep that evening and all day Sunday that by Monday morning I felt almost restored to health. Well enough anyway to make my way to my new post at the Éleuthèrian Mills in the chemical laboratory of Monsieur Vernet, with no one the wiser.

I never said a word of the episode to anyone until long after my time at the powder works had ended. And although I was no more bothered by the brutish Danny Boyle, it would not be the final end of him.

Not just yet.

"To Fail is to Learn"

I went to work in the DuPont laboratory under Monsieur Vernet alongside two proper chemists whose chief task was the formulation of a smokeless gunpowder that could be manufactured safely and at scale, which is to say in quantities that could supply an army. And although that goal would not be achieved in my time on the Brandywine (guncotton proved devilishly difficult to harness) the work was energizing and intense, and not without reward for the DuPont Company some years later.[27]

Mornings started with a baguette and coffee—the dark French roast for which I soon acquired a taste—and quickly moved to the preparation of the chemical samples upon which experiments would be conducted that day.

I cleaned and sterilized the equipment; measured, sifted and stirred the compounds; applied heat to the samples; calculated ignition speeds; recorded temperatures; and trapped and calculated the volume of smoke given off by the reactions, all the while taking careful note of unintended consequences in the experiments.

And oh were there unintended consequences, Watson!

It was for that reason our testing was conducted out of doors in a clearing on the other side of the creek. On afternoons when the weather was fair, we would troop across a disused railroad bridge to a point well away from the works, where guns could be fired and eprouvettes[28] employed and the results observed on the spot.

But whatever the weather and wherever I worked, above all things, I observed Monsieur Vernet.

---

27 *DuPont #1 Smokeless Gunpowder revolutionized warfare when it was introduced in 1894.*
28 *A portable device to measure the throwing distance of a prescribed unit of gunpowder.*

Impatient, temperamental, insecure, egotistical, self-absorbed and impossibly opinionated about those things of which he was knowledgeable, he proved—unlike most men in my experience—curious and open-minded about anything he had not yet learned. Indeed, when presented with information that was new to him, Monsieur breathed it in like Mr. Hoover's vacuum cleaner, and once absorbed into that brain of his, it was locked inside forever.

One other trait distinguished Monsieur from other men, Watson. Failures in our work never appeared to bother him in the least. Indeed, he often appeared more delighted by the failure of an experiment than a successful outcome. When I inquired about this mindset after one particularly discouraging afternoon at the test range had left the rest of us dragging but Monsieur ebullient, he shrugged his shoulders.

"You learn nothing when you are proven right, you know. But you learn everything when you are proven wrong."

I would later refine this precept into a somewhat grandiose maxim you have heard me say more than once, Watson: Eliminate the impossible; what remains must be the truth. But Monsieur stated it far more simply that afternoon. "To fail," he said with a smile, "is to learn."

And much did I learn, Watson!

The days went by as swiftly as the waters of the Brandywine.

I Encounter a Famous Thespian

The Éleuthèrian Mills operated every day but Sunday and ten hours every other day except on Saturday, when the closing whistle sounded an hour early. Mondays always proved the busiest, for Monsieur would be bursting with ideas from his Sunday *pensée*, and by Saturday we were sagging, tired and ready for a day of rest.

I began attending Sunday services with Monsieur and his wife at St. Joseph, where I acquired my first taste of the Latin language upon hearing the Mass. It was here that I also began to play my violin alongside Monsieur and his flute as he led the Éleuthèrian Players at the fete after services.

As I became more efficient at my work in the laboratory, I found myself less tired at the end of the work day, and so took to exploring Wilmington to utilize an unanticipated benefit of my employment at the DuPont Company: the pay I received for my labours. One evening I saw a promising outlet for my spare funds in the form of a troupe of local players billing themselves as Unparalleled Interpreters of the Works of Wm. Shakespeare.

I had always fancied myself something of an actor, Watson. Survival in the streets of London demanded it, and my little improvisation of a match-striking doomsday machine in the roll mill had given me a taste for the power of the craft. So I paid my half-dollar and stepped inside.

The accommodations were dreadful—old stables converted into a gaslighted theatre—and the actors were more enthusiastic than accomplished, but I enjoyed myself immensely, for theatre in America was something of a Roman sport in those days.

The audience hissed when Claudius strode onstage, clapped approval when Hamlet stabbed poor Polonius to death and pelted the players with apples and peanuts when Hamlet's father became so entangled in the mosquito netting intended to convey his ghostly shroud that the "dead" Polonius suddenly restored himself to life and vigorously cut away the netting with Hamlet's knife so the production could resume.

The evening proved a most excellent release after a long day in the laboratory, and by the end of the troupe's run I was being called upon by the players to assist in their wardrobe, for the war had created a scarcity of glues and dyes used in makeup, and my facility at devising substitutes from the chemicals in our laboratory became highly demanded in the green room.

It was all great fun, and of course the skills I learned with the makeup kit would prove of considerable benefit later in my career.

But it was not until a derailment on the Baltimore & Ohio caused a first-rate company to overnight in Wilmington and stage an impromptu Julius Caesar at the Indian Queen Hotel that I grasped the full powers of the craft—and set my eyes upon a man whose path I would cross, both literally and figuratively, not many months later.

He was tall and lean, a black-haired dervish, and his mustachioed face held the most piercing blue eyes I have ever encountered. To this day, Watson, I recall how they flashed—even in the dim light of the gas flares—when his cry of "Thou shalt see me at Philippi!" so shook the rafters that it was met with startled silence from the poor fellow playing Brutus, a local thespian who fled the stage in terror.

Pandemonium ensued until a substitute was found, but the effect of the scene was mesmeric. Mere words could not describe the face of the man who played Caesar that evening, but I can see something of the power and depth in his photograph even now, for it was an image that would become famous—or, more accurately, infamous—around the world.

You see, Watson, the man who played Julius Caesar with volcanic fire that evening was none other than the leading tragedian of the day, Mr. J. Wilkes Booth.[29]

Now, it has been written in the histories of the times that Wilkes Booth possessed many flaws in addition to his maniacal hatred of the Negro—among them, that he was a debauched libertine and a seducer of women.

And yet that is not quite accurate, Watson. In truth he was as much seduced by the fair sex as they by him, for women (and not a few men, as his own tragic enterprise was to show) were drawn to Booth like moths to a flame.

Indeed, I saw it with my own eyes the morning following that

---

29 *Holmes follows the custom of the day of identifying Booth with the initial of his Christian name, rather than the full name as he is known today: John Wilkes Booth.*

unforgettable performance.

I was making my way to the horse trolley, bound for the powder works, when two women passed me by, one bearing flowers and the other a cake. From snatches of conversation I understood that Booth and his troupe were resuming their train ride to Baltimore, and these women were making for the station to see him off.

I changed direction and followed—this was too good to miss, Watson—and soon I came upon a scene one might have expected if Admiral Nelson had climbed down from his column in Trafalgar Square and gone horseback riding in Hyde Park.

It was a mob of men, women and children, at the center of which could be seen the tall figure of J. Wilkes Booth walking serenely to the platform while all around him was mayhem. Women thrust gifts upon him and sought to kiss his hand. Businessmen pressed their cards upon him and sought to shake his hand. Boys fought over the right to carry his costume trunk.

The remainder of the troupe followed unmolested, carrying their own luggage.

I would have stayed to watch Booth's departure, but as it was readily apparent the train would not leave on time, and as Monsieur insisted upon punctuality much as he insisted upon finding the truth, I turned my back on the commotion and began making my way to the powder works.

And yet the scene had made an impression, Watson! I dare say that as I toiled away in the chemical laboratory that day, my impressionable young mind kept returning to that scene at the depot and the thought that Mr. Booth's occupation was one very much worth aspiring to.

As it was, I would soon have a chance to test my skills along those very lines.

I Learn Something of the
Underground Railroad

It was a Saturday, almost a month since my arrival at the Éleuthèrian Mills, when I was called away from my workbench to the office of General Henry. There his secretary handed me a train ticket to Washington City and a telegram from Edwin M. Stanton summoning me to an interview next morning in the study at Franklin Square.

I was not surprised. Mr. Stanton had let it be known that I would be expected to return on occasion to bring him my impressions from the DuPont works. Indeed, I was rather pleased, for I determined to spend the journey practicing my newly intended vocation.

With my talent for mimicry and some few skills at makeup, I decided I would set out to fool the passengers in a Baltimore & Ohio carriage just as I had fooled poor Denny Boyle in that roll mill.

That evening I conjured up the character of an oyster boat roughneck from the Chesapeake Bay setting out to join his cousin's boat on the Potomac, for I had spent enough time observing the roughnecks at the Christiana docks to mimic the peculiar inflections of the Tidewater. Next morning, while my landlady was in the kitchen, I set out with a sunburnt face and unkempt hair, wearing a seedy and well-used pea-jacket found in a closet, and at the depot boarded the train for Washington.

Taking a seat beside a sympathetic-looking Quaker woman, I struck up a conversation and found that my ability to take her in with talk of the tide tables and their influence upon various species of bivalve mollusks, without eliciting so much as a raised eyebrow, proved an intoxicating experience—at first.

But as the train rumbled on and I learned of the reason behind her own journey, my enthusiasm began to wane.

You see, Watson, this good lady was travelling in the company of a freed slave (although, to be sure, her companion was riding in the "Negro carriage," as it was called, at the rear of the train). They were on their way to visit the Freedman's Village that had been constructed upon the old

Arlington estate of General Robert E. Lee by order of Edwin M. Stanton
for the security and development of slaves emancipated by Grant's Army
on his march to Richmond.

They hoped to find the young woman's family there.

Along the way, the Quaker said, she planned to visit the White House in
the expectation of an audience with Mr. Lincoln—she had heard he met with
all visitors—for the purpose of convincing him to stand down the Northern
armies and thus end this terrible Civil War.

I could not imagine for a moment that President Lincoln would spare
the time to meet with her, Watson, for I had seen how vast was the press
of business outside Mr. Stanton's own modest study. But as the train rolled
on and this Quaker woman spoke ever more fervently of her mission, my
admiration for her determination grew and my interest in my own little
deception diminished, and I fell silent.

The Quaker woman began to eye me with some little curiosity. The
oystermen she had met were all slave owners, she observed. Might she ask a
question or two? Then she began:

Did my family own slaves? How many? How did it feel to own a fellow
human being? Were the slaves allowed to read? To attend church or a
Quaker meeting? To marry? Had I ever seen a slave auction? Had I ever
watched a mother being separated from her child?

My conscience would not allow me to speak words I did not believe to
this kindly woman, Watson. I quickly unmasked myself, laying out a true
history of my background, my journey to America and my residence in
Wilmington, and the admittedly selfish origins of my impulse to employ
fakery in her presence. Rather than condemning me for playing her falsely,
however, the woman's face lit up at the mention of my rooms at Shipley
Avenue.

"Shipley!" she cried, gripping my hand with some emotion. By my
expression she could see that I did not grasp its significance. "Why, 227
Shipley is the most famous address in the North!"

It was, she explained, the home of Thomas Garrett, a Quaker
merchant who had made it a crucial stop on what was called the
Underground Railroad. Runaway slaves who reached 227 Shipley were

almost certain to make it to Philadelphia, where the population was uniformly friendly to their cause, or to Canada where their freedom was assured.

I now understood the furtive activity which took place at all hours at the brick home several doors down from my lodgings, invariably prompting clucks of disapproval from my landlady who kept a watchful eye from her front parlor window while muttering darkly about "mixing the races."

Mr. Garrett had helped nearly three thousand souls escape the bonds of slavery by way of that unprepossessing house, the Quaker woman said.

"Have you met him?" she asked. "No? That is a shame. He is as great a man as exists on this earth. You'll not be closer to such a great man in your life, I'm sure."

She would be wrong about that, Watson—very wrong.

But neither of us had any way of knowing how wrong she would be.

A MOST PECULIAR INSTITUTION

Perhaps, my dear Watson, it would be well to say a word or two here about the "peculiar institution"—as slavery was euphemistically termed by its apologists—and the debasement inflicted upon the Negro race by it, debasement so shameful it could prompt the Thomas Garretts of the day to invite ruin upon their heads by actively working to free men and women from its wretched grasp.

After all, no Englishman—save those who crossed the Atlantic Ocean as I did—ever witnessed the degradations extant in America (separate railroad carriages for Negroes, to name just one), and that is a great shame, inasmuch as the institution of slavery owed a good measure of its establishment to the Liverpool cotton merchants who had promoted the vile trade and the Lloyd's syndicates that profited handsomely by insuring the English ships which carried the human cargo.

So, let me briefly hold up a mirror, as it were, to my fellow Englishmen, that they may see what they, in no small measure, wrought.

I had encountered slavery's unsavory hold upon the Negro almost immediately upon my arrival at the train depot in Washington with young Eddie Stanton. A porter there—a grey-headed Negro man—approached us, lifting his cap and bowing as if we were imperial rajahs. He repeatedly addressed us as "Marse" (a shortening of the term "Master," as Eddie informed me with a laugh—yet another considerable shock, Watson), and generally acted in a most abject, subservient manner that I found not a little distressing.

My distress turned into profound dismay, however, when, as we walked to the Stanton carriage, a Negro woman curtsied and gave us the sidewalk—and young Eddie took it! Understand, Watson, that the filthy, unpaved, mud-churned streets of Washington City made the cobblestones of Pall Mall seem like magic carpets, so this wretched submission—from a woman I would never have allowed to step in a street in London—seemed inconceivable. Yet there she stood, bowing low in the mire, waiting for us to pass.

It was a picture of humiliation to which I never reconciled my mind, then or since.

And although such pictures were not on display at the DuPont works—the free Negroes employed by General Henry in the family's stables were treated in no different manner than the powdermen—the Éleuthèrian Mills proved a small island of equanimity in a larger sea of debasement, for Delaware was still a slave state back then and the cruelties unleashed upon the African races there were not limited to an insistence upon bowing and curtseying before whites.

Indeed, my next—and quite horrific—exposure occurred at the Christiana wharves only some few days later, during my first week at the mills.

I had accompanied Bell, the DuPont teamster, and his wagonload of powder to the docks at mid-day to take in the process of how the kegs were transferred to ships. We were seated well away from the dock, watching from a safe distance as the experienced handlers rolled the kegs on beds of straw from the wagons to the ship, when I noticed, on a distant wharf, two overtaxed Negros unloading sacks of potatoes from a sloop in the blazing sun.

One was a boy not much older than I, the other a man of indeterminate age. Nearby, on the same wharf, a white man in a broad hat and waistcoat was leaning against a hogshead of tobacco, talking to a slouching deckhand, chewing and spitting out sunflower shells upon the dock. It took some few moments of studying the scene before I worked out that those hatless black figures handling the heavy burlap sacks, their bodies glistening in sweat, were slaves—and the white man was their overseer.

I had never seen such a contrast between men working as hard as those two slaves and the overseer doing no work at all, and was on the point of remarking upon this when suddenly something happened, and the Negros began to move in great animation about the wharf.

What had happened was this: a sack of potatoes had been dropped and its contents had spilled out—mostly upon the dock, but some had tumbled off into the water. They were potatoes, Watson, not gold bars, but the pair scrambled after them as if their entire beings depended upon retrieving each one.

And very soon I saw why.

Out of the corner of my eye I noticed the white man in the broad hat calmly removing from his waistcoat something thin and black, which I took at first to be a very long tobacco pipe—but as he flexed it in his hands and waggled it above his head, I saw it for what it was. Striding swiftly over to the frantic Negroes he began raining lashes down upon the boy with that black whip while the older man groped ever more frantically for the spilled potatoes.

I could scarcely believe my eyes, or my ears, for the wharf upon which this violence was being meted out stood some little distance away from us—the powder wharf being isolated from the other docks—and the sound of the blows coming across the water reached us with a slight delay after they were struck. But when that sound reached us, the hair upon my neck turned up, and I jumped to my feet.

I had to do something, Watson.

I had no plan, mind you, but my eyes had already begun seeking the quickest route to the wharf where that malevolent beast was taking his pound of flesh when I realized I was being restrained by a strong grip on my collar. It was Bell, the teamster. "We have work to do, son, and there's nothing you can do about that."

My anger and frustration were compounded by my incredulity at the thickness of this man. "But he's whipping the boy."

"And he's within his rights, he is," said Bell, who, I noticed, nevertheless winced as the sound of each blow came across the water.

I—well, I can say no more about it, Watson. The words catch in my throat. I can only report that the lashings finally did cease, but not because of any sympathy for the boy, mind you. Only from the evident exhaustion of the overseer.

And so, my dear Watson, should you encounter an Englishman who speaks lightly and delicately of the "peculiar institution" that his forebears helped to incorporate in a distant land, take care to remind them that slavery was no mere eccentricity. It was a heavy hand that meted out tragedy and suffering.

Nothing less.

Mr. Lincoln's Detective

Upon our arrival in Washington City, I said goodbye to the diminutive, perceptive Quaker woman and wished her luck on her mission as she went to retrieve her companion from the rear carriage. In the depot I washed off the last vestige of my oysterman guise—keeping the pea-jacket as a reminder of my inability to fool the good woman—and then, once again an assistant chemist at the Éleuthèrian Mills of Wilmington, Delaware, I boarded the horse-trolley to Franklin Square.

I was not chagrined at my failure in the train, Watson. Failure, as Monsieur had taught me, was my learning, and I had learned that it is not enough to be merely familiar with the character one is attempting to inhabit—one must know his entire history. It was a lesson that would strongly inform my own small efforts in later years, during our cat-and-mouse pursuits of Professor Moriarty and his agents.

But to a far more welcome effect.

At the White House stop I descended from the trolley and was bypassing the eternal crowd of office seekers and supplicants gathered at the gates when I spied a familiar face among the guards.

It was young Eddie Stanton, in uniform.

He separated himself from his comrades and greeted me with far more conviviality than our moments together had merited—I suspected he saw a chance to shirk his duties—and after offering me a cigarette (which I declined, having not yet acquired the habit), he self-consciously modeled his crisp blue uniform for me.

"I was enlisted. Father demanded it. But," he added with a wink, "I swung the guard duty at the President's Mansion. Pretty dull stuff."

"How can guarding the President be dull?" I asked with some wonderment.

"Oh, we only man the gates. The President has his own fellow inside."

"I should hope."

"Aye, and the best fellow in all the world. Allan Pinkerton!"

You can imagine my astonishment at this, Watson. "Pinkerton, the detective?"

"The very same. Why, at this moment he's meeting with Father in the house about some secret mission."

This was news, indeed. My boyhood hero, at the very house to which I was walking! I was about to ask Eddie whether he had met Pinkerton in the flesh, when his sergeant let out a sharp whistle and my companion acknowledged the order with a wave. "Miserable cur," he said under his breath. Then he brightened. "I say, Holmes! Our company guards the Navy Yard Bridge,[30] and those fellows know how to have a time! Come to the guardhouse there tonight, you'll see."

With another wink, he strolled back to the Presidential gate, and I went on my way. I had no intention of taking part in the after-hours antics of soldiers on guard duty, Watson, whatever those antics might be. My mind was on something else: catching a glimpse of the man whose exploits had captured my young imagination and whose likeness I had seen only in books.

Very soon I was seated outside the War Secretary's study, well ahead of my scheduled interview.

It was some little time, however, before I would meet the famous Allan Pinkerton. The crush of business seemed even more intense than

---

30 *Bridge adjacent to the Navy Yard in southeastern Washington, later used by John Wilkes Booth in his flight after assassinating President Lincoln.*

during my first visit, and messengers came and went with even greater frequency. Occasionally, raised voices could be heard from within the study, before subsiding.

The clock in the hallway chimed away two quarter-hours, and still I waited.

At noon, Mrs. Stanton entered the house, evidently returning from church services with guests from Ohio. Ever solicitous, she saw that I was served coffee and encouraged me to partake of the library as I waited. This I did gladly, for in addition to dry legal tomes, the War Secretary's collection offered a vast selection of history and literature, and I meant to educate myself.

I was immersed in one of Gloucester's speeches[31] when the voices from within subsided, "Guard!" was called, the door was opened and there emerged from the study a short and stout man in the dress of a workman, his beady black eyes peering out from a heavily bearded face.

It was none other than Allan Pinkerton.

Evidently he was meant to be in disguise, Watson, much as I had been in the train from Wilmington—only less convincingly, if such a thing were possible, for he was wearing a theatrical moustache and the most ridiculous, ill-fitting wig I had ever seen upon a human head.

I stood and offered my hand, but the detective-in-disguise brushed past me without a glance. He grabbed a workman's cap from the peg and was about to leave, whence he turned back, shoved me aside, re-entered the study, leaned across the desk and spoke some few final words to Mr. Stanton in a low, imperious brogue before bringing down his fist upon the desk for emphasis.

Then he straightened up and with a stiff bow to the War Secretary— which only served to shift his wig even more askew—left the study and the house.

His abrupt, rude manner, his unsoiled "workman's uniform" and the ridiculous wig and beard—they would not have fooled a blind beggar, Watson—had so suddenly and completely smashed my boyhood image of Allan Pinkerton as the supreme manifestation of the rational detective, I found myself smiling in amusement as I entered the study.

31 Holmes would have been reading from Richard III.

Edwin M. Stanton did not, however, return my smile. Instead, he began asking questions.

I Am Interrogated

The questions began even before I had taken a seat, without preamble or courtesies, and, quite unlike my previous—and exceedingly brief—interview, Mr. Stanton put down his pen and fixed his gaze upon me as he launched into them:

Can you describe the process of making gunpowder, briefly?

Describe the layout of the powder works—how many entrances and exits? Are they gated? Are the gates manned? At all hours? Are all visitors challenged?

The hogsheads of sulphur and saltpetre imported to the works—where are they stored before the contents are processed with charcoal and turned into black powder? Is every hogshead accounted for? By whom?

How many kegs of finished powder are produced in a day? Are the kegs taken directly to the docks or stockpiled in magazines? How many magazines? Are the magazines locked and guarded? At all hours? Where might the DuPont works be corrupted—that is to say, where might a thief find them vulnerable?

Now, to the teamsters: how many wagonloads of powder are taken to the docks each day? How many kegs in each wagon? Is every wagon inspected before leaving the gates? How long is the wagon ride to the docks? Are the teamsters DuPont men or outsiders? How often do they rest their horses? Could a wagon be waylaid before reaching the docks?

Describe the process of loading the ships at the docks...

It was fortunate, Watson, that I had worked in all parts of the Éleuthèrian Mills my first week there—also that I had become accustomed to riding with the teamsters of an evening as I returned to my lodgings—for I was able to answer most of his questions with some little confidence.

Mr. Stanton listened intently to my answers, interrupting only to clarify certain points until he possessed the facts squarely in his mind. Then, when he had finished his questions, he sat back in his chair, scratching his sideburns and nodding in silent contemplation. Finally, he stopped scratching.

"It's settled. Guard!"

The man stuck his head in the door. "Sir?"

"No interruptions."

"Yes, sir."

When the door had been firmly shut again, the War Secretary's narrow eyes bore down upon me as he spoke words that provided me with the greatest shock and surprise of my young life.

Gunpowder was disappearing from the DuPont powder works, he explained, and he wanted to find out how it was being stolen and who was responsible.

And I was to be his spy.

The Mystery of the Disappearing Powder

In that year of 1864, the Éleuthèrian Mills of the DuPont Company supplied to the government of Abraham Lincoln some four million pounds of gunpowder—half of all the powder consumed by the Union armies. The balance came from three smaller mills: Hazard's in Connecticut, the Oriental in Maine and the Laflin works at Saugerties, in New York.

But not all the powder produced by these mills was reaching the supply depots of the Union armies.

Gunpowder thieves working surreptitiously and treasonously within their gates were diverting many thousands of kegs of powder each year to the armies of the Confederacy, which had few mills of its own and made up for its deficiency by smuggling foreign supplies through the Union blockade of southern ports or by stealing powder from the North.

And the largest source of the illicit powder, Edwin M. Stanton had reason to believe, was the Éleuthèrian Mills on the banks of the Brandywine.

DuPont gunpowder was, after all, of the highest quality, and Union commanders knew when the rebel soldiers were firing it. Empty DuPont kegs left behind by Confederate batteries on the battlefield had only confirmed the treachery.

When the matter had come to Mr. Stanton's attention in his first few days as War Secretary, however, he had determined the amount in question too small to pursue. It was simpler to increase production to make up for the lost kegs, he reasoned, than to risk disrupting the DuPont works by pursuing the thieves at such a delicate time in the conflict.

But now that the tide of the war had turned—Meade had repulsed Lee at Gettysburg; Sherman was marching on Atlanta; Grant had captured Vicksburg, freed Chattanooga and was closing in on Lee's Army outside Richmond—Mr. Stanton had decided it was time, as he put it to me in that uniquely American turn of phrase, "to scratch the itch."

He meant to resolve the question of the disappearing powder for all time.

You may think it inconceivable, my dear Watson, that the most powerful man in the American government would assign such a task to a youth not yet in his majority and just a month off the boat from England.

I certainly did.

But the shrewdness of Mr. Stanton's lawyerly mind became evident to me as he explained the ruthless practicality which lay behind the scheme, for it was the very improbability of my role which caused me to be useful to him.

Gunpowder, he explained, was not only dangerous to manufacture—as I well knew—but it was exceedingly dangerous to transport. Railroads would not carry it, merchant ship captains would not allow it in their holds, and no teamster would carry so much as a thimbleful in his wagon unless he was experienced in the trade.

It was, therefore, a certainty the powder was being diverted from the DuPont yards before it could be put aboard the ships on the Christiana. And yet, as I had affirmed, every hogshead of sulphur and saltpetre sent through the gates of the DuPont works—and every keg of gunpowder manufactured behind those gates—was being accounted for.

This meant a more complex scheme was in place, for powder was unquestionably disappearing—but how?

Mr. Stanton allowed with grim humour that his preferred method of dealing with the situation would have been to dispatch to Wilmington a military detachment that would arrest half the powdermen on the spot and string them up in front of the other half.

But that would not do in this case, for nothing must interrupt the business of the DuPont mills—and, anyway, there were not enough soldiers north of the Potomac to spare for such a venture. General Grant had called up every available man to serve in the field.

His second thought, he said, had been to employ an American spy—just such a course had been urged upon him by the bearded figure in the wig I had seen leaving his study, whom he identified only as "a friend of the Government"—but this would have aroused suspicions, for every able-bodied man of age in the North was now expected to be in uniform, not mixing chemicals in a laboratory on the Brandywine Creek.

And so, when word had reached him that Mycroft Holmes—saviour of the Éleuthèrian Mills and trusted custodian of young Eddie Stanton in London—had offered the services of his younger brother to the DuPont chemical laboratory, why, the role had immediately suggested itself.

No suspicion would attach itself to a young chemist from Bart's in London.

It had been necessary, of course, to evaluate my fitness for the venture. Happily, my observations on the workings of the DuPont mill in response to his barrage of questions had more than satisfied him. I was, therefore, ordered to return to Wilmington next morning, go about my business as usual and keep my head down, so to speak—but my eyes and ears open.

And when I had something to report to him, to do so at once.

Mr. Ford's Theatre

I left the Secretary's study in something of a daze, Watson. How long
I had sat there I did not know, but it could not have been as long as it
felt, for the sun was still high overhead when I took my cap, descended
the front steps and began to walk. With no appetite for food but a great
thirst for fresh air—and an afternoon free of responsibilities—I wandered
the wide boulevards and saw the sights of Washington City, replaying the
conversation with Secretary Stanton in my mind.

And working out the task before me.

My perambulations took me far that afternoon—seven miles in all, I later
calculated. I walked all the way from the prison next door to the Capitol,
where a great many Confederate prisoners were housed (disconcerting,
Watson, to see those hollow-eyed men taunted by passersby like monkeys at
the zoo), to the Old Soldier's Home north of the city, where wounded Union
soldiers recuperated and President Lincoln himself conducted business on
summer days when the fetid grounds around the Executive Mansion (and the
swarms of office seekers) made the White House unbearable.

Along the way, I stopped in at the magnificent Smithsonian
Institution to study Hare's electrical machine, bought a ticket for the
evening's performance of King Lear at Mr. Ford's Theatre and climbed
to the roof of the Naval Observatory for a glimpse of the rebel territory
across the Potomac River to the south.

It was not a little thrilling to stand on the parapet and imagine
the sights and sounds of armies clashing somewhere over the horizon,
Watson, but what positively struck me sober was much closer at hand: the
Freedman's Village that my Quaker friend in the train had been planning
to visit with her Negro companion.

The village had been built on the grounds of the family home of
Robert E. Lee—the Confederacy's leading general—after its confiscation
by the Union Army as a rebuke to Lee for siding with his home state of
Virginia (and, therefore, with the Confederacy).

And the stately, columned Lee mansion still stood there among the
jumble of whitewashed structures of the village, not a mile from President

Lincoln's bedroom.

I arrived back at Franklin Square just as the lamps were being lighted, not a little tired and very hungry, to find Ellen Stanton in the front hallway, anxiously awaiting my return.

"It is about young Eddie," she said in a confidential tone, drawing me into the dining room and shutting the door behind her. She feared, she said, the boy was mixing with a bad lot since his enlistment, for he had taken to spending nights at the Navy Yard Bridge, which, she had it from Mrs. Seward,[32] possessed a reputation among the guards for drink, and worse doings.

Would I visit Eddie at the bridge before returning to Wilmington, she wondered, wringing her hands with intense anxiety. She wanted to know what Eddie was doing there, more particularly whether he was engaged in behaviour that would reflect poorly upon her husband.

What else could I do, Watson? With the greatest enthusiasm I could muster, I said that, as it happened, Eddie had invited me to the bridge that very evening—I did not mention the hint of mischief, of course—and that I had planned to go there after attending Lear at Ford's.

Her face brightened and she thanked me profusely, but with the admonition that I not say anything to her husband. "He has so much on his mind," she explained. Then, after gripping my hand with a warmth that bespoke her womanly anxieties, she returned to her guests in the sitting room while I went upstairs to wash and change my linen.

Soon I was off again, and after a hearty dinner at a nearby tavern, I made my way to Mr. Ford's famous theatre.

I found it to be large, clean and well-lighted—nothing like the dark, malodourous playhouses I had patronized in Wilmington—and considerably less boisterous. In fact, the production, which remains one of the more sublime Lears I have ever attended, was brought to an unplanned halt only once.

It occurred late in the first act, when a tall man with a trim beard and high collar was seen entering the upstairs box. The rumour swept the hall that it was President Lincoln, and soon all eyes were fixed upon the box. The actors stopped speaking their lines and had begun making their bows

32 *Frances Seward, wife of William Seward, Secretary of State in Lincoln's cabinet.*

and curtsies while the orchestra struck up "Hail to the Chief"—only to discover the man was a Major General (Hancock, it was said[33]).

I left at the interval—American productions in those days offered patriotic readings and songs between acts, and entertainments extended late into the evening—and set out for the Navy Yard Bridge as the crowd was singing "Yankee Doodle" with fervour.

And it was well that I did, Watson, for a scandal would be avoided that might have brought no little discredit to young Eddie Stanton, and to his most powerful father.

I Make a Friend

The Navy Yard Bridge resided alongside the poorest and most dangerous section of Washington, called "the Island" in those days, being roughly a triangle bounded on one side by the Potomac River, on the second by the Eastern Branch of the Potomac and on the third by the same fetid canal that ran alongside the White House.

So poor and dangerous was the Island that I had been warned against walking there by Mr. Stanton's groomsman. No gas lamps were lighted in that quarter, for it was a squatter's camp of Negros who had escaped from the Southern states before the Freedman's Village had been established. "As desperate and dangerous a place as you'll ever find," he said, shaking his head.

But I chose to walk—I had experienced the worst London had to offer and found the journey no great hardship. One simply followed the old towpath alongside the reeking canal. Within the hour I reached the Negro metropolis of which I had been warned and found it far less of a threat than the groomsman's description.

Amid the ramshackle huts were children playing, women nursing babies, men engaged in cards and dice games, and dogs and pigs rooting through the sewer troughs. It was a desperate place—that much was true—but I found no danger there, Watson.

---

33 Unlikely: "Hancock the Superb" was serving under Grant outside Richmond.

Rather, I found a friend.

It came about in this way. I had stopped, unsure of the route to the bridge, when out of the shadows there emerged a Negro boy, perhaps ten years of age, thin as a rail and dark as the night, wearing nothing more than torn trousers held around his waist by string.

He approached cautiously, with the deference to which I still had not grown accustomed. "Lost, Marse?" his quiet voice inquired.

"Looking for the Navy Yard Bridge," said I, holding up a half-dollar coin.

His eyes fairly gleamed at the sight of the coin, and with a smile and a nod he pointed into the darkness to the north, away from the encampment. Then he dashed off so quickly, whistling a tune all the while, that I had to run to keep up.

It is a memory that still causes a catch in my throat, Watson, for in my mind I see that boy—he has a name, as you shall find—dodging carts and mules, mudholes and ruts with such sure steps that never once did he miss his footing, and it forever reminds me of how I once dashed through the streets of London, messages in hand, with the same sureness of foot, the only thought in my head being to please my brother Mycroft.

I made after the boy, and soon we arrived at the high brick wall of the Navy Yard.[34] This we followed to its end, where, up ahead in the moonlight, I could see the bridge.

It was a simple, wood-trestle affair with only a single empty wagon plodding across the Eastern Branch of the Potomac River to Maryland, where the lights of a small village twinkled. A tollgate barred the entrance, and next to this stood a guardhouse. Past the guardhouse were the stables, where a boy was brushing a horse.

There was no sentry at the tollgate, and none emerged from the guardhouse to challenge us. My young pathfinder appeared anxious and subdued as I called out several times. Finally, a shuffling was heard from within, and a soldier appeared on the porch in a disheveled state, carrying a tallow candle unsteadily in one hand and a rifle in the other.

"Who goes?" he called out in the thick voice of a man attempting to mask the effects of strong drink, pointing his rifle uncertainly into the

---

34 *The Navy Yard was Washington City's largest employer; the USS Monitor ironclad was repaired there after the "Battle of the Ironclads," March, 1862.*

night. Before I could answer, my pathfinder suddenly and without a word vanished from my side as swiftly and silently as if he had never been there.

I had turned to go after him when there came a crashing noise from behind me. The guard had fallen down the steps, his rifle clattering to the ground, the tallow candle somehow still in his hand. I rushed forward and found the guard fast asleep, the sharp stench of alcohol from his breath so thick in the air that I became momentarily lightheaded.

I removed the candle from his hand and raced up the stairs and inside the guardhouse, and what I saw by the light of the candle alarmed me considerably.

Three young men in uniform were seated around a table, each slouched in various states of incoherence and immobility. The source of their unconscious state was immediately evident: a nearly empty growler of some foul liquid clasped in the hands of the guard who appeared the most stupefied of the three.

It was young Eddie Stanton.

I pried the bottle from his fingers and tried to rouse him, but his skin was cold to the touch and his face almost as blue as his coat. Having seen my own father in the same condition—and watched my brother revive him more than once—I shouted for water in the hopes that the stable boy was at hand and began to haul young Eddie out of the chair and onto his feet.

He was fully dead weight, Watson, and not responsive to shouts or ear-pulls, so I employed a technique of Brother Mycroft: I knuckled the fingers of my free hand into Eddie's sternum with some little force. This is highly painful and quite effective, and it brought young Eddie instantly awake with a violent start just as the stable boy appeared with a bucket of water.

Together we marched Master Edwin Lamson Stanton outside onto the porch and propped him against the railing, and there followed the most unpleasant business of alternately stabbing a finger down his gullet to expel the poisons within and ladling cold water down his throat and forcing him to drink.

It was a close thing, but after some little effort he stabilized, and the other guards eventually revived themselves, in a manner of speaking. As a church bell across the river chimed one o'clock, I was much relieved to see fresh guards arrive for duty—until I realized that they appeared not at all surprised by the state of their fellow guardsmen.

Indeed, the sergeant, one Silas Cobb (another name to remember, Watson!) seemed rather crestfallen that the carousal had ended.

It was not until I showed Cobb my pass signed by Edwin M. Stanton, the father of the incapacitated young Eddie, that he shed his sullen informality and began barking orders to his men. They were quick to assume their proper duties and I was finally able to slip away on a horse provided by the stable boy, leaving the son of the most powerful man in the country stripped of his clothes and sound asleep on the porch.

Had I been granted the ability to see into the future, Watson, I might have lingered there at the bridge that night, but the only thought in my head was that the son of my host had very nearly died in a manner entirely unbecoming a soldier—and that my host's wife would want to know what I had seen.

Approaching the Negro camp, I halted near the setting of my encounter with the young pathfinder, and almost at once, as I had hoped, his now-familiar figure emerged from the shadows.

"Lost, Marse?"

"Not this time," said I, removing my cap so that he would recognize me on the horse. "But I owe you payment for taking me to the bridge." As he took the coin with some little surprise and an overabundance of gratitude (evidently he had expected I would not make good on my promise), a thought occurred to me. I patted my mount. "You can ride a horse?"

At this he laughed—he had a most infectious laugh, Watson—and nodded vigorously.

"Good. I have borrowed her from the stable boy at the bridge and am riding to Franklin Square. If you'll come with me and then return her—"

His smile disappeared and he backed away, shaking his head.

"You won't have to worry about the guards," I said, recalling how he had vanished from my side at the sight of a soldier waving a rifle. "They're in enough trouble on their own to make any for you. You'll just take her straight to the stable boy. And you'll earn this—" I pulled another coin out of my pocket and held it up. After a moment's consideration, he swung himself up behind me and we were off.

In less than a quarter-hour we had arrived at the Stanton carriage house. As I was dismounting and handing over the reins, and the dollar coin, I asked, "What is your name?"

"Abraham, Marse."

"Abraham, my name is Johnnie."

"Yes, Marse," he said in the same soft voice. And, after giving the horse her head, he was off for the Navy Yard Bridge as one born in the saddle, whistling that tune.

Abraham would become my companion and fast friend during my time in America, and I would learn something of that vast, young country with him at my side. We shared food and shelter, rode long days side by side, swam creeks and sailed rivers. There would even be times—as with you, my dear Watson—that I would put my life in his hands, and he would put his in mine.

And yet he would never call me anything but "Marse."

You May Call Me "Abe"

I spent a restless night in my bed turning over in mind what I might say to Mrs. Stanton about the events at the Navy Yard Bridge, and it was well that I did, Watson, for upon descending to the dining room next morning I found the lady waiting for me, alone but for the cook pouring coffee, an anxious look upon her face.

Her Ohio guests had yet to awaken, she said, and her husband was at the War Department telegraph office monitoring the results from the convention in Baltimore where President Lincoln had evidently been nominated to a second term.[35] When the cook had departed, she searched my face with some little anxiety. "Well? What news of Eddie?"

As you know, Watson, I am exceedingly skilled at deceiving my enemies, but not at lying to a woman in distress. I allowed that I had seen young Eddie at the bridge, and I was attempting to find my way to

---

35 *Lincoln was nominated for a second Presidential term at the National Union Convention in Baltimore on June 8th, 1864, placing this encounter early in the morning of Thursday, June 9th.*

describing the events of the evening—hesitantly and with some few words of preamble—when Mrs. Stanton caught up my wrist.

"What happened there? Be frank with me, now. I know there was bad business last night. You must tell me what it was—for my husband's sake."

I was cornered, Watson, and yet still I hesitated, for there was little I could say without getting young Eddie and the other guardsmen in trouble—very grave trouble, at that. Once again, Mrs. Stanton seemed to read my mind. "My husband will not punish anyone. I shall see to that. But you must tell me."

What else could I do? I began, slowly, to tell the story, recounting my encounter with Abraham and our unchallenged approach to the guardhouse, the guardsman's drunken stumble off the porch and Abraham's disappearance from the scene, my lifting of the candle from the guard's hand and rushing inside.

But before I could describe the scene at the table and the used-up bottle clasped in young Eddie's fingers, there came an excited shout from the front door.

"His Excellency!"

The cry was quickly taken up within the house by the girl and the cook. "His Excellency! His Excellency!"

Mrs. Stanton sprang from her seat. "The President is here!" she exclaimed, half aloud, half to herself. "I must go." And without another word she left the room.

My relief at being interrupted before getting to the most unsavoury details of the previous evening was not unmixed, Watson.

The lady would of course need to be told what happened at the bridge, but I had a train to catch for Wilmington and new responsibilities there. The only thought in my head was to get to the depot before I could be impeded by the many guards who, I imagined, accompanied the President on such excursions. I dashed upstairs, retrieved my cap and pea-jacket and swiftly descended with the expectation that at any moment I would meet a phalanx of soldiers blocking my way.

I found instead only Mrs. Stanton.

She was standing on the porch, her fingers fidgeting with her dress, watching an elegantly fitted four-wheeled barouche[36] come to a halt at the curb. I stopped several paces behind my hostess, unsure what to do while the groomsman calmed the horses and a young attendant scrambled down from the box to open the half-door to the carriage.

Then, as I watched over Mrs. Stanton's shoulder, there emerged from the carriage the longest trouser legs I had ever seen, swiftly followed by the rest of His Excellency, President Abraham Lincoln.

Standing to his full height beside the diminutive attendant, wearing a black frock coat and black waistcoat over a white shirt, he cradled a silk hat that seemed as long as the arm holding it. His face wore the same fatigued expression that I had seen in the photographs and appeared so deeply etched with lines of worry that it seemed impossible to imagine he could ever smile.

And yet his weary face did just that when his eyes lit upon Mrs. Stanton.

"Ellen!" he cried, taking the stairs two at a time with ease to greet her. She curtseyed in return, a gesture he dismissed with a wave. Then, grabbing her hand, he bent to kiss it, causing her face to turn an even brighter shade of red. "Your husband is on his way from the War Department," he said, in a voice rather more high-pitched than I had expected from such a tall frame. "He brings the latest cables from Baltimore and we are to breakfast alone in your dining room, if that suits you."

She tried to respond, but was quite literally speechless, which only caused the smile upon the President's face to widen. Then, suddenly, his attention shifted to me, for in my fascination with his expressive face and the genial familiarity it expressed towards Mrs. Stanton, I had forgotten to move out of the way of the front door.

"Now, who is this, Ellen?" he asked, nodding at me. "One of your Ohio relations?"

Yet still she could not bring herself to speak, and before I could get out any words myself, the President stepped forward and gripped my palm with the most swollen, calloused hand I have ever held—more like a smithy's glove than a hand—but possessed of a surprising strength.

"Your name, sir?" he asked.

36 *An open carriage that accommodated four passengers.*

I found myself as speechless as Mrs. Stanton, and now he laughed at me. "We'll find a name for you yet!" Then, peering down at my face with the most penetrating eyes I had ever beheld, he added, "But you may call me 'Abe'."

"I think not!" A pale, thin, dour-looking young man—I later came to know him as John Nicolay, one of President Lincoln's secretaries—was now ascending the steps. "He'll call you 'Mr. President'."

But the tall, friendly man shook his head as he held my eyes with his. "That's all right, Nicolay. He may call me by my Christian name. The newspapers call me worse!"

And with that, Abraham Lincoln released my hand, bowed to Mrs. Stanton and walked straight inside the house, ducking his head under the lintel with practiced ease.

Nicolay approached the still-speechless figure of Ellen Stanton. "There is some little business from the Baltimore convention that needs to be discussed," he said in a brisk, confidential manner. "His Excellency is to confer with the Secretary on the matter in private."

"But I have nothing prepared!" she burst out in considerable agitation.

"Coffee and bacon would suit us very well, thank you." And with that, Nicolay excused himself, brushed past me and followed the President inside. Mrs. Stanton raised her hands in exasperation and dashed after him, and soon her voice could be heard calling for the cook, the maid and the servant girl.

I took my leave, walking down the steps and past the carriage, its horses twitching away flies as the driver and the groomsman smoked cigarettes and chatted in a most idle fashion, whence I made for the train depot, still marveling at the astonishing grip of that rough, swollen hand.

I have no recollection of the train ride back to Wilmington, Watson. My mind—as you might imagine—was rather preoccupied.

In all my days running messages down the corridors of White Hall, I had never so much as glimpsed a Minister. Their precious, exalted persons were hidden away behind doors I was never allowed even to set my eyes upon. Yet here, in America, I had shaken the hand of the President.

It seemed inconceivable, and yet it had certainly not been a dream.

And while I pretend no gift of prophecy, Watson, my mind did wonder that I—just four weeks off the boat from Liverpool—had encountered this most famous, this most powerful, this most human figure with not so much as a soldier or marine or guardsman in sight.

Why, not even the famous Allan Pinkerton—the flush-faced and bewigged Allan Pinkerton—had been by his side! Only a punctilious secretary, an idle driver and his boy.

"Doctor! Doctor!"

I awoke with a start, blinking my eyes against the bright sunlight streaming in through the window of the railway carriage. The train to Eastbourne had come to a sudden halt, the door to the corridor was opened, and a hand was shaking me roughly by the shoulder.

"You *are* a doctor, are you not?"

It was the genial ticket inspector from Victoria Station, except now his bearded face was a mask of horror and his voice trembled with emotion.

"Yes," said I, pushing away the hand. "Yes, I am Doctor Watson. John H. Watson, M.D. What is the meaning of this?"

"Thank God!" The man closed the door. "Saw the stethoscope sticking out of your bag at Victoria—thought you must be a doctor. Name's MacManus sir."

"MacManus, eh? What station is this? It can't be Eastbourne."

"No, it's Berwick, sir. And we need your help. It's a terrible state, sir. Terrible!"

"What is it? There's been an accident?"

Now fully awake, I sprang to my feet—the instinct to rush to the injured never leaves a doctor—but the excited ticket inspector pushed me back against the cushions and pointed to the next compartment.

"Murder, sir," he hissed. "*There has been a murder in this train.*"

END OF PART I

II.

MURDER ON THE SOUTH COAST RAILWAY

"There is a strong family resemblance about misdeeds, and if you have all the details of a thousand at your finger ends, it is odd if you can't unravel the thousand and first."

—Sherlock Holmes
A Study in Scarlet

THE SOUTH DOWNS

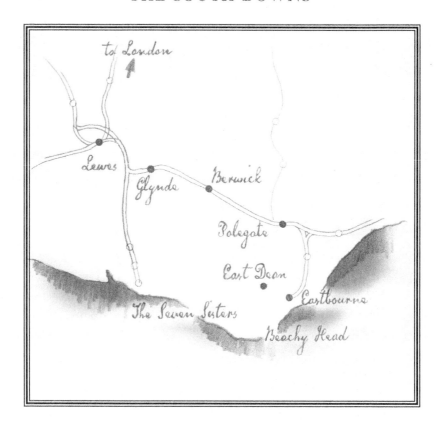

Chapter One

A DEATH IN THE TRAIN

"Murder!" I cried.

"Yes sir, murder sir, in this very train!" The ticket inspector's bearded face was horribly contorted, the eyes wide and frightened. "It's a dead body, sir! There's blood everywhere!" He pointed wildly next door. "Morrison found the lad dead! Poor old Ivan. He's in a terrible state. Come sir!"

He rushed out into the corridor and I followed him to the next compartment, where it was immediately evident a crime of great violence had been committed, and not very many minutes previously.

Fresh blood was everywhere—on the floor, the cushions, the table and the curtains. I hesitated to enter, so thick was the blood upon the floor, but MacManus pulled me inside and shut the door behind us, and so I found myself face to face with the victim.

He was a young man of perhaps twenty-five, dressed in civilian clothes but with no shoes upon his stockinged feet, and he sat slumped against the armrest in the far corner by the window, his head bent down upon on his chest like a puppet whose strings have been cut. Upon the lifeless face was an expression of shock and surprise, with wide-open eyes and clenched jaw, and his skin was white as a sheet from the loss of blood.

I drew the curtain across the window, for bystanders were now gaping from the station platform, then rolled back my right shirt-cuff and gently lifted the head with my left hand while probing the neck with my right for a pulse, if any trace could be felt.

What I felt instead was the death wound.

Somewhat startled, I withdrew my hand and carefully tilted the head further back, now perceiving a half-inch stab wound in the throat where blood still glistened and the white cartilage was visible within.

The carotid artery had been entirely severed.

"Is the poor lad dead?" The voice came from behind the ticket inspector, and glancing behind me I beheld an old, thin figure in the uniform of a railway guard.[37] He had been seated in the opposite corner of the compartment, as far away from the body as possible, and he was rocking back and forth and fanning himself with his hat. His face was nearly as white as the dead man's.

"I'm afraid so," said I, closing the eyelids and muttering a prayer for the victim's soul.

"Dear God!" the old guard cried. "Dear God, what shall be done!"

"Steady on, Ivan," said the ticket inspector, patting the man's shoulder. Then he turned to me. "That's Ivan Morrison. He found the poor lad."

"He seems quite undone," I said quietly. "Can you remove him to the station while I attend the body?"

"Ivan!" said MacManus brightly, taking the man's arm. "What say we go inside and clean that blood off of you?"

"No!" cried the guard, shaking off the offending hand. "This is my train! I have thirteen years on the South Coast Line, and I ain't leaving now! Who is this fellow to tell me I should be off?"

"I am a doctor, sir."

The old guard seemed surprised by this. "You got here right quick for a doctor."

"He was in the compartment next door, Ivan. Lucky thing, too."

"Yes, and I must attend the body. Just draw those curtains shut beside you." Passengers from the other carriages were gathering now to peer in the

---

37 In England, train conductors are called 'guards' from the stagecoach days.

corridor window. The old guard did as I instructed, then, glancing at the body once more, resumed rocking in his seat.

"Dear God, MacManus! Yesterday it was vandals on the line, and now a murder!"

"This fellow is of no use here," said I to the ticket inspector, for I did not have my friend Sherlock Holmes's ability to shut out distractions. "Can he not be moved?"

"I ain't leaving, sir!"

"How about a touch from your flask, Ivan?" MacManus said with a wink at me.

"Now there's a thought," said the old guard, his features pallid in the dim light. "Fetch it from my locker in the van,[38] like a good lad."

"Right, Ivan. You sit tight."

"And bring the newspapers from my compartment," said I. "That way we might cover this floor. And get this train moving so I can open the curtains and get some light in here!"

"Right, you are, Doctor." MacManus swung open the door to the platform with some difficulty against the crowd. "Oi! Back!"

"He's a good lad," said the old guard as the door slammed shut. "Helps me out at every turn, he does. Blind as a bat, or he'd be in France, fighting like the rest of the lads. Happy to have him, though. Too many women ticket inspectors, if you ask me. Be glad to see 'em go when the boys come home..."

While the old man prattled away, I removed the lampshade to bring some light to the dim carriage, and at once discovered the reason for the dead man's civilian dress.

Clasped in the fingers of his right hand were a pair of gold-rimmed spectacles, evidently the only object in the room that had not been splashed with blood, and I saw that the fingers in which they were clasped—the middle and forefinger—had been fused together by an accident of some kind. I unclasped the spectacles from the red and scabby fingers, wrapped them in my handkerchief and placed them in my watch pocket for later inspection.

---

38 The brake van housed the train guards and supplied braking to the entire train.

Stepping back from the body, I now noticed a gash in the seat cushion at the very height the blade would have entered the man's neck. Probing the slit in the cloth with my finger, I discovered it went all the way to the wooden back. It was evident, therefore, that the weapon had pinned the body upright while the thief went about his business. Once the weapon was removed, the blood was released and the body slumped over in its current position against the armrest.

But what type of weapon could have done this? The gash in the cushion was too thick for a knife. Scissors, perhaps? I would have to wait until we had pulled away from the station to draw back the curtains and examine it in the light. Whatever the weapon, it had been brutally effective, and a most vicious attack.

Most vicious and cruel, indeed.

MacManus now returned with newspapers and the flask. He handed the flask to his grateful comrade, then together we laid the papers across the seat cushions and upon the floor. When this was done, we felt a vibration of the carriage.

"We're getting up steam now. Be pulling out soon." He pointed to the stockinged feet of the dead man. "What do you make o' that, guv?"

"I make nothing of it except that whoever killed the poor man also stole his shoes."

A thought appeared to cross MacManus's mind.

"What is it?" I asked.

"I remember him!" he said, snapping his fingers. "Had his feet resting on the seat cushion. I told him to get 'em off, but he didn't take too kindly to that. I noticed the shoes, though. Nice-looking shoes, they were. Real leather! French, from the looks of 'em."

"And stolen by whomever did this. Was he seated with anyone?"

"Bloke with a ticket to Polegate." His eyes widened. "Ivan! That must have been our jumper!"

"Eh?" said the old guard, who had been preoccupied with his flask.

"At the Selmeston curve! We were in the guard van, and Ivan looks out the window and says, 'We got a jumper!' Right he was. The bloke hit the ground rolling and came up running, eh Ivan?"

"Oh. Aye!"

The ticket inspector checked his watch. "Beg pardon, guv. I'm to signal the driver. We're making for Polegate."

"Polegate!" said I. "This train isn't going on to Eastbourne?"

"Not now sir, no sir. The nearest constabulary is at Polegate."

"But I have urgent business to attend!"

"More urgent than that dead fellow there?" the old guard cried, considerably revived by his drink.

"It may well be, as a matter of fact," said I.

"Where you making for, guv?" said MacManus.

"East Dean."

"You're in luck, then. Easy cab ride from Polegate. Five miles up the Jevington Road, and that's a good road, that is. The military keeps it tidy to get their pilots to the Airship Station."[39]

"Aye," said the old guard. "And when you get to East Dean you'll say 'ullo to Jack at the Tiger for me!"

"I have rather more pressing business than saying hello to the landlord for you." I was bitterly disappointed and not a little anxious about this turn of events, but I comforted myself that Sherlock Holmes was in good hands by now thanks to my wires from London. "Still, I suppose it will have to do. As soon as we leave the platform, I can open the curtains and get enough light to finish my examination."

"Right you are, sir." MacManus opened the door to the corridor and herded the onlookers off the carriage. "Last stop, Polegate! Oi, back!" I heard him shout.

Soon the whistle sounded, and the train jolted on its way.

When we had left the platform well behind, I drew back the curtains, filling the compartment with sunlight. Even to my hardened eyes this brought fresh horror to the bloody scene, but I steeled myself and set to work. I began by unbuttoning the dead man's shirt collar.

"Dear God. Dear God!" the guard cried, losing his composure at the sight of the bare chest. After several more exclamations in this vein, I

---

39 *The Polegate Royal Naval Airship Station, from which airships patrolled the southern coast of England.*

thought to distract him with questions, as I had watched Sherlock Holmes do in similar situations.

"How long to Polegate?" I asked as I continued my examination of the body.

"Dear God! The poor thing!"

"I repeat, sir, how long to Polegate?"

"Eight minutes from Berwick," said he by rote.

"May I ask how you discovered the body?"

"Saw the door open! Found him sitting that way, bent over. Dear God—"

"You entered from the corridor?"

"Aye."

"Why did you inspect the train at Berwick?"

"On account of the jumper. MacManus said we ought to 'ave a look. I didn't think nothing of it. We get jumpers all the time." He took another drink from the flask.

"And he jumped from this carriage?

"Aye."

"Did you get a good look at him?"

"Not much to see. Ordinary bloke," he said vaguely. "One minute he was there, next minute he was gone."

I paused from my task and assessed the proximity of the door to the body. "So, after stabbing this poor fellow and robbing him, he fled by the corridor and jumped from the carriage. That seems clear enough. Did you move anything or touch anything in here after you found the body?"

"By the mass, no! What do you take me for? A sneak thief?"

"I only wished to know if anything had been altered."

"Not a button on his jacket, sir."

"Anything like this ever occurred before?"

"No sir! I've been thirteen years on this line, and we've had babies born and soldiers get into rows and old men just close their eyes and die, but never nothing like this."

The effect of this conversation was as I had hoped, for it allowed me to finish my examination somewhat undisturbed, although I struggled to make sense of what the bright sunlight had brought to the scene in the carriage.

The surprise upon the dead man's face suggested a sudden attack, and purple bruising of the skin surrounding the entry wound in the neck clearly indicated the weapon had possessed handles.

That would mean scissors, most likely—but what scissors would have been long enough, with a sharp enough point to impale the man against the cushion? I could only think of the embroidery scissors Margaret once used in her needlework. They were long-bladed and sharply pointed, with rather ornate handles.

I dismissed this notion—it seemed too fantastic—until the voice of my old friend came to me as I considered what I saw in that carriage:

"Eliminate all other possibilities, Watson, and one arrives at the truth, no matter how improbable!"

The words brought a new light to the scene before me.

Accepting the deduction that embroidery scissors had been the murder weapon, the inference suddenly became very clear to me: this had been an unplanned crime—a burst of passion by an individual with embroidery scissors in his coat, most likely attracted to the shoes, which appeared to have been of considerable value.

The further inference was clear: a tradesman had done the deed.

I gazed at the body with growing confidence in my reasoning, whence I was struck by its peculiar position upon the cushion. Shifting the dead man's torso slightly to one side—which was quite difficult to do without smearing blood upon myself—I discovered an object lodged beneath the thigh.

It was a bronze Mary Box[40], and in excellent condition.

"Had a Mary Box, did he?" the old guard said as I held it to the light of the window. "He was a Tommy, then! Poor lad. Got in a row, I'll wager..."

I nodded my agreement, but upon opening the engraved lid I found to my surprise a pack of Gauloises cigarettes and three franc-notes inside. I said nothing as the guard went on about the "Poor Tommy," and simply shut the lid and slipped the box into my coat pocket.

---

40 A bronze or silver cigarette case distributed to British troops in France at Christmastime, 1914. They contained cigarettes, a square of chocolate, and a Christmas card from Princess Mary.

My inspection was now complete—and just in time, for the steam whistle blew and the carriage slowed as Polegate station came into view. I drew the curtains shut as we approached the platform, for it was crowded with people. The train lurched to a halt, and after some little wait there came an authoritative rap at door, which was then opened by a portly, white-bearded sergeant. He peered inside, removed his hat at the sight of the deceased and stepped carefully within, followed by MacManus, who shut the door behind them both.

"Right. Hullo! Trouble again, Ivan?" the sergeant said to the flustered guard, who was slipping the flask inside his jacket. "Yesterday it's vandals on the line, today it's a murder in the carriage?"

"Aye, sir."

The sergeant turned to me with difficulty in the crowded compartment. "You must be the doctor. Pleased to meet you. Sergeant Vincent Furnier."

"John H. Watson, M.D."

The sergeant's face changed in an instant from bland officiousness to a look of astonishment. "*Doctor* Watson?"

I half-bowed and allowed a slight smile at the deference in his voice.

"Why, this is an honour indeed, sir. Indeed! Have you loungers any idea who you've been hosting here? Say hullo to Doctor Watson of Sherlock Holmes fame!"

The sergeant's introduction did, I admit, give me some little pleasure, but at the same time he could read my disinclination to chat.

"I'm sorry, Doctor. MacManus here tells me you have a pressing engagement in East Dean. Have you had time to inspect the body?"

"I have." I carefully handed the Mary Box by its corners. "This was caught under his left thigh when he slumped over. The thief missed it."

"Ah, then the boy was a Tommy."

"No. You'll find the contents are French, not English." I handed him the spectacles, which I had been also able to examine in the sunlight before reaching Polegate. "And these possess the mark of a French optician—there," said I, pointing at the inscription.

He frowned. "No blood on the specs—you didn't wipe them, certainly."

"No."

"A bit odd, don't you think? Everything else here seems pretty well drenched."

"It was an arterial hemorrhage," said I. "Rather like a fire hose. It could have easily missed the spectacles."

"Ah, no doubt that explains it. I say—his *shoes* were nicked?"

"Yes, and his purse. MacManus says the shoes were quite fancy."

"That's right," said the ticket inspector.

"Very good, Doctor, very good. Our men will take over from here. The coroner is on his way, so if you'll proceed to the station-master's office, the inspector will take your statement and you can be on your way."

"Of course."

"But you'll return for the inquest?"

"Most certainly."

"Thank you, sir. Most kind of you. We are shorthanded these days. You being here is a most fortunate occurrence. Most fortunate indeed."

"May I get my things from my carriage first?"

"By all means, Doctor. Just use the corridor please. The platform is a fright." He touched his cap and opened the door for me. As I departed, I heard him instructing the old guard to leave the carriage, but the poor man's pants were stuck to the cushions by the dried blood, and the fellow had relapsed into moaning.

It was good to be released from that stuffy death chamber, and I took several deep breaths of fresh air in the corridor. Upon entering my own compartment, however, I immediately sensed something was amiss.

My valise was on the floor—I had almost certainly left it on the seat—and my walking stick was on the seat, not up in the rack. My Burberry was still on the hook, but upon thrusting my hand into the inner pocket, I discovered my purse was missing.

Then, glancing around the compartment, I realized something else was missing, too—and of far greater importance than my purse: *the manuscript of Sherlock Holmes.*

Chapter Two

A CONFRONTATION

I was beside myself.

I frantically inspected my valise and turned the compartment upside down, but Holmes's typewritten manuscript on "The Art and Science of Rational Deduction" was nowhere to be found.

I cudgeled my brains to think of what could have happened to it.

I had fallen asleep reading it, that much was certain, but I had no memory of holding it in my hands when I was shaken awake by the ticket inspector, nor when I followed him into the corridor. It must have been removed from my compartment while I was asleep—when my purse was also stolen—and almost certainly by the same thief who killed the poor young Frenchman next door.

I sat on the cushions and berated myself. The great Dr. Watson! Of Sherlock Holmes fame! So careless with a document entrusted to him that he has lost it in the train!

I went on in this way for how long I don't recall, until a familiar hand was felt upon my shoulder and a familiar voice came to my ear.

"*Self-pity will not return the manuscript, Doctor,*" I heard the voice of Sherlock Holmes saying. "*Observe and reflect.*"

I conscientiously began a detailed and systematic inspection of the compartment for any signs of the missing papers, turning over the cushions, looking underneath the seats, scrutinizing the overhead racks and even examining the corridor the length of the carriage. When this turned up nothing, I emptied the entire contents of my valise upon the seat cushions. There were Holmes's packet with the map and timetable, my old syringe in its morocco case, and a bottle of carbolic and one of morphia in their velvet pouches.

Also, and to my great surprise, I found my pistol was still wrapped in my linens.

It seemed incomprehensible that a thief would overlook a pistol but take a manuscript of no possible value to anyone else but me, but there it was.

Reluctantly, I reassembled my things, put on my coat and hat, and with my valise securely in one hand and my stick in the other, departed the carriage.

Outside, the day was warm and still. Clouds of steam rolled down from the engine's chimney and settled lazily upon the platform, which was now a hive of activity. Curious spectators tried to get past the constables ringing the carriage while disembarked passengers impatient to give their statements milled about, and fresh ticket holders had formed a long queue at the booking office inquiring for the next train to London.

Sergeant Furnier hailed me and led me to the station-master's office, where I wrote out my statement while the tearoom next door was turned into an investigation chamber. When I had finished, I was admitted and found a comfortable room with a fireplace and two men already seated at a deal table. One was a constable who was to take notes. The other was a tall, thin, taciturn man, introduced to me as Inspector Cummings of the South Coast Railway. He had been investigating the previous day's incident of vandalism on the line when MacManus brought news of the murder, and he was now charged with its investigation.

Upon the table before the inspector lay the Mary Box, the spectacles and the contents of the victim's pockets, which included a piece of licorice, a box of Swan Vestas[41] and a return-ticket to Lewes. The constable, I could not help but notice, stared at my card with wide eyes, while the Inspector studiously ignored it, preferring to examine the items upon the table.

Sergeant Furnier excused himself. "I must greet the coroner, but I'll be back. Meantime, you're in good hands with Inspector Cummings."

And with that, he touched his cap and closed the door behind him.

It quickly became apparent, however, that I was not at all in good hands with Inspector Cummings.

About the same age as Sherlock Holmes in his prime and possessed of the same gaunt appearance—even down to the hawk-like nose and jutting chin of the great detective—Cumming's attempt to imitate my friend's cerebral bearing by effecting a haughty demeanor and never letting a long-stemmed pipe leave either his hand or his clenched teeth was quite familiar to me. I had encountered many such imposters over the years. By adopting the trappings and the suits of Sherlock Holmes's dress and mannerisms, they thought they could achieve the same magnificent results. But without Holmes's mastery of the fundamental elements of detection and his encyclopedic knowledge of the history of crime, they only ever achieved disappointment and dejection, and it showed in their work.

In Cummings's case, I spotted the warnings signs immediately. His welcome was little more than a slight nod of the head, and he glanced at my statement with a raised eyebrow and a cynical curl of the lip.

"Dr. Watson, is it?" said he, finally.

"John H. Watson, MD—retired."

"Yes, the sergeant gave you quite an exalted status. '*Associate of the great Sherlock Holmes*' et cetera, et cetera."

"I was indeed associated with Mr. Holmes for almost two decades—"

"Yes, his fame has reached us even here, thank you. I have only one or two questions."

"Of course."

Just then the charwoman entered with a tray of tea and biscuits, and Cummings tapped the table impatiently with his pipe while she served us. When she had finally departed, he blew a cloud of blue smoke to the ceiling reflectively.

---

41 *A brand of matches.*

"Now, Doctor, you speculate the victim was a Frenchman—"

"I deduce that, yes."

"Until we can identify him, of course, your *deduction* remains a speculation."

"Perhaps, but—"

"And you insist upon this even though the victim was found with a Mary Box upon his person?"

"A Mary Box containing Gauloises cigarettes and several French francs, yes."

"But a British soldier could have acquired those items in France, surely."

"Our boys weren't paid in francs and they did not gallivant to Paris to buy spectacles."

"Then how do you explain the injury to his fingers, if not from the battlefield?"

"It is common enough among field hands working with tractors. I have read the case studies in the medical journals. The mufflers burn very hot—"

"You put the time of death at 10:35 o'clock," Cummings said, abruptly changing the subject. "How do you reckon that, Doctor?"

"The train departed Haywards Heath at 10:30 and arrived at Lewes at 10:38. A return ticket to Lewes was found in the deceased's pocket. He must have been murdered after Hayward Heath, but prior to our arrival at Lewes."

"How do you know the ticket was not a plant?"

"The murderer was seen jumping from the train shortly after Lewes."

"By whom?"

"By the guards, from the van."

"But how do the guards know it was the murderer?"

"He jumped from the carriage in which the murder took place, and the door from the corridor to the victim's compartment in that carriage was found open. *That* is how they know."

Cummings again changed the subject.

"You say he was killed by a knife of some sort?"

"No. I make very clear it was *not* a knife. The wound at the point of entry was more of a gash, inconsistent with a knife—"

"Could it not have been a knife with a dull blade?"

"Yes, but that would not explain the ability to pierce the neck and penetrate the seat cushion. Then there were the bruises on the neck, which are consistent with a weapon possessing handles. I think you are much more likely to find the weapon was a—"

"There's no need to speculate on the weapon. We will find it."

"I believe I can tell you precisely the type of weapon you are looking for, if you will only listen!"

He glanced at the constable with a smirking smile. "Something covered in blood, I should think, wouldn't you?"

With that remark, I had had enough.

I rose from my chair and gathered my coat and hat.

"A friend requires my urgent assistance, and you have delayed me long enough with this childish interrogation. You have my statement. I leave you to it."

At that moment, the sergeant entered. Seeing me standing, with my coat on and valise in hand, his face clouded. "What is it, Doctor?"

"I'm leaving. I am not accustomed to having my professional opinions contested in so offensive a manner."

"Please, Doctor," said he in a soothing manner, looking daggers at the inspector. "I would greatly appreciate it if you would stay and continue with your findings."

"Not if I am to be subjected to these affronts." I put on my hat.

"You'll have no more trouble, Dr. Watson, I assure you."

"You're right, I will not. Good day."

"Doctor!" Sergeant Furnier stood between me and the door with a beseeching look upon his face. "Please. We have a dead man in the train and there is panic in the station. They think a lunatic is escaped and on the loose here, and I've got only three spare men to look for him. I need you to tell us who it is we should be looking for."

I glanced from the sergeant to the inspector, who would not meet my eyes, and to the constable, whose pen was poised to take down my words.

"Very well, then. The man you are looking for is between forty and forty-five years of age, is left-handed, is of average height and build, and hails from Polegate." I picked up my valise, nodded at the sergeant, strode to the door and delivered my parting shot.

"And he is very likely a tailor."

With that, I left the room.

Polegate station was now a madhouse. Regular service had been cancelled and the booking office was overflowing with angry ticket holders. Reporters from the Eastbourne newspapers had arrived and were confronting passengers from "The Polegate Murder Train," as it was already being called.

Outside, the platform was swarming with all manner of spectators trying to make their way around the cordon of constables to view the "Death Carriage." There were no cabs at the taxi rank, and I had just set down my valise to await the next when Sergeant Furnier caught up to me, an apologetic look upon his face.

"The Inspector's behaviour was uncalled for, Dr. Watson. Please accept my humblest apologies."

I shrugged my shoulders and glanced at my watch. "I know the type, Sergeant. As soon as a cab comes, I must be on my way."

"Of course. But please, Dr. Watson. I need to understand your theory. You say the murderer was left-handed. I assume that is because of the nature of the entry wound? Good. But why do you say he was of average height and weight? And how do you determine his age?"

The sergeant's manner was earnest, and his supplications were, I admit, pleasing. I dropped my icy guard.

"His age is self-evident," said I, feeling within me something of the deductive powers of Sherlock Holmes as I had seen him at the peak of his art. "Any younger than forty and he would be fighting in France—"

"Of course!"

"Yet he could not be too old to jump from a train with the agility described by the guard. Hence, he must be in his early forties."

"Why, that seems clear!" the sergeant exclaimed, with the deference of a student to his teacher. "But why of average height and weight?"

"Because both the guard and the ticket inspector saw him jump, yet neither man could describe him. Nothing distinctive stood out in their minds. He must, therefore, be of average height and weight."

"Well, I never." The sergeant shook his head. "And why do you say he was a local man, from Polegate—and a tailor?"

Here I felt the full weight of Holmes's reasoning at work within me.

"By the surprise upon the dead man's face, it is evident the attack came from an unexpected quarter—and what would be less expected than an unassuming tailor, using the only weapon he had at hand? As I tried to tell that bore of a detective, it was *not* a knife that left behind that wound. It was a pair of scissors with long, pointed blades and a thick handle. Embroidery scissors. My wife has a pair. But what man would carry embroidery scissors in a train? Someone who works with them in the course of his trade. It must be a tailor."

"I see it!"

"Speculative to be sure, but the missing shoes confirm to my mind that the murderer was attracted by the man's clothing. A tailor would know their value and find them easy enough to sell in the course of his business. If a tailor, well, he would have a shop nearby. Berwick is a hamlet, too small for a tailor to ply his trade. It must be Polegate—and the ticket inspector said the murderer had a ticket to Polegate."

"Brilliant! Why, you might have been Mr. Sherlock Holmes himself the way you worked that out."

I felt no little pride at the sergeant's kind words, but now the conversation turned in a less comfortable direction.

"I have one more question, Doctor. You said your own purse was stolen. Nothing else? Nothing from your kit—no drugs or...?"

"No, nothing from my kit," said I, with some hesitation. "But, as you ask, a manuscript I had been reading was also taken, although it was of no great importance."

The sergeant scratched his chin. "If it was of no great importance, why do you imagine it was taken?"

"I cannot think, except that the thief grabbed whatever was at hand—"

"But did not bother with your luggage?"

"My valise is rather conspicuous."

"And yet he stole a pair of shoes, which are also rather conspicuous."

"Well, he would not have had much time to inspect my valise to determine its value. He would have had to enter my compartment—"

"While this French lad was pinned against the seat, yes." There was a subtle trace of condescension in the sergeant's voice. "And, yet, instead of taking a valise full of medicine, he took a manuscript of *no great importance*." The sergeant studied my face. "Perhaps you can tell me about this manuscript of such little value that it was snatched from your hands by a murderer while you slept?"

"Well, if you must know, it was a manuscript from Mr. Sherlock Holmes."

The sergeant did not appear at all surprised. "Another story, was it?"

"Why, yes, but a very personal story. It would be of no value to anyone else."

"I see. May I ask where Mr. Holmes is keeping himself these days?"

"Quite nearby, at East Dean. I am on my way there directly."

This was met with a confused smile on the sergeant's part.

"Surely Mr. Holmes moved away!"

"I hardly think so," said I, but coldness gripped me as he returned my gaze with a blank look. "I received a letter from him this very morning."

Just then, a cab pulled up, depositing a passenger. The sergeant approached the driver's open window.

"Tony—does Mr. Sherlock Holmes still live out at Went Hill?"

"You know he doesn't, Vince," said the cabman. "Moved out after the French set up training on Frost Hill across the Birling Gap."

The sergeant nodded. "That's as I recalled."

"But I have a note from Holmes calling me to that address!" I pulled out the foolscap and waved it before them, but they merely shrugged, and their bewildered faces shook me to the core. After the loss of the manuscript and the unspeakable tragedy in the train—now this.

I scarcely knew what to say.

The sergeant put a kindly hand upon my shoulder. "Now that's just like Mr. Holmes, isn't it? *Vincent,* he'd tell me, whenever I tried to worm out of him what he was thinking, *the only secret is one that is never shared.*" He turned to the cabby. "Tony, this is Dr. Watson of Sherlock Holmes fame! He's lost his purse, but you'll take him where he needs to go? Doctor, please give Mr. Holmes our best when you find him. Tell him we miss him 'round here. And thank you. It was most kind of you to delay your journey to accommodate us."

He touched his cap and walked back to the station while the cabman eyed me with suspicion.

"Lost your purse?"

"Yes, but I'll be able to pay you when we arrive at Went Hill."

"At the home of Mr. Sherlock Holmes?"

"Yes."

"Mr. Sherlock Holmes who moved away?"

"I never heard of that," said I. "When was this?"

"When the Army set up camp on Frost Hill, like I told the sergeant. Be right with you milord," he said to a well-dressed man standing impatiently nearby.

"But that's impossible! This note arrived from Holmes just today—"

"Well it didn't come from these parts, guv. When the French started their practice guns blazing day and night, Mr. Holmes packed up and moved. Bad for the bees, he says."

"For the bees?"

The cabby nodded.

"What absolute bosh. I never heard such a thing."

He eyed me narrowly. "Drove Mr. Holmes to the train myself, didn't I, guv? Now, if I may attend to this other gentleman—?"

"You go right ahead, Tony, I'll get to Went Hill without you."

"Give my regards to Mr. Holmes when you find him!" he said insolently before speeding away with his new passenger as I considered my options.

With my purse gone, however, these were few.

It was then that Providence at last favoured me in the form of MacManus, the ticket inspector, who came rushing from the station to greet me like a long-lost friend.

"Dr. Watson! There you are—may I have a word?" He guided me away from the cab rank behind a water fountain. "I wanted to thank you for your help today. Without you, I don't know what we'd have done."

"Not at all," said I, somewhat distractedly, for I was still considering my options. "It was the least I could do."

MacManus glanced about furtively as he slipped from his jacket a folded document. "Wasn't able to get this back to you, until now."

My heart leapt as I recognized the familiar sheaf of onionskin paper. "The manuscript!" I cried, snatching it from his hand. "You found it!"

The dark melancholy which had oppressed my mind since leaving the train was lifted. In an instant, a day that had grown dark indeed was light again.

"Yes. Sorry, guv—couldn't get it to you 'til I finished up with the sergeant."

"I can scarcely believe my eyes! But how did you find it? *Where* did you find it?"

"On the floor in your compartment. At Lewes. While you were sleeping."

"I had been out all night on a case," I said sheepishly.

"Well, the pages were everywhere. I picked 'em up fast as I could before the whistle blew. Jumped in the guard van and we were off. Then that bad business with the Frenchman happened, and it slipped my mind."

"I can't thank you enough."

"There might be a page or two missing," he said apologetically. "They were all about the carriage, and when the door was opened, well, the wind carried a few pages under the train before I could grab 'em."

My heart sank at this, but as I read the dejection upon MacManus's face, I reasoned that a few missing pages were a small price to pay for having the manuscript back in my possession.

"That's all right, my good man. Better most than none at all. Again, sir, I really must thank you."

He touched his cap as the whistle sounded. "Least I could do after all you did for us. Must be off now, we're getting up a special for London."

A thought now sprang to my mind.

"Can you first show me the road to East Dean?" I turned over the manuscript and handed him my pen. "Such a beautiful day, I have decided to walk it."

It was true. I was determined to reach Holmes's cottage even if it meant walking. Despite the testimony of both the cabby and the sergeant, I found it hard to credit the idea that Holmes no longer resided in East Dean. I had in my pocket the desperate note calling me to his aid, and in my valise was the map with his cottage so precisely circled. Who but Holmes could have sent them?

MacManus nodded, took the pen and quickly drew a simple map. "It's a good road, like I said. You won't have any problem!"

The whistle sounded again, and he quickly handed back paper and pen and moved off, with, I noticed, something of a limp in his gait.

I glanced at my watch. It was close on one o'clock.

I was nearly two hours behind schedule, but I was confident the Eastbourne constabulary would have attended to Holmes by now, and my spirits had been considerably revived by the return of Holmes's manuscript. My body, too, felt quite refreshed from the charwoman's tea and scones, and my stamina was certainly up to the task, for even in my advanced years I walked to my London club almost every day, in bad weather and blackouts.

I filled my flask with water from the fountain, folded Holmes's manuscript and placed it safely in the innermost pocket of my coat, rested the strap of my valise comfortably upon my shoulder, set my face to the southern hills and began my walk to the cottage of Mr. Sherlock Holmes.

The ticket inspector's words were quickly proven correct.

As the rough cobblestones of the Polegate High Street gave way to the smooth tarmac of the Jevington Road, I found the gentle uphill grade made for easy walking. Aside from the occasional military lorry or farmer's tractor, there was almost no traffic, and the tall hedgerows scented the air with the pleasant aroma of sweetly rotting grape clusters and offered a cooling shade. The only inconvenience proved to be the muck-covered crossings where cows or sheep were led to pasture.

I decided the truculent cabman had done me a favour. A long walk seemed just what I needed after the excitement of the morning, and I began turning over in my mind this idea that Sherlock Holmes had moved away from Went Hill.

Certainly, it was not out of character for my friend to act in such a decisive and secretive fashion, even if the notion that it had been out of concern for his bees seemed utterly absurd to me. But what purpose did it serve to call me to Went Hill if he had, in fact, moved away?

The deception, I decided, was more likely being practiced upon the locals.

But towards what end?

The answer, I realized, might be found in Holmes's manuscript. I removed it from my coat and unfolded it as I walked. Some of the pages were dirty and others out of order, but to my considerable relief the missing pages numbered only three, and they were in sequence, just after the very point at which I had fallen asleep. It appeared they had concerned young Holmes's mundane daily activities at the DuPont powder works, and little else.

I placed the portion of the manuscript I had already read in my valise to make handling the rest more manageable. Then, with a good two hours of easy walking to occupy my feet, and an occasional halt for a drink of water from my flask and a bit of scone while a farmer and his weary team passed me on the narrow road, I was soon once again absorbed in the remarkable narrative of Mr. Sherlock Holmes.

Chapter Three

THE MANUSCRIPT OF MR. SHERLOCK HOLMES, CONTINUED. . .

And in this way my responsibilities in the laboratory grew, almost as swiftly as my admiration for Monsieur Vernet's skills of observation and deduction.

It helped considerably that I seemed to need no sleep in those days— my irregular habits in that regard were even more pronounced back then, Watson—and after working sunup to sunset six days of the week, most Saturday evenings found me attending theatre productions, some as far away as Baltimore. During the week, however, it was quite enough to retire to my rooms and fall asleep reading a book from Mr. Stanton's library after playing my fiddle for my landlady and her other boarders in the Shipley Avenue parlour.

Of the combustible Denny Boyle, I saw very little, for my work in the laboratory kept me away from the powdermen, a fact which considerably hindered my efforts to ferret out the perpetrators of the gunpowder thefts.

It did not help matters that upon those not infrequent occasions when I *did* attempt to trace the thieves, I brought an amateurish and unsystematic method to my actions—also, that the thieves possessed an uncanny ability to cover their tracks, despite the fact that nobody at the works but General Henry had knowledge of my clandestine visits. These took place after-hours when the weather seemed propitious for thieves moving kegs off the property—which is to say, when the sky was overcast, with no moon—and yet I failed to discover anything untoward in any quarter of the mills.

Even the magazines, from which it seemed evident the thieves must be stealing the kegs, proved quiet upon these visits.

Indeed, the only lesson a half-dozen such outings had taught me was that the night watchmen were exceedingly good at their task, for I had found myself spending the majority of my after-hours within the gates dodging their lanterns.

There was no doubt Denny Boyle was at the heart of the matter—that kegs could disappear without his knowledge seemed impossible—but never could I find a link between him and the thefts. Not a man dared speak ill of him, no matter how subtle my inquiry.

Soon my evening forays declined in number as my days at the chemical bench grew longer. We had begun to formulate working strains of smokeless powder, and the afternoon experiments at the testing range had become more serious and intensive.

It was not until I applied the signal precept of Monsieur Vernet—eliminate all other possible explanations, and that which remains *must* be the truth—that I was finally able to place my hand upon a thread that would ultimately unravel the entire mystery of the disappearing gunpowder.

WHAT SUNSHINE BILLY WAS CATCHING

It was a hot afternoon late in August, my third month in the Brandywine Valley. The DuPont works had only recently returned to its normal state after yet another disruption from one of the panics caused when Confederate soldiers—usually Mosby's men[42]—splashed across a ford somewhere on the Potomac to throw a scare into the citizens of Washington

---

42 *Confederate cavalry under the command of John S. Mosby, who was called "The Grey Ghost" in Northern newspapers. They operated on the Virginia Neck and conducted guerilla raids around Washington City.*

City.

I was returning to the laboratory from the testing range when I spotted Sunshine Billy and his dog—you may remember their appearance, Watson, my first day at the mill with General Henry—searching the pools and eddies for a place to drop his fishing line.

I had seen Billy and his dog many times in the months since, of course, but my responsibilities at the laboratory had always taken precedence over my curiousity as to his fishing abilities. On a whim, however, I decided that afternoon to introduce myself and perhaps learn his secrets.

His reaction, Watson, was extraordinary.

As I approached, he gathered up his wicker basket, whistled for his dog and before I could introduce myself, the pair had fled upstream and disappeared over the rocky outcrop to the north of the Éleuthèrian Mills, where his family's cooperage turned out kegs for the DuPont Company.

I returned to the laboratory and mused upon this strange behaviour while writing up my notes from the afternoon's experiments. After quickly completing that task, I determined to set down my observations of Sunshine Billy in a systematic fashion, rather along the lines that Monsieur would have demanded of me if the subject had been an errant chemical reaction and not a mysterious fisherman.

These observations proved remarkably few, however.

Billy was young and in robust health, although evidently too young to be apprenticed in the family cooperage. He owned a single pair of brown trousers and a ragged shirt of spun cotton and always wore a straw hat upon his head. He carried the same pole and the same wicker basket each time he appeared, and he moved frequently from place to place in the course of the afternoon.

Always in the afternoon. And only in the sunshine.

Any hint of a cloud in the sky—even if the clouds rolled across late in the afternoon of an otherwise glorious day—would send him and his dog back up the rocky cliffs.

And, speaking of the dog, Watson, it rarely strayed from Billy's side despite the numerous rabbits and squirrels in those woods—yet its sense of smell was exceedingly acute for a hound that refused to chase rabbits.

She could sniff my presence well before ever I appeared at the bridge, and she always kept a sharp eye upon me as I crossed, even though I never came anywhere near the pair.

But it was the fish caught by Sunshine Billy that puzzled me the most. He rarely seemed to catch any.

I recalled an old couplet the hopeful men on the Thames used to sing as they cast for eels alongside me on wet, overcast days: *"With southern wind and cloudy sky, the fisherman his luck may try!"*

If the empty wicker basket of Sunshine Billy was any indication, that sage old verse seemed as applicable on the Brandywine as it had been on the Thames, where I had learned by hard experience that fish didn't much bite in the sunshine.

As I glanced over my notes, it seemed suddenly quite evident that in some fashion I was unable to readily deduce, Sunshine Billy played a role in the gunpowder thefts.

But what role?

If he was signaling to the powdermen across the creek, it was not evident from his appearance, which never varied. The straw hat always remained upon his head, the basket always hung upon his left side and the pole was always carried in his right hand. Nor did his aimless meanderings appear to favour any particular spot along the creek.

I walked to my rooms that evening, turning over these observations— and others less relevant—but to no avail. It was not until after supper, while scraping away at my fiddle upon the sleeping porch, that my observations yielded deductions worth examining.

I had not consciously set about to imitate Monsieur Vernet and his flute-playing *pensées*, Watson, but as I played the melody I had heard Abraham whistling the evening of our first encounter and watched the soothing colours rising from the strings of my violin, I found my mind floating away from the calculations of smoke volumes and propulsion rates with which it was normally occupied to the image of Sunshine Billy walking with his dog in his casual but alert fashion along the banks of the Brandywine.

And I recalled a conversation I once had with Brother Mycroft which made their entire enterprise known to me.

It was upon the evening I had fled Bart's chemical laboratory in shame, when Mycroft had confided in me the full scope of our father's villainy towards our mother. I had asked him how it happened that our father was never at home when the debt collector came banging on the door, leaving her to that man's evil intents.

"Did you never wonder, Johnnie," he had said, "why our father never bought matches when the match boy appeared at our door? No? Well that was no match seller, Johnnie—that was a *lookout*. He wasn't selling matches. He was the signal for father to clear out."

At that moment, of course, I understood that Sunshine Billy was no fisherman—as I suspected—but neither was he engaged in sophisticated communication with the powder thieves.

His very *appearance* was the signal for them to act.

One week later, on a warm, sultry Saturday—the first sunny day following a week of poor weather—we had finished our afternoon experiments at the testing ground, and I was returning to the laboratory when I spotted Billy's dog eying me warily as I crossed the bridge.

It was their first appearance since my new insight, and I resolved to test my theory.

I gave no indication as to my intent, of course. I made my way to the laboratory, as usual, and wrote up my notes, as usual. I said goodnight to Monsieur and left the powder works as I always did—by the path through the woods to the front gate. There, my clothes were inspected for powder, as they always were, and I hitched a ride with a teamster to the docks, as I often did.

I arrived at my lodgings on Shipley Avenue for dinner and afterwards played a few tunes for my landlady and the other guests while they drank their coffee. Then I retired to my rooms. When the sharp click of the latchkey in the front door sounded at ten o'clock, I was prepared. Wearing my dark pea-jacket and moccasins, I let myself down into the alley from my sleeping porch and made my way back to the DuPont works on foot.

I went not down the Barley Mill Road to the front gate, however, but by the private carriageway to General Henry's office. There he handed me a wooden key to the magazine, whence I descended the hillside steps into the powder works. All was quiet but for the soft murmur of the creek waters and the rustle of night creatures in the brush. I moved slowly and cautiously so as not to add to the sounds and I kept well in the shadows, for it was a cloudless night and the moon was rising.

As I say, Watson, this was not the first time I had kept such a vigil, but it was the first time under a clear sky. Within a few minutes I found myself at the magazine, and I was surprised and not a little disappointed to find nothing untoward.

The doors were latched shut, and no noises could be heard from within.

After some indecision I settled in the shadow of a nearby tree to ponder my next move while keeping out of the view of the watchmen— except that no watchman could be seen! Not a single lamp flashed among the trees, and not another step but my own was heard for the next two hours, even as I shifted my position so as to stay hidden when the moon rose high and bright overhead.

I was, as you can imagine, Watson, becoming not a little discouraged that my new theory had failed to yield a positive result. But then, suddenly my patience was richly rewarded.

A discordant sound came to my ears—not, however, from the vicinity of the magazine, but from a building closer to the roll mill. Indistinct at first, I came to discern a kind of muffled drumming and soon perceived it was coming from the packing house, where empty kegs were packed with finished powder and sealed before being taken to the magazine.

With careful maneuvering, I was in view of the doorway. And there, illuminated by the silver light of the risen moon, I saw the familiar form of Mr. Denny Boyle, his back to me, watching the activity within.

After some little time, Boyle disappeared inside, and I retreated to the shadow of the roll mill, where I could watch the packing house entrance unobserved. Very soon Boyle's figure reappeared, only now he was carrying powder kegs—25-pounders they looked to be, one under each arm. He was followed by two other men doing the same.

They walked slowly across my field of vision, past the roll mill and out of sight to the banks of the creek behind me.

The next sound I heard was of kegs splashing in the water, and after some few moments the quiet of the night was broken by the barking of a dog from the far side of the creek. It was a familiar bark, and as the three figures reappeared, scurrying empty-handed across my line of sight on their return to the packing house, all was clear to me.

I was seated outside Mr. Stanton's study the next day.

On my previous visits to Franklin Square, Watson, I had been kept waiting as long as three hours before being admitted—and even then, my time with the War Secretary was frequently interrupted by grim-faced messengers with urgent telegraphs and letters, and long waits while he crafted his replies.

But on this third day of September, of 1864, I felt something very different in the air as soon as I entered the house.

The guard—normally a stone-faced fellow—grinned as I announced myself and waved me to a seat in the library, where the other fellows waiting their appointments no longer possessed the solemn faces of men facing an inquisition. The messengers, too, were smiling as they dashed into and out of Mr. Stanton's study.

An even bigger surprise came when I was called into the War Secretary's office, for I was greeted at the door by Mr. Stanton himself— his hand extended, a broad smile upon his face.

"Take a seat! Take a seat!" said he in a booming voice, waving me to a chair. "You have something to share, by the looks of General Henry's wire. "*When sorrows come, they come not single spies but in battalions,*' eh? Well, I reckon good news comes likewise!"

I took my seat, puzzling over this display of good humour, when another messenger was admitted. In contrast to the strict formality exhibited on my previous visits, the War Secretary grabbed the envelope out of his hand, ripped it open and smiled as he studied it, his eyebrows arched high above the rims of his spectacles.

"Good news is general across the land!" he erupted. "Sherman entered Atlanta at daylight. Get this to Nicolay for the President," he barked, fairly pushing the fellow out the door. Then he strode behind his desk and gazed out the window at the Executive Mansion, which stood tall and white across the park. "Until this moment I didn't see it. I didn't see the math. But now...I see it now. *I see the math.*"

I didn't understand what he meant by "the math," Watson (I later came to understand he had been speaking of the upcoming election and "the math" required to assure the re-election of President Lincoln), but I knew enough to wait patiently as he contemplated this evidently important business.

Finally, the clock upon the mantel chimed noon and broke his reverie. "Forgive my confidences," he said, turning to face me. "If I seem somewhat overfamiliar to you, it is because of that business at the Navy Yard Bridge with my son."

He twisted around a picture frame that stood upon his desk. It was a photograph of young Eddie as a boy, holding a pinwheel, and my host's manner was transformed from ebullient War Minister to that of an anxious father.

"Mrs. Stanton told me everything that happened that night."

Removing his spectacles, he polished them thoughtfully with his handkerchief, exposing eyes that revealed the debilitating effects of the strains his enormous responsibilities had placed upon him.

"If I may speak frankly, I would admit that Mrs. Stanton is more, let us say, *discerning* of my son's inclinations since he came under the influence of those guards at the bridge, and it was well that she pressed you to go there. They proved a bad lot. A bad lot. I could have had them all strung up, of course, but that would have broken my promise to Mrs. Stanton, who is more forgiving than I." He smiled grimly. "I sent them to Grant instead. As for Eddie, well, I will find something else for him."

He returned the picture frame to its place and replaced his spectacles upon his nose. Holding up the cable from General Henry, his face returned to its familiar steely gaze.

"Now, to the gunpowder thieves," he said, unrolling a map of the Delaware Basin across his desk. "You have unmasked them, it would appear?"

I nodded and proceeded to explain precisely how Boyle and his men sent the kegs floating across the Brandywine to a shallow sandbar just above a dam, where they were detected by the powder-sniffing dog of Sunshine Billy and retrieved by its master, who delivered them into the hands of an accomplice with a boat to be taken across the Delaware River to the New Jersey side.

"The perfidy! The *perfidy!*" Edwin M. Stanton glanced up from the map and fixed his terrible glare upon me. "And you have no doubts about what you saw? None?" His brow furrowed and he pounded the desk so hard the photograph of young Eddie fell over with a clatter. "The *perfidy* of it!"

I realize now, Watson—in the clarity of the years since those fast-moving days in America—that Mr. Stanton was not so much astounded by the scheme as he was embarrassed by its simplicity.

"Very clever. D--nably clever." He scratched his whiskers and considered the entire scheme for a moment. "You saw no watchmen inside the gates? They must be in league. One of them, anyway." He cast a sideways glance at me. "You say General Henry appeared surprised and upset? Of course he was. He's a good man. A Union man."

His voice regained a glint of his earlier merriment as another thought came to mind. "You have made a fool of Allan Pinkerton, it may interest you to know."

That *did* interest me, Watson, and greatly, too.

Ellen Stanton, you see, had been keeping me apprised of the blustering Scotsman's unceasing efforts to have me replaced at the powder works with one of his own agents—but I said nothing in the presence of the War Secretary. He seemed to read something of my true thoughts, however, for a smile crept to his face, and he regarded me with some little amusement.

"Your brother Mycroft underestimated you. '*A little seasoning is all he wants,*' he wrote me." Mr. Stanton fairly chuckled. "*A little seasoning,* indeed!"

When his eyes returned to the map, however, his smile quickly vanished and once more he began tracing his finger across it. "You say there's no indication where it goes after crossing the Delaware, eh? I see a dozen creeks in this region of New Jersey. They could be taking it anywhere." He removed his spectacles and bent his nose inches from the map, moving his finger hither and yon. Then he looked up, his eyes opened wide.

"Why, they cross New Jersey to the sea!" He bent once more to the map and ran his finger on a line across that state. "The telegraph road runs straight across the Pine Barrens to the Atlantic! *There!*"

His finger had come to rest upon a narrow stretch of the Atlantic coast marked *Cape Island*.[43]

There was a sparkle in his eye as he glanced up from the map, his finger tapping the point reflectively. "Mr. Boyle and his accomplices will keep, for now. There must be no disruption at the powder works until the war ends. But it might do well for you to see how far you can trace these thieves across New Jersey."

As he rolled up the map, he studied the photograph of young Eddie on his desk and another one of those scheming thoughts seemed to have entered his mind. "You'll need a sturdy accomplice, I should think, to help you." He glanced from the photograph to my face. "I have just the one."

It was evident whom he had in mind, Watson, and my heart sank.

In Memory of Kenneth and Daniel

It was a dark, windswept evening of an unusually warm day in October, almost one month after that meeting in Mr. Stanton's study, during what the Americans call an Indian Summer and we call a Saint Luke's—a warm turn of the weather after the first hard frost. My companion had jumped down from my shoulders after peering into the greasy window of a whitewashed shanty on a marshy inlet of Cape Island, New Jersey. A massive grin was spread across his face.

He nodded silently. There was no question about it.

After three weeks of the most cautious and careful movement tracing the marks of the powder thieves' wagon wheels across the sandy soil of the telegraph road through the Pine Barrens of southern New Jersey, we had found the terminus of their dangerous cargo.

It was an undertaker's shack, filled with coffins.

---

43 *Now Cape May.*

But they were not coffins lined with fabric and holding preserved corpses, Watson. They were coffins lined with hay holding 25-pound DuPont Company powder kegs, ready to be loaded onto a fast packet ship and sent on their way south to Bobby Lee's Army.

We began our return to Wilmington that very moment.

It was two days later, and the sky was threatening. We were barely halfway across the Pine Barrens to Wilmington, moving by foot, and our eyes scanned the woods for a concealed spot to bed down for the night. We always stayed well off the public road at night, for we made a rather conspicuous pair in that hardscrabble territory of New Jersey—I in moccasins borrowed from the DuPont works for just such a purpose, and my companion, a barefooted black-skinned former slave named Abraham, in his bare feet.

You see, Watson, I had not taken "young Eddie" along on this venture, after all.

As I had feared, Mr. Stanton did indeed suggest I take his son with me. But with a bit of help from my secret ally in the Stanton household, I managed to convince him it would be best to bring Abraham instead and to employ him at the du Pont stables so we could slip away together—well, let me finish one story at a time, Watson, and get back to that evening in the Pine Barrens.

We were two days out of Cape Island, as I say, and in search of shelter when the stars stopped shining and the wind turned, blowing sharp from the northeast. This was an ominous sign. As I had learned in our previous journey across these barrens, the fierce storms they called "nor'easters" brought high winds and torrential rain.

Soon enough a streak of lightning lit up the woods around us, followed by a booming thunderclap. Abraham tugged at my sleeve and pointed to a small settlement we had never noticed. It was perhaps three hundred yards off the telegraph road, deep in the pine woods. We made a run for it as lightning crashed all about us, illuminating a barn, a corn crib, a pigpen and a smithy, until we found ourselves at a small cabin with a single light in the window.

A lone horse hitched to a nearby tree was rearing and pulling against its lead, its eyes wide in terror. I was about to knock when the cabin door suddenly burst open and a hatless man with the large shoulders and muscular arms of one who worked a forge emerged, halting abruptly at the sight of us.

"Who the devil are you?"

"Heading to Glassboro, sir, for work!" I said, having been cautioned by General Henry himself never to mention the name of the DuPont Company in this region.

"Well you missed the Glassboro road!" the man shouted as the wind picked up. "That your boy?"

"No, sir. He works with me."

"Can't speak for himself?"

"No, sir. Mute." Abraham was by no means mute, Watson, but in America, in those days, trouble for the Negro could come from any quarter.

He eyed Abraham skeptically. "If he's a runaway, he'll be tracked down."

"He's no runaway," said I. This was met with a raised brow and a brief inspection, circling Abraham as if studying a horse. "You'll find no markings, sir. He was born free."

In fact, the brand with which Abraham had been marked—a most ugly, most disfiguring "W"—was on his thigh, hidden beneath his trousers. But before our inquisitor could get to that, lightning struck a tree near the barn and sent the horse into hysterical bucking. The man uttered an oath—the terror upon his face was striking, Watson—and he shoved us to the door.

"Get inside! It's fifteen miles to Glassboro. You'll have supper and sleep in the haymow. Get!" And, shielding his face from the slashing rain, he made for the terrified horse while Abraham and I stepped inside and shut the door behind us.

The cabin was pleasantly warm and dry, and the welcome scent of home cooking met our noses. A slight, stoop-shouldered woman was filling plates of game and potatoes at the wood stove. She froze at the sight of us and seemed to examine us as if we were ghosts.

"Who are you?" Her voice was soft, almost too soft to hear, and possessed of an unspeakable sadness. And though she could not have been older than forty years of age by her eyes, her wizened face appeared as ancient as the cabin—the hair shot with grey and held in a bun and the taut, sunburned face bespeaking years of labour out of doors.

"Beg your pardon, ma'am," I said. "Labourers from Wilmington. On our way to Glassboro."

"You'll be staying the night?"

"Your husband offered the haymow, and we would not refuse it."

"You have eaten supper?"

"No ma'am."

"Sit yourselves down. It's rabbit and potato."

I saw there were four place settings upon the table. "You are expecting other guests, ma'am?"

This was not the innocent question I hoped it sounded, Watson. I had seen enough evidence in the yard to suspect we had found ourselves in the cabin of an accomplice to the powder thieves, and I expected an answer that would confirm my deductions, for I had become quite full of my capabilities in that department.

To my surprise, the woman burst into tears, grabbed my wrist and unleashed a sudden torrent of words in such a jumbled manner of speech, and so interrupted by sobbing, that I could not hope to express them as she did.

The extra places were for her boys, she said, twin boys who had volunteered for the Union Army the day they came of age and hadn't been heard of since the battle in the Wilderness. Letters to their congressman, senator and the War Department inquiring of the twins' whereabouts had gone unanswered.

But they would come home one day, she was certain. And every Sunday, she set two extra places at the table for them.

At that moment the door shot open, bringing wind and rain and the master of the house. The woman let go of my wrist—her fingers had left white imprints, so tightly had she held it—and her husband glared at her as he shook off his waterproof and hung it upon the peg beside the fireplace.

"It's a nor'easter, woman. You have enough for these boys? All right then."

But we did not take her sons' places at the table, Watson. The woman set out fresh plates for us, and those for her twin boys would remain untouched throughout the meal.

Then, without further ado, we ate.

Or, rather, *we* ate while our host devoured his food with the grace and manners of a starved dog. He picked out the best meat for himself, sopped up the gravy from the communal bowl with a hunk of black bread and poured his own liquor from a bottle kept at his elbow, all the while eying Abraham suspiciously and barking commands at his poor wife.

At times, I noticed, his gaze would fall upon the two empty plates, and his face would cloud until he returned to his food. When he had more or less finished, he offered forth a series of loud belches, evidently to prepare himself for dessert, then directed his voice at me. "Where you from? Not around here by the sound of it."

"Delaware now. England before."

"And what kind of work did you and your boy expect to find at Glassboro?"

I shrugged my shoulders. "I've heard there is plenty of work and good wages there."

"Well you hear a lot of things that ain't true," he snarled, his eyes fixed on the two empty places set for dinner. "You hear Grant's men cheered him at the Wilderness, but you never hear about the boys who died there." On this last he brought the bottle down with such ferocity I thought it would break, and his wife began to sob noiselessly at her place.

"Hush, woman." He refilled his glass and drank it with a single gulp.

Had I been older and considerably wiser, Watson, I would have deduced by this outburst the entire scope of the man's betrayal and spent the remainder of the meal in silent contemplation of how to extract myself and Abraham from that cabin without alerting him to our true mission.

But I did not.

As I say, I had become rather full of my abilities in observation and deduction from my months with Monsieur Vernet, and with the special breed of arrogance and lack of foresight only youth possesses, I decided now to employ them—my previous inquiry of his wife having failed in that regard. "You distill your own excellent spirits, I observe." said I, nodding at the bottle.

"And what makes you observe that, mister glass-man?" A sudden trembling of his hand made itself visible in the liquid as he held his glass, poised to drink.

"Well, of course the bottle at your elbow is typically used for medicines. That suggests a homemade liquid, and it would have been difficult not to identify the scent of sour mash in the air when we passed the barn."

"And how might you know what sour mash smells like?" There was something akin to fear in his voice now.

"My father was in the trade," I said, shrugging my shoulders. "I tended his pots as a lad." My father had been in no such trade, of course—he merely drank whatever liquor he could lay his hands on—but I thought it might cause our host to drop his guard. "Perhaps we could tend your pots and do any odd work you might have around here."

"I have no work to spare for other hands."

"You would have considerably more time for repairing the wagons."

As soon as these words were out of my mouth, Watson, I saw they had hit their mark. Our host set down his glass, for the trembling in the liquid had become quite pronounced.

"And how would you know that I repair wagons here, mister glass-man?"

"The iron hoops in the yard." I did not mention the size of the barn, where he evidently kept more horses than necessary for his own use, nor the bucket of grease that could only have been meant for wagons which he did not possess. It was not necessary to display ALL my cards, Watson, for I already had my answer: the blood drained from his face as he poured out the last of the bottle and drank it in one gulp.

"Get that pie now, woman," he croaked. Then, at me: "You'll find, mister glass-man, I take work any way I get it in these parts. I repair a lot o' wagons that break down on the telegraph road, and I make my own whiskey, you're right enough about that. But I don't share it with strangers."

His wife set out the pie and he ate his slice in three bites, then pushed back from the table. "I'll ready the barn. You boys eat your pie."

We did as he instructed—it was exceedingly delicious pie—and I thanked our browbeaten hostess, but her mind was elsewhere as she cleared the plates. After some little time when our host had not returned, I asked her kindly, "What are their names, madam?"

"Kenneth and Daniel," she blurted out, tears filling her eyes.

"We will ask for them, ma'am."

"Thank you."

The door opened and our host entered, the worry and distrust upon his face replaced by a hint of smugness. "Barn's ready. You'll spend the night there."

"The storm is past," said I, pointing at the window, where the rain had stopped. "We'll move on if you can spare a horse."

"You won't be moving anywhere. This is just a calm. Be raining again something fierce soon enough. You'll get settled in the barn while you can."

He was right about the storm, of course. The wind soon shifted, and by the time we were inside the barn and settling down in the straw bed of the haymow, the sky had opened up again.

"Hear that?" said our host as the rain beat down with the sound of horses galloping across the wooden planks above our heads. "At daybreak, you'll have breakfast and be on your way to Glassboro." Then, before taking with him the oil lamp hanging from a beam and descending to the barn below, he delivered a stern warning. "*Don't* strike a match in here, or you'll set the place afire."

And with that, the haymow was in complete darkness.

But not in complete silence, Watson. To the sound of howling wind and thundering rain there was soon added the thin brass tinkle of a bridle being removed from a wall and the thump of a horse stirring in its stall. Then came the creaking of the barn door being opened and shut, and the sudden clank of a bolt sliding into place.

"He's locked us in," I hissed. "We must not lose a moment."

But Abraham was already feeling his way to the hay door. Throwing it open, we could see by the flashes of lightning the figure of our host, mounted and riding hard for the telegraph road in a driving rain.

We jumped down to the muddy ground and came to our feet as the rider turned onto the road, east, in the direction of Cape Island, where a certain undertaker's cottage filled with a quantity of caskets stuffed with kegs of DuPont powder awaited transport to the battlefields of Richmond.

He was lashing his horse for speed.

Abraham and I circled the barn in slashing rain and unbolted the door. Making our way inside, we inspected the stalls for a suitable mare, and I understood at once our host's extreme reaction to the lightning that had flashed near his barn as we first arrived upon his doorstep—and his warning against using matches inside that dry space.

Inside the first stall, on beds of straw, lay a quantity of 25-pound DuPont powder kegs. In addition to his role in mending the powder thieves' wagons, our host evidently offered his barn as a waystation on the journey to Cape Island.

A stray match would not merely have touched off a fire, Watson. It would have flattened the barn, the cottage and a good many trees for half a mile around—and neither Abraham nor I would have been seen again.

We took the calmest of the three horses and were soon on the same road as our host, but riding in much the opposite direction: west, for Wilmington. So bad was the weather and so churned up the road that it would take us two full days to reach the Delaware River. Once there, we traded the horse for a ferry ride and, after a roundabout walk, arrived at the stately home of General Henry du Pont in the late hours of a Saturday night, in a rather bedraggled state.

Next morning we were in the train bound for Washington City.

I Cross a Line

By noon I was in the study of Edwin M. Stanton, with Abraham this time, tracing upon the map the route of the powder thieves across the pine barrens of New Jersey to the undertaker's shack at Cape Island. Mr. Stanton gave me his full attention, asked his usual measure of sharp questions and then pondered my answers for some little time while scratching his whiskers and nodding.

"Clever," said he, finally. "Very clever. I thank you both. This will keep, for now. You'll return to Wilmington, as if nothing happened. *Nothing.* Understood? Both of you? Good."

Before he could call for the guard, however, I begged the favour of a private word.

When Abraham had left the room, I broached the question—which I had expected Mr. Stanton would not refuse—of whether it would be possible to reward Abraham for his assistance in tracking the gunpowder thieves by providing his mother in the Island with a proper shack, in the place of the leaky shelter that kept her wet and miserable all year round.

To my delight, Mr. Stanton readily agreed—in fact, he would send a carpenter over that very day. Then, to my surprise, he asked whether there was anything he could do for *me.*

I was at a loss for words, Watson. Never had I expected anything more than a "thank you'" from the War Secretary. As I reflected upon his question, however, and the sincere manner in which it had been expressed, a thought came to mind. It was a ticklish business, I knew, but he awaited my response with such friendly anticipation that before I could consider whether it was an appropriate subject to broach, the words had left my mouth.

It would have been far better had they stayed in!

In very brief terms—and in a most exceedingly polite manner, with all proper terms of respect—I described for the War Secretary the uncertain fate of the twin sons of the treasonous wagon-mender in the pine barrens of New Jersey and wondered if it might not be feasible to determine what had become of the two brothers, Kenneth and Daniel, in the Wilderness. For the sake of their poor, browbeaten mother?

It did not take long to have my answer.

And while I had heard some rather volcanic eruptions coming from behind the closed door of that study on previous visits to the Franklin Square, Watson, the tongue-lashing I received that day in the confined space of that small, cramped room was more fierce, more fiery, more potent than anything I had ever experienced.

You might have thought I had requested a private lunch with Jefferson Davis.

"What the deuce does it matter to a citizen of Great Britain what

has become of the sons of an American traitor? Why on this earth would
a boy in your position expect the Secretary of War of the United States of
America to waste even a single telegraph flimsy for the peace of mind of
a traitor's wife? Who the devil are you to dare SUGGEST such a thing?"
Etc. etc.

When he had finished—it seemed like an hour, but it lasted no more
than a minute—Mr. Stanton glared at me while he recovered his breath,
those steely eyes narrowed to pinpoints behind the spectacles.

Then, with a shout of "Guard!" I was dismissed.

I departed the study in a daze. A funereal hush had descended upon
the occupants of the library, and you might have thought I had contracted
a highly contagious jungle fever by the way they buried their heads in
their newspapers and avoided my eyes. But curled lips told me that they
not only had heard, they had all very much enjoyed the volcanic eruption
of Mount Stanton at my expense.

All except Abraham, who stood holding out my cap and pea-jacket
on the expectation that we would leave at once for the next train to
Wilmington. These I gratefully accepted, and we scurried out of the
library and were about to exit the front door when a voice called after us.

It was the voice of Ellen Stanton. She had emerged from the dining
room to ask if we would join her for lunch.

I hesitated, Watson. My only thought was to flee that house. But of
course I could not refuse her kindness, and so we turned back and ate
our lunch with her. The conversation was entirely inconsequential—
the household preparations for the new holiday of Thanksgiving to be
celebrated shortly, as I recall—and I left the house in some perplexity
as to why she had insisted we join her.

It was Brother Mycroft who explained her kind intercession—in his
rooms in Pall Mall some months later—after I had told him the story
of the traitorous wagon-mender, the twin brothers and the eruption of
Mount Stanton.

"Why, it's quite obvious," he had said with the patient wisdom of an
adult. "She overheard her husband's outburst, she understood how deeply
shaken you would be and she meant to soothe you."

And looking back on it, she had done exactly that, Watson.

But it was more than that kind gesture from Ellen Stanton which I have cherished ever since. It was the tenderness she always showed Abraham in our time at Franklin Square. She treated him more like the son of one of the Ohio friends she was forever hosting than the mere acquaintance of a houseguest. Indeed, it was she who had coached me in how to approach her husband about taking Abraham along on the powder-thieves journey rather than young Eddie, after I had fretted over the command in her presence.

"My husband is a man who rarely hears the truth," she had said, gently and with her characteristic kindness of expression, when I had finished enumerating with some frankness the many weaknesses of the War Secretary's son, as I saw them. "I would tell him precisely what you just told me." Then she had patted my hand. "Mr. Stanton will understand."

And he *did,* Watson—in fact, he went so far as to procure Abraham work at the du Pont family stables for the duration of our efforts so that we could disappear from the powder works together when need be!

In any case, after our soothing lunch with Mrs. Stanton, we caught the next train from Washington and arrived back in Wilmington at dusk. Abraham returned to his loft at the du Pont stables, I to my rooms in Shipley Avenue. As for the War Secretary, I never dared to cross that invisible line again.

But to this day I wonder what became of those two boys from New Jersey, and I feel some little guilt as to what might have become of their mother.

She deserved a kinder fate.

THE GREAT 'MANCIPATOR

As absentminded as I have become in my declining years, Watson, certain dates spring naturally to mind. I shall forever recall the 8th of November, 1864, for it was election day in America—a most important day to that still-young country.

And no less important to the future of young Johnnie Holmes.

The DuPont works had been closed for several days to allow the men to vote, and I had returned to Washington City with Abraham, for he was homesick to see his mother and it was not a good idea for a young Negro (actually, *any* Negro) to travel alone in America in those days.

Abraham's mother was overjoyed by his arrival and so proud of the tidy cabin erected for her by the War Department carpenters that she insisted we stay for a pig roast being held in anticipation of the election outcome. (Imagine, Watson, if you can, the notion that all one's freedoms might vanish because of an election in which you played no part—astounding, is it not?)

It seemed to me an unnecessary burden to place upon this woman whose cupboard possessed barely sufficient food to supply the vermin that ran underfoot, but of course I accepted. And I was forever glad I did, for it was on that evening that I became a witness to the most remarkable display of—well, I can think of no other way to describe it, Watson, than in the poetry of scripture: of faith and hope and love.

A fire pit had been prepared, and a single, lean pig was produced—with not a garnish in sight. But as the savory scent of roasting pork began to spread throughout the neighboring shacks, the root cellars were scoured and pots began to boil. By the time the dinner bell sounded, every portion of that pig had been cooked—ribs, knuckles, cheeks, tongue—and makeshift tables groaned with dishes of potatoes, corn, yams, peas, beans, cornbread, biscuits and gravy, as well as jugs of cider and other, harder spirits to wash it all down.

"And they did all eat, and were filled," as the Gospel writer said. And to my young eyes, what occurred that night was no less a miracle than the feeding of the five thousand on the shores of Galilee.

But it was not merely the abundance of food that made an impression that evening, Watson. It was the gratitude, expressed continually and without reservation, through prayer. Prayers—spoken, shouted, and sung—were given for *everything* that night: for the pig and the potatoes, the beets and bread; for the rain that poured down, quite hard, throughout the evening and for the fruits of the earth it would yield; for Sherman taking Atlanta and for Grant pressing

Richmond.

A prayer of gratitude was even spoken for the safe return to the Island of young Abraham and his white friend.

But above all else—above all things, Watson—thanks were given for Freedom. And throughout the evening fervent prayers were sung and shouted that Father Abraham, the man they called "the Great 'Mancipator," would be victorious.

And for much of our time there it appeared that prayer would be answered.

But as the rain continued, biting and cold, and darkness descended upon the Island, rumours began to arrive thick and fast from all quarters that the state of New Jersey had gone to McClellan.[44] How this news managed to reach the Island, Watson, I could not deduce at the time, for no horse messengers dared venture there.

But reach the Island it did, and the adults spoke of this surprising turn in low, anxious voices. Soon even the children caught the subdued spirit of their elders and stopped playing games. When Abraham and I departed for Franklin Square (we were expected to be at the DuPont works next day), we left behind many grim, anxious faces.

They would not be that way for long, however!

We had reached the government district and were making our way past the stump of the Washington Monument when a great shout went up from the anxious crowds filling the streets that New York State was reported good for Lincoln, and his reelection was assured. Caps and gloves filled the air, and huzzahs were shouted.

Then came the thunder of booming guns firing in salute from the forts on the outskirts of the city, and in an instant the streets became impassible. We could do nothing but join the serenaders singing "John Brown's Body" and follow the mass moving inexorably towards the gates of the White House. Once inside the gates we were swept along the curving driveway directly underneath the looming mansion, where lights began to appear in the upper windows, and the singing around us turned into a sustained cheer.

I had not a thought in my mind about what was to come, Watson—I

---

44 *General George C. McClellan, who had failed Lincoln so often at crucial moments in command of the Northern armies, was the Democratic candidate for President.*

was, of course, entirely unfamiliar with the custom of election evenings in America (or in Washington City, anyway)—but the cheers grew louder and shouts of "SPEECH!" filled the air until suddenly, and with no fanfare, there appeared in the upper window a familiar silhouette.

And pandemonium erupted.

I cannot recall a single word spoken by Abraham Lincoln from that window, Watson—his remarks were brief and modest, spoken in a thankful and hopeful tone, with not a single warlike word—but I vividly remember his face, for it was illuminated by a candle which he was holding to illuminate the pages in his hand.

And it was *not* the face of a triumphant victor, as those around me had evidently expected.

It was, rather, a thin and tired face, deeply lined and worn down—very much the face of the man I had seen striding up the steps of the Stanton house before catching sight of Ellen Stanton and smiling—and when he had finished reading his pages, he simply removed his spectacles, gave thanks to the Almighty and retreated from the window.

The crowd, I must admit, seemed crestfallen. A half-hearted "three cheers" were given for Old Abe, then all began moving *en masse* in the direction of Secretary Seward's residence across the park, evidently in search of a more warlike speech.

But as Abraham and I veered away towards Franklin Square, I

discovered there was at least one among the listeners who had not been disappointed, for I could hear the soft voice of my friend, awestruck and disbelieving.

"*Marse Abraham*," he repeated in wonder, over and over. "*Marse Abraham*."

We found the Stanton house to be eerily quiet.

Mr. Stanton was at the War Department telegraph office gathering election results, the girl told us, and Mrs. Stanton had gone to the White House to keep the President's wife, Mary Lincoln, company—an act of kindness on the part of Ellen Stanton entirely in keeping with her character, for it was well known in the Stanton house that she felt rather intimidated by the First Lady.

Anticipating an early train ride back to Wilmington, Abraham and I climbed the stairs to my room and, there, fell soundly asleep.

A shout from the groomsman and the jangling of a horse team awoke me some time later. I went to the window to see what had excited the lazy groom and found myself looking down upon the splendid figure of the President's carriage, its two high-stepping horses in the shafts being brushed and fed while the driver made use of the privy[45] alongside the stables.

This was not the first time I had seen the Presidential carriage beneath my window at odd hours, Watson—the President often visited Mr. Stanton in his study when there was delicate business to discuss—but it was new to Abraham, who had sprung from his bed and nudged me aside, eager to study every detail.

We stayed there until dawn began to lighten the sky and the warm, tempting scent of freshly baked bread drifted up to our window from the kitchen below, when I suggested we dress and breakfast before the house had stirred, for we had an early train to catch. Soon we were descending the stairs with no other thought in our minds than to cadge a hunk of bread and a cup of hot coffee from the cook before making our way to the train depot.

But as often happened during my time in America, Watson, Providence had quite a different intention in store for us.

---

45 *British term for 'outhouse.'*

A Most Intimate Audience

Upon reaching the bottom of the stairs, we tiptoed past the library and made our way to the dining room, only to find the gaslight turned up and—to my great surprise—Eddie Stanton seated at the table, in uniform, a cup of coffee at his elbow and his rifle leaned against the wall nearby. He had been absorbed in a magazine, which he abruptly closed and slid beneath his cap when he noticed us. Then he rose and greeted me in a friendly fashion, without a glance at Abraham.

"Father is in the study with the President on some serious business," he said, in a low, conspiratorial whisper. "They stayed all night at the telegraph office for the election reports. The results were delayed on account of winter storms in the West." He nodded at Abraham. "Found yourself a pickaninny, I see."

I could have struck the lout, but a sudden commotion from the hallway caused Eddie to snap to attention just as the door opened.

It was President Lincoln.

He was glancing backwards over his shoulder at a flustered Ellen Stanton, who was in her nightdress and had evidently been urging the President to remain in the study, where he could be served his coffee.

"I thank you, good lady, but your husband is occupied with a pressing issue that needs a response, and I smell breakfast being cooked. Besides, it's cramped in there and I need to stretch out a bit—" The President had twisted himself around and a look of surprise crossed his face as he caught sight of the three of us standing at attention.

"Oh no!" Mrs. Stanton cried, seeing us now. "You boys mustn't be here!"

"Oh, yes they must!" the President exclaimed as a broad smile overcame the deeply etched lines of care and worry. "Surely your cook has got bacon and cornbread enough for me and these hungry young men!"

Mrs. Stanton wrung her hands, her face a mask of indecision. "Yes, of course, your Excellency—"

"*Mr. President* will do," he said, eyeing us thoughtfully. "If you'll see how the cook is making out, Ellen, I will set myself here and become a little more familiar with this pair." He nodded at me and Abraham.

"Yes, your—. Yes."

She disappeared into the kitchen talking to herself, while the President chuckled and tossed his stovepipe hat upon the table, where it happened to displace young Eddie's cap, revealing the magazine beneath. Eddie snatched up the publication and stuffed it inside his jacket while attempting to salute.

A wry smile replaced the jovial look upon the President's face.

"At ease, son. Drink your coffee and get back to that...*literature* you're always studying." Young Eddie flushed crimson and he remained at attention as the Great Man, in his kindly way, changed the topic entirely.

"You know, Eddie, my boy Tad and I watched from the window while you and the other guards voted yesterday—and I meant to thank you for your ballot!"[46] He let out a high-pitched laugh and turned to me with those thick eyebrows arched high, a look of merriment in his eyes.

"Now sir, you are familiar to me—the houseguest I met on the porch here some months ago? I thought so." He held out his hand, the texture of which was as thick and coarse as I had remembered it. "You had something to do with tracking those gunpowder thieves, I understand. Don't look surprised! Mr. Stanton speaks quite highly of you."

I was too flustered to do anything more than nod my head at this, Watson. He winked and turned to Abraham, who was standing beside me open-mouthed, eyes big as saucers. "And who is your friend, here?" He reached for Abraham's hand. "What is *your* name, son?"

"Abr'am, marse."

Lincoln smiled. "Abraham, I am pleased to make your acquaintance. I'm told that quite a few thousands of your brethren have been given my name. I think it's the finest compliment I have ever received." He let go Abraham's hand, pulled out a chair and sat down, one arm resting upon the chair back and one leg thrown over his other leg. "—Although, in truth, it may be the only one!"

He laughed at his own joke as the door from the kitchen opened and the girl entered bearing covered dishes. She was nervously placing them before the President when Mrs. Stanton entered and once more attempted to shoo us out.

---

46 *Americans did not vote in secrecy in Lincoln's day. Different coloured ballots were handed out by party representatives at the ballot box, and soldiers often cast their votes in the field, in full view of anyone watching. Lincoln may well have seen his own guards voting from the White House windows.*

"Now, you boys must eat in the kitchen. Mr. Stanton will be in here shortly—"

"These boys must do nothing of the sort, Ellen. The callers at the White House are already a hundred deep and the gates don't open for three hours. I ain't in a rush to get home, you know." The President nodded agreeably at the dishes of eggs, bacon, cornbread and stewed apples set before him.

"Besides," he said, glancing at Abraham as he was served a plate. "I want to learn a little something from this boy."

And learn something he did, Watson.

It would be the first time I heard my friend Abraham tell his story—indeed, it would be the first time I had heard him say more than ten words in a row. But there was something about the Great Emancipator that brought out a hundred times that number at the breakfast table that morning. They came out in a torrent that was sometimes quite difficult to grasp, being in the peculiar *lingua franca* of a freed slave who had grown up among a mixture of dialects while being forced to learn the vocal inflections of the whites he once served.

But President Lincoln listened to every word.

Abraham's Story

It was New Year's Day. Abraham was not sure of the year, but it was before the Marse's oldest boy went off to fight—I will call him Marse, Watson, as Abraham did, because this is Abraham's story—which means it was before Secession and the war.

Abraham was happy because the chores were light on New Year's Day. Marse and the Missus always went calling that day, and Abraham's mother had only to empty the slop jars and sweep the kitchen before she returned to the cabin.

Abraham's father was gone because he was the coachman, so he drove Marse and the Missus on their New Year's Day visits. He was the only slave Marse trusted to drive them, and he wore a frock coat and a top hat while driving the carriage—and he always carried a mouth organ with him to entertain his passengers and to announce his return to the plantation.

Abraham's father was the most valuable slave on the plantation. Abraham had heard that said about his father, and although he did not know what that meant exactly, it had made him proud until later, when he understood.

His father loved being coachman—and he loved playing the mouth organ. He played the instrument like he was singing it. He played Abraham and his sister to sleep each night, and he played for the other slaves when they all snuck out for prayers at the hush harbour.[47]

But most of all, his father played while driving the carriage, and he had a way of announcing his return to the plantation with a song about a Balm in Gilead. His father's song could be heard long before the carriage came over the rise. The dogs would hear it and start barking, and Abraham knew he would soon be seeing the carriage—his father somehow steering the team while playing and smiling and waving.

Abraham couldn't wait to hear the song that New Year's Day, for his father had said he was going to bring back a real mouth organ for Abraham. Abraham's hands were too big for the tiny one his father brought home the year before, and it was time Abraham played a grown-up mouth organ.

Abraham was excited, but his mother was not. When she returned to the cabin she fell into bed weeping, and stayed there. When Abraham pestered her with questions about when his father was coming home, she just cried, and she didn't get out of bed. Didn't fix lunch for him and his sister. Just lay there, listening. She knew what Abraham hadn't yet learned.

New Year's Day was sale day.

It was the day the speculators came calling, looking for slaves to buy, offering slaves for sale. It was the day Marse could get rid of a problem slave—an injured field hand or a barren female or a lame boy—or just raise cash.

Abraham did not know this, and his mother didn't tell him. But something in her manner caused him to stop pestering her. He took his

---

47 A secret location such as a smokehouse or forest clearing where slaves could hold religious services.

sister outside to play in the yard. A long time went by while their mother stayed in bed.

And then the dogs started barking.

Abraham called for his mother to come outside to watch for the carriage, but she did not even get out of bed. And when no song could be heard coming over the rise—only the rattle of a carriage being driven by Marse—Abraham could hear his mother start to wail.

His father had been sold that day for nine hundred and eighty dollars. Marse had put in a big tobacco crop that year and the bottom dropped out when the Yankees gave up tobacco to hurt the slave owners. Marse needed the money.

It was rumoured he'd sold Abraham's father to a planter in the islands.[48] When they were sold to the islands, the other slaves said among themselves, they never came back.

Life changed after that day.

Abraham's mother was always crying and laying in bed. The overseer would come by—a huge man, the meanest man he'd ever seen—and drag her outside and whip her for missing the chores. His little sister was taken to another shack to be cared for by an old slave grandmother, and Abraham was put to work in the fields.

He didn't mind working in the fields, but whenever the dogs started barking he'd look to see the wagon coming over the rise, expecting it was his father playing that song about a Balm in Gilead.

It was never his father.

Freedom came a few years later, after Secession. Abraham was working in the fields with the others. All day there had been a sound like thunder on the horizon, only he knew it wasn't thunder because the sky was blue and the other slaves were excited, not scared. They were telling stories about Moses and the Exodus—the stories Abraham's father used to tell him.

Then he saw his mother come to the door. She was not crying. She was listening to the thunder.

That night Marse and his youngest boy were seen burying trunks in the flower beds. Dug the holes themselves! Buried the silver and plate, it

---

48 The West Indies.

was said. White neighbors brought furniture to hide in the old tobacco barn, too.

Next day the thunder was closer—just across the river, it sounded like— and even the dogs acted different. They didn't bark. They hid under the porch. Next morning, the thunder started early. And loud. Then it stopped.

It would never start again.

After the thunder stopped, Marse came out on the porch and started shouting orders at the slaves. "Dig up the trunks and load 'em on the wagon, N----rs! Don't bother to clean off the dirt, just load 'em up!" Then the overseer drove the carriage away down the Richmond road and never came back. Marse and the Missus watched the carriage go, and then they went upstairs.

To pray, someone said.

About noon the dogs crawled out from under the porch and started barking again, like when the carriage would come over the rise.

But it wasn't the carriage. It was Freedom on horseback, a Yankee soldier—a tall man in a blue uniform—riding hard up the public road, bridle jangling, sword slapping. He brought his horse to a sudden halt alongside the first slaves he came to in the fields, touched his cap and said, "You are free now. You are all free to go."

None of them moved. Nobody could believe a white man could say such a thing and mean it. So they just stood there while he moved on to the next group, telling them the same thing: "You are all free now."

But they didn't move either. They were watching Marse, who was on the porch eyeing the soldier, and they were waiting to see what Marse would do.

Marse, however, did nothing. Just watched the soldier now turning his horse into the carriageway.

And when the soldier reached the house and got down off that horse, it was a strange sight. He didn't do the usual things a caller did. Didn't remove his hat for Marse, didn't hand him a card. Didn't shake hands. Just walked up the steps to where Marse stood all quiet and scared, "like a slave, like a n----r," they remembered, and spoke something they couldn't hear. And Marse just took it. Just stood there nodding and saying, "Yes, sir," over and over, "like a n----r."

Then the soldier watched while Marse rang the dinner bell and yelled like he used to yell for the overseer to start whipping—only he was crying. And shouting.

"You all free now. You n-----s all free."

And that's when they believed it, and they moved fast. Abraham's mother had her things in a burlap sack, and she went to get his sister from the old grandmother. Then the two of them walked across the field and his mother grabbed Abraham's hand—he'd been standing with the old men and women who were crying and shaking and hugging and praying—and they began to walk north, to Washington City, to the Island.

How long it took, Abraham couldn't say, but when they got there, Abraham's mother gave him his new name.

Abraham did not remember his old one.

The coffee had remained untouched in the china cup; the eggs and bacon had turned cold upon the plate. President Lincoln had listened with one elbow set upon the table, his spectacles dangling from his fingers, his mouth a thin line of grief.

And never once had he removed his eyes from those of my friend.

After some few moments of silent contemplation, he reached out with his free hand and covered Abraham's, which were clasped together on the table before him. "Your mother lives in the Island?"

Abraham nodded.

"Do you know where your father was sold?"

Abraham shook his head.

"Well, we will see if we can find him for you." The President put on his spectacles and turned his hat over, revealing the inner band. Inside the band were inserted telegrams, letters and folded pieces of foolscap. He removed one of these and asked Eddie Stanton, "Might I have a pen?"— not noticing that young Eddie had fallen asleep during Abraham's story.

A swift boot under the table from me brought Eddie awake with a start, and he retrieved the ink stand from the desk in a corner of the room. "Thank you," said the President. "And might I ask you to trouble the cook for hot coffee?"

As Eddie disappeared into the kitchen, the President turned his great, sorrowful face towards Abraham's. "Now, what is your father's name?"

Abraham shrugged his shoulders.

"What was your master's name?

"Marse Weeps."

"Master Weeps. Well that is an appropriate name for a slave master," the President said sourly. "From Ashcake, you say? I have an Attorney General who is well versed in these matters. We will see what he can do." He finished writing on the paper, in a precise hand, then folded it and slid it inside the hatband.

"Now, sir," said he, turning his attention towards me. "While young Edwin brings us coffee and finishes his forty winks, perhaps you'll tell me something of this gunpowder business."

A Name, Interrupted

I was surprised, Watson, and not a little intimidated, but the President's manner was so genial that my stuttering response quickly fell into the manner of a conversation with him. It was nothing at all like the inquisitions I had endured at the hands of Mr. Stanton.

I began at the beginning, of course—my introduction to Sunshine Billy and his dog that first Sunday at the mill—and continued straight through to Abraham's discovery of the coffins loaded with powder kegs in the undertaker's shanty at Cape Island. The President listened to it all, sipping coffee and chewing bacon as I talked, nodding and chuckling at various points.

I had just begun to describe our near entrapment in the barn of the villainous wagon-mender when the door flew open and Edwin M. Stanton burst in, telegrams clutched in his hand. He stopped short with a startled look upon his face as young Eddie snapped to attention.

"What the devil is this?" cried the War Secretary, looking from the President to me and to Eddie.

"Your English guest is telling me about the powder thieves that bedeviled poor Mr. du Pont, Edwin. Join us."

The War Secretary waved his fistful of telegrams. "We have work to do, sir."

"And four more years to do it!" Stretching one long leg under the table, the President pushed out the chair opposite him. "Have a seat, Edwin, and get those telegrams in order while I hear this out. Now, sir," said he, turning his expressive face to mine, "it's not clear to me what it was about this 'Sunshine Billy' that got your hackles up in the first place."

The War Secretary rolled his eyes—he was remarkably unabashed in the presence of the President, Watson—and began to leaf through the flimsies while I recalled for Mr. Lincoln the old adage of those fishermen on the Thames.

"*With southern wind—*" I began, but the President smiled and raised his great, swollen hand to stop me.

Then he tilted back his head and, in that high voice of his, recited: "*With southern wind and cloudy sky, the fisherman his luck may try!*" He dropped his hand to the table and laughed a great guffawing laugh. Mr. Stanton's expressive eyebrows arched in evident pique, and the President regarded his War Secretary's countenance with no little amusement.

"Fish don't like the sun, Edwin. Makes 'em easy to spot. I expect you never had to fish for your supper in Ohio!" Mr. Stanton pursed his lips and shook his head as the President turned back to me. "I get why you smelled a rat with that 'Sunshine Billy,' but how did those powdermen fool General du Pont's bookkeeper? Mr. Stanton here tells me every ounce of material that went into and out of those mills was counted."

Before I could answer, however, the door from the hallway opened and the grim, businesslike figure of John Nicolay appeared bearing fresh telegrams. "Begging your pardon, Excellency. From Springfield."

The President brightened, put on his spectacles and stretched out a hand. As he studied the flimsies, the shadow that always seemed to cloud his eyes lightened measurably, and a very pleased smile crept to his lips as he tossed them without comment across the table.

His War Secretary glanced through each, then stood abruptly. "These require a response," he barked, marching off through the door to the kitchen, whence he was followed by Nicolay.

The Great Man sighed, unfolded himself from his sitting position and rose slowly to his full height. "I am called away, gentlemen. Young Abraham, I have your old master's particulars in my hat, and we'll see if we can't but find where your father was sold. As for you, sir," he said to me, "I haven't forgotten the promise I made to give you a name. If your friend here can take mine for his, I reckon you can take another fellow's just as well!"

He studied my face for a moment with those penetrating eyes, then clapped me upon the shoulder. "You remind me mightily of a boy I met on the Mississippi. Kept us off that sandbar where old Jim Bowie fought his duel. He was mighty clever about it, too. Knew we couldn't hear him shouting at us across the water, so he swam out against the current and stood up on the bar so we could see how shallow it was right there in the channel! Saved our little expedition, I can tell you. Quite a fellow he proved to be. His name was—"

Mr. Stanton had reappeared at the kitchen door, eyes ablaze. The President dropped his hand and chuckled.

"Until next time," he said, bowing. Then he picked up his top hat and left the room, followed by a flustered Eddie Stanton, who was trying to jam the magazine into his coat pocket as he went.

Abraham and I finished our breakfast, gathered our coats and found Mrs. Stanton at the front door turning away serenaders gathered at the curb in apparent hopes of seeing the President. We said our goodbyes to her, passed through the disappointed crowd and walked all the way to the railway station.

Abraham, you see, was not allowed on the horse trolley.

It was some time later that I learned from Eddie Stanton, the family gossip, that the telegrams which had caused the President to leave the breakfast table that morning in such good spirits had come from his old law partner, Herndon, in Springfield, Illinois. They carried news that the final vote count had given Mr. Lincoln a majority of the votes in his home state.

It meant as much to Abraham Lincoln as being re-elected President.

THE WAR ENDS AND MY AMERICAN ADVENTURE FAIRLY BEGINS

It was a cold day in February of 1865—three months after Mr. Lincoln's re-election and nine months after my arrival at the Éleuthèrian Mills—and Abraham and I stood together in the office of General Henry to receive our letters of dismissal.

It was nothing to do with our performance, however, or any embarrassment we had brought to Mr. du Pont or Edwin M. Stanton. It was that the end of the war was finally in sight.

Sherman's Army of the Tennessee (named for the river, Watson, not the state) had completed their "March to the Sea" through Georgia and was racing upwards through the Carolinas, the birthplace of Secession, to join Grant's Army of the Potomac for the final destruction of Bobby Lee and his Army of Northern Virginia, now trapped in the rat-infested trenches surrounding Petersburg and Richmond.

Only Joe Johnston's battered Confederate Army of the Tennessee stood in Sherman's path.

As a result, General Henry explained, the call on gunpowder for the Union armies had dropped by two-thirds, and he was making cutbacks wherever he could.

He told us all this while pressing envelopes thick with dollar bills into our palms and shaking our hands warmly as the greyhounds sniffed our trousers one last time. We then departed from the Éleuthèrian Mills, but not before saying our goodbyes—I to Monsieur and the other fellows in the laboratory, Abraham to Mrs. du Pont and the children—and hitched a final ride to the Christiana wharves, from whence we made for my rooms to clear them out.

A curious mood was in the air, Watson. From General Henry to Monsieur to the wagon teamsters and the roughnecks at the docks, a tinge of melancholy sounded in their voices. There was certainly great relief that the fighting was almost over, of course. And great pride that more than a million slaves had been freed by the Union armies, and that a vast country that had been split apart in a most literal fashion would be joining back together.

But no one seemed in the mood to celebrate just yet. Four years of war had brought much suffering—what would peace mean?

Even my dour landlady seemed affected by the apprehension of what was to come. That woman, who had never parted with so much as a piece of bread without payment up front (and who never took her suspicious eyes off Abraham when he was in her house) thrust into our hands three fish sandwiches and a jug of her own cider for the trip to Washington.

"Just in case," she said, without explaining what that "case" might be.

I felt no such apprehension towards the future, however. Now that my usefulness to Mr. Stanton was ended, I expected to be sent back to England on the next available steamship. My only concern was whether Abraham and I would be allowed to visit at least one of the great battlefields of the war before my ship sailed.

Imagine my delight, then, when upon my arrival at Franklin Square, I was informed—in a meeting so brief I was not even invited to take a seat—that a boom of sea commerce unleashed by the prospect of an end to hostilities had made berths difficult to secure at a reasonable expense to the U.S. Treasury.

My return to England would be delayed, perhaps as long as two months.

"Until such time as a berth may be obtained, you are a guest of this house," Mr. Stanton said, in a not unfriendly manner while handing me a pass. "You will have use of our stables, and this pass will let you on any road or bridge north of the Potomac. May I suggest Gettysburg?" he added thoughtfully. "The newspapers call it the high watermark of the Confederacy, and for once, the newspapers are not far wrong."

Then, "Guard!"

And with that I was dismissed, and I made immediately for the Island to retrieve Abraham. To Gettysburg we would ride.

We set out on Inauguration Day—March 4th—because the city was swarming with sightseers and Mrs. Stanton was hosting several Ohio families for the occasion. Abraham and I would have been required to share our room with five other boys, all for the prospect of witnessing a rather dreary ceremony from afar.

We chose instead to witness a battlefield—*the* battlefield—up close.

It was a wet morning and the roads were slick with mud from the end of the winter frost, but we made good time. We rode the two fastest horses from the Stanton stables, and although I had learned how to handle a horse during my time in America, Watson, it was on that journey I learned to *ride*, for Abraham was fearless in the saddle, and I had no choice but to follow his lead.

And what a lead it was!

Rail fences, stone walls, fast-rushing creeks and slow-moving wagons—nothing was an obstacle to Abraham. Our ride was so intense and exhilarating, the hours went by in minutes.

Indeed, as I jotted down my first notes for these memoirs, I recalled the journey to Gettysburg being a speedy overnight ride. Consulting my atlas, however, I see that the distance from Washington City is no less than eighty miles—a three-day ride in those conditions—and I conclude that Abraham and I must have been gone at least a full week.

In any case, we made the most of our time there at Gettysburg, filling our pockets full of Minié bullets—just kicking the topsoil would stir them up—and reenacting in our minds the famous battle scenes that had unfolded everywhere around us: in the Devil's Den, upon Cemetery Hill, in the Peach Orchard and the Wheatfield, on Culp's Hill and Little Round Top—*especially* Little Round Top.

I say "we" and "our," Watson, but with the clarity of years, I concede that although Abraham tramped the fields and hills alongside me, and although he employed his remarkable ability to read the messages of the tracks in the dirt as I narrated the action of which I had read so much, he was not there to see the sloping fields and barren hilltops where a great battle had been fought.

Abraham was always and everywhere looking for his father.

I BEFRIEND A CERTAIN FAMOUS SON

Our return to Washington found a changed city.

Sherman's Westerners were marching through the Carolinas with such speed that sentiment was universal they would soon unite with Grant's

Easterners and together end the stalemate with Lee. Then Richmond would fall and the Confederacy would be a relic for the history books.

Uncertainty had been replaced everywhere by a bully confidence.

And that confidence was evidently shared by General Grant, for it was rumoured that he had invited President Lincoln to visit Army headquarters at City Point—a bustling supply depot one hundred miles south of Washington, just outside Petersburg—to confer with himself and General Sherman to map out the final steps of the war.

Lincoln, it was said, had instantly accepted, so delighted was he at the chance to get out of Washington City and meet with Grant, who had been given overall command of the Union Armies not even a year before and yet was now on the verge of complete victory. Plans were being drawn up under a cloak of utmost secrecy.

The source of this "confidential" information, as you might have guessed, Watson, was Eddie Stanton. He spilled the story at supper one evening while his father was at the War Department. I thought nothing of it—young Eddie was possessed of an unhealthy showmanship, always aimed at impressing his wary stepmother—and so I went to bed that evening with only memories of the ride to Gettysburg in my head.

Next morning, however, I was summoned to the War Secretary's study before breakfast, where I learned that not only was Eddie's story true—the President and Mrs. Lincoln would be leaving for City Point in two days—but that I would be going with them.

Mrs. Lincoln, you see, insisted upon taking their young son Tad with them, and I was to be the boy's keeper on the journey.

Now, this commission was not the honour you might think, Watson.

I had never met him, but it was well known in Washington City that Tad—his given name was Thomas, but it is said his father had thought him "wiggly as a tadpole" as a baby—was immature (even for his eleven years), exceedingly attached to his parents and prone to misbehaving when not strictly supervised.

In England, I fancy, he would have been a titled Lord by birth and sent off to schooling in Germany or some distant land, well hidden from view. But in America he was left to his own devices, and those devices were legendary.

Ink stands might be overturned, postage weights tossed rattling into spittoons, doors latched shut and the keys hidden—yet no punishment was ever bestowed upon the boy by his indulgent parents. They had lost his older brother, Willie, you see, to typhus contracted from the foul White House water, and their grief had never left them. (The oldest Lincoln son, Robert, was a Harvard graduate serving on the staff of General Grant, and very well liked).

The potential for disruptive behaviour during the President's visit to Grant's headquarters was real enough, in fact, to have caused no little discussion between Mr. Stanton and Secretary of State Seward, and the two men had conspired to bring a friendship into the boy's life—one that could act as a caretaker on the voyage.

And that caretaker would be me, provided I met the approval of the most difficult figure in the Presidential household: Mary Lincoln.

"Make yourself known to Mrs. Lincoln," Mr. Stanton instructed me, "and be a friend to Tad."

Next morning, I found myself passing through the White House gates in the company of a uniformed Eddie Stanton, who led me past the lines of office seekers, up the stairs to the great veranda and inside the doors of the august Presidential Mansion.

It was a scene I shall never forget, Watson.

Even at eight in the morning, the vestibule was a barnyard of activity. Men were smoking, expectorating and talking of potential appointments like racing touts. *Postmaster of Southport...Harbourmaster for York... Westerly Lighthouse Keeper...*It was Hamlet's "convocation of politic worms" in the flesh!

Eddie steered me past the worms and up the stairs to the upper floor, where the President worked and lived, and I was handed off to a guard in the vestibule outside the library to await my call from Mrs. Lincoln.

Now I should tell you, Watson, that it was not an easy thing to become known to Mary Lincoln. It was no secret that she had something of Lady Macbeth in her, and not merely in the great ambitions she held for her husband. An element of madness had descended upon the poor lady when Willie died in their first year in the White House.

He had been taken sick, you see, only days after an elegant ball Mrs. Lincoln had hosted for the elite society of Washington. She took the boy's death as a sign of disfavour from Providence, and never recovered from the loss. (Nor did her husband, I might add, for it was widely known that young Willie had been the President's favourite.)

Like Banquo's ghost, the dead boy's spirit seemed to haunt the great mansion, placing a terrible burden upon young Tad, who, it was said, possessed none of his dead brother's personable qualities.

Indeed, I took pity upon the boy at first sight.

Short, black haired and with an elfin face, Tad was possessed of a cleft palate that made his enunciation difficult to follow. He took one look at me and quite literally disappeared into his mother's skirts, refusing to come out while Mrs. Lincoln—a short, handsome woman—looked me over with a wary eye.

I thought my assignment had ended before it had begun, Watson, and so made a meaningless remark about the boy's skill at hiding himself. To my surprise, this caused her face to brighten—I suppose my Pall Mall inflections caused her to take me for the son of a noble duke or some such—and she instructed Tad to come out and shake my hand.

This he would not do until I drew from my pocket several of the Minié bullets Abraham and I had retrieved from the fields at Gettysburg—I knew what interested young boys, Watson!—and held them out for his inspection. Tad at once lost his shyness and was soon displaying for *me* the tattered Confederate battle flags collected at Gettysburg and given to his father upon the occasion of his famous speech there.

Mrs. Lincoln, delighted by our rapport, announced she was taking her leave, whence young Tad abruptly abandoned his flags (and my bullets) and followed her out of the room. I found myself alone with the guard, a friendly, bearded fellow who smiled and shrugged his shoulders.

"She'll be back on her own time," said he. Picking up a book from the desk, he handed it to me. "Something to read in the meantime."

Then he, too, disappeared.

I turned the book over and studied it. The leather was old and black, but the title was almost as grand as the subject himself:

The Life of George Washington,
With Curious Anecdotes, Equally Honourable To Himself
and Exemplary To His Young Countrymen

Written by a man named Weems.[49]

Leafing through the book, I found it offered a rather compelling—
if somewhat fanciful—recitation of the life of America's first President.
It also contained remarks and notes written in rough pencil upon almost
every page, sometimes so densely printed as to render the book passages
unreadable.

They were the markings of a young boy, and it occurred to me that
young Tad must be a savant of sorts. I could not fathom where a boy with
such childish mannerisms had acquired the youthful wisdom to have
devoured such a book in so comprehensive a manner, but upon turning to
the title page, I discovered, to my astonishment—in the same crude block
letters as elsewhere on the pages—the following inscription:

THIS BOOK PROPERTY OF A. LINCOLN.

Imagine my horror, Watson, at the realization that I had been
handling a keepsake of President Lincoln from his youth! And imagine my
embarrassment when, as I made to return the book to its place upon the
desk, the door opened and in walked President Lincoln himself, holding
hands with Tad.

The President smiled as the boy introduced us (in Tad's peculiar lisp,
"Johnnie" came out as "Honey"), then took my hand in his great leathery mitt.

"Yes, Tad, I have met 'Honey' before. In fact, I have promised him
a *name*." But as he was trying to recall the name of his companion on
the Mississippi, he spied the book in my hands. "Ah! Weems! That's a
good 'un. Take it with you—you might learn something about our first
President they don't teach in your country!"

I had no intention of taking the book, of course. Tales of souvenir

---

49 Mason L. Weems, better known as Parson Weems. His was the first biography of President George
Washington.

hunters scavenging the White House were legion, and nobody would believe the President had given me such a precious book, so I set it aside and at Tad's urging brought out the Minié bullets from Gettysburg.

The President was almost as taken with them as the boy had been.

He picked them out of my palm one by one and inspected each with intense curiosity. To my young eyes, Watson, he appeared to witness in the nicks and dents of these small lead cylinders the very bones of the men they had killed or maimed—and I believed he was about to make a comment in that vein when the door opened and the familiar figure of John Nicolay, serious and businesslike, appeared with telegrams to be read.

And with that I was dismissed.

CITY POINT

Of President Lincoln's remarkable sixteen-day visit to the headquarters of General Grant at City Point during the final weeks of the Civil War, I must naturally be circumspect.

This owes itself as much to the peculiar nature of my role—which was as something of a nursemaid to young Tad, not as a participant in the events I would witness—as it does to the sensitivities of Brother Mycroft even to this day, fifty-some years later, as it pertains to the history of Anglo-American relations. (England was a neutral party to the conflict, after all, and I was merely its citizen.)

But a witness I was, and the diary of that voyage—I thought it well to maintain a firsthand account for Mr. Stanton in case anything went awry— now sits upon my lap as I speak these words. Someday these notes may be reproduced in their entirely, but certainly not, as Brother Mycroft has advised, until every person involved in that remarkable journey has passed away.

A bare-bones recital of the highlights must make do, for now. Our journey began midday on Thursday the 23rd of March, 1865, at the 6th Street wharf, where we boarded the steamboat *River Queen,* whose Captain Penrose ran a tight ship, commanding a dozen sailors, deckhands and cooks.

The President was accompanied only by William Crook, the bearded officer who had handed me the Weems book in the family quarters, and the ever-present John Nicolay. Mrs. Lincoln, to her husband's embarrassment, brought not only her maid, but a large wardrobe and several unexpected attendants, causing no little delay in our casting off.

Once underway, however, we found the breeze refreshing and the Potomac bustling with traffic, and the voyage promised a welcome break from the close, dirty streets of Washington. Tad kept up an excited commentary upon the passing ships and sloops for his father, who held the boy's hand as they stood together upon the deck. Upon reaching the deeper waters of the Chesapeake, a giant Navy warship steamed past us, its wheels churning the waters, its crew lining the decks in salute to the familiar figure upon our deck.

Tad was beside himself, and the President thoroughly enjoyed the display.

Soon afterwards, unfortunately, the President was sickened by tainted water on the ship and spent the rest of the voyage at the lower railing. After a time the weather turned foul, and I removed Tad to the stables below decks, where his main delight came in snapping the horses' tails and hiding among the stalls, while I took the opportunity to practice my voice-throwing technique, which was greatly enhanced by the confined spaces— to the groomsman's annoyance and young Tad's amusement.

We reached City Point, at the junction of the James and Appomattox rivers, at nine o'clock the evening of the 24th. It was too late to go ashore.

Next morning we were awakened not by the sound of buglers blowing reveille but by the sudden clap of booming cannon fire—a thunder of indescribable percussive effect that nearly rocked us out of our beds. We were ordered to stay in our rooms as the firing kept up, but it had already begun to die down when the President's son Robert boarded the ship to inform his father that the "little rumpus," as he cheerily described it, was, in fact, a last gasp attack by Lee's Confederates on nearby Fort Stedman that had been quickly repulsed at a heavy cost to the Confederates.

When we finally emerged from our cabins—the President was recovered from his stomach ailment by now—the aroma of fresh bread from what was said to be the largest bakery in America reached our noses across the water and we beheld the astonishing site of a veritable city newly constructed along the banks of the James.

A sea of white tents, wooden barracks and stables crowded the bluffs above the river, while on its banks stood mountains of coal and wood, pyramids of cannon balls and powder kegs, crates of cracker boxes and hogsheads of food for the men and hayricks of fodder for the horses—all being fed by ships and schooners lined up at piers a half-mile long, the piers fitted with railroad tracks to move the matériel for Grant's Army ashore from the ships lining the piers.

And chief among the ships, Watson, were DuPont powder vessels!

President Lincoln, who surveyed all this from the deck while holding hands with Tad, could not have been more impressed or more delighted. After a hearty breakfast and a welcoming ceremony onshore, he was taken by railroad carriage to confer with Grant and his generals a mile inland, near the Petersburg lines.

And I was off with Tad to explore the camp.

For the purposes of these reminiscences, Watson, it can be said that young Tad proved to be—well, let us say that it was well I accompanied him. But only once did he get into serious trouble, and that trouble happened on the very first day, when a group of Confederate prisoners were marched past us to ships bound for Northern prisons.

In his excitement at seeing up close a "real-life, honest Injun Confederate!" Tad reached out to touch one of the poor fellows in the impulsive manner of a child, only to receive the shock of his young life when the prisoner—a dusty, emaciated, lice-ridden fellow—suddenly clutched at the boy's jacket and attempted to pull him into their ranks.

A guard brought his baton down on the fellow's hand and he dropped his hold on Tad, but the lesson was learned. Young Tad never bothered the prisoners after that.

Mrs. Lincoln, however, would prove far more difficult to contain.

There were many minor perturbations in the wake of that headstrong, highly strung woman, Watson, but the history books do not do justice to

her infamous *contretemps* with the handsome, demure wife of General
Ord at the ceremonial parade next day. To have seen it with my own eyes—
and to have witnessed the embarrassment it caused General Grant, General
Ord, their staffs and President Lincoln, and the humiliation it brought
Mrs. Ord and her friend Julia Grant, the General's sturdy wife—was
something I would never wish to repeat.

Nor would I embellish upon it in these memoirs.

Still, that unfortunate incident, which caused the parade to be
canceled and sent Mrs. Ord to her husband's tent in tears, had one
surprisingly welcome effect: Mrs. L retreated to her stateroom aboard the
River Queen and would spend the next few days locked away pouting.

This afforded the President the chance to spend his days doing what
he enjoyed most: conferring with General Grant (and Sherman, too,
when he boarded the River Queen one memorable afternoon for a long
conference), visiting the lines near Petersburg, exchanging wires with
Secretary Stanton from the telegraph tent and spending time with his
eldest son Robert, who, as I say, served on Grant's staff.

And, as Tad chose to spend the next few days closeted with his
brooding mother, I was afforded the chance to tag along on a Presidential
visit to General Grant's headquarters. I even set eyes upon Lieutenant
General Ulysses S. Grant—the first general given that exalted rank since
George Washington—himself.

A more modest, yet impressive, soldier I never encountered in
America.

He was seated outside his headquarters tent upon a wooden camp
chair, studying a map spread across his knees, his hat pushed back upon
his head and an unlit cigar rolling from one corner of his mouth to the
other. He wore none of the trappings of his rank—only a plain blue
jacket, unbuttoned—and but for the simple stripe of four stars upon the
shoulder, you might have thought him a surveyor examining property
lines.

So thoroughly engrossed was General Grant in his map, in fact, that
he did not hear the President announced, and he remained seated until
Mr. Lincoln called out to him, when he rolled up the map and stood to

welcome the man who had brought him east and given him command of all the armies of the North.

Grant's size was surprisingly diminutive—even allowing for President Lincoln's height—and he greeted the President warmly but without the fawning familiarity that I had seen others employ at City Point. After only a few moments in their presence, Watson, it became clear that what had been written about Grant—that "he could be silent in several languages"—rang true.

But the firm brow and steady gaze revealed purpose of character and decisiveness of manner, and as he opened the flap of his tent to admit the President, it was clear that much important business was to be discussed within. This left the gawkers gathered nearby without much to do, and I decided it would be well to return to my charge on board the *River Queen*.

And just in time, too, for Mrs. L had emerged from seclusion and Tad was soon back to his antic ways.

We spent several days exploring the wharves and warehouses of City Point, studying the machinery of war, while the President visited Grant so they could draw up their plans together—Grant's for destroying Lee's Army, Lincoln's for the reconstruction of the country.

Mr. Stanton later told me these days were the best of the President's life.

And yet City Point also provided some of his worst experiences, I have no doubt—even leaving aside his wife's tantrum on the parade grounds— for his time was not limited to meetings of high command and the settling of great questions. There was the matter of life and death spilling out of the nearby trenches around Petersburg, made manifest by the trains bringing the wounded soldiers to the City Point hospital tents—or, for those for whom medical treatment was no longer necessary, bringing their bodies for burial in the Union cemeteries springing up in the old tobacco fields all around City Point.

It was the railway carriages full of wounded men, Watson—they arrived at the City Point depot day and night—that weighed most on the President. You could hear their screams wherever you were, even below decks on the River Queen: *Oh God! Oh Dear God! Kill me, please! Oh my God, kill me now!*

Hardest to bear were the men crying for their mothers. Their screams rent the air and made one want to clap one's hands over one's ears—young Tad often did just that—but President Lincoln, of course, could not shy away.

He would leave the River Queen and go ashore to meet those trains and shake the hands of those men—men missing fingers and limbs and eyes and jaws, men walking with crutches, their heads wrapped in bloody bandages—and return to the *River Queen* so bowed down he could scarcely lift his head.

It was General Sherman who said, "War is cruelty, you cannot refine it."

And he was right, Watson. Terribly right.

"THANK GOD I HAVE LIVED TO SEE THIS"

Before the end of our first week in City Point it had become clear something big was up.

The sound of booming guns from the Federal lines around Petersburg increased each morning, as did the number of trains bringing back the dead and wounded from the lines at night, and all around us the activity on the wharves was intensified. The cannons, guns and powder kegs were being unloaded from the ships as fast as they came in.

Suddenly, too, the President's daily routine was abruptly altered.

There were no more visits to the General's tent, for Grant had moved his headquarters twenty miles inland, and the President began to spend long hours in the telegraph tent instead, exchanging messages with Secretary Stanton in Washington and receiving reports delivered by horse messenger from General Grant in the field.

And Tad was often with him.

I never purposely eavesdropped on the President's telegraphic communications, of course, but Tad loved nothing more than to brazen his way inside the tent to watch the telegraph operator at work. And as the communications with Stanton were no longer in cipher (the lines being secure to Washington City), I couldn't help but make out what was being transmitted thanks to those years I had spent beneath my brother's telegraph desk.

And what I made out was the President telling Mr. Stanton, "Grant means to end the business here."

While Sherman kept Joe Johnston's men bottled up outside Raleigh, in North Carolina, Grant would prod Bobby Lee's Army out of the Petersburg and Richmond trenches, engage it in battle and destroy it before the Confederates could flee west to supply depots at Farmville and Appomattox, or, worse, all the way to Lynchburg, where they might scatter into the mountains and carry on the war for who knows how long.

To finish off Lee, of course, Grant needed every man at hand and all the matériel Stanton could provide—hence, the stepped-up activity all around us.

Now it is well documented in the history books, Watson, that on March 29, Grant unleashed six infantry corps and Sheridan's cavalry against Lee's defensive lines southwest of Petersburg; that battles at Lewis's Farm, White Oak Road and Dinwiddie Courthouse were inconclusive but cost Lee soldiers he could ill afford to lose; that the fighting moved inexorably towards Five Forks, a strategic crossroads on the White Oak Road which would give the Federals control of the Southside Railroad, the main supply route for Lee's Army, if they captured it; and that Phil Sheridan's Union horsemen whipped the Confederates at Five Forks on the first day of April, 1865, while two of Lee's best generals—George Pickett and Fitzhugh Lee, a nephew of Bobby Lee—were attending a shad bake out of hearing of the cannon fire.

It is also in the books that Grant followed up Five Forks with a general assault all along the Petersburg and Richmond lines, driving what remained of Lee's Army out of the trenches and in flight west for Appomattox Station, where railroad cars loaded with Confederate rations awaited them; that Sheridan and his hard-riding cavalry beat Lee's starved and barefoot soldiers to Appomattox, confiscated their supplies and closed off their escape into the mountains; and that on Sunday, April the 2nd, Lee telegraphed Confederate President Jefferson

Davis to abandon Richmond—which Davis and his cabinet members did later that night, with the last reserves of the Confederate treasury in a train bound for the Carolinas.

And it is a fact that President Lincoln visited Richmond just two days later, walking through that vacant and smoldering city to what had been the Confederate White House, where he sat in the very chair from which Jefferson Davis had directed the government of the Confederacy until eight-and-forty hours before.

It has not been recorded, until now, that I was privileged to be with him.

It happened in this way, Watson. The evening of April the 1st was by my notes, a clear, windless night. President Lincoln was pacing the deck after dinner, awaiting news on Grant's progress from the field—as he did every night—when a messenger dashed up the gangplank waving two fistfuls of regimental flags captured from the rebels at Five Forks just hours before.

A look of vast relief came to the President's face as he unfurled the tattered and mud-splattered flags. "Here is something material," said he, handing one to Tad, who immediately began to parade about the deck with it while his father sat down and mused over another flag in his lap, his face aglow with colour such as I had never witnessed. "This is something I can see and feel. I understand this," he said. "This means *victory*."

And he was right, Watson. First thing next morning Grant sent word that Richmond was once again in Union hands, and before we had even breakfasted it was being arranged for the President and his party to board an Army warship for a short but treacherous journey up the James River to visit the fallen capital of the Confederacy.

President Lincoln wanted to see Richmond.

Rear Admiral David Porter, who had been on hand for a meeting with Grant, Sherman and Lincoln on board the River Queen in recent days, supervised the voyage to Richmond. The deckhands employed long wooden poles to sweep away mines and torpedoes and other detritus of war, until our way became blocked by two ironclads that had been sunk by the Rebels. Then we were transferred to a single large rowboat manned by marines and rowed past the charred and vacant waterfront to the remains of what had been the Confederate Navy Yard.

The landscape before us seemed to lose all colour. What must have once been a busy and bustling district was now an eerie and barren forest of stunted chimneys and collapsed brick walls, the smoke still rising from the embers where entire buildings had once stood.

It seems madness in hindsight, knowing what would befall President Lincoln two weeks hence in his own, friendly city, but when our barge made landfall and it was evident there were no Union soldiers to greet the President, he simply stepped onto the charred wooden pier with the marines at his side, remarking fervently as he looked about him, "Thank God I have lived to see this."

Then, after asking the way to the Confederate White House, he clapped his hat atop his head, gathered himself to his full height and began to walk swiftly and with purpose in his stride, his eyes taking in everything, all weight and care seeming to be shed from his being.

The rest of us hurried after him.

It was a most nerve-wracking journey, Watson. A determined band of armed Confederates—even an unarmed mob—could have overwhelmed the half-dozen marines and killed or captured the President in that first half-hour. And had Mrs. Lincoln been with us that day, I have no doubt she would not have let the President step out of that boat.

But Mrs. L had returned to Washington on account of a dream the President had had, in which the White House had caught fire. Both she and her husband believed strongly in the power of dreams, Watson—"It worked for the Magi," as Mr. Stanton later told me with some amusement—and she had left City Point the day before, so there we were on our strange procession, the President leading while the rest struggled to keep up.

I gripped Tad tightly by the hand—it was his twelfth birthday and he was in an even more antic disposition than usual—and was keeping my eyes open for any danger that might come his way when, on each side of the street, I discerned the movement of Negroes scavenging among the ruins.

Dusty and barefoot, they very soon began to take notice of our procession—especially the very tall, very famous civilian in his very recognizable stovepipe hat at the head of it. And suddenly, as if on a signal, they abandoned their scavenging and raced to join us.

They came from every direction, Watson, from seemingly out of nowhere, and they came rejoicing. They made straight for President Lincoln, their hands outstretched to touch him, to touch his sleeve or his trouser—the analogy to the suffering woman grasping the Saviour's cloak is exact—and cries of thanksgiving for "Marse Abraham" filled the air.

Crook, the President's guard, became increasingly apprehensive as the congregation gained size and slowed our pace, and he attempted to fend off the admirers while pushing the President from behind to move faster. But it was no use. Their ranks swelled as if some invisible telegraph wire connected them with kith and kin, so swiftly did they materialize to exalt this man with cries and loud wailing.

Their adulation might have pleased a lesser man, Watson, but it did not please Lincoln. The President instead became increasingly agitated, and when a shout of "Great Messiah!" filled the air, he shook off the hands grasping his coat and admonished the crowd. "Do not kneel to me!" he cried, with some little emotion. "Kneel to your Creator and thank *Him*!"

But his remonstrations only fed their fervour, and the shouting and crying and singing continued until we found ourselves in the shadow of a long brick building several stories high that was still intact although its windows had been smashed. It was Libby Prison—I recognized it from the engravings, for the Northern papers had carried horrific stories about the terrible conditions there—and now the crowd went silent as the President stopped to stare at it.

After some few moments, a new cry went up: "Pull it down! Pull it down!"

But the President shook his head as he continued to study the building. "No," he said finally, in that high, clear voice, "leave it as a monument to all that has gone before." Then he dropped his head and resumed his quick march.

It was that way of his, Watson, that singular gift that allowed him to see clearly beyond the emotions of the moment.

Always the long view.

A blue-uniformed Union cavalryman now appeared in our midst. "Is that Old Abe?" he shouted to Crook. Assured that it was, the man galloped off and returned minutes later with a mounted and heavily armed escort for the President. For the first time since we had left City Point that morning, we felt at ease, and we moved quickly. Within minutes we had arrived at the porticoed brick structure of the Confederate White House.

The President's eyes fixed upon it for a moment, studying the building much as he had studied the prison. Then he stepped decisively forward, leaving behind the soldiers and the swelling crowd, climbed the steps and entered.

Tad raced in after him, and I, of course, followed.

The President was making straight for Davis's office at the end of the corridor. There he surprised a pair of Union soldiers examining boxes in the closet. They jumped to attention, their eyes wide as they watched him glance at the furnishings for some few moments before sitting down at the desk, which still held Davis's ink stand, pens and blotter.

Each of these items the President picked up and set back down, as if assuring himself of their materiality, then he watched with a dreamy disbelief as Tad gamboled on the carpet with a Confederate flag wrapped about him like a shawl.

It would have surprised no one, Watson, if President Lincoln had allowed himself a moment to gloat.

Indeed, the soldiers had been remarking upon the ignominious midnight flight of Jefferson Davis when we entered. But he uttered not a word of exultation. Instead, in a quiet, tired voice he said simply, "I wonder if I might have a glass of water?"

Soon thereafter General Weitzel, the Union Commander who had taken the surrender of Richmond the day before, arrived to greet the President and Admiral Porter. After a private lunch with his distinguished guests in what had been the Confederate White House dining room, Weitzel conducted the President and Tad on a public carriage tour of the city. As you might imagine, Watson, our carriage encountered such a press of freed slaves seeking to see and touch the

"Great 'Mancipator" that a mounted escort was required to keep us moving.

At sunset the President departed for City Point, never to return to Richmond. But the visit had left its mark. President Lincoln seemed transformed, his face no longer possessed of that indescribable sadness that had underlain his every frown and smile. That, at least, is as I saw it.

Others may say differently, Watson. I cannot speak for them.

"Nothing Can Touch Him Further"

We remained several more days at City Point—the President evidently wished to be at hand in case of Lee's surrender—but with Grant's Army on the move and out of telegraph range, there was little for the President to do but to await horse messengers bringing updates from the field and to exchange telegrams with Mr. Stanton in Washington.

And, as always, to meet the trains of wounded now returning in ever-greater numbers from the front lines.

Our last day at City Point was perhaps the most exacting on this score. Mrs. Lincoln had returned from Washington City and brought with her Charles Sumner, the abolitionist senator from Massachusetts, and several other rather self-important political men evidently seeking to bask in the success of Grant's final offensive by touring the empty Petersburg trenches.

The President appeared restless in their presence and eventually excused himself to visit the giant field hospital that had sprung up along the James in the week since Grant began his chase of Lee across the Appomattox watershed. Tad and I went with him.

I can say with confidence, Watson, that President Lincoln did not depart that hospital until he had visited every wounded soldier in every ward—including no small number of Confederates—and had shaken the hand of more than six thousand men, for Tad and I counted each one. I thought it would be an effective means of keeping the boy occupied in a space in which no horseplay could be tolerated, and I may say it succeeded (but perhaps too well, for the swelling and disfigurement of the President's hand afterwards was incredible).

Upon our solemn return to the *River Queen* that evening, we began the two-day return to Washington City.

Next morning dawned pleasant and fair on the Chesapeake. It was the ninth of April—Palm Sunday—and the President was in a jovial and expansive mood. He spent the daylight hours seated on deck of the *River Queen,* entertaining his distinguished passengers with readings from Shakespeare—in particular, eerily enough, the melancholic speech Macbeth makes after hearing of the murder of his rival, Duncan:

> *...Duncan is in his grave;*
> *After life's fitful fever he sleeps well;*
> *Treason has done his worst: nor steel, nor poison,*
> *Malice domestic, foreign levy, nothing,*
> *Can touch him further.*

It was as if he were speaking of himself, Watson—and of what was to come.

We reached Washington City at sunset and tied up at the 6th Street wharf in a hard rain, but the weather didn't dampen anyone's spirits. All of Washington City knew that Grant was closing in on Lee. What we didn't know—nobody in Washington City knew yet—was that Lee had already surrendered.

It had occurred earlier that day after the final battle of the campaign, now known as the Battle of Appomattox Courthouse, and it had taken place in the front parlor of the house of a slave owner named Wilmer McLean, who, as it happened, had moved his family two hundred miles south from Washington after the first great battle of the Civil War was fought in his front yard in Manassas.

The first report of Lee's surrender, along with several other messages from Grant describing the terms of the surrender, had departed Appomattox at four o'clock in the saddlebag of a horse messenger riding hard for the Union encampment at Fredericksburg, Virginia.

At Fredericksburg, those messages were transmitted by telegraph to the War Department in Washington and the news reached Mr. Stanton at about eight o'clock, when all the Union forts surrounding the city fired their cannons—and all the residents turned out for the celebrations.

All but me, Watson!

Relieved of the duty of minding the President's son, I found the bed at the Stanton house so comfortable after two weeks of cramped quarters on the *River Queen* that I fell asleep despite the fireworks and the cannon fire, to dream of a reunion with my friend Abraham and the battlefields to be toured now that the Confederacy was no more.

And those dreams were answered almost literally when I awoke next morning, in the form of an envelope slipped under my door with a note from Mr. Stanton expressing thanks for my assistance during the Presidential voyage, and a fresh pass for the Potomac bridges.

My heart fairly leapt when I saw that the pass would allow us to visit the Virginia battlefields as far south as Fredericksburg. I dressed and descended the stairs, expecting a quick breakfast and a fast ride to the Island to retrieve friend Abraham and make our plans—only to find Mrs. Stanton waiting for me with a very different idea in mind.

She wished, she said, a more suitable role model for young Eddie, in place of the guardsmen at the White House, and she wondered if I might use my remaining days in America to stay close to Franklin Square and become better acquainted with her son.

It was a most awkward moment, Watson, as you might imagine.

I felt a great tenderness towards this woman, but I could think of no other way to confront the matter than to employ the same frankness which she had encouraged me to show her husband in that business of taking young Eddie along on the track of the gunpowder thieves. And so I showed her the pass signed by her husband and explained that I had no intention of staying close to Franklin Square—indeed, that I was already on my way to the Island. Abraham and I would soon be riding south.

She nodded—there was a glistening in her eyes that very nearly caused me to change my intentions, Watson, but I held firm—and then she clasped my hand with some little warmth.

Abraham and I crossed the Long Bridge for Arlington next day.

THE GRAPEVINE TELEGRAPH

I have mentioned my fascination with the old Lee estate across the Potomac, Watson, but I have failed to mention that Abraham's fascination with that estate exceeded even mine, although for an entirely different reason.

While I was intrigued by its heritage as the ancestral home of the Confederacy's supreme general, Abraham's interest was in the Freedman's Village that had been constructed upon the grounds of the old mansion for the care and feeding of the slaves emancipated by Grant's Army on his march to Richmond.

Abraham's mother was convinced that her husband—Abraham's father—might very well be found there.

As it was on the road to the battlefields of Manassas and Fredericksburg that I hoped to see, we stopped there after crossing the Long Bridge to Arlington—I in search of the ghosts of Robert E. Lee, and Abraham, as ever, in search of his father. And although neither of us would find what we were looking for there, our three days at the Freedman's Village would inform the rest of our time together.

And have some little bearing upon our adventure to come.

The Freedman's Village was a crowded assembly of white tents and whitewashed clapboard buildings spread out incongruously below the tall Lee mansion over hundreds of acres of lawn that sloped gently down to the lazy waters of the Potomac River.

We were directed by the provost guard[50] to an admitting tent, expertly examined by a Negro doctor—many of the freed slaves suffered from exposure, Watson, not to mention the untreated wounds from years of maltreatment— and finally allowed to enter by the main gate. There, a white woman in the modest garb of a Quaker approached us with a wide smile upon her face.

"The oysterman!" she exclaimed.

Yes, Watson, it was she—the kindly Quaker woman who had seen through my disguise in the railroad carriage early in my days at the DuPont works. I felt my face flush, whereupon she embraced me kindly and introduced herself to Abraham.

Her name was Miss Nichols, and she had come to the Freedman's Village

---

50 *Forerunner of the military police.*

with her Negro companion on that trip to Washington City, she said, after
a brief but inconclusive meeting with Mr. Lincoln. Almost the moment they
had entered the gates of the village her companion had discovered a sister, and
so they had decided to stay to help reunite others.

And now Miss Nichols listened intently as Abraham explained his
own reason for coming. Then she took him in hand and led us to a long
wooden building where the midday meal was being served.

Inside was a dense sea of noisy humanity. Men and women, girls and
boys of every age and state of dress stood in long lines at the cooks stations
waiting to fill their bowls with chowder and biscuits before taking seats
at one of the dozen long tables where hundreds were already eating. As we
took our turn in line, however, all talking around us ceased and we were
waved ahead with much bowing and curtseying in that deferential manner
I found most uncomfortable.

I felt a squeeze upon my arm from Miss Nichols. "They think you
must be Abraham's overseer," she whispered.

I scarcely knew what to say, Watson. The notion made me positively ill.
I was determined to leave so that at least Abraham could eat, but the firm
grip of Miss Nichols guided me instead to a grey-headed man at the head of a
long table. After she had spoken some few words to him, he took my hand in
his—the roughness and wrinkles reminded me of a certain other Great Man,
Watson—and he spoke kind words of welcome to me and friend Abraham.

Somehow—the signal was too subtle for my eyes to see—the chatter
around us resumed, and we once again took our place in line, this time with
no commotion.

Soon we had filled our plates and were seated on either side of
this gracious man, who was, evidently, a pastor of renown, and clearly
the most respected figure in the Freedman's Village. He led a blessing
that extended several minutes, evoking the exodus out of Egypt, the
Emancipation Proclamation of "Marse Abraham" and the troops of
General Grant who had seen the Proclamation enforced and the slaves of
Virginia freed.

He ended with a kind word of thanks for the good Miss Nichols, and,
finally, all around us began to eat, whence the good pastor turned to my

companion. "Looking for your father, I hear. Tell us 'bout him."

And this Abraham did, although his story required substantially more time in the telling there among the inhabitants of the Freedman's Village, Watson, than that memorable morning in the Stanton dining room.

For Abraham's story had been *their* story, too.

Instead of listening in silent attention as President Lincoln had done, cries of "*Shame!*" and "*Cruelty!*" erupted as Abraham spoke. Prayers were spontaneously shouted, and tears were shed—as were words of encouragement, and great love—and before he had finished, the crowd around us had swelled in the same inexorable manner in which those men and women had surrounded President Lincoln as he walked the empty streets of Richmond.

When Abraham finally fell silent, all around him fell silent, too. Then the pastor gripped him by the hand and promised their help, much as President Lincoln had done, come to think of it—although their methods were not quite the same, Watson!

The machinery of a vast government was not theirs to utilize, of course, and they had no secretaries to dispatch, no telegraph operators at their command, no Attorney General to summons.

Their method was much cruder and far more ancient, but highly effective all the same.

I had witnessed it that day in Richmond, I now realized, when those freed slaves materialized seemingly out of the ether to gather around the Great Emancipator; and on the evening of Election Day, when the voting tallies in distant states came to the inhabitants of the Island faster than any horse messenger could have carried them.

You and I would call it "word of mouth," Watson, but they called it "the grapevine telegraph," and it was their means of transmitting information person-to-person, but in so subtle a manner as to escape the ears and eyes of their masters.

And it began humming across the Freedman's Village that very moment in search of Abraham's father.

My friend did not find his father on that visit, Watson—I will not keep you in suspense—but he did find a new family there, one that lifted his heart with the promise that somewhere, somehow, a connection would be found, and that they would one day be reunited.

As for me, it was enough to have been granted a respite from the responsibility of caring for the President's son and to spend some little time exploring the old Lee mansion (there was not much to explore, admittedly, for it had been converted into a Union hospital), while Abraham and Miss Nichols engaged the grapevine telegraph.

My respite ended, however, when a War Department messenger bearing a more material form of telegraph—from the War Secretary himself—found me.

I was wanted back at Franklin Square.

I Am Given a Book, Which I Have Kept

It was three days later. Friday, April 14th. Good Friday. A mood of unrestrained jubilation gripped the crowds of Washington City as I pushed my way from the Stanton home to the White House to fulfill my new assignment from the War Secretary.

That assignment once more involved young Tad Lincoln, and although it did not seem nearly so adventurous an assignment as that boat trip down the Potomac, Watson, it would shortly overwhelm my memories of the Richmond voyage, as you will see.

The President and Mrs. Lincoln—as the entire city of Washington knew—were to attend *My American Cousin* at Ford's Theatre that evening in the company of General and Mrs. Grant. And as General Grant and President Lincoln were the most popular figures of the day, and as they had never appeared together in public, it was expected to be the most sensational event of the year.

Mr. Stanton wanted nothing to go awry.

"I want you to keep that boy out of the Chief's hair," he had told me upon my return from the Freedman's Village, handing me two tickets to a performance of *Aladdin* at Grover's Theatre, a few streets from Ford's. "You'll take him to this show, and until the President and Mrs. Lincoln have returned General and Mrs. Grant to the Willard Hotel for the night, you will not bring that boy back to the White House. Under *any* circumstances."

The crowds at the White House gate were thicker than usual—everyone in Washington, it seemed, wanted to shake the President's hand, or beg a favour of him, or steal a souvenir—but soon enough I was admitted upstairs to the family quarters, where I came upon the President engaged in a wrestling match of sorts with Tad, who was delirious with joy at having his father to himself.

"Your charge is here, Tad," said the President, raising himself slowly to his feet, a great unfolding of limbs that brought him a full two heads taller than myself. He dismissed the guard and frowned at his disheveled son. "Best tuck in that shirt and tell Mother your companion is here."

When the boy had dutifully scampered away into Mrs. Lincoln's parlour, I found myself alone with the President.

He was gazing thoughtfully at the bookshelf, whence he picked out a book—the Weems book, I could see—and began to glance through its pages. "I can't seem to get Tad to read this," he said with some regret. "Prefers 'Wild West' stories, you know." He turned to face me. "I said you ought to have it. I meant it."

Just then the door from the President's office opened and John Nicolay entered, fuming. He handed a telegram to the President, who studied it briefly, shrugged his shoulders and handed it back to the incredulous aide before turning once more to the book in his hands.

"Oughtn't you respond?" Nicolay fairly barked. "That d----d scoundrel Davis is making for Mexico!"

"Godspeed to him!" said the President. "We should all hope he makes it."

"Dear me!" It was Mrs. Lincoln, at the parlour door, with Tad at her side. "I blush to hear such language, Mr. Nicolay," said she in her scolding, high-toned manner, hugging her son protectively.

"It's only Shakespeare, Mother," said the President with a wink at his secretary, who turned on his heels and left the room.

"It is not for a boy to hear such language."

The President chuckled. "Tad heard a good deal worse from the deck of the *River Queen*, I expect."

Mrs. Lincoln gave a scolding cluck, then turned to me. "This

young man will see our Tad is returned safely?" she asked, as if we
had never met—indeed, as if I had not spent sixteen days shepherding
her son around City Point, pulling him to safety from Confederate
prisoners and keeping him from unraveling giant pyramids of cannon
balls!

"Well, Mother, seeing's how he returned Tad safely from City Point, I
expect he'll manage Grover's well enough."

"Then the boy will get dressed."

This oddly formal inquisition completed, Mrs. L retired to her room
with "the boy," and the President sat down in the cane-backed chair at
the desk. He put on his spectacles and began to leaf through Weems by
the light of a lamp—smiling, evidently, at the notes he had written in the
margins as a boy.

"He's a bit fanciful, Weems is. But he prints General Washington's
farewell address word for word, and it still scours." He glanced at me over
his spectacles. "I mean to say, it's mighty good."

He took up a pen from the inkstand and found the title page. After
pausing to study the portrait of Washington that hung upon the wall
above the desk, he began to write—with no explanation to me—two or
three lines across the page. Then he returned the pen to the inkstand
and was waving the book to dry the ink when Nicolay reappeared with
more messages in hand and a grim look upon his face.

"What is it, Nicolay? Bobby Lee hasn't changed his mind, has he?"

"No, but General Grant has. Sends his regrets. Says he and Mrs. Grant
must take the evening train to visit family in New Jersey if he is to return
in time for his conference with Sherman on Sunday. He begs your pardon
and thanks you for your kind invitation, etc. etc."

Lincoln nodded, then shut the book and handed it to me. He appeared
not in the least surprised at this news, but a cloud had descended upon his
features, and lines of fatigue and care returned. "This will not go over well
with Mother," he said in a somber voice.

At that moment, Mrs. L appeared at the doorway with Tad, now
dressed for the evening. "What news, Mr. Nicolay?"

"General Grant sends his regrets—"

Nicolay's words were cut short by a hideous screech and the sight of the President's wife tearing off her gloves, flinging them to the carpet and stamping on them like a child. The imprecations that woman heaped upon poor Julia Grant were such that I would blush to repeat them, Watson—and no publisher would print them. The President said nothing, but slumped ever more deeply into his chair. Nicolay grabbed Tad decisively by the hand and motioned me to follow him into the President's office, shutting the door behind us.

I found myself in a large room with tall windows—the window from which the President had spoken to the serenaders the night of his re-election was the one in the corner—and walls lined with shelves of books and displays of regimental flags. Several bell pulls hung from the ceiling, and in the center of the room was a long, oval table covered in maps and surrounded by a half-dozen chairs, all beneath a bright, many-globed gas chandelier. The President's desk in the far corner was piled with books, letters and documents.

Mrs. L's screams were still somewhat audible through the library door, and Tad exhibited a manic nervousness that I had witnessed on the River Queen during similar episodes, so I occupied the boy by drilling him on the regimental flags while Nicolay sent messengers to find a suitable couple to take the Grants' place.

Eventually he secured the services of one Henry Rathbone, an Army major who, with his fiancée, had accompanied the Lincolns on similar occasions. By that time, the fires of Mrs. L's tirade had burned themselves out, so I escaped to Grover's Theatre with Tad while father and mother prepared to see *My American Cousin*.

Without General Grant and his poor, abused wife.

"They Killed Papa!"

It should have taken us only a few minutes to reach Grover's, it being a mere two streets away from the White House, but so crowded was Pennsylvania Avenue and so jubilant were the celebrants that we would have missed the curtain rising but for the foresight of Nicolay. Seeing the crowds from the window of the President's office and fearing for Tad's safety, he had insisted we be accompanied by the White House doorkeeper—a tall, burly policeman named Donn.[51]

And it was well that Donn came with us, Watson, for Tad very nearly lost himself more than once on that short walk, so full of energy and excitement was he. "There's Pa!" he would shout as the serenaders marched by, waving portraits of the President and General Grant, whence he would disappear into the crowd until Donn pulled him back.

We reached Grover's just before the curtain rose, and Donn excused himself that he might take dinner at the tavern across the street. Tad was soon engrossed in the fairy-tale story upon the stage whilst I, as was my habit, employed the time to make an intensive study of the actors—and of the tools and techniques they employed.

Needless to say, *Aladdin* was by no means a work of distinction, but the adventure was portrayed with some little competence, and the evening passed swiftly enough. It was what occurred between the second and third acts, however, and not the play or those who performed it, that is forever etched in my mind.

It was, as I have said, common for theatre performances in America in those days to be interrupted with patriotic songs and poetry readings. During one such interval at Grover's an actor stepped up to the gaslights to recite a rousing poem he called "The Flag of Sumter."

I remember being impressed with the fiery delivery, which brought the men in the crowd to their feet, stamping and whistling in approval— but my recollection of the poem's contents has been erased in the aftermath of what was to come, when the cheers and whistles were

---

51 *Alphonso Donn, a former Washington City police officer.*

interrupted by a new sound, discordant and out of place, emanating from somewhere in the darkness of the theater behind me.

It was the voice of a man in distress.

His cries were hoarse and indistinct at first—and masked somewhat by the actor's recitation from the stage—but they persisted until the actor became flustered and paused, allowing the words being cried from the back to ring throughout the theatre, blasting the ears of everyone in their seats:

"President Lincoln is assassinated in his private box at Ford's!"

I write the words precisely as they were shouted, Watson—although I cannot adequately portray the manner in which the man's voice fairly choked on the passive verb, nor can I convey the profound hush that fell upon the audience as the full import of that horrible word reverberated in the very air.

Next—well, the history books tell us that pandemonium erupted, but that is not what happened next. No, what happened next, Watson, was this: nothing. And for the very simple reason that almost nobody in the theatre believed what they heard. Confused silence lingered until another voice, a reassuring voice of authority, cried out:

"Pay no heed! It is a ruse of the pickpockets!"

A murmur of approbation arose from the crowd—in those days, Watson, pickpockets were never far from any gathering in Washington City—and all around me the men and women settled their children in their seats for the resumption of the entertainment.

And who might blame them?

The words seemed impossible, unbelievable, absurd. After four years of insurrection and war, subterfuge domestic and foreign, could anyone believe America's Great Man had been taken away only days after the very moment his vision, so strongly held and so firmly pursued, had finally triumphed? In something so prosaic as a theatre box? Watching an entertainment so lightly thought of that no one would remember the point of the play—only what happened during it?

Who could believe it?

But I believed it, Watson. And not because of the skills of observation

and deduction I had been practicing since my days in the laboratory with
Monsieur Vernet.

It was the instincts of a street urchin that told me it was so.

No pickpocket would have thought to raise such a cry in such a place
at such a time. Merely shouting "fire" would have cleared the theatre
and provided ready prey for the cutpurses. Nor would he have spoken
with such precision—*in his private box at Ford's* was a detail only an
eye-witness would have known.

Without a second thought I grabbed my charge by the wrist, pulled
him out of his seat and raced him to the lobby, where a knot of anxious
men had gathered around the stranger who had brought the news.

The men included, to my relief, Donn, the White House doorkeeper.
He had finished his meal and was smoking on the steps of Grover's when
the man had begun shouting, and he was interrogating the man now—
rather roughly, I thought, holding the poor fellow by the throat and
shouting, "It's *not* so!" But the man—hatless and disheveled, with a face
whose spectral pallor was streaked with real tears—insisted that it *was* so.

And so forcefully that Donn let go the man and listened as he told the
entire, horrible story.

He was an usher at Grover's, he said, sent by Mr. Grover to Ford's as
a spy to count the house. He had been watching the President's box when
the explosion occurred; had seen the puff of smoke billow from the box;
had heard the commotion and watched an actor—J. Wilkes Booth—leap
from the box to the stage; had seen him come down hard on one leg before
rising awkwardly to his feet, brandishing a knife and shouting wildly as
he limped off through the wings.

Donn listened carefully to each detail, repeating them to himself to
make certain that even in such a trying circumstance he had ascertained
precisely what this fellow had seen. Then he set about to question the
man, whose answers sent a chill to my heart.

No, the man said, he didn't know if Booth was holding a gun—he
only remembered the knife; yes, Booth had been followed—by a major
named Stewart; no, the major had not been able to stop Booth from
his flight; yes, President Lincoln was being attended to by a doctor, an

Army doctor. No, he didn't know the doctor's name. Yes, he *knew* the President was dead.

"*How?*" pressed Donn.

"Mary Lincoln screamed it."

At this last, Donn nodded gravely and turned away, taking Tad's hand and hissing an emphatic command to me: *"Get to Franklin Square and tell Mr. Stanton what you have heard, at once!"* Then he picked up Tad and trotted away down the steps.

As they disappeared into the surging crowds I could hear Tad screaming, "They killed Papa! They killed Papa!"

I pushed and ran my way to Franklin Square as quickly as I could manage, though my progress was slowed by the crowds, for I was intent on helping in whatever way was necessary.

I could never have imagined, my dear Watson, what form that help would take.

THE GREAT MAN BREATHES HIS LAST

To my utter astonishment after the excitement at Grover's, the Stanton house was dark.

Mrs. Stanton had retired for the night, the girl informed me, and Mr. Stanton had just departed in the carriage for the home of Mr. Seward, across the park. It seemed the Secretary of State had been injured in some sort of attack just half an hour before.

It is a plot, I thought to myself, and without another word I turned on my heels and raced down the steps and into the crowded streets, once more dodging still-joyful groups of drunken men. Reaching the Seward house some few minutes later, I found Mr. Stanton in conversation with Secretary Welles,[52] who had evidently just arrived to pay a visit to the wounded Secretary of State within.

"Mr. Seward's condition is bad, but not fatal," I heard him saying. "The son is injured as well, but Mrs. Seward was not harmed... No villain has been apprehended... A visit from you would be most welcome. Most welcome."

---

52 *Navy Secretary Gideon Welles.*

When Secretary Welles had rushed inside, I approached the War Secretary. He stared at me with evident confusion, then gave a startled gasp. "Why the devil are you not with young Tad?" he exclaimed.

I told him quietly what had occurred at Grover's, and the facts Donn had elicited from the eye-witness to the events at Ford's Theatre. His face blanched in the gaslight, and he gripped my arm with some little force.

"Wilkes Booth? The actor?"

"Seen by everyone at Ford's, instantly recognized," said I.

"He was captured, then!"

"No. He fled by horse, pursued by an officer named Stewart."

Mr. Stanton relaxed his grip. "Major Stewart, I know the man. That is like him, to pursue a fiend."

His eyes now took in the crowd gathered outside the White House gates, just across the park, and his mouth tightened as the enormity of what was unfolding seemed to reveal itself to his mind. Then he removed his spectacles, bowed his head and began to scratch his whiskers in that attitude of deep reflection I had come to recognize.

When he lifted his head and replaced his spectacles, his eyes met mine with such intensity as I had never before witnessed. He nodded several times—as if he had just made up his mind about a great many things—and called over a knot of guardsmen standing nearby, pointing his finger into the chest of each man as he spit out his instructions with such force and brevity that they could not but be instantly obeyed.

"You, to the War Department, tell Meigs[53] to close the bridges! You, to the White House, secure it! You, to the Kirkwood House—find Vice President Johnson there and guard him!"

As they dashed off, Secretary Welles emerged from the Seward home. "The Secretary is safe, Edwin!" he called out with relief.

"The President is not," said Mr. Stanton gravely. "He is shot at Ford's."

Welles staggered backwards. "Dead?"

"I can't say." Mr. Stanton had whistled for his carriage and the two men now climbed in, Stanton pulling a nearby adjutant in with them. I had started to make for the Stanton house when the War Secretary called after me. "Where the deuce are you going?"

---

53 *Montgomery Meigs, Quartermaster General of the Union Army.*

"To Franklin Square, to tell Mrs. Stanton."

"She'll hear soon enough, and I need your swift legs. Get in." I climbed in and we jolted away.

The carriage ride to Ford's was the blackest twenty minutes of my life, Watson.

First singly, then by couples and then by groups the news spread like a wildfire burning in a stiff breeze, turning the exuberant crowds into gatherings of grief before our eyes. Men dropped suddenly to their knees and wept. Woman cried out, pulled their hair, screamed. Soldiers burst forth from taverns, prowling for 'secesh' to string up from the lamp posts.

On that brief ride, I watched the mood of an entire city turn from unabated joy to utter despair.

So thick with grieving, angry citizens did the road become that Mr. Stanton finally ordered a halt at Tenth Street. We exited there and the adjutant cleared a path to Ford's, where a guard informed the War Secretary that the dying President had been taken directly across the street.

To a house owned by a fellow named Petersen.

Finding its steps blocked by spectators jostling to see inside the windows, Stanton ordered them flung aside and we quickly entered. Its hallways were crowded with the curious and grieving, and its atmosphere was heavy with the sour, oppressive odour that accompanies death. Stanton and Secretary Welles made for the rear bedroom where the President lay dying.

I waited in the hallway with the adjutant and the other guardsmen.

After only a few moments, however, Mr. Stanton reappeared, his face possessed of a curious mixture of sadness, anger and determination. He set about taking control with much-needed firmness. The hallways were cleared, the entrances secured and, yes, Watson, as the history books have written, the order was given to escort "that woman"—Mrs. Lincoln—from the death room.

But this was not the heartless command it has been made out to be. The poor woman was quite literally out of her head—understandably so—and her repeated intrusions into the bedroom interfered with the doctors

attending the dying President. (These included, as I later learned, the
very same Negro surgeon who had inspected Abraham and myself at the
Freedman's Village days before.[54])

Next, Mr. Stanton commandeered the front parlor for an office. A
candle table became a desk, and a military adjutant soon arrived with the
necessary telegraph blanks, pens, seals and cipher books. In short order
the War Secretary had begun dashing off messages to the War Department
telegraph office for transmission to military and political leaders around
the country.

It was vital, he said, to affirm the government's control over the land, for
nobody yet knew how vast the conspiracy unfolding that night might be.

General Grant was recalled from New Jersey; guards were ordered to the
homes of every Cabinet secretary and high official in Washington; Union
cavalry (more than a thousand men) were dispatched across the land to join
the manhunt for Wilkes Booth and his accomplices, whomever they might
be; and every Union fort, battery and warship was placed on the alert.

And all these went out in just the first few minutes!

Over the next several hours, messages would be sent ordering all trains
out of Washington stopped and searched; harbourmasters in Baltimore,
Wilmington, Philadelphia and New York to inspect every outgoing vessel;
and the Governor of Maryland to place militia in control of Baltimore,
for it was believed—mistakenly, Watson, as we shall see—that Booth was
making for that city, where he had family and from whence the rail lines
ran north to Canada.

In addition, witnesses to the assassination at Ford's were called before
the War Secretary and interviewed, provost marshals were sent out to follow
leads, and extra manpower was requested from police departments as far away
as New York City.

Never have I seen a man work harder and with greater purpose than
I saw Edwin M. Stanton work that evening and through the following
morning, Watson.

And never did I work harder in my life.

I was drafted, along with a half-dozen soldiers and guardsmen, to run
messages and telegrams to the War Department telegraph office all that long,

---

54 *Anderson Ruffin Abbott, a Canadian-born physician.*

rainy evening. I made fourteen trips in total, although I remember little of them except the cold, slashing rain and the increasing panic and confusion in the faces in the streets—and that with each return to the Petersen House, the atmosphere within had grown darker and sadder in the interval.

Upon returning from my last run, at about six o'clock Saturday morning, Mr. Stanton closed the telegraph book on the candle table and shook his head. "No more messages will be sent from this house. I am going to sit with the President."

The meaning was clear.

"Good God! Andy Johnson is now President!"

For some little time, Mr. Stanton had been in the bedroom where the dying President lay surrounded by mourners and his doctors. I sat in the front parlour with several wet and tired guards, hearing only the soft voices and gentle sobs from the bedroom as the grey dawn lightened the sky outside the windows.

Quite suddenly the sobs were halted, and it became intensely quiet in the house. Now the long, laboured intake of a breath by the dying President could be heard. It was held an almost impossible length, until a harsh exhalation followed, and the long breath was once more taken.

This was repeated—how many times I can't recall—until, suddenly, shockingly, the harsh exhalation was replaced by a loud, choking gurgle.

It was the death rattle. President Lincoln had breathed his last.

The utter silence that now prevailed was broken swiftly and harshly by Mrs. Lincoln—she had been admitted to the chamber for her husband's last—with screams that rattled the house. *"Live but one moment, my love!"* as I remember it. Then, *"Speak to me and to our children!"*

Now came a rustle as two guards carried her from the room, for she had fainted. Then a solemn voice from within was heard: "He is gone," it said. "He is dead."

Another voice spoke—one of the doctors, by the sound of it: "On this, the morning of April the Fifteenth, President Abraham Lincoln" (he had no middle name, Watson) "expired at twenty-two minutes after seven o'clock."

Silence again, then Mr. Stanton's voice was heard asking the Reverend Gurley (the Lincolns' pastor) to lead a prayer. Though moving and powerfully spoken, I remember not a word but the final "Amen."

It is at this point in the histories of that terrible evening that Edwin M. Stanton was said to have bowed his head over the body of the dead President and solemnly proclaimed a most fitting and respectful epitaph: "Now he belongs to the ages."

But I never heard those words, Watson.

What I heard was, "Good God! Andy Johnson is now President!" and the footfalls of Edwin M. Stanton as he raced from the bedroom and appeared before us, his face a mask of shock. Then, pulling one of the guards close, he hissed, "Keep Johnson sober for the swearing-in. *Don't let him drink anything but cow's milk!*"

As the guard dashed off, Mr. Stanton instructed the next man to send for the coffin bearers—they had been waiting in the street for several hours with the hastily built pine coffin—and dismissed me and the others with a wave of his hand before picking up his telegraph book and departing for the War Department, adjutant in tow.

Until that moment, Watson, I had resisted the impulse to look in on the death chamber.

I had seen too much vulgarity throughout the evening—spectators pushing their way past the guards under the guise of kinship or grief to gawk at the dying man in his bed; orderlies rifling drawers for souvenirs before they were sent on their way; and worse. I had too much respect for the deceased man to be associated with such opportunists.

But I was overcome by the strongest desire to honour him—not only for myself, but for my friend, his namesake Abraham—and as a lull descended over the house and the weary mourners filed out of the room, it seemed the right and proper moment to do so.

With an approving nod from the guard, I entered.

The room was stuffy and warm with the odour of death—it was my first exposure, Watson, and I can smell it even now—and the mourners who remained were quite silent, their attitudes of shock and grief broken only by the sounds of the doctors gathering their instruments. I took a position behind Robert Lincoln, who had returned to Washington after Lee's surrender at Appomattox. He was seated at the bedside, noiselessly sobbing, still holding his father's lifeless hand, and beside him was Senator Charles Sumner, whom I recognized from the journey on the *River Queen*.

There I stood, and looked.

It was a shock, of course—and it seemed a double-shock to know I had watched this now-lifeless form wrestle with son Tad only some few hours before. The tall frame had been set strangely askew across the bed, for it would not have fit lengthwise, and the sheet draped across his body was darkly mottled with bloodstains. The head was grossly swollen, and the exposed face was black and blue above the cheekbones.

But what shook me most, Watson, was the presence of two silver dollars, one placed over each of the Great Man's sightless eyes. Such a savage joke they seemed to play on a man whose vision had been so much keener and more penetrating than his peers!

I had not long to meditate upon this, however, for the coffin bearers soon arrived and the bedroom was to be cleared. I left the Petersen house for all time, and found myself in the street where the oppressive grey light of a rainy, gloomy day revealed a city turned upside down. Last night's jubilation had become profound grief. Buildings that only yesterday displayed flags and gay bunting were today being draped in black. Everywhere in the streets, the military guards and fire brigades had been called out to keep order.

As on the previous evening, I found the Stanton house unduly quiet. The cook was in mourning, the coachman on duty with the War Secretary and Mrs. Stanton was at the home of her friend Mrs. Seward to help tend to the Secretary of State. Young Eddie Stanton had been called to duty at the White House.

I climbed the stairs, removed my clothes and fell instantly asleep.

ONCE MORE, PROVIDENCE

Out of the world of dreams I was taken by a sharp knock upon my door. Daylight still shone through windows, and I felt as if I had only just gone to bed, so I turned over and tried to go back to sleep, but a loud, insistent voice called my name.

I was wanted in Mr. Stanton's study.

For one brief, glorious second, Watson, I wondered that the events of Good Friday had been a dream. I stared at the ceiling and told myself it was impossible to have been at Grover's seeing an inconsequential entertainment one minute and running telegrams to the War Department the next.

But when I roused myself from bed and saw my mud-spattered trousers upon the floor and the Weems book there upon my night table—I had carried it all night in the inner pocket of my coat to protect it from the rain—the awful memories of that evening returned, and I knew the terrible truth.

I splashed my face, put on fresh linen, and left my room.

At the head of the stairs I encountered Ellen Stanton in mourning clothes, with young Eddie in uniform by her side. She was red-faced and scarcely able to speak without crying. Eddie, to my considerable surprise, showed an uncommon tenderness towards his stepmother—a protectiveness, I might call it.

Gone was the reckless guardsman who had nearly died with a growler in his fist. Gone too was the smirking affability with which the son of the War Secretary had masked a not over-bright intellect. And, for the first time in our association, he made an inquiry other than whether I would like to participate in some dubious recreation or other: he wondered if I would be attending church services with them, as it was Easter Sunday.

I realized with a start that I had slept a full day.

"May I give you a lift, sir?"

The voice that startled me out of my reading from the manuscript of Mr. Sherlock Holmes was possessed of a clipped French accent and belonged to a youngish man with a clean-shaven face almost entirely hidden beneath a riding cap, muffler and goggles. He was seated behind the wheel of a dusty pre-war Wolseley Colonial which he had brought to a halt not three feet in front of me on the Jevington Road.

A small French Tricolour was affixed to its hood.

It took some few moments to get my bearings and respond to this Good Samaritan, so immersed in Holmes's story had I been. To my right, I saw a friendly looking public house, the Eight Bells, with a parish steeple rising behind it. To my left, a row of attached brick houses abutted the road. From the doorstep of one of the houses, a mutt of indeterminate breeding had arisen to inspect our encounter.

By the steeple clock, I realized to my great surprise that two hours had elapsed since I had left the Polegate station, and I now realized, too, how tired I was. My feet were swollen, my hips ached, and my shoulder throbbed from the Jezail bullet wound that had been so long dormant.

"Why, I would be most grateful, sir!" I said with no little gratitude to the figure who had been watching me patiently from his car. "I fear, however, that I am headed to East Dean—the direction from which you have already come."

He considered this for a moment, then gave a Gallic shrug.

"The war is almost over. I can be late to a staff meeting." He eyed the dog warily as it trotted to the rear of the motorcar and began to growl. *"S'il vous plait, monsieur.* Put your bag inside and I will take you to East Dean. I am not a lover of *les chiens,* you see? Climb in!"

"Thank you!" said I, hastily folding the manuscript and placing it in my inner pocket. "You are a Good Samaritan indeed!"

"No, monsieur, only a humble officer in the French forces." He spoke in a rushed manner, as the dog's barking stiffened. "With haste, if you please."

I tossed my valise in the back and climbed as swiftly into the front seat as my weary bones would allow. But even before I could sit down, the driver put the car in reverse and sped backwards, turning abruptly into the carriageway beside the Eight Bells. There he brought her to a sudden halt, threw her into gear again and spun the wheel sharply, causing the Wolseley to lurch southward onto the Jevington Road and begin the final ascent of the Downs.

Not until the dog's barking had died away did the driver relax the car's pace.

"*Pardonnez-mois*," he shouted over the growl of the engine, "I have not a coat or goggles for you."

"But you have saved me a long walk!" I exclaimed, pulling my hat down tightly upon my head. "I cannot thank you enough!"

"*C'est rien, monsieur.*"

And with that, he fell silent, while my thoughts turned to Mr. Sherlock Holmes and what I might find when at last I reached his cottage.

The Wolseley, with its big, powerful engine, climbed the hills with ease, and after not even a quarter-hour we had attained the summit where the old Friston windmill announced the long descent of the southern headlands to the English Channel. At the junction with the coast road, my Good Samaritan steered the car left towards Eastbourne. As we rumbled downhill past the old telegraph house, I motioned him to take the next right, onto Upper Street, for East Dean.

This he did, and we soon passed the stone cottages that marked the edge of the village green, where a small wooden barracks now appeared, newly built since my last visit, its presence explained by an anti-Zeppelin gun that stood rather incongruously in the center of the green beneath a camouflage netting.

Happily, the familiar whitewashed walls of the Tiger Inn stood as ever on the northeast corner of the green, and from behind the old tithe barn on the corner opposite the Tiger rose the lofty bell tower of the East Dean parish church. The driver steered the Wolseley around the green and made for the red lamp box[55] where, at last, we arrived at Went Hill Way.

As we turned down the lane I sat up, my heart racing in anticipation that we would soon be at the cottage of Sherlock Holmes and I would finally be reunited with my old friend, for his carriageway would be visible at the sharp curve just a few hundred yards ahead. But when the Wolseley passed the old bake-house and began to bump and jar on the rut-filled road, a cold fear gripped me.

Suddenly nothing was familiar.

---

55 Royal Mail mailboxes, used in rural areas, affixed to lamp posts.

No longer did a commanding view of the Downs present itself ahead of me. Instead, on both sides of the road rose a tall, impenetrable yew hedge!

Where once I would have seen the distant figure of the Belle Toute lighthouse perched at the edge of the great chalk cliffs known as the Seven Sisters, standing sentinel above the English Channel, unseen but ever-present beyond, I now saw only thick green hedgerow.

And at the curve where Holmes's carriageway would have been marked by a telegraph pole, there was no carriageway—and no telegraph pole. Just the tall yew.

I motioned for the driver to stop the car, which he did. Then he glanced at me sideways, awaiting my instructions.

"I am sorry," said I, removing my cap and scratching my head. "This yew hedge is all new. Can you reverse her?"

He nodded and complied, driving us in reverse all the way back to the lamp box, where he again brought the Wolseley to a halt and waited patiently.

"There is the lamp box," said I, "and that is the bake-house. This *must* be Went Hill."

"There have been many changes with the war, monsieur."

"Yes, but lighthouses and telegraph poles don't disappear! Make your way again, please. Slowly this time."

He shrugged and complied, but I could see nothing in the unbroken yew indicating where Holmes's cottage lay. At the curve, he once more brought the car to a halt and waited while I thought back to the remarks of the sergeant and his cabby friend at the Polegate station.

Could they have been speaking the truth? Was it possible that Holmes *had* moved away—without alerting me, his oldest and closest friend? And if so, what kind of trick was he playing with his note requesting my aid?

I had left the car to inspect the road on foot as these questions played in my mind, when I became aware of a bustling from the hedgerow behind me.

"Good heavens!" I cried, turning around. "What the devil—?"

A tall woman in a soiled white cloth coat and thick leather gloves had burst out of an unseen break in the hedge. She wore a menacing look upon her sunburned face and cradled in one arm an odd, blown-glass contraption, rather like a hookah, while in the other arm she held a growling, squirming Jack Russell, its teeth bared, its ears flattened.

"Why do you linger here?" she shouted above the murmur of the engine and the growling of the dog.

"I am Dr. Watson!" said I, my walking stick at the ready. "I come to aid my friend, Mr. Sherlock Holmes!"

"Then you have come to the wrong place. There is no such person here." She set down the glass contraption to better control the dog as it snapped and wriggled to get free. "Now be off!" Her brow glistened from her exertions and her eyes blazed at me, but behind the fierce countenance I detected a certain haughtiness one would not expect in a farm girl.

"Surely Mr. Holmes's cottage is beyond this hedge—please call off your dog!"

"You are mistaken. There is no one here with that name. You must leave."

"Not until I have seen Mr. Sherlock Holmes!"

The struggling dog suddenly burst free and leapt to the ground. I raised my stick, but it dashed past me and made for the car, barking ferociously and snapping at the wheels. The Good Samaritan seemed quite unstrung, for even before the dog had reached the car the man had begun slapping his cap against the door and shouting "*Non! Go away! Allez-vous en!*" at the top of his voice.

But this only had the effect of provoking the Jack into more vicious snapping and growling, which, in turn, incited ever more frenetic pounding upon the door by the driver and more screams of "*Go away!*" and "*Allez-vous en!*"

"Please, madam!" said I. "Call off this dog and show me to the cottage of Sherlock Holmes, or I shall—"

My words were cut short by a sudden racing of the engine and the spinning of tires as the Wolseley was thrown into gear. I turned in time to see my Good Samaritan waving his cap and crying "*Au revoir!*" as he drove the car down Went Hill at high speed, the small dog in frantic pursuit, barking and snapping.

"Where the devil are you going?!" I cried. "Come back!" My heart sank as both car and dog vanished out of sight beyond the curving yew hedge.

A more disjointed, disheartening end to my journey, I could not have imagined.

I turned back to the woman, who seemed amused by my predicament. "Now see here," said I sharply. "I have been to the cottage of Sherlock Holmes *many* times—"

"Since the war?"

"Well, no, but—"

"Of course not. He moved away when the military came to Eastbourne."

"But he *summoned* me here this very morning!"

"Impossible. Mr. Holmes has left the district."

The dog had given up its pursuit and was returning in a slow, panting trot. The woman knelt down to gather the Jack into her arms, and when she stood up, comforting the dog, I detected an erectness to her bearing that presented a singular contrast to her working clothes.

If Sherlock Holmes had taken an assistant here on Went Hill, I decided, it would be just such a woman.

I pressed my case now in a more friendly tone of voice. "If Mr. Holmes tells me to leave, good madam, I will be on my way. All I ask is to see my friend."

"I'm sorry," she began, "but you must not stay here—"

Suddenly the dog cocked its ears, wiggled loose and jumped to the ground, barking as it dashed through the same unseen break in the hedge from which the woman had emerged, and soon a voice sang out from the hidden side of the yew—a familiar voice, somewhat huskier than last I heard it, but well-remembered all the same.

"Toby! Toby the Second!"

The dog's barking ceased, and now there was a rustling in the hedge followed by the appearance of a hand parting the hedgerow with an odd, flat trowel dripping with honey. The hand and trowel were soon followed by their owner, a tall, thin figure dressed in a well-used lab coat similar to that worn by the woman. As the dog joyfully circled his heels, he set down the tool and extended his hand.

"My dear Watson," said Mr. Sherlock Holmes, with a smile and, dare I say, a glistening in his eyes. "Forgive the rather unwelcoming nature of your reception. It is so good of you to come."

"Holmes!" I cried, taking his outstretched hand in mine. "Holmes!"

Chapter Four

MR. SHERLOCK HOLMES
OF WENT HILL

He looked older in appearance by somewhat more than the four years that had elapsed since our last adventure together and was now possessed of a slight, rheumatic stoop to his previously erect stance, which only served to exaggerate the effect of the angular cheeks and hawk-like nose. But it was to my considerable relief that the tall, lean figure standing before me did not look anything like a man hopelessly addicted to a narcotic.

Indeed, the keen grey eyes fixed upon me with a twinkle, and I could detect in them no sign of the pinprick compression of the pupil such as an addict would possess, nor were the eye sockets hollowed out from muscle loss that would have also marked him in that way.

His skin, though not ruddy, was not sallow either. In fact, for the first time since I had known Sherlock Holmes, his hands were altogether clear of the staining caused by the chemical experiments with which he had occupied much of his time when he was not working on a case. Most important, his smile revealed a healthy set of teeth altogether free from the debilitating effects imparted to the mandible in the addicts I had seen in my surgery.

Such indications, coupled with the rich, if greying, hair peeking out from beneath a workingman's cap, gave Sherlock Holmes the look of an active beekeeper, not a man addicted to opium or cocaine. Had I not been keenly aware of his remarkable abilities with a makeup kit and the suggestive fact that, despite the balmy temperature, Holmes wore a long-sleeved smock with a high collar—which of course prevented me from observing the state of his arms for needle marks—I would have been entirely convinced the morning's note had been a fake.

"This is not an awkward time for a visit, I hope?" said I, continuing to look for clues as to my friend's state of health.

"Not at all, dear doctor." He picked up the strange, flat-bladed tool the dog had been licking as we stood together. "I was scraping combs into the centrifuge while Miss Colvin here was tending the hives."

"Then you did not expect me?"

"Oh, I expected you, but not quite so expeditiously."

And with that somewhat ambiguous remark, Holmes nodded to the woman.

"You have already met, but I fear you have not been formally introduced. Miss Honoria Colvin, this is John H. Watson, M.D.—my Boswell, I call him—of whom you have heard some rather fulsome reminiscences upon my part. It is to this man I addressed the words of the manuscript which you so ably typed for me."

I was deeply gratified by the warmth of Holmes's introduction, and the woman seemed relieved to no longer be carrying on a deception. She removed her thick gloves and we shook hands—a new experience to me, but not uncommon thanks to the war, with so many occupations filled by women.

"In addition to her ability to cook excellent meals with a French flair from limited rations, Miss Colvin is something of an expert on bees and the farm life. She appeared on my doorstep one morning with a new queen bee I had ordered from Mr. Sturgess at the local apiaries, whence she happened to make several keen-eyed suggestions regarding my hives, and I have enjoyed her assistance ever since—"

Holmes paused as the dog began barking madly and made a sudden dash across the road, disappearing through a small hole in the hedge.

"And that Jack Russell now taking off after a rabbit is her dog, Toby.

I took the liberty of christening him 'Toby the Second' in memory of the bloodhound whose assistance was of some importance in that case which had been brought to us by your first wife, Watson—"

Holmes stopped, for in his characteristic manner he had read the grief upon my face, and he now put a comforting hand upon my shoulder.

"But I see that memory still touches your heart, Watson. I owe you an apology. Mary succumbed to illness after, what was it, four years of marriage?"

"Five."

"Five. Indeed. And how is Margaret, if I may ask?"

"Doing as well as can be expected, though she remains confined to the house by her asthmatic condition."

"I should think a fortnight in the fresh air of the Downs would do her wonders, Watson. You must bring her with you next time."

"I shall, now that I know that you DO live here!" I exclaimed with a rueful laugh. "Everywhere I turned, Holmes, I was told that you had moved away. I thought I had lost my mind!"

"That is what I want visitors to think," he responded with the utmost seriousness. "It is far safer that way."

"You are in some danger, then?"

"Brother Mycroft's agents on the Continent picked up a rather too credible threat in my direction from the Kaiser's *Preußische Geheimpolizei*[56] after our little run-in with his man Von Bork on the eve of this war." Holmes gestured at the tall yew hedge on both sides of the road. "As I refused to leave behind my winged friends, Mycroft had the landmarks removed and the hedges installed as a compromise."

"But how are you supplied without the carriageway to your door?"

He nodded down the road, where my Good Samaritan had vanished some minutes before. "By way of Miss Colvin's farm, which lies along the Birling Gap road at the base of Went Hill."

"Well, you certainly had me confused, Holmes. And you certainly fooled the cabby at the station. He refused to drive me! Claimed he took you to the train in his cab when you moved away!"

---

56 *The Prussian Secret Police, forerunner of the Gestapo.*

Holmes smiled. "Tony is not easily fooled, Watson. He is well paid to deny my existence here."

"What? You mean to say you *pay* him to tell that story?"

"Tony and a few others in Polegate—and a handful in Eastbourne as well."

"One second, Holmes. How did you know I came here from Polegate? My ticket was to Eastbourne."

"My knowledge of the timetables is admittedly rusty, Watson, and I was not able to work backwards from the time of your arrival," said Holmes in his familiar, didactic manner. "But your shoes told me all."

"My *shoes?*"

"The walk from the Eastbourne station is quite scenic, being up through the old golf course and along the chalky footpath over the Downs. From Polegate station, on the other hand, one takes the Jevington Road, which affords a smooth, dry path with only the occasional muck-covered crossing." He pointed at my feet with his trowel. "Your shoes display no chalk upon them, but the heels are well splotched with mud. Inference, you came from Polegate."

"Holmes, you are a magician."

"Magic has nothing to do with it. It is a matter of observation," he said sharply. But his crisp, firm voice and the evident delight he took in displaying his powers of observation and deduction brought a strong emotion to my heart, and I clapped him on the shoulder.

"You have no idea how relieved I am that I did not travel here in vain."

"I know my Watson. An old campaigner like you would not let a tight-lipped taxi driver and a stone-faced constable stand in his way."

"So the police are paid for their silence as well?"

"Not with cash, of course. But I assist the local constabulary from time to time when a sheep goes missing or some other trifle disturbs the peace, and they return the favour by making certain we remain unmolested here at Went Hill."

"You have done much more than find lost sheep, Mr. Holmes!" cried his assistant. "The Lord Mayor of Eastbourne—"

"Tut, tut, Miss Colvin. Which is the verse that warns against sounding one's own trumpet? Matthew, is it not? I rather think some tea and biscuits for friend Watson would not go amiss."

"Of course, Mr. Holmes." Her cheeks reddened at this gentle remonstrance, and she retrieved her odd glass contraption from the ground.

"I take it that is some sort of device to smoke the bees?"

"Excellent, Watson! You scintillate, as in the old days! Yes, it's my own little invention. It is, or was, a hookah. Except the smoke is not inhaled at the mouthpiece, here—it is expelled by way of that valve, there. Please stay a moment, Miss Colvin, and demonstrate the smoker for my friend while I retrieve Toby."

As she lighted the device, Holmes put his two forefingers between his teeth and whistled shrilly for the dog, which was soon wriggling back through the hedge. Then he turned his attention to the smoker with no little pride.

"It allows us to experiment with differing mixtures of combustible materials to find what works best in soothing the colonies without tainting the flavour of the honey. A blend of lavender and rose hips works exceedingly well, wouldn't you say, Honoria?"

She nodded, and I watched her set about manipulating the odd contraption. After some few minutes, I came to feel Holmes's keen eyes upon me.

"You have been studying me, Holmes," said I, meeting his piercing grey eyes. "What do you see?"

"I see what anyone can see, should they look closely enough."

"And that is...?"

"I see that your trouser cuffs have been taken up somewhat more than half an inch, but your waistcoat has not been altered. Inference: your weight is approximately the same as the last time we were together, yet you have lost half an inch in height—"

"Wonderful!" I cried.

"Elementary. I suppose you would express amazement if I asked how far your walk took you from the Polegate station before you were picked up and deposited here by automobile?"

"My dear Holmes! How in the name of all that is wonderful did you deduce that I was driven part of the way?"

"Good old Watson! Your ability to be amazed by a very ordinary inference has not been dulled by the years."

"Now see here, Holmes. It is true that I walked a good distance until a Good Samaritan offered me a ride, but as you didn't see him or his car, I fail to understand how you deduced it."

Holmes's eyebrows rose in amusement.

"Is it not obvious, friend Watson, that a man who has walked the entire route from Polegate would have somehow found his way through the hedge and simply knocked at my front door?"

"Well, yes, I suppose—"

"And as your arrival was announced by the dog, which can hear road traffic a mile before it reaches our premises, it stands to reason you were deposited here by a motorcar."

"But why a car and not a farmer's wagon?"

"Because the back of your coat is free of road dust. You could not have been seated in an open wagon. Is it not obvious?"

"Yes, it does seem rather obvious." I felt a twinge of embarrassment in the presence of his assistant, who stood smiling at our exchange. "I should have known there was a clue I had failed to notice."

"In point of fact, Watson, you provided no fewer than six clues, but I mentioned only the most patent." Holmes's irritation at perceived slights to his skills at observation and deduction had not diminished with the years.

"My admiration is complete, Holmes. You have divined my journey as if you had walked alongside me." I could not restrain my joy at seeing the old Sherlock Holmes in all his decisive reasoning, and so took his hand once more and squeezed it. "My dear Holmes...I don't know what to say."

"Then say nothing and let us provide you refreshment. A three-mile walk under a warm sun will make even an old campaigner tired and thirsty. Honoria, please lead the way, thank you."

As she started through the hedge with the glass contraption in her arms, the dog at her heels, Holmes added, "You brought no clothes, Watson, I see?"

With a start, I remembered my valise and whirled about.

Then suddenly it came back to me.

"Holmes, what have I done—I left my valise in the car!"

"Gone with that Good Samaritan, eh? Tut, tut, Watson!" Holmes adopted the same soothing tone with which he had calmed many a flustered client. "Miss Colvin will find a clean shirt and toothbrush for you."

"It is not those items that concern me," said I, with a sidelong glance after his assistant, who had disappeared through the gap.

"I take it," Holmes responded quietly, "You had packed your revolver along with your toothbrush?"

"I thought it best to take no chances, as I was carrying precious cargo."

"And what cargo was that?"

"Your manuscript, of course."

"Ah, the manuscript! You have read it, then? Well, we will have something to discuss over tea."

"But I'm afraid it was in my valise, Holmes."

"On the contrary, Doctor, I observe a portion of it never left your person." Holmes nodded at the breast pocket of my coat. "The outline is quite plain in your damp clothing."

"What!" I felt my coat. "Why, you are right! Thank goodness!"

"Then all is not lost," said Sherlock Holmes wryly, motioning me through the hedge. "Let us hope your Good Samaritan returns the valise without peeking inside."

Chapter Five

THE EIGHTH SISTER

With an apology to those readers already familiar with the appearance of the cottage of Sherlock Holmes from the published casebooks of our adventures,[57] I should like briefly to convey a true impression of the house to which he had retired, for it was there, in the heart of the South Downs, that my friend found a measure of the peace and tranquility necessary to write not only his *Practical Handbook of Bee Culture*, but also the remarkable remembrances of his years in America—some portion of which has already been shared in this narrative.

Holmes's cottage was a timber-framed farmhouse dressed in local stone and set in the southeastern face of Went Hill, a gentle slope of green and gold fields that descends for a mile from his backyard and comes to an abrupt end at the Seven Sisters, the great chalk cliffs that stretch from Seaford Head to Eastbourne.

Two chimneys poked through a red roof of Wealden clay, which now appeared, to my eyes, somewhat the worse for wear, being patched in one corner where lightning damage or some other mishap had occurred since my previous visit. Otherwise, the cottage looked entirely familiar to me.

The landscaping, however, was more considerably altered.

---

57 *Watson is mistaken. The cottage, though mentioned by Watson in* His Last Bow, *was never described in that story or in any of Watson's published writings.*

The well-tended rose gardens that had adorned either side of the gravel pathway to the front door had become entirely overgrown, and the carriageway that once led around the side to the stable block had almost entirely disappeared under an undisciplined mass of stinging nettles, horseweed, sheep's sorrel and other plants I did not recognize.

"Not a very English garden, Holmes," said I, picking cockleburs off my trousers as we followed Miss Colvin and the dog along what had once been the carriageway. "What happened to your roses?"

"Oh, their utility is mainly limited to making tea, so we let some more useful varietals take their place."

"What utility is there in stinging nettles and cockleburs, if I may ask?"

"A rag soaked in the boiled stem of a nettle once saved my leg, as Miss Colvin can attest."

"Indeed! I take it, then, that each of these ragged-looking weeds has a practical use?"

"Most certainly, Watson. Horehound to soothe the throat, hyssop flower for the relief of angina, peppermint to cure dyspepsia—"

"The thistle is not for the goldfinch, then?" said I, spotting a bright yellow and black bird plucking the seeds from a plant nearby, sending puffs of white, feathery hairs into the breeze.

"On the contrary, Watson, the thistle is entirely for the finches." Holmes stopped to admire the industrious bird. "But the stems *do* make a most excellent emetic in the case of mushroom poisoning."

"Goodness, Holmes, I hope you have not been experimenting on yourself!"

He chuckled and shook his head. "In my younger days, perhaps—but no, Watson, it was the dog." Holmes pointed to a raspberry bramble into which the creature had disappeared. "Toby the Second gets into everything, as you can see."

We continued around past Holmes's bedroom window to the old stable block. It stood apart from the cottage and had been given a new roof and fresh coat of paint since my last visit. Miss Colvin held open the door for us.

"The stables now house our beekeeping endeavors, Watson—please, Honoria, after you."

I followed Miss Colvin inside, and the atmosphere that met my nose smelled of cloyingly sweet honey and overripe apples. Sunlight slanting through the windows illuminated a low table upon which sat several buckets and a metal cylindrical contraption with a spinning device atop it, looking much like an ice-cream maker. Upon the walls were hung all manner of tools, from pruning saws and rakes to specialized implements evidently used in beekeeping.

At the far end of the stables sat a small, mud-spattered tractor.

"Holmes! You drive a tractor now?"

"That is Miss Colvin's department, Watson. She is our mechanical expert." He held up his trowel. "I handle the simpler tasks. As I said, I was uncapping honey from the frames when Toby sounded your arrival. The wax cappings are scraped into this bucket, to be delivered to our candle-makers in Eastbourne."

"So you are a candlestick maker as well?"

"Beeswax makes exceedingly fine candles, as Miss Colvin pointed out shortly after her arrival, and ours was going to waste. Once the cappings have been removed for the candlemakers, the frames—laden with honey—are placed inside this centrifuge and given an energetic spinning. Voila! Twenty pounds of a most excellent honey."

Holmes placed his trowel into a large metal sink and removed his coat, which he hung upon a peg next to Miss Colvin's.

"During the summer months we send at least five tubs of honey a week to the brewer, also in Eastbourne. He fills the jars and handles the tradesmen."

"Honey, candles—why, this is a thriving enterprise, Holmes!"

"Needs must, Watson, needs must. When the Kaiser's submarines halted imports of sugar along with much else, Miss Colvin here suggested my hives might cease to be a hobby. In short order she pruned my rather ramshackle orchard, installed several more hives and made the arrangements with the brewer. We have added colonies every spring, yet the demand continues to overtake my capacity to produce. Our bottles, I am assured, sweeten tea and toast from Whitehall to John O'Groats."

He handed me an empty jar with a mischievous smile.

"*Eighth Sister*," I read. "Why, this is the very jar in our pantry!"

"I should think so! Brother Mycroft's agent keeps your cook quite liberally supplied."

"My dear Holmes! I must tell Margaret. But why this name, *Eighth Sister*?"

"Well, I could not afford any association with my own name, but—"

"But you could not resist your own little joke. The Seven Sisters stand a mile from your cottage, so naturally..."

"Once more, you scintillate, Watson!" Holmes gestured to the door. "Come, let us show you the hives."

I was impressed.

Sherlock Holmes's backyard had been transformed from a scattering of beehives among a few apple trees into a well-organized collection of neatly spaced white boxes amid a tidy orchard that stretched to the sheep pasture at the limit of Holmes's property. There, through the line of trees, one could now see all the way to the Birling Gap, where the tiny figure of the old Belle Tout Lighthouse rose from the fog like a stout candle.

"Magnificent, Holmes! You have created your own postcard here!"

"It is not the view that interests me, Watson. Bees require a clear path to their feeding grounds—hence the more symmetrical orchard. The view of the lighthouse was a happy consequence."

He had been studying the sky visible between the row of trees, and I could see that something in the scenery that was quite invisible to my eyes had met with his own satisfaction.

"What do you observe, Holmes?"

"I observe a thousand tiny creatures returning from their routes, their baskets full of pollen. The feeding has been good today."

"You can *see* this?"

"In a manner of speaking. When the pollen sacs are full, the sky looks a touch darker, their movements a trifle slower. The screens will be heavy tomorrow, Miss Colvin."

"The sky does seem alive with the creatures, Holmes, but I can make out nothing from their appearance!"

"I expect not, Watson. It comes from the many days I have spent at that window—" He nodded at a large bow window which now jutted from the back of the cottage in place of what had been a small leaded glass fixture. I could see Holmes's old desk within and the hulking figure of a typewriter upon it.

"I can monitor my friends while Miss Colvin and I work on my manuscript, and any other little project keeping me indoors. It has also proven exceedingly helpful in an emergency," he added somewhat ruefully.

"Emergency? Then you *are* in danger here!"

"Oh, it was nothing like our old adventures, Doctor, I can assure you." Holmes chuckled. "*The Case of the Philandering Farmer*, you might have called it in one of your story books. A young farmwife asked me to track her husband on nights when he claimed to be attending his cows in their labours. They had been exceedingly promiscuous cows, evidently, for he was gone quite almost every night. Anyway, the fool's boots led straight to the neighbor's hayloft. For my modest exertions I was given a dozen eggs by the wife and paid an angry visit by her husband—with his pitchfork—late one evening. I managed to escape by that window with my nightshirt on."

"He did not catch you, I hope?"

"No—and thank the bees for that, Watson. He followed me out the window and ran straight into a hive! Thirty-seven stings rather put an end to his midnight ramblings. Never knock over a beehive at night, Watson, I can tell you that."

Holmes now gestured at a small, prim hut where the privy once stood. "Our candlemaking shed. That went in at the same time as the bow window."

"So, you installed plumbing at last!"

"Yes, Watson—and you may thank Mycroft for that touch of civilization. He refused to visit otherwise."

"But you can't possibly manufacture your candles in that tiny shed?"

"No, we experiment with new designs there. Our brewer handles the production. We needed a space some distance from the cottage—risk of fire, of course."

"Of course."

Miss Colvin now excused herself to prepare our refreshments, and as I watched her and the dog enter the kitchen by the side door, I noticed a large mound of fresh compost atop a thick loam of black dirt nearby.

"What is that, Holmes?"

"My compost bed, Watson. The farmers refresh it after the harvest season, and I add to it with my tea leaves throughout the year. These limestone hills possess only a thin layer of chalky topsoil, and it would not do to let the natural properties of our kitchen waste be squandered. Come spring, that dirt will fertilize my apple trees most delightfully."

He studied my shoes.

"Speaking of dirt, Watson, I think it best if we entered by the front door. Miss Colvin keeps a tidy house, as you'll see, and the boot-scrape will be more than a match for that Jevington mud." We completed our circle of the cottage by working our way through the bramble to the doorstep, where I employed the boot-scrape as Holmes watched.

"Thank you, Watson. That will do—I should think your boots are clean enough! Pray, friend, cross the familiar threshold. You have had a long journey and I hear the kettle whistling..."

Holmes opened the door and continued talking as I entered, whereupon a familiar aroma met my nose. It was a peaty, powerful aroma of old shag tobacco and the vinegary scent of chemical experimentation, with perhaps a sulphurous hint of gunpowder and the wintery odour of a smoky fireplace, and I suddenly felt myself carried back across the decades to our rooms at Baker Street and the memories of our life together, even as Holmes continued to chatter.

"...and now let me take your coat—I say, Watson, your knees buckle! Steady on, old friend, take my arm! There is strength enough in these old bones to support you! *Miss Colvin!* Please come at once! The doctor faints!"

When I opened my eyes I found myself seated in my old armchair before the fireplace, the face of Sherlock Holmes studying me from inches away, with no little alarm upon his brow. In his hand was a flask of brandy and in his eyes a tenderness I had rarely witnessed in all our years together.

"You are revived, Watson?"

"Yes, Holmes, thank you. Not a very gracious entrance to an old friend's house, I'm afraid."

"The nose is a singularly powerful instrument, Watson. It is a time machine that can carry one back in a moment."

"It certainly did for me, Holmes. All our days together at Baker Street—Mrs. Hudson, Lestrade, the Baker Street Irregulars—they all seemed to return to my mind at once. I was overwhelmed..."

"Steady on, old friend. Take this." He offered me the flask. "Another sip should help."

"Yes, thank you, Holmes."

His assistant now entered with the tea tray. It held a large pitcher of water, a steaming cup of tea and a plate of croissants with a dripping piece of honeycomb across each.

"Miss Colvin has prepared the house specialties, Watson." Holmes waved his hand across the tray with the flair of a waiter as she set it on the side table. "I recommend first a refreshing glass of water to rejuvenesce your muscles, then a cup of tea and a croissant, both dressed of course with a most excellent piece of honeycomb. After you are revived, we may reminisce. Thank you, Honoria. I believe my friend will soon be recovered from the excitements of the day."

A quarter-hour had passed by the chiming of the clock upon Holmes's mantel, and I felt considerably better. My old companion was gazing at me from his armchair through half-lidded eyes and smoking his black clay pipe in a contemplative manner, while from the kitchen came the sounds of Miss Colvin busy at the stove.

As I cast my eyes about the high-timbered room, I saw much that looked familiar.

On one side of the fireplace stood the tall bookcase filled with old casebooks, while on the other was the entry to the kitchen. Upon the mantelpiece stood the clock and other well-remembered artifacts of

Holmes's life from his days as a consulting detective, including the pipe rack with Holmes's favorite pipes and the Persian slipper filled with tobacco.

And above the mantelpiece still hung the print of Holmes's struggle with Professor Moriarty atop the Reichenbach Falls—into which I and the rest of the world believed Holmes had vanished, along with the professor, only to find Holmes in my consulting room three years later, hale and hearty, with the shocking news that he had used his widely reported "death" to draw out into the open the professor's underlings, Colonel Sebastian Moran among them, and that the time was ripe to round up the elusive gang.

Twisting to my right I saw Holmes's flat-top desk in its usual spot facing the south wall of the cottage (with its new bow window). Turning the other way I glimpsed the front threshold where I had fainted, while behind me was the old settee, and further back, on the wall opposite the fireplace, was the door to Holmes's bedroom and, in the far corner, the old chemical table.

As I say, at first glance, much was familiar.

But as I rose from my chair and began inspecting each of these things, my mind clear of the fog that had descended upon it during my fainting spell, I found much that had changed.

Upon the mantelpiece, in addition to the familiar mementos from Baker Street, there now stood a quantity of beeswax candles in varying states of depletion, while the casebooks on the bookshelves, I could see, were no longer scrambled about but had been quite neatly arranged and stood in order row upon row. The old settee was altogether bare of the newspapers and magazines that once made it hazardous to sit upon, while the old tin box at Holmes's feet—which once overflowed with handwritten notes and paper clippings from our cases, awaiting a burst of energy and a rain-soaked week of indoor habitation to be organized and cross-referenced by Holmes—now held only a neat stack of the current newspapers and magazines Holmes was evidently reading.

The new bow window, I could see, had utterly changed the southward view from Holmes's desk, affording a splendid panorama of the hives, the orchard and the great sweeping Downs beyond, while Holmes's desk lacked the piles of books and papers that once made it difficult to even find space to write out a check. In their place sat a Remington typewriter neatly encased in a dustcover that gave it rather the impression of the hunched shoulders of a man. Next to it stood a small bust of Abraham Lincoln atop a stack of fresh onionskin paper, and an old honey jar full of pencils, erasers, brushes and other tools for the typist.

And nothing else.

My greatest surprise, however, was reserved for the old chemical side table. It had evidently been transformed into a type of weather station, with thermometers and barometers in place of the microscope, Bunsen lamp, test tubes and retorts that had once cluttered its surface and engaged my friend for days on end. Also, a large chalkboard had been hung upon the wall above it, bearing temperatures, barometric readings and other unfathomable figures written in Holmes's familiar, precise hand.

"You are a weatherman, now, as well as a beekeeper?" said I.

"One must be both, Watson." Holmes had been following my movements from his armchair, puffing evenly upon his pipe. "The bees live by the weather, and so must I."

I noticed with a start that the beam above the chalkboard had been scorched and the ceiling newly plastered, evidently remnants of the accident which I had observed from outside the cottage.

"Holmes!" I cried. "What on earth happened?"

"A near-calamity, Watson," he said grimly. "I was experimenting with blasting powder, as in my old DuPont days, preparatory to the excavations of an old barrow I had discovered atop Went Hill. It is fortunate the ancient builders employed oak beams in these cottages, for they do not burn easily—"

"Blasting powder? To excavate an ancient burial chamber?"

"No, my dear Watson, I would never be so crude. A farmer had bricked up the entrance to keep his sheep out of harm's way, and it required rather more force to clear in order to access the barrow than a sledgehammer could bring to bear. Anyway, I was preparing a solution of guncotton when something caused a spark, and the spark did what sparks will do in the presence of a highly combustible material." He shook his head at the grim memory.

"How were you saved?"

Holmes pointed his pipe at the center of the room. "Miss Colvin found me seated upon the floor, dazed and not a little confused, just as the bees were gathering."

"The bees?"

"Yes, Watson, the bees. The force of the blast had knocked out the old window—thankfully it was much smaller in those days—and the bees merely acted upon their instinct to attack the point of danger."

"Goodness! How did you fend them off?"

He nodded at the fireplace. "Miss Colvin had the wits to close the flue. The room was soon filled with smoke and the bees pacified, but not before I had received a dozen or so stings. Less than the philandering farmer, more than I get during the season while tending the hives. Nothing a poultice of tea leaves couldn't cure."

"You were not injured by the blast?"

"Oh, you did not notice?" Holmes turned the left side of his face to the light of the lamp at his elbow.

"I see no disfigurement," said I, approaching him.

"It is a credit to the surgeon." Holmes set down his pipe and touched his earlobe. "The beaker exploded within a yard of this ear, scarring the pinna and rendering me deaf for a month on this side. Fortunately, my back had been turned and I was wearing my smock, so the flying glass stung quite a bit less than the bees."

"Goodness, Holmes! Where were you treated?"

"In London, under an assumed name. Brother Mycroft procured the services of a refugee Dutchman who had made remarkable advances in reconstructive procedures during the German occupation. My recovery took a year of plasters and ointments, but it is altogether a testament to the creation of man to contemplate how one's body adjusts. The reconstructed pinna and a rather annoying case of tinnitus are the only relics of my misadventure."

He pulled a small blob of wax from his watch pocket and held it out for my inspection.

"Beeswax makes an excellent earplug, Watson. I remain sensitive to certain sounds, and these come in handy."

"Dear me, Holmes!"

"I deserve no sympathy, Watson. I had forgot the lesson of my DuPont days—chemicals are a dangerous game. Why, the good Lammot du Pont was killed in a nitroglycerin explosion not long after I left America. In any case, as you can see, the weather station has replaced the chemical table, and I have not fired the Bunsen stove since."

"Well, thank goodness for that!"

On the table at Holmes's elbow I noticed a familiar object—a small black and white ivory box that I had not seen in years.

"The deadly cigarette case sent by Culverton Smith!"[58] I exclaimed. "I trust it has been rendered harmless?"

"Quite harmless, unless you consider the cigarettes it now houses."

I picked it up and studied the tiny hole where a poisoned spring had once been ready to prick the casual admirer.

"Scotland Yard finally saw fit to return it, then?"

"Not officially, Watson. It was a gift from Lestrade upon his retirement."

"Quite a thoughtful one! He rose quite high, did your old friend. *Commissioner Lestrade.*"

"Yes, well, the competition in the official force is not so stiff, of course."

"Now, now, Holmes. Surely you can afford to be more charitable than that! By the way, whatever became of Culverton Smith?"

"Oh, he died in prison—of natural causes. Quite unlike Colonel Moran," Holmes added.

"Yes, I saw that notice in the *Times* this morning," said I, placing the ivory box upon the mantel. "Quite a coincidence, that happening and us being reunited days later."

"Yes, wasn't it?" he said dryly.

I gently pulled the bottom of the etching of the Reichenbach Falls away from the wall, expecting to find the familiar "V.R."—the royal

---

58 *Told in* The Dying Detective.

cipher of Queen Victoria—stenciled in bullet holes in the wall, as at Baker Street.

But the wall was unbroken.

"The cipher is not there, Watson."

"So I see, Holmes. But why? Don't tell me it's the bees!"

"Ah, but it IS the bees, Doctor. After that chemical blast, indoor shooting practice became a thing of the past." Holmes lit a cigarette, his eyes fixed upon my face. "Now, Watson, you have quite studied my lair. What do you make of the changes here at Went Hill?"

"It is certainly less cluttered than my last visit. I suppose your winged friends taught you something of their methods of organization?" I said sardonically.

"The bees can claim no credit in the matter, nor can I. Miss Colvin is unable to enter a room without straightening out so much as a misplaced matchbox. Speaking of the bees, however..."

Holmes rose from his chair and walked to the recess of the bow window, where he unlatched the center casement and threw it open. A sultry breeze filled the room, and the gentle sounds of an autumnal meadow reached my ears. Holmes cocked his head and closed his eyes in an attitude of the utmost concentration.

I was about to ask what he was doing when he held up an admonishing finger. Then, after a moment, he opened his eyes.

"The bees, Watson! I am listening to the bees. Their mood is a trifle unsettled, I perceive. It will be best they not be disturbed tonight. A change in weather is coming."

"You judge this by listening to their *mood*?"

"My dear Doctor, bees are as moody as any of God's creatures, and quite a bit more volatile, living as they do in such a confined space. The disposition of the hive is an ever-changing thing. The slightest provocation, well, ask my farmer friend..."

He held up his hand to arrest further conversation, cocked his ear once more and, after some few moments, nodded decisively. "Yes. Winds from the north tonight will bring scudding clouds and temperatures well below normal, I should think."

"You'll find the wind is from the south, Holmes. The papers are calling for a mild evening."

He shrugged his shoulders. "We shall see."

Something in his condescending manner annoyed me.

"At least have the goodness to tell me how the bees perform this service for you, Holmes!"

"They do what you and I might do on a brisk day, Watson—they take exercise. Bees require a consistent temperature in the hive. Sensing a cold front, as they evidently do now, their activity increases. It's quite audible to the trained observer. *Let anyone with ears*, you know."

He pointed to the chalkboard scrawled with his figures. "I have monitored their activity against the weather these last three years, and they are never wrong. I would trust the bees before I would trust the Met Office."[59]

"Holmes! You have entirely gone over to the bees!"

"Quite out of necessity, thanks to you, Watson."

"Thanks to me?"

"The fame brought upon my head by your books and stories proved a two-sided coin. On the one side, satisfied clients; on the other side, unhappy criminals brought to heel. To maintain anonymity in a hostile world, I required a supplement to my diminished income during these retirement years."

"To pay the constables and cabmen for their silence?"

"Precisely. And the newspapers, too."

"The newspapers?"

"Most certainly. An enterprising reporter could easily expose me here, so I keep their publishers well compensated to keep that from happening." He retrieved an edition of the *Eastbourne Gazette* from the tin box and handed it to me without comment. I leafed through its pages in growing astonishment.

"Why, Holmes, between your honey and your candles, you must be one of their largest advertisers!"

"Third largest. That influence extends to Brighton, by the way."

---

59 *The Meteorological Office, the national weather service of Great Britain.*

"Ingenious, Holmes! I congratulate you."

"Suggested and carried out by Mycroft, actually." Holmes nodded at the hulking form of the Remington upon his desk. "I've got quite a bit else to occupy my spare time."

"Which reminds me, Holmes. Your manuscript! I am eager to—"

But he cut me off with one of his sharp glances as the figure of Miss Colvin appeared at the kitchen door. Knowing Sherlock Holmes did nothing without good reason, I said no more, but I did wonder at his evident reluctance to speak about the manuscript in her presence.

"There is onion soup in the pot and bread in the pan, Mr. Holmes," said she. "I must attend to Uncle's dinner now."

"Excellent, Honoria, thank you. Miss Colvin cares for a destitute uncle, Watson. He is rather ill, the poor man. Will Toby the Second be joining you?"

At this, the dog rose from his place between the fire grate and Holmes's violin case and stretched languidly. Then he trotted slowly to his mistress's side.

"And there is our answer!"

"Shall I light the lamps on my way out?"

"Thank you, Honoria—just the candles on the mantelpiece. There remains an hour or so before sunset."

"Dear me, Holmes! Still no electricity? I recall you were intent on installing it—quite enthusiastic about it, in fact."

"You remember correctly, Watson. But I had to forgo those plans."

"It wasn't laid through East Dean?"

"No, the line is quite nearby. Miss Colvin's farmhouse has it, in fact."

"Don't tell me, Holmes," I said with some asperity. "The electric light would disturb the bees."

"It is not the light that would bother them, Watson. It is the *vibration*. The extension line would have come up Went Hill through the orchard, and bees are highly sensitive to strong vibrations."

"I suppose your friends sent a delegation to discuss the matter?"

Holmes chuckled.

"In a way, they did, Watson—when that beaker exploded."

"I had no idea the bees were so sensitive, Holmes! Vibration, smoke, heat, cold... their catalogue of discomforts is almost human."

"They're more human than you might ever dream, Watson. I may say they are every bit as intelligent in their way as you or I." Holmes bowed at his assistant as she finished with the candles. "Thank you, and good night, Honoria."

"Good night, Mr. Holmes."

When we heard the kitchen door shut, I turned to my friend, who had moved once more to the recess of the window.

"Now, see here, Holmes, you have put off my questions at every turn with this incessant chatter about your bees. Would you please explain—"

But Sherlock Holmes held up a cautioning hand. He was staring intently out of the window, his eyes following Miss Colvin and the dog as they made their way past the beehives and through the orchard. Finally, the pair had reached the stile, crossed to the meadow and disappeared from view.

Only then did he shut the window and latch it.

Then he strode to the mantelpiece and recharged his clay pipe with the utmost concentration. Soon great puffs of smoke were curling slowly upwards to the high, beamed ceiling as the mantel clock chimed the half-hour. Finally, taking his seat in his old armchair, Holmes waved his hand towards my chair. When I was seated, he fixed his inquisitive grey eyes upon me and uttered words that positively amazed me.

"Now, my dear Doctor, we are quite alone. First, you must tell me what brought you to Went Hill in such a hurry and in such a disjointed frame of mind. Then you will provide every detail of the murder in the train. Who died? How did he die? And, above all, who did the deed?

"Leave out nothing."

For a moment, I had not the clarity of mind to respond to this astonishing series of questions, but by the seriousness with which he held my eyes, I could see that Sherlock Holmes had intended no surprise.

"My dear Holmes!" I cried. "How in the name of all that is wonderful did you guess there had been a murder on the train?"

"I never guess, Doctor, you know that."

"Your friends from the police alerted you, then?"

"Not at all," he said sharply. "I deduced it. Besides, the wires are down. I couldn't possibly—"

"But if the wires are down," said I, in some confusion, "then the Eastbourne police never received my telegrams!"

"Why on earth would you have cabled the Eastbourne police?" Holmes's surprise appeared as great as my own.

"Because of this note you attached to your manuscript."

I pulled from my pocket the folded piece of foolscap and handed it to Sherlock Holmes.

He slipped his spectacles from his watch pocket and settled them upon his nose, adjusted the lamp at his elbow and began to study the note.

Another quarter of the mantel clock would chime before he would stir.

END OF PART II

III

FIRST CASE...AND LAST

"He is the Napoleon of crime, Watson. He is the organizer of half that is evil and nearly all that is undetected in this great city. He is a genius, a philosopher, an abstract thinker. He has a brain of the first order. He sits motionless, like a spider in the center of its web, but that web has a thousand radiations, and he knows well every quiver of each of them. He does little himself. He only plans. But his agents are numerous and splendidly organized...

"This was the organization which I deduced, Watson, and which I devoted my whole energy to exposing and breaking up."

—Sherlock Holmes on Professor Moriarty
The Final Problem

Chapter One

AN INTERROGATION

Sherlock Holmes sat in silence, puffing at his pipe and gazing into the fireplace, his eyebrows knitted in the deepest thought. Upon one knee lay the lens with which he had conducted with the utmost care his examination of the note summoning me to Went Hill.

Upon the other knee lay the note. It read, as will be remembered, as follows:

> *Watson—*
>
> *That I have become addicted to a particularly malignant class of opiates is the inescapable conclusion to which I have arrived after a brief but intensive period of self-examination, and it is in this moment of lucidity I call upon you to come to my aid.*
>
> *Bring your medical kit, and please, come at once.*
>
> *—Sherlock Holmes*

Holmes stirred as the clock chimed the quarter. Then he nodded with the air of a man who has quite made up his mind on some matter, set down his pipe and turned to face me.

"Very effective. Very effective indeed. One thing is certain, Watson. This is no university prank, as your first instinct told you. It is a forgery by the hand of a professional, designed to bring you here to Went Hill with all due speed."

"Why a professional, Holmes?"

"The first indication is the pen, of course. A broad-tipped 'J' pen is common enough, but this one has been dipped in the very finest ink. Why employ such a common nib with such costly ink? Because the wide tip masks the individuality of the writer, making the forgery more difficult to detect. That is the mark of a professional. Also, I perceive a slight hesitation at the start of each sentence. Inference: the author is consulting a template as he writes."

"But a prankster would have done the same, surely."

Holmes shook his head and handed me the note. "Feel it, Watson! It is of a fine, creamy stock, is it not? Such paper has disappeared from public trade these last few years, impossible to purchase at any price. What student would have it lying about his rooms?"

"I suppose you are right, Holmes."

"I *know* I am right. You will also see it carries no watermark—another sign of the professional." Holmes rose from his chair, handed me the lens and then knocked his bowl against the grate. "Of course, there is one quite obvious clue that this is a forgery, and one you might have noted even before setting out for my cottage this morning."

"Yes?"

"The penmanship is rather more precise than a man under such evil influence—as I am purported to be—could have achieved."

"Of course that occurred to me, Holmes," I said, with some asperity, "but I could not risk being in the wrong."

"Quite so, Doctor," he said kindly. "Quite so. But, pray, let us set aside the note and turn to the murder in the train."

"Yes—and just how did you deduce a murder, Holmes?"

"By observing one of those trifles that forever escape your notice."

"And what might that trifle be?"

"All those years we worked together, Watson, and yet you are quite unable to follow my train of reasoning?"

"Some blood on my sleeve, no doubt?"

"There was no blood on your sleeve, Watson, although there was a copious amount of dried blood upon the soles of your shoes. But I only observed that later, when you were scraping your boots at my door. I had already deduced a murder by the state of your cuffs."

"And what did you see in the state of my cuffs?" I glanced at my sleeves and saw nothing unusual.

"What I would expect to see after your medical skills have been called upon. Your right shirt-cuff is unbuttoned, you see there? And yet the left cuff is intact. The inference is plain."

"I'm sorry, Holmes, but I fail to see it."

"It was your habit, Doctor, whenever we chanced upon a victim requiring medical assistance, to remove your jacket and turn up your right cuff with three quick folds before checking the pulse at the neck with the first two fingers of that hand."

"Why, I never gave it a thought!"

"But I did. And the fact that your cuff was still unbuttoned when you arrived at my doorstep told me that whatever you had encountered in that train, it was quite out of the ordinary. When you admitted coming from Polegate, well, what else could it have been but a murder?"

"What had Polegate to do with it?"

"Dear me, Watson, do you not see? You have always taken the express to Eastbourne. To leave the train at Polegate meant something highly unusual had occurred *en route*."

"Unusual things happen in a train without it being a murder, Holmes. Engines break down, cows wander onto the tracks—"

"Nothing like that would have accounted for your distracted demeanor, Watson. Your valise and revolver had been carried away by that 'Good Samaritan,' as you call him, and yet you did not think of it until I mentioned the absence of luggage. There was something far more sinister on your mind than cows on the tracks."

"Is that is why you were hesitant to speak in front of Miss Colvin—in the event she was somehow involved?"

"Precisely so."

"You have reason to suspect her, Holmes?"

"Not a bit. But it would not do to overlook the possibility."

"You are as keen as the day we met, Holmes."

"I think not, Watson. No, I am rather a dull fellow." Sherlock Holmes stirred the fire reflectively.

"Why do you say that, Holmes?"

"Because I cannot deduce the hand behind it."

"You think there is some sort of mastermind?"

"I *know* there is. But I can't find the thread that will lead me to him." Holmes settled back in his chair, put his elbows upon the arms of his chair and pressed his fingertips together, as always when he would devote his entire attention to a matter.

"Now, to the murder in the carriage, Watson. I wish to hear every detail. Leave out nothing."

Then he closed his eyes and listened with the utmost concentration as I began my story, stirring only to ask a pointed question or offer an occasional interjection. When I had finished, he opened his eyes fully, cleared his throat and began an interrogation every bit as rigorous as that which he had described in his memoirs at the hands of Edwin M. Stanton.

"The packet in which you received my manuscript and the other items, Watson, which you said bore the seal of the Diogenes Club. The seal was unbroken, or else you would have remarked upon that fact?"

"Yes, now that you mention it."

"And you say that the map and timetable were marked in the same hand as the forged note?"

"Yes."

He held up the note. "At the top corner here I perceive a curious indentation. Can you see it in the light? It would appear the four items had been held together by a rather large paper clip of some kind?"

"Yes, come to think of it. It was oddly shaped, a kind of 'W,' or triangle."

"You interest me exceedingly, Watson." Holmes set aside the note.

"Now, the driver of the cab to Victoria—you recall nothing about him save that he tapped his watch in remonstration when you entered the hansom?"

"Nothing. I paid very little attention to him. I was anxious to reach the station."

"Quite so. Did he say anything to you?"

"Not that I can recall."

"Not even 'goodbye'?"

"No. I simply sprang out and dashed into the station."

"That is of significance."

"What does it signify, Holmes?"

He ignored my question. "And there you sent off a second telegram, bought the newspapers, entered the carriage and were about to read my manuscript when the ticket inspector entered?"

"Yes. I put it away and did not take it out until Clapham Junction—"

"Whence you began reading until, after a period of time, you fell asleep and did not awaken until Berwick station, where shouts from the ticket inspector reached your ears. But how did this ticket inspector know you were a doctor?"

"He had seen the stethoscope sticking out of my valise at Victoria."

"So he said. Do you recall that it was so?"

"I don't recall, no, but why would he—"

"Never mind. Now, as to the scene in that compartment—you were the first to enter, after this distraught guard and the ticket inspector?"

"Unquestionably. The blood was fresh, and the body had not been moved."

"Slumped over against the armrest, you said. And it was upon checking for a pulse that you discovered the fatal wound. Embroidery scissors, you deduce?"

"Yes. As I said, Holmes, the blade was too thick to be a knife, and the weapon had possessed handles, judging by the bruising to the neck at the point of entry."

"But wielded by a man?"

"So it would seem. The point was driven straight through the neck with exceptional force, pinning the body upright."

"And it was while the victim was so transfixed that the murderer carried out the robbery?"

"So I presume."

"Before Lewes, you say?"

"Without question. A return ticket to Lewes was found in the victim's watch pocket. Surely he would have been killed before his stop!"

"Yes, how clumsy of me." Holmes changed the subject. "You say it was the Mary Box that first led you to conclude the victim was French?"

"Yes. I found it contained franc coins and Gauloises cigarettes in place of the British articles."

"Quite so. And this French identity was confirmed by the spectacles?"

"Yes, they bore a Parisian maker's mark."

"You are certain the spectacles were for reading?"

"Yes, I *did* examine them, Holmes," said I with some little irritation at his clipped manner.

"But how is it possible they were not also tainted by blood, if, as you say, he had removed them upon being interrupted by the murderer?"

"With a swift piercing of the carotid artery the blood would be released like a fire hose rather than a spray. The spectacles were simply missed."

"I see. And what had this 'Frenchman' been reading?"

"An Eastbourne timetable was found on the floor at his feet."

"A timetable," said Sherlock Holmes, his thick eyebrows raised. "Nothing else?"

"No, but I see nothing odd in that. It is natural to consult a timetable when one's train approaches the platform."

"But it is hardly natural for a Frenchman to be riding in an English train without a French newspaper—*Le Temps*, say—or a pocket Voltaire."

"I hadn't thought of that."

"Clearly not. Now, these fingers clasping the spectacles—disfigured in a farming accident you say?"

"Yes. Forefinger and middle finger were fused together. I have read

studies in which the mufflers of the new tractors heat to enormous temperatures, and their placement astride the engine is such that a stray hand can
become trapped when attempting to access the oil bin."

"Quite so. Miss Colvin is exceedingly careful handling our little Ford. It
was not a recent wound?"

"At least a year by the look of it."

"Hum! I am not clear, Watson, why you concluded the motive was
robbery? Young men from war-torn countries are not typically flush with
pound notes."

"Why, he was stripped of his purse, his watch and also of his shoes,
which must have been of some value to the thief!"

"Who was a tailor, you inferred."

"Yes, or somebody who works in the trade and would naturally carry
embroidery tools."

"But how do you deduce that this tailor intended to *rob* the poor man,
rather than merely to make his identification more difficult?"

"Well, as I say, my own purse was also stolen."

"Yes, but it would have taken an exceedingly cool tailor to viciously kill a
man, strip him of his shoes and purse, and *then* visit the compartment next
door to see what might be worth taking before returning to the dead man's
compartment, removing the scissors from the neck and leaping from the
train. Would he not flee the murder scene at once?"

"Goodness, Holmes, I suppose you're right."

"Of course I'm right. Now, you say both the ticket inspector and the
guard saw the murderer leap from the train, just after Glynde?"

"Yes, they saw him from the guard van."

"And which of the two discovered the body at Berwick?"

"The old guard."

"Whence the ticket inspector roused you from the next-door carriage to
attend the body. That is clear enough. How long had the train been stopped
at Glynde?"

"But nothing happened at Glynde, Holmes!"

"Unless I am mistaken, Watson, Glynde was where you were robbed."

"Dear me, Holmes, why do you say that?"

Sherlock Holmes again ignored my question. "As I recall, it was the ticket attendant who told you the manuscript pages had been blown about at Lewes?"

"Yes he found the manuscript on the floor of my compartment, but several pages had blown under the carriage when he opened the door from the platform."

"That seems conclusive. And you say these pages concerned my work at the DuPont powder works?"

"Yes, I'm very sorry, Holmes—"

"Never mind about that, Watson. Miss Colvin keeps a copy of everything she types. I was only interested in what was *in* those pages." Holmes sat back in his chair and began recharging his pipe.

"Do you make something of it, Holmes?"

"You find these events unconnected, Watson?"

"What events in particular?"

"This forged summons, the train ride, the murder, the missing manuscript pages?"

"I had not considered it."

"Evidently."

"Well, what is your theory, Holmes?"

"I cannot yet say that I have a theory, Watson. Only inferences that warrant further inquiry." He lit his pipe and lapsed into silence, puffing thoughtfully as he gazed into the fire.

I knew Holmes's mind was cataloguing every observation drawn from my memory, weighing each upon its merits and searching for that 'path of least resistance' that would lead him to the thread connecting a series of occurrences which had appeared entirely unrelated to my less discerning mind.

In all our days together, I had never broken my friend's meditative silences, and I did not do so now.

The fire's embers had dimmed and the sky outside was showing the first red tints of sunset when Sherlock Holmes came out of his reverie. He picked up the foolscap and studied it for a moment before glancing up at me with a thoughtful countenance.

"This note was exceedingly clever, Watson. I'm honoured it caused you to rush to my rescue even though its premise was entirely false! But before we examine the reasons why somebody wanted you here at Went Hill, what must I do to assure you and," he added with a knowing smile, "your dear wife, that I have no addiction to opium or cocaine, or anything else, for that matter, excepting, perhaps, my pipe?"

"There is no need of that, Holmes," said I, with some embarrassment. "I saw it the moment you appeared at the yew hedge, looking every bit as hale as our last time together."

"But you had your doubts, surely."

"Well, your skills with makeup *are* so extraordinary, Holmes..."

"Thank you, Doctor. That may be the kindest compliment you have ever paid me. Here..." He set down the note, turned up his cuff and stretched out his bared arm in the light of the lamp. "Let this set your mind at rest, for all time."

"Surely that is unnecessary, Holmes!" I protested.

"I insist, Watson. Being a doctor, you will note the remnants of the odd bee sting, but no needle punctures. Not fresh ones, at any rate," he added with a rueful smile.

And as he exposed in a similar fashion his other arm, I felt an immeasurable relief flood over me.

"Dear God!" I cried. "This is wonderful, Holmes! Wonderful! The note *was* entirely fiction! You have no idea how the thought that you had relapsed weighed upon me."

He smiled as he returned his dress to its normal state.

"A weight has been lifted from my shoulders, too, Doctor. The addict leaves behind many injuries besides those he does to himself." He nodded towards the window. "My colonies did not survive their first harsh winter here when I selfishly indulged myself once too often and failed to pack the hives with honey before the temperatures dropped. I knew I had to change—and for all time—but I could not have done it without your wise counsel."

The sense of relief was so great that my eyes now blurred with tears. Until that moment I did not appreciate how heavily I had felt the stress of the day's events.

"I have been through much today, Holmes. I hardly feel able to understand what it all means."

"It means we must clear our heads with a brisk walk to the Seven Sisters," said he with decision, "and then repair to that barrow I was telling you about and give this matter our full attention."

"This barrow—you have excavated it, then?"

"Indeed. I once told you that a concentrated atmosphere helps a concentration of thought, did I not?"

"Yes, you did, Holmes! You said it might lead so far as climbing into a box to do your thinking!"

"Well, I stumbled upon a far more amiable method of concentration than a box, burrowed into the top of Went Hill a few thousand years ago. It is where I now go to relax my brain. Knowing your interest in the ancient burial mounds of the Salisbury Plain, I think you will find it quite respectable."

He rose from his chair and stretched out his hand to me.

"But first, the bees will be expecting me to say good night. If you have quite recovered from your exertions, Watson, let us take our leave. The soup will keep for our return."

With Holmes's help, I rose slowly to my feet. It felt good to stand up and stretch my legs, but he frowned as I put on my coat.

"That will never do, Watson."

"The bees would not approve of my Burberry, I suppose?"

"It's not the tailor that would distress them, Doctor, it is the colour. Their primordial predator was the black bear—and a grown man in a dark coat approaching the hives at dusk would not go unchallenged. Take this instead."

He removed from the peg a bright yellow waterproof that matched his own. I put it on, chuckling at my friend's enthusiasms.

"I see my precautions amuse you, Doctor—but I would rather be free to set my mind to this little mystery that has brought you to Went Hill than scraping stingers out of your flesh. Just grab that torch—and please, bundle warmly, for it will blow sharp along the cliff."

Then Holmes donned his familiar hunting cap, wrapped a scarf around his neck, took up his stick and stepped outside with his quick, familiar stride.

I took my own cap and stick, and the torch, and followed.

The sky was losing its last shades of yellow and red to the grey hues of evening, and the air was cool and clear. For me, this contrast with the dirty brown smoke of the city could not have been more refreshing, and the bees evidently agreed, for the white boxes were crawling with the creatures just returned from their day's rounds. Holmes made a curious, weaving route among the hives, speaking in a soft, easy manner while his eyes made those quick, darting glances by which I knew he was observing far more about his colonies than I could make out.

Occasionally he halted to examine the carcass of a dead bee or to inspect the entrance to one of the boxes, whence he would make a note on his cuff before resuming his stride.

When Holmes had finished, he nodded in satisfaction and spoke in the manner of one quoting scripture:

"*And the Lord inspired the bees to make hives, and from out of their bodies comes a drink of a different colour in which there is a cure for mankind.*"

He smiled at my questioning glance.

"From the Quran, Watson. The Prophet certainly understood the worth of the bees."

Now he pointed his stick through the orchard toward the unseen Channel.

"Are you up to a brisk walk? Good. First to the cliffs, then we shall repair to the barrow. Southward, and quick march!"

Holmes set a fast pace, and soon we had left behind the orchard and gained the footpath across the sheep meadow that sloped towards the sea. A rising moon now peaked above the fog that was settling upon us, illuminating a village of white hospital tents spread over the eastern hills beyond the road to Birling Gap.

"Summerdown, they call it," said Holmes, in answer to the question already forming on my lips. "First the French trained there, then the Army put in hospital tents when the influenza began its march through the trenches. New tents had been going up there every day until recently."

Closer at hand, several hundred yards down Went Hill from us, I noticed a farmhouse rather garishly lit with the electric light.

"And that brightly lit cottage is Miss Colvin's," said Holmes without pause. "Her uncle is bedridden—he may not survive the winter. Tread carefully, Watson, the limestone gravel grows slippery in this fog."

A dog's high-pitched bark reached our ears as we walked.

"Good old Toby the Second!" Holmes called out over his shoulder. "I sleep better at night knowing he is keeping watch over Miss Colvin and the uncle."

In less than half an hour we had arrived at the crumbling edge of the great limestone cliffs overlooking the Channel. We stood in silence amid the swirling fog, England's eternal moat hidden from our eyes, and listened to the inexorable rolling of the breakers onto the shingle beach a hundred feet below. My foot slipped suddenly, sending a small shower of limestone gravel over the edge, and Holmes seized my arm in his characteristically strong grip.

"Beware the edges, Watson. They take more than a few sheep every spring. The poor devils cannot perceive the loss of the cliffs during the winter storms."

"Surely you exaggerate!" I took several steps backwards, nevertheless.

"Not in the least. That clump of gorse on the brink yonder was a dozen feet from the edge when I first arrived at Went Hill."

"Why, that would mean the cliff has lost almost a foot every year!"

"Precisely so, Watson. In another five thousand years or so, my cottage will be washed into the sea."

"That is a rather gloomy sentiment, Holmes."

"It is not sentiment, Watson. It is arithmetic." Holmes gazed at the shingle becoming visible far below as the fog slowly retreated.

"Well, Holmes. We are together now, and that is enough for me."

"Good old Watson!" he said, and I thought I discerned a catch in my friend's voice.

As the wind quieted down, the fog continued moving out to sea, revealing the black shingle beach and the dark waters of the great English Channel.

"The wind shifts," said I. "Your bees may not be far wrong, Holmes."

"They are nature's weather forecasters, Watson. We will know if mankind's dominion over the earth has put the natural order at risk when the bees start to follow the path of the dinosaurs to extinction."

"Surely, we count for more than a mere insect, Holmes!"

My companion was studying a seagull that had suddenly appeared before us, rising from the shingle on an unseen current, a dead crab limp in its beak.

"*Behold the fowls of the air,*" he intoned, with mock solemnity. "*They sow not, yet your heavenly Father feedeth them. Are ye not much better than they?*"

"I beg your pardon, Holmes?"

"It is one of the lapses in Christian scripture that never ceases to disappoint me, Watson—I believe it was Saint Matthew." Holmes shook his head. "He was no biologist, that is certain."

"And what would a biologist say about that seagull?"

"Why, that it scavenges the beach, adds nutrients to our soils and disburses the mustard seed that becomes a mighty tree! My bees would not exist without that bird, Watson. Nor, I suspect, would we."

The gull veered off on a sudden gust, and I dismissed this overly morbid reflection of Holmes's and began to the contemplate the invisible shore across the great Channel. It was a somber thing to imagine the fields of Flanders, Verdun, the Marne, all filled with the graves of a million of our men killed in a cruel war.

And for what purpose? To what end?

"You are right, Watson," said Sherlock Holmes, breaking in suddenly upon my brown study. "It is a pity to have lived to witness such cruelty practiced among men."

"Yes it is, Holmes. Mustard gas, box barrages, machine-guns...Afghanistan was nothing like that—" I suddenly realized how completely my friend had traced my innermost thoughts, as in the old days. "My dear Holmes! How on earth—?"

"Your features are as transparent as ever, Watson."

"But I was merely staring into the fog!"

"It's your eyes, Doctor. They told me all. You were not my aid and companion all those years because you lack compassion, you know. Quite the contrary! I rather think you brought to our adventures a touch of humanity which I lacked," he added in a surprisingly gentle voice, before relapsing into a more cynical vein, as was his wont. "Besides, what else could an old soldier be thinking of, staring at the hidden battlefields of France!"

Holmes tightened his muffler and turned his back to the sea.

"Are you rested, Watson? Would your legs stand a sharp climb to the top of Went Hill? Good. Let us repair to the barrow. I suspect the secret to our little mystery lies in my manuscript. It was, after all, the device which prompted your visit. Perhaps if you would read it to me, as in the old days—at least, that portion which remains in your coat—I can turn my mind to the puzzle whose solution eludes me. What say you, Watson?"

"The wind blows sharp from the north, now, Holmes. I say your bees were right."

Chapter Two

THE BARROW

"Why Holmes! This is worthy of the National Trust!"

My companion rubbed his hands in delight as I ducked beneath a lintel of Horsham stone and stepped between two ancient, upright stones to find myself inside a narrow but comfortable burial chamber.

"I thought you'd find it worth a visit, Watson, given your studies in the field," Holmes remarked, squeezing past me. Then, setting aside his torch, he lit a ceiling lamp that illuminated a Neolithic tomb of remarkable authenticity, with arched stone walls defining a central tunnel some two dozen feet in length along the classic east-west orientation, nearly high enough even for Sherlock Holmes to stand erect upon the rough stone floor.

Four small burial chambers branched off at intervals, and Holmes ducked into the first of these, which had been fitted out as a sort of kitchen. He lit a spirit lamp and filled a teapot from a cistern that was fed, he explained, by a dew pond atop the hill.

"Remarkable, Holmes! Just remarkable!" I had visited many barrows and other ancient burial sites over the years since my retirement, and this was as striking as the best of them. "But surely you did not perform this excavation on your own?"

"Not by any means, Watson. Once I determined the farmer had blocked up a genuine Neolithic burial chamber, Brother Mycroft called in a team from the British Museum, aided by one of the boys from the village—and, on occasion, Vicar Evans and myself. The artifacts all went to the museum, of course, and I was left with a place of rest and solitude, and a testing ground for my own little theories on scientific methods of skeletal identification."

"It is every bit as impressive as Avebury, Holmes. Just magnificent."

"Thank you." Sherlock Holmes's eyes gleamed as he took in my admiration of his discovery. "I dare say it was worth a reconstructed earlobe."

The overhead lamp cast a cheery glow inside what was, by its nature, a rather gloomy place, and the heat from the spirit lamp soon warmed the air, bringing a welcome coziness to the barrow. Holmes cleared a wooden bench of various tools of the archeologist's trade and several *Eighth Sister* honey jars filled with flint arrows and iron hooks, then together we sat down.

"You have made quite a little snuggery here, Holmes."

"I find the discipline of piecing together fragments of a lost race quite relaxing after a day of labour with the honey business and whatever case I may be consulting on."

Holmes poured the tea and raised his mug in a toast.

"Your health, Doctor."

"And yours," said I, with some little warmth. "It is good to be with you again."

"And with you."

Sherlock Holmes now set aside his mug and retrieved the lens from his pocket. "Might I glimpse the manuscript, Doctor? Thank you."

He held the thickly folded document to his nose, then unfolded it and smoothed out the pages upon his knee. Leafing through them, he inspected several with his lens, emitting his characteristic grunts and exclamations as he worked.

"Yes. Hum! Quite!"

Finally, he set aside the lens and returned the manuscript to me, his eyebrows knitted, his lips pursed.

"What is it, Holmes? You have discovered who is behind this?"

"On the contrary, Doctor. It makes the thing rather less clear than before. There was absolutely nothing of importance in the missing pages—a rather dull description of my workaday duties at the DuPont works, as you rightly inferred, and some discussion of my apprenticeship at the elbow of Monsieur Vernet. Nothing of Lincoln, or what came after. Certainly nothing worth killing for."

"What do you mean, Holmes, when you say, 'of Lincoln, or what came after'?"

Holmes smiled.

"You hold the answer in your hands, Doctor."

"And what do you propose we do with it here in the barrow?"

"I propose to sip my tea, smoke my pipe and listen with the utmost concentration as you read aloud from wherever you left off." Holmes took an old briar pipe from the shelf and began to charge it. "I have never heard the finished text spoken aloud—and, as you know, I much prefer listening to reading. Doctor, if you would?"

"It will be an honour." I glanced through the document, seeking my place. It seemed weeks, not hours, since I had read the pages I held in my hands. "All these years, Holmes, and you never once let on about your remarkable youth!"

"It was a pleasure to finally be released of that burden, I can tell you."

"I suppose Mycroft was the only other person who knew of this American adventure?"

"Certainly he was the only person in whom I *confided* it. But if I told you Professor Moriarty had picked up rumours from his American affiliations, I'm sure it would come as no surprise."

"Professor Moriarty?" I asked, much puzzled. "How could your tracing of a few gunpowder thieves in the last century have been of interest to a criminal such as he?"

Holmes smiled and lit his pipe.

"The powder theft business was a scouting adventure by comparison to what came after, Watson." He nodded at the manuscript and sent a cloud of blue smoke drifting upward to the ancient stone ceiling. "The explanation is there in your hands, and I beg of you to pick up where you left off on the Jevington Road."

I found my place.

"Here we are... Now, Holmes, you have been summoned to the office of Mr. Stanton in the aftermath of the assassination, and you have encountered Mrs. Stanton and young Eddie on their way to church services. You learn it is Easter Sunday—"

"*Black Easter*, it was called." Sherlock Holmes fairly shivered at the memory. "If ever a whole kingdom was contracted in 'one brow of woe,' Watson, it was America in the days after that terrible evening. But excuse my interruption. And pray, proceed."

He leaned back against the crude stone walls of the barrow, his eyelids half shut, puffing languidly upon his pipe.

And with pauses only to soothe my throat with sips of tea sweetened with honey, I read aloud the most remarkable chapters of this most remarkable account of the very first case of my friend, Mr. Sherlock Holmes.

THE MANUSCRIPT OF MR. SHERLOCK HOLMES—CONTINUED

I declined their invitation, however, explaining my summons to the War Secretary's study, and so we said our goodbyes.

These took the form of a warm hug from Mrs. Stanton and a handshake from Eddie Stanton that was surprisingly firm and manly. Such was the change in his demeanor since the assassination of President Lincoln, Watson, that from that day forward I would never again think of him as "young Eddie."

But it was not only Eddie Stanton whose demeanor had changed.

Descending the stairs of the Stanton home, I found a most serious and fearful mood had taken hold in the four and twenty hours since Black Friday. A veritable cesspool of political machination even in normal times, the intrigue and nervous agitation in that house seemed magnified a hundredfold. The number of officials, messengers and guardsmen crowding the front hallway was incredible, and while attempting to enter the library I was stopped by a guard demanding my credentials. The note from Mr. Stanton sufficed, of course, but I was searched top to bottom before being allowed a seat on a freshly installed bench outside the study door, between a nervous Congressman and a Treasury official, to await my turn.

And from the reports in the newspapers being shared as we waited, the reason for the new security measures—and the oppressive mood among the men around me—was plain.

That J. Wilkes Booth had been so thoroughly aroused in opposition to the Emancipation Proclamation of Abraham Lincoln that he had plotted to kidnap or kill the President in recent months had been attested to by a score of friends and acquaintances tracked down by detectives hired by Mr. Stanton. That he had also planned the attack upon the Secretary of State (and one on the Vice President that had not been carried out) was also confirmed by Mr. Stanton's agents. That he had fired the bullet that killed Abraham Lincoln in the box at Ford's Theatre was undeniable—a thousand eye-witnesses at the theatre had heard the shot and watched him jump from the President's box—and a reliable stableboy had watched him flee the alley behind Ford's on a one-eyed horse. Finally, Booth's arrival at the Navy Yard Bridge on that same horse not fifteen minutes later was sworn to by the sergeant on duty at the bridge, Silas T. Cobb—the same sergeant, as it happened, who had come to relieve young Eddie Stanton after my intervention that fateful evening at the Navy Yard Bridge.

But what had become of Booth after he crossed into Maryland was entirely unknown. A hundred Federal cavalrymen had combed that region, known as Anacostia, in the days since the assassination without turning up a single lead.

It was as if a gigantic hot air balloon had lifted Booth and his horse and vanished in the sky.

PINKERTON, AGAIN

Rumour, Watson—as Shakespeare put it—is a pipe blown by surmise, jealousy and conjecture. And the newspapers were playing that pipe with enthusiasm.

The Philadelphia Inquirer reported Booth turning west from Anacostia and crossing the Shenandoah River at Harper's Ferry, disguised as an American Indian. The New York Herald had him bound for New England by train, calmly reading a newspaper at the Philadelphia depot. The Washington Evening Star claimed Booth had never left Ford's Theatre at all, but was hiding in the stables behind Ford's, waiting for the manhunt to die down, whence he would rendezvous with Jefferson Davis and resurrect the Confederacy!

I had been seated outside the study, reading these and other, wilder speculations as to Booth's whereabouts, when Mr. Stanton's door opened and there emerged a cavalryman—a major, by the looks of his uniform—in the company of a man dressed in the guise of a roughneck.

The roughneck, I swiftly perceived, was none other than Allan Pinkerton (his way with makeup still lacked the professional touch, Watson) and he was boasting, in a voice loud enough that everyone could hear, that his man in Baltimore had found a one-eyed horse at the train depot that morning.

The one-eyed horse of J. Wilkes Booth.

His further boast—that Edwin M. Stanton had just dispatched him with the major and a cavalry detachment to that city to capture Booth— was heard by every man in that waiting room, as were the last words from his lips as he departed with the major: "We'll have him by supper."

You can imagine, Watson, how cheerful a thing this was to hear when compared with the wild speculations of the newspapers. The heart of every man in that room was lifted by this seemingly incontrovertible proof of Booth's whereabouts from President Lincoln's most trusted detective. By the time I was admitted to the War Secretary's study an hour later, Pinkerton's boast had acquired the legitimacy of a settled fact among us, as stories do when they are passed with hushed confidence from one stranger to the next.

We did not yet know that Pinkerton and the major were on a fool's errand, and that his placement of Booth in the vicinity of Baltimore would set back the manhunt for the assassin of Abraham Lincoln by a crucial week, creating an infinity of trouble for the man I was called in to see.

He was seated behind his desk signing papers being set before him by a secretary I had never seen before. A slight tremor was now present in the War Secretary's shoulder that he appeared unable to control, and when at last he glanced up at me, I could see by the length of his unkempt beard, the soiled collar and the dark rings beneath his eyes, that he had not been to bed since the events at the Petersen house.

If Pinkerton's boast had brought any light to the War Secretary, as it had done to the men waiting their turns outside his door, Watson, I did not see it. Nor did I hear it in his voice, which was hoarse and subdued.

"With the President's assassination, all commerce has paused, and space is now available on the transatlantic lines," he said, holding out an envelope for me that quivered in his hand. "This contains a berth for Southampton, departing New York one week from today. Guard!"

I took the envelope and had turned to leave when he called me back. "Your aid at the Petersen house was most appreciated. Most appreciated. You will find a fresh pass in there for yourself and your friend, to go where you wish in the meantime."

Before I could thank him, however, a new messenger had burst in with a telegram that required an immediate response, and my host was once more engaged in far more important business than the travel schedule of a houseguest.

TALES OF THE PATTERROLLERS

Upon its issuance the first day of January, 1863, the Emancipation Proclamation of Abraham Lincoln—which proclaimed all persons held as slaves in the rebellious states "are, and henceforward shall be free"—was celebrated in most quarters of the North, and, as word spread over the "grapevine telegraph," in the fields and kitchens and smokehouses of the South.

It was derided, however, in other quarters, and not just by Negro-hating whites, the likes of J. Wilkes Booth among them. Cynical Northern newspaper editors and political rivals of Lincoln called it an utterly toothless declaration. How, they asked in scornful tones, could slaves in the Confederate states be freed by a proclamation that possessed no authority in those states?

The answer to this weighty question had come not eighteen months later in the implacable form of Lieutenant General Ulysses S. Grant and the one hundred twenty-thousand soldiers of his Army of the Potomac under the command of General George Meade, whose relentless pursuit of Confederate General Robert E. Lee and his Army of Northern Virginia from the Wilderness to Lee's surrender at Appomattox recaptured the territory of Virginia for the Union, thus freeing some half a million human beings thanks to President Lincoln's "toothless" proclamation.

And although many of those freed slaves possessed neither the means nor the ability to leave their poor domiciles, enough had found their way to the Freedman's Village on Bobby Lee's old homestead in Arlington that its population had more than tripled since Abraham and I first visited.

It was my friend Abraham's idea that the expanded population of the Freedman's Village might now include his father.

And so once more we rode our horses over the Long Bridge to the Freedman's Village, this time with our saddlebags full of provisions and a pass signed by Mr. Stanton that would allow us to continue south to explore Manassas and Fredericksburg—the battlefields forbidden to us until Lee's surrender.

As before, Watson, I will not hold you in suspense, nor will I prevaricate. Once more we failed in our efforts to find Abraham's father—failed most miserably, in fact—although our visit was not without benefit in all that would soon follow.

We failed not because the Freedman's Village wasn't bursting at the seams with new residents from Grant's success in Virginia, however. It was. We failed because those residents were in no frame of mind to discuss anything other than the assassination of President Lincoln and to lament the incompetent manhunt for his killer.

It had been three days since Wilkes Booth had killed President Lincoln and ridden off on his one-eyed horse, "time enough for Jesus himself to be resurrected and on the road to Emmaus!" they cried.

Why, they demanded to know, was Booth still free?

They hooted and laughed when I tried to explain the various reports of Booth's whereabouts from the Northern papers. That anybody could think Booth had fled north to Baltimore seemed the height of madness to these people—had anybody ever known a runaway slave to flee south? they would ask (and not very politely, Watson!)

In fact, the notion seemed worse than madness to them. There must be treachery in it.

We heard this again and again: there was treachery in the killing of Abraham Lincoln; treachery in the escape of Wilkes Booth; treachery in the manhunt.

Especially the manhunt.

Keep in mind, Watson, these were people accustomed to being hunted—hunted by "patterrollers," they called them: white men with dogs who had patrolled the roads and rivers of the South at night for runaway slaves. Every inmate of the Freedman's Village, it seemed, had had a brutal encounter with a patterroller, and they showed us the welts upon their backs and the rope marks upon their wrists and ankles to prove it.

Why then, they would demand, their eyes flashing, did Mr. Stanton—the man who built this village for them!—not send the patterrollers after Booth?

And they would answer their own question this way: treachery!

I was ashamed, Watson. By allowing myself to be taken in by Pinkerton's tale of the one-eyed horse in Baltimore—ridiculous as it now seemed in the light of day at the Freedman's Village—I had utterly failed to employ the independence of thought demanded by Monsieur Vernet during our chemical investigations. The first move of any thief on the run in Wapping was to get across the Thames as quickly as possible—not to run in the direction of the nearest constable!

Why on earth would the man who had killed Abraham Lincoln flee northward into the arms of a thousand Union cavalrymen searching for him?

It was fruitless to remain at the village any longer. Our mere appearance upon a doorstep—my appearance, as I bore a pass signed by Mr. Stanton—only served to excite the inhabitants within. Near sunset, we said goodbye to Miss Nichols and rode our horses out of the gates.

But we did not head south to the battlefields, for Abraham was in no mood to visit Manassas or Fredericksburg after failing yet again to find any trace of his father in the Freedman's Village, and I had no stomach to push my friend to exploring battlefields in such a defeated state of mind. Instead we turned our horses north, back over the Long Bridge into Washington City.

And there we quickly discovered that Edwin M. Stanton was now the most sought-after man in the country.

Andrew Johnson might be President, Watson, but Mr. Stanton ran not only the machinery of war, he was also in charge of the manhunt for Wilkes Booth and the funeral service of the late President. And every man of want and means sought his ear.

Those crowds of petitioners, supplicants and swindlers that had once formed outside the gates of the White House now besieged the house on Franklin Square, and in such numbers that a provost guard had been enlisted to hold them back. Abraham and I found it necessary to steer our horses farther along Franklin Square to an alley that would take us around to the stables in back of Mr. Stanton's house.

It was only a slight inconvenience. But it would change my life forever.

Mr. Stanton's Privy Council

Before describing the following encounter—important as it would be in my life to come—I must explain how exceedingly conscientious of making the most efficient use of his time was Edwin M. Stanton. I have already said that when the War Department was closed on Sundays, he conducted business from his study following church services—and yet even that does not describe the full measure of his commitment to the responsibilities heaped upon him.

He dictated letters in the bath, on the short walk to his War Department office and on the walk home late at night by candlelight. He read correspondence at the dinner table, after dinner and after retiring to bed, often late into the night. Not infrequently, when the press of business proved too great, he simply worked straight through to the morning without returning to Franklin Square.

In fact, so pressed for time was the War Secretary that he refused to interrupt his meetings for anything—even trips to the privy. He simply continued them, on the way to and from. Both at the War Department and at home.

"Mr. Stanton's Privy Council," the household staff called these sessions at Franklin Square.

So it was no surprise, then, that as Abraham and I steered our horses behind the kitchen to the stables in the gathering twilight upon our return from the Freedman's Village, the door from the kitchen flew open and Edwin M. Stanton himself burst forth and charged down the stairs.

"There's no time, Allan! No time!" Mr. Stanton was yelling while unbuttoning his waistcoat in such a preoccupied manner that I was compelled to jerk my horse's reins to avoid trampling the War Secretary as he stepped in front of my horse without breaking stride. Then he opened the privy door and, with a final shout of "NO TIME!", slammed it shut behind him.

The fellow to whom he was shouting these words now came huffing down the stairs, and in the kitchen fanlight I could see that it was none other than—did you already guess it, Watson?—Allan Pinkerton.

Out of disguise and in even worse humour than the War Secretary, Pinkerton was so intent upon his quarry that he walked straight into my horse. "Watch yourself!" he cried in his gruff brogue, letting out an oath and smacking my mare on the rump, which startled the creature and gave me some little difficulty in bringing her under control. At this, Abraham leapt off his horse to help me.

"Got a n----r friend now, have ye?" snapped the Scotsman with a nod at Abraham.

I had heard this epithet in the vicinity of my friend many times during our journeys together, Watson (indeed, it was common for slaves to refer to themselves in that manner), but hearing it from the mouth of this coarse, grasping man caused to well up within me a rage that I managed to restrain only with the greatest effort, for I knew that the last thing the overburdened War Secretary needed was a pair of bickering guests outside his privy door.

I kept my silence, therefore, while Abraham and I made our way to the stables and Pinkerton turned his attention to the figure inside the wooden shack, aiming his pleas at the door.

And most abject pleading they were.

If one ever wanted to grasp the depths to which a commonplace man might sink, Watson, one could have done no better than to listen to Allan Pinkerton request a position of prominence from Edwin M. Stanton, as Abraham and I heard him do while we unsaddled and watered our horses in the stables that night.

Pinkerton, of all things, was asking to be put in charge of the hunt for J. Wilkes Booth.

His argument—if begging might be given such a name—took this line: with Allan J. Pinkerton devoting all his powers to the task of finding Wilkes Booth, the War Secretary would be spared considerable time and effort that could be better employed towards his War Department duties and the planning of President Lincoln's funeral. And had he stopped there, Watson, I believe he might have been handed the job that very evening.

But he did not stop there.

No, he promised to deliver J. Wilkes Booth and his conspirators to the War Secretary before the funeral of President Lincoln, not three days hence.

"Just say the word, Edwin! Say the word and we will get him!"

By now, Abraham and I had finished brushing the horses, and we exited the stables just as the War Secretary emerged from the privy with a humourless smile upon his face. This was too good to miss, Watson. We took a discreet position near the woodpile.

"By the funeral, eh, Allan?" Mr. Stanton buttoned his waistcoat in a nonchalant fashion as Pinkerton eagerly anticipated his reply.

"Just say the word, Secretary!"

"Oh, I'll say the word, Allan. I say a score of words. I'll say this: it's Monday night, Allan. Funeral's Thursday. That gives you forty-eight hours. Now, I have thirty-eight eyewitnesses, starting with Sergeant Cobb—a drinker, who says he let Booth cross the Navy Yard Bridge fifteen minutes after the deed—and finishing with a correspondent from Chicago who claims Booth was seen in a brothel in that city, dressed as a woman...this morning."

Stanton was not a tall man, Watson, but Pinkerton was of even shorter stature, and the War Secretary fairly towered over him now.

"So tell me, Allan, how do your men plan to be in thirty-eight places in eight-and-forty hours?"

"Booth is neither in Harper's Ferry, nor in Chicago, nor across the Navy Yard Bridge," the detective said smoothly. "He is in hiding in the Baltimore harbour—"

"I sent a cavalry detachment to Baltimore on account of your last report, Allan. That one-eyed horse belonged to the sexton at Old Paul's Church! Never been within fifty miles of Ford's Theatre!"

Pinkerton didn't flinch. "Ah, but my man in the harbourmaster's office saw Booth stealing pickles from a barrel this afternoon!"

The idea of J. Wilkes Booth—who had coolly fired a single bullet into the brain of President Lincoln in the presence of a thousand witnesses—rooting inside a pickle barrel in Baltimore harbour, with Federal cavalry scouring the republic for any trace of him, evidently struck Abraham as ludicrous a notion as it did me, for my companion began to laugh.

And Abraham, as I have said, had a most infectious laugh.

I found myself joining in, until quite suddenly—and to my great shock—I heard our laughter being taken up by the War Secretary a dozen yards away. I had never seen Edwin M. Stanton laugh, Watson, but there he was, bent over, hands upon his knees, laughing such a laugh as no man had ever done.

In the hindsight of the years, of course, I see it for what it was—a sudden release of the unbearable strains brought upon him by the terrible events of Black Friday, and not a personal affront to Allan Pinkerton. But the display infuriated the beleaguered Scotsman, and his response was much as any bully would make in such a situation.

He confronted not the War Secretary—he confronted my friend, Abraham. Bullies pick on the least powerful, Watson. It is their way.

"Why you little pickaninny!" he fairly screamed, making for us by the woodpile. "You'll get back in that stable and tend those horses or I shall whip your skinny hide!"

Once again, however, the War Secretary surprised me.

"I think not, Allan!" he barked, a stern grimace replacing the smile upon his worn, lined face. "The boy is all right. You'll get back here, Allan, right now. Back! That's better." He placed a firm hand upon the shoulder of the red-faced Scotsman and turned him around towards the kitchen door. "Tell me, Allan, what do think is going on inside my house at this very moment?"

As Pinkerton studied the door in evident confusion, a wry smile played upon the War Secretary's lips.

"Come, come, Allan. You are the Great Detective, so called. Can you not detect what is occurring there at my study at this very moment? No idea? Then I will tell you, Allan. Now, the time is—" He glanced at his watch but could not make out the time. "What o'clock is it?"

"A quarter past eight o'clock, sir," said the subdued Scotsman.

"A quarter past eight o'clock, sir, and there are eight men seated outside my study at this very moment. Probably more since you hounded me to the privy. And I must see each of those men before I retire for the evening. Why? Because they all want something from me. There's a man who wants the flower contract for the funeral—seems I can't place just any flowers around the President's casket, I must use this man's flowers. For the good of the country, don't you know!"

Stanton held up his hand to forestall Pinkerton's remonstrance, then pointed his finger at a second imaginary figure inside the house.

"And that gentleman there, why he handed his card to Mrs. Stanton at the communion table on Easter Sunday, if you please, so that she might present me with his scheme to sell copies of Mr. Lincoln's death mask! To defray the war debt! For the good of the country!"

Again he held up his hand.

"I know, Allan! I've heard it all! It's for the best of reasons! For the good of the country! For the memory of our fallen President! For the welfare of his grieving widow!" Mr. Stanton's voice had reached a paroxysm of indignation. "And you'd waste my time badgering me to be put in charge of the manhunt! For the good of the country! No, don't speak, Allan! Don't say it!" Stanton's eyes blazed in steely countenance at the silent Pinkerton.

"Save it for the privy, man."

In the silence that followed this lengthy rebuke, the War Secretary motioned for Abraham and me to join them. Then he put his arm about my friend and pulled him to his side.

"See this boy, Allan? Take a good look. While you were bellyaching to get charged with that DuPont business last summer, what was this little *pickaninny* doing? He was tracking a wagon loaded with the finest DuPont powder bound for Bobby Lee's Army across ninety miles of New Jersey swamp. Just went and did it! And what did he get out of it? Nothing but a roof over his mother's head in the Island!"

The War Secretary's eyes bore in upon the diminutive Scotsman, whose stature seemed to shrink before us.

"So here's a thought, Allan. If Wilkes Booth is in Baltimore, why are you in Franklin Square begging for a grand title, eh? Why aren't you hiding inside that pickle barrel to catch him next time he comes 'round? Don't answer me, Allan! Don't say a thing. Just get Wilkes Booth wherever you can find him and bring him to me—alive, mind you—and I'll make you the highest and mightiest constable in the land."

Pinkerton's countenance seemed revived by this modest encouragement. "I'll have him by—"

"Save it, Allan!" the War Secretary barked. Then he glanced at Abraham and back to Pinkerton, and his eyes fairly gleamed as an idea seemed to cross his mind. "You know what I will do for you, Allan?"

Pinkerton came alive again. "Hey?"

"I'm going to make it a race. You and your men against this 'pickaninny' and my houseguest. Let the best trackers win."

The Scotsman stood staring, his face flushed even darker than its normal red, his teeth clenched and jaw set. Then he gave a slight bow and stalked off to the stable calling for his horse.

The War Secretary watched him go with evident relief and placed a tired hand upon each of our shoulders. "There's no race, boys. I only wanted to send him on his way. Now, before I take my leave, a word, please. I had a thought…"

And a most powerful thought it would prove to be, Watson.

ALL THE SOLDIERS IN CHRISTENDOM

It was close upon nine o'clock when Mr. Stanton bade us good night, turned his back upon us and wearily climbed the steps to the door of the kitchen at Franklin Square, where he was met by the enthusiastic death mask salesman, who immediately began to describe his bizarre scheme to the exhausted War Secretary. As they disappeared inside the house, Abraham and I retrieved our horses and fitted them with the saddlebags that were still full of the provisions we had expected to need for our abortive journey to the southern battlefields.

Then we rode straight to Ford's Theatre. We would begin our ride where Booth had begun his on that famous one-eyed horse.

The street outside Ford's was dark, for the gas lamps remained unlit to discourage souvenir hunters—although that was not stopping men from climbing the steps to peer in the curtained windows and paying the newsboys fifty cents to show the blood spots in Tenth Street where Lincoln's brains were said to have spilled out as he was being carried to the Petersen house.

Abraham and I were not, however, interested in such ghoulish relics. We were interested in horse tracks.

Our instructions from Edwin M. Stanton, which we received as we stood watching Allan Pinkerton ride away from the stables in a rage of indignation, had not been nearly so glamorous as Pinkerton undoubtedly feared, Watson. As always with Mr. Stanton, it was the shrewdness of his mind—even in that exhausted state—which had led him to perceive a facet of the manhunt that had never before crossed his mind.

And it had occurred to him upon hearing Abraham's laughter.

In that moment, he later told me, he had understood that although slaves and freed slaves never spoke unbidden to a white, they nevertheless saw and heard everything around them, just as Abraham had witnessed Pinkerton's abject mewling outside the privy and had burst into laughter as a result. With Abraham's laughter had come to Mr. Stanton the notion that the field hands of Anacostia must know something of Booth and his whereabouts—perhaps even whether he had in fact turned north to Baltimore, as Pinkerton and most of the press seemed to believe, or south to the Potomac and the safety of Virginia, as the inhabitants of the Freedman's Village were convinced.

And in the same manner in which he had found an unconventional use for me during my time in America, Watson, Mr. Stanton saw a use for Abraham.

"Your friend can go places and hear confidences which all the mounted soldiers in Christendom cannot," he had said to me outside the privy, while glancing at Abraham. "And I expect the Negros in the fields of Anacostia know a great deal more than they've been willing to tell a white cavalryman in a blue uniform. With any luck, you may learn something of Booth's trail that those cavalrymen couldn't."

(Many years later, Watson, I would adopt a similar stratagem by employing the street urchins we called "the Baker Street Irregulars" to do my scouting for me—and yet another secret behind my methods is revealed!)

Anything we learned, Mr. Stanton stressed, we would report to the nearest Union cavalryman and return at once to Franklin Square—but we were not to return until we had learned something. He wanted no rumours and no secondhand sightings. "I have had too d----d many rumours to be useful," he said. "I want proof. Incontrovertible proof."

And so we had set off.

Our first decision, of course, had been where to start. With the undeveloped foresight of youth, I reasoned the place to begin was Baptist Alley, where Booth had fled Ford's Theatre, and so find the tracks of Booth's horse—utterly failing to reason that this same thought had already occurred to the hundreds of cavalrymen who had gone before us.

And did we find tracks, Watson!

Every Federal horse in the North, it seemed, had churned up the mud of Baptist Alley in the hours after the assassination when it was still wet, and hundreds of indecipherable tracks had been preserved when the ground had dried in the days since. Abraham saw it was impossible without even dismounting, and so we departed Ford's at once, riding hard onto F Street. We cut through the crowded streets of the government sector, past the White House, the swamp and the half-chimney of the Washington Monument and onto the old towpath alongside the fetid canal that led to the Island.

Within fifteen minutes we were at the Navy Yard Bridge.

The "Other Fellow"

This was not the first time I had returned to that bridge since my little adventure involving young Eddie Stanton and a growler of bad liquor, Watson. Abraham and I had ridden far and wide outside Washington City in the weeks after our discharge from the DuPont works, and those rides had included several crossings of this very bridge, for the Anacostia district of Maryland had remained Union territory, and it held fertile ground for both our interests.

I spent those rides gaping at the Union forts that had been erected along the Potomac to ward off Confederate raiders—Mosby's Rangers, from the Virginia Neck—while Abraham rode among the farms and fields of Anacostia to inquire after his father.

I had quickly discovered that one earthen fort looked very much like the next, and Abraham had learned the depressing fact that his father had never been heard of in those parts—worse, that his father could have ended up anywhere, from Cuba to Vicksburg. The speculators who bought and sold slaves were in the business of making money, not keeping families together.

Nevertheless, it had proven a pleasant place to escape the crowded, noxious city, and we knew the main roads well and most of the guards at the Navy Yard Bridge.

We had not, however, been back since the assassination.

Upon our arrival that evening, we found much had changed. Gone was the simple wooden turnpike pole and in its place a spiked gate. Gone too were the lackadaisical sentries. We were challenged immediately upon our approach. My pass was taken, our haversacks and saddlebags were searched, and while Abraham tended our horses, I was marched into the guardhouse to be interviewed by the sergeant on duty.

The sergeant on duty, as it happened, was Sergeant Cobb. This was most fortunate, Watson, for I had become familiar with the man since our meeting that fateful evening of young Eddie's malfeasance, and my affiliation with Mr. Stanton always made him nervous and talkative.

He was seated alone at the table with the morning's newspaper and a stack of freshly printed War Department proclamations at his elbow—and a bottle he stashed under the table as I entered. He recognized me at once.

"It's all right, Lydon. This is the joyrider that likes to look at forts," said he, dismissing the guard and fingering my pass until we were alone. "So, what is it now? You can't see them forts at night, you know. I suppose Mr. Stanton sent you on the manhunt, too?"

When I nodded at this he jerked his head in surprise and uttered an oath. "D—n me! Stanton thinks you'll find him when all those cavalrymen didn't? A hundred men been across that bridge and they couldn't find Booth anywhere in Anacostia! Now they don't even believe I seen him that night!"

He shook his head. "But I saw him. I know it. He crossed here and I had him!" He tapped the newspaper with its photograph of Booth. "That's the man. Same moustache, same eyes. He wore a slouch hat to hide his face, but those were his eyes. Now Pinkerton's saying he's in Baltimore? Booth ain't in Baltimore. I watched him cross here! Couldn't keep his left foot in the stirrup, you know. That leg flapped like some angry goose when he galloped away across the bridge. In mortal pain, he was. Cursed something fierce. 'D--n this' and 'D--n that.' But very fine boots, he wore. Knee-high collar. Brass spurs. Very fine."

"Did he say where he was headed?" I asked when he fell silent.

"Beantown!" Cobb laughed bitterly. "Said he was going to Beantown. Beantown! No account nothing town. But I know better. Fellow with a bad leg like that can't ride long. He'd make for St. Mary's on the Chesapeake. Take a fast boat to the Atlantic—with that other fellow, I expect."

"Other fellow?" said I.

"Herold. Davey Herold."

Just fifteen minutes after Booth had ridden across the bridge with his leg flapping, said Cobb, there appeared another rider, a young man named Davey Herold, who had been so nervous he could barely speak to Cobb when challenged.

"He finally told me he was seeing a girl on the other side, so I let him go. But now I ain't sure..."

Cobb may not have been sure about Davey Herold, Watson, but I certainly was. His appearance just minutes after Wilkes Booth could not have been a coincidence. The two men must have been in league. Must have planned their escape from Washington City across the Navy Yard Bridge, most likely to get south of the Potomac into friendly territory.

Like any thief in Wapping.

I asked permission to leave and Cobb nodded, handing me my pass and dismissing me with a snort. "Your funeral, son."

Abraham and I were across the bridge by ten o'clock, riding by the pale light of a cloud-covered moon—riding with the conviction that J. Wilkes Booth was not in a train bound for Canada, he was not hiding in the stables behind Ford's Theatre, and most certainly he was not rooting for pickles alone on the Baltimore docks. He was bound for Virginia with Davey Herold.

And I had not the slightest doubt we would find their tracks.

We halted just over the bridge in Unionville—a small village in the vicinity of Fort Stanton—and bedded down in the shadow of the large earthworks.

Abraham would need sunlight to find the trail.

FIRST SCENT

In setting out this record of our involvement in the manhunt for J. Wilkes Booth over the following seven days, I have relied upon the private diary in which I recorded our progress through Anacostia and beyond.

Keeping a record was one of several conditions laid down by Edwin M. Stanton during that brief interview outside his privy, and it is a good thing I did, Watson, for our movements in the following week were disjointed, our sleep intermittent and our meals mostly unsatisfactory. In a sense, it was not unlike the experience of men in war: long stretches of inconsequential movement followed by brief moments of intense—and, in a least one case, life-threatening—activity.

Thanks to these notes, therefore, I can say with certainty that it was at sunup on Tuesday, April 18th that we were awakened by the sound of reveille from Fort Stanton and resumed our ride on the public road.

The traffic was against us—slow-moving wagons carrying wood or crates of chickens or sacks of potatoes to Washington City—and we did not ride hard, as on our previous journeys in that region. Rather, we carried ourselves in the manner of a lark, so as not to draw attention to ourselves, for we could never know when we were sharing the road with an ally or conspirator of Booth.

Abraham ignored the first turnoff—it was the River Road to the earthen forts erected along the Potomac, and Booth would certainly not have taken that route. We therefore continued east into the rising sun and soon attained the summit of a hill that overlooked the awakening countryside, whence Abraham halted at the junction with the old Branch Road.

Here we faced a crucial decision: whether to continue east towards St. Mary's on the Chesapeake Bay, where a fast ship could be waiting to take Booth to the Atlantic Ocean, as Sergeant Cobb had speculated; or to turn south towards the Potomac, a day's ride away, where Booth could cross to the Virginia Neck and disappear among the last holdouts of the Confederacy.

Whichever route we chose, there was no easy way to alter our course in case it proved wrong. One road ended at the Chesapeake, the other at the Potomac. The stakes were high.

So, while we rested our horses, Abraham scoured the ground for clues in the unique fashion which, I freely admit, I came to make my own. Crouched like a bloodhound, he moved back and forth across the ground, on his knees or flat upon his stomach, eyes intently focused upon details in the dirt that scarcely appeared perceptible to my eyes.

But the public road proved as overrun with dried hoof prints as Baptist Alley had done, and so Abraham altered course. He followed a short path into the woods that led to a creek where we had sometimes stopped to refresh our horses—and where we had once come upon a pair of lovers who evidently used the place for their assignations.

Abraham studied the ground here, his pace slowing as he seemed to find tracks that told a story. When at last he rose to his feet, he was smiling.

There had been a meeting between two riders in this clearing, he said, some time before the ground had hardened. One rider's horse was fitted with a bar horseshoe[60] on the off-foreleg, and this man had waited a short time for the second rider (the length of the wait indicated by the evidence that "bar horseshoe" had relieved itself but once), whence they returned to the public road.

It was a slim reed to hang upon, but we chose to take it. Returning to the public road, Abraham studied the tracks, this time knowing exactly what to look for.

The bar horseshoe had galloped off down the Branch Road, to the south.

Much later, when retracing for Edwin M. Stanton our progress across the map upon his desk in Franklin Square, we learned that the prominence where Abraham had found the print was called Soper's Hill—and it had proved to be the very spot at which J. Wilkes Booth had waited for Davey Herold after crossing the Navy Yard Bridge, not an hour after the assassination of Abraham Lincoln.

But at that moment, Watson, we knew only that there had been a rendezvous at that junction some time before the roads dried—probably but not definitely the evening of the assassination—and that after a brief parley the two riders had turned towards the Potomac.

---

60 A circular shoe with a bar across the middle, typically used to mend cracked or weak hooves.

We mounted our horses and followed 'bar horseshoe' down the Branch Road south.

Traffic thinned as we made our way past the corn cribs and tobacco barns that dotted the bottomlands of Anacostia, and soon roaming cows and sheep were turned out in the green fields. As the sun climbed in the sky, the field hands appeared, beginning their daily labours of turning the soil to make it ready for the spring planting.

And Abraham spoke to them all.

As the War Secretary had suspected, these forgotten people proved eager to share what they knew with Abraham, once they had been assured that I was Abraham's friend and not his overseer. Unfortunately for our efforts, however, few possessed anything useful in the way of exact knowledge. None admitted to seeing Booth, or any other white man for that matter, in flight on the public road the night of the assassination, or any time thereafter.

And how could they, Watson, since they never ventured out of their shacks after sunset? The fear of the patterrollers had never left them—and of course there were the laws still on the books against Negros venturing outside after dark.

We pressed on south into the less populated region of Anacostia, where tobacco crops had leached the richness out of the soil and the fields were sickly or abandoned. Here, old logging trails branched off from the public road through sparse woods, and at each trailhead we halted while Abraham scoured the ground for signs of the bar horseshoe. It made for slow, frustrating going, and as the sun climbed overhead it became evident to me how Wilkes Booth seemed to have disappeared from the face of the earth.

A healthy man on the run might get lost in Anacostia for half a lifetime.

But Wilkes Booth was not a healthy man. He was possessed of a leg so badly broken that even Sergeant Cobb had noticed it flapping out of the stirrup. And a man in that condition surely could not remain hidden without first getting help. Where, I wondered, in that quiet countryside, in the middle of the night, might Wilkes Booth have found a doctor?

It took some time to answer that question, Watson—the field hands were not allowed use of a so-called "white man's doctor," and the man who killed Marse Abraham would surely never have allowed his leg to be fixed by anyone else. After conversing with many field hands and drovers, however, Abraham found one who knew of just such a doctor.

The fellow didn't know exactly where this doctor lived, but he knew where we could go to find out.

It was a tavern owned by a notorious secesh by the name of Mary Surratt.

A Doctor Named Mudd

It was noon when we reached the tavern—a shabby-looking clapboard house with several horses tied out front at the pump, nearby outbuildings in various stages of decline and a gristmill that evidently serviced the farmers in the area. The only sign of life came from the rear of the tavern, where a fat, greasy man was cutting into a pig roasting over a firepit.

This was the local post office and tavern where, it was said, the doctor in question sometimes drank. The tenants who ran the tavern for Mrs. Surratt, the field hand had said, could point us to his place. We dismounted at the pump and Abraham remained behind while I entered.

It was dark inside, with only a handful of tallow candles and oil lamps for light, and malodourous, too, thanks to the unwashed men drinking whiskey at a long table. A young black boy who had been sweeping the floor suddenly vanished out the rear door, whence he soon reappeared with a hard-bitten woman wiping her hands upon a filthy apron.

"What'll you have?" she said, doubtfully.

I told her I would have bacon for two and the name of a doctor, holding up coins and affecting a limp as I handed her the money.

She looked me up and down with suspicion, but took the coins. "What happened?"

I explained that a horse had stepped on my foot and that it required some attention. Her frown vanished.

"Oh, well, then. Lloyd!" she screeched out the rear door. "Bacon! Two!" She gave the boy a kick and he dashed outside, returning with cuts of bacon wrapped in newspaper, which I accepted thankfully. Then she indicated where I might find this doctor. I returned to Abraham, and as we ate Lloyd's bacon and shared the dipper from the well, I noticed he was tapping his bare foot upon the ground. Glancing down, I saw why.

In the dried mud beneath his foot was the impression of a bar horseshoe.

I was careful not to change the expression upon my face, for I had observed old Lloyd watching us from the firepit, but I swiftly perceived the shoe was on the off-foreleg. Upon finishing our bacon we remounted our horses, left the tavern behind and returned to the public road.

Whoever had rendezvoused on Soper's Hill that night had also stopped at Mrs. Surratt's tavern.

Two more hours of easy riding found us at the junction described by the crone, whence we turned off the public road and made our way up a gentle hill, past tobacco fields being worked by Negros—dust-coloured men in grey cloth who stopped to watch us pass by in silence—until we reached the doctor's homestead.

We turned in at the gate and followed the carriageway past several decrepit, windowless shacks (Abraham pointed them out as the old slave quarters), then a tobacco barn, two corn cribs, several woodpiles and finally the stable block alongside a whitewashed farmhouse at the crest of the hill.

Our horses sniffed their way to the water trough beneath a chestnut tree, and there we dismounted. Abraham remained with the horses while a muscular Negro man stopped splitting wood at a pile next to the porch long enough to point me to the front door in response to my inquiring after the doctor.

Before I could knock, however, the door was opened, and the master of the house appeared.

He was not older than forty, of middle height and corpulent, with more hair upon his chin than upon his head. He wore woolen pants and

a woolen waistcoat, and he fingered a thick gold watch chain as he stared
down upon me with the friendly manner of a kindly bookshop proprietor.

I felt instantly that Dr. Samuel Mudd was not to be trusted.

Everything about his mannerisms, Watson, from the courteous
greeting and the affectation of kindliness to the ostentatious toying with
that watch chain brought to mind a long-buried memory of the most
detestable man I had ever known.

That man's name was Mr. Neville Heath, and his appearances at
our wretched garret I had only later come to understand when Brother
Mycroft explained to me my father's iniquities that evening in his
telegraph room. A flood of sickening memories returned as I stood before
his embodiment here in America, in the form of Dr. Samuel Mudd, and I
momentarily forgot my intentions.

"What is the matter, young man?" Mudd repeated, in a smooth,
make-everything-easy voice.

"Sore throat," said I, coming back to my surroundings and affecting a
cough. (I had altered my symptoms from the tavern, for I presumed Mudd
would have spotted at a glance that there was nothing wrong with my
foot.) "Hurts something bad."

"Indeed?" His voice maintained its friendly tenor, although I read
suspicion in his eyes as he glanced over my shoulder, eying Abraham in the
yard. "You look in rude health."

"If you have a salt gargle, I could manage."

"Drink this." He removed a flask from his trousers and thrust it into
my hand, his eyes fixed upon Abraham.

I feigned a drink, blocking the liquor with my tongue, and returned
the flask. "Thank you."

"What's that n----r doing?" He spoke in the peevish manner that many
whites spoke of Negroes—as of a wayward dog—but his eyes reflected
some little wariness. I turned to follow his gaze and saw my friend walking
slowly around the water trough, head down, kicking a stone ahead of him
with his calloused foot in utmost absorption.

"Kicking a rock, is all. We'll be off, now."

"Mind you are."

We mounted our horses and rode away, but not before I had been able to discern what my friend had spotted once more in the dirt—this time alongside the well of Dr. Samuel Mudd.

The bar horseshoe.

But there was were new marks, puzzling to Abraham, and they had caused his seemingly aimless perambulations around the trough as he attempted to decipher their meaning: pairs of shallow holes poked in the ground, separated by about the width of a man's shoulders.

And each pair of holes alternated with the mark of a single bootheel.

Abraham had never seen a man on crutches, Watson, but I had— and a great many of them, in fact, during my stay at City Point with the President. Those holes in the dried mud and that single bootheel between them meant one thing: the unctuous Dr. Mudd had fashioned crutches for a broken-legged rider sometime during the rainy evening of Black Friday, before the ground had dried.

I now had a burning sensation on my tongue from Dr. Mudd's whiskey, and the conviction that J. Wilkes Booth had been at the doctor's house for treatment of his broken leg. We had only to find Mr. Stanton's proof.

But this would not be so simple to accomplish.

I Make an Inference

The sun was low, the shadows long, and Abraham's eyes remained fixed upon the trail.

The going should have been swift. There seemed no question we were following Booth's horse, and Abraham could spot the bar horseshoe without leaving the saddle now, for the public road in those parts was lightly travelled. But since leaving the Mudd house the tracking had become more difficult, not less, for the fugitives had taken to varying their route—at times taking the public road, at times cutting through thick woods on old trails. They were hiding their tracks well—too well, for Abraham's taste.

He suspected Booth and Herold were now being guided by a patterroller.

Such a man would be well armed and exceedingly dangerous, and Abraham was in no mood to take undue risks. Our progress slowed to a crawl. And as the sun declined in the western sky and the public road reached a miry, overgrown region not many miles from the Potomac River, it stopped altogether.

We had entered the Great Zekiah Swamp, according to a nearby field hand, and a more decrepit netherworld could scarcely be imagined, Watson. Pools of thin black water stretched to the eastern horizon, broken only by gnarled, dead trees and pine-covered hillocks that rose like ancient, forbidden islands out of the rank water. The ground became spongy here, and the imprints difficult to read. Abraham moved this way and that, following one false impression after another, trying to recover the trail.

At last, he found it.

The bar horseshoe had turned off the public road onto a narrow, raised path through the mire that entered a thick stand of pine trees atop a hillock several hundred yards away. We steered our horses towards this strange, wooded cathedral and had proceeded perhaps a hundred yards across the mire when the horses suddenly halted and refused to continue.

Horses are sensitive creatures, Watson, and one does well to heed their instincts. Abraham dismounted at once, calming them while fixing his gaze upon the pine thicket, dark and mysterious at the end of the curving trail.

If the horses wouldn't go there, he decided, neither would we.

And it was well that we didn't, for upon retracing our steps to the public road and returning to the field hand who had identified the swamp for us, the fellow became greatly agitated as Abraham described the pine thicket at the end of the fishhook path.

"The hush harbour!" he exclaimed. "The ol' hush harbour!" He used to listen to a preacher there, he said. It was a perfect hiding place. If Booth and Herold were in there, he reckoned they could kill any man who tried to enter before that man knew a bullet had hit him.

The sun had set and there seemed nothing to do but find shelter for the night. We retreated to a well-hidden clearing across the public road where we fed and watered the horses, ate some of our provisions and admired a display of shooting stars that lit up the sky like a full moon on a cloudless night, before sinking into a deep sleep.[61]

Next day saw us spend many more hours in the saddle exploring hidden trails—and avoiding dangerous pools of quicksand that threatened to pull us down into the swamp forever if we were not careful—but those hours brought us no closer to unlocking the secrets of that pine thicket in the Zekiah Swamp. Never could we find a pathway across the mire that did not cause our horses to stamp their hooves, flatten their ears and halt.

And yet, in the end, Watson, we didn't need it.

Whether it was the warmth of the sun upon my shoulders or the gentle rocking of the horse's gait as I followed Abraham from one dead end to the next—or a combination of the two—my mind began to discern an entirely different means of finding the proof of Booth's whereabouts demanded by Edward M. Stanton.

And next morning we set out at first light, leaving J. Wilkes Booth and Davey Herold—if they were indeed in that hush harbour—to their hiding place in the old Zekiah Swamp just two miles from the Potomac River. I had decided we would return north, in the direction we had come.

To the house of Dr. Samuel Mudd.

Had I known the risks we would be taking, however—well, I didn't, did I? All I knew was that the boot of J. Wilkes Booth must be inside that house.

That was the inference I had made during our ride, Watson—the very first inference I ever made in the manner of my mentor at the Éleuthèrian Mills. It had come to me as I sat on horseback, watching Abraham search for safe passage to the pine thicket, and thinking back to the crutch marks in the dirt and the single boot mark.

Suddenly, in my mind's eye, the scene at the Mudd house had revealed itself to me.

Sometime in the middle of the night of Black Friday—how long after the assassination? One Hour? Two?—Mudd had been roused from bed by a desperate banging at his door to fix a man's broken, bleeding leg. Probably there had been a prior arrangement with Mudd—how else would Booth have known where to find a doctor in the middle of the night in the

---

61 *The Lyrids peak in the Northern Hemisphere the third week of April.*

countryside of Maryland well off the public road?In any case, Mudd would fix the leg—but first, the boot would have to be removed.

And if the damage to the leg had been anything like that described by Sergeant Cobb, the boot could not have been pulled off. A knife would have been required to cut the leather legging from Booth's swollen and distorted leg, and it seemed obvious that a boot of such fine leatherwork must have caught the eye of a miserly man such as Dr. Mudd—why, his decrepit slave quarters lacked even windows!

This meant the boot would not have been discarded.

Somewhere on the grounds of that house, I had realized with a start, there existed the boot of J. Wilkes Booth, sliced and bloodied, but more valuable than gold. And it was probably close at hand, for Samuel Mudd would not want whispers of a stray boot to leave his property. Such evidence of treachery could get him hanged.

Stanton's proof existed.

The boot only had to be retrieved.

A Very Close Encounter

"You again? What is it this time?" The portly, bewhiskered figure gazed warily at me from behind the half-opened door. All pretense of kindliness was gone, and the eyes of Samuel Mudd now looked past me with suspicion to the yard, where Abraham was tending the horses.

"You brought no one with you? Just the n----r?" His wary eyes intently surveyed the carriageway. Evidently seeing no one else but Abraham, he nodded. "All right then, come inside."

And with that, I entered the house.

Standing in the hallway, however, I realized just how difficult was the task I had given Abraham—and how much risk I was taking upon myself. Doctor Mudd was now very much on his guard, and our knowledge of the layout inside the house was limited to the rough map that had been scratched out in the dirt for Abraham by one of the doctor's field hands moments before.

"Throat got worse, has it?" Dr. Mudd gazed at me through narrow eyes as the sound of wood-chopping came in through the opened window. "How is it you could find no other doctor in all of Anacostia?"

I shrugged my shoulders and explained we had inquired elsewhere but had found no one.

"Where else did you inquire?" he asked, casually.

"Beantown," said I.

This was risky, Watson. I knew nothing of Beantown except that Cobb had mentioned it as the destination Wilkes Booth had claimed the evening of the assassination. Still, it was the only village I could name in this region of Anacostia, aside from Bryantown—and I could not mention Bryantown in the presence of Dr. Mudd.

Bryantown was where the Union cavalry was headquartered.

Fortunately, my answer seemed to satisfy my wary host. He smiled and nodded in approbation. "That settles it." And with that odd comment, he motioned me into the dining room, dismissing a Negro girl clearing the breakfast dishes with a harsh word and indicating a seat while he retrieved a velvet-lined leather case from a side table. He set down the case before me and glanced through it, picking up and discarding various instruments.

"And what brings you boys to these parts?"

"Powdermen from Wilmington. Looking for work."

He shook his head as he picked out a slender item. "There's no such work around these parts."

"We heard the oyster boats need men."

"Well, that much is true." Mudd gave a wry smile as he unsheathed a silver tongue depressor. "And you are right to get your throat attended. A fellow ought not to have a sore throat if he wants to work on the river."

There was a sinister hint in his voice as he bade me to tilt my head back, and my reluctance to follow his instruction brought a soft chuckle from him. "Well now, if you won't show me your throat then I can't help you," he said as the wood-chopping continued outside the window.

"What do you intend to do with that?" I asked.

"I intend to hold down your tongue so I may inspect your throat."

I feigned a coughing fit. I was playing for time, Watson—Abraham's as well as my own. If all was going as anticipated, Abraham would have been through the kitchen door and up the back stairs while Mudd's wife was occupied in the cellar, for we had been told she always packed away the butter after breakfast.

The field hand who had provided us this bit of information was the fellow splitting wood, and he had promised to keep up the noise long enough for Abraham to search upstairs for the boot. It was common knowledge among the servants that Wilkes Booth had spent the night in the front bedroom of the house of Samuel Mudd the same night that Abraham Lincoln had been killed.

And his discarded boot, it was whispered, still lay beneath the bed.

Mudd waited for my coughing to subside, smiling with such evil intent I still shake my head that I did not bolt from his chair at that very moment. Why I allowed him to insert the tongue depressor is an even greater mystery, Watson, but I did—and the suddenness with which he mashed the blade down onto my tongue caught me by surprise, as did the strong grip of his free hand, with which he now pressed my shoulder to hold me in the chair.

"The thing is," said he in a whisky-tinged whisper, his spectacled face bending slowly towards mine as I attempted to free myself from the unnatural grip, "this is Beantown. And I, sir, am the only doctor in Beantown."

All pretense was gone. I was trapped.

I struggled mightily but found myself powerless to gain any advantage. His grip was strong, and the tongue depressor cut off my breath. Again he hissed into my ear.

"But I already knew you were up to no good, boy. Old Lloyd up at Surratt's place told me you hurt your foot. Horse stepped on it, Lloyd said." The pressure against my throat was incredible, and the smile turned into a scowl. "Now, suppose you tell me why you come here?" His face reddened and his voice rose above the sound of the wood-splitter, filled with fear.

"Why? Why? Why?"

I tried to call out for Abraham, but I could not even exhale. I grabbed for a knife, a fork—anything that could be used as a weapon—but the table had been cleared.

You have often been piqued, friend Watson, at the secretive and meticulous care with which I planned my campaigns during our years together at Baker Street. Such forethought goes back to that day in America, in that dining room, with that duplicitous doctor. My plan—to keep him occupied in the examination of my throat long enough to allow Abraham to find the boot that had been cut away from the leg of J. Wilkes Booth—had come to ignominious grief.

I found myself trapped, with no alternative means to my end, and very quickly the lack of oxygen began to affect the clarity of my thinking.

I mistook the villainous Dr. Mudd for the villain of my childhood— Mr. Neville Heath seeking payment in my mother's bed—and wondered why Brother Mycroft would not come to my rescue. I now heard screams, my mother's screams, and I wondered why Mycroft would not even come to the rescue of our mother.

Can he not hear her? There, she screams again! Where is Mycroft?

I was struggling in desperation for some way to aid my poor, abused mother when—with no warning and no explanation from the villainous Neville Heath—I found the pressure upon my throat had suddenly eased, and I could breathe. As the oxygen returned to my brain, I became aware that I was not in the Wapping garret of my childhood, but in Beantown, in America. And the screams were not my mother's—but they were real.

And they were coming from a woman somewhere in the house of Dr. Samuel Mudd.

All pressure to my throat now ceased and the grip upon my shoulder was relaxed. Dr. Mudd had turned away from me. He was peering at the front hallway, alert and tense. The woman screamed again. "What are you doing?" she cried, and now Mudd abandoned me altogether. It took some few seconds to catch my breath before I could rise from the chair and follow him outside the dining room.

Whereupon I encountered a strange tableau.

Dr. Mudd was standing with one foot upon the bottommost stair, peering up at a slight, middle-aged woman standing at the head of the stairs. She had her hands raised and a look of horror in her eyes—eyes which were fixed upon the figure of my friend, Abraham, who stood framed in the doorway of the front bedroom.

He was holding a long black object in his outstretched hands, and a very broad smile was spread across his face.

The object was a knee-length riding boot of fine black leather, crusted with dried mud and mottled by what must have been bloodstains. A foot-long slit ran along one side of the boot, where it had evidently been cut from its owner's leg.

At the heel were brass spurs.

It was no little thrill I felt, Watson, to see that my deductions during those long hours in the saddle had resulted in this most tangible proof of the flight of Wilkes Booth!

My host, however, did not feel the same way. From the drawer of a nearby candle table he removed a small pistol and pointed it at Abraham.

"I will handle this, Frances," said the doctor in a low, ominous voice. "Get away from the boy." As the woman retreated from my friend, Abraham stood frozen, his eyes fixed upon the pistol in the doctor's hand. "Thought I wouldn't hear you sneaking around with the wood-chopping, eh, boy? You can't keep that, now. It is not yours."

"Nor is it yours, I'll wager," said I. "Whose is it, Abraham?" I called. "Is there a mark?"

"Doesn't matter if there's a mark," Mudd snarled, "it's on our property, and not for a n----r to steal." He waved the gun at Abraham and gestured for the artifact. "Give it here, boy."

"Don't use the gun, Samuel," his wife cried. "You're a Christian man."

"And that n----r's a thief. I have my rights."

"But you've never shot a man, Samuel!"

"Never caught a thief in my house, either." Still, I perceived the doctor's hand waver.

His wife was in tears now. "What would Father Hoskins say?"

The doctor scoffed. "He'd say—"

"You won't need to use that gun," I said quietly, for I had seen a way out. I took a step alongside the staircase and held out my hands. "Pass it down,

Abraham." Abraham gladly let the boot drop into my arms. When I turned over the collar I found a New York City bootmaker's mark in the yellow leather.

And below this: *J. Wilkes.*

"It's Booth's!" I shouted to Abraham. "This'll fetch a nice price in Richmond!"

How that improvisation had come to me, Watson, I never could say, but it was a flash of instinct that considerably altered the mood in that house and possibly saved Abraham's life, as well as my own.

The doctor started. "You mean to sell it?"

"What else?" said I.

"Let them take it, Samuel!" Mudd's wife shrieked. She was pushing Abraham down the stairs. "Just get that dreadful thing out of here. If the Federals find it here, you'll hang."

By the look upon his face, it appeared to have dawned on Samuel Mudd that his wife was right. He nodded dumbly. Then he stepped aside as Abraham clattered down the stairs and dashed past him out the door.

I followed.

Thanks to the perverse ministrations of Dr. Samuel Mudd, I now possessed a genuinely sore throat and the cast-off boot of J. Wilkes Booth in my haversack. We had only to hand it over to the Federal cavalry in Bryantown, and we would be on our way back to Franklin Square.

THE WISDOM OF ABRAHAM

It was Shakespeare, Watson, who wrote that there is a divinity that shapes our ends, rough-hew them how we may. And I have always felt that such divinity works through human interventions. That day, the divinity that shaped our ends came in the form of my friend, Abraham.

Let me explain.

Bryantown was an easy two-hour ride from the Mudd farm. Once there, we were directed by a provost guard to the weather-beaten hotel that served as Union headquarters for the cavalry in the Anacostia region and taken to a private room. There we found

Lieutenant Lovett, a handsome, sandy-haired, clean-shaven man dressed in civilian clothes, as were most of his men (in order to blend in with the locals, it was said, although they fooled no one in that secesh region of Maryland).

Lovett eyed us with no little amusement as I placed the boot upon the table before him—and I can't say I blamed him, Watson!

Abraham and I made for an odd pair wherever we travelled. And turning up out of the ether in Bryantown as we did, with a story out of the pages of a Boy's Own adventure, seemed all too incredible to the cavalryman. But when I showed him the pass from Mr. Stanton and explained briefly our commission from the War Secretary, he became curious and picked up the boot. It was mud-spattered, bloodstained and still damp, with the slash down the side, and as he turned it over his bemused smile vanished.

"From Mudd's house, you say? Samuel Mudd? The cousin of the fellow here in Bryantown?[62] Samuel Mudd of Beantown?" With each nod of my head, Lovett's voice rose in anger and disbelief. "But I questioned that man two days ago! Claimed he knew nothing of Wilkes Booth!" Lovett studied the boot, muttering to himself with mounting animation. "Left-footed, yes...cut from the leg...of course...and what's this?"

As he turned the leather collar inside out, his eyes fell upon the inscription.

"'J. Wilkes'!" he shouted. "By God! This is Booth's."

He twisted around at the men peering over his shoulder, an astonished look upon his face. "Samuel Mudd fixed him up! Mudd fixed him up! Mudd, a d----d liar! A traitor!"

This and other oaths aimed at the doctor were repeated as the men passed around the boot and Lovett set about questioning me regarding the exact circumstances by which we had retrieved it. He grew hotter with each detail, and his men began dashing this way and that, retrieving their sidearms and ordering their horses saddled as it became evident that they would be riding once more to the house of Dr. Samuel Mudd.

---

62 *Dr. George Mudd, Samuel Mudd's second cousin. He was a Union man and unaware of Samuel's actions.*

It was to no avail that I explained how we had traced the horses of Booth and Herold to a pine thicket in the mire of the Zekiah Swamp, and that, as of that morning, we believed they were still there.

"No man in that kind of pickle would spend five days in a pine thicket doing nothing." He handed me back my pass and held up the boot triumphantly. "Give Mr. Stanton our compliments when you get to Washington City. We're going to pay the doctor another visit. He'll lead us to Booth."

And, with that, Lieutenant Lovett ordered the bugler to call "boots and saddles" and swept out of the room muttering imprecations for the soul of Dr. Samuel Mudd. Soon all the men were mounted and riding fast down the road to Beantown.

After we watched them ride away I ventured into the tavern to buy a plate of fried oysters, our first hot meal since leaving the Stanton House. We ate the oysters under a willow tree, for Abraham was not allowed to eat in the tavern. This turned out to be no great loss, however, for we could eat without being under the watchful gaze of the unfriendly patrons of the inn.

And Abraham had an idea of his own to discuss.

It involved the stories his mother had told him all his life of runaway slaves, those who had made it across the Potomac and those who hadn't.

The ones who made it, she had always reminded him, were the ones who took their time.

They might stay hidden for a day or two—even a week if necessary—in lightless cellars or abandoned haymows or in the remote forest glade of a hush harbour. They would wait until just the right moment—until the bloodhounds had lost the scent and the patterrollers gave up, until the weather turned bad and the moon disappeared from the evening sky. Then they would make their move to cross the river. And it was always a river—not a creek or a wood or a swamp. They never felt safe until they had put a river between themselves and the patterrollers.

They had only one chance, his mother always said, and they would not risk that chance by moving precipitously.

Now Abraham came to his point. It had been clear skies since the assassination, he reminded me. Big moon, bright stars, even meteor showers! No runaway slave would have dared cross the Potomac on nights like that. He would have waited. For a cloudy night, with no moon and no stars, and no meteor showers.

Our horses were right, he concluded. Booth was still in that swamp.

We finished our meal, mounted our horses and rode south.

By nightfall we were once more on the public road at the edge of the great mire, once more gazing at the pine thicket that rose from the swamp at the end of the long, curving pathway, and once more soothing our agitated horses.

They had refused to enter, as before—nostrils flaring, ears flattened and forelegs pawing the turf—and when the fog rose from the cooling mire in the gathering dusk and crept across the pathway around our feet, the instincts of our mounts and the wisdom of Abraham were confirmed in a most unpleasant fashion, for we were downwind of the pine thicket and the fog carried with it an odour of the vilest essence.

It was the scent of unwashed men.

Now, the odour of a man who has been on the run for a week is truly incredible, Watson. We could only retreat before it, and so we returned to the clearing where we had spent the night previously. From there we could watch the public road where the footpath veered off into the swamp, without being seen and out of range of the stench of the fugitives. We fed our horses and bedded down, munching silently on biscuits and apples as the whippoorwills began their plaintive calls from the marshes.

We were prepared to wait for days this time. Our saddlebags were filled with extra provisions purchased in Bryantown with greenbacks provided by Mr. Stanton. A nearby stream would keep us washed and the horses sated. After drawing straws, I prepared to keep watch while Abraham found a soft bed of pine needles on which to spread his blanket, and he fell asleep there almost at once.

But he would not sleep for long.

THE MAN IN THE GREY CAPE

A cloud cover had crept across the sky, and the thin silver moon was soon entirely effaced, bringing upon our little encampment a darkness so profound I could barely see our horses a dozen feet away.

It was a perfect night to make for the river—almost too perfect, Watson. I had begun to fear we would miss our quarry should they move. As my eyes became accustomed to the darkness, however, I found I could distinguish the public road from the shadows of the woods around us and the narrow shade of the footpath tracing into the fog-shrouded swamp. And so I waited, alert, listening for foreign sounds above the chorus of bullfrogs and the stirring of night creatures around us.

Then it came to my ears—the dull plodding of a horse upon the public road.

Even before I could rouse him, Abraham had sprung from his blanket and moved to calm the horses, for they might have given us away. From my vantage point I could now make out the figure of a lone man in a dark cape riding a mare, the black steel of a rifle poking out of his leather saddlebag. He halted his mount at the pathway into the swamp and waited some little time, head cocked to the sounds around him.

Evidently satisfied he was alone, the man swung down from his horse and led the nervous animal along the trail with exceeding care, pausing every few paces to reassure the beast or to cock his head at some sound or other before resuming his careful gait towards the great pine thicket.

I watched the shadow of his figure until it had blended into the fog covering the swamp and I could no more hear the tread of the horse. Then, suddenly, from within the fog, a distinctive call sounded. It was something like the harsh "chick" of a mockingbird: three notes, repeated twice.

Then all was silent again.

For at least an hour nothing more could be heard from the direction of the thicket, and I had begun to suspect the man in the cape had led the fugitives out of the swamp on a different path, when, once more our horses stirred.

Soon low voices were heard from within the fog, and a figure materialized in the grey mist.

It was a lone man on foot—the same man who had entered an hour before, now holding his rifle but no longer wearing his cape or leading his horse. He moved towards us in the same careful, noiseless manner in which he had entered the swamp, and upon reaching the public road he stopped and stood motionless for several minutes. Then there came from his throat the same chick we had heard when he had entered the pine thicket: three notes, twice repeated.

The tread of a horse was soon heard and there suddenly emerged from the fog the shape of another man on foot, leading the guide's horse. Upon the horse was seated a hatless figure wearing the dark cape of the guide who had preceded them. The rider appeared severely agitated and barely able to sit still. At every step of the horse, a cry of pain would spring from his lips, which was met by the guide with a wave of his rifle and a caution for the man to hush himself.

But the groans and whimpers continued as the horse was led to the public road and reunited with the guide. And it was at that very moment the moon broke through the clouds, and my companion gripped my shoulder and pointed at the figure upon the horse.

Even in the brief, uncertain moonlight, there was no mistaking the face of J. Wilkes Booth.

NIGHT FLIGHT

The thick, drooping moustache had evidently been shorn off during his stay at the house of Dr. Mudd, but the eyes that flashed in that glint of moonlight would have given him away even had he grown a full thick beard in his time on the run. They were the eyes in the photograph—and the eyes that had flashed from that small stage in Wilmington, when his cry of "Thou shalt see me at Philippi!" so shook the rafters that the poor amateur playing opposite him was struck dumb.

His left leg hung limply against the flank of the horse, and with no little satisfaction I could see that the bootless foot wore something like a slipper and that across his lap were slung a pair of crude wooden crutches.

The crutches of Dr. Samuel Mudd.

It was in vain that the guide hushed the suffering rider as he and the third man—evidently Davey Herold—led the horse away from us, southward down the public road, for the yelps and cries continued even after they had disappeared in the foggy darkness. But it was well that those cries did continue, Watson, for the only way we could track them in that dark, foggy evening was to be guided by the sounds of the crippled rider.

We left our horses and followed very slowly and very, very carefully.

There would be frequent halts by the cautious guide, and one long wait while he left Booth and Herold for some little time—to retrieve food and supplies from a farmhouse off the road, we later discovered. So it was altogether two more hours before we found ourselves on the firm, sandy banks of the Potomac, watching from the shelter of the underbrush some distance away as the guide dragged a rowboat from its hiding place in a stand of willows to the water's edge where Booth and Herold waited, a flickering candle now illuminating their shadowy figures.

The river was barely visible under the dense cloud cover, but the strange moaning of its powerful current made its presence felt as we watched the fugitives prepare their flight—and listened to their conversation, for, being upwind from us, their voices came to us quite distinctly.

They were conferring over a map, and there was some little discussion about the route they should take. By the candlelight I could now see the face of the guide. He was a gaunt, older man, and he spoke to the fugitives with rough command, pointing through the darkness to an unseen landmark on the opposite bank.

Then he and Herold lifted Booth—who was holding his crutches—into the boat and pushed the little boat off the muddy flat into the water. The guide let go while Herold jumped in, causing a violent rocking that provoked from Booth the loudest, vilest oaths I had ever heard a man utter. When he had calmed down, Herold took up the oars and began to stroke as Booth held the flickering candle over the map and called out his thanks to their guide.

The guide did not respond. He turned his back, slung his cape over his shoulder, picked up his rifle, cocked an ear intently, then disappeared from our view into the willows alongside the riverbank.

The rowboat moved slowly out into the Potomac, Booth holding the candle and shouting instructions while Herold rowed silently but with great strength for the unseen Virginia shore some two miles distant. The boat stayed on course in the shallows, but once it reached the channel, it was caught up as if by an invisible hand, twisted by the unseen, powerful current and carried upriver by the incoming tide, seemingly possessed of its own will.

A stream of invective in the now-familiar voice of J. Wilkes Booth carried to our ears across the water, and it grew ever more vituperative as the point of candlelight illuminating the shadowy fugitives was lost in the gloom of a dark and foggy night.

When we could no longer hear the bickering voices, Abraham and I climbed the steep clay palisades that loomed over the riverbank and made our way cautiously and silently back to our encampment, our eyes peeled for any sign of the guide and his horse.

Booth had been swept away by the very river that he had been attempting to cross, probably back to the Maryland shore. He had missed his chance, for now.

As for Abraham and me, our wisest course seemed to be to get some sleep. There was no telling where this guide in the dark cape lived.

And what other friends he counted in this region.

American Brutus

We awakened next morning to the sound of birds in full voice and the dawning light of a clear eastern sky, for it had rained during the night and the fog and mist had cleared. After bathing in the creek, we led the horses onto the pathway into the pine thicket, for I meant to inspect the hush harbour where Booth and Herold had hidden themselves.

This time the horses did not resist.

We moved, nevertheless, with exceeding caution, and as the curving pathway took us into dense pine woods, we discovered that it was well we had not tried to enter when Booth and Herold had occupied this sanctuary. The old field hand had been right. From within, one could easily watch the sunlit pathway without being seen, and a well-placed bullet would have dispatched an intruder before he even understood he was in mortal danger. The sanctuary in the pines was a most perfect hiding place.

It was also a most disgusting habitat.

In length and width not much larger than Mr. Stanton's dining room, every inch of the soft pine floor—save two nests where the two men evidently slept—was littered with human refuse. There were bloody rags and opened tins, empty whisky bottles and discarded newspapers, and the appalling odour of unwashed bodies hung so thickly in the still air that even pressing our sleeves to our noses we could not keep the smell from invading our lungs.

Abraham set off in search of the fugitives' horses—he meant to find that bar horseshoe, Watson!—while I examined the debris for anything that might be of interest. I quickly found it in the newspapers. They had not been used to wrap food, as I had anticipated. They had been used for reading.

And, evidently, by Wilkes Booth himself.

It seems the man in the dark cape had kept Booth exceedingly well supplied with news of the assassination and Booth's flight. There were multiple editions of the Washington papers (the Chronical, the Evening Star and the Intelligencer), several more of the Baltimore Sun, one of the Philadelphia Inquirer and one each from the New York Herald, Tribune and Times. All had been well thumbed, and many were marked up in Booth's own hand, with sentiments of appalling self-congratulations and not a little vanity.

It was evident that Booth had taken much satisfaction in the misplaced accounts of his whereabouts, but less well received had been the essays portraying his act as a cowardly, treacherous killing—the "American Brutus," he was called by the Northern writers—and the reports from correspondents in the South that many Confederate loyalists regarded the assassination as a terrible mistake.

His aggrieved scribblings covered some of the pages more completely than even the newsprint, and I saw that these papers must be gotten to the nearest Federal soldier at once. I gathered them up and packed them neatly in my haversack, then set off out the rear of the thicket to find Abraham.

He was standing at the edge of the soft, watery ground of the swamp, which the occupants had evidently used as their privy. It was there the

prints of the poor beasts, bar horseshoe included, had disappeared in
the muck, and Abraham was staring at a black cloud hovering over the
mire, perhaps a dozen yards away. I was at a loss to understand what this
cloud consisted of until Abraham's foot slipped and his leg was gripped
by quicksand. As I grabbed his arm to pull him back to safety, the black
cloud rose up in a body—they were a swarm of bluebottle flies, Watson—
to reveal the withered legs protruding from the upturned, gas-filled bellies
of the two dead mares.

They had been herded into the mire and shot.

We did not brood long over this beastly act, however, for our attention
was now drawn to a welcome sound coming to us through the woods of
the pine thicket.

It was the sound of thudding hoofbeats on the public road and
the high jangle of bridles and slapping of scabbards that could only
signify Federal cavalry on patrol. I grabbed the haversack with Booth's
newspapers safely inside, and together we mounted our horses and rode
hard out of the pine thicket to intercept them.

It would perhaps have been better had we let them alone.

We Are Not Believed

They were a six-man detachment from the 3rd New Jersey Cavalry,
and they were making for the river at speed, in precisely the direction
Booth and Herold had moved the previous evening. I had no doubt they
were on the trail of the fugitives—probably Mudd had confessed all to
Lieutenant Lovett—and rejoiced that Booth's route was now known and
the cavalry were finally going to get their man.

When they spotted us, however, their major shouted a command
to halt, bringing his mount to such a hard stop the creature sat on its
haunches. "The river road to St. Mary's!" he barked. "Where is it?"

I recognized him, Watson. He was the major I had seen with
Pinkerton outside Mr. Stanton's study, shortly after the assassination.

"The river road!" he cried impatiently. "Quick! Which way?"

My answer—that there was no river road in these parts—was met
with disbelief and a sharp tongue.

"Come, come, boy. The river road to St. Mary's. Where is it?"

Again, my answer in the negative was not believed, and so I drew out
our pass and handed it to his adjutant, who let out a whistle.

"Signed by Mr. Stanton, Sir!"

"And why would these boys have a pass signed by Mr. Stanton?" The
major leaned on his pommel and stared at me with a sharp glint in his eye.

By way of answer, I opened my haversack and began to display the
newspapers—undeniable evidence of Wilkes Booth's occupation of the
pine thicket, as I saw them—but he shook his head and fumed.

"Funny game!" he cried, jerking the reins and spurring his horse. "The
hag at the tavern plays a deep game, fellows! We've been tricked! Tricked!
That d----d hag tricked me!" And with that, the major galloped northward,
his men following.

With our pass.

It was Edwin M. Stanton who would explain the major's behaviour,
Watson, some few days later, as I was seated in his study with the
newspapers. "Two boys materialize from the woods of Maryland with a pass
signed by the War Secretary? Carrying a collection of odiferous newspapers
with pencil marks on them? Why, I would have dismissed you as he did!
Two boys on a lark who found the pass in a tavern somewhere, got a hold of
the newspapers and marked them up to have a laugh at his expense."

(This would not stop the War Secretary from stripping the major of
his rank after the manhunt, however, for reasons that will be made clear
shortly, Watson.)

In any case, we were without a pass, in a Confederate-friendly
territory of Maryland, and very hungry. We decided to eat breakfast
before settling on our next move. But first, we made our way to the
Potomac, to the scene of the night flight, to see if we could learn anything
from the marks left behind in the sand by the fugitives.

How differently did the river look in the bright morning sun, Watson!
The broad waters, which had been so dark and mysterious the previous
evening, were now alive with the white sails of sloops and oyster boats

tacking swiftly among the large hulks of the paddle-wheelers moving slowly against the current.

While I admired the variety of sailing vessels, Abraham examined the marks in the mud left behind by Booth and Herold, but they revealed nothing new to my friend. As he rose to his feet, however, his keen eyes spotted a rack of silver fish drying in the sun a half-mile downriver, being tended by a man mending his nets—a Negro.

We could satisfy our hunger, Abraham said brightly, and perhaps learn something about his father from the grapevine telegraph before returning to Washington with the newspapers in my haversack. I readily agreed.

At that moment, Watson, I thought our journey was almost over, but in truth it had scarcely begun.

Freeman

The barking of a dog reached our ears even before we began leading our horses carefully down the palisades on a narrow path cut into the face of the red clay cliff overlooking the Potomac. Where the path bottomed on the sandy riverbank, the dog appeared—a one-eyed female mongrel— and sniffed us warily, whence her demeanor changed, and she became our escort, leading us past a shallow creek[63] and a neatly kept vegetable garden to the clearing Abraham had spotted from the upriver shore.

In the middle of the clearing stood a whitewashed shack, the defining feature of which was a door frame tall enough to accommodate a veritable giant. And that giant was now standing on a small wooden dock at the river's edge, fishnet in hand, his bald head gleaming in the morning sun, his smile wide and inviting.

"You a little past your time," he said in a voice as deep as the river. And with that enigmatic statement, he gestured at the clear creek water. "Take off your shoes and stand a while in that. It's mighty cold, and you'll wanna holler, but it'll do you a world."

We tied our horses in a stand of willow trees and did as he suggested.

---

63 Most likely what is called Pope's Creek today.

The effect was instantly soothing. Until that moment, Watson, I had not contemplated how far our travels had taken us the previous five days and the toll they had taken upon our limbs. Even now I feel the icy water gripping my ankles and the soft cold mud under my feet.

Our host had set aside his netting and now he indicated where a half-dozen shad were grilling on the fire and onions and potatoes sizzled in a frying pan.

"I know all about you boys from the grapevine telegraph. Heard 'bout you buying bacon at the Surratt place from Lloyd's boy there. He said you was headed this way. Then old Jimmy watched you tryin' to find a way into that hush harbour for a couple days. When I saw you at the bend this morn' we made ready for you. Only thing I don't know is your names."

We told him.

"Nice to meet you," he said. "Now, time to eat."

And so we ate, while he talked.

His name was Freeman Sheels—a name famous in America in those days, Watson, for his grandfather was Christopher Sheels, the manservant who had tenderly comforted George Washington, the first American President, during his final illness.

The affections of Freeman's grandfather had not extended to that late President's wife, however, for Christopher Sheels had been a so-called "dower" slave—owned by Martha Washington, not her husband—and by the maddening laws of slavery, Christopher Sheels and his offspring remained her property even after the slaves of George Washington had been set free upon his death by the terms of his will.

Freeman Sheels was, therefore, born a slave. But he had earned enough by fishing the Potomac to buy his freedom from Bushrod Washington— nephew of Martha Washington and, by all accounts, a harsh master—and the freedom of his wife, Sarah (who was, he indicated, still sleeping).

The couple had left Mount Vernon long before Secession and crossed the Potomac to put the water between themselves and their old master. They had found this abandoned shack and made it their own. The dog had been rescued by Sarah one morning while out gathering firewood along the river, and they had named the dog Martha, after the woman who would not set Christopher Sheels free.

Abraham was now playing with Martha, and our host had turned his gaze to the river. Ships of all sizes and white sails of all shapes moved in the breeze.

"You know they didn't make it 'cross last night," said our host quietly.

I was startled, Watson. How did this man know what had brought us to his doorstep?

He chuckled at my surprise. "You think I didn't know Booth was headin' this way? This here secesh territory! Ol' Tom Jones ran the Confederate mail in these parts—always expected he'd be the one to run Booth across the river."

He turned very serious as he watched Abraham gambol with the dog. "You boys lucky. Heard about the trouble at Doc Mudd's place, fetchin' that boot. And good thing you stayed outta Ol' Tom Jones' hair last night. He wouldn't a thought twice to kill your friend if you got in his way."

After absorbing this sobering news, I asked where Booth and Herold might have landed if they didn't make it across the Potomac.

Freeman shook his head. "Ain't heard yet. The current was mighty strong last night. Chapel Point, maybe. Port Tobacco. Nanjemoy Creek, if they missed those."[64] He pulled a stick from the fire. "Show you."

And with that, he began to draw a simple map in the sand.

I have reproduced the map with the help of my atlas, Watson—and in a more formal manner and with such addendums as to make plain the route of our journey and that of Wilkes Booth and Davey Herold for the clarity of these memoirs.

Freeman studied the lines in the sand and shook his head, a look of pained sadness upon his expressive face.

"When I heard Ol' Tom Jones put 'em in the hush harbour—my hush harbour—Lord I had a pain in my heart!" He grabbed the stick and poked it in that spot. "I hid runaways in those pine woods! Said church there. Mighty fine place to sing, too." He broke out in a sad, deep voice that rang out across the river:

---

64 Booth and Herold landed near Blossom Point, on the Nanjemoy Creek.

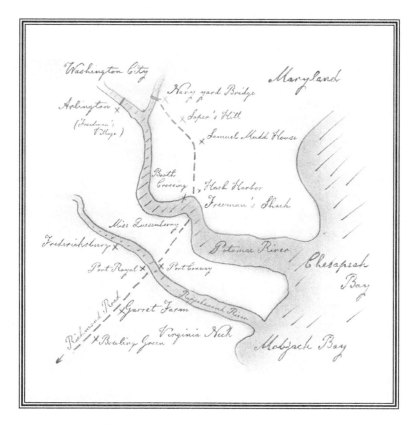

"There is a balm in Gilead to make the wounded whole, there is a balm in Gilead, to heal my sin-sick soul..."

It was, I realized with a start, the tune Abraham had been fond of whistling. Suddenly another voice joined in. It was Abraham's. He had stopped playing with the dog.

"Sometimes I feel discouraged, and think my work's in vain, but then the Holy Spirit revives my soul again."

When they had finished, Freeman gave Abraham a great, enveloping hug. Then he looked out at the river, studying the water with the intensity of one reading an especially difficult book.

I asked what Booth and Herold would do next.

"Wait again. Wait for the right time. They in no rush. Plenty of secesh in these parts to help 'em."

I asked where they would go if they made it across the Potomac.

He smiled. "You like to ask questions. Get some rest. Grapevine telegraph tell us when they move. Right now the current's running. I got to set my nets."

Freeman stripped off his shirt and walked into the river. The sunlight shone upon his back, and the shocking sight of livid purple welts crisscrossing his spine bespoke a life far more arduous than his own modest self-history had admitted. The welts disappeared with each step as the water rose slowly up his back, until it had reached his neck.

We were watching him work when the dog suddenly jumped up from the sand and dashed to the cabin. The giant door now opened, and a very tiny woman emerged carrying a basket in the crook of her arm.

Sarah Sheels possessed gray hair and carried her small frame in a stooped manner I had never before witnessed. Evidently she had been much abused by the same overseer at Mount Vernon that had left the scars across Freeman's back, for she proceeded to walk in a limping, swaying fashion among the vegetables in the garden set alongside the creek, collecting potatoes and onions such as we had eaten with our fish, all the while stealing glances at Abraham with a kind, motherly face.

She was not able to meet my eyes, however—for reasons I could only imagine.

THE RICHMOND STAGE ROAD

Freeman was working his nets and his wife was gathering her harvest, dog at her heel. Abraham had fallen asleep on the sand. I studied the river, which was alive with all manner of craft. The current was powerful indeed, judging by the slow movement of a large passenger steamboat headed upriver against the tide, but the waters did not slow Freeman.

He moved easily and gracefully, even with the water at his neck. When he had finished with his work, he made his way to shore in a manner that gradually revealed his massive scarred body until he emerged towering and wet, his great domed head reflecting the sun. He sat on a log to dry himself and studied Abraham.

"So, this is the boy looking for his father." He picked up a sweet potato roasted black in the fire and began munching. "Ain't we all."

I asked if Abraham would ever succeed, and our host shook his head grimly. "We been scattered like seeds, my friend." Then he pointed to the sky. "Marse Abraham Lincoln himself, ascending to his glory, would not be able to find that boy's father, even now, looking down on all Creation." Studying my friend again, he added, "But don't say nothing to the boy."

I asked our host why his people referred to President Lincoln as Marse Abraham, as Lincoln had never been a slave master himself.

Freeman stopped eating. "Deliverance to the captives, my friend. As Moses led the people out of Egypt, Marse Abraham led the people out of bondage."

"So, it is a term of respect."

"Of great and holy respect, my friend." He nodded at young Abraham, who was evidently dreaming in his sleep. "Why else his mother name him Abraham? Marse Abraham stands high—most high and mighty."

A large Navy vessel now steamed downriver, paddlewheel churning, black smoke billowing from its funnels. I thought of Booth and his flight to Virginia.

"Could he make it?" I asked. "Booth, I mean."

"I know who you mean. Under cover of the night, with the right tide? Yessir. He could."

"How will we know if he tries again?"

"Grapevine telegraph hears all. You just—" Martha had begun barking and dashed from the garden to the water's edge, running back and forth in wild agitation. Freeman wiped his hands and stood up, gazing across the river, smiling.

"And here it comes!" He turned to his wife and waved her over. "Jacob comes!" he shouted.

A small white sail had separated from the others in the channel, growing larger as it made its way towards us. Soon, a trim little oyster sloop was bumping against Freeman's modest dock, its sail gone slack. The sole occupant was a short and muscular man, possessed of an athletic bearing that saw him leap into the water and haul the sloop to shore as easily as if it were a child's toy boat. Martha greeted him with licks.

"Jacob!" Freeman's voice boomed.

"Freeman! Sarah! Hey! Brought the pigs!" The two men met, and the diminutive Jacob embraced the enormous Freeman. "Marse in a whippin' mood, brother," said he, in a high, excited voice. "Had us lookin' all night for two men crossin' the river."

"They make it?"

"No sir." Jacob shook his head, one eye warily on me until Freeman spoke some words of comfort in his ear, whence he resumed his excited speech. "Don't know who they expectin', but Ol' Miss Quesenberry herself was waitin' on the porch! All night! Marse in a mighty rage this morn'. Sent us up and down river at first light, but we didn't find no boat."

Jacob continued in this vein while Abraham and I retrieved several pigs from the hold of the skiff, so freshly killed they were still warm. When we had finished carrying them to the kitchen shed at the back of the shack, Freeman whispered some few words into his friend's ear, then the two men hugged goodbye and Jacob pushed back the skiff, swung himself on board, poled her out to the current, raised the sail and was carried away.

The entire transaction had consumed not five minutes.

"I told friend Jacob to keep a sharp eye out for those two men, that one of 'em is on crutches, and that Ol' Tom Jones was helpin' 'em, so take care," Freeman said as he watched Jacob's sail become lost among the others on the river. "Grapevine telegraph needs be real careful now."

"Why did you not tell him it's Booth who's crossing?"

He shook his head gravely. "Jacob get a whipping if he knew that. Ol' Miss Quesenberry's the biggest bootlegger on the Neck. She don't tell her boys a thing, and she don't expect 'em to know a thing. Problem with Jacob is he can't keep his mouth shut. Jacob better off not knowing, my friend."

"If Booth does make it, across, where will he go? Where would you go if you were Booth?"

"I'm a Negro, sir," said he with a most serious demeanor. "Booth a white man. I can't go where he go."

This was a condition I had never considered, Watson. Once again, the peculiar institution seemed to warp all boundaries of common sense.

"But I tell you this." He pulled his stick out of the sand and drew another line across the map. "A white man who killed Marse Abraham and got 'cross the Potomac would take the Richmond stage road to the Rappahannock. It's a good road—the secesh ran their mail down that road."

"Why the Richmond road? Booth wouldn't go to Richmond, surely—the Union Army is in Richmond!"

"No sir—he wouldn't go that far. He'd take it 'cross the Neck to the Rappahannock, then 'cross to Port Royal and make his choice." Freeman studied his map. "From Port Royal, he can go east to Mobjack Bay and get to sea—here. Or go south to Bowling Green—here. That's still secesh. Then he take the old plank road west and make for Swift Run Gap. Be half way to Mexico before they know it." He looked out at the Potomac.

"But he got to get 'cross the big river first."

A Curious Preponderance of Oyster Shells

We slept that evening on the porch on beds of hay and next morning awoke to the succulent smell of roasting pig and the unexpected sensation of a dog licking our faces. It was Martha, encouraged by the looming figure of Freeman Sheels smiling down upon us, almost unrecognizable in a black suit and white shirt, and clutching a very large black Bible.

"Putting you boys to work," said he, pointing the Bible to the spot where Abraham and I had cooled our feet upon our arrival the previous day. "Creek needs dammin' up. Got us a baptism this morning."

Soon enough we had blocked up the stream using stones piled nearby—evidently for this very purpose—creating in a short time a pool some two feet in depth, which Freeman regarded with much satisfaction. "Wish I had you boys about this place all the time. Now help the missus, if you wouldn't mind."

And with that, Freeman's wife took control.

She had lost some of her shyness around me, Watson, once my relationship to Abraham had been explained, but she was as a mother to my friend. Under her direction we cleared the porch of hay and set up an old barrel that Freeman would use for an altar—and we finished just in time, for the woods atop the palisades now came alive with voices.

Martha dashed off to investigate, and soon there appeared, in couples or singly, men and women dressed in bright clothing and making their way down the side of the face of the red clay bluffs to the swollen creek, laughing and talking as the dog bounded alongside them.

Their laughter froze in their throats when they saw me, however. Immediately their pace slowed, and in that curious, deferential manner they avoided looking my way while they quietly deposited upon the porch the various foodstuffs they had carried with them—potatoes, leeks, carrots and onions, as well as a curious preponderance of oyster shells.

Then they stood aside, eyes fixed upon the ground.

I made to leave—I was prepared to go anywhere, Watson, to avoid such a scene—but Freeman's wife grabbed my wrist and pulled me close. "Before Freedom," she said, in her low husky voice, "we hadda have a white man, like a overseer, watching whenever they was three of us together. They think you the man come to watch the baptism."

Now she held up my hand in hers and shouted, "He ain't no overseer! He's this here boy Abram's friend!"

I can't say they entirely lost their shyness about me, Watson, but not many minutes later we were gathered together at the porch in a half-circle facing Freeman as he clapped his hands, bowed his head and began to pray.

I say he "prayed," Watson, but a more fervent cry to the Lord—a Lord that had once been forbidden to these people, remember—I have never heard, and it was followed by preaching of such a heartfelt intensity that we were swept from the story of Exodus to the Sermon on the Mount to the raising of Lazarus from the dead to the Passover feast seemingly without pause.

I was drawn in and captivated, no longer a self-aware and detached spectator, but fully immersed. As the pace quickened and Freeman's voice rose in strength and volume—rather like a quiet, lazy river moving towards a powerful waterfall—the story of Christ's trial and condemnation and of the soldiers gambling for Christ's clothing and their fashioning a Crown of Thorns for His head tumbled forth, and the very ground beneath us seemed to shake. His voice now surged with a power I had never experienced, rooting me to the spot as Freeman cried the last recorded words of Christ on the cross:

"My God, my God, why hast thou forsaken me?"

All around me, the men and women shouted "Amen!" while I—well, I admit, Watson—I was puzzled. I found these words hard to fathom.

Why such a hopeless cry at the hour of His death? Did He not believe He was the Son of God? Did He not anticipate his own resurrection? Had He no faith?

But I was left with no time to ponder such questions, because Freeman had not finished. He had merely paused to recover his breath. Now he tramped back and forth across the porch, his body stooped like a tired pilgrim, telling with somber voice the story of Mary of Magdala.

He told of how she carried her oils to the tomb to cleanse the Saviour's body but found the tomb empty, and how she rushed to tell the other disciples but they believed not. He told of how she sat down in the garden to weep over what she did not yet understand, and how the resurrected Saviour now showed himself to her, saying, "Woman, why weepest thou?"

Then, with his voice rising once more to an incredible pitch, Freeman drove his point home with the power of a ship's horn blasting across the water:

"Weep not, sisters and brothers, for this miracle of the Redeemer and Saviour, risen from the dead and showing himself to the faithful Mary of Magdala is the story of Marse Abraham, a Son of God and the Redeemer of Christ's forgotten children, saved for all time."

Then he lowered his head and whispered a barely audible, "Amen."

Fully spent, the preacher leaned heavily across the barrel, his great bald head bowed down, his white shirt grey with sweat, as men and women gathered around him murmuring their "amens," the children among them watching in silence, knowing by the tears upon their mothers' and fathers' faces that something profound and worthwhile had been said.

In comparison to my other churchgoing experiences in America, Watson—at St. John's in Washington City with Mr. and Mrs. Stanton, and St. Joseph's on the Brandywine with Monsieur Vernet and his wife—it had been as a hurricane to the gentle breeze of a summers' day.

And I vowed that one day I would strive to understand those last words of Jesus Christ.

But now it was time for the baptism, and at a signal from Mrs. Sheels, a raven-haired, barefooted girl of perhaps twelve was escorted to the creek, where the pool of frigid water awaited. As Freeman helped her step in, she gasped an involuntary "Oh my Lord!" and everyone laughed. Freeman steadied her tenderly. Then, holding his Bible above her head and gazing directly into her eyes, he began.

"Do you believe in the resurrection of the Lord Jesus Christ?"

"I do!"

"Do you accept the Lord Jesus, your Saviour?"

"I do!"

"Are you prepared to be born again in these waters as in the waters of the Jordan, so help you God?"

"I are!"

"Sister Ruth, be now baptized in the holy water of our Lord and Saviour."

And, gently, with one big hand upon her shoulder, Freeman allowed the face of Ruth to be briefly submerged, whence she bounced up whooping and dripping wet, a most beatific smile upon her face. Friends and family joined her in the water, whooping and crying, and then they brought her to the porch and dried her off while the waters were released by the dismantling of the rocks, and Mrs. Sheels handed out the oyster shells.

They were to be our spoons for the feast.

And what a feast it was, Watson! Well, for all except Abraham. He was seated alone on the porch, petting Martha, seemingly rooted to the spot in a disaffected manner that might have been taken for rudeness were it not for the intensity of the look upon his face as he watched young Ruth.

He had not taken his eyes off the girl from the moment she had stepped into the cold waters of the creek and gasped "Oh my Lord!"

I had retrieved a ham hock for my friend when Freeman's dog suddenly jumped off the porch and ran to the waterside barking wildly at a now-familiar sail wagging its way towards the dock. Soon the animated figure of Jacob was visible, arms waving, yelling words that were indistinguishable until the skiff had reached the dock and he had jumped out into in the shallow waters, dragging his skiff to shore.

"He land!" Jacob was yelling. "He land!"

"The devil," said Freeman, breaking away from the crowd and greeting his friend. "Where?"

"Machodoc Creek, brother! This morn'! They go straight for Ol' Miss Quesenberry's place!"

"Who?"

"Young man and a cripple!"

"Cripple?"

"Man on crutches!"

"The devil."

A Fisher of Men, and of Women, Too

The Potomac waters were broad and powerful, her deep channel busy with traffic—but no longer was I observing the variety of sails and ships from the distance of the shore. Abraham and I were among them, in the oyster skiff captained by Jacob, crossing to the Virginia Neck.

We had pushed away from Freeman's dock—Jacob, Abraham and I—within minutes of Jacob's frantic alarm. The crossing was slow, for the current was strong, but this allowed Jacob to tell us something about Freeman Sheels that had not been revealed during our time with that good, honest man himself.

Freeman and Jacob, you see, had been partners in a most dangerous enterprise. They had helped runaway slaves escape from Virginia.

Jacob's skiff would carry them from a hidden inlet near Gambo Creek on the Virginia Neck across the Potomac to the very spot on the Maryland shore we had earlier departed. From there, Freeman would take them by horse or wagon or on foot—any way he could—to the famous brick house of Thomas Garrett at 227 Shipley Avenue in Wilmington, Delaware. From there, Mr. Garrett would shepherd them east to Philadelphia or north to Canada to Freedom.

"Fishers of men," Jacob called their days together, "and a whole lotta women, too," he added proudly.

He then did something uncharacteristic in my brief time in his company: he stopped talking, for we had left the heavy current of the river behind and were approaching his favoured spot near Gambo Creek. This was just upriver from the point where the excitable young man called Davey and the miserable older man with the broken leg and the bad temper had landed early that morning.

Unfurling the sail, Jacob steered the skiff into a seemingly impenetrable thicket of willow branches which formed a dark, quiet hollow. Then he stepped out into the shallow water and put a cautioning finger to his lips. "Don't move, and don't say nothin'" he hissed. He was off to fetch a guide who knew every inch of the Virginia Neck.

We were a half a day behind Davey Herold and J. Wilkes Booth.

MOSBY'S MEN

Our guide turned out to be half Negro, half Cherokee, of indeterminate age and possessed of a most evocative name: Birdsong Vance.

Tall, and slender as a sapling, of impassive face and piercing brown eyes, he wore self-made deerskin moccasins and carried a leather purse around his neck. His long, unwashed hair fell like braided rope down his back, enhancing the impression of leanness about him, and he possessed an animal smell that befitted a tracker who had escaped the infamous Alexandria slave pen.[65] He had spent his days since his escape helping other runaways cross the twenty miles of the Virginia Neck from the Rappahannock River to Gambo Creek, where a voyage in Jacob's oyster sloop awaited them.

As you might imagine, Watson, I was thunderstruck to meet an Indian in the flesh. Until that moment I had only read about them in the penny dreadfuls of my youth! Unlike the "red savages" portrayed in those storybooks, however, our guide's skin was no more tinged with red than was mine (it was, rather, the shade of a mahogany tree) and he was no more savage than you, friend Watson.

Also, quite contrary to the depiction of vocal natives forever emitting war chants in those stories, Birdsong rarely uttered a sound, for, as Jacob had confided in me, the Alexandria overseers had taken to whipping the boy whenever he was heard speaking Cherokee.

---

65 *The Price, Birch & Company slave traders of Alexandria, Virginia.*

Our guide did, however, possess one attribute played up by the storybook writers.

I may have learned something from Abraham in the ways of tracking a horse, Watson, but it would be from studying Birdsong that I learned the tracking of men. Every bent twig, misplaced stone and chattering mockingbird meant something to his keen senses, and it was he who would show me how to follow a man without that man ever knowing I was on his trail.

But that first evening tracking of Booth and Herold across the Virginia Neck—well, it did not go as even our guide had anticipated.

Rather than make straight for the Rappahannock River—a day's ride across the Neck on the Richmond stage road—the fugitives, Birdsong discovered on his first scouting foray, were making for an estate called Cleydael, the home of a doctor named Stuart.

There seemed nothing odd in this to me, Watson—the bloody rags in the pine thicket had told me Booth's leg had not mended, and he needed a doctor. But Birdsong was quite unsettled. He had brought many ill and abused runaways to Dr. Stuart over the years—under cover of the night, of course—before handing them off to Jacob, and he could not believe the good doctor would aid a man like Booth.

On his next scout, however, Birdsong confirmed that not only had Booth and Herold arrived at Cleydael, but they had been admitted to the house, evidently for the evening.

There was nothing to do but wait and watch. We followed our guide to a hidden campsite nearby, one of several he maintained across the Neck (another device I later adopted, Watson, when I took apartments throughout London, where I might take refuge or change costumes during a case), and there we waited.

Time dragged in those woods. One's thoughts turned to food— but something other than the hazelnuts Birdsong carried with him in his purse. And so, when the mouthwatering aroma of roasting chicken suddenly drifted our way upon the evening breeze—evidently from the direction of the old slave quarters at Cleydael—Abraham was eager to pay the cooks a visit.

Our guide, however, would have none of it.

There was no chance so delectable a meal was being prepared by servants, he declared. More likely they were Confederate soldiers returning home, or, even worse, Mosby's rangers. Mosby's men had been Birdsong's keenest adversaries during his time moving runaways through these woods, and bounties had been hung upon his head by Mosby himself.

But I thought back to Lovett and his men, and that detachment of Federal cavalry Abraham and I had encountered outside the pine thicket, and wondered aloud why soldiers at a campfire might not be Federal cavalry? After all, Federal patrols were everywhere in the manhunt for Booth, and if these men were Federals, why, we could lead them straight to Booth and be back in Washington City for breakfast!

At this, however, our guide's impassive face offered the only smile I would ever see from him. Union cavalry never ate in the field, he said flatly. Not with all the food they could want at the Federal camp at Fredericksburg.

Our discussion went back and forth for some little time. In the end, however, with Booth only a half mile away and the voice of Monsieur ringing in my ears—"Investigate all possibilities, and that which remains..."—Abraham and I set out to investigate while our guide remained behind, seated against a pine tree, silently munching hazelnuts.

He would not risk an encounter of his own with Mosby's rangers.

The campfire was soon visible flickering through the trees. We had approached to within fifty yards, being careful to remain downwind, and I counted five figures seated by the firelight. Their conversation carried distinctly to us. They were Confederate soldiers, as Birdsong had anticipated. More than that, there were Mosby's men among them, as he had feared.

And they were in heated discussion.

Mosby, it seemed, had issued a call for his men to disband that very day, and three of the men were bound for Winchester, Virginia, to sign an oath of allegiance to the Union. The remaining two, however were in no such frame of mind. They were not, it seems, officially under Mosby's command—they identified with the 9th Virginia Cavalry—and they were for keeping up the fight. After some little remonstration, the recalcitrant pair stood up, strapped on their sidearms, picked up their saddlebags and made for their horses.

When they had safely disappeared, I stepped tentatively out of the darkness and into the firelight, with Abraham lingering in the shadows.

The three men did not seem surprised by the appearance of a stranger materializing from the woods. After looking me up and down a moment, their leader introduced himself as Willie Jett of Mosby's command, then invited me to partake of their dinner. (I could feed Abraham from my share, he allowed when I called my companion from the darkness, and this I would do, Watson, for it was most excellent fowl).

Then, without introducing me to his companions or evincing the slightest interest in me and my friend, he resumed the discussion they had been having. It was evident they were not sorry to see the other two soldiers leave—it would mean a faster ride to Winchester, for one thing—and there was even some jesting that they might stop in Fredericksburg on the way, to partake of the vast foodstuffs at the Federal canteen there!

I listened attentively but discreetly as I ate, for there was every possibility they knew something of Booth's flight or were in league with the fugitives in some way, but when the subject came up in the course of their discussion it was evident they had been unaware of J. Wilkes Booth's presence in these very woods.

"I hope they catch him soon," Jett spoke solemnly. "That business brings us nothing but trouble, gentlemen. Nothing but trouble."

When Abraham and I had eaten our fill, I thanked Jett for his hospitality, and we returned to our campsite, weary from the day's adventure. Birdsong was out on a scout, however, and so we lay down without awaiting his return. Sleep came quickly.

It was still dark and not many hours later when I was awoken by a rough shake from our guide. Booth and Herold were on the move.

Dr. Stuart had turned them out.

CONSPIRACY

There is no need to relate every false start and fitful detour Booth and Herold took upon their journey across the Virginia Neck, Watson.

For purposes of this memoir, it would suffice to say we remained close upon their heels all the way to the Rappahannock and that our efforts were made considerably easier when the pair switched from horseback to wagon transport after being turned out by Dr. Stuart, who evidently had done nothing to fix Booth's leg. By noon next day we found ourselves standing in the shade of a hazel tree on a promontory overlooking the Rappahannock River.

The Rappahannock was a thin, lazy ribbon snaking across our field of vision a mile or more in the distance, busy with schooners and skiffs, although not nearly so majestic as the Potomac—but our guide cared nothing for the scenery. He was gazing intently through his field glass at the ferry landing in the center of this scene, where a knot of men were gathered around the ferryman.

After some little time, he handed me the glass with a worried look upon his normally impassive face, and as I peered through it, I quickly understood why.

Wilkes Booth, instantly recognizable in his civilian dress, black hair and slouching posture, was seated uncomfortably on a horse next to the ferry—actually little more than a raft. From the stables nearby there now emerged a young man leading a fresh horse to join Booth. He was also familiar. Clean shaven and quite tall, it was Davey Herold.

Near Booth, talking to the ferryman, were three men all in soldierly dress. And the man doing the negotiating with the ferryman was Willie Jett.

I watched in cold disbelief as Jett finally gave a nod and the soldier standing next to him handed the ferryman something—a fistful of paper, it looked like— which the ferryman took before gesturing to Booth and Herold to get aboard.

So impatient was Booth to cross the river, however, that he bolted onto the primitive ferry on his horse. That impatient—and reckless— behaviour drew gestures of disapproval from the ferryman and clucks from Birdsong, whose very fine eyesight had allowed him to take it all in even without the field glass.

It would also, as you will see, Watson, be Booth's undoing.

But, for now, J. Wilkes Booth and his horse were onboard the ferry and quickly followed by the other men, who walked their horses with care onto the flat-bottomed raft. Willie Jett went on last, and the ferryman pushed away from the slip.

I handed the glass to Abraham and told Birdsong we needed to alert the nearest Federal troopers in the fastest possible time.

Booth and Herold were in the company of Mosby's men. Willie Jett had played me false.

An hour later found us at the ferry slip.

Booth, Herold and Mosby's men were already across the river at Port Royal, a small hamlet of little account, and barely visible to us on the other side. Abraham was on his knees examining the mud about the ferry slip, while Birdsong disappeared inside the stables to procure horses for the ride to Fredericksburg.

He returned empty-handed, however, for Booth and Herold had taken the last two serviceable mounts, leaving behind a team of old draught horses entirely unsuitable for our purposes.

We would have to walk.

ADDERS FANGED

Abraham, Birdsong and I set out upon the well-worn towpath alongside the Rappahannock for the Federal camp at Fredericksburg.

Birdsong maintained a grueling pace, but it was not until the sun was descending beyond the western hills ahead of us that we glimpsed the first sign of the Federal encampment—a pontoon bridge across the Rappahannock.

It was from those hills beyond the bridge that Bobby Lee had directed his "masterpiece" two years previously—a smashing Confederate victory over the bumbling and incompetent Ambrose Burnside (Burnside's legacy was more stylistic than military, Watson, being in the form of the long "sideburns" he made popular). The old village of Fredericksburg had been reduced to brick and rubble in the fighting, but from the surrounding fields and hills there had arisen a bustling military base reminiscent of City Point, with acres of white tents and stockpiles of the matériel of war, along with cook wagons, their chimneys emitting a most tantalizing smoke.

Birdsong did not, however, stay around to sample the food.

The moment a sentry emerged from the guard hut to challenge us our guide turned on his heels and walked swiftly away down the towpath from whence we had come, his hand raised in goodbye. I had not even time to offer my thanks, however, still less to dwell upon his leaving, for my surprise at his sudden departure was now replaced by my surprise at the sentry standing before me.

It was the guard who had fallen off the porch the night of my first visit to the Navy Yard Bridge.

He did not recognize me, of course—I doubt he remembered anything from that unfortunate evening—but it was plainly evident by his diligent manner that he had suffered a harsh lesson at the hands of Edward M. Stanton, for he inspected our saddlebags with the utmost thoroughness, and when I was unable to show a pass, we were marched to the tent of the camp commander.

The commander, as it happened, was away on an inspection, and the sentry was about to place us in the custody of the provost guard until the commander's return when I received yet one more surprise, in the form of the major who had relieved me of our pass two days previously—with none other than Allan J. Pinkerton by his side.

Both men were mud-spattered and evidently fatigued from riding, and they had been on their way to the mess tent when we crossed paths.

A look of startled recognition came upon the major's face. This was followed by a smile and a hearty handshake, and the dismissal of the sentry with crisp authority. "See here, Pinkerton, the fellow who retrieved the boot!" the major boomed, placing a firm hand upon my shoulder in a most familiar manner while Pinkerton, who had been gazing at me with venomous eyes, managed to stop grinding his teeth only long enough to nod curtly.

"What brings you boys to Fredericksburg? Still got those newspapers of Booth's in your haversack? Not talking? Can't say I blame you. Hungry? Come along to the canteen. Get some food in you. Yes, the boy can eat too," the major said in an unctuous tone, condescending to wink at Abraham.

If we were to be played for fools, Watson, I decided we might as well be played on a full stomach.

Soon we were inside the tent, and gloriously rewarded, too, for the mess tables were as well stocked as Belshazzar's feast. Pork, lamb, beef, fried oysters, steaming plates of sweet potatoes and potatoes mashed with butter, green vegetables of all kinds, pickled onions, sardines and cheese—all these did Abraham and I scoop onto our plates and soon were eating, seated between a voluble major and a silent, spiteful Allan Pinkerton.

The major's name was Hardaway S. Morris, and he had learned of Abraham's retrieval of the boot during an encounter with Lieutenant Lovett, shortly after galloping away with our pass in his adjutant's jacket. "No hard feelings taking your pass, I hope." Then, in a confidential voice: "Dr. Mudd is a scoundrel of the first order. When Lovett presented the boot, Mudd confessed all. He has been taken to the Capitol Prison and I should think he will hang."

This was not true, of course—Samuel Mudd never confessed "all" in his life, to my knowledge—but I did not know it at the time. I did, however, recognize adders fanged when I saw them, and I saw them there at the mess table. So I said nothing.

And the less I said, the more the major spoke.

He spoke—to Pinkerton's evident annoyance—of their wild goose chase to Baltimore, of leaving Pinkerton behind in Baltimore and making for Anacostia where the crone at the Surratt tavern sent his men the wrong way to St. Mary's, of reuniting with Pinkerton (who had finally given up on Baltimore!) and their return to Fredericksburg to refresh their mounts and await orders from Mr. Stanton.

Still, I gave away nothing. Not about Booth's Potomac crossing, or his movements across the Neck, or his rendezvous with Mosby's men. Nothing. My silence unnerved the major, Watson—he could not keep his eye off my haversack—and it finally led him to change his approach altogether when we had finished our dinner.

"Come to the telegraph tent with me. Both of you." Then he winked at Pinkerton. "It wouldn't do for this fellow not to have some share of that reward money, would it, Allan?"

Pinkerton looked aghast but held his tongue. I had no interest in the money, of course—I only wanted to present the newspapers and tell my story to the camp commander—but it was evident this was the major's last card in buying my cooperation. We followed him out of the canteen and up a hill to the telegraph tent, where he motioned for us to remain outside while he and Pinkerton disappeared within and engaged the operator.

In short order, messages were being tapped out on the wire to Mr. Stanton at the War Department from the major, who evidently never dreamed that I could make out everything the operator was transmitting.

And a greater collection of lies could not have been imagined.

An hour later found us standing before the camp commander, Lieutenant Colonel Lucien Goodridge of the 61st Massachusetts, who had returned from his inspection.

Morris vouched for my bona-fides and was dismissed, and Colonel Goodridge swiftly turned his attention to our story, listening carefully to my account of what we had witnessed since crossing the Navy Yard Bridge three days after J. Wilkes Booth.

I found Goodridge to be an upright man, Watson, although—like Morris and the other soldiers we had encountered—he took Abraham for my "boy" rather than a comrade and paid him no mind. After inspecting the markings on the newspapers and questioning me about the Confederates accompanying Booth and Herold, he handed the papers to an orderly with instructions to carry them to Mr. Stanton at the War Department at once.

And when the orderly had departed, he provided me with the greatest surprise of a day which had already provided its share.

"You could identify Booth if you saw him again?" he asked, and I nodded. "And Mosby's men? Good." He turned to the telegraph book on his small camp desk. "I'm notifying the War Secretary that you will accompany Morris to identify Booth and Mosby's men. Be at the stables before sunup and follow Morris's orders to the letter. He rides at dawn. Wilkes Booth's days are numbered, I should think."

He scribbled out the telegrams and handed the flimsies to his adjutant. "Take these to the operator, then find a bed for this fellow and his boy."

Upon reaching the telegraph tent, however, it was discovered that the operator had gone to supper. While the adjutant set off to find him,

Abraham and I stayed behind to await their return. With no soldiers nearby and Abraham keeping watch, I ducked inside.

The equipment was quite familiar to me.

A FAREWELL

Abraham and I were up with the birds before dawn, walking by moonlight past silent tents and smoldering campfires along a well-worn path. It was with a chill I realized that we were following the Sunken Lane, where six thousand Confederates under Longstreet had held off forty thousand Federals for five hours, leaving the fields of Fredericksburg so littered with Union dead that it was said you could walk from one bend of the Rappahannock to the next—a half mile—without touching the ground.

At the stables we found the horses being saddled and made ready for the ride. Morris insisted Abraham would have to ride with me if I wished to bring him (I had expected some petty slight from Morris, Watson, and was not altogether surprised). "*Boots and saddles*" was called, and soon we were riding east with Morris's detachment—the very same men we had encountered outside the pine thicket in Maryland—plus the sullen figure of Allan Pinkerton.

Morris set a fast pace, and the first hint of sunlight had begun to illuminate the fog rising from the cool waters of the Rappahannock as we found the river road. It was a two-hour ride to Port Royal, but Abraham and I lagged badly on a single horse, and we reached our destination a good twenty minutes behind the detachment.

We found them resting their blown horses and listening as Morris instructed them on the next stage of the ride. The chase would be south, he said, down the Richmond road to Bowling Green. Booth must be taken alive, etc. etc.

But before he could finish his exhortation, Morris received a shock.

On the opposite side of the Rappahannock, at the ferry slip at Port Conway, there now appeared Federal cavalry, and in quite a large number.

"Sixteenth New York Cavalry, d--n 'em," muttered Morris, peering through his field glass at the soldiers leading their horses onto the ferry. "Doherty's men." He uttered some rather choice oaths about this Lieutenant Doherty—evidently, they had had dealings in the past— and with no little determination handed the field glass to his adjutant, shouting "*Boots and saddles*, men! *Boots and saddles!*"

But the horses were not ready, and the major stewed and fumed as the ferry made its way to our side of the Rappahannock. Within a quarter-hour it had deposited the first of the New York cavalrymen in our midst.

And Lieutenant Edward P. Doherty was the first man off the ferry.

He was a tall, red-moustached Irishman with a friendly demeanor. "Morris," said he, extending his hand to the major and acknowledging Pinkerton with a touch of his hat. "Secretary Stanton sends his compliments. Have you fresh word on Booth?"

Morris maintained a façade of cool confidence. "Wilkes Booth and Davey Herold were placed at this spot yesterday, in the company of three of Mosby's rangers. I expect they are well along the Richmond road by now, probably past Bowling Green, possibly making for Orange Courthouse."

Doherty's hazel eyes twinkled as he listened, then he stroked his moustache as if he were deliberating whether to share a most intimate secret with Morris. "Booth and Herold ride east," he said finally, and with some authority. "They make for Mobjack Bay."

Morris started. "Who told you this?"

Doherty nodded at the ferry. "The ferryman overheard Mosby's men on the crossing yesterday. Their idea all along was to feint south for Bowling Green and send you that way, then make for Mobjack instead. A fast packet there is expecting to rendezvous with Booth, bound for Cuba."

Pinkerton waved his cap and slapped Morris on the shoulder. "I knew it! I knew it! Didn't I tell you, Morris? Didn't I? He's making for the Chesapeake! Hey!"

Morris ignored Pinkerton. "Why are you not after them?" he asked Doherty, with some little suspicion.

Doherty began a lengthy explanation of the fast, hard ride that had taken his men from Belle Plain that morning on orders from Stanton, the blown condition of his horses and the several more ferry crossings that would be required to get the rest of his men across the river. A glint came to Morris's eyes at this, and when Doherty stroked his moustache and allowed that his horses might be in condition to send a detachment after Booth in as little as, oh, one hour, Morris lost his caution altogether.

"Ours are fresh enough!" Morris cried. "*Boots and saddles*, men! We'll track him down and you'll be in time for the capture! The chase is on, boys!"

Pinkerton climbed onto his mount and winked at me. "You and your darkie have a fine ride home, son." With that, he spurred his mount and followed Morris and the blue riders galloping hard east—or, as hard as their tired horses could take them, anyway—along the river road towards Mobjack Bay and the Atlantic Ocean beyond.

And out of the hunt for J. Wilkes Booth for all time.

It was quite evident, Watson, that my late evening visit to the telegraph tent at Fredericksburg had not been wasted.

Lieutenant Doherty watched the riders disappear beyond a bend of the river, then turned to me with a satisfied grunt. "So much for Major Morris and the great Allan Pinkerton, eh?" He touched his hat with formality. "Mr. Stanton sends his compliments and thanks you for the reports received last night. The 16th New York Cavalry now commands the manhunt. You are directed to return by way of Fredericksburg to Washington City, where you will report to Mr. Stanton."

But we would not leave just yet.

It would take three more trips to carry the rest of his detachment across the Rappahannock, Doherty said, and in the meantime he wanted to hear everything I could tell him about J. Wilkes Booth, Davey Herold and the three of Mosby's Confederates who appeared to be accompanying them on their flight. Abraham and I could fill our stomachs while we talked, for a shad-bake was being organized by his men while they waited for the rest of their comrades. Then he and his men would ride south for Booth and Herold while Abraham and I departed for Washington City by way of Fredericksburg—where, he added with a friendly wink—we would be given a tour of that battlefield by the camp commander, arranged by

Secretary Stanton as thanks for our assistance in the manhunt for Booth.

If, however, you have already divined, friend Watson, that Providence would send us on a different path to Washington City, well, you are entirely correct.

Ghost Walkers of Appomattox

Three hours had passed before the last of Doherty's twenty-six men arrived on the Port Royal side of the Rappahannock. Now that they were assembled the air filled with the sound of leather creaking, bridles jangling, scabbards slapping and soldiers chattering and laughing as their mounts snorted and pawed the dirt.

Man and horse were ready for the chase.

Doherty thanked me—and Abraham, mind you—with a touch of his hat, then he spurred his horse, and soon all twenty-six cavalry men were pounding south down the Richmond road, past the old, decaying buildings of Port Royal and up the long incline into the wooded hills that overlooked the river valley.

I invited the old ferryman to partake of the remaining shad now cooling on the rack—Abraham and I had eaten our fill—and he said he wouldn't mind if he did. As he walked over to help himself, I mounted our horse and was waiting for Abraham to climb up behind me, when I heard an exclamation and saw Abraham staring down the road where the cavalry had disappeared in the dusk just moments before.

A man, dust covered and barefooted, was walking our way.

He bore no weapons and carried nothing but a limp haversack hanging from his shoulder and a canteen swinging from his belt, and he was picking lice from his scalp in a most absent-minded fashion as he walked, paying no attention to anything but the bugs, inspecting each before crushing it with his fingers and flicking it aside.

We had seen such men on our journey, Watson—Confederate soldiers making their way home in tattered grey uniforms turned white from the road dust—"ghost walkers," Birdsong had called them. And that is indeed how this poor fellow appeared upon materializing out of the dusk. As he came near and Abraham pointed to the fish rack where the ferryman was enjoying a meal, however, a smile broke the white pallor of his face, and our ghost walker spoke.

"Thank you kindly. Private Rob Fraim, Company K. Virginia 30th. Fought for Marse Robert"—he meant Robert E. Lee, Watson—"from Second Manassas to Appomattox."

I dismounted and we joined him on a log. And as he devoured his meal, he told us his story.

It was a story of hopeless battles against overwhelming Union numbers and barefoot slogging in mud and rain; of rancid meat and green corn and sweet-potato coffee; of the lost race to Appomattox Station and of Marse Robert surrendering at the McLean house while his men waited outside; of Marse Robert emerging from the McLean house telling his men they were surrendered and they should go on home to their families; of Marse Robert mounting old Traveler, his famous horse, and riding away while his men cried and the Yankee officers made off with every stick of furniture in that house for souvenirs.

Even the chamber pots.

"I didn't lay down my rifle because we was whipped," he wanted me to know. "I laid down my rifle because Marse Robert surrendered us, and now I am going home to the Neck, because Marse Robert told us to go home. And I am taking the oath because Marse Robert done it."

He leaned into my face, his eyes showing that blue light that came from deep within. "Know this, sir," said he, in a quiet and gruff voice. "Marse Lee is a great man, sir. A great man."

At that moment, the ferryman whistled, signaling the last crossing before nightfall. Our ghost walker prepared to leave, but he had a question for me.

"That Union cavalry flying down the road to Bowling Green—they after Booth, ain't they?" He chuckled. "I expected so. But they won't find him in Bowling Green, and that's a fact. Mosby's men left Booth behind on the Richmond road."

You can imagine my surprise at this, Watson. "But I thought those men were in league with Booth and Herold!"

He slapped his leg and laughed. "In league? No sir. Willie Jett's my cousin! He ain't in league with nobody but John S. Mosby. Booth and that boy Herold asked Willie to take 'em to Mexico, but they didn't even make it to Bowling Green! Couldn't stand the riding! Willie left 'em at a farmhouse along the way."

"Do you know where?"

"Nosir."

The ferryman whistled again, and the soldier started his walk to the ferry, telling the lice as he picked them about those greedy no good Yankees looting the McLean house at Appomattox.

The ferry soon pulled away and Abraham and I mounted our horse. She was frisky—evidently eager to return to her stables. But we would not be riding to Fredericksburg, out of the manhunt.

We were riding south, to find Doherty.

Unless, of course, we came across Booth first.

Tuesday April 25th Evening

The Richmond road climbs out of Port Royal to a plateau overlooking the Rappahannock River that is heavily wooded with occasional clearings. In those clearings, the marks of human habitation were visible at nightfall only by their shapes: tobacco sheds, corn cribs, log shacks. I kept my eye upon these for signs of life, while Abraham's eyes were fixed on the road itself.

I have said, Watson, that Booth had unwisely ridden his horse onto the ferry at Port Conway, so impatient was he to leave the Neck behind and cross the Rappahannock, and that it was an impulsive gesture that would seal his fate—but I have not explained why.

Booth's impatience meant that his was the only horse not walked onto the ferry by a man. That meant its prints would be unaccompanied by a man's boot marks. And Abraham had found that horse's prints precisely where Booth had spurred his mount onto the raft.

Once more it was the off foreleg that marked Booth's mount—but not with anything so distinctive as a bar horseshoe. This time it was a plain horseshoe, but cracked in such a fashion that Abraham thought he could trace it anywhere, so long as the ground would hold the impression.

Unfortunately, the Richmond road had hardened in the dry weather, and our pace slackened in the gathering darkness as we were forced to halt at every clearing and horse trail where Booth might have left the road, so that Abraham could inspect the sloughs and creek beds for signs of the cracked shoe.

This went on for at least an hour—each time Abraham rising to his feet and shaking his head—until we came upon a large, well-fenced clearing extending half a mile on the left side of the public road. It was there at the gate, where a thin trickle of groundwater was revealed, that Abraham rose from his inspection of the damp earth and smiled. Booth's horse had entered here.

And by the looks of the tracks, it had not left.

We removed our horse to a sheltered swale across the road and tied her securely, then returned to the gate. There we slipped between the rails and made our way towards the house, always keeping downwind from the stables and staying off the carriageway. After skirting a pond, several woodpiles and the old slave quarters, we came upon the rear of a two-story wooden structure, the most prominent feature of which was a porch or veranda on three sides.

The occupants appeared to be at supper. Lights illuminated the kitchen and dining room, and voices could be heard from within, but no conversation could be distinguished. We found a tall woodpile that afforded a view of the kitchen as well as the stables and also the pump—and behind this we awaited developments.

They were not very long in coming.

A young Negro woman soon emerged from the kitchen with a bucket and hurried down the steps to the pump that was not fifteen feet from us. To our surprise, she was met there by a horse that had nosed its way from the stables, trailing its bridle. It nuzzled the young woman in competition for the water splashing into her bucket, and the girl cooed and patted the beast as it lowered its snout into the bucket and drank.

After letting the horse have its fill, the girl filled the bucket once more and began making her way back to the house, hunched over and trailing water splashes as she trudged up the steps. A harsh voice from the kitchen door told her to make haste.

To my alarm, Watson, I noticed the horse was attempting to follow her.

Abraham saw it, too, and when the girl had entered the house, he squeezed my arm and vanished from my side, moving swiftly and silently to the mare, calming it with his low, soothing voice before tying it to the pump, whereupon he dropped to his knees and examined the telltale leg in the moonlight. Soon he was back at the woodpile, smiling.

The shoe was cracked. The horse was Booth's. He must be inside the house.

Again, Abraham squeezed my arm. It was the signal that he was to return to our horse and fetch Doherty—we had spent considerable time during the ride from Port Royal discussing what we would do in this event—but as my companion moved to leave my side, there was a commotion from the pump.

The horse had begun to buck and pull away in an attempt to follow Abraham. This attracted the attention of an old dog that emerged barking from beneath the porch. Suddenly the kitchen door was thrown open and a dark-featured, wild-eyed man appeared, hobbling forth on a single crutch, wielding a lantern.

Even in the uncertain light, Watson, I recognized those flashing eyes.

They seemed to gaze directly into mine, despite the darkness of the evening, and their mesmeric effect held me in thrall even as he set down the lantern and drew from his belt an object, black and metallic.

I watched in the manner of a disinterested observer as he lifted the strange object and brought it carefully to eye level. My eyes saw that it was a pistol, of course, but my mind dismissed it as a harmless toy, and even as he cocked the weapon and took aim, those blazing eyes held me in their grip. My body was frozen. I could not move, and I would not have moved but for the hand that grabbed my arm and pulled me down sharply to the ground at the very moment the figure upon the porch let fly a bullet with a deafening crack.

George Washington, in that famous letter to his brother, describes the "charming" sound of a bullet whistling past his ear in the heat of his first battle. Rest assured, Watson, I found nothing charming in the bullet that crashed into the very log over which I had been peering a half second before, exploding the wood into a thousand splinters. I knew instantly that I would have been dead had Abraham not pulled me from its path.

The bullet did have one welcome effect, however: it served to snap me out of my strange trance.

It also sent the dog back under the porch, which helped cause the horse to settle down. Abraham and I now huddled together, motionless and alert as the sound of another figure was heard upon the porch. Peering through a gap in our improvised battlement, I could see in the haze of gun smoke the same figure who had stood with Booth all during their journey.

Davey Herold.

The pair conversed in hushed voices until an older gentleman appeared—I judged him to be the man of the house—inquiring as to the cause of the gunshot. "N----r horse thieves!" Booth barked, letting fly one more loud, percussive shot into the branches above us, as if to prove his case. An oath was shouted, there was movement on the porch and the door was slammed shut. Silence fell upon us.

With a third squeeze of my shoulder, Abraham vanished from my side. I was on my own, and my vigil had begun.

My recollection of the time spent behind that woodpile is not easy to mark, Watson. In the quiet countryside there were no parish clocks chiming the quarters, only the sounds of a household at supper and then in preparation for bed. From the dining room window, male voices occasionally rose in some little heat, then quieted down. The kitchen door was opened several times for visits to the privy, and, as the evening wore on, wood was retrieved from the very woodpile behind which I remained hidden and water was fetched once more from the pump. After what might have been two hours, lights appeared in two of the upper windows, then were extinguished.

This I took to mean the inhabitants had gone to bed.

Suddenly, however, there came the sound of a heavy door banging open followed by raised voices, including Booth's. The voices came from the front porch on the far side of the house. At once I began to maneuver to a new hiding place from which I could observe this development.

It took some little time, and very stealthy movement, but I settled on an empty corn crib amid a stand of locust trees halfway between the house and a tobacco barn. Upon letting myself in, I found the crib would serve my purposes admirably, for through its slats on one side I could watch the front porch of the house, while from the other side I could keep an eye upon the carriageway to the public road.

I paid no attention, at the moment, to the tobacco barn one hundred feet away.

Three figures were now on the porch and in animated discussion: Booth, Herold and a third man—John Garrett, as I later learned, son of the elderly gentleman I had seen at the kitchen door.

And John Garrett was a severely agitated man.

Booth and Herold, it seemed, had been masquerading as Confederate soldiers—Booth claiming his leg had been shattered at Petersburg—and calling themselves "the Boyd cousins." But John Garrett had been a true soldier of the Confederacy, recently returned from Appomattox, and he had found them out.

Now he meant to turn them out. Booth, for his part, was in a fit of anger, gripping the back of a rocking chair and sputtering indignities in that ferocious voice:

"Why, sir, I spent the night in that very room with you and your brother! What do you mean denying me a second night of hospitality? Will the cock crow upon a third denial? What kind of a man refuses the request of a Confederate gentleman for succor and rest? How will you hold your head up in company again?" Etc. etc.

But Garrett appeared unmoved, and after much grumbling, Booth suddenly changed his tactic. He prodded Herold to offer a wad of greenbacks for a carriage to drive the pair to a doctor who could fix his leg.

Garrett refused. "I can spare no one to drive it."

Booth now adopted a low, menacing snarl and fingered the gun on his belt. "Well, then, you must allow us the porch."

Garrett may have been indignant at Booth's masquerade, Watson, but he was no fool. "I can put you in the tobacco barn, if that will do."

This Booth accepted, and while Herold retrieved a carbine and blankets from the house, Booth followed Garrett to the tobacco barn—passing not ten feet from my corn crib! He moved slowly, emitting grunts and cries with each swinging step on the crutches, but upon entering the barn he seemed satisfied with the accommodations.

Soon I could hear him giving instructions to Davey Herold to pile hay for a bed.

The pair had finally settled down when Garrett shut the door—but he did not leave the barn just yet. He stood motionless outside and listened to the sounds within for some little time. Tobacco barns being built with open slats to air the leaves, he could hear every sound they made.

And so, Watson, could I.

Booth fussed and cursed, and Herold responded to each command like an anxious waiter. From the scraping and shuffling noises, it was evident that there was some form of barricade being made from furniture stored by neighbors to keep it out of the hands of Union troops. When, finally, all was silent within, John Garrett tiptoed past my corn crib to the house, where he was joined on the porch by another man—younger by perhaps five years and clearly his brother by the nature of their conversation—and together they sat upon the steps, speaking in urgent, hushed voices about the men in their barn.

If these "Boyd cousins" were not soldiers, they wondered, what were they? Horse thieves? Highwaymen? They were trouble in any case, for both were armed, and it was obvious the man with the broken leg would stick at nothing in the event of a confrontation. After some little deliberation, the elder brother retreated into the house and re-emerged with a large skeleton key.

Together they moved stealthily to the barn, halted outside the door and listened carefully for sounds from within. The only sound, however, was heavy snoring. And so, while one brother kept watch through the slats, the other acted.

And with a click of the latch, the fates of J. Wilkes Booth and Davey Herold were sealed for all time.

TUESDAY APRIL 25TH MIDNIGHT

All was quiet from the "Boyd cousins" inside the tobacco barn, but the Garrett brothers were taking no chances. They retrieved blankets and sidearms from the house and made their way on tiptoe to a second corn crib closer to the barn and not thirty paces from mine.

Silence now descended over the farm, and my mind turned towards Abraham. Where was he? When might he return?

There was no moon to work out how long it had been since he had left my side, and in any case it was impossible to calculate when he might return without knowing how long it had taken him to catch up to Lieutenant Doherty and his men.

Then, of course, there was the possibility my friend had lost his way on the unfamiliar road, or worse. I began to imagine fantastic schemes that all seemed to end with the capture of my friend by patterrollers, and soon convinced myself that every one of the strange circumstances which had brought me to the dusty wooden floor of this corn crib, with the assassin of President Lincoln snoring gruffly in his sleep not a hundred feet away, had been towards the entrapment of young Abraham.

Why even the "ghost walker" might have been part of some devious plan!

My mind was ablaze in a most distracted fashion. Dark images of my friend in captivity swirled in my head, and I cursed myself for sending him out alone. What was I thinking letting a freed slave boy ride alone on the public road in the Virginia woods with Mosby's raiders still lurking? Where could he be? What should I do?

These thoughts were suddenly interrupted by strange sounds coming from within the barn. They were the sound of nightmares, Watson, chilling shrieks and cries for "Mother." It was Booth's voice, of that I had no doubt, and the cries seemed to me to be the pleadings of a soul that had peered deep within itself and had found remorse for what its hands had wrought. But the crying ended as abruptly as it had begun, and, again, all was silent.

Then I perceived a new sound. It was the sound of distant thunder.

The storm grew in strength and clarity, finally revealing itself as the pounding of horses' hooves on the Richmond road, and above the low rumble came the high-pitched slap and jingle of bridles. This meant cavalry, Watson—Federal cavalry, riding hard—and all my senses were now on alert.

I pressed my face against the slats to glimpse the carriageway as the angry trill of a mockingbird from the road indicated the riders had broached its territory. At that moment, all grim, fantastic thoughts vanished from my mind as I spotted the shadowy figure of a fast-flying horse taking the front gate in one stride and galloping up the carriageway at full speed.

A moment later the horse was brought to a halt, and off leaped Lieutenant Doherty.

He trotted up the steps to the porch and was about to pound on the door when the Garrett brothers intercepted him, having emerged from their corn crib protesting the sudden invasion of their property, even as more horsemen filled the yard, the upstairs lamps were lighted, and a general alarm arose across the property.

A most welcome sight now greeted my eyes when I saw Abraham leaping from the back of a mount. I exited the corn crib and we were quickly reunited—and only just in time, Watson, for as the yard filled with horsemen, the situation was becoming somewhat beyond the control of the good Lieutenant Doherty.

Two rough-looking men in civilian clothes—detectives from New York City by the names of Luther Baker and Everton Conger, I later learned—had dismounted, weapons drawn, and charged past Doherty and the Garrett brothers into the house. After knocking about inside with much noise and shouting, they reappeared with a badly frightened and confused old man between them—the senior Garrett, in his nightdress—followed by the man's terrified wife.

The pair proceeded to bully the elderly Mr. Garrett—a pitiful spectacle, for he clearly knew nothing of the true identity of the "Boyd cousins," or even their whereabouts on his property—until his sons jumped between them, objecting loudly to this treatment of their father.

The situation deteriorated until Doherty put himself between the detectives and the brothers and began quietly questioning the brothers for a minute or two, whence the elder son produced the skeleton key from his trousers and held it up for Doherty.

"We have them locked in the tobacco barn. They can't get out."

It was as if a starter's pistol had been fired, Watson. Suddenly, every man in the yard was racing to the barn, with Baker and Conger in the lead. Abraham and I departed from the vicinity of the corn crib—it seemed as well to get out of their way—and made for the house, where the elderly Garretts stood together on the porch, alone and badly confused.

I helped the old man into the rocking chair while his wife fetched a blanket, and then we all watched the scene at the tobacco barn not a hundred yards away, where—to quote Milton—all hell broke loose.

Much has been written, Watson, of the events that transpired at the Garrett farm in the early morning hours of Wednesday, April 26th 1865—twelve days and ninety miles removed from the murder of Abraham Lincoln in Washington City—and nearly all of it is false, for the histories of those tragic hours are based, in the main, on the prevarications, embellishments and sheer fabrications of the participants, whose motivations were not feelings of patriotism towards their country or loyalty to their fallen leader.

They wanted the reward money.

It amounted to a mighty sum, and the thought of gaining even a piece of it is what caused a shambles to be made of what should have been a relatively simple problem for the soldiers outside the Garrett tobacco barn that early morning: how to get J. Wilkes Booth out alive.

That was the most fervent wish of Mr. Stanton, of course, for he believed Booth was part of a vast Confederate conspiracy, and he meant to prove it.

And, really, Watson, it would not have been a difficult thing to draw Booth and Herold out. The smoke from a few pine boughs, set just upwind of the barn, would have quickly disabled the inhabitants within, rather like a bee colony. The pair could have been taken without a shot, and Edwin M. Stanton would have had his man.

But it did not go that way.

Baker and Conger, the two so-called detectives, first attempted to get Booth out in a variety of unproductive ways—mainly threats and abuse, but also, at one point, sending a trembling John Garrett inside the barn to negotiate with the fugitives!

Poor Davey Herold finally gave himself up, but Booth resisted—the threats only stiffened his resolve, of course—and it was finally decided to set fire directly to the barn with a pile of hay. The barn caught fire in a whoosh, but as the wood did not smoke, Booth was not disabled, and he continued his resistance while Doherty turned his attention to putting out the blaze that he could see would destroy the very man Edwin M. Stanton wanted alive.

It was in the midst of this distraction that Sergeant Thomas Corbett, an undisciplined glory-seeker, took it upon himself to fire his revolver through a gap in the boards, mortally wounding J. Wilkes Booth with a bullet to the neck.

The end result is well known: Booth was removed from the burning barn to the porch of the Garrett house, where he died at almost precisely the same time of morning as Abraham Lincoln had done, twelve days previously. And with him died the ability of Edwin M. Stanton to conduct one of his rigorous interrogations to learn what links, if any, J. Wilkes Booth might have had to the Confederate administration of Jefferson Davis.

Booth's corpse, wrapped in a bloody blanket with only the sightless face—shorn of its moustache—exposed, was taken by wagon to Belle Plain on the Potomac and then to Washington City by steamer, under heavy guard, for viewing by Secretary Stanton.

Conger and Baker, meanwhile—charlatans both—raced ahead of Doherty's detachment to present their version of Booth's capture to Mr. Stanton in person, setting in motion a mad scramble for the reward money. And although their actions had caused the death of the very man Stanton wanted to save—and had turned to ashes whatever clues to the assassination of Abraham Lincoln had been left behind in that barn—the unscrupulous pair would, in time receive the bulk of it.

Just as bad: Sergeant Corbett would become famous overnight for his much-embellished story of the shooting of Wilkes Booth, portrayed by the press as an act of heroism rather than the impulsive act of a not-over-bright attention-seeker that it had been.

Lieutenant Doherty would go on to lead an honourable life—his report of the manhunt, in my view, remains the only one worth reading, if accuracy rather than drama is desired—but he received only a fraction of the reward money.

And poor Davey Herold, an impressionable young drug store clerk who made the fatal mistake of allowing himself to be taken in by the bitter ravings of a mesmeric stage actor and then stayed loyal to the man on his flight to safety, would be hung by the neck along with six other conspirators sentenced to death by a military tribunal that allowed the wily Dr. Mudd to escape hanging.

As for Abraham and myself, while the soldiers were gawking at the corpse on the porch (and clipping snippets of Booth's hair for souvenirs), we busied ourselves assisting the Garrett brothers in their attempt to extinguish the fire by carrying water buckets up from the pond until it was evident the barn could not be saved.

And although our efforts failed, the brothers were immensely grateful.

Indeed, when the wagon train to Belle Plain had been readied and we said our goodbyes to the stunned and exhausted pair, John, the elder brother, offered me his hand, and it was only then that I noticed, in the light of the rising sun, that two of his fingers had been fused together in rather a painful-looking looking manner.

With no little pride in his voice, Garrett explained that the injury had occurred at Gettysburg during the cannonade prior to Pickett's famous charge. A cannon had misfired, the barrel had split, and a long section had crushed the leg of a comrade, trapping the poor man beneath a caisson.

Garrett had instinctively grabbed the hot metal to lift it from the leg, whence the heat of the barrel melted the two fingers together

"Holmes!" I cried, glancing up from the manuscript with a start. "This hand injury! The fused fingers—!"

Through the blue tobacco smoke that hung thick in the barrow, I could see the piercing grey eyes of Sherlock Holmes gazing at me with an expression that combined amusement and the utmost concentration.

"Bravo, Watson. It is indeed the very same injury as that young man in the train, and not uncommon among soldiers handling cannons in battle. I don't blame you for being unfamiliar with it. Your medical experience in Afghanistan was, as I recall, limited to bullet wounds and the occasional slashings of a scimitar."

"But that would mean the fellow in the train—"

"Precisely."

"—was not a civilian injured in some farming accident, as I supposed? He was a soldier, injured in battle!"

"Quite so."

"But surely, he *was* French?"

Sherlock Holmes shook his head. "Very likely another faulty deduction on your part, Watson."

"But the Parisian spectacles! The French francs!"

Holmes chuckled softly. "Have you not noticed an overabundance of Gallic influences during your travels today? Think Watson."

"Well, the spectacles, of course, and the francs. And the Gauloises cigarettes in the Mary Box. But—"

"Don't forget the 'Good Samaritan' who drove you to my cottage. You said he reverted to fluent French, did you not, when the dog approached the car?"

"Why, yes, but he was in the uniform of a French officer! I thought nothing of it."

"Did you think nothing of the fellow who drove you to Victoria station?"

"What about him?"

"You said that he tapped his watch in exasperation at your tardiness—is that not a Gallic gesture?"

"A gesture is hardly conclusive, Holmes."

"Then, pray tell me, what did he say when he deposited you at Victoria?"

"Why, he said nothing."

"Quite so."

"But what of it?"

"He was *French*, Watson. He could not speak English without an accent, so he avoided speaking altogether. And he was in league with the murderer— his job was to get you to Victoria Station in time for that Eastbourne train."

"Then the murderer was a Frenchman!"

"Almost certainly, Watson."

"But the dead man was *not*?"

"By no means."

"Why, then, was he outfitted as one?"

"To obscure his identification, using whatever the murderer had at hand."

"But how do you explain the missing shoes, Holmes? Why had they been removed?"

"Because they were *army* boots, Watson. Every de-mobbed soldier wears them. Had they remained upon the dead man's feet, even the most feeble-minded inspector of the Southcoast Line would have marked him as a Tommy, and his identity would have been traced within an hour of your arrival at Polegate station. The murderer could not afford to let them be found."

"Then you brought me to this barrow and invited me to read your manuscript merely to send me up?" My voice trembled with some little emotion.

"Not at all, Watson. My request that you read it to me was heartfelt. And hearing it spoken in that familiar voice of yours, well, it sent me back in time. I was reliving my days in America and had entirely forgotten the hand injury to John Garrett until you arrived at that point in the story."

I thought back to the self-importance with which I had regaled the police with my misguided deductions, and a hot flush came to my cheeks. Sherlock Holmes placed a gentle hand upon my shoulder.

"You are not to blame, Watson. It was exceedingly cleverly done."

"But I really have been the most foolish—"

"No, Watson. You mustn't condemn yourself. Once the French contents of the Mary Box were confirmed by the mark of the Paris optician on the spectacles, all your thoughts turned that way, precisely as the murderer intended. It was a blind, to make you believe you were attending a Frenchman bound for Lewes, missing a rather expensive pair of shoes. That the poor fellow was, instead, a de-mobbed soldier traveling to Eastbourne could never have crossed your mind."

"But why go to such lengths to deceive me, Holmes?"

"That is the question that I have been turning over in my mind ever since learning of the clues so conveniently placed for your discovery. False clues have been employed since Cain slew Abel, of course, but this fellow took the time—at no little hazard of being interrupted, mind you—to plant enough evidence to make the French connection quite inevitable. And yet he took the even *more* considerable risk of jumping from the train and fleeing on foot..."

Holmes's jaw set, his eyes glinted by the light of the lamp and his body became tense and alert. I, who knew the significance of his every movement, recognized their meaning at once.

"You have solved the puzzle, Holmes?"

"Answer me this, Watson," said he, emphasizing with his pipe each point as he made it. "What murderer, alone in a railway carriage, takes the time to plant five false clues upon his victim, *then* ventures into the next compartment to steal a different man's purse—*then* leaps from the train in the middle of the English countryside to disappear in the reeds and marshes of Sussex?"

"I cannot think."

"A murderer who never left the train, of course."

"I do not follow you, Holmes. Are you saying the murderer was not the fellow who jumped from the train?"

"No, Watson. I am saying there never *was* such a fellow."

"But the old guard swore to it!"

"The power of suggestion, Watson. It was the ticket inspector who reminded the guard they had seen a man jumping, was it not? You said the old guard merely agreed, as would any man in his position. It makes him feel important, when, in truth, he was probably too busy fixing his tea to notice anything."

Holmes sat back and puffed thoughtfully at his pipe, the blue smoke ever denser in the barrow, and a further light came to his eyes.

"Was it not also the ticket inspector who said your stethoscope had been sticking out of your bag, Watson? And told you the victim had placed his fine leather shoes upon the seat?"

All the vague surmises lurking in my mind now seemed to arrange themselves in a new image of the ticket inspector. I recalled the manner in which he had engaged me at Victoria Station and had shaken me awake at Berwick. And how he had returned Holmes's manuscript at the cab rank with such fawning assuredness. And had even written the directions to East Dean on the manuscript!

"That would mean the return ticket for Lewes was also a plant," I ventured to remark.

"Quite so, and easily done by a ticket inspector."

"So the ticket inspector conspired with the murderer!"

"No, Watson," said Sherlock Holmes, speaking words that sent a chill to my heart. "I rather think the ticket inspector *is* the murderer."

My mind raced with this new image of the smiling, bearded figure in the railway uniform.

"But what of the Good Samaritan, Holmes? He, too, was French—do you mean to say they were in league together?"

"Did it not occur to you, Watson," said Holmes, setting aside his pipe, "that the ticket inspector and your Good Samaritan might be one and the same?"

I started.

"It is not possible! The ticket inspector was bound for London when I left Polegate station—"

"So he said. But nothing would have prevented him from riding on to Eastbourne—or wherever his lair may be—to change his costume before hiring, or stealing, the car with which he met you on the Jevington Road."

"But the Good Samaritan looked nothing like the ticket inspector!"

"Oh, pshaw! You said yourself he wore a heavy muffler and driving goggles. What do you know about his appearance beneath that disguise? I have performed the same makeup tricks too many times to count!"

"But how would he have had time to kill the poor boy and plant all that evidence to cover his tracks, and yet still perform his duties in the train?"

"Easily enough, I should think. He simply stayed in the carriage after the murder and performed his duties from there—without returning to the guard van. The stops between Lewes and Polegate are rather rural, are they not? I doubt there was any traffic in the first-class carriage. He would have had all the time in the world to arrange the scene to the desired effect. Then he simply returned to the guard van, invented the jumper and caused the old guard to inspect the carriages at Berwick, whence the body was found and you were awakened."

I shook my head. "Well, I must admit he took me in."

"He took *everyone* in, Watson. It was cleverly done. No—it was *expertly* done. I would not have been so easily fooled, of course..." Holmes returned to his pipe and relapsed into a brooding silence, puffing thoughtfully for some few minutes.

"Why did you tell me you thought I had been robbed at Glynde?" I asked. "How did you know the murder had occurred *after* Lewes?"

"Lewes is a rather important junction. I argued that a body in the carriage would have been discovered there. It was not. Therefore, the murder and robbery must have occurred afterwards."

"But if you knew this all along," I said with some bitterness, "why did you say nothing at the time? Why did you let me go on about the French student and the tailor and my grand theory of the missing shoes?"

"I had no proof, Watson. Only a series of deductions that led to the ticket inspector."

"And what were they?"

"Oh, well, you know my methods. Fit the theory to the facts, not the facts to the theory."

"What facts? I suppose it was the wound to the soldier's hand?"

"No, Watson. As I say, I did not grasp the significance of the crippled fingers until you read from my manuscript. It was the missing pages that gave me pause as to this ticket inspector."

"But you said there was nothing of importance in those pages!"

"There wasn't, Watson. It was his tale of how he had *found* them. He told you the manuscript had been blown about at Lewes, and several pages had been lost beneath the carriage, did he not?"

"Yes, but I don't see—"

"Yet you told me the steam was settling upon the platform when you exited at Polegate, just minutes after the Lewes stop. Inference, it was a windless day."

"Holmes!" I cried, "what a fool I have been!"

"This is not a time for self-reproach, Watson. We must keep our wits about us and think this through." Holmes turned his attention to his pipe, knocking out the ashes against the stone shelf and filling the bowl once more. "There was absolutely nothing of value in those pages—and yet they *are* missing. That is of significance, is it not?"

"What does it signify?"

But Sherlock Holmes said nothing. He sat back against the cold stones of the barrow wall and puffed in silent thought for some little time.

I have been subject to many friendly gibes over the years for the manner in which I accommodate the moods and habits of my friend Sherlock Holmes when he is working out the solution to a mystery. But to Holmes, my "grand gift of silence," as he once called it, allowed his brain to work out problems at hand without interruptions from a less-practiced reasoner, and once more I gave him that gift as we sat silently together in the barrow, each in our thoughts, the silence punctuated only by the faint chiming of a parish clock and the gentle puffing of Holmes upon his pipe.

Finally, he removed the pipe from his mouth, briefly considered the state of the bowl, and, with one of the archeological tools on hand, proceeded to scrape it out with some assiduousness, indicating that he had smoked his final bowl in the barrow.

"You have arrived at a solution, Holmes?"

He chuckled softly and shook his head. "No, Watson. An impasse. With each door that opens to my feeble brain, it seems another closes." He rose and stretched, placed his cleaned pipe upon the shelf and set about returning the tea service to the improvised kitchen, talking to himself as much as to me.

"We have the missing pages of a manuscript, the murder of a de-mobbed soldier in a train and the forged note which led you to that train, the connection of which requires a solution...."

He had put away the cups and was now standing, hand to his chin, dissatisfaction written upon his face.

"May I see the note once more, Doctor? Thank you."

"Why, Holmes, upon my arrival at your cottage, did you say you had expected me to come, only 'not so soon'? Why did you expect me to come at all?"

"Because of the note which I had attached to the manuscript—*my* note, not the forgery you received," he said, glancing up with a wry smile. "I had invited you to cast your eyes upon my manuscript and bring your wife and your thoughts on my memoir to the Sussex Downs at your leisure, that we might renew our acquaintance now that this dreadful war appeared to be coming to its end. I did not expect to see you forty-eight hours later!"

His eyes clouded as he studied the foolscap.

"I might have known to have expected you here after those telegraph lines went down..."

"Why should a dead telegraph wire result in a visit from me, Holmes?"

He glanced up with some little annoyance.

"Coming so soon after the death of Colonel Moran at Pentonville prison, I should think the reason is self-evident."

I started. "But the death of Moran was a coincidence, surely!"

"So you say, Watson. So you say. I say it is another thread in the great web that ties all these occurrences together."

He turned back to the foolscap and spoke to himself as much as to me.

"When my oldest living adversary is stabbed to death in the confessional by a substitute prison vicar, I know something is up as surely as a spider senses the faint vibration of a fly hitting a distant thread. And when those telegraph lines went out the very next day, I ought to have deduced that we would soon be reunited..."

"But why, Holmes?"

"Because that telegraph station hums night and day! What with the airfield at Polegate and the hospital tents all over the hills across the way, it's a rare thing for the lines to go down, Watson. A rare thing..."

His glanced up from the note and looked keenly into my eyes.

"Describe once more the paper clip that held this to the other documents."

"You have a solution, Holmes?"

"The paper clip! Describe it!"

But before I could answer there came the frantic barking of a dog in the distance. Holmes held up his hand, his ears cocked. "That is undoubtedly Toby the Second," he said with tension in his voice. "I wonder what the deuce has unstrung him?"

"Perhaps he hears a car?"

"A car...." Holmes's face assumed an intense concentration. "Watson— the car that deposited you outside my yew hedge today. Was it French-made or British?"

"It was a pre-war Wolseley Colonial," said I, proud to be able recall such detail. "I remember it distinctly—"

"A Frenchman driving a British-made car. Curious, is it not? Did you notice whether he had trouble with the gear stick being on the left hand?"

"None that I recall. He handled it rather expertly, in fact."

"I thought as much. Now, good Watson, pray tell me this. The ticket inspector—when he wrote the directions to East Dean upon my manuscript for you, did he do so with his right hand or his left?"

"He used his left, as I recall."

Sherlock Holmes took up his waterproof and the key to the barrow, then placed the torch in my hand. "Accept this as a gift from one of the greatest fools in England, Watson."

"Why do you say that, Holmes?"

The dog's barking had become more agitated, and Holmes's expression had become grim, the jaw set, the eyes narrow—the piercing grey eyes of old.

"You have not worked it out, Doctor?"

"No, I'm afraid I don't see, Holmes. You have deduced who is behind it?"

"Too slowly, Watson. Too slowly. How my powers have diminished! But, of course, I had been assured by Mycroft's agents that he remained trapped in Paris behind the German lines, and that was wrong. Very wrong."

"Who is it you speak of, Holmes?"

"In all the world, Watson, there can be only one man alive who could have pursued me like this, over all these years, with not merely the energy of youth, but the cunning of his bloodline."

"Who, Holmes?"

"You will meet him before the night is over, Watson. I have no doubt."

When the full moon rises above the English Channel, it shines oversized and bright, a great silver disk illuminating the grassy headlands of the Sussex Downs and everything put upon them by God and man. Emerging from the barrow, we saw the white tents of Summerdown shimmering ghostlike across the valley and the tower of the old Belle Tout lighthouse throwing a blue shadow to the edge of the cliffs that overlooked the unseen waters of the Channel.

Closer at hand and partway down the slope of Went Hill, the apple trees of Holmes's orchard cast strange, moving shadows in the moonlight, while farther down towards the Birling Gap road, the Colvin farmhouse was still brightly lighted.

And from its vicinity the dog was still barking.

"Toby the Second is sounding particularly agitated tonight," said Holmes as he struggled with the iron grate that secured the barrow. "Might I have the torch here, Watson? Thank you...this latch is not so—"

His words were interrupted by the loud crack of a pistol shot that rent the sky, followed almost instantly by the piercing cries of an injured beast.

"By God, he has shot the dog!" Holmes forced the latch shut and pocketed the key as the dog's yelps ceased. "Did you see the lights have gone out in the farmhouse, Watson?"

"I did, Holmes. What does it mean?"

"If I am not mistaken, Watson, it means the same fiend who killed the dog now threatens Miss Colvin and her uncle. If I have placed them in mortal danger, I should never forgive myself! Extinguish your torch, Doctor. The moonlight will suffice. We must move with haste, but pray, have a care. The footpath is wet with the fog!"

Our descent upon the chalky footpath proved far trickier than the ascent had been, for the crumbly limestone pathway was indeed quite slick. We had not gone ten paces when another gunshot sounded—but muffled, and without an accompanying flash of light.

"That came from inside the farmhouse, Holmes!"

"It did, Watson. We must hurry!" Holmes abandoned all caution and fairly flew down the path as quickly as his rheumatic knees allowed.

A third shot sounded, quite like the second. Then all went quiet.

"The brute! The brute!" Holmes cried as I struggled to keep up.

"Who is it?" I called after him.

"Work it out, man! The—" Holmes missed a step on the chalky gravel and his feet flew out from beneath him. He came down hard, with a violent twist of his ankle. "Help me up, Watson. We can't stop now."

I lifted Holmes to his feet, and with his arm across my shoulder we continued down Went Hill and past Holmes's orchard, slowly and with effort. It was some little time before we arrived in the courtyard of the darkened farmhouse, and when we did we were met by a sad sight.

It was the motionless body of the unfortunate dog.

"The entrance to the kitchen is there—I shall try it," Holmes whispered, letting go of me as we skirted the dead beast. "We must beware, however. He is armed, very likely with your own pistol. And he has three bullets remaining."

"He has *my* pistol? Surely you don't mean it is the Good Samaritan!"

Holmes chuckled grimly as he removed something from his pocket. A small derringer glinted silver in the moonlight.

"Yes, Watson. I mean the Good Samaritan."

"But who is he, then?"

Holmes ignored my question and gently tried the latch. "Locked. We must break it down. I have no leverage with my foot, Watson. Pray, put your shoulder into it, while I cover you."

"But who is this man, Holmes?"

"The *door*, Doctor!"

I slammed my shoulder into the thick wooden door, but it did not give.

"Again!" Holmes hissed.

I put my shoulder into it, harder, but again it held.

"Once more, Doctor! It will give if you bend to it!"

I gave my all, and this time the door flew open. I stumbled inside, carried by the force of my own charge. All was dark.

"Your torch, Doctor, hurry!" Sherlock Holmes maneuvered past me into the kitchen as I flashed the torch ahead of him, and it was then that he uttered a name that startled me.

"Moriarty!" he cried. "Where are you?!"

"Moriarty?" said I, stunned and blinking at Holmes. "You don't mean to say the professor has been alive all this time!"

"No, Watson. It is not the professor."

"Who then?"

"Why, it is his son."

Chapter Four

THE FINAL REVENGE

Sherlock Holmes and I inspected every room of that farmhouse, which was unusually spacious and well-appointed, but neither the man he sought, nor—as Holmes had feared, the bodies of Miss Colvin and her uncle—were to be found. Only a splintered armchair covered in feathers unleashed when its cushions were shredded by gunfire.

"Clever," said Holmes with a wry chuckle when we came upon the wrecked chair. "Very clever. He fired into the cushions, twice, to make me think he had shot the woman and her uncle. But it was a blind, Watson! And thank goodness for that."

"And yet the dog is most certainly dead, Holmes. Why would he shoot the dog?"

"To silence it. He was deathly afraid of dogs, and Toby could be rather aggressive in his own way."

"But why only *pretend* to shoot Miss Colvin and her uncle?"

"Because he wanted us here, of course."

"This is a trap, then?"

Holmes was silent for a moment, scratching his chin in deep thought. Then his eyes recovered their familiar sharpness.

"No, Watson. It is a diversion."

"From what, Holmes?"

"From my cottage, of course. Quick, Watson!"

Holmes dashed out the door with something of a limp but no longer requiring my support. The path, however, was as slick going uphill as it had been coming down, and our way was made the more difficult by a pronounced shift in the wind, which now brought only fleeting glimpses of moonlight through the racing clouds.

Several minutes passed before we reached the stile and entered Holmes's orchard. The eerie, windswept shadows of apple trees flashed in the intermittent moonlight, and Holmes now slowed his pace, eying each tree as if expecting an ambush. Then he took a position behind the candle hut so as to observe the rear of the cottage. Suddenly he squeezed my arm and pointed towards his vine-shrouded bedroom window at the far end, and I saw that the sash had been thrown up and a light was flashing within, giving the strong impression of a thief searching all corners of the room.

"He is after the Weems book, I'll wager," said Holmes in a low voice.

"The book from America? Why on earth...?"

But Holmes was absorbed in a study of the house. Finally, he nodded.

"I think we can surprise him, Watson, but you must carry out my instructions to the letter."

"Yes, of course, Holmes. What are they?"

Five minutes later found me alone at the front door of Holmes's cottage.

As the parish clock began to sound the tenth hour, I stamped my feet and rapped my stick upon the stones, in accordance with Holmes's instructions.

"You will approach the threshold as if you are just returning from a stiff walk and I am expecting you," he had said. "Be noisy about it! Light the torch, scrape your boots, drop your stick—do whatever you can do to let him know you are coming."

"But to what end, Holmes?" I had asked.

"To this end: when the parish clock sounds the last bell—and not a second before, mind you—throw open the latch and have your stick ready.

I will have entered by the kitchen and will take him when he is preoccupied with your arrival. Am I clear?"

Now, as the seventh, eighth and ninth bell tolled, I made ready.

On the tenth, I reached for the latch.

To my considerable surprise, however, the door swung abruptly inward and I found myself face-to-face with a bearded, well-dressed young man with a smile upon his face and my pistol in his hand.

It was the ticket inspector from the train, and I could see—now that he no longer wore the goggles and muffler that had shrouded his face in the Wolseley—my Good Samaritan.

They were indeed one and the same person.

"Do come in, Dr. Watson," said he, in a familiar voice that bespoke a French ancestry. "And have a care with that stick."

I stepped across the threshold with the unfamiliar sensation of being welcomed into Sherlock Holmes's cottage by a familiar stranger, if such a thing is possible.

Holmes was seated in his armchair by the fireplace, the lamp upon the mantelpiece illuminating a rueful smile upon his face.

"He surprised me, Watson. That light we saw in my bedroom window was a diversion. The lamp had been hung from the hook and given life by the open window to make us think he was prowling about my bedroom. I was ambushed at the kitchen door. It was very neatly done."

Our host latched the door behind me as Holmes continued.

"Dr. Watson, allow me to introduce Thomas Adam Moriarty, ticket inspector for the South Coast Railway, French lieutenant impersonator and interceptor of strangers upon the Jevington Road. And, most relevant to our ill-omened meeting here, the youngest and last living son of the late Professor James Moriarty."

Dressed in an expensive-looking suit, with the neat triangle of a handkerchief peeking just so from the breast pocket, and wearing rich leather shoes, my "Good Samaritan" possessed more the appearance of an artful dandy than the vengeful son of Sherlock Holmes's greatest enemy.

The soft, sensitive face and delicate mouth that regarded us with some amusement suggested a rather more libertine lifestyle than befits a criminal, and yet his hands were large, for his palm enclosed my pistol as if it were a toy gun, and the arms and shoulders bulged with the well-defined muscles of one who exercises with weights, which explained how he had so effortlessly pinned that poor soldier against the seat cushions in that carriage.

His eyes, no longer hidden by spectacles, cast a look of triumph as he waved me to the armchair opposite Holmes.

"From now on, Mr. Holmes, I will do the speaking, if you please," said Moriarty.

"There is a certain Gallic rhythm to his English, eh Watson? You now understand the thread that was woven through all those clues planted in the train—"

"As I *said*, Mr. Holmes, I will do the speaking."

"And there is, perhaps, just enough light to observe the high forehead and deeply lined temples of his famous—but far more intelligent—father? But I forget myself, Watson, you never met the professor. You only glimpsed his person during a brief encounter, as I recall."

Sherlock Holmes was, I knew, testing the young man's mettle, but his provocations were met only with a smile and a smug, satisfied voice.

"And yet there you sit, Mr. Holmes, under my command."

"Yes, here I sit. May I at least ask what you propose to do with us?"

The young man pointed the pistol at the settee. With a start I saw my valise resting upon the cushions, but when I rose to retrieve it, he waved me back with the pistol.

"You will stay seated until I command you to move."

I glanced at Holmes, who responded with a subtle nod. As I returned to my armchair, our host shifted slightly off his keel.

"Mr. Holmes is not in charge here!" said he sharply, and I noticed that as his voice rose, the pronunciation acquired a brutish, Slavic inflection. "Now, doctor, you may take the valise—no sudden moves—and return with it to your chair. Very good. Now open it. You will find everything in its place. Well, almost everything."

My eyes once again met Holmes's for the briefest moment, and from the faintest shrug of his shoulders it was evident his thoughts reflected my own: that our position was quite desperate and our host was a most unstable human being. It would be best to do as he demanded.

Opening my valise, I found my linens, syringe case, the bottle of carbolic and one of morphia, and the package with the Diogenes Club seal containing the Ordnance map, timetable and the remainder of Holmes's manuscript. Everything was in its place.

Everything, of course, except my revolver, which was now pointed at me.

"May I smoke, young Moriarty?" Holmes asked with the utmost politeness, nodding towards the ivory box upon the mantelpiece.

"*Doctor* Moriarty," said our host, nodding.

"*Doctor*," said Holmes. "Forgive me."

The young man covered Holmes carefully with the revolver as my friend rose and retrieved the case.

"Watson, would you care to smoke? No? I would offer one to our host—who is also a doctor, evidently—but of course he is partial to the pungent Gauloises of his adopted homeland." Holmes lit a cigarette, blew a perfect O and admired its shape until it broke against the ceiling beam. "Pray forgive me," said he, with a friendly smile at young Moriarty, who had been watching him carefully as he returned the case to the mantelpiece. "But you are a Doctor of...?"

"Psychoanalysis."

"Ah, yes. You studied with Herr Freud himself, I believe?"

"Two years. With Simmel for three. My studies were completed under Ferenczi in Budapest—"

"Dear me," muttered Holmes. "What on earth is so difficult to understand about human nature that three scholars are required to educate a person upon the matter for six years? I should think your mother's work in the streets of Paris would have taught you everything you needed to know about this cruel world?"

Moriarty sprang to his feet, his face a mask of rage.

"And what would you mean by *that*?" he screamed, the pistol shivering at my companion, who nevertheless maintained his most imperturbable façade.

"I meant no disrespect, my boy. I merely know the history—"

"I am *not* a boy, Mr. Holmes. You would do well to remember that."

I marveled at Holmes's composure in the presence of the quivering rage which he had provoked, a gun barrel aimed at his head. He sat back in his armchair, calmly ignoring the outburst, and set aside the cigarette. Then, with his fingertips pressed together, he proceeded to speak of the history of our unstable host in his familiar, precise fashion.

"See here, Watson, what the human urge to procreate has wrought! The father of our rather unexpected guest here at Went Hill was none other than Professor James Moriarty—mathematician, art connoisseur and astronomer of no little repute, and, of course, master criminal, or I may say *the* master criminal of his day, commanding an empire of evil that stretched from the docks of Liverpool to the Winter Palace at St. Petersburg, until, of course, he fell to his death at the Reichenbach Falls in May of '91."

The gun barrel was slightly lowered as curiosity replaced the rage upon young Moriarty's face, and he nodded and took his seat upon the settee when Holmes raised a questioning eyebrow that he might continue.

"Thank you," said Holmes, resuming his didactic manner. "The mother, if I may be so frank, was a Parisian *respectueuse*, a lady of the evening, as it were, for Professor Moriarty possessed a rather gigantic appetite in that line—" Here Holmes interrupted himself with another glance at young Moriarty. "Once again, Watson, I perceive agitation at my reference to the unfortunate woman, but no doubt you would assure our host that my trade lies in the observation of the natural world, without prejudice as to the circumstances which may have given rise to its composition. Rational deduction is impossible otherwise."

It seemed a wonder our host did not put an end to Holmes's disquisition then and there, but something in Holmes's masterful voice, and his seemingly encyclopedic knowledge of the elder Moriarty's life, intrigued the younger Moriarty as much as it did me.

"I may proceed, then?" Holmes asked politely. "Thank you. The professor, as I say, was possessed of a large appetite in matters of the flesh—and, of course, the means to satisfy it—but he was careful to limit such relations to French-speaking women with no family, in order to keep the secrets of his criminal enterprise, well, secret. This required, not infrequently, trips to Paris for the... let us call it 'the replenishment of the stock,' because the unfortunate young ladies in his service would invariably pick up enough of the English language over time to become a danger to the professor."

Holmes picked up his cigarette and smoked pensively for a time.

"Their disposal through a trap door over a tidal flat on the Thames makes for a rather dark tale, Watson, I am sorry to say. A certain depraved Lascar was responsible—you may recall him from that *Twisted Lip* episode—but enough of that ugly business, Watson, for I perceive renewed agitation in the barrel of that pistol.

"He named his third son Thomas Adam Moriarty—I correctly state your name for my friend, do I not?—after the doubting saint and the first man, whose bite of the apple brought sinfulness to the human race. This was done by your father in a most ironic vein, for the professor was an atheist of the highest order, and the intellectual motivation behind his criminal enterprise was, I believe, nothing less than the undermining of organized religion, beginning with Christianity—"

"Holmes!" I exclaimed. "Is this true?"

But he ignored me and continued without pause.

"The professor's turn in this regard had come early in life, upon witnessing the ill treatment of textile labourers at the family mill in Manchester by his church-going father. This struck the young man—not without reason—as hypocrisy of the highest order, and he renounced his legacy, whence he was shipped off to Leipzig University with no very great expectations. Being of a mathematical bent, however, the publication of his masterpiece upon the Binomial Theorem six years later resulted in a chair at Durham, in the north of England.

"It was there he became 'Professor Moriarty' and seized upon the idea of using his legitimate chair to subvert the benevolent interpretation of the Bible, beginning with the much-abused fragment of Saint Paul's letter to the Ephesians ('Servants, be obedient to your masters,' etc. etc.), from which his father had frequently quoted to justify his harsh treatment of his millworkers—and which I had often heard during my days in America to justify the slave trade, as it happens.

"In time, the professor's efforts would encompass the entire Bible—both Old and New Testaments, *and* the apocrypha—in something he referred to as the 'Anti-Bible,' which attempted to lay bare every inconsistency of logic, biology and science contained within the holy writ, starting with Genesis and progressing to the virgin birth, the empty tomb and Christ's rising from the dead.

"Undertaking such a task—and he meant to eventually take on *all* the world's great religions, mind you—required funds much greater than a professor's salary could provide, of course, and so a criminal enterprise was begun which became an end in itself, causing his exit from Durham. There was a shocking and destructive break-in at the Vatican archives in '78, never disclosed to the public, but I have always suspected who was behind it."

I was much astounded by these revelations, but the attentive look upon young Moriarty's face told me he already knew them—and was impressed that Holmes did, too. He smiled and nodded.

"I thought as much, Watson. Now, our Thomas Adam here was one of three boys. There were no female offspring I could trace, and the middle brother, as I recall, had been entirely disinherited when he took up the Methodist faith and became an itinerant preacher?"

"Yes, my network has not entirely lost its effectiveness.

"The eldest brother, born to a different mother, had been given a name—Judas Iscariot—I may say with confidence has never been given to a mortal man since. It was upon him that the expectations of the father naturally fell, and yet is it any wonder the boy proved utterly incapable of fulfilling the crushing weight of those expectations?"

Here Holmes spoke directly to young Moriarty.

"You are aware that the gun with which poor Judas blew out his brains had been conveniently placed upon his bedside table by Colonel Sebastian

Moran, your father's chief lieutenant? Yes, I expected as much. And *that* is why you killed Colonel Moran on Sunday of this week at Pentonville, disguised as a prison vicar."

"Holmes!" I cried, "it was *he*?"

Young Moriarty answered. "*Quite so*, Doctor—as your friend would say—quite so. And bravo, Mr. Holmes." My gun now lay upon the settee beside him. Like me, he seemed entirely entranced by the narrative being spun by his father's oldest adversary.

"Thank you. Your brother's premature demise left only you, still in your minority, as a threat to Colonel Moran when he managed to take control of the professor's criminal empire upon the professor's death after our struggle at the Reichenbach Falls.

"When you reached your majority, Colonel Moran sent you to Russia, allegedly to learn the family business in a sleepy backwater of the syndicate. Very likely Moran expected you would be swept away in the rubble of the coming revolution there, but I dare say he severely underestimated your abilities."

Young Moriarty gazed at Holmes with a look of studious concentration playing upon his features, but I could see he was flattered.

"You easily ingratiated yourself with the Tsarist aristocracy thanks to your father's old network of contacts in the art world as well as your command of the French language, which was spoken in the court of St. Petersburg. Quite contrary to the expectations of Colonel Moran, you turned the Russian outpost into a thriving enterprise by providing a means for the Russian aristos to discreetly pawn a Sterov portrait or Fabergé egg when their cash ran low.

"After Bloody Sunday in '05 your business positively boomed thanks to the even *more* lucrative trade of helping your customers smuggle their valuables out of Petersburg to bank vaults in Zurich and Geneva when revolution appeared inevitable.

"I understand you even helped Herr Fabergé escape to Lausanne?"

Young Moriarty smiled. "And was well paid for it, I can assure you."

"In priceless eggs, I don't doubt. My research indicates you earned something on the order of one million Swiss francs from the Russian trade during those years? Yes, well, it is best to be discreet in such matters. In any case, it was from those courtiers, I imagine, that you learned of the poor health of the Tsarevich[66] and the rot that had set into that regime—hence, your decision to leave Russia in 1910 and reclaim the Paris base of your father's operation from Colonel Moran, who remained behind bars at Pentonville and was content to let you operate across the Channel while he exerted control of things here in England.

"By the time the Tsar and Tsarina were strung up last summer, your syndicate in the Rue d'Eglise was powerful enough and rich enough to seek the reclamation of your father's old operation here in England—but for one problem: it remained under the strong arm of the wily Colonel Moran from his prison cell at Pentonville."

Holmes tossed his cigarette in the grate and eyed young Moriarty, who returned his look with a steely gaze that bespoke the white-hot fire that evidently kindled the young man's ambitions, belying his somewhat bookish exterior.

"To that point I am on solid ground," said Holmes. "But here I must make several inferences, because until this evening, I was under the mistaken impression that you had never left France." Holmes paused and gestured at the ivory box with a questioning glance. "May I?"

"But of course."

"Thank you." Holmes retrieved another cigarette and lit it.

Young Moriarty nodded with magnanimity. "It you please, go on."

"When Foch and Haig began the Hundred Days Offensive along the German front and an Allied victory seemed inevitable, you began to plot a return to England. How you managed to be admitted into Pentonville as a prison vicar will probably never be disclosed by His Majesty's government, but no doubt it involved a convincing outfit and the liberal dispensation of cash."

Young Moriarty shrugged his shoulders. "Who would search a vicar?" His face clouded. "I merely repaid Colonel Moran for what happened to my brother."

"Quite so. However, your plot against *me*—involving, as it did, drawing

---

66 *Alexei Nikolaevich (1904-1918), the only son of Tsar Nicholas II, was born with hemophilia.*

Dr. Watson to my cottage without suspecting any intrigue—proved far more intricate! Probably you placed a confederate in the Eastbourne post office who intercepted my manuscript, whence you replaced my original and quite harmless note to Dr. Watson with that cry for help, along with the map and timetable? I thought as much. Might I ask what that young soldier in the train had done to deserve *his* fate?"

"He was reading your manuscript, which he'd found on the floor of the doctor's compartment, and making a great fuss about it. 'Look! A Sherlock Holmes mystery!' he cried, waving it at me as I took his ticket. I told him he must return it but he shook his head. 'It's mine now.' I had no choice. He would have taken it to the pub to show his mates while your doctor here was summoning the police to find it."

"So you stabbed him and grabbed the pages. Your weapon of choice was...?"

With a sly smile, young Moriarty half-drew from his coat a silver-bladed letter opener with an ornate handle.

"A gift from Tsar Nicholas. It is always readily at hand."

Holmes chuckled. "A rather far cry from embroidery scissors, eh Watson? That leaves only the three missing pages to clarify."

"You can't 'work out' that little mystery on your own, Mr. Holmes? Please, you have come this far!"

Sherlock Holmes accepted the challenge, blowing a cloud of smoke to the ceiling as he pondered the notion for some little time.

"As Dr. Watson and I have discussed, it could not possibly have been the content of those pages that mattered to you. There was nothing of interest a half century on. What *was* it about those pages...?"

As he worked towards an answer, Holmes studied young Moriarty. Then he shut his eyes and he shook his head, again in self-reproach.

"Of course. *Blood!* The soldier had been reading the manuscript when you stabbed him—surely some of the pages would have been spattered with blood. You couldn't possibly return those pages to Dr. Watson, so you destroyed them."

"*Précisément*, Mr. Holmes."

"Well, there you have it, Watson—all that my diminished powers were not able to deduce. Each one of these disconnected intrusions into my quiet life here upon the Downs were, in truth, the result of the careful planning of a poor, broken boy—"

"*A poor, broken boy* who found it easy enough to lure your dull-witted friend here to complete my design," Moriarty broke in hotly. "You would do well to learn that a chain is only as strong as its weakest link, Mr. Holmes. As for your diminished powers, I can promise you they will be reduced to nothing, shortly."

A slight but tragic smile played upon Sherlock Holmes's lips. It was an acknowledgement, I thought, for the first time, of the impossible predicament we were in.

"And pray tell me, how do you intend to fulfill that promise?"

"Oh, *I* will not," said the young man with a thin smile. Then he spoke words that gave me the shock of my life. "Dr. Watson will."

"Never!" I cried.

"I thought as much," muttered Holmes.

Moriarty picked up the gun and swung it towards Holmes so suddenly that I expected to see a flash of gunfire from the barrel.

"Oh, you did, eh? Then let us employ that little trick of yours! *You* will tell *me* how Dr. Watson will accomplish this, and I will tell you where you have gone wrong!"

"By all means," said Sherlock Holmes, calmly tossing the cigarette stub in the grate and sitting forward in his armchair, his brow knitted.

"You wish to eliminate me," said he, resuming his didactic manner of speech. "*That* is your goal. It is also, I may say, a necessary condition for the continued existence upon this earth of your criminal syndicate. And, of course, by disposing of me, you will have not merely avenged your father's death, but you will have caused yourself to be placed ahead of even the most exalted of criminals—if there can be such a thing—by becoming forever known as 'The Man Who Killed Sherlock Holmes.' That, I suspect, without unnecessary self-glorification, has become your *raison d'être*."

"*Très bien, Monsieur Holmes!*" A strange giggle emanated from young Moriarty's lips as Holmes continued.

"You are quite aware, however, that you cannot accomplish this feat without also extinguishing the life of my closest friend, Dr. Watson, for the very simple reason that if my life ends in a manner that does not involve dying quietly in my sleep at a supernumerary age with Watson at my bedside, his own *raison d'être* would become the tracking down of the murderer of Sherlock Holmes."

"Very good. 'Spot on,' as you might say." Again, that awful giggle.

"And yet the occurrence of *both* our deaths in a compressed span of time—no matter how well fixed up—would be even riskier than mine alone. Mere suspicion of your involvement would become the absolute certainty of it. Brother Mycroft would bring the entire resources of the state crashing down upon you. You *and* your enterprise would be broken. A more subtle and devious means is required.

"You determine to lure the doctor—with his kit, mind you—to my cottage by a cleverly forged message which my unfortunate history with alkaloids will render utterly credible in the mind of the doctor, and there you will ensure, at the point of a gun if necessary, that *he* administers the fatal injection—"

"What are you saying, Holmes?" I cried. "That I would—"

"Do you not see it, Doctor? The note—in my handwriting—will be found in your pocket! To what other conclusion will the authorities reach than that I accidentally killed myself with a fatal dosage while the loyal Dr. Watson was rushing to my rescue at Went Hill...and upon discovering my body, took his own life in an agony of grief?"

"Bravo, Mr. Holmes."

"Never!" I cried.

"Tut, tut, Watson. It is really quite clever—almost unique in the annals of crime. My namesake in Chicago[67] was reputed to have carried out a similar scheme in '88, but not so cleverly conceived."

Something akin to respect, even awe, perhaps, showed itself in young Moriarty's eyes. It was as if he saw in Holmes's unparalleled reasoning an intellect to challenge his own late father's.

---

67 *H.H. Holmes, one of the first American serial killers.*

Holmes sensed this, I think, for he retrieved another cigarette, this time without asking permission, lighted it with deliberation and exhaled a contemplative cloud of smoke before returning to his armchair.

"Might I ask what you have done with Miss Colvin and her uncle?"

A look of smug satisfaction replaced the admiration upon young Moriarty's face, like the cat that has caught the canary.

"What makes you think I have *done* something with them, Monsieur Holmes?" said he, fixing his eyes upon my friend's with an assuredness that I had only seen before on one man.

And that man was Sherlock Holmes, at the height of his powers.

As Holmes returned the gaze, his grey pupils narrowed beneath his furrowed brows until a stricken look crossed his features and the cigarette dropped from his fingers to the floor.

"I see," said he in a soft voice. "Yes, I see it all now."

"What do you see, Holmes?"

"I see now what my declining powers did not permit me to see, Watson."

"Yes? *Pray tell us,* Monsieur Holmes!" Moriarty leaned towards my friend with an extravagant smile.

"That Miss Colvin has been in the employment of young Moriarty here all along."

Moriarty sat back and frowned in mock chagrin.

"I am disappointed Mr. Holmes. You do not exactly 'see it all,' I'm afraid."

Holmes started. "But if she is not *employed* by you, then..." Another train of thought seemed to reveal itself to Sherlock Holmes, and his eyes widened in genuine surprise. "Why, then she must be..."

"Go on, yes."

Holmes slumped back in his armchair, fists clenched in self-reproach. "Dear, Watson, what have I done? All Mycroft's warnings about Miss Colvin, ignored. And now this."

Young Moriarty grinned extravagantly at my friend's evident distress.

"What is it, Holmes?"

"You haven't worked it out, Watson?"

"Why, no, Holmes, I cannot—"

"She is his *sister*, of course."

"Sister? You can't mean it, Holmes!"

"But I can and I do, Watson. As I said, I was never able to trace any female offspring of the professor—and yet I thought it highly improbable that none existed. It must be so."

"Is this true?" I asked Moriarty.

By way of answer, he raised a delicate hand to his lip and with finger and thumb carefully gripped one tip of his moustache and began slowly to peel away the thick moustache and beard from the raw skin, leaving behind traces of gum Arabic on his face while a growing astonishment showed itself upon that of Sherlock Holmes. When the false hair was entirely removed from cheek and chin, the visage that remained bore a striking resemblance to that of Miss Colvin.

"*En fait*," the giggling voice exclaimed triumphantly, "she is my twin!"

Holmes looked as stricken as I had ever seen him.

It took him some few moments to recover his voice.

"I thought I had anticipated every possible maneuver by my enemies in the years since my retirement, Watson, but that one eluded me." He shook his head slowly. "I congratulate you—" Holmes was about to say 'my boy,' I believe, but he refrained "—I congratulate you, Doctor."

Young Moriarty acknowledged the respectful tone in Holmes's voice with a nod.

"Your planning was, I may say, meticulous, your implementation nearly flawless and your improvisations quite inspired. I dare say your father would be proud."

"Holmes!" I exclaimed. "This fellow needs no congratulations. He intends to do us both in!"

"Tut, tut, Watson. To the logician, all endeavors must be evaluated upon their merits, and this one has been very cleverly done. Besides, I said it was *nearly* flawless," said Holmes, recovering somewhat a measure of his self-assuredness. "There are several points at which the entire operation was threatened by a failure to anticipate all eventualities, reflecting a certain defect of the mind. Four points, to be precise—"

Holmes's speech was interrupted by a burst of laughter from our host.

"Very good, Mr. Holmes! Very good indeed. But the delaying tactics have gone on long enough." He turned the gun on me. "Doctor, would you please open your valise and extract your syringe?"

"I beg your pardon?" said I.

"Your syringe. Extract it."

"Never."

"I think it is for the best, Watson." Holmes gave an encouraging nod.

Still I hesitated, and now Holmes spoke more forcefully.

"Please, Doctor, do as he says."

With no little trembling in my hands, therefore, I retrieved the morocco case, opened the cover and exposed my old-fashioned three-piece syringe.

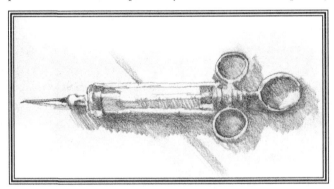

It was a monstrous contraption compared with the sleek modern versions, admittedly, but the large dimensions fitted more comfortably in my arthritic hands, and so accustomed was I to the cylinder's proportions that I could have administered any dosage with my eyes closed.

I removed the three separate pieces—the glass cylinder that held the solution, the needle that screwed into the base of the tube and the plunger that fitted to the top—and these I placed before me.

"Now," said he, waving the gun, "you will assemble those pieces and fill it with five hundred milligrams of morphia."

"*Five hundred?*" I shook my head in defiance. "That I cannot do. I *will* not."

"But you must, Watson."

"I won't, Holmes. No doctor would intentionally harm a patient, and I will certainly not harm you."

Young Moriarty pointed the gun at my head.

"It will be one way or the other, Doctor."

"I'm afraid he is right, Watson. And the needle will certainly be the least painful way."

"That may be, Holmes. But if this fellow thinks he will get away with this...surely the men of the Yard will see a connection with the murder in the train! There will be something—stray fingerprints, the dead dog! *Something* will lead them to the ticket inspector and the death of that soldier!"

Holmes shook his head. "There will be no stray fingerprints on the gun but yours, Watson, and none on the syringe but mine. And I have no doubt the dog's corpse will disappear from the yard as completely as young Moriarty's fingerprints will disappear from the lamp still hanging in my bedroom. As cleverly as he staged that compartment in the train, Watson, the scene here will be set. Then our host will vanish without a trace."

"Once more, bravo, Mr. Holmes," said young Moriarty in a flat, deadly voice. "You have just solved your last case."

He stood up and pointed the pistol directly at my face. "The syringe, Doctor."

With extreme reluctance, I began to assemble the components.

But do not believe, dear reader, that I intended to carry out this most appalling command! When I had assembled the pieces, I placed the syringe upon my lap, crossed my arms and stared with the utmost resolution into the villainous eyes of young Moriarty, refusing each of his increasingly obstreperous commands until I found the cold metallic point of a pistol—my own pistol, from my own valise!—pressed into the center of my forehead.

"*Fill it, Doctor.*"

And yet, even with that gun to my head and that hot, giggling voice in my ear, I would not comply. I shook my head and resigned myself to die.

It was then that the voice of Sherlock Holmes, quiet but firm, broke the stillness.

"I beg of you to cooperate, Watson. There is no other way."

"There *is* another way, Holmes—to make this coward pull the trigger himself."

"You heard that poor dog die, Watson. All your doctorly instincts must know that a needle will prove a far less painful death to me than a bullet."

I gazed into Holmes's eyes and saw he was being quite sincere. Indeed, there was a helplessness which I had never seen in my friend's face that considerably startled me. I nodded reluctantly and began to slowly extract the brown bottle of sulfate of morphia from its velvet pouch while my mind raced with desperate schemes.

The simplest and most direct, of course, would be to attack Moriarty with the syringe. When I glanced at Holmes in what I thought was a casual and innocent manner, however, he seemed to have read my train of reasoning as swiftly as that thought traced itself across my brow, and he evinced his disapproval by the most discreet lifting of an eyebrow and the faintest shaking of his head.

And it was well that he did so, for, in my heart, I knew that under no circumstances could I have overpowered young Moriarty.

I removed the glass stopper, therefore, and it was then, as the not-un-pleasant odour reminiscent of extract of vanilla filled the air, I felt a sudden glimmer of hope, for the sweet, familiar scent of the morphia told me that the contents had not been tampered with.

To my medical mind, this gave Sherlock Holmes some chance of survival.

It was a very slim chance, to be sure, but if the purity of the morphia remained intact—and it evidently had not been mixed with any other substance by our host as I had feared—Holmes might survive an injection if I could somehow limit the dosage that reached his bloodstream.

With this in mind, I began slowly to fill the glass cylinder under the watchful eye of young Moriarty, who hovered over me in a most nerve-wracking manner, giggling as he squinted at the rising column of brown liquid against the striated glass.

An excited *"C'est ça!"* sprang from his lips when it had attained the dosage he had demanded, which was more than ten times that which I knew would send my friend into a respiratory failure from which he would not recover. I set down the half-emptied bottle and held up the lethal syringe for young Moriarty's inspection. He nodded with satisfaction and in return handed me a bootlace, which I was to tie around my friend's arm. While attempting to obey this dreadful command, however, my hands trembled with such apprehension that I could not even loop the bootlace around the bare arm, let alone tighten it.

Once more, Sherlock Holmes appealed to me with the soft voice of reason.

"You must know, Doctor, that a plump vein will make the thing easier."

"For you, Holmes, perhaps, but not for me."

Nevertheless, I took several deep breaths to steady myself and then set about the task. It took some little time to accomplish—time which allowed me to consider the situation, and as I fumbled with the bootlace, a new notion came suddenly to my mind.

Far subtler than my first, this scheme held an equally uncertain outcome and offered no little risk to Sherlock Holmes—but anything that might increase the odds of survival in the favour of my friend was well worth the candle.

I finished tying the knot with renewed confidence, therefore, and positioned Holmes's elbow upon the lamp table with a practiced eye. Picking up my syringe, I spoke to young Moriarty in a sharp, commanding voice—much as any doctor would speak to a nurse in attendance.

"I will need a fresh towel, of course."

"And for what do you need a fresh towel?"

"To shield the syringe from the patient. The temptation to glimpse the needle as I seek a vein often results in discomfort."

Moriarty let out a harsh laugh. "Your *patient* was in the habit of injecting himself three times a day for months on end! He needs nothing to shield him from the sight of a needle."

"I have performed this task in precisely the same manner my entire career," I answered coldly and with no little irritation, as Holmes studied my stern face. "It is my way."

Moriarty turned his suspicious gaze from me to Holmes—who nodded as if he had heard me say this many times in our years together—and yet still Moriarty hesitated.

Finally, I snapped.

"If you would compel me to put my friend to death in this appalling manner, you cannot begrudge me the opportunity to be competent in the task so that I may see him dispatched without undue discomfort." Then I shrugged my shoulders. "But it is all the same to me. If the authorities find a botched injection, then I have no doubt they will see through your scheme."

I had him.

He pulled his handkerchief from his breast pocket and fairly tossed it at me.

"This will do."

I took it somewhat hesitantly. "Is it clean?"

"Clean enough." He pointed the gun at Holmes's head. "Proceed at once, or we will do this the *unclean* way."

With some little reluctance I wrapped the handkerchief carefully around the syringe and put forth the evident effort to make certain the needle within was screwed tightly into the cylinder. Then, when I had finished, I nodded at the lamp upon the mantel and spoke once more with all the rude authority I could muster. "Now, place that lamp by his arm."

Moriarty frowned. "Why?"

"So that I may see the vein clearly, of course. The light from the fireplace has faded."

He muttered something in French but placed the lamp as I had asked. In its wavering light, the cephalic vein showed as a clear blue line running down Holmes's ghostly white forearm.

"The hour approaches, Doctor," said our malevolent host, placing the revolver against the back of Holmes's neck and nodding at the sharp, silver needle sticking out from the handkerchief. "It will be that way, or *this*."

As he cocked the revolver, the grim voice of Sherlock Holmes cut through the gloom pervading that desolate cottage.

"I know all your instincts cry out against this, Watson, but—*if it were done when 'tis done, then 'twere well it be done quickly."*

I took a deep breath and ran my finger along the bare stretch of Holmes's illuminated arm to find the most advantageous entry point for the shrouded syringe in my hands.

Our eyes met, briefly, and Holmes gave a sad smile.

"Pray, proceed, old friend. And know that you were ever my Horatio, the best of men upon this earth."

"No, Holmes, it was you—" My throat choked with unfeigned emotion. "You who gave me a life worth living—"

"Oh, end these wretched vanities, if you please!" cried Moriarty. "Doctor, when the clock strikes eleven, you will press that trigger in your hands or I will pull *this* trigger. The choice is yours."

Holmes smiled wanly, his face a mask of exhaustion and relief.

"You had better do as he says, Watson. And know that I forgive you."

Fighting back against a paralyzing fear that had suddenly welled up within me, I hovered the shrouded needle over the bare arm, begged forgiveness from my maker, and, with a single swift movement, plunged the needle home.

Holmes's limbs began to tremble uncontrollably even before the entire dosage had been fully discharged, and when the cylinder was emptied—but before I could withdraw the needle—his entire body convulsed, causing him to jerk his arm clean away, taking the lamp crashing with him onto the stone-flagged floor and plunging the room into darkness.

"Holmes!" I cried, as the enormity of my actions seized me and I, too, collapsed, the syringe smashing beneath me upon the floor.

"Holmes!"

Chapter Five

INSTINCT AND DEATH

"It's no use, Watson." The familiar voice of Sherlock Holmes broke the silence all around me. "He knows."

I opened my eyes and saw Holmes seated once more in his armchair, nursing his bare, swollen arm, and the figure of young Moriarty placing upon the mantel the lamp he had evidently just retrieved from the bedroom.

"It is, as he says, no use, Doctor Watson. Your little trick did not fool me. You may give me my handkerchief and take your seat."

I sat up slowly, my head reeling from the syrupy odour of the morphia soaked into my shirt, and sheepishly handed Moriarty his handkerchief, which was now damp with morphia and stained brown.

"Thank you, Doctor. No, leave what's left of your your syringe there on the floor, just as it is—with the needle so cleverly loosened, yes. Now take your seat. Good."

The hair upon Holmes's head was disarranged and there was a rather dazed look upon his face.

"Holmes! How do you feel?"

"A touch woozy, Watson, thank you, and the beginnings of a pulsing headache, which heralds worse to come."

"It is no matter, Doctor. He will not be alive long enough to feel the effects." Moriarty spoke with commanding firmness, brandishing the gun practically under my nose. "Your little *tour de force* failed to impress me. As for you—" he nodded at Holmes "—proud actor that you once were, you could not deceive me."

"I'm sorry my performance was not up to snuff, Watson. Yours, however, was superlative," said Holmes in a rather disjointed fashion. "To unscrew the needle under cover of the handkerchief...the morphia leaking out as you jammed the plunger—it was admirably done! And smashing the evidence beneath you as you fell to the floor—a touch, Watson! A very clever touch!"

"And yet," said young Moriarty dismissively, folding his wet handkerchief with disdain, "all in vain, Mr. Holmes. All in vain."

And for once, I feared, young Moriarty was right.

The dosage that had reached Holmes's veins—though greatly diminished thanks to the quantity that had leaked from the loosened needle into the handkerchief—already seemed to be taking its toll upon him, judging by the swelling of his arm and a sudden lethargy that reminded me all too much of my early years with Holmes when he was in between cases and seeking stimulation in other, more dangerous forms.

For my own poor efforts I had acquired cuts on my arm from shards of glass, abrasions in my side from the twisted metal of the handle, a shirt redolent of extract of vanilla and the depressing recognition that we were back to where we had started not ten minutes before—except, of course, that Sherlock Holmes now possessed a potentially dangerous measure of morphia working its way through his system.

The only relief I could feel was that I had steered the loosened needle into the anterior muscle of Holmes's arm rather than directly into his cephalic vein, which would further diminish the impact of whatever amount of morphia had made its way into his system.

"If I may ask," said Holmes, "what caused you to perceive my friend's plan?"

"His eyes, Mr. Holmes. 'Men lie with their mouths and speak the truth with their eyes.' My father wrote that in his last letter to me."

"Bravo, my boy. Bravo."

"Your attempts to provoke me with that epithet failed some time ago,

Mr. Holmes. I am not a boy, and I'll wager you learned that tonight."

"No, sir, you are not. It is a figure of speech we English have, that is all. A figure of speech."

"Well, in my French we also have a figure of speech, '*C'est tout finis.*' *Comprenez-vouz?*"

"*Oui, monsieur.* Very well."

"*Bon.*" Moriarty stepped back, taking in the room and our positions in the chairs as scudding clouds brought intermittent bursts of moonlight through the window, enhancing the flickering light of the lamp.

"And what will be your final improvisation?" asked Sherlock Holmes politely.

"Oh, that is simple enough," said Moriarty with the utmost coolness. "I will shoot you in the head. Then I will shoot your friend."

I started from my chair.

"You can't possibly expect to get away with it!" I said hotly.

Moriarty shrugged his shoulders. "I will be very far away when your bodies are discovered."

"I dare say he will, Watson." Holmes's voice was subdued, and his manner had turned to one of utter exhaustion. "Might we have one last cigarette while you prepare the scene? Condemned men and all that."

Moriarty smiled with the confidence of a card player who has seen his opponent's hand.

"A cigarette would be most appropriate."

"Thank you. Would you retrieve it for me?" Holmes nodded towards the mantelpiece. "I suddenly feel too tired to stand."

"No, I shall stay right where I am, with this gun pointed at your head."

Holmes smiled wryly. "You anticipate my every move. Your father would be proud."

"Such flattery does not move me. Do not dawdle."

Holmes rose from his chair with some little effort. "Watson, would you care for a cigarette?"

"No, thank you, Holmes. How do you feel now?"

"The headache is quite debilitating, and I anticipate worse to come."

Holmes retrieved the ivory box and held it open for me. "Take one, Watson, you deserve something for that effort. But for the rather over-dramatic collapse on my part, I dare say we might have gotten away with it. Come, come, Watson. I insist."

I took a cigarette and Holmes did likewise. Then he held out the lighted match, and as our eyes met, I could see that he was not yet done.

"I am watching!" Moriarty shouted as moonlight briefly illuminated the room. He was standing at the desk now, his back to the bow window. The clouds once more shrouded the scene briefly, then the light reappeared.

Holmes smiled and held up the box. "I may return this to its place?"

Moriarty cocked the pistol and nodded.

"Thank you." Holmes returned the ivory box to the mantel, then picked up the water pitcher and turned to Moriarty. "I suddenly crave water. May I?"

"No tricks, Mr. Holmes."

"No tricks but one!"

And as the moonlight once more disappeared behind the fast-racing clouds, Sherlock Holmes swept the lamp, the clock and everything else upon the mantel crashing to the floor with one hand, while with the water pitcher he doused the fireplace embers in a sudden hiss that sent the room into a most complete darkness.

"Dive, Wats—!"

Holmes's cry was cut short by a thunderous explosion. The bullet crashed into the chimney with incredible effect, and a sulphurous cloud of spent gunpowder smoke billowed through the room.

I found myself upon my knees, crawling toward the fireplace, waving my hand at the space where I had last seen Sherlock Holmes, but my fingers touched only the warm metal of the fire grate and the leather cover of Holmes's violin case. My heart went cold, and as the ringing in my ears subsided, I heard that awful, excited giggle coming from young Moriarty.

"Is he dead? Have I killed him?"

"Holmes!" I cried, sweeping my hand feverishly about the floor. "Holmes!"

But my cries were answered only by that strange giggle and shouts of, "*Is he dead?*"

"Holmes!" I shouted. "Holmes!"

"Is he dead?"

I feared the worst. "Holmes!" I cried again, but the choking smoke was settling all around me and I found it difficult to catch my breath.

It seemed only a matter of time now before Moriarty came for me.

But then a new sound came to my ears—a small, sharp cough from the vicinity of the bedroom door.

"Holmes! Is that you? Holmes!"

The cough erupted into a fit.

Moriarty uttered an oath. "He lives! But not for long..."

I could see Moriarty's figure outlined against the window, pistol extended, moving cautiously towards the bedroom door on the far side of the room.

"Be careful, Holmes! He comes for you!"

Sherlock Holmes did not reply, but the sound of coughing had moved inside the bedroom.

"Holmes! Hide yourself and I will take him!" I was on my feet and about to rush young Moriarty when a strong, bony hand suddenly grabbed my arm and pulled me down to the floor.

"Not a sound, Watson," whispered a familiar voice into my ringing ear.

"Holmes!" I hissed. "Can it be you? But how—?"

He pressed a finger to my lips.

"The ability to throw one's voice possesses a far more practical aspect than ever I had dreamed, Watson. Take these—" I felt a pair of soft, waxy lumps pressed into my hand. "Plugs of beeswax, such as I wear for my tinnitus. Place them in your ears when I leave you. That pistol has two bullets remaining, and he means to use them. These will preserve your ears—and you will require your hearing to survive."

"You have your derringer, I expect?" I spoke as softly as I could manage.

"No, Watson. He took it when he surprised me at the kitchen door."

"Then he has two guns and we have nothing."

"Ah, but we have our wits, Watson, and that has always proved a better match!"

And with a squeeze of my hand, Sherlock Holmes was gone, silently and with those cat-like instincts which had served him in so many difficult situations over so many years.

I placed the wax lumps into my ears and pressed them home. Silence came upon me, and when the moon was once again shrouded by clouds, the darkness seemed complete. With only the faint shadows of my surroundings visible, I was left guessing as to where my friend had vanished and what he had up his sleeve.

Fortunately, young Moriarty seemed no wiser than I.

He had been knocking about in Holmes's bedroom all this time, and when he reemerged, he banged into the old chemical table, sending one of the instruments crashing to the floor. He shuffled cautiously back to his post at the desk and I could see his silhouette once more framed by the bow window, the gun in his outstretched hands, twisting this way and that.

"I can see every threshold of this room, Holmes!" His disturbed voice came softly through my earplugs. "Kitchen, front door and bedroom—if your shadow crosses one of them, I will see it! You cannot leave this room. Escape is impossible!"

"We shall see!" Holmes's familiar, high-pitched cry rang out—from the kitchen door!

Moriarty whirled in that direction—my direction!—just as Holmes's laughter sounded again, but now from the *front* door!

Moriarty emitted an oath and darted forward, but an even greater surprise awaited him, for as he reached that threshold, the bow window he had left behind was thrown open with a sudden, sharp thrust.

"What the devil?" Moriarty screamed, whirling about as a draft of cool, fresh air entered the room.

Now the shape of a hunched figure rose above the desk and hurtled out through the opening, crashing onto the patio outside, and Sherlock Holmes's voice rang out once more, from among the beehives!

"*The father could not stop me at the Reichenbach Falls—and so it is with his son at Went Hill!*"

Moriarty let out such a cry of frustration as to be inhuman. He raced to the open window, leaned out and let fly a pistol shot—loud and violent even to my muffled ears—that shattered something in the yard.

"Did I hit him?" he screamed, standing in the recess of the window, shrouded by swirling gun smoke, his head swinging this way and that. "I hit *something*. What moves there—is that Holmes among the trees?" His eyes fixed upon an object in the orchard. "Yes! I see you now! There, you may run, but cannot outrun a bullet—!"

And with that, he cocked the pistol one final time, took deliberate aim and fired.

As the echoes of the deafening explosion died away, the yellow smoke swirled about his shoulders, making him appear for all the world a devilish fiend seeking dominion over the earth, and it was with a vile, jubilant voice he bellowed out the window the words that turned my heart to stone.

"*Sherlock Holmes is dead!*"

I had but one thought now—to take the brute myself by force.

I may not have been his equal in physical strength, but so filled was I by a sudden wellspring of anger at seeing this demon gloating at the window that I was willing to wager that if I could take him by surprise, it would compensate for my physical deficiency.

I removed the earplugs to ready my senses—the distant chiming of the parish clock sounded incredibly loud to my fresh ears—and I felt confident in my chances. He was clearly deafened by the explosions and fixed solely upon the fate of Sherlock Holmes.

But even before I could rise to my feet, I once again felt my arm seized by that strong hand and heard in my ear that familiar voice!

"Stay down, Watson," the voice hissed. "It is life or death."

"But Holmes! I saw you leap from that window! How—"

"I leapt out of no window, Watson. That was my typewriter heaved through the—but hush!" He clapped his hand over my mouth. "To the floor, Doctor," he whispered intently, pushing me down with an unexpected brusqueness. "And not one word. Your very life depends upon it. Hark!"

I could hear nothing, but Holmes evidently knew some danger was coming, for he had placed himself atop me and was pressing me tightly against the floor.

"Forgive my shielding you in this fashion," he said in a barely audible voice, "but the scent of morphia upon your shirt is enough to bring them our way."

"Bring who, Holmes?"

"The bees, Watson. Do you not hear them?"

I did not, for my ears had only been partially protected by the beeswax plugs, and were still ringing.

"No? Well, my mind may be dulled by the effects of the morphia, but my hearing remains excellent, and if I am not mistaken those are the scouts."

"Scouts? What scouts, Holmes?"

"From the hives, Watson. They seek the source of the explosion that destroyed their nests. Listen!"

Straining my ears, I could discern a low murmur from the window, punctuated now by grunts and cries from young Moriarty.

He was no longer giggling.

"Ah! What is that sticking me? Ah! What the devil? Is that a needle?"

"The scouts have found the source," Holmes whispered gravely. "With each sting they emit a scent that alerts the rest of the hive. We must remain *absolutely still*."

Just then I felt a sharp pinch on my jowl. I gave a jerk, but with my arms pinned by Holmes I could not brush it away.

"You were stung Watson? Press your face to the floor and expose no skin—that is most essential. Above all, remain motionless, *no matter what*."

The cries and yelps from Moriarty swiftly grew in volume and frequency. Evidently he had come under the delusion that an invisible Sherlock Holmes was jabbing him with a syringe.

"Needles, Holmes? You stick me with needles?! And again! Holmes, you stick me?! How do you manage it?"

All my professional instincts urged me to rush to the man's aid, but Holmes's keen grip and the pressure of his wiry frame kept me pinioned against the cold floor.

"You must resist the impulse, Watson," he hissed, his lips pressed to my ears. "Any movement on your part could prove fatal—to you and to me."

An ominous moan now swelled inside the room.

"The colonies swarm, Watson—" Holmes paused his commentary as the shouts and screams from Moriarty began to come without pause.

"How do you manage it, Holmes? How do you stick me?! Stop it! *Stop! Please! STOP!*"

There was a welcome lull, but it was brief. Too brief for young Moriarty.

"Holmes! The needles! How do you do this? Where do they come from, these needles? Needles! More needles! *Oh, God! MY GOD!*"

Poor Moriarty was *in extremis* now, incoherently so. His cries and screams came faster as the room darkened and the sound of the swarm intensified, and his pleadings took on a frantic, desperate nature, mixing French and English in an almost incomprehensible blubbering that I will do my best to indicate.

"I see it now Holmes! You have unleashed your bees on me! *Des abeilles! Ils son partout!* In my mouth! My nose! My eyes! *Mon Dieu! MON DIEU.*"

There came a heavy thud upon the floor.

"The poor devil has fallen," whispered Holmes. "He must shield himself—"

Holmes ceased talking as the din attained an intensity that seemed unbearable. It was as if a motorcar had entered the room, its engine racing and its gears grinding into a higher and angrier pitch, punctured again and again by the high-pitched screams and the crash of flailing limbs against table and chair of a desperate man who cannot escape his fate.

"The worker bees have arrived, Watson. They will attempt to finish off the threat to their queen. No, Doctor! You must stay your conscience!" I struggled to break free from Holmes's grip, but it was impossible.

"Watson! Do...not...move."

Young Moriarty's cries now reached a fevered pitch as all around us the air pulsed with the synchronous movements of thousands of tiny wings.

"Oh God! Why can't I die? Why don't I die? *Mon Dieu! S'il vous plait!* Make this stop! Oh *mon Dieu*—my tongue! My ears! They crawl in my ears!

Oh God! Oh Mother! Maman! *S'il vous plait*!! Oh, MOTHER! *MAMAN! MON DIEU HELP ME.*"

And then he screamed no more.

Yet even when the last bee had discharged its stinger into young Moriarty and the thrashing convulsions of his body had ceased, still I felt Holmes's ironclad grip holding me down.

"Not yet, Watson," he hissed. "Not yet."

It was only when the air had become absolutely still and the buzzing had ceased entirely and all was silent to my ears but for the soft mewling of young Moriarty on the stone floor that my friend's keen hearing told him it was safe to move.

But when it did, he moved with an urgency such as I have never witnessed.

"Grab your kit, Watson!" he cried, leaping to his feet and pulling me with him. "I will get the torch. Hurry! We must save him!"

The sight in that cottage was one I shall never forget.

Tables and chairs were upended, books flung about, the weather station equipment smashed, and everywhere, on every inch of that floor the dead bees were strewn so thickly they felt like an uneven carpet beneath my feet.

The victim of these poor creatures' instinct for death, Thomas Adam Moriarty, was lying in much the center of the room, between the desk and the settee, curled up in a ball with his arms covering his head, his knees tucked into his chest, and all his fine clothing so clotted with dead bees that it appeared as if he had been rolling in Holmes's cocklebur garden. Yet as we turned him over, it was evident how ineffectual had been his effort to shield himself.

His face was puffed and swollen, like a boxer after a bloody and bruising match. The lips were inflamed, the mouth swollen shut and neck and throat so bloated that it was difficult to distinguish where the neck ended and the chins began. And every inch of skin was so grotesquely blackened by the tiny stingers matting his face that it gave the appearance of a thick, quivering beard.

His arms and legs twitched, I now perceived, and so swollen were the hands and fingers that Holmes could not remove the gun—my gun—from his grip.

I loosened the collar and felt beneath the ear as Sherlock Holmes abandoned his attempt to extract the pistol and watched anxiously by torchlight.

"Is he gone, Watson? Is there no spark left?"

"He has a pulse, Holmes, but it is very weak. His blood pressure is dangerously low. It is fortunate he wore such expensive clothing. It likely shielded him from a good deal worse." I lifted a puffy eyelid, and the eyeball stared back vacantly with only the briefest flicker. "There is life here, Holmes, but...have you your old syringe?"

"Alas, no."

"Then I cannot administer morphine."

"He must be saved, Watson." I had never heard Sherlock Holmes speak with greater urgency. "He *must!*"

"We'll fashion a poultice—Holmes, what are you doing?"

Sherlock Holmes had produced the pocketknife with which he habitually cleaned his pipe bowl, whence he had begun scraping the stingers from the young man's face.

"This man needs a poultice, Holmes, not to have his face cleaned!"

"The stingers release venom even after the bees have died, Watson. They are best removed by scraping. You might fashion a poultice from the leaves in the teapot."

"That is hardly enough for this man, Holmes! Those we'll save for your arm." I had observed in the torchlight a harsh red wound flaring on Sherlock Holmes's forearm where the needle had entered the anterior muscle.

"This is not the time to think about *me*, Watson. We must save *him*," said Holmes, who scraped away the stingers with feverish energy.

I recalled the compost bed by the kitchen door. "A cold mud bath should do the trick, Holmes. You boasted of the excellent minerals in your compost. I think it will be just what he needs."

"Then prepare the bath while I scrape! Quickly, Watson! He is the last of his line, and there is so much I have yet to learn from this boy!"

The "boy"—and young Moriarty did indeed look very much like a boy when he had been stripped of his fine clothing, laid out in the kitchen tub and coated with the finest mud that Went Hill had to offer—would live.

Still, it was a near thing.

Upon comparing notes with Sherlock Holmes later, not even ten minutes had elapsed from the time the first gunshot exploded among the hives to the moment the attack had ended, but in all our adventures together, I could not recall witnessing such a close brush with death. Fortunately, the cold mud bath worked as I had hoped in drawing the bee poison from the body, but it was Holmes's quick thinking to scrape away the venomous stingers from the exposed flesh that had saved young Moriarty when his life hung in the balance.

Within the hour, his face no longer possessed the appearance of a grotesquely bearded circus performer, his breathing was regular and his pulse had regained its strength. It only remained to bring his temperature up and get him to hospital.

I had sent Holmes to gather all the blankets he could find while I heated water on the stove, but he had been rummaging about his rooms for so long that I had begun to wonder what was keeping him, when a strange knocking could be heard upon the cottage door.

It was a series of sharp, distinct taps, as if a woodpecker were hunting for insects.

Coming so closely upon the heels of the evening's strange adventures as it did, the sound had caused my every instinct to be on alert when Sherlock Holmes stuck his head in the kitchen, blankets piled high in his arms, his eyes fairly gleaming with delight.

"I dare say Brother Mycroft has arrived!" he cried. "That is his telegraphic signal from the old days. May I leave you?"

"Yes, but I should like those blankets now, Holmes." I turned back to young Moriarty. "The boy is stable, but I will need to get his temperature up—"

I glanced up and realized Holmes was gone, blankets and all.

I was about to call after him when I heard the latch being thrown open, followed by voices in conversation. There was Sherlock Holmes's voice when he was in high spirits and the low rumble that could only be Mycroft Holmes. After some little discussion, and to my great surprise, these were joined by a high, thin, woman's voice that sent my spirits soaring.

"Margaret!" I cried, and soon my wife had entered the kitchen ahead of a surprisingly thin Mycroft Holmes and his ebullient brother, still holding the blankets. I had to resist the impulse to clasp her in my arms, for my own clothing was damp with mud and clotted with dead bees.

"Thank God, John, you're safe," said she, looking me up and down with relief in her eyes but concern in her voice.

"And you, my dear! How on earth did you make such a journey in your condition?"

"Mr. Holmes hired a special," she said, nodding at Mycroft. "It was quite comfortable, and I have found the country air quite soothing to my lungs." She studied my hands, mottled with red marks. "But you, John! You were stung!"

"Only a handful of times. Nothing like poor Moriarty here."

"I was so worried about you, John—"

"Yes, there will be time for that, madam," interrupted Mycroft Holmes, ever the gruff man of state. "But how is the boy, Doctor? My brother tells me he will survive?"

"Yes, but we must raise his temperature, and he should be removed without delay to hospital."

"That is easily done. An ambulance will soon be on its way from Eastbourne."

"Indeed?" said I, taking the blankets from Sherlock Holmes, who seemed to have forgotten he was still holding them. "That was quick."

Mycroft chuckled. "Lestrade and I expected no little excitement where Sherlock was involved."

"Lestrade is here, then?"

"I sent him to the farmhouse with his men to round up that Miss Colvin and her so-called uncle."

Sherlock Holmes shook his head.

"I fear he won't find them at the farmhouse, Mycroft! I rather think he will have greater success at the Belle Tout lighthouse. Better send a locksmith, as well."

Mycroft turned to his brother in some puzzlement.

"Why on earth would they be at the old lighthouse?"

Sherlock Holmes laughed—a bit too long a time for my medical instincts not to be on alert—and told, in an abbreviated and somewhat jumbled fashion, of the shooting of the dog and our search of the empty farmhouse. "I have reason to believe young Moriarty abducted Miss Colvin and her uncle to the lighthouse," he concluded breathlessly, "and has left them chained to the foghorn. They will be deaf, dumb and blind if they are not rescued—"

"But surely it is a tearoom now?" said Mycroft, with confusion written upon his face. "Has been ever since the Beachy Head lighthouse went in."

Sherlock Holmes started, then blinked several times and offered an apologetic smile.

"Please do forgive me, Mycroft. A momentary lapse of reason." He looked his brother up and down as if seeing him for the first time. "Why, you are skin and bones, my dear brother. I hope it is your diet that has brought you to this state and not a condition more in the doctor's line of work?"

"I have been practicing some of your own asceticism, Sherlock. I abstain from alcohol and beef and take no tobacco but snuff. In any case, we ought to—"

"Indeed? I should think life not worth living without your favourite indulgences!"

"Ordinarily I would agree, Sherlock, but when one receives a personal appeal from His Majesty[68] to alter one's lifestyle in order to maintain one's services to the Crown, one does not take half measures. As he phrased it, the choice was to maintain my unsound diet or my relevance to the Crown, and I chose relevance. But we must attend this boy—"

"And you chose wisely, Mycroft," said his brother with sudden emotion, and so unsteadily that Margaret took his hand and led him to a chair at the kitchen table.

---

68 *King George V.*

The pot was at the boil and Margaret offered to fix tea, but Sherlock refused, pointing to young Moriarty in the tub.

"He needs it more than I, madam."

"Yes he does," grumbled Mycroft impatiently. "Please see to it, Doctor!"

"There is hot water enough for both," Margaret said with a kindly pat on Sherlock Holmes's hand. "And I should think some soup would do you no harm, either."

It was well after midnight and we were seated around the kitchen table with Lestrade, who had returned to Went Hill in the ambulance which had come to take away young Moriarty to hospital, sharing a welcome meal of the onion soup and croissants left by Miss Colvin.

In a corner of the kitchen sat the mud-streaked tub, empty but for the remnants of dead bees.

Sherlock Holmes ate hungrily, a poultice on his arm and a wet towel wrapped around his forehead, listening intently as Lestrade gave us the remarkable account of Miss Colvin, whom his agents had found *not* chained to a foghorn at the Belle Tout lighthouse with the man who had been posed as her uncle, but unharmed, although in a hysterical state, at the Eastbourne Police Station.

She had driven there after a brutish encounter with young Moriarty at the farmhouse, evidently while Holmes and I were snug in the barrow. She was eating dinner with the old man when Moriarty burst in, waving my gun and shouting orders until he realized she did not know who he was because he was no longer in his French lieutenant uniform and she did not recognize him as the "Good Samaritan" who had fled the brief encounter with her Jack Russell outside the yew hedge.

Changing tack, Moriarty proceeded to calmly explain to Miss Colvin that he was both her twin brother and the anonymous relation who had supported her after the death of her adopted parents (and later sent her to England to care for the mute figure she supposed was her uncle). Then he handed the stunned woman the keys to the Wolseley and ordered her to drive the old man into Eastbourne and discard him at the train station before returning to the farmhouse with the car to await his instructions—presumably providing his getaway after he had sprung his trap upon Holmes and myself in the cottage.

When she refused, Moriarty shot the poor Jack Russell to demonstrate what would be done to the 'uncle' if she disobeyed his command, and so she rushed the confused old man into the Wolseley while two more shots rang out from within the house. But instead of depositing the poor fellow at the Eastbourne station, she had driven to police headquarters, where she began telling the bemused officers the bizarre story of the deranged fanatic at the farmhouse who claimed to be her twin brother.

It was at that point that Lestrade arrived, and he was able to piece together her story with what Sherlock Holmes had briefly informed him when he had deposited Mycroft and Margaret at Holmes's cottage door.

Sherlock Holmes nodded vigorously when Lestrade had finished. "I told you, Mycroft. I knew she couldn't have been involved!"

"She was placed here to *spy* on you, Sherlock."

"But she never knew that, and Lestrade proves it! When she found out what her brother was up to she went straight to the police!"

"What of her so-called uncle?" I asked. "What was his role?"

"An excuse to place Miss Colvin in that farmhouse down the hill, I expect," said Lestrade. "She thought she was attending the old man for the same benefactor who sent her to a finishing school in Lausanne after the death of her parents."

"But how is that possible?" said Margaret. "Surely she would have conversed with the poor old man!"

"He is a mute," said Lestrade. "Our men could not get a word out of him."

"And very likely he possesses no living relatives," said Mycroft. "It was quite cleverly done."

Sherlock Holmes was now staring at his brother in sudden confusion.

"What on earth brought you here tonight, Mycroft?"

His brother smiled and produced from his coat the early edition of the *Evening Standard* with the flaming headline, "*Murder in the Southern Train! Elementary, My Dear Watson!*"

"Apparently we still count for something, Watson!" cried Sherlock Holmes with rather an excess of hilarity.

"And thank God for that, Sherlock. One glance at this headline and I ordered up a special for Eastbourne. Next thing I knew, Lestrade appeared at the door of the Diogenes Club with two of his best men. He had seen the same headline."

"You each suspected some sort of intrigue?" I asked.

"They *knew* there was intrigue! Think, Watson! A murder is committed in the very carriage in which John H. Watson, M.D. is riding to the Sussex Downs of Sherlock Holmes! What are the odds the circumstances are unrelated? They don't exist!"

"Precisely so, Sherlock," said Mycroft. "We were about to leave the club when a commotion in the lobby announced the arrival of Mrs. Watson. So we all departed together, at once."

"But not before I had been denied entry by one of your more misogynistic members," said Margaret, replacing the towel upon Sherlock Holmes's forehead with a fresh, damp cloth.

"Not our finest hour, madam. Still, the confusion was quickly cleared up."

"And what caused *you* to venture out of doors to the Diogenes Club, madam?" asked Sherlock Holmes with feverish intensity.

"Oh, I had been fretting ever since John left. Something in the note gnawed at me. And then—"

"And then she saw the same headline that brought Lestrade." Mycroft Holmes chuckled. "We tried to stop her, Doctor, but she insisted upon making the journey. In the end, we got you here safely, did we not, madam?"

"You did, indeed, sir. I thank you."

"And I thank *you*, madam." Sherlock Holmes let his spoon drop into the empty bowl with a clatter, and I noticed his shirt was mottled with spilled soup. He grasped my wife's hand with an expression of affection such that I had never seen from this supremely cold logician. "I owe you my life."

"But I sent John into a trap that almost killed you, Mr. Holmes!"

"Tut, tut," he replied, with sudden cheer. "That young fellow was intent upon doing me in, and if your husband had not answered the call to my aid, he would have found some other means—but not by Miss Colvin, eh Mycroft?! I always said she was true!"

"Yes, yes, Sherlock." Mycroft raised an eyebrow and glanced at his brother. "And I always said there was something too clever by half in her appearance at your door with those queen bees, did I not?"

Sherlock Holmes fairly bristled at this.

"How was I to know?" he snapped in an uncharacteristic display of peevishness. "She worked with Mr. Sturgess for two years before ever appearing on my doorstep! Came with the recommendation of Sturgess himself! And might I add, Mycroft, your men could never find a *hint* of scandal with her!"

"Steady on, Sherlock, I meant no censure. The brother played a very long game," said Mycroft calmly. "Very long and patient. He knew it was only a matter of time before you met."

"But how did you come to suspect her in the first place, if I may ask?" Margaret asked, as Sherlock Holmes continued to sputter his indignation.

"I dare say I had my eyes on her from the day she appeared at Went Hill, madam," Mycroft said. "She seemed too well tailored to my brother's requirements. But, as he indicated, all my inquiries reached a dead end. I could never confirm my worst instincts."

"They are far better instincts than mine, Mycroft," said Sherlock Holmes, once again subdued. "I should have trusted your judgment above my own."

"Tut, tut, Sherlock. Younger brothers always think they know better!" Mycroft glanced at his brother's arm with alarm. "That doesn't look well. Doctor, would you cast your eye once more upon that wound?"

Sherlock Holmes's entire forearm was now swollen the size of a squash, and the bandage holding the poultice was stained a sickly yellow. Margaret put the kettle on while I helped Holmes to the sink and began to unwind the cloth.

"Never mind about me, Watson," said Sherlock Holmes in a jittery voice, his facial expressions interrupted by a persistent blinking of the eyes. "When do you expect young Moriarty will be well enough that I may interview him?"

"A week at the earliest, I should think—stay still, Holmes, please—his injuries were terrible."

Mycroft looked on gravely. "And when do you and Mrs. Watson plan to return to London, Doctor?"

"Oh, that can wait," said I.

"But I'll want to review your witness statement in Polegate tomorrow, Doctor," said Lestrade. Then, glancing at his watch, he amended himself. "Or should I say *today*, for it will soon enough be morning."

"We must tell the Bard!" cried Sherlock Holmes with frantic merriment. "The *morn, in russet mantle clad, walks o'er the dew of something rotten in the state of Denmark*!"

Mycroft Holmes looked from Lestrade to me with an expression of the gravest concern.

"I think the Doctor's statement may stand as it is, don't you, Lestrade? And as for yours and Mrs. Watson's essentials, Doctor, I'll have them sent on from London at once. I rather think my brother requires your best attention, for now. The excitements of the evening appear to have caught up with him."

"On the contrary, Mycroft, I leave anon for a tête-à-tête with young Moriarty! The walk will do us all wonders!" There was an edge of hysteria in Holmes's voice that quite alarmed me, and Lestrade and I moved to restrain him. "He is the end of his line, you see! Now, at last, we can fill in the gaps in my knowledge of the professor and his gang!"

"Not tonight, Sherlock," said Mycroft firmly, helping us hold his brother still while Margaret daubed the infected wound with boiled water. "And certainly not without the approbation of Scotland Yard. Meantime, you will remain in the doctor's care until you are quite recovered. Then we can see about a visit with young Moriarty—under the auspices of Mr. Lestrade, of course."

"Excellent, Mycroft, excellent. We shall make an end of the Moriarty enterprise once and for all—if he will talk to me. He *must* talk to me!"

"Yes, well..." grumbled Mycroft, as we guided his brother from the kitchen to his armchair by the fire, past the mounds of bees that had been swept up by Margaret. "But first, is somebody going to dispose of these dead bees? I find them positively revolting."

Sherlock Holmes sat down heavily and gazed at the fuzzy grey heaps.

"A show of sympathy for my valiant friends would not be inappropriate, Mycroft. They did, after all, give up their lives for me..."

And with that, Sherlock Holmes's eyes rolled upwards until the grey iris disappeared, and he was gone.

Three days would pass before Sherlock Holmes had fully recovered from the ill effects of the morphia and the other strains of that evening. I estimated that the dosage which had made its way into his arm had been somewhat less than half that necessary to induce heart failure, and the drug had been rendered even less potent by having been injected into the muscle.

Miss Colvin returned to the cottage the day after that strange encounter with her brother—she didn't know what else to do, she told Margaret—and soon she was cleaning out the dead bees and fixing Holmes's meals in addition to caring for the old man at the farmhouse.

Sherlock Holmes accepted her return to his cottage with a tenderness not often expressed by my friend, and was soon back to his usual self, following with keen interest the press reports of the inquest into the death of the poor soldier in the train.

The victim was identified as Lance Corporal John Richard Baldwin of Eastbourne, and the coroner swiftly reached the appropriate conclusion from the testimony of the medical examiner who had conducted the autopsy.

It had been death by stabbing.

I am forever grateful that Lestrade had the good sense to withhold my witness statement from the inquest (and from the murder trial of young Moriarty months later at the March assizes[69]), for it meant that my grandly

---

69 French for "sittings," the assizes were circuit courts that heard criminal cases at certain times of the year. They were replaced by the permanent Crown Court of England and Wales in 1972.

misguided deductions about the victim being a French soldier done in by a shoe-stealing tailor were known only to Lestrade, the dour Inspector Cummings and the Polegate constabulary—and to Sherlock Holmes, of course, who quite enjoyed teasing me about them.

It is also fortunate that inquests are for the sole purpose of determining the cause of death, for no mention was made of the remarkable manuscript of Sherlock Holmes that had been at the heart of the day's terrible events, nor of the excitement at Went Hill that same evening.

In fact, thanks to Mycroft Holmes's arrangements with the local press, only a single account of the bizarre encounter at Holmes's cottage ever reached the public.

It ran in an early morning edition of the *Eastbourne Gazette* under the headline, "The Curious Incident of the Bees in the Night-Time," and it contained a much-embellished account of a vicious attack by a swarm of bees upon an unidentified guest in the cottage known to have been the residence of Mr. Sherlock Holmes before his sudden departure from the vicinity.

The edition was recalled shortly after reaching the news-venders, however, and the offending account was later traced by agents of Mycroft Holmes to the village greengrocer, who had glimpsed the bee-strewn bathtub in the kitchen when he resumed making his rounds to Holmes's cottage a morning or two after the affair (it being no longer necessary to promote the fiction that Sherlock Holmes had left the area now that Colonel Moran was dead and young Moriarty was behind bars).

Unfortunately the voluble man gleaned enough of our encounter with young Moriarty from Miss Colvin—who was still in something of a state of shock from the surprises of that fateful evening—to imagine the rest.

It will no doubt disappoint readers of that edition to learn that the unidentified guest of Mr. Holmes suffered two hundred and forty-eight bee stings, not ten-times that number, as was the claim in the paper. And although there was no denying the report that the young man's life had been saved by the frantic efforts of Sherlock Holmes to scrape away the poison-filled stingers from the man's skin, and, happily, my own modest improvisation of the mud bath as a poultice, one other correction to that story demands my attention here, and it concerns the preposterous notion that five wheelbarrow loads were required to take away the volume of dead bees swept up by Margaret.

Miss Colvin had accomplished the task with only two trips of her Ford tractor.

After the inquest was concluded, Mycroft returned to London and Margaret and I moved into a room at the farmhouse, for Holmes was eager that I be close at hand to assist him in his preparations for the interrogation of young Moriarty, which was to occur under a cloak of secrecy by the authorization of Mycroft Holmes.

"I must learn his father's secrets, Watson," Holmes said earnestly, directing me to the garret above his bedroom to retrieve some of his old notebooks from amid a vast trove of books, newspapers and periodicals.

And he would do just that.

Chapter Six

THE SINGULAR CASE OF
THOMAS ADAM MORIARTY

It was a bleak forenoon upon the last day of October, and the rain of a late autumnal gale lashed the bow window of Holmes's cottage as I sat alone by the fireplace in a distracted frame of mind, awaiting the return of Sherlock Holmes and Brother Mycroft from their third and final visit to the hospital bedside of young Moriarty, the first two attempts to interview him having ended in failure.

I alternated between reading accounts in the *Times* of the influenza sweeping the trenches of the opposing armies, now bogged down in a stalemate, and staring absently out the bow window at Holmes's beehives. They had been repaired and packed for the winter, and once more stood white and sturdy beneath the swaying branches of the bare apple trees.

It was with a start that I noticed the movement of the branches gave rather the impression of a figure dashing through the orchard—and that it was no doubt this effect which had convinced young Moriarty he was seeing Sherlock Holmes fleeing the cottage before he unleashed his final shot into the hives!

So thoroughly had my thoughts become enmeshed in the memory of that peculiar evening that it was Margaret who heard the commotion at the door, and she bustled in from the kitchen to greet the jovial figure of

Sherlock Holmes, followed closely by Mycroft and a gust of rain that swept inside the warm cottage before the door could be shut.

"Thank you, Mrs. Watson!" my friend exclaimed, removing his waterproof as his brother set out the streaming umbrella to dry. "Our pure Sussex air suits you most admirably, madam. Most admirably!"

"This miserable rain does not suit *me*, Sherlock," grumbled Mycroft Holmes as he removed his coat. "Give me the dry reading room of the Diogenes Club any day."

"Ah, but not *this* day, Mycroft!" cried his brother, taking down the black clay pipe from the rack upon the mantelpiece.

"You have had success, then?" said I.

"Success at what, Watson?" The glint in Sherlock Holmes's eye was answer enough, but I let him play his game as they settled in before the blazing fire, Holmes with his pipe, Brother Mycroft with his despatch box upon the settee between our armchairs.

Margaret disappeared briefly and returned with tea and refreshment, and soon Mycroft Holmes was tucking into a croissant while his brother charged his pipe in the meticulous fashion which I knew always preceded a lecture.

"Young Moriarty finally spoke, then?" I prodded, lighting a cigar in anticipation of a long and satisfying answer from my friend.

"Yes, Watson, he spoke. Most admirably, he spoke." Holmes lit his pipe with some little relish, letting go a blue cloud and chuckling softly while removing his notebook from his inner pocket with the satisfaction of a magician pulling the rabbit out of his jacket.

"It's all in here."

"Yes, and quite a haul, too," said Mycroft. "The dam certainly broke today."

"He was a scalded cat," said Sherlock Holmes. "Alone in the world, save his sister—who thinks him mad and refuses to have anything to do with him—he expected I would want to destroy his father's reputation for all time. But today I found the key to that latched door…"

"And what was that key?" asked Margaret.

"It was your husband, madam. The good Dr. Watson."

"Me?"

"Yes, *you* Watson." Holmes opened his notebook and glanced at the pages. "It had become evident after our previous sessions that I must alter my approach entirely before Mycroft put an end to these clandestine affairs. As we were riding to Eastbourne this morning, I thought back to the unexpected death of your brother. It left you, I recalled, without any close relations, and you began courting an estranged aunt in order that she might fill in the gaps in your family history."

"Why, yes, but how did that help you?"

"I reasoned I might be able to draw out the boy if he viewed me not as his father's *enemy*, but as his last link, much like your estranged aunt. The yin to his father's yang, as it were."

"And about time, too," the thin, drawn figure of Mycroft Holmes grumbled as he took a sip of tea to wash down the last of the croissant. "I was quite wondering when you would change tack, Sherlock." Mycroft now gathered a great pinch of snuff from his tortoiseshell box. "The pressures from on high were becoming unbearable. If word had gotten out that we were circumventing Scotland Yard by letting you interview that boy—" He interrupted himself with an emphatic sneeze into his handkerchief.

"But all's well that ends well, eh Mycroft?" Sherlock Holmes sent another triumphant circle of blue smoke to the ceiling. "And this ended exceedingly well, if I may say so."

"Too well," said Mycroft Holmes, glancing at his watch. "I missed the evening express, and I fear I must impose upon Mrs. Watson again."

"That is no imposition," said she. "There is always a spare room in the farmhouse, and the table here can be set for four."

"Madam anticipates all our wants!" cried Sherlock Holmes. "You should have moved to the country long ago, Doctor—Mrs. Watson grows more robust every day!"

"And I grow more impatient every minute," said I. "Did you learn nothing from young Moriarty today?"

"Quite the contrary, Watson. Today I learned *everything*."

And with, that, he sat back in his armchair and began to relate the remarkable story of Thomas Adam Moriarty.

"Amid the detritus shaken loose by the vast human struggle known as the Great War, one well-fed young man moved with a will and determination not shared by his haggard, dust-cloaked counterparts, for he had a dream to fulfill. It was a dream he confided in no one—the risks were too high and the consequences of failure too great—and a dream of such unbridled ambition as to appear almost incredible to anyone but him.

"He dreamed of the reunification of an empire. Not a political empire, mind you, but the criminal kind. That of his late father, Professor James Moriarty, who, you will recall, had tumbled to his death when I finally got the better of him as we came to grips on that narrow ledge above the Reichenbach Falls on a clear spring day in May of 1891.

"It was an empire that had been in the hands of Colonel Sebastian Moran, the professor's trusted chief of staff, ever since Moran watched from a hiding place above the falls as the professor perished while I scrambled up the cliff face to a narrow ledge to consider my options.

"I learned today that even as I lay on that ledge and decided I would fake my own death for purposes of drawing the professor's subordinates out of their cover, Colonel Moran had glimpsed the means to take the professor's place at the head of his syndicate by pretending the professor had *lived*.

"I know now that Moran was *not* attempting to kill me when he set those rocks loose upon me on that ledge, as I naturally presumed, Watson. He was *chasing me away*."

"Which would explain why such an expert hunter did not track you down as you fled across the mountains!"

"Excellent, Watson! You scintillate tonight. Moran had *no* intention of tracking me over the mountains to Florence—he needed me gone so that he could set the scene at the Falls before you returned with the official police."

Sherlock Holmes spoke with crisp authority as he replayed the scene in his mind.

"After I hastily departed that ledge and made for the pass at Grosse Scheidegg, bound for Florence, Moran began searching the base of the Falls for the professor's body. He found it in a quiet pool and recovered it with the help of a local farmer—no doubt passing himself off as an English sightseer whose companion had accidently fallen into the chasm—for which the poor farmer would pay the supreme price.

"They brought the body via oxcart to the farmer's barn, whence the farmer sent his son for the police. While the son was gone, Moran bashed the poor farmer to death with his stick—a most heavily weighted specimen— then called the unsuspecting wife and daughter to the barn, where he repeated his savagery.

"The barn is a most combustible shelter, of course, and all the ingredients were at hand for a bonfire that would consume the bodies—including the professor's—and cover up *both* Moran's crime and the professor's death. But there was a problem...."

Sherlock Holmes shot a questioning glance at the three of us.

It was Mycroft Holmes who answered it.

"Why, the professor's skull would have been crushed by the fall on the rocks, of course, and his dental plate smashed. Even the most simple-minded *gendarme* could not fail to notice it in the ashes."

"Quite so, Mycroft. Moran therefore set about smashing the dental plates of *all* the bodies before striking his match. By the time the farm lad had returned with the *gendarmes* Moran was seated in the train to Zurich, and when I reached Florence days later, he was back in England as the professor's *locum tenens*."

"But how did he convince his confederates the professor was still alive?"

"By employing the same forger whose handiwork would bring you to my cottage some years later, Watson. The fellow concocted a handwritten memo 'From the Professor' along the lines of, 'I miraculously fell into the deepest pool beneath the falls; I am bruised and battered, but not dead; and I will be for some time in Montreux at the clinic of Dr. Henri-Auguste Widmer.'

"That detail, incidentally, was the most compelling of the entire deception, as Dr. Widmer had treated the professor from time to time during bouts of melancholy and other worse symptoms of the physical illness caused by his...let us say, *indiscretions* with the fair sex. Widmer's office manager was well paid to redirect the mail back to Moran in London, and no one was the wiser.

"Colonel Moran now held all the strings. He sent young Moriarty off to Paris with the boy's French mother and was free to purge the ranks, which he did with speed and decision, leaving him in control of every aspect of the professor's criminal empire—corrupt bankers in the City, smugglers here and on the Continent, arms dealers and worse."

"And where was the boy's sister all this time?" asked Margaret.

"Geneva. On her birth the professor had secreted her to a childless Swiss couple, one of his art dealers. Told the mother the baby had died. He had no interest in raising a girl, so she grew up 'Miss Colvin' and never knew her true paternity. Nor did she realize she had a twin brother."

"Dear me! May I ask what turned the boy against Colonel Moran?"

Holmes smiled and studied the bowl of his pipe. "Once again, your husband."

"My John!"

"Yes, madam: *your* John. You recall he published that *Adventure of the Empty House*, describing my return from three years of playing dead? Well, young Moriarty read it in *The Strand* along with the rest of your husband's loyal readers, and so learned the true story of the professor's death years earlier. Until that moment, the boy had been quite happy in Paris. He had been schooled privately, enjoyed the freedoms of a foreign city, learned to speak fluent French and became very attached to his mother, especially when the poor woman came under the disfiguring influence of a terrible disease, which took away first her beauty and then her sanity."

"The syphilis?" I broke in.

"Precisely, Watson. And when I made the mistake of uttering that diagnosis aloud in the presence of young Moriarty this afternoon, he abruptly pronounced our conversation over. It took some little coaxing before I was able to convince him to renew the dialogue, which will account for the hourlong gap in the transcript."

"Transcript?"

"It's in here," said Mycroft Holmes, tapping his red despatch box. "Bound for Whitehall. We pledged the results will not be used in the trial. There is much that must remain secret, of course."

"In any case, the boy, who was now of age, vowed revenge upon Moran. He requested a post in the family enterprise, as it were, and was sent to St. Petersburg. Quite to Moran's surprise, of course, he turned Russia into one of the more profitable arms of the syndicate before returning to Paris to take control of the professor's entire continental operations from Moran, which he soon accomplished.

"To Mycroft's agents he appeared to be a libertine in Paris, always seated at the same table in Les Deux Magots, drinking bottles of absinthe and sending the waiters out for cigarettes and women—but it was all a ruse designed to deceive Mycroft's informers (and anyone else intent on breaking up the syndicate) into thinking that he had no involvement in his father's old business. The absinthe was green apple juice, the waiters were messengers in his pay, the women his agents. It was quite a successful deception, I might add."

"Yes, quite, Sherlock." Mycroft Holmes shook his head ruefully and took another pinch of snuff as his brother continued.

"From that table he ran the continental syndicate and hatched his plan to reunite it with his father's old British operation, which remained in the clutches of Colonel Moran, who had continued to operate it by way of coded messages in his laundry at Pentonville Prison.

"It was during that period, I have learned, that young Moriarty sought to make amends with his father's mistresses—or at least those who had survived. He spared no expense in his ministrations to them, and I may say—at the risk of causing Brother Mycroft to arch his eyebrows—the tender mercies shown by young Moriarty to such poor creatures engendered no little empathy between the two of us."

Mycroft Holmes sneezed, wiped his nose and emitted a peevish grunt. "You veer from the matters of state to matters of the flesh with alarming speed, Sherlock. Please dispense with the softer passions so I may get back to my papers before I am compelled to turn in."

"But when did he learn he had a twin sister?" Margaret asked.

"In his twenties, when he was helping the Russians aristos smuggle their wealth out of the country. He crossed paths one day with the Swiss art dealer who had raised the girl for Professor Moriarty. The poor fellow recognized young Moriarty as his daughter's twin and was quite undone. Not long after...well, let's just say there was a tragic accident and he and his wife were never heard from again. The young woman—now Miss Honoria Colvin—was sent off to finishing school, where she learned the various arts her brother expected might appeal to me, beekeeping among them."

"Dear me! What a devilish mind!"

"Yes, madam. As Mycroft says, young Moriarty played a *very* long game. When his sister had been sufficiently groomed towards his ends, he placed her at the farmhouse with the elderly mute under the pretense of getting one of her adopted relations from France out of harm's way. He judged it was only a matter of time before she caught the eye of Mr. Sturgess at the East Dean apiary and began learning my habits during visits to my cottage.

"That she would be taken in by me when my Scottish housekeeper returned to Skye was an entirely unexpected boon to his scheme on my part, I'm sorry to say. In any case, as long as the war kept him bottled up in Paris, young Moriarty would have to wait his chance. Plans were devised and recast as circumstances changed, until finally the time was ripe.

"One day in September he collapsed at his table and was removed from the café by ambulance—to Dr. Widmer's clinic, the word went out in the street, for treatment of his cravings for absinthe. Hours later, however, on a dark and moonless night, he set out from Dieppe in a small fishing boat for the harbour at Eastbourne, where he was rowed ashore by his French valet—the man who drove you to Victoria Station, Watson—and taken to a flat practically next door to the Eastbourne station.

"From there he found employment with the South Coast Railway— easy enough to do with false papers to present the railway company and all our young men fighting in France! Then he placed his confederate in the Eastbourne post office to monitor my mail in search of the appropriate device to trick friend Watson here into flying from London in a South Coast carriage.

"That same fellow, by the way, masqueraded as the doctor who attended Miss Colvin's 'uncle' at the farmhouse. In this way he could learn my habits while in casual conversation with the unsuspecting Miss Colvin." Sherlock Holmes's grey eyes dimmed at the recollection of that singular failure in a carefully lived life. "She had not an inkling the 'doctor' was passing on the information to a man who meant to use that knowledge for my destruction."

He sighed and stared morosely into the fire.

"Still, it was an error of judgment my younger self would never have made."

Mycroft patted his brother on the knee. "My brother is hard enough on himself, and sometimes deservedly so. But this is not one of those times. The boy planned it with meticulous care. Our agents never suspected a thing."

"But what was his *end*game?" I asked. "After killing Colonel Moran and drawing me here and—well, that business with the morphia and my pistol—what did he plan to do next?"

"If that poor soldier in the train had not disarranged his plans you mean?" said Sherlock Holmes. "He would leave his sister and the *non-compos mentis* uncle behind and return to France on that inconspicuous fishing boat with the Weems book in his pocket."

"The Weems book, from Lincoln!" I exclaimed. "He *knew* about it?"

"Oh, yes. His father had made several attempts to find it over the years. Moran too. That is why I had no doubt he was searching for it in my rooms that evening, Watson."

"But why would he not simply stay in England and reclaim his legacy? Why go back to France with the book?"

"To establish his alibi, of course. The bodies—*our* bodies, Watson, yours and mine—would be discovered by the unsuspecting Miss Colvin next morning and reported to the police. Even before the newspapers were running the shocking story of the grotesque murder-suicide of Mr. Sherlock Holmes and his trusted companion and biographer, young Moriarty would be back at his table drinking Evian water at *Les Deux Magots* and making himself quite visible to Mycroft's agents, his stay at the sanitorium evidently a success.

"He then would have waited—weeks or months, however long it took—for the Armistice, whence he could enter England through the front door, as it were, on the Channel ferry with the other refugees returning from Paris. By then, presumably, the dust would have settled on the bizarre deaths at Went Hill, the Weems book would have been sold for an exorbitant sum—a king's ransom, you might say, knowing his customer list—and all his adversaries removed from the scene.

"The ascendency of Thomas Adam Moriarty over the dark empire of the late Professor Moriarty would be complete."

We all sat for some little time in silent contemplation as the enormity of the plot settled upon us, the rain beating against the bow window.

"Do you believe he could have achieved all that?" I asked. "Did he have the temperament?"

Sherlock Holmes shrugged his shoulders and knocked out his bowl against the grate.

"Well, he didn't achieve it, did he? The site of that soldier reading my manuscript set him off, and from then on it was all improvisation. The boy is a curious mixture of his father, the professor, and what I imagine his mother might have been. As bloodless as any man who ever drew mortal breath, but quick to reveal a fiery, temperamental nature when a line has been crossed—witness his reaction to that young soldier in the train. Unlike his father, however, he had none of the habits of the flesh that took their toll on the professor."

"Ah, so the professor did *not* manage to avoid the disease he inflicted upon those poor women he secured for his pleasures?" said I, tossing the stub of my cigar in the fire grate.

"Excellent, Watson. Your medical schooling has not deserted you the way my criminal training did me! Had the professor's life not been cut short at the Reichenbach Falls, he would have likely suffered a much longer, more grueling fate. If you had read something of his treatise on the Bible, you would see a strain of brain fever unequaled outside the court of King George III."

"You have read it, then?"

"It was found in young Moriarty's rooms, along with a quantity of the disguises he employed during his stay, and returned to him at the hospital.

He allowed me to study it while he napped. The thing is quite long—six hundred and sixty-six pages, to be precise, for obvious reasons—and barely coherent in its ramblings. The 'analysis' devolves into little more than a diatribe, for a kind of monomania had taken hold by then, and the professor had begun to confuse the stories of the Bible for a literal history, which of course made it easily debunked."

Mycroft Holmes nodded vigorously.

"Our handwriting experts detected in the professor's correspondence a severe deterioration in mental acuity during the last three years of his life. Why, it was evident in his philatelic collection! The arrangement of the stamps becomes increasingly erratic from '86 on, until in '90 he stops filing them at all!" Mycroft's eyes opened wide at a thought that still seemed to astonish him. "My men found a dozen sheets of mint condition Penny Blacks—from plate 11, no less—stuffed in a chest of drawers!"

He glanced at his brother.

"I take nothing away from your victory in that struggle at the Reichenbach Falls, Sherlock, but the professor's mental faculties at that point were likely well off their zenith."

"And I am forever grateful for that, Mycroft." Sherlock Holmes smiled ruefully. "Unfortunately, the estimably cunning Colonel Sebastian Moran took his place, putting me in even greater danger than before. Hence my perambulations to Tibet and Arabia before returning home."

"Yes," said I. "And as Margaret will attest, the blackest years of my life were the three I spent thinking you had vanished down that chasm."

Sherlock Holmes once more shrugged his shoulders.

"It was the only way I could think to draw Colonel Moran and the rest of his gang out into the open, Watson. And as your own rather flowery account of it attested, I may say it worked." He looked me over with a critical eye, and the didactic toned softened somewhat.

"But the wound remains fresh, I see."

"You have no idea how difficult was that period for John," Margaret said, patting my hand to break my mood, which had fallen as dark as the sky outside. "Shall I put the kettle on?"

"A fresh cup would not go amiss," said Mycroft Holmes. "Thank you, madam."

Margaret excused herself and for some few moments we heard only her movements in the kitchen and rain slashing at the window.

I used the opportunity of her absence to raise a question that had been bothering me ever since Holmes had revealed to me the true identity of my 'Good Samaritan,' the answer to which I believed could only embarrass my friend.

"You will excuse me from saying so, Holmes, but it seems obvious from the start that the force behind this rather complex plan to kill you must have been young Moriarty. Why were you blind to that possibility?"

Sherlock Holmes frowned and studied his empty pipe bowl.

"I suffered the fate of old men, Watson. I had an idea stuck in my head and I refused to look at new facts as they presented themselves and to adjust my ideas accordingly. Young Moriarty was a mere figurehead, according to Mycroft's agents—a libertine in Paris! Suffering an addiction to absinthe and recently sent off to a clinic to recover! I was certain my fate would one day lay in the hands of Colonel Sebastian Moran."

"But surely Moran was in prison—"

"Prison walls have never stopped men of wealth from having their orders carried out, Watson. *Shikari* that he was, my expectation had always been that the colonel would one day be smuggled out of prison, unearth his old safari rifle and track me down right here on Went Hill, bagging me from a thousand yards one bright spring afternoon while I gathered honey from the hives—steady on, Watson! Mycroft's men were prepared for every eventuality."

"My brother does not exaggerate," said Mycroft Holmes gravely. "Colonel Moran could not butter his toast in his prison cell without one of Melville's men[70] knowing he had used a dessert knife instead of the butter knife."

"But why could they not stop young Moriarty from getting at him in prison?" I asked, causing Mycroft to purse his lips.

"It was a most singular failure on our part, I will admit."

---

70 *Mycroft refers to William Melville, one of the founders of the British Secret Service.*

Now it was Sherlock Holmes's turn to reassure his brother.

"There, there, Mycroft. It was, as you say, very cleverly done. And it is a reproach to my faculties of logical synthesis that I did not deduce the hand of young Moriarty pulling the strings all along. The entire operation displayed an inventive quality that I had never known the colonel or his associates to have possessed."

Mycroft stirred. "One could go further than that, Sherlock. One might say it demonstrated some of the same devilish subtleties of the old professor himself."

"I *did* say that, Mycroft—to young Moriarty today. Needless to say, he was considerably flattered. It brought him out of one of his pouts, and from then on I could barely get him to stop talking."

"He did have one very fortunate bit of luck, Holmes," said I.

"Yes?"

"Those vandals taking down the wires. If my cables had reached the Eastbourne police, none of this would have taken place."

"That was not luck, Watson, and those were not vandals. It was Moriarty and a strong pair of bolt cutters."

"Why, he anticipated everything!"

"Everything but the late lamented John Richard Baldwin reading my manuscript in the first-class railway carriage, Watson, I'm afraid."

"That poor boy," said Margaret, who had returned with the tea. "What on earth made him snatch it from John in the first place?"

"Here we enter the realm of speculation, madam," said Sherlock Holmes as he recharged his pipe, "but I have spoken with the parents and I believe we can construct a reasonable case. The young man was on the disability scheme lately approved by Parliament and had been to London for an appearance before the medical board. His battery had been caught in mustard gas at Ypres, you see, and temporary blindness had resulted in that terrible hand injury.

"As you know, de-mobbed soldiers are allowed to occupy first-class carriages. No doubt young Baldwin entered, saw the doctor here asleep with the manuscript in his hand or scattered upon the floor, saw my name on the pages—his mother told me he had been an avid reader of your books, Watson—and could not resist. He removed himself with the manuscript to the empty compartment next door and was engaged in reading it when the ticket inspector—Moriarty—happened upon him."

"And there was the poor boy's undoing."

"Quite so, madam. Young Moriarty's reaction upon seeing the manuscript in the soldier's hands was instantaneous. He told me that even before the blade had penetrated the unfortunate young soldier's neck he had foreseen the means by which he would create a mistaken identity for the boy, recruit Dr. Watson to the investigation and then—by way of flattery and subtler means—encourage a faulty conclusion."

"I was an utter fool," said I, shaking my head. "A Frenchman killed by a tailor!"

"You were not a fool, Doctor. You were *fooled*. There is no need to condemn yourself. He planted his own reading spectacles with the French mark in the dead man's fingers, placed upon the body other clues readily at hand and removed the telltale Army boots from the feet—making sure to invent a fanciful tale concerning expensive shoes when you first arrived on the scene. To what other conclusion could you have arrived?

"For good measure, he alerted the police that the famous Dr. Watson happened to be seated in that very train, and they more or less took the bait—although Sergeant Furnier was wise enough to set your statement aside on account of that business with my lost manuscript. In his mind, it was an unthinkable coincidence that a murder occurred and a document such as that was stolen—although he never deduced it was the ticket inspector all along.

"In any case, after seeing you off on the Jevington Road, young Moriarty made his way to his rooms in Eastbourne, where he kept a quantity of disguises precisely for such a contingency. He adopted a military uniform and drove the very route he knew you must be walking, picked you up in front of the Eight Bells and brought you to my doorstep, where his plans were once more disarranged by an encounter with Toby the Second outside our yew hedge. He is, you see, deathly afraid of dogs—"

"So that was not an act, as with the rest of his disguise?"

"Not a bit, Watson. He had been attacked as a young boy, in the presence of the professor—who, in the way of odd and evil geniuses, watched the attack for some little time before calling off the dog."

"No father would do that, Holmes!"

"None but Professor Moriarty, Watson. He was fascinated by the manner in which the dog—another Jack Russell, by the way—went for the boy's ankle. You may have noticed the slight limp?"

"Yes! I recall it now."

"Anyway, his fright was real, and he returned to his rooms with your valise and the knowledge that he needed to alter course once more. Upon inspecting your bag, he found it not only contained the medications, but your revolver as well, so he changed into his regular attire while we were having tea and saying goodnight to the bees. Then he waited for nightfall when he knew Miss Colvin would be preparing dinner for the old man, drove to the farmhouse with the intention of getting them out of the way before he dealt with us...and here we are."

"And all because I fell asleep in the train," said I, feeling no little remorse.

"You could not know, Watson. Nobody could. But we avenged the boy. '*On ne doit aux morts que la vérité.*'"[71]

"And very glad am I that we did, Holmes. I could not have lived with the knowledge that I had harmed you—" and here I faltered "—even at the point of a revolver to my head."

"Your quick thinking saved the day, Watson. Had you strictly obeyed young Moriarty's command, well, five hundred milligrams of morphine—I cannot imagine! Even in my more robust youth I would have been found dead with a needle mark in my arm; you with a bullet in your head from your own revolver. In your pocket would be found the forged note calling you to my aid. The men of the Yard could have reached no other conclusion than you had come across me in an overdosed state and had been so consumed with grief that you had shot yourself."

"But surely the absence of a quantity of needle marks in your skin would have dispelled the notion that you had relapsed!"

---

71 *Holmes quotes from Voltaire's axiom, 'One owes respect to the living; one owes the dead only the truth.'*

"Oh, that objection would be simple enough to overcome, Watson. A dozen or so pricks to my arms and, for a flourish, between my toes, would have done the trick."

"Dear me. He certainly has a devious mind," said Margaret. "Who in this world thinks such thoughts?"

"Men without proper role models," grumbled Mycroft Holmes without glancing up from his papers. "Loosed from the moorings of civility, adrift with the flotsam and jetsam of the tide, nothing to tie them down..."

"It is fortunate indeed that *I* had a proper role model," said Sherlock Holmes, gazing at his brother with no little admiration. "Was there anything else, Watson?"

"One final detail, Holmes. What caused the realization that it was young Moriarty? We were in the barrow, as I recall—"

"It was the paper clip."

"The paper clip!"

"Yes, Watson. You will recall that when you handed me the manuscript, I held it to my nose? The pages were redolent of Gauloises tobacco—"

"You mean to say you recognized the particular scent of the tobacco?" Margaret asked, with some little astonishment.

"Even in my retirement, madam, I have not let go *all* my skills. The scent of the French Gauloises is unique, and, as your husband had told me the ticket inspector produced the manuscript from his coat, it was evident the ticker inspector had planted those cigarettes in the Mary Box. Therefore, ticket inspector and murderer were one and the same."

"But what of the paper clip?"

"And therein lies the hinge upon which the entire case twisted, Watson— and quite literally, I might add." Holmes roused himself from his chair and, after a polite, "May I?" rummaged through his brother's despatch box, producing the manuscript. He held it up, pointing to an indentation in the upper corner.

"I had a large and varied correspondence from some of the reigning houses of Europe before the Kaiser's war closed the borders, and this peculiar style of paper clip is exceedingly common in St. Petersburg, where young Moriarty first learned his trade. I should have known it was he the moment I saw that same curious mark upon the forged note as we sat here after your arrival. But then again..." he glanced at his brother, who shifted uncomfortably upon the settee.

"You had been assured by our agents the boy had not left Paris. Quite."

"Of course, by now even the most blind beetle could see it. Colonel Moran and the soldier died within days of one another, each by the point of a—well, not embroidery shears, anyway! The clues planted everywhere in the carriage to divert friend Watson had all possessed a French character. Who else could it be but young Moriarty seeking to avenge his father's death at the Reichenbach Falls all those years ago?"

Outside, the rain had slackened and a half moon was attempting to break through the clouds. Mycroft was immersed in his papers and Margaret in her needlework—the hobby she had resumed since our move to the Downs, for her asthmatic attacks had all but disappeared.

Sherlock Holmes stood up, stretched his limbs and made his way to the window. He stared out of the glass for some little time before throwing it open to admit a blast of fresh air.

"That we survived, of course, is thanks in no small measure to the native instincts of my friends out there, whose ranks, I fear, were severely diminished in the process. I can only hope that, come spring and the flowering of the land—and with the addition of a few new queens—my hives will be restored to their health."

His brother glanced up from his reading in some annoyance, as the wind had blown one or two papers from the settee.

"I take nothing from the instinctive behaviour of your winged friends, Sherlock, but I rather think it was Dr. Watson's stratagem of loosening the needle under cover of the handkerchief that saved your life. May I ask, Doctor, how you conceived of that?"

"I saw no other way out," said I. "Still, it didn't fool the man. He saw through it immediately."

"But it bought my brother *time*, Doctor, and that was all-important." Mycroft Holmes chuckled at a memory. "By the way, Sherlock, that night upon our arrival, Lestrade, Mrs. Watson and I circled the house, as things seemed a little too quiet and we feared a trap. When we came upon your smashed typewriter, I inferred that you had attempted to alert your bees by tossing your machine out the window. It never occurred to me that Moriarty would sign his own death warrant by blasting the hives!"

"I only hoped to draw him into firing a shot, Mycroft, and so rouse the colonies," said Sherlock Holmes ruefully. "I did not anticipate a direct hit."

"I take it you finally found employment for that juvenile voice-throwing technique of yours?"

"Yes, Mycroft, but at a very great cost to the bees. It will require all of Miss Colvin's skills to resume production this spring if *Eighth Sister* is to remain in the pantries of England."

"I don't doubt she is capable, Holmes, but I wonder that you would reward her with such responsibilities," said I. "Her brother nearly killed you!"

"She knew nothing of his plans, Watson. Think of the innocent hound that is raised and trained for purposes of giving chase to the fox. Miss Colvin was groomed by a man she never met, for a purpose she never contemplated."

"He is right, John. The poor girl did only what was asked of her."

"And made my life considerably easier in the bargain!" added Sherlock. "Her patience at the typewriter was indispensable, and the income from those hives more than made up for the absence of work elsewhere. Not only that, she looked after a declining old man with the tenderness of a relation."

"I would hardly describe you as a declining old man," said Mycroft Holmes with a wink at Margaret.

"I was speaking of the uncle, Mycroft."

"Begging your pardon, Sherlock."

Mycroft Holmes had returned to his papers, and Margaret to her needle-point, but Sherlock Holmes's kindly words about Miss Colvin had put me in something of a brown study.

It was Holmes who broke the silence, demonstrating once again his unique ability to read the inner workings of a mind from the features upon one's face.

"She was my *typist*, Watson. Not my most trusted confidant, as you have been."

"And yet you confided the innermost secrets of your life to her!" I fairly snapped. "And in the bargain, you told the world what an utter fool I had been to believe that tale of your family tree!"

"Well, really, Watson—it was the thinnest of stories. The greatest surprise of my days with you is that I was never unmasked. Surely a week's worth of investigation must have yielded the truth."

"You underrate me, Holmes. I did precisely that, and more than once, as Margaret will attest. Why, on our voyage to the Mediterranean for her health, I arranged to stop in Avignon that I might pursue your heritage!"

Holmes frowned. "Avignon?"

"You told me your grandmother was related to Vernet, the painter. When I learned he was from Avignon, I—"

Holmes burst out laughing. "My word, that *is* dedication. I merely took his name from Monsieur at the DuPont works because it was the best I could come up with at the time, and it happened he was a great-grandson of Vernet of Avignon. But I gave you no other reason to think Avignon was somehow a hotbed of my ancestry, surely?"

"On the contrary, Holmes. You said you visited Montpelier during your three lost years, and Montpelier is close by Avignon. It gave a certain logic to the tale."

Holmes nodded thoughtfully. "I dare say it did, Watson, although I must admit, that was purely serendipitous. I never made the connection."

"Well, *I did*, and spent considerable energy attempting to work out the linkage."

Margaret had risen from the settee and had taken my hand in that soothing fashion of hers.

"In any case, I should have thought my efforts to bring your methods of observation and deduction to the world deserved a measure of confidence in me, not deception."

"Ah, but the deception was quite necessary, Watson—"

"Then you admit it!" I exclaimed hotly. "You admit the deception!"

"Allow me, Sherlock." Mycroft Holmes put down his papers and removed his spectacles with no little deliberation.

"Did you never stop to think, Doctor, that not all your readers were innocents like that boy in the train? That every master villain in England, and on the Continent, for that matter, was also reading your stories—and cataloging my brother's living habits for their future ends?"

"Dear me!" Margaret exclaimed, her face ashen.

"Yes, madam. *Dear me*. Every time one of those little adventures was published, our foreign desks reported a new line of threats against my brother. It became imperative to provide misdirection, as the magicians would say, to put his enemies upon the wrong scent. 'Country squires' did the trick." Mycroft Holmes fixed a solemn gaze at me. "The deception was not intended for you, Doctor. It was intended for your readers."

"Quite so," said Sherlock Holmes.

The pride and bitterness that had welled up within me dissipated and was replaced with remorse.

"I'm sorry, Holmes, I never knew."

"And I am sorry I could never tell you."

"But why did you allow John to continue publishing the stories of your cases?"

"Oh, the benefits far outweighed the costs, madam, as I'm sure Sherlock would agree."

"Indeed they did, Mycroft. The aura of invincibility projected by those tales considerably amplified my own small powers of observation and deduction, and of course brought me to the attention of a rather influential clientele."

"*Highly* influential. My brother's assistance to the Crowns of Europe has proven no small benefit to His Majesty's government for many years."

Sherlock Holmes touched my shoulder with a kindly hand. "Still, Doctor, I should not have mocked you for accepting my fake heritage. I owe you a thousand apologies."

Seeing Holmes thus chastened, I felt much assuaged.

"Perhaps, then, you can now tell me what you were doing those three lost years while I was mourning your death. I never believed your story of researching coal tar was enough to fill a thousand days for a man of your talents!"

"Excellent, Watson. Yes, the coal tar research was something of a detour from my wanderings in those years. It came about that Monsieur Vernet had returned to France late in life, and I had taken the opportunity to visit his laboratory at Montpelier. I was helping supervise his own experiments in coal tar derivatives the day he died at his bench—which was the way he had wanted to leave this earth, I might add—and so I stayed on to help his widow organize the funeral Mass. Several of the du Ponts attended, of course, and then it was up to me to tell his bees."

"Tell his *bees*?"

"One always tells the bees when their caretaker has passed on, Watson."

"I've never heard anything so ridiculous!"

"Actually, John," said Margaret softly. "It is quite a well understood thing. Otherwise they scatter."

"Yes, madam, and I expect your husband will do it for me here at Went Hill when that day comes."

"Surely not, Holmes!" I cried.

"You had better," said Mycroft Holmes gruffly. "I'll have nothing to do with those creatures."

"But that day is surely too far off to be discussing it now," I protested.

"The final judgment is up to God, not to me, Watson." Sherlock Holmes had been once more gazing out the window, and now he turned to face me. "Was there anything else about my manuscript that left a bad taste, Watson?"

"Not a thing. I quite enjoyed it. Your story is remarkable. Unique, really."

"Thank you."

"But what caused you to write it now, if I may ask?" inquired Margaret.

"I wanted to tell the unvarnished and absolute truth of my life, madam. It was a relief no longer to be in the clutches of a false history, however necessary it had been to maintain that fiction."

Holmes turned back to the window, but I could see in the reflection that his eyes were glistening. I returned his emotion with some feeling of my own.

"A weight has been lifted from me, as well, Holmes. Knowing you intended to deceive the world, not your most loyal companion."

Sherlock Holmes shrugged his shoulders and responded with the kind of backhanded slight that had once stung.

"Well, of course, I have had to keep my wits about me even when others did not."

It still stung, but I accepted it now.

END OF PART III

IV

THE AMERICAN
RETROSPECTION OF
SHERLOCK HOLMES

"It is a capital mistake to theorize before one has data. Insensibly one begins to twist facts to suit theories, instead of theories to suit facts."

Sherlock Holmes
—*A Scandal in Bohemia*

Chapter One

THESE ONEROUS TERMS

November saw a harsh winter descend upon the Downs. The sun rose late and set early, and the winds from the north brought blistering gales that allowed only occasional breaks in the clouds, keeping us indoors most days.

Yet our mood was not nearly so gloomy as the weather.

The Hundred Days offensive formulated by our Field Marshal Sir Douglas Haig and France's Marshal Foch had pushed the German troops back to the Hindenburg Line and made a surprising breakthrough at Cambrai. Then came rumours of a shocking mutiny among sailors of the German Imperial Navy and peace overtures from the new German Chancellor.

Even the cold weather was doing its part, for it appeared to be taking a toll on the influenza. One could see it in the reduced number of white hospital tents on the hillside across the Birling Gap.[72]

Margaret, I was delighted to see, was positively flourishing in the countryside. The pure Sussex air so assuaged her lungs that she was as active as the day she had arrived from India. She had even taken over the kitchen duties, leaving Miss Colvin free to plan the rejuvenescence of Holmes's

---

72 *Watson repeats a commonly held belief that spread of the 'Spanish Flu' diminished in cold weather. He would discover that this was not the case.*

candle and honey operations with the help of a young man from the village just returned from France.

For Sherlock Holmes, the hearty curries and exotic breads of Margaret's childhood in India provided a welcome change from the French fare prepared by Miss Colvin and the heavy Scottish recipes of his previous caretaker, and he had renewed work upon his manuscript with vigour, although in a quite secretive vein. Most days found him seated alone at the typewriter, which had been speedily repaired following its flight out of the window, slowly pecking away at the keys, with frequent pauses to stop and correct his work.

I spent the days seated in my armchair by the fire, reading up on the practice of beekeeping from Holmes's own remarkable treatise.[73] Upon occasion, Holmes and I took excursions along the cliffs, but these were infrequent and often abbreviated, for the rheumatic aches in his bones had increased with the cold, damp atmosphere, whilst my old war wounds had never fully recovered from that long walk up the Jevington Road and the exciting events of our encounter with young Moriarty.

Evenings were spent together before the fireplace, with Margaret engaged in her needlework and Holmes and I combing through old casebooks to gather material for publication. Now that the war was nearly over, it was expected that demand for entertainment would soon return, and Holmes was amenable to the requests from my publisher to help supply it.

Mycroft Holmes had not visited since that final interview with young Moriarty, for the reason, we later learned, that he had been deeply involved in urgent discussions at 10 Downing Street, where a request for terms of surrender had been received from German authorities through backdoor channels and negotiations were underway for an armistice.

It was the afternoon of November eleventh, 1918—how could I not remember the date? —and Sherlock Holmes and I were seated on either side of a blazing fire talking over an old case while Margaret prepared dinner in the kitchen, all three of us anxiously awaiting news from the negotiations between France and Germany that were rumoured to be taking place in a forest near Compiègne.

---

73 "The Practical Handbook of Bee Culture, with Some Observations upon the Segregation of the Queen."

I had removed an old newspaper clipping from one of the casebooks in preparation for our evening's work and had chanced to remark upon the almost pristine condition of the linen newspaper when a mischievous light came into Holmes's eyes. After a glance towards the kitchen door, he rose from his chair, still wrapped in the muffler that had become customary during his waking hours, and disappeared into his bedroom. Soon I heard his steps in the garret above my head, evidently rooting among the books and memorabilia.

When he returned some minutes later, he carried a cracked and faded leather satchel.

"My old haversack," he said quietly. "From America."

"Good Lord, Holmes! Do you mean it?"

By way of answer, and with one eye on the kitchen, Holmes unbuckled the flap and carefully removed a newspaper from within—one of several, all evidently very old—and handed it to me with particular care.

I found myself holding a *Baltimore Sun* edition, dated April 18, 1865.

"Holmes!" I exclaimed, pointing to the masthead. "Not one of Booth's, surely?"

My friend touched a finger to his lips and nodded discreetly.

"Goodness, Holmes!" I found it a chilling thing to hold in my hands an object once removed from the assassin of Abraham Lincoln, its pages somewhat greasy to the touch and still possessed of a most unpleasant scent.

"It certainly is redolent of unwashed men, Holmes. Puk!"

"Stick two men in a space smaller than my kitchen for five days and you will cook up a most unsavory aroma, Watson!" Holmes chuckled as he pulled out a second newspaper, the *Philadelphia Inquirer*, for himself.

"Five days! Why, that would mean Booth was on the run for more than a full week?"

"Twelve days, Watson."

"Twelve days!"

"Yes, and it felt like twelve years to Mr. Stanton, I can tell you that."

"I find it hard to understand why it should have taken so long to find him, Holmes."

"Nobody in Washington understood it, either. The pressure on Stanton was indescribable. But America is a vast country, you know. It was no easy thing to find a man who didn't want to be found—especially one who could count on the likes of Samuel Mudd for succor!"

I marveled to behold this most tangible, most indisputable token of my friend's adventures in America. Turning its pages, I found the margins filled with pencil marks, exclamation points and indecipherable scribbles.

"These markings, Holmes. Surely they can't be Booth's?"

"Read them and judge for yourself, Watson."

And so I did.

They were Booth's.

So engrossed had we become in the dramatic accounts of the assassination and Booth's feverish pencil scrawls in the margins, that neither of us heard the telegraphic tap-tapping at the front door.

It was Margaret who admitted Mycroft Holmes.

This was his first return to Went Hill in some time, and my companion's reaction considerably surprised me. Instead of rising to greet his long-absent brother, Sherlock Holmes snatched the newspaper from my hands and hastily stuffed both it and the *Inquirer* into the haversack, which he then dropped into the tin box at his side before casually letting his muffler fall on top just as his brother entered the room.

Mycroft paid no attention to his brother's machinations with the tin box, however, for he was—quite out of character—all smiles and good cheer, and the reason was quickly evident in the newspapers he waved above his head.

They were the day's latest editions from London, with the first accounts of the armistice beneath large-point headlines.

"Glorious!" said I, taking the *Evening Standard*, while Sherlock Holmes snatched the *Times* from his brother.

"Yes, it is," said Mycroft, depositing his despatch box upon the desk and glancing out the window at the spare, wintry landscape and the white hospital tents still visible across the Birling Gap road through the bare apple branches. "The men will be coming home soon."

"Your friend Mr. Law will be pleased."[74]

"Yes, Sherlock, and so will the health ministry. Those camps don't *cure* the influenza. I dare say they merely spread it around."

He turned away from the window with a frown, accepted a cup of tea from Margaret and opened his despatch box. In place of the normal bundles of red-ribboned papers and wax-sealed envelopes, however, it now contained several thick books, one of which he removed.

"I fear you will see even less of me than you have been, Sherlock. The hard work of rebuilding now begins."

To his brother's inquiring glance, Mycroft Holmes held up the book. "*America and Reconstruction*," he said, taking his seat upon the settee. "I am reading up on the lessons of your friend Mr. Stanton and his American peers after their civil war. How we manage the peace will be *the* issue of the age, as it was in America after Appomattox."

"You'll find no helpful lessons in there, I suspect," said Sherlock Holmes dryly. "Andrew Johnson was no Abraham Lincoln, that is for certain."

"Then it will be well to learn from his mistakes," said Mycroft with the utmost seriousness, turning to his book. His powers of concentration were, I had found, even greater than his brother's, and he was quickly absorbed in the text. Sherlock Holmes and I turned to the London papers in our hands and feasted our eyes upon the news we had been waiting for throughout four years of blackouts, rationing and death notices.

It was not until darkness had settled upon the Downs and Margaret announced dinner that we brought ourselves to put down the papers. Even then, the news they had carried to Went Hill was all we could discuss as we ate.

Mycroft fretted that the dissolution of the monarchies of Italy and Austria-Hungary provided an opening for the Communists now overrunning Russia, while the flight of Kaiser Wilhelm to neutral Holland could only mean anarchy in Germany.

"Wilhelm is, after all, Victoria's grandson," he observed before taking another mouthful of chicken. "He imparted something of the rule of law on that country."

---

74 *The Right Honourable Andrew Bonar Law, Chancellor of the Exchequer (the British Treasury) in 1918.*

Margaret, as was her wont, was considerably more optimistic.

"Surely the rebuilding of France and Belgium will employ the men returning to their homes from the battlefields? Why, it might even lift the world from chaos to prosperity!"

But Sherlock Holmes shook his head gravely.

"I fear there will be nothing left to lift, madam. And as for your monarchs, Mycroft—I've met them all! Not an original thought in their brains! In any case, I dare say nothing good can come of these terms being imposed on Germany." He nodded grimly at the *Times* by his elbow. "These onerous terms."

"What of them?" said I.

"Why, is it not obvious, Doctor? France is demanding the Rhineland and control of Germany's railroads—and yet will allow no lifting of the Allied blockade! What good will come of such harsh measures?"

"*Harsh?*" I exclaimed. "What of the desecration of Flanders? Was that not harsh? Have you forgotten the Rape of Belgium already?"

"I forget nothing, Watson. But tell me how such terms can right such wrongs? Be specific, now. Tell me: how will the Germans feed themselves with their industry seized, their ports closed, their railroads commandeered by the French? You have no answers, and neither do the Allies, I suspect. And this talk of reparations! If the Germans can't feed themselves, where will the Deutschemarks to pay us come from?"

"What concern is that of ours?" said I, rather hotly. "Surely the Germans brought it upon their own heads."

"You sound the old Northern war cry from America, Watson: '*The South brought it on their own heads!*'" My friend smiled as he pushed back from the table to charge his pipe, nodding at the book at Mycroft Holmes's elbow. "Brother Mycroft, *you* have been studying the American failure in that department. What say you?"

"I say you have a very fair point, Sherlock. Without Mr. Lincoln to bring cooler heads to bear in that way of his, the radical elements in the North— led by our old friend, Mr. Stanton—set about to punish the South, and it came back to haunt them. Still does."

"And how?" asked Margaret.

"By making Jefferson Davis a sympathetic figure," said Sherlock Holmes.

"That is difficult to imagine!"

"Imagine it, good madam. Mr. Stanton slapped him in chains and made a pitiable spectacle of the man—even something of a martyr. He was pardoned within the year! *Pardoned!* Imagine Cromwell pardoned, if you please!" Sherlock Holmes frowned. "Why do you look at me like that, Watson? I'm telling you, Davis was resurrected! His memoirs secured his family's fortune—every good Southern home had a copy—and his book tour of the South was as a church revival. He became the beloved figurehead of the Lost Cause. His passing was a day of mourning in the very states he had led in rebellion. Roads were named for him, statues erected in his honour. Reconstruction worked well for Jefferson Davis. It did not work so well for the black man."

He glanced at his brother.

"Mycroft, you have been reading up on this. Do I exaggerate?"

"By no means, Sherlock. Andrew Johnson set about dismantling everything Lincoln had worked for. Refused to endorse the Freedman's Law signed by President Lincoln the month before he was assassinated![75] It would have given slaves the land they'd been working at the point of a lash!" Mycroft shook his head. "But Johnson gave it all back to the slaveowners. Said the Negros were happier under slavery."

"Precisely, Mycroft. Mr. Stanton had it right when he screamed 'Good God, now Andy Johnson is president!'"

"And what happened to Mr. Stanton?" I asked.

"The good Mr. Stanton went the way of all flesh without so much as a statue erected in his name in the city he had helped save. Died before he could be sworn a Justice of the Supreme Court—the only title he truly coveted."

Sherlock Holmes lit his pipe, filling the kitchen with clouds of blue smoke that set Margaret coughing. As I cleared the plates, his discourse returned to the present.

---

75 *"An Act to establish a Bureau for the Relief of Freedmen and Refugees," approved March 3, 1865.*

"Mark my words. These terms will do no good, and probably much bad that we cannot yet comprehend."

"It would be difficult to imagine anything worse than the last four years, Holmes."

"Then your imagination is limited, Watson. I fear for Germany. I fear for France. I fear for my country. Madam, I beg your pardon. I will retire to the den."

And with that, Sherlock Holmes took his pipe and his newspaper and left the kitchen.

"Certainly, we have much to look forward to!" I called after him.

"Good old Watson! Ever the ray of sunshine on a cloudy day!"

With the plates and silverware put away, we joined the two brothers by the fireplace for tea and the distinctive *shahi tukda* sweet breads Margaret had prepared.

Sherlock Holmes sat gazing deeply into the fireplace, smoking his pipe in the utmost concentration, the *Times* edition upon his lap. As he absently reached down to pick up his muffler from the tin box, Mycroft Holmes spotted the haversack now exposed at his brother's feet.

"Well, Sherlock, what have we here?" Mycroft said, retrieving the haversack from the tin box and placing it beside him on the settee. Upon removing the *Baltimore Sun*, his eyes widened as they fell upon these headlines:

THE NATIONAL CALAMITY
DEATH OF PRESIDENT LINCOLN

"By the Lord Harry! How on earth did you manage this, Sherlock?" Mycroft exclaimed, glancing through the pages with increasing astonishment.

"Manage what, Mycroft?" Sherlock Holmes turned away from the fireplace to face his brother. When he glimpsed the haversack, he smiled, and his face took on a look of feigned innocence. "I surely don't know what you mean."

"This newspaper! The pencil markings! Why, these are Booth's papers! You brought them back!" Mycroft removed his handkerchief and pressed it to his nose. "The linen paper is most odiferous! But how did you manage it, Sherlock? You didn't abscond with them, I hope?"

Sherlock Holmes chuckled and shook his head. "No, nothing like that. Mr. Stanton wanted them burned, you see, and—"

"Burned!" Mycroft dropped his handkerchief. "I don't believe it."

"Believe it, Mycroft."

"Why on earth—"

"Because he had expected to find a conspiracy between Wilkes Booth and Jefferson Davis, and he meant to prove it. But these showed precisely the opposite. You see that writing just there, where the editor claims an understanding between Booth and Davis?"

Mycroft Holmes held the paper to his eyes.

"'*Who but I alone?*' Booth has written."

"Quite so. Other notations say much the same. Mr. Stanton wanted nothing to do with them."

"And yet he would *burn* history?" Mycroft Holmes could barely contain his chagrin.

"Ah, but it was not *history* then, Mycroft. It was merely a damp, smelly newspaper with Booth's ravings scribbled upon it."

"But surely he could have seen the value in preserving this!"

"You must understand, Mycroft—all was confusion after Booth's capture. Such a calamity had never happened before! There was no system, no order. Soldiers were clipping locks of hair from the corpse...a guard exchanged his jacket with Davey Herold for a souvenir! Everything was an improvisation. And these papers did not prove what Mr. Stanton expected they would prove, so..."

"And so he simply *gave* them to you?"

"No, Mycroft, it was not quite like that. This was Edwin M. Stanton—and you of all people knew his shrewdness of mind. It happened that I had been called into his study the day after our return from the Garrett barn. The newspapers were laid out across his desk and he started in on me in his usual fashion: *Where had I found them? Had anyone else handled them? Had any gone missing?* That sort of thing.

"When he finished, he handed three of them to me, told me to toss them into the grate. I instead found myself asking whether I might not have them for keepsakes, rather fearing another eruption of Mount Stanton. But to my delight, he acquiesced. Said it was fair recompense for the efforts Abraham and I had made, so long as they never saw the light of day."

"Remarkable, Sherlock. Even more remarkable that you kept them hidden away in your garret all these years."

"You understand why I could not have shown them to you, Mycroft?"

"All too well. You never would have seen them again."

"I trust there are no wounded feelings?"

"None in the world, dear brother. I'm delighted to finally hold them in my hands. And in such excellent condition fifty years on. The advantage of linen paper cannot be denied—but for the odour!" Mycroft again pressed the handkerchief to his nose while shooting a glance at the tin box. "No sign of the Weems book in there?"

Sherlock Holmes smiled and resumed his expression of innocence. "I'm sure I don't know what you mean."

Mycroft glanced from Margaret to me. "He hasn't brought out that book of Mr. Lincoln's for either of you, has he?"

Our faces bespoke our ignorance.

"I have my answer," he said, shrugging his shoulders. "Any other secrets you have been keeping from me, Sherlock?"

"None in the world, my dear brother."

"Then I have one for you," said Mycroft, and he began to describe a most remarkable exchange of telegrams between Whitehall and Washington City in April of 1865, which caused his brother to nearly start out of his armchair.

"*What!*" Sherlock Holmes exclaimed with as surprised a look as I had ever seen upon his face, as Mycroft paused to take a pinch of snuff. "Edwin Stanton consulted *you?*"

"Yes, Sherlock. On the very day you reached Washington City with the corpse. We exchanged half a dozen cables, as I recall."

"Why in the devil—?"

"He wanted to know what had become of Cromwell's remains."

"*Cromwell's* remains?" I exclaimed. "What on earth for?"

Sherlock Holmes had recovered some of his equanimity. "Well, as Mr. Stanton was making preparations to dispose of Booth's corpse..."

"Precisely so, Sherlock. He was anxious to learn how we had managed to keep Cromwell's grave from becoming a shrine to the revolutionary elements of the underclass."

"Oh, and how did *we* manage that?" said Sherlock Holmes, a gleam in his eye at his brother's conjugation of himself with the entire British government.

"Well, Sherlock as every schoolboy knows—and since you were not a schoolboy, it does not surprise me you don't know it—some years after Cromwell's rather grand funeral at Westminster, the body was exhumed, the head stuck on a pole for display and the rest of him so widely dispersed that no one ever knew where to find him."

"But nothing so grisly was done to Booth, surely?"

"No, Doctor, certainly not. My advice to Mr. Stanton was nothing along those lines. I simply told him he must establish beyond all doubt that the corpse was Wilkes Booth's and no other. This had not been done with Cromwell, you see, and the rumour persisted—to this day, I might add—that Cromwell's remains had been secreted elsewhere."

"Well, now, that explains a great deal," said Sherlock Holmes, sitting back in his chair, thoughtfully puffing upon his pipe and nodding in evident satisfaction. "A very great deal."

"And what does it explain, Sherlock?"

"It explains why Mr. Stanton arrived at the wharf with a half-dozen men of various backgrounds, all of whom had known Booth in life. There was a doctor, as I recall, and a stage manager, and several others. Stanton required each to sign an oath attesting to Booth's identity."

"At my suggestion, dear boy," said Mycroft proudly.

"Indeed! We all wondered what the fuss was about. Stanton was evidently not aware that Booth possessed a tattoo—the mark *J.W.B.* was plainly visible on his knuckles." Sherlock Holmes held out his own bunched fist to demonstrate.

"You underrate Mr. Stanton, Sherlock. He was quite aware of that tattoo, and he was also aware that any fool could have had himself branded on the knuckles with the same letters. It was also my suggestion to have photographs taken. For absolute proof."

"Ah!" Sherlock Holmes nodded. "That would explain the photographer setting up his box camera and fussing with his plates while Booth's clothing was removed, the corpse being twisted this way and that with each new exposure. Made for a long and gruesome spectacle, I must say."

"Where was the body finally taken?" I asked.

"The family claimed it in the end. It came to rest in a cemetery outside Baltimore."

"And how many conspirators were eventually rounded up?"

"There were, I believe, seven, Watson, tried by the military tribunal—"

"Eight were tried, four hanged, Sherlock." Mycroft Holmes held up the book he had been reading.

"I stand corrected."

"But Samuel Mudd was spared the noose?"

"Yes, Watson! That's the pinch! The fiend escaped hanging by a single vote of the commission. 'It is no crime to set a man's broken leg' was his barrister's defense, and it worked well enough to send Mudd to prison for life in the Dry Tortugas, instead of to the gallows."

"Life in prison is not inconsequential," observed Margaret.

"No, but Samuel Mudd did not even suffer *that* fate, thanks to the spineless Andrew Johnson." Sherlock Holmes's voice soured at the memory. "The saintly doctor was pardoned for ministering to his fellow inmates during an epidemic of yellow fever."

"Well, surely that counts for something."

"In my opinion, good madam, it counts as a man trying to salve his conscience and save his skin. Mudd *knew* Booth! Why, they'd met over a hairbrained plot to kidnap President Lincoln the year before the assassination! I don't believe there was *any* confusion over who appeared at

Mudd's door that evening, whose leg he was fixing, whose moustache he was shaving off, whose figure climbed into his spare bed that night. And yet he prevaricated every step of the way."

Sherlock Holmes shook his head. "Lived out his days denying any connivance with Booth like a dog trying to keep an old bone buried."

The silence that followed this impassioned outburst was broken by a soft chuckle from Mycroft Holmes.

"All that may be so, Sherlock, but I rather think justice was served when the very name of 'Mudd' received a more timeless condemnation than a life sentence."

"Perhaps, Mycroft. Perhaps."

"Speaking of condemnation, Holmes, what became of Allan Pinkerton?"

"Written out of the history books, Watson, by order of Edwin M. Stanton. On account of those telegraphs from Fredericksburg I had managed to get off."

"My very favourite story from your manuscript, Sherlock!" cried Mycroft. "I was never more proud to learn how you had put your skills in that department to use. But what exactly had you written in your messages to Secretary Stanton?"

"Oh, they contained a rather frank correction of the missives from Major Morris. You may recall the major claimed he had sent the War Secretary a recommendation that Abraham and I receive a share of the reward money? Stuff and nonsense! He took credit for the newspapers I had just presented to Colonel Goodridge—and the boot we had handed Lovett as well."

"Good Lord!" exclaimed Margaret. "How could a man, an *officer*, stoop so low?"

"He was stooping for the reward money, madam. It was enough for several lifetimes."

"Does it not seem remarkable," said I, "that the War Secretary would side with the word of a young houseguest against a major in his own Army?"

"A major who had confiscated a pass signed by the War Secretary himself!" Sherlock Holmes shook his head. "Morris could have been court-martialed for that alone, Watson. And when I revealed that the major was in league with Allan Pinkerton to steal the reward money from other, more deserving parties, well..."

"Rosencrantz and Gildenstern, that pair," said Mycroft Holmes. "Hoist with their own petard, and smartly done, Sherlock."

"My conscience rests easy on Allan J. Pinkerton. He was a bluffer and a bully, no more."

"But I recall that you spoke rather well of his detective agency in one of our cases, Holmes.[76] Did you reconcile with him?"

"I never saw him again, Watson—but you remember aright. My acquaintances in the American police circles credited one of the Pinkerton men in that matter of the Long Island smugglers."

"I take it you and your friend Abraham never received a share of the reward money?"

"We never asked for it, Watson."

"But surely you were given some recognition for what you had done?" said Margaret.

"No, madam." Sherlock Holmes shook his head. "We had no standing, you see."

"No standing? Why? Had you done something to upset Mr. Stanton?"

"Quite the contrary," Mycroft Holmes spoke up with some little pride. "Johnnie's efforts paid dividends to Her Majesty's government for many years to come."

"Then perhaps your brother's name is mentioned somewhere in the history books? When you took the journey to Richmond with President Lincoln, or pulled young Tad out of that theatre?"

"That was not *me*, madam," said my friend with a wry smile. "It was a young orphan named Johnnie. What possible relation could he be to the great and famous detective named Sherlock Holmes?"

It was late, and a mellow mood had settled over the cottage as the storm outside dwindled. Sherlock Holmes and I lit cigars while Margaret brought out the claret. It was she who broke the silence with a question for Sherlock Holmes.

---

76 *The Valley of Fear, set in the late 1800's.*

"Mr. Lincoln's question was never answered in your manuscript."

"Ma'am?"

"How the gunpowder thieves managed to fool Mr. du Pont and his accountant. Was the accountant in league with the thieves?"

Sherlock Holmes shook his head.

"No, madam. It turned out that the accountant was right—no powder was missing."

"And yet you witnessed the thieves removing the kegs!"

"Oh, yes. DuPont powder was being secreted from the mill. Quite a bit, in fact. But it turned out the bandits weren't *stealing* the powder. They were simply making extra supplies during their off-hours with the aid of that thuggish Irish foreman and some homemade saltpetre smuggled in from the cooperage upriver."

Holmes studied his cigar before knocking the ash in the grate.

"And *that* is why Mr. du Pont's accountant could not find any missing quantities—none were missing! As was often the case when your husband and I worked together, the simplest explanation proved the correct one."

"Indeed!" I exclaimed. "But who else was in on it?"

"Three powdermen and two watchmen, and of course Sunshine Billy and his family."

"Quite extraordinary thinking for a bunch of common rogues," said Mycroft Holmes, taking a sip of claret from his brother's glass, rolling it on his tongue and exhaling with a wistful sigh.

"Why did you never explain all this in your manuscript?" I asked.

"Because General Henry had requested the particulars never be discussed, else others might attempt them. And I gave him my pledge."

"But surely the statute of limitations on that promise has expired fifty years on!"

"Yes, Watson, I suppose it has." Sherlock Holmes studied the dark red liquid in his glass. "It's an odd thing to feel such loyalty to that family as I do, even to this day. General Henry risked his life, you know, living there above the roll mills. A half-dozen men of the du Pont line went 'across the creek' over the years. Lammot included."

Holmes turned to his brother.

"I wager you never met an industrialist willing to share the fate of his labourers like that, eh Mycroft?"

"No, Sherlock, but as Dr. Watson says, the statute of limitations on your promise has certainly passed."

"Yes, I suppose it has. Well, and there you have it."

"What became of the thieves?" Margaret asked.

"Boyle and his gang were rounded up the morning after Lee surrendered at Appomattox, and Denny Boyle sang like a bird. Like a very scared bird."

"Were they tried?"

"There was no trial, madam." Sherlock Holmes said, with a glint in his eye. "You may, however, recall the infamous midnight explosion of an undertaker's shack in the tiny hamlet of Cape Island, New Jersey in the final days of the Civil War? No? Well, it was never determined what set off the kegs stored in that shack. But several powdermen and two of the night watchmen from the DuPont works were rumoured to have been among the bodies blown to pieces in the blast, and I fancy the hand of Edwin M. Stanton was behind it."

"Surely not! That is a most dreadful way to settle a score."

"So you may think, madam. But it was most assuredly the safest way to avoid public exposure of the crime, and with it, the DuPont methods of manufacturing, which were the envy of the world. And it would certainly have caused anyone else even remotely involved in such a scheme to have second or third thoughts."

He glanced at his brother.

"A rather *Stantonian* solution, wouldn't you say, Mycroft?"

"Quite so, Sherlock," said Mycroft Holmes approvingly. "Quite so."

Chapter Two

THE GRAND REVIEW

Near midnight I walked Margaret to the farmhouse and bid her goodnight. When I returned to Holmes's cottage I found the decanter upon the mantel substantially drained in my absence, an empty glass next to Mycroft Holmes upon the settee. His abstinence pledge evidently abandoned for the evening, Mycroft snored as he sat nodding over the ancient *Baltimore Sun*, which collected stray grains of snuff as they fell from his shirt front.

Sherlock Holmes gently slipped the newspaper from his brother's lap, shook off the grains and gazed at the front page as he puffed reflectively on the last of his cigar. I poured myself the dregs of the claret and studied my old companion for some little time as I stood at the fireplace, absorbing the warmth from the embers.

"How did it end, Holmes?"

He glanced up from the newspaper. "I beg your pardon?"

"Your time in America. How did it end?"

"Alas, I had forgot—you never finished the manuscript that evening in the barrow."

"Yes, and it had entirely slipped my mind until Margaret raised this business of the gunpowder thieves tonight."

I took my seat and pressed my questions upon him.

"How long did you remain in America? Did your friend ever find his father? And when exactly did you return to England?"

"Brother Mycroft has the manuscript in the bottom of his despatch box," he said, tossing the last of his cigar in the grate, stretching out his hand

and shaking his brother's knee.

"Mycroft! Would you be averse to Dr. Watson reading the last few pages aloud? We left off at page ninety-three or thereabouts, as I recall."

Mycroft Holmes yawned, shook himself awake and revived himself with a huge pinch of snuff. "One moment, Sherlock." He placed his spectacles upon his nose and began to leaf through the remaining pages of the manuscript.

"You can't possibly still be worried your brother might have written something he shouldn't have?" said I—but it was quite evident he *was*, for he ignored my question.

"That looks fine," said he gruffly, handing me the manuscript.

"Right, then!" said Sherlock Holmes. "Now, before you begin, Watson, I must first set the scene."

And with that, he turned his gaze to the ceiling and called forth his final memories from the days he was still known as Johnnie.

"It is the 24th of May of the year 1865. One month after that bad business at the Garrett barn and two weeks after Jefferson Davis was finally captured in a pine woods outside Augusta, Georgia—just a day's ride from the Atlantic Ocean, incidentally.

"A return to business has settled upon Washington City, and I am to set sail for England two days hence.

"There is, however, time for one last hurrah with friend Abraham: to watch the 'Grand Review' of the victorious Northern armies being staged to celebrate the end of the American conflict. One hundred fifty thousand soldiers have gathered in the farms and fields outside the government district for a march down Pennsylvania Avenue to a viewing stand in front of the White House. After saluting the President and various dignitaries there, the units will be dismissed, and the men will be civilians once again.

"Yesterday it had been General Meade's Army of the Potomac; today it will be Sherman's Army of the Tennessee, and Abraham and I have secured a prime viewing spot up a large tree directly alongside the grandstand.

"President Johnson, General Grant, Mr. Stanton and Mr. Seward are there, of course, as well as many lesser lights, including some whom I recognize from their anxious appearances outside the study of Mr. Stanton during various crises of the past year. The stores are shut, the taverns open, and the sidewalks and alleys are filled with flag-waving patriots eager to see these soldiers from the West.

"And to watch what Sherman will do when he meets Mr. Stanton.

"You see, Watson, after Lee's surrender at Appomattox, only one Confederate Army of significance had remained in the field, that under Joe Johnston. It had been brought to bay by Sherman's men outside Raleigh, North Carolina—but when Sherman proposed terms of surrender, they proved so broad and so generous that the War Secretary accused Sherman of treason! In the papers! Sherman who, more than any other, had helped Grant defeat the Confederacy!

"And today, Sherman and Stanton must meet, for they will share that platform.

"At ten o'clock, the signal cannon thunders and the air fills with the sound of drums beating and bugles calling. The ground begins to tremble with the tramping of tens of thousands of feet, and the rolling thunder of wagon trains sends up a massive cloud of dust in the region of Washington's Monument.

"Sherman's Army is on the move!

"It is a full quarter of an hour before they come into sight, but as the cloud rolls ever closer and the drums and bugles ring ever louder, a cheer arises from the throats of the spectators anticipating the general they all have read so much about but have never seen in the flesh—the general named for the great Shawnee warrior, the general whose 'gift' of the captured city of Atlanta to President Lincoln in the dark days of 1864 secured President Lincoln's reelection.

"And now that general appears! He rides alone and erect at the head of a mighty column of infantry, twelve men across! All around us the cry goes up, 'It is he!'"

Sherlock Holmes paused, his eyes glistening. He nodded at the manuscript in my hands, and one last time I read aloud from the remarkable text of Mr. Sherlock Holmes the words I reprint here:

Abraham and I gripped the sycamore branch with both our hands, for
the tree was shaking as the crowds pressed for advantage. "It is Sherman!
It is Sherman!" was the cry, and we strained to make out the figure on
horseback leading his men as they marched in step, their fixed bayonets
glinting in the sun and swaying to the beat of the drummer boys.

There was no mistaking him, Watson: William Tecumseh Sherman,
whose March to the Sea has been recounted in every magazine from *Leslie's
Weekly to Harpers*—"Old Cump" in the newspapers, "Uncle Billy" to his men.

And every inch a general.

I watched transfixed as he brought his mount to a halt not twenty
paces away, so stiff-necked and upright, with such a demeanor of the
utmost seriousness to his slightly crossed eyes, unkempt hair and
dust-covered uniform that one could not but be impressed.

All eyes were upon him as he dismounted, handed the reins to an adjutant
and strode up the steps to the grandstand. Everyone around us—soldiers
and spectators, reporters and clerks—now seemed to hold their breath in
anticipation of what the fiery red-haired conqueror would do when he met
the brilliant and irascible War Secretary upon the viewing platform.

We watched as Sherman shook the hand of President Johnson;
watched as Sherman bent down to grip the hand of Seward, who was
seated, not having fully recovered from the attack in his bedroom on Black
Friday; watched as Sherman came to the outstretched hand of the Edwin
M. Stanton...and brushed right past it.

He instead made straight for Grant, whose hand he gripped with
warmth and fervour. Grant, of whom Sherman had said, "Grant stood by
me when I was crazy, and I stood by Grant when he was drunk, and now
we stand by each other."

It was a snub Mr. Stanton deserved, of course—much as I admired the
man, and as kind as he had been to me during my time in America—but it
was shocking all the same, and that shock was now reflected upon the faces
of everyone who had seen it. Everyone but Grant's, anyway, for Grant's

smile made it known that he still stood by his favourite general. Sherman ignored the gasps and grins and raised eyebrows—and the bright red burn upon Mr. Stanton's face—and took his place next to Grant.

Then together they turned to face Sherman's men, and together they watched them march.

They were lean men, Sherman's Westerners, sunburnt and sturdy— nothing like the finely uniformed soldiers that had been Meade's Easterners. Their shirts were patched, their hats askew, their boots mud-splotched like their general's, and they broke ranks, these men from Wisconsin and Minnesota and Iowa and Illinois and Michigan, when they reached the grandstand to give a proud roar and a toss of their caps for the man they called "Uncle Billy."

And how the tears flowed from that man's eyes, Watson!

Onward the Westerners marched, column after column, even as the sun climbed overhead and then began its descent; even as the dignitaries became restless and deserted the platform for nearby taverns; even as the crowds grew hungry and thinned. First marched the infantry, and then the cavalry, and then the artillery, until the last regiment of the last brigade of the last division of the last corps of the last army of the American Republic had saluted their Uncle Billy.

But even then, Watson, it wasn't over!

Now came the "bummers"—the sutler wagons and the ambulances, the farriers and blade sharpeners, the cooks and undertakers, cattle and the drovers that kept such an army on the move. And after these came the most surprising assembly of all.

The camp followers.

These were the slaves freed by Sherman's men during his march through Georgia and the Carolinas, and they rode muleback or strode barefoot—dressed in black clothes, for the most part, and wearing black armbands or black ribbons in their hair, for they were still in mourning for Marse Abraham—and they fairly electrified the crowd.

It seemed we were watching Freedom in the flesh.

And Freedom was singing that day, Watson! From their throats came a most joyous noise, despite their mourning dress, and that joyous noise was joined by fiddlers and harmonica players, and their step was as lively as their song.

And, yes, Watson, their song—it was the song about a Balm in Gilead.

When it reached our ears, friend Abraham nearly started out of the tree. I caught hold of him that he would not fall, but as he leaned further from its branches, straining his eyes at the swaying and singing and clapping figures moving across our field of vision, I realized with a start that Abraham was, in fact, struggling to be freed.

And so, Watson, I let him go.

In an instant he had leapt down and disappeared among the top hats and frock coats crowding the sidewalks, until—there!—he re-emerged in the Avenue, whistling that song while dodging the camp followers and their horses and pigs and mules, just as he had done that first evening in the Island, and a catch came to my throat just as it had done that evening, until I realized he was not merely running to take part in the festivities.

He was making for a particular wagon with a particular coachman. A coachman who sat tall and erect with a top hat upon his head and a mouth organ to his lips as he steered his wagon straight down the center of Pennsylvania Avenue.

How this coachman controlled his team I know not, for he was playing in such a lively manner that he required both hands to manipulate the instrument even as the wagon team plodded on, and still he kept playing loudly and clearly, even as Abraham caught up to the wagon and hoisted himself onto the step and clambered onto the seat beside him. Only then did the coachman stop playing—and I could see disbelief and joy upon his expressive face and the kind of passion one sees when a great thing happens that seemed impossible and might vanish if it is not embraced.

Now the two were entwined, and as the wagon rolled on past the viewing stand and disappeared into the crowds filling the Avenue, the harmonica sounded again, and it sounded to my ears, Watson, as if two were playing as one. Abraham was together with his father once more.

And I was alone.

Alone, although not in isolation, for the revelers were still vast, and the camp followers made a colourful procession. But as their numbers dwindled and their ranks were infiltrated by drunks and schoolboys on a lark, my attention turned to the grandstand.

Sherman was still there, standing with Grant, although looking much fatigued. He seemed to have aged in just the few weeks since I glimpsed him boarding the *River Queen* at City Point.[77] No doubt the public rebuke from Mr. Stanton had taken its toll upon him, but there were still pride and valour in his face, reflecting the crowd-pleasing performance of his men on their final day under his command.

And now that the parade was nearly concluded, he and Grant had begun to talk in earnest.

I say "he and Grant" talked, Watson, but of course Grant mainly listened and Sherman mainly talked, while a growing crowd of lesser men encircled the two Americans who, more than anyone except the dead Lincoln and the still-mortified Stanton, had preserved the Union.

Then the military band took up a rousing "John Brown's Body" to signal that the Grand Review was ended, and suddenly the platform was overwhelmed by a rush of reporters and preening Congressmen eager to make themselves known to General Grant.

Sherman soon found himself outside a pack of sycophants surrounding his friend.

This seemed not to bother the man, however, for he now took his leave. Without a backward glance, he walked swiftly down the steps, accepted the reins from his adjutant and swung himself into the saddle as he had no doubt done a thousand times before. He was about to give the horse its head when a man with the dress and bearing of a Congressman stepped in his path, waving a program and pencil, beseeching the general for his signature.

It was then that I witnessed an act that any man thrust into a position of eminence would do well to emulate, Watson: the cross-eyed man in the dusty uniform waved off his admirer.

"I did my duty, sir," he said. "That is all."

And with that, the tall, spare figure spurred his horse past the sputtering Congressman, against the surging crowd and away down the Avenue, whilst I

---

77 *Holmes refers to the famous meetings of Lincoln, Grant and Sherman with Admiral Porter on the River Queen at City Point on March 27th and 28th, although his description of those encounters was evidently withheld from this manuscript, probably upon the insistence of Mycroft Holmes.*

jumped down from the sycamore tree and began to make my way to Franklin Square.

I had much to prepare before my journey home.

Early next morning, I said goodbye to my hosts, or, at least, to Mrs. Stanton and Eddie, for Mr. Stanton had worked through the night at the War Department. Mrs. Stanton, if I may say so without evoking vainglory, cried as if losing a son—and you may believe me, Watson, when I say the feeling was much reciprocated on my part.

Eddie Stanton spoke of a plan to return to law studies in London, and he asked whether he might look me up when in England. I told him I would be delighted, and we shook hands warmly. I handed him my note to his father, in which I made explicit my thankfulness for my host's many kindnesses, and was then driven by the Stanton's groomsman to the depot, where I boarded the train for Jersey City.

The carriages were full of men who had been soldiers until that very morning.

They were heading for their homes—many for the first time since they had donned their uniforms—but their mood was somber, not celebratory, as if they had lost something of themselves in putting an end to the war. Some were in their cups, of course, and occasionally one would rise unsteadily in the swaying carriage and call out "Three huzzahs for Grant!" But when no one had joined in, he would sit back down and resume a gloomy stare out the window.

At each stop the train was met by marching bands and wagons bearing family members, which made for very slow going. At the terminus in Jersey City I was met by Mr. Stanton's detective. We ate dinner at the same tavern where he and young Eddie and I had supped the previous May. Then he accompanied me and my trunk across the Hudson and saw me aboard the ship bound for Southampton on the next tide.

In a fortnight I would be reunited with Brother Mycroft.

It was, of course, Mycroft whose modest ambitions for his younger brother had led to this great adventure in America, but I dare say even he could not have foreseen the grand ambition that had been kindled within me as I boarded the ship!

And it was in the cabin on that ship—Mr. Stanton had kindly booked passage with no expense spared—that I resolved to embark upon the systematic study of the necessary branches of science and of the history of crime in order to make myself the greatest consulting detective that England, and, perhaps, the Continent, had ever known.

I had already taken the first step upon that long path, Watson, just before leaving dry land, when it had come time to enter my name in the ship's register.

I had written *"Mr. Sherlock Holmes."*

As the Buddha said, "What we think, we become."

THE END

I removed my spectacles and sat for some little time before folding the manuscript and handing it back to Mycroft. My mind raced with questions, but it seemed churlish to break the pensive mood that had settled upon his brother. When I rose from my chair to stir the fire, however, it was Sherlock Holmes who broke his own reverie, in a voice that spoke of somber, distant thoughts.

"Might I trouble you to hand me my violin, Doctor?"

"Of course, Holmes."

I retrieved the antique instrument and its bow and handed them to my friend. He nestled the body between chin and shoulder, lifted the bow and began to play a mournful air that was instantly familiar to me.

"You recognize it then, Doctor?" he said, gazing intently at my face while he continued playing.

"I would be remiss if I didn't, Holmes. You played it in our rooms at Baker Street too many times to count. Whenever a somber mood was upon you, it seemed to me."

He now sang in his soft, pleasing tenor to the melody that sprang again from his bow:

"*There is a Balm in Gilead to make the wounded whole, there is a balm in Gilead, to heal my sin-sick soul—*"

"Holmes!" I cried, as he brought the song to a halt, smiling at my astonishment. "Why—I thought *you* had composed that tune! Do you mean to tell me *all* those melodies you played in Baker Street were songs learned in America?"

"A good many of them, in any case."

"Why, I gave you credit in my stories for being their composer!"

"I sought no credit, Watson. I simply could not tell you where I had learned them." Holmes resumed his playing, his voice harmonizing soothingly with the sweet tones from his Stradivarius:

"*Sometimes I feel discouraged, and think my work in vain, but then the Holy Spirit revives my soul again.*"

He abruptly stopped his playing and gazed with concern at my face. "What is it, Watson? You think me a thief? A mountebank? Come, come, old friend. Dvořák appropriated the spirituals for several of his greatest symphonies, you know."

"No, it's not that, Holmes. I'm trying to understand why that song held such a sway upon your friend Abraham and his people."

Holmes smiled. "Let me finish it, then." He resumed playing, and his quavering tenor rose above the pleasing sound of the strings:

"*If you cannot preach like Peter, and you cannot pray like Paul, you can tell the love of Jesus, and say 'He died for all.'*"

"Ah. Lincoln," said I, as he laid aside the violin. "He died for all."

"Precisely so. It was a common enough tune among the slave population before the assassination, but as you might imagine, those words took on quite a new significance afterwards."

Holmes now removed his muffler and placed it atop the snoring figure of his brother Mycroft stretched out upon the settee.

"I think it is time we get you home to Mrs. Watson, wouldn't you agree, Doctor? It is quite late, and I have not said good night to the bees."

The night air was cold, and the light of the half moon was diffused by fog. Sherlock Holmes wore a pea-jacket buttoned to the neck. It hung loosely from his thinning frame, and he walked slowly with a limp and relied upon his stick, for his tumble upon the footpath had given his hip a soreness that had not gone away.

Holmes spoke softly to the bees. He spoke of the new varietals he would plant in the garden for the nourishment of his winged friends come spring, of his plans for the construction of several new hives, of the queens Mr. Sturgess would soon be delivering to restore *Eighth Sister* honey into the cupboards of England.

When he had said good night to the last hive, we strolled beyond the apple trees to the stile, where I said good night to my friend and then walked carefully down the moonlit footpath to the farmhouse, a haunting melody playing softly in my mind above the shrill call of a mockingbird as I entered its territory.

The melody of *A Balm in Gilead*.

Chapter Three

SPRING

The seasons turn differently in the country than in the town, and seemingly overnight.

It was one morning in early February that I was making my way to the cottage of Sherlock Holmes before dawn, bundled up against the cold, when I felt something different in the air from the morning before and the morning before that.

I felt the absence of the sharp rawness in the morning chill.

I loosened my muffler and carried on.

Such was the beginning of spring upon the Downs—and the rhythms of life in the countryside, though new to me, became evident as the days lengthened. Fields were tilled and planted, hayricks were assembled, empty sheep pens were filled with bleating and hungry sheep. As the early shoots began to break upwards through the warming soil, green hues effaced the brown earth of the countryside, while from the branches of Holmes's apple trees and the dense thicket of the yew hedges there sprouted the pink and yellow blossoms that would soon feed his hungry charges.

Across the valley, the hospital tents of Summerdown were being removed—the influenza epidemic having subsided almost as mysteriously as it had begun—and in their place, a demobilization center for the troops returning from France was being erected.

With warmer temperatures, too, came the return of the greengrocer to Holmes's kitchen, for Margaret was eager to prepare a new variety of meals from his fresh bounty and she had convinced Holmes to forgive the talkative man's indiscretions regarding the episode of the bee encounter.

I, of course, was anxious to begin the practical application of my winter beekeeping studies upon Holmes's hives, for the new queens were due any day.

Mycroft Holmes had not visited since Christmas, so occupied had he been in the Government's preparations for the upcoming peace negotiations at Versailles, but our old friend Lestrade came by regularly to brief us on the upcoming Moriarty trial. He often stayed for dinner and took great pleasure in supplying the missing details of several of our more obscure but instructive cases which I had been preparing for the publisher.

Sherlock Holmes, when he was not reliving one case or another with Lestrade and myself, spent long stretches at his desk slowly pecking away at his typewriting machine, or intently studying what he had typed, pencil in hand, making corrections. His natural secretiveness precluded me from asking him to share with me the contents of this portion of his work, but I gathered he had moved beyond the autobiographical details and was hard at work upon that which he had set out to write concerning *The Art and Science of Rational Deduction*.

It was in the third week of February that Sherlock Holmes, after working diligently all morning at the typewriter, simply keeled over at his desk.

I was in the yard preparing the smoker when the greengrocer who had been taking tea in the kitchen with Margaret, burst from the door shouting for help. They had heard a noise and found Holmes slumped against his typewriter, his forehead dangerously hot. Together we were able to get him into his bed, where he lay alternately wracked by fever and chills.

Fearing the influenza, I sent at once for his brother from London and began the administration of fluids while Margaret assisted in the refreshing of his linens and bedding.

Mycroft Holmes arrived less than two hours later in the company of a specialist from Harley Street whose discretion could be relied upon. Mycroft was considerably taken aback by his brother's appearance and blamed the greengrocer (irrationally, I felt, for the epidemic appeared to be receding), muttering that the fellow's rounds throughout the village and his proclivity to stop for "chin-wags" along the way, had, he surmised, turned the man into an exceedingly efficient carrier of the lethal flu.

Sherlock Holmes missed nothing, of course, even in his reduced state, and smiled wanly as the doctor examined him while we watched with anxious faces.

"I look better with my hair combed," he said with a soft chuckle, after the doctor had removed the thermometer from his mouth.

"Your hair hardly enters into it, Sherlock."

"You mistake my levity for vanity, Mycroft. It was a habit of Mr. Lincoln to make that self-deprecating remark to place visitors at ease when they found themselves gaping at his rather forlorn appearance."

"Mr. Lincoln had a quote for every occasion, it seems."

"It was his way, Mycroft." Sherlock Holmes coughed several times for the specialist, then resumed his line of thought in a halting manner, interrupted by chills. "He told stories the way a honeybee uses its dance to indicate the route to the best flowers. He made his points without orders or bluster. It was highly effective."

"Well, I am not so fortunate as to work for a genial storyteller, Sherlock. My taskmaster is rather less patient and takes my absences unkindly. I must get back to town for supper at Downing Street. The negotiations are bogged down in some rather petty business. Dr. Watson will keep you well in hand, I should think."

"I would ask this specialist—" Holmes nodded at the tight-lipped little man, who was checking his pulse for the third time "—to look after *you*, Mycroft. I dare say they are running you ragged."

"The wages of peace, Sherlock, the wages of peace. I am trying to impart something of the sensibilities of Mr. Lincoln to the jackals who wish to tear Germany apart."

"Our country is the better for your efforts."

Mycroft Holmes gripped his brother's hand, his own eyes moist. "Thank you, Sherlock. It goes without saying our green and pleasant land is much the better for you."

Soon, Sherlock Holmes had fallen asleep, and Mycroft Holmes departed for London, specialist in tow. All were agreed that there was nothing to do but to see that Sherlock Holmes got rest and fluids.

Word of Holmes's condition spread quickly throughout that small village. The next morning brought no end of farmwives to the kitchen door bearing freshly laid eggs, warm bread and fattened ducks for the man to whom they all referred, with the utmost respect, as "Mr. Sherlock." The afternoon brought the menfolk, including several I had gotten to know since our move to Went Hill.

There was Tony the cabman from Polegate; Jack, the landlord of the Tiger Inn (his son was the fellow helping Miss Colvin with the honey-making preparations); and, of course, Vicar Evans from the parish church. The vicar was a kindly man who, like Holmes, kept bees and was quite an expert in the Neolithic artifacts turned up by the farmers upon the Downs.

By evening Holmes had recovered enough strength to sit before the fire, and I could not help remarking upon the day's intrusion of polite and thankful neighbors, each of whom had shared with us their stories of Sherlock Holmes's assistance in the minor mysteries that befall the inhabitants of a village in the countryside.

"Now, Holmes," said I. "You once told me the countryside filled you with horror. *More sins are committed in these villages than in the vilest alleys in London*, you said. And yet there you sit, eating biscuits from the baker to whom you supplied honey when the sugar disappeared from the shops and drinking your tea with cream from the farmer whose stray cows you once traced—hardly the stuff of vile alleys! What say you now?"

My friend smiled somewhat ruefully.

"I *was* rather didactic in those days, wasn't I, Watson?" said he in a soft, weak voice. "Well, the road to the truth is indeed a long road, and I was barely started upon my way when I made that rather over-broad assertion."

"But where did you find the time to run hither and yon to clear up all their minor little cases?"

"Minor to *you*, Watson, but not to *them*, I can assure you."

"All right, but, still, how did you do it?"

Holmes turned his gaze to me, his grey eyes recovering something of their merriment.

"You've seen my lair, Watson. You know my habits. Deduce it."

It had been some years since Sherlock Holmes had put me to such a challenge, and I felt quite put on the spot. But Margaret was looking on with an expectant face, and I did not wish to disappoint her.

"Well," said I, thinking back upon that which I had witnessed of Holmes's life at the cottage, "we can eliminate the idea that you scurry around the village. Tracking footprints in barns and hayfields with your lens at this time of your life, and with a manuscript to write and bee colonies to maintain, is surely impossible."

Holmes nodded. "Good, Watson! Excellent!"

"Your clients are likewise hard-working men and women. They can't very well leave their ovens and fields to consult with you here. You must have some other means to accumulate the facts—"

"Bravo, Watson! You scintillate!"

"Miss Colvin, perhaps?"

Holmes said nothing.

"A stable boy? The charwoman?"

Holmes glanced at Margaret, a slight smile playing upon his lips.

"I doubt a charwoman or a stable boy would be able to spy upon a whole village, John," said Margaret. "And Miss Colvin would certainly stand out among the townsfolk."

Holmes nodded approvingly. "Well said, madam."

"Then it must be someone who knows everyone in the village, and to whom confidences are given willingly," said I, thinking through the many visitors who had come to our door while Holmes glanced from Margaret to me between sips of tea.

I had it! "The vicar!" I cried, with some little triumph.

"Really, Watson. Do you believe Vicar Evans is so indiscreet a fellow as that?" Sherlock Holmes shook his head. "I would no more rely upon his kindly eyes and trusting manner to keep me up on the earthly sins of his flock than I would ask you to inform upon your patients."

"Then how do you do it, Holmes? I am at a loss."

A mischievous twinkle came to his grey eyes.

"I will let you and Mrs. Watson in on my secret, but it must go no further than this cottage."

"You have my word."

"And mine," said Margaret.

"There is no confidant who brings me my cases. Nor do I run hither and yon to investigate, as you correctly divined. In point of fact, I go no further than the Tiger."

"The pub! Of course!"

"Yes, it has been a hobby of mine during these retirement years to spend an evening or two of a fortnight getting my supper at the Tiger, dressed in a different guise as the mood suits me—now a ship's carpenter, now a brick-layer, now a blind fiddler, but never as Sherlock Holmes. I take the window seat, I listen, and I observe."

"You mean to say no one ever recognizes the man beneath the disguise?" Margaret said, with more skepticism than I would have dared muster.

"My skills in that department are, if I may say so, madam, somewhat better than the commonplace actor."

"And by sitting in the window seat," said I, "you keep your face in shadow!"

"Precisely so, Watson."

"But why take up a disguise in the first place?"

"Because I mean to *observe*, madam. And observation without disguise is impossible—thank your husband and his busy pen for that! Undisguised, I could not take my seat at the Tiger before all conversation would cease and the patrons would begin settling up with Jack."

He saw Margaret's skeptical face and smiled knowingly.

"No, madam, that is not my conceit, as you surmise. It is my understanding of human nature. The very act of posing as an observer causes behaviour to change, you see, rendering the observation faulty. It is a principle upon which I have considered writing a monograph..."

Holmes drifted off as a chill gripped his body and so Margaret replenished his tea while I took his pulse. After several minutes, the chill passed, and he was able to resume.

"Anyway, there I sit in my window seat while the unsuspecting subjects go about with their pints and their darts. I hear it all!" A gleam came back into his eye. "A sheep disappears from Mrs. Smith's pen—I *know* upon whose table its shanks furnished dinner! A horse is nicked from Mr. Weiss's stable block, and I can tell him whither the tracks lead. I'll take you both one day, when the weather turns."

And he did.

It was upon the following Saturday, when Holmes had recovered enough strength for the short walk into the village, that he and I made for the Tiger. Margaret stayed behind, fearing the smoky atmosphere of the pub would inflame her asthma. Sherlock Holmes went undisguised, for his days in bed had sapped his stamina.

And it was well that my companion was not gotten up! Before we were even able to take our seats, he was greeted with warmth and a certain respectful familiarity by the regulars of the Tiger, which much pleased him.

We settled in—Holmes in the window seat, I opposite him—and I could see that he commanded not only an unobstructed view of the bar and the dartboard, but the entry to the snug as well. As we sat and drank our pints, Holmes kept up, under his breath, a running commentary upon each new villager who entered—his name, the size of his farm, number of cows or sheep owned, injuries suffered in the fields, sons lost in this terrible Great War, etc. etc.

When the girl arrived with our shepherd's pies, however, his attention turned to his food, for he had quite recovered his appetite. Still, he ate very slowly, and I had finished my meal and turned to a copy of the *Eastbourne Gazette* nearby while he continued to nourish himself.

After a time, I felt Holmes's keen eyes upon me as I turned the pages.

"You do jump around there, Watson," he observed between mouthfuls.

"It is these accounts of the peace conference. I am trying to stay up on the negotiations."

"Any mention of Brother Mycroft?"

"You don't mean to say he has been called to Versailles!"

"Not yet, Watson. But any day I expect to see it. He would bring a quite rational atmosphere to the proceedings by his formidable person."

I put down the paper and met my friend's eyes. "You are fortunate to have had such a brother, Holmes. You seem to have absorbed every lesson in life from him."

"I stood upon Mycroft's shoulders, certainly. But there were others."

"That chemist at DuPont, I suppose?"

"Monsieur Vernet, yes, very much so. I'm afraid I rather copied so many of his methods and mannerisms it is hard for me to say where his teaching left off and my own development began."

I sensed Holmes had others in mind as well. "Mr. Stanton, perhaps?"

Holmes shook his head. "No, Watson. He was far too busy to offer advice, and I only ever saw him on Sundays. His prodigious work habits *did* set a good example, of course..." He had set down his fork and lapsed into silence, but the glint in his eye told me he had another, particular figure in mind.

"Not Lincoln, Holmes?"

"It was quite serendipitous, Watson—"

"But surely the President was ten *times* as busy as Mr. Stanton!"

"Undoubtedly so, Watson. It was a mere flash of illumination—expressed in a minute. But it has lasted me a lifetime."

"Holmes, I pray! Tell me!"

"Well, now, it was some few days into our Richmond journey. I was outside the stateroom waiting for Tad—his mother often kept me waiting when I was to take the boy for some amusement or other—and the President emerged looking for Crook, the guard. When he spotted the book in my hand, however, he forgot entirely about whatever business he was on.

"*Hamlet!*" Holmes adopted an American voice in a high treble key. "'*He's a good 'un. But have you read the Bible yet?*'

"I shook my head and a look of disapproval crossed the expressive face of Mr. Abraham Lincoln. He made a motion with his hand, of a farmer sowing corn, and gave me the lesson of a lifetime.

"'*Don't scatter yourself like wild seed, boy! Plants grow best when they grow in relation to one another. Row upon row, sharing nourishment and shade. So it is with knowledge! But, even better, knowledge builds on itself—it compounds, like money in the bank. So read the great ones, in order, row upon row. To understand Shakespeare, you must know the Romans and the Greeks—but it starts with the Bible. Begin with Genesis. Read both testaments, straight through. Then read them again, more slowly. Then a third time—and you'll find you've learned a thing or two.*'

"Then, Watson, he tilted his head up and recited,

"'*In the beginning God created the heavens and the earth—*'

"Now he stopped and smiled that great, sad smile.

"'*They say I tell stories, by jingo, and they're right. But the Saviour spoke in parables, so I guess I'm not in bad company!*'

"By then, Mrs. Lincoln appeared, and my lesson was over." Holmes sat for some few moments, evidently moved by the memory. "I had already taught myself how to read, Watson, but it was upon that evening I was taught how to *learn*. It was a principal I carried with me the rest of my life."

"That was quite a gift, Holmes."

"And not the only gift from that man. By no means was it the only one."

"The Weems book?"

"Yes, Watson. The Weems book."

"Why did you presume young Moriarty was trying to steal it that night? What makes it of such value?"

"Because it is entirely unique! Lincoln read it as a young boy—and well into manhood—and almost every page is marked in his hand. Of course there is his signature as well. And then there is—well, let us just say that any collector would want it."

"But why have you kept it hidden from Mycroft?"

"For the same reason I never gave him the Booth papers. It would have gone straight to the Prime Minister and I would never have seen it again."

"I expect you keep it with your bank in London?"

"No, Watson, it is far too valuable to entrust to anyone else. I keep it quite close at hand."

"What, at the cottage? It must be very well hidden. Neither Margaret nor I have ever come across it!"

"Well, it is, rather," said Sherlock Holmes slyly.

"In your garret, I presume."

But he had turned his attention to the dart players assembling for a match, and our conversation ended.

For some time we sat in silence, absorbed by the proficiency of the Tiger darts-men—*Plunk! Plunk! Plunk!*—and the chaff and teasing as they waited their turns. Sherlock Holmes showed no signs of tiring. Indeed, he seemed quite refreshed by the pleasant meal and was following with keen interest the debate among the darts-men about the leading figures of the recent war and which man ranked above the others—our man Haig or Joffre of France or "Black Jack" Pershing, the American.

It was Haig who received the most vocal support, of course, but I now put the question to Holmes. He smiled thoughtfully, as if he had been expecting my question.

"General Sherman said that of all the men of high office he had ever met, Lincoln combined more elements of greatness and goodness than any he had come to know. I suspect, Watson, that none has risen so high as Lincoln. Even one of our own."

"And yet Sherman was a rather controversial figure himself, was he not, Holmes? You wrote fondly of him in your memoirs, I know, but was he not responsible for the burning of Savannah?"

Holmes chuckled. "I take it you've been reading some of those books on the Reconstruction that Mycroft left behind?"

"Yes, I thought it well to learn something of that period."

"Excellent, Watson! But it was Columbia, South Carolina, that burned, not Savannah. And it was Sherman's men who put *out* those flames. The Confederates had torched their own stores of cotton bales to keep them from Sherman's Army."

"Well I don't know about that, but—"

"Ah, but *I* do, Watson. And it is a fact."

"What, then, of Sherman's 'March to the Sea'? Was that not rather cruel—taking the war to civilians?"

"'War is cruelty, and you cannot refine it.' Sherman said that, too, Watson. He understood better than the politicians that to end the war, the North had to end the South's willingness to fight."

Holmes now lit a cigarette, despite my protestations.

"I feel better by the hour, Watson. Whatever knocked me down is on the retreat."

"I don't approve, Holmes."

"You change the subject, Watson. We were talking about Sherman, of whom you also disapprove."

"Yes, well, he was rather intolerant of the Negro, was he not?"

Holmes's eyebrows arched.

"Are you speaking of the same Sherman as I? The General who freed some hundred thousand human beings on that march to the sea through Georgia? It is quite true, Watson, Sherman was no more genial towards the Negro than many of his peers. I wouldn't suggest otherwise. But I take it there was no mention of his Special Order 15 in these books? I see by your face there was none. Pity. It granted miles of coastland to the slaves who had been farming it for their white masters. Did those authors also fail to mention the thousands of freed slaves who followed Sherman and his men all the way to Washington City and marched in the Grand Review?"

Sherlock Holmes shot a scornful glance at the newspaper on the table.

"Beware what you *read*, Watson. Too often a writer seeks to satisfy his readers—not challenge them. And those books you've been reading suffer that very affliction, I'm afraid."

"Then what of Lincoln, Holmes? I have read so much of him and yet you make me feel I know very little."

Sherlock Holmes tossed his cigarette stub in the grate and smiled.

"I can help with that."

He lit another cigarette and puffed meditatively for some few moments, his eyes glinting.

"If you won't take General Sherman's kind words about Mr. Lincoln, perhaps those of Frederick Douglass[78] would do, Watson?"

"I should think so! They were close, then?"

"Not exactly. Early in the war Douglass had expressed dissatisfaction with Lincoln's management of the emancipation question, quite publicly, too. So Lincoln did what he often did when presented with a dissenting view—he invited Douglass to talk about it. Several times, in fact. The two men developed quite a mutual respect. Remarkable, really, when you consider that prior to Lincoln, Negros had only gained admittance to the White House as valets and waiters."

Some little time went by as we watched the darts match and I turned over in my mind Holmes's observations.

"You evidently believe there is no other man could have accomplished what Lincoln accomplished, then?"

"I *know* it, Watson. There were times I waited outside Mr. Stanton's door with men who would come to grace those history books you've been reading—and you would not let one of them woo your sister. They had not a strand of moral fiber in their being. None could have done what Lincoln did."

"What, exactly, did he do?"

"Why, he kept the Union without compromising on the slavery question."

"And that was difficult because...?"

"Pressure, Watson. Incredible pressure. Pressure to give in, to give up, to be done with the war. Pressure to cut the South free and let them be."

"But he was the President! Surely he could do what he thought right."

"Easily said, not so easy to do when the newspapers are bringing pictures of dead soldiers into the taverns and the homes." Holmes studied the

---

78 *A former slave who became an abolitionist newspaper publisher, activist, author and human rights leader, and would also become the first African-American nominated for Vice President of the United States. The motto of one of his newspapers read, "Right is of No Sex – Truth is of No Color – God is the Father of us all, and we are all brethren."*

cigarette in his fingers. "Tell me, Watson, how many soldiers did Wellington lose at Waterloo—three thousand? Four? And how many Northern soldiers died in Mr. Lincoln's war from bullets and disease? Do you recall from the books? Five thousand? Twenty-five thousand? Fifty? No, Watson, it was more than *three hundred thousand*."

Holmes exhaled a ring of smoke and shook his head.

"If my little scouting trip with Abraham across the barrens of New Jersey taught me anything, it was that feelings ran high against the war in surprising corners of America. Mark my words. Had any other man stood in Mr. Lincoln's place, the North might well have let the South go. America as it stands today would not exist. And slavery would still be with them!"

"But what made him so uncommon?"

Holmes studied the dart players as they prepared for another match. The darts disappeared in their giant hands as they were pulled from the cork.

"Well of course, physically Lincoln was quite a robust specimen from his log-splitting days. His grip was not of this world—"

"Yes, your description was quite vivid."

"And he neither smoked nor drank spirits." Holmes glanced ruefully from the cigarette in his thin fingers to the empty pint glass before him. "I rather think such abstinence gave his mind a peculiar lucidity not common to men of that era, who frequently started their days with some form of punch—the water being so unreliable. And, of course, he was one of the best-read men of his day."

"But surely there were many fit, well-read men in America, Holmes!"

"Yes, but they hadn't read Weems the way Mr. Lincoln had read it."

"What, tall tales about George Washington chopping down the cherry tree?"

"No, Watson, not those fanciful stories of boyhood years. It was Washington's farewell address. Weems quotes it verbatim—the portion devoted to the Union, anyway. And Lincoln had marked up nearly every sentence when he was just *a boy*."

"Indeed!"

"Yes. A most forceful address it was, too. Washington didn't mince words. It was the Union over everything—*everything*—and quite

compellingly reasoned. Lincoln memorized it and he never forgot it."
Holmes smiled. "There was no mention of Weems in those books you've
been reading, either?"

"No, Holmes."

"I don't doubt it. I've never seen its influence commented upon in
the serious histories of the times—although it was known to be Lincoln's
favourite book."

"Well, I should like to study it someday."

Holmes considered this for a moment. "Mycroft is not here to object—
perhaps I will read a selection when we return to the cottage."

"I should like that, Holmes."

Plunk! Plunk! Plunk!

We watched the darts for a time, but I sensed Holmes's eyes
studying me.

"Do those books mention the Gettysburg Address by any chance,
Watson?"

"Of course..."

"Dare I ask what they say about it?"

"Well, it was a good speech, certainly. But—well, it was just a speech, I
should think."

"If Magna Carta was just a *contract*, yes," said Holmes, with no little
asperity. "Gettysburg was a speech that changed the American cause,
Watson. For all time."

Plunk! Plunk! Plunk!

"How?"

"By declaring that all men are created equal—as Jefferson had set out in
the Declaration of Independence. You'll recall the American Constitution
had decreed the Negro worth only three-fifths of a white? Well that notion
ended at Gettysburg. Lincoln turned three-fifths of a man into a whole man.
In a three-minute speech. Quite a leap for one speech, don't you think?"

"Why, then, did his Emancipation Proclamation fail to free the Negro—"

I was stopped short by a look from Sherlock Holmes such that I had
never seen.

"I beg your pardon, Watson?"

I blushed hotly as I attempted to recall the criticism I had been reading. "The Emancipation Proclamation was, in practice, a rather empty document, as I see it."

"Indeed, Watson, is that how you see it?"

"Well, as it freed only slaves in the South, where the Union Army held no sway, it was an empty promise, was it not?"

"The worst travesty ever promulgated by the anti-Lincoln scolds, Watson. You really ought to expand your reading list." Sherlock Holmes lit a third cigarette. "That proclamation was a promise that was ultimately redeemed all across the South. Did you *not* read my manuscript?"

"I did—but surely the slaves weren't freed until the Union soldiers won back those states!"

"Did you think the slave owners were going to give up their legal rights without a fight? Until the Thirteenth Amendment, Watson, slavery was *legal* in America." Holmes shook his head severely. "You disappoint me, Doctor, parroting inanities."

"Well I am sorry, Holmes. Naturally, if I had had your experiences in America—"

"You would have heard Abraham's mother tell of the day the Yankee horseman appeared at the edge of her master's field. *The day Freedom come*, she called it."

Holmes's sharp, grey eyes held mine.

"Think about that, Watson: the mere *appearance* of a blue-clad soldier meant Freedom for every slave on the plantation. It was, without exception, the greatest day of her life. *Their* lives. They thrilled to tell the story—every person at the Freedman's Village. 'I worked for marse for such-and-such years, until *Freedom*.' 'My mother worked on such-and-such plantation until *Freedom*.'"

The passion in Holmes's voice rather took my breath away.

"I should know better than to express opinions with an incomplete understanding of the facts behind them," I meekly apologized.

"You're not the first, Watson. You won't be the last!" Holmes studied me for a moment out of the corner of his eye, and his voice softened. "I have one rather large advantage over you and the scolds."

"You saw it firsthand."

"Precisely so. Look to it, Watson. Without the Proclamation, there would have been no freedom when the Union soldiers appeared on those plantations. And without Lincoln, there would have been no Proclamation."

"I am quite satisfied, Holmes."

"So too was Abraham's mother!" said he with a chuckle. "She changed her son's name to Abraham the moment they reached Washington City!"

Holmes turned his gaze out the window behind him, where the moon was rising bright and full above the green. I was relieved at no longer being lectured by my friend.

"Mycroft grasped my friendship with Abraham at once. 'You were kindred spirits!' he said when I had recounted that first visit to the Navy Yard Bridge. 'Lost fathers, maltreated mothers, a childhood without mirth and spirit.' And he was right, Watson. Not to be maudlin about it, but we were two of a kind—if an ocean apart."

A tone of immeasurable regret had crept into Holmes's voice, and I did not need his extraordinary ability to follow a train of thought backwards to its station of origin to guess what was going through his mind. After some little hesitation, I took it upon myself to ask the question which, until that moment, I had dared not ask.

"Whatever happened, Holmes?"

He did not respond. Did not even turn away from the window.

"I meant, to the boy. To your friend, Abraham."

"I know what you meant, Watson," he said quietly, still staring out the window.

It was a good five minutes before his shoulders dropped and he turned to face me. His expression was one of ineffable sadness.

"History was not kind to the sons and daughters of slavery, Watson— as I hope those books you have been reading make clear. So-called 'Reconstruction' became a kind of, oh, a reincarnation of the very suppression of one skin shade by another that Lincoln's Proclamation had sought to end."

"And Abraham?"

Sherlock Holmes shook his head.

"The reunion with his father was sweet, but very brief, I'm afraid. I don't know exactly what took the father back to Augusta, where he had been sold, but there were obligations at the old homestead. As for Abraham..." Holmes became very grave. "He made the fateful error of catching a runaway horse carrying a terrified young white girl in the presence of her brother, who was too paralyzed with fear to move. This embarrassed the brother, of course, and he made the outrageous claim of an impure motive on the part of my friend—"

Holmes stopped talking as the barmaid came by to clear the dishes, and I engaged her in conversation while Holmes busied himself attempting to light yet another cigarette.

When she had departed, Holmes put aside the unlit cigarette and fixed me with his eyes. "*A lynching*, they called it, Watson. *A lynching*!"

His eyes were grey, piercing and cold, his voice distant.

"As if it were something other than murder."

Holmes winced as the *Plunk! Plunk! Plunk!* sounded from the cork.

"A most beastly, inhumane murder."

"I am sorry, Holmes. I am very sorry."

After some few moments, I excused myself and left Sherlock Holmes alone with his thoughts.

"Jack wanted you to have this," said I, returning from the bar and placing a glass of sherry before my friend, whose mood by that time appeared to have been considerably revived by a dramatic conclusion to the darts competition.

"Thank you, Doctor. I have quite shaken off my brown study." He applauded the winner and acknowledged the darts-men's hearty appreciation, for one or two of them had evidently sought his help in the past.

"Then perhaps you will indulge me one more question, Holmes? About the night of the assassination?"

"Good old Watson! Here was I thinking how excellent is the Tiger mutton once again now that this war is behind us—and you want to take my mind back to the worst night of my life!"

By the satisfied look upon his face, however, I knew that Holmes meant nothing of his jibe.

"Well, really, Watson, I enjoy nothing more than taking my mind back to America in those days. What is it you wish me to clarify?"

"You write that Mr. Stanton knew nothing of the assassination when you reached him at the Seward home—but how is that possible? I should think such terrible news would have been brought to the War Secretary at once."

"An excellent question, Watson. Mycroft did not understand it, either. But to get news to Mr. Stanton that night, one had to *find* him, and that was not an easy thing in those primitive days. There were no telephones, of course, and no cars—and the streets were at a standstill, with the crowds still in rapture over the great news from Appomattox. Four years of war was ended! Lincoln had saved the Union! To think, somehow, that he was now gone? By a single pistol shot? Fired by an *actor*? In front of a thousand spectators? It was unimaginable. Impossible! Even when people heard the news, they couldn't bring themselves to believe it."

"But why wasn't Mr. Stanton at the theatre with the President in the first place? From all that you say about him, he had a rather ruthless instinct for power. Surely an evening in public with President and Mrs. Lincoln, on the heels of the great victory of the Northern Armies, would have been quite a feather in his cap."

"Yet another excellent observation, Watson. The Tiger sherry improves your mind by the minute! That very question was raised in some of the less savory Northern newspapers at the time as proof Mr. Stanton had a hand in the killing."

"What? I don't believe it, Holmes!"

"Believe it, Watson. One must never doubt the tendency of the crowd to ascribe the most lurid of motives to the most innocent of explanations."

"And what *was* the explanation?"

"Ellen Stanton was morbidly afraid of Mary Lincoln. Simple as that. The Grants declined for precisely the same reason. Julia Grant could not be in the same room as Mrs. L."

"So, the lives of Stanton and Grant were possibly spared from assassination thanks to their wives?"

"Absurd, Watson, is it not? But such was the perverse influence of Mary Lincoln—not that I fault the poor woman. Her family were Confederates, slave-owners, and she had always been viewed with mistrust in the North. Then she lost two sons. She was a painful case. Ellen Stanton, though..."

A look of fond remembrance came to Holmes's face.

"She was such as any boy would have wished to have called his mother."

"Did you remain in touch with her?"

"No, Watson. Her husband died not long after the war ended, and she moved back to Ohio."

"What became of young Eddie?"

"I never saw him again—although he did return to his studies at Cambridge and made some effort to contact me through Mycroft at the time."

"Mycroft refused to allow it?"

"Well, there was still some tenderness with that American business."

"Or perhaps Eddie was in some sort of trouble and needed your help again!"

Sherlock Holmes shrugged his shoulders. "I like to think he was a changed man after the assassination—that perhaps he set out to make something of his life."

"He hardly seemed the type, Holmes."

"One has to climb the mountain, Watson. A very wise man told me that."

"Mr. Lincoln, I suppose?"

"No, Watson. Not he."

Something in the glint in Holmes's eye gave me pause.

"Who, Holmes?"

"You might recall where my travels took me during those three years I spent *incognito*?"

"Yes, something of them. To Mecca and Khartoum I believe?"

"There was a third destination. Do you remember it?"

I shook my head as Holmes savored the last of his sherry, then put down his glass.

"Well, perhaps it is a subject for another day, Watson."

"Ah! That must be what I have seen you working on at your typewriter, then!"

But Holmes did not answer me.

We said good night to Jack and the regulars of the Tiger, bundled ourselves tightly against the evening chill and took our leave, the moon lighting our way across the village green, past the long shadow of the zeppelin gun. At the lamp box, Holmes stopped and studied the sky full of silver stars shining brightly over the Channel to the south.

"It was on a night such as this I sailed out of New York harbour with my violin and sea chest, Watson."

"A sea chest full of some very valuable keepsakes!"

"I wouldn't call this pea-jacket terribly valuable," said he, glancing down at his coat.

"Surely that is not the coat from America, Holmes."

"Surely it is, Watson. Do you not perceive the sulfurous odour of rotten eggs?"

"Not especially."

"Ah, but it is dry tonight. When the air is damp, the Brandywine comes back to me every time. Quite a pleasant remembrance, too. Speaking of which," Holmes said, resuming his walk, "let me go on ahead so that I may fetch the Weems book. We shall have a short reading before bedtime."

I watched him disappear past the bake-house and then followed at a slow pace. Upon entering the cottage by the kitchen door, I found Margaret preparing tea.

"Where is Holmes?" I asked.

"In the living room, stirring the fire. He sent me outside in his old, brusque fashion, no explanation, then called me back in after a minute. Asked me to fix tea and join him by the fire when you had returned." She paused from straining the leaves. "He seemed quite himself, John."

"Yes. And he has a reading for us."

"I should like to hear it!"

We found Holmes seated in his armchair, leafing through a thick brown leather volume, which he handled delicately, even reverently, as Margaret set out the cups.

He held up the book as an auctioneer would display for a select audience his rarest manuscript, then read out the title page:

The Life of George Washington,
With Curious Anecdotes, Equally Honorable To Himself
And Exemplary To His Young Countrymen

Next, he turned to a page that appeared so heavily marked—with sentences underscored and comments jotted down in the margins—as to be difficult to read.

"Watson, are you comfortable? Madam? Excellent. Lend me your ears, for I have in my hands the Farewell Address of the late President Washington—much studied and memorized by a young boy who would himself become President. I think you will find it most illuminating."

Then, speaking slowly and distinctly, Sherlock Holmes read with reverence and respect the words that he believed had impelled the man who had saved a country from self-destruction.

For reasons both historic and personal I reprint them in the manner Holmes accented them, as they were highlighted by Lincoln himself. The excerpt is brief, and yet its import is enduring:

"Citizens, by birth or choice, of a common country, that country has a right to concentrate your affections. The name of AMERICAN, which belongs to you in your national capacity, must always exact the just pride of patriotism, more than any appellation derived from <u>local discriminations.</u>

"With slight shades of difference, you have the same religion, manners, habits and political principles. You have, in a common cause, fought and triumphed together. The independence and liberty you possess are the work

of joint councils, and joint efforts—of common dangers, sufferings and successes.

"But these considerations, however powerfully they address themselves to your sensibility, are greatly outweighed by those which apply more immediately to your interest. Here every portion of our country finds the most commanding motives for <u>carefully guarding and preserving the union of the whole.</u>

"The NORTH, in an unrestrained intercourse with the SOUTH, protected by the equal laws of a common government, finds in the productions of the SOUTH, great additional resources of maritime and commercial enterprise, and precious materials of manufacturing industry.

The SOUTH, in the same intercourse benefiting by the agency of the NORTH, sees its agriculture grow, and its commerce expand.

"The EAST, in a like intercourse with the WEST, already finds, and in the progressive improvement of interior communications, by land and water, will more and more find a valuable vent for the commodities which it brings from abroad, or manufactures at home.

"The WEST derives from the EAST supplies requisite for its growth and comfort: and what is, perhaps, of still greater consequence, it must of necessity owe the SECURE enjoyment of indispensable OUTLETS for its own productions, to the weight, influence, and the future maritime strength of the Atlantic side of the Union, <u>directed by an indissoluble community of the interest, as ONE NATION.</u>

"While then every part of our country thus feels an immediate and particular interest in union, all the parties COMBINED cannot fail to find, in the united mass of means and efforts, greater strength, greater resources, proportionably greater security from external danger, a less frequent interruption of their peace by foreign nations.

"In this sense it is, that your <u>union ought to be considered as a main prop of your liberty,</u> and that the love of the one ought to endear to you the preservation of the other."

Holmes closed the book and glanced from Margaret to me with twinkling eyes.

"Remarkable!" said I. "Just remarkable, Holmes. That is the very line President Lincoln took throughout the Civil War!"

"Precisely so, Watson. He had learned the lesson at a young age, and it never left him."

"And this is one of those books your brother left behind?" Margaret asked.

"No madam. This was President Lincoln's own. I brought it with me from America."

She gasped in surprise.

"It is the Weems book, then, from your journal?"

"The very same, madam."

She appeared much perplexed.

"And you have kept it hidden on the shelf among the cookery and housekeeping books all this time?"

Now it was Sherlock Holmes's turn to be surprised.

"Why, yes—but, as you did not see me retrieve it, may I ask how you deduced this?"

"You sent me out of the kitchen, and I have used every inch of that kitchen excepting the cookbooks, which are out of my reach. Where else could it have been hidden?"

"A woman after my own heart, Watson!" Holmes chuckled. "My cottage has been ransacked three times over the years—young Moriarty was only the latest—and they always went for the garret. It's a fine thing you were not here to point the way, madam!"

"You never worried that I would come across it?"

"Your childhood in India has given your cooking a distinctly Eastern cast," said Holmes, with a shrug of his shoulders. "I judged the Scottish recipe books would hold no interest for you."

Margaret gazed at my friend with no little admiration written upon her face.

"I understand why John holds you in such esteem, sir."

Sherlock Holmes coloured, but then, as was his custom, turned the topic away from himself.

"You seem rather introspective, Watson."

"I just can't help but wonder that you have kept that book hidden all this time, Holmes. Surely any historian would wish—"

"Sometimes, Doctor," said Sherlock Holmes, yawning as he closed the cover and held the book in his lap, "great knowledge is merely a thing worth knowing."

He declined Margaret's offer of tea.

"Thank you, madam, but I feel suddenly very tired. I must get an early start on my manuscript tomorrow, for the new queens arrive this week, and your husband and I will be inspecting the hives before lunchtime. Please take the torch as you see yourself out. Watson, tomorrow before lunch, if you are ready for your test, you will smoke the hives, and I will examine them!"

Margaret and I put on our coats while Holmes sat in his chair, fingering the book and casting his eye about the room.

I had no doubt he would find a new hiding place for it once we were gone.

Almost certainly in the garret.

Chapter Four

A SECRET REVEALED

It was the first day of March, and the warm impulse of spring was making itself felt all across the Downs. I had spent the morning in the shed preparing the smoker while Sherlock Holmes worked on his manuscript. At the appointed time, Holmes entered the shed and donned his white smock.

"Are you ready, Watson? We must determine which of the queens survived the winter—and young Moriarty's bullets! And of course check the colonies for mites and other infestations."

He eyed me critically, arms akimbo as I held the smoker in nervous anticipation. Then he shook his head.

"Gloves, Watson? Please remove them, thank you. I never use them. You'll want to *feel* the presence of the bees, else you might crush one without knowing it. And a crushed bee is not a happy bee. Believe me, it is actually safer this way."

I followed Holmes bare-handed with some little trepidation to the first hive, whence he began to direct me with his stick, much as an army colonel would use his baton.

"You are well practiced with the smoker by now? Good. Touch the match there. Yes, it smells of lavender, does it not? Now, approach the hive— not from the front, Watson! *Never* from the front, unless you want a short, sharp lesson in territorial manners. The foragers have been out all morning gathering pollen, and should they find you blocking their threshold, they will not hesitate to make their displeasure known. Always from the back, like that. Yes, very good.

"First, a gentle puff across the entrance neutralizes the guard bees— that's right. Now lift the cover—it sticks? Smoothly Watson! Avoid the jerky hand movements of the novice—else they'll sense your nervousness and make you pay. Just so. A few puffs over the frames will calm them. Excellent!

"Yes, set the cover down. Now, brush aside those fellows on the top of the frames—gently, but without hesitation. The bees will move if you are gentle. That's it. You see how the frames within are exposed? Time to inspect them!

"Set aside the smoker, good, and slide out that first frame. Lift it straight up, Watson, smoothly and not too quickly. The poor fellows go from darkness to sunlight and it disturbs their sense of time—and a disturbed bee is an angry bee. No, I am not joking, Watson. I never joke when it comes to my friends. Yes, those frames weigh something with all that wax clinging to the combs, do they not? That is a good sign! It signifies a healthy queen, thank God. Now it is my turn to work."

And with that, Sherlock Holmes whipped out his lens from the pocket of his smock and bent to the task, examining the combs and extracting drone larvae between his fingers to study them for mites, all the while muttering a constant stream of observations. "Hum! Yes! Hum! Excellent!"

He stepped back and pointed a long thin finger into a quivering mass of bees.

"There she is, Watson. You see this one with the abnormally long abdomen and the several drones courting her? Naughty drones! It is the queen."

I made a comment and Holmes nodded approvingly.

"Yes, Watson, she *does* lack the crosswise markings of the others. That is because she is stretched full of eggs—an excellent observation! Dear me, what is that spot there—a mite? No, the colony is healthy, I perceive, and let us move on..."

In this way we worked until lunchtime, and so immersed did I become that by the time we finished I had lost my fear of the creatures—at the expense of a few stings, I must admit—and had even become competent in spotting mites. Three of the hives would need new queens, Holmes had determined, but there was no sign of the *Acarapis woodi* mite infestation that had devasted the beehives on the Isle of Wight.

It was an excellent first start, he felt.

And so did I.

Mr. Sturgess appeared upon Holmes's doorstep next morning, shortly after breakfast, bearing three new queens. He was a sturdy man of the Downs, as immersed in beekeeping as Holmes had once been in criminal detection, and I followed him as he worked, wielding the smoker at his direction. He performed his task quickly, with an ease and confidence I found remarkable, much like Sherlock Holmes upon a scent.

When he had finished, he told me in a gruff, matter-of-fact manner that we would know within the week if the queens had taken.

"How will we know?" I asked.

"If fresh eggs are being laid in the comb, she is alive and happy, otherwise she is quite dead."

And with that, Mr. Sturgess departed.

Such was the harshness that underlay the country life—a frank acceptance of nature's way—which always took me by surprise when it surfaced there on the Downs. I remarked upon this over lunch, as we were seated outside, and Holmes nodded thoughtfully.

"Death is *the* fact of life here, Watson. I rather think it becomes submerged in London beneath the trappings of civilized society. Out here, I dare say it rather stares one in the face."

Holmes then proceeded to inquire in the most detailed fashion as to the placement of the new queens. When I had finished answering his questions to his satisfaction, Holmes gazed out at the hives, alive with the buzzing, crawling, flying creatures.

"It is well we look after them, Watson. They are mankind's truest friend."

"You have quite gone over to the bees, Holmes!" I chuckled and turned to Margaret. "Holmes once told me that he cared not whether the earth revolved around the sun or the sun around the earth—what mattered to him was his work. Now he attributes all the goodness of the earth to the bees!"

"I was selfish, Watson. I thought of no one but myself and my clients. Here on the Downs I find myself responsible for the care and well-being of many thousands of these delicate creatures, and they look after the rest of God's handiwork." He gestured at the orchard. "Look at my yard, Watson. The apple tree, the thistle, the purple heather—without bees to pollinate them, what is this island but a bare pile of chalk?"

"Oh, Holmes, surely you don't mean to suggest we must exalt the bees!"

"But I *do*, Watson. How would the flowers propagate without them? How then would the apples grow? Without apples and their kin, how would the beasts of the earth or creatures of the sky exist? How, indeed, would *we* exist?"

I was irritated by this paternalistic homily. "I suppose we ought to glorify the cockroaches and the ants as well?"

"Ah, but ants and cockroaches do not *create*, Watson. They destroy. And the older I get, the less use I have for the destructive forces of nature, and of man. Besides, bees are *logical*—you have seen their hives, Watson— and you know my predilection for logic."

He nodded approvingly at an image in his mind.

"And of course they are ruled by their queen, which propagates the species while the workers make their honey for me. It is easy, and I am lazy."

"Then you are the most successfully lazy beekeeper in all the British Isles!" said Margaret. "But you do not fool me, Mr. Holmes. A man who rises to the heights of his profession as you did is not a lazy man."

Holmes looked sideways at me.

"I dare say your wife knows me as well as you, Watson! Yes, madam, I admit it. I planned a quiet retirement to focus on my treatise upon the art of detection and perhaps the publication of one or two modest works upon the lives of my small friends—but my engine never seems to stop running."

He gazed through the orchard at the tiny image of Belle Tout poised upon the edge of the cliffs a mile or two distant.

"I suppose it will slow down only when these fires have been extinguished, much like the old lighthouse..."

"That is a dismal thought," said I.

"Not in the least!" Holmes nodded at Margaret with a kind smile. "Why, only yesterday Mrs. Watson and I discovered we share a favourite passage along those lines from the Bhagavad Gita, while you were practicing with the smoker. '*The soul is neither born, nor does it ever die,*'" he began, then nodded at my wife.

"'*—nor having once existed, does it ever cease to be,*'" she concluded.

"There, you see, Watson? Not dismal in the least! Thank you, madam."

"I thank *you*, Mr. Holmes," said she.

Such was the mellow state of Sherlock Holmes's mind that upon returning to the cottage later that afternoon, after my exertions with the pruning shears among the apple trees, I was shocked to find him seated at his desk, fingering my newly mended syringe in its old morocco case.

"Good God!" I cried. "I hope you aren't—"

"No, Doctor. I was merely admiring the craftsmanship behind your antique device." Holmes twisted himself around to glance at me, and a smile sprang to his lips. "That look upon your face is priceless, though. You have aged ten years in an instant."

"I do not find it so amusing, Holmes."

"Nor do I!"

It was Margaret. She had entered with tea, and now set down the tray with a clatter. "John spent many an evening pondering how to rid you of that habit, sir."

"Yes, madam, and I owe him my infinite thanks for seeing it through. I could never have done so, left to my own devices."

"But *why*, Mr. Holmes? Why, *you*, of all people? Why the need for constant stimulation?"

"You have read my memoirs, madam. Cannot you deduce a cause for the effect?"

"You acquired the habit in America, then?"

Holmes shook his head.

"I never encountered it there, no. But I was all of sixteen-some years of age when my grand adventure took place. Does that not suggest some future crisis of confidence?"

"Crisis of conf—what are you saying, Holmes?" I asked.

Sherlock Holmes retrieved his pipe from the mantel, then sat back in his armchair and charged it with some little care before speaking.

"Doctor, you've known me in my worst days. Surely, you have worked it out? No? Dear me, I should have thought it quite obvious!"

He lit his pipe and watched the blue smoke curl upwards to the high-beamed ceiling for some little time. When he finally spoke again, it was in such a bloodless tone that I felt a chill myself.

"Has it never occurred to you, Doctor, that throughout my 'brilliant' career as a consulting detective I might have been consumed with the gnawing fear that I would never again experience a case as sublime as the hunt for J. Wilkes Booth? That every time the fresh footfalls of a new client sounded upon our stairs at Baker Street, I silently prayed *this* was the case that would lay to rest the ghost of Wilkes Booth from my youthful past and lift me from my eternal melancholy? By your face, it is evident the thought never crossed your mind."

He blew another long cloud of blue smoke to the ceiling.

"Anyway, that case never came."

"But if I had known, Holmes—"

"If you had known, Watson, then what?"

"Well, surely I could have helped in some way."

Holmes shook his head.

"Nothing you could have said or done could have effaced that memory. Compared to the hunt for J. Wilkes Booth, those little mysteries brought to us at Baker Street seemed not even worthy of Allan J. Pinkerton. The *wunderkind* who traced the assassin of Abraham Lincoln across the countryside of Maryland to a tobacco barn in Virginia with the help of a boy named for that Great Man receded further into the past each time a new client entered our rooms."

The silence that hung in the air after this remarkable admission was broken by Margaret, who spoke with some little emotion.

"But Mr. Holmes, you saved lives, and reputations! You rescued eminent *careers* from ruin. You solved the unsolvable!"

"Unsolvable to Lestrade, perhaps..."

"Is that why you were offered the Grand Cross? For solving mundane cases? Yes, John told me about that honour, Mr. Holmes. Surely it stands for something!"

"A palliative to an aging relic, madam, instigated by Brother Mycroft, I have not the slightest doubt—although he denies it. The boy Holmes deserved it. The adult Holmes most certainly did not. Which is why I declined it."

I rose from my chair in some little agitation. "Was it the *boy* Holmes who saved a noble woman from the vilest blackmailer in England? Who stopped a scheming doctor from killing his stepdaughter for her inheritance? Was beaten senseless by thugs for his efforts to stop a ruthless killer from marrying a naïve young lady? Who poisoned himself almost to death with that Devil's Foot toxin in order to solve the Cornish murders that so baffled the police?"

From the mantelpiece, I retrieved the ivory box that once contained a poison-tipped spring and held it to the light.

"Did the *boy* Holmes receive this deadly contraption to prevent him from avenging a young man's death?"

"Perhaps not, Watson—"

"There is no 'perhaps' about it, Holmes! You have no equal in the world!"

"John is right, Mr. Holmes. And never forget that it was you who brought John together with my sister. She was forever grateful, as I have been."

Holmes gave a snort and inspected his pipe. "I may as well be remembered for playing Cupid as for solving a few mysteries, I suppose."

Something in his dismissal of my wife's tender memory infuriated me, and the words were out of my mouth before I could contain myself.

"Is *that* how you will be remembered by those thousands of the London poor you fed and clothed with the proceeds from our books these last thirty years? A silly Cupid?"

Now it was Holmes's turn to show agitation and annoyance, as Margaret started.

"What! Is this true, Mr. Holmes?"

He did not meet her eyes, but rather fidgeted with his pipe and glared at me.

"I'm sorry, Holmes. I could not help it. You were rather crass with Margaret just now."

He shrugged his shoulders and nodded with resignation.

"I suppose I deserved it, Watson. And there's no harm done. It was bound to come out eventually."

Margaret appeared confused. "But John had told me all the profits went to *you*, Mr. Holmes."

"It was the only way your good husband could explain why you saw no monetary windfall from the books he laboured over, short of revealing our secret."

Margaret gazed upon my abashed friend with and spoke with tenderness.

"I should think you have laid to rest the ghost of J. Wilkes Booth for all time, Mr. Holmes. *'As you have done these things unto the least of my brethren, you have done it for me,'* you know. And you have evidently done much for the least among us."

Sherlock Holmes coloured, and once more busied himself with inspecting his pipe until his old, joking manner returned, as it always did when an emotional turn threatened his cool, logical nature.

"Best get cracking on the new publications, then, Watson."

"Now that the hives are replenished Holmes," said I, "I shall do just that!"

Margaret had returned to her needlework. Sherlock Holmes was puffing meditatively on his pipe and seemed absorbed in his own thoughts. I took the opportunity to retrieve my syringe from the desk and was tucking it away in its case when Margaret glanced up at the device, and a look of revulsion crossed her face.

Sherlock Holmes, who had followed her with his keen eyes, now broke in upon what he had deduced were her thoughts.

"You are wondering, madam, how I managed to inject myself as frequently as I once did with those deadly toxins?"

"No, Mr. Holmes," she said, putting down her needlework and speaking to my friend with utter frankness. "I was wondering how you managed to be supplied with them."

I believe Sherlock Holmes was as startled as I.

It was a question I had turned over in my mind many times during my years at Baker Street, of course, and yet I had never been able to summon the courage to ask it of Holmes.

Something in the sordidness of the subject seemed to hold me back each time.

Perhaps more to the point, I was afraid of what the answer might be.

But Margaret had asked the question in the straightforward manner that was her wont, and with such candidness that Sherlock Holmes could not take offence.

Nor could he ignore it.

As he set himself to answer her, however, he was overcome with such uncharacteristic shifting in his seat and clearing of the throat that I knew not what to expect. And when the answer came, it proved even more shocking than I had ever dreaded.

"The truth is, madam, all my wants along those lines, both here and when I lived in London, were procured through my brother Mycroft."

I was speechless.

Margaret was livid.

"Why, your brother should be ashamed, Mr. Holmes. Heartily ashamed! That is conduct unbecoming a gentleman!"

"So you may think, madam. So you may think."

"So I know, sir! So I know! No gentleman would do such a thing. And a brother at that!"

"Madam, if I may, please—you must understand that, in his own way, Mycroft was looking after his younger brother, as he had always looked after me throughout my life."

"I would hardly call procuring an addictive material whose destructive qualities are beyond dispute a way of 'looking after' you, Holmes!" I exclaimed.

"Ah, but the purity and safety could never be doubted, Watson, coming as it did from my brother's impeccable sources. And, knowing I was going to use it anyway, he wanted at least to be assured it was not tainted."

I shook my head. "I cannot agree."

"No, and that is why I never told you, Watson. I knew it would never have met with your approval."

The somber grey eyes of Sherlock Holmes held Margaret's some little time. Then he spoke to her in a soft voice.

"But I rather think you had guessed it all along, madam."

Chapter Five

THE STATEMENT OF MR. MYCROFT HOLMES

I had been asked some time ago by Dr. Watson to provide for these pages a personal perspective upon the life of my brother, Sherlock Holmes, with perhaps some mention of my own "feelings" towards him, and any corrections I might put forward regarding either my brother's remarkable manuscript, or the somewhat flowery embellishments attached by Dr. Watson.

Without time to spare for such an enterprise, however—the call upon my small abilities from His Majesty's Government remains supreme, even at my superannuated age—nor the inclination to discuss "feelings" with anybody, let alone with the common lot of readers who find such trifles of interest, I naturally refrained from doing so.

Until now.

The exposure of this admittedly unflattering aspect of my relationship with my brother (let us call it, simply, "procurement"), which had lain unexamined in the many published stories of my brother's adventures over the years—even though its existence would surely have been deduced long ago by a mind more supple than Dr. Watson's—naturally forces my hand.

And inasmuch as I must now put pen to paper to assure that my standing with His Majesty's Government does not become unduly tarnished by the doctor's sensational (but incomplete) disclosure, I have decided to take a further moment to offer, in addition, one or two perspectives upon the life of my brother which are, by definition, entirely unique, coming as they do from the only surviving relation of Sherlock Holmes.

First, as to my involvement in securing the vegetable alkaloids consumed by my brother during the years in question, let me point out that his attachment to such stimulants was an established fact before ever I became involved in their acquisition upon his behalf.

The habit had been acquired at Bart's, I understood, during the later years of his self-education, well after his return from America, when he had taken up the pursuit of an especially intensive investigation into poisons as part of that self-directed and exceedingly disciplined period of study which would culminate in his career as a consulting detective.

Once I learned that it had become a habit—which, by definition, is not easily broken—I immediately and without hesitation set about to establish a method of supply that would be both impeccable and secure, for I (and I alone) understood the unique history at the root of my brother's alarming compulsion, and, therefore, how difficult it would be to cure him of it.

My paramount conviction was that he must be kept as safe as possible while the thing took its course.

Ought I have turned a blind eye? Ought I have allowed my brother to continue fetching his supplies from some back-alley peddler? More to the point, should I have stood fast while his fledgling habit led where all of London's underground narcotics supply led in those days: a lice-infested berth in an airless, smoke-filled opium den managed by a Malay underling of that Napoleon of crime, Professor Moriarty?

I kept Sherlock supplied, yes. But I also kept him safe and alive, thanks to the assured purity of the substances, which came thoroughly vetted from the most outstanding Harley Street specialist in the field.

Had my brother been allowed to continue attaining his wants through the usual channels, I strongly suspect we would not be discussing this remarkable document of his—or, indeed, any other manuscript from his hand, save, perhaps, the besotted scribblings of a common opium-eater who had long since passed on from this world, unknown and uncared for.

For that alone, I dare say my actions deserve praise, not censure.

Second, let it be known that despite my role in that dark business, I never stayed my hand from frequent and forceful attempts to discourage the practice. And while it was Dr. Watson who finally cured my brother after many years of diligent effort, the good doctor did so with substantial encouragement and assistance upon my part.

I simply never wished to detract from the encomiums he deserved for his efforts.

No, I am not proud of my role in that sorry chapter of my brother's otherwise exceptional life story, but I would state unequivocally that it was necessary not merely in my view, but—more important—in the view of the distinguished personages upon whose behalf my brother expended no little portion of his remarkable talents.

They include, for the record, one glorious Queen, two superlative Kings, and too many Prime Ministers to mention here.

Moving on to the manuscript itself, and in particular my brother's revelation of the events leading up to that extraordinary year in America, I wish to state plainly that the role I am said to have played in "saving" the DuPont Company—and, by implication, the American Union—has been vastly embellished in the telling.

It is true that I happened to be on duty that fateful evening when Mr. Lammot du Pont entered the Whitehall telegraph office in a disturbed frame of mind, fretting aloud that the Prime Minister's refusal to grant access to the India wire might cause the DuPont mills to be shut down.

It is also true that my decision to open the India line to Lammot that evening (and for the next several as well) enabled him to secure every pound of saltpetre necessary to keep the DuPont Company mills producing gunpowder—and that, as a result, my name would become familiar to many within the corridors of the American War Department and, in a more modest way, a certain figure inside the White House.

But I was by no means the swashbuckling hero portrayed in my brother's manuscript.

The impulse to aid Mr. du Pont that evening might be considered

remarkable in an age when men back from war write poetry debating
the meaning of existence and demeaning the honour of fighting for their
King, and the fleeting attainment of fame seems to be of greater moment
than simply doing one's job well. But I am confident that any Englishman
in my position (the Prime Minister, of course, excepted!) would have made
the same choice that night, so clear was the need and so right was the
cause.

Indeed, I am quite more proud—if I may admit to that un-Christian
vanity—of the services rendered to the world at large by my brother as a
result of his work for Mr. Edwin M. Stanton, the American War Secretary,
which I cheerfully admit would never have occurred had I not sought a
position for my brother at Bart's in the first place and, later on, arranged
his journey to America.

Mind you, I had no grand design in mind when I encouraged Johnnie
to learn the chemistry trade. I merely wanted my little brother the chance
to escape his fate—much as the invention of the telegraph had given me
the chance to escape the rigid strictures of Victorian England—and to see
what he might make of it. It was a happy chance that Mr. Stanton, who
possessed one of the shrewdest minds I have ever encountered, had been
looking for a means to resolve his nagging little problem at the DuPont
works when my brother came to his attention.

That Johnnie's abilities showed through to such uncommon effect was
a testament not to any foresight upon my part, but to the remarkable gifts
of my brother—and his very good sense to befriend a boy whose instincts
in tracking and survival made them, together, quite a useful combination
to Mr. Stanton even after the gunpowder thieves had been unmasked.

It must be said, however, that the risks Johnnie faced during his
time in America were substantially greater than he ever realized. Any
blunder on Johnnie's part—any blunder at all—and he would have been as
dispensable to Edwin M. Stanton as the blustering Allan J. Pinkerton.

Yet, though I prayed fervently for his safekeeping during each one
of those three hundred and eighty-eight days he was away from my snug
telegraph office in Whitehall, I had absolute faith in his abilities. I never
for a moment doubted that Johnnie would accomplish whatever Mr.

Stanton desired of him—although the scope of his accomplishments was, as might be imagined, quite a bit more sublime than ever I had dared conceive.

One final perspective I will share, at the risk of overfilling a narrative already overstuffed with the kind of psychological porridge that has turned the brains of a youthful generation to mush, for it is a perspective of my brother that the good Dr. Watson did not—indeed, could not—provide.

Unspoken in my brother's remarkable memoirs—and, therefore, an omission of considerable interest to me—is the absence of any mention that Johnnie was, in fact, born a twin. Perhaps the memory is too painful for him to recall to mind.

Or, perhaps he has chosen to forget.

In either case, I would maintain that the hard shell which Johnnie often presented to the fairer sex owed itself not to any inherent distrust of women on his part, but to having watched the girl who was, biologically speaking, his copy, fall victim to depravities of the flesh at the behest of our father—a wretched man, taken from this world by a just Providence and presumably cast into the lowest circle of hell—who had thought nothing of offering Johnnie's twin for twopence to the wastrels prowling the alleys of London until, one day, she did not return.

And neither Johnnie nor I could ever learn what happened to her.

It followed then, that while I took to sowing no few wild oats before settling into the life of a man married to the Crown, Johnnie drew an impenetrable veil around himself even during those years when a young man might be expected to run riot.

Such a disposition, of course, allowed him to remain on a far more productive path—a certain dangerous habit aside—than any man I have ever known, but I am pleased to say it did not keep him from presenting a most chivalrous demeanor towards the weaker sex, even when his considerable fame would draw to his sitting room maidens both pure and otherwise, as moths are drawn to the flame.

Indeed, I have always thought most highly of my brother not for his remarkable contribution to the American Union, nor for the several times his skills saved our Crown from the devious schemes of a deviant world. No, it was Johnnie's kind manner towards the poor young girls who had been held captive, in a fashion, by the lecherous chemists of Bart's, that I thought most profoundly noble, and right.

And I am pleased readers of this manuscript will now, and ever, know it.

In looking over these few pages, I see that I have allowed myself to be drawn into the speculations of the mind which I had pledged to avoid at the start. Let me conclude, therefore, by returning to the point at which I began, to more forcefully address the admittedly tawdry aspect of my relationship with my brother that has been dredged up by the well-meaning Dr. Watson.

That I supplied Sherlock Holmes with his needs in the way of morphia and cocaine for almost the entire course of his career—save in the earliest days of that dark practice—is, and shall remain, a black spot upon my soul.

I engage in no prevarication upon that point.

But do not think that I approved of what my brother was doing. I had seen far too many a "coming man" tucked away in an obscure room at Whitehall for whom an excessive appetite for alcohol or opium had wrecked a brilliant career to ever wish to come across Johnnie in such a state.

Then consider, as I did, many times and during many a grave crisis, what might have transpired had my brother's not-inconsiderable abilities been forever lost to Crown and Country because a single, impure particle—whether by accident or by malevolent intent—had made its way into his veins.

And then judge my actions.

Mycroft Holmes
Diogenes Club
London
April 5, 1919

END OF PART IV

V

THE DEATH OF
SHERLOCK HOLMES

It was on a bitterly cold and frosty morning during the winter of '97 that I was awakened by a tugging at my shoulder. It was Holmes. The candle in his hand shone upon his eager, stooping face and told me at a glance that something was amiss.

"Come, Watson, come!" he cried. "The game is afoot. Not a word! Into your clothes and come!"

John H. Watson, MD
—The Adventure of the Abbey Grange

Chapter One

BECOMING
SHERLOCK HOLMES

I come now to the last week of April, 1919, when the distressing events that help give name to this book unfolded before my eyes. So exceedingly difficult has it proven to set down these memories in my own hand, however, that I have turned to my wife to help me complete the narrative.

It is she who transcribes by hand the words I dictate of the events described herein, and my final interviews with my friend, Mr. Sherlock Holmes.

The days at Went Hill had acquired a familiar and pleasant routine about them.

Most mornings I tended the hives, overseen by Sherlock Holmes, who watched either from his desk at the bow window, or, if the weather was fine and he had finished his writing for the day, from the basket chair outside, with a blanket upon his lap and a cup of tea and a piece of honeycomb at his elbow.

He had quickly and, it appeared, fully recovered from his strange collapse at the typewriter, which I had put down to exhaustion and overstimulation after a private consultation with Major Graeme Gibson, one of the military doctors across the way at Summerdown.

I had known of Gibson from my medical reading, for his reputation reigned supreme: it was he who had been the first to identify the particularly deadly strain of influenza that was killing troops on the Somme with no rhyme or reason, and it was he with whom I had toured the camp to learn more about this mysterious strain and to discuss the best course of action should my friend's fainting episode herald worse to come.

He had warned me there was nothing I could do once a diagnosis had been confirmed but to keep the patient comfortable, and that the best remedy was not to be exposed to the virus in the first place. When I explained that my companion never ventured out of doors except to speak to his hives and to stroll along the cliffs, however, he said he thought it unlikely Holmes's fainting spell signaled an exposure.

"Then I should not be too worried," Gibson had said. "Besides," he added with a smile, pointing at the few remaining tents around us, "the cold weather seems to have knocked it flat."

The cold weather had not bothered Holmes's beehives, fortunately.

So well had the new queens attracted fresh swarms, in fact, that the honey-making operations of *Eighth Sister* recommenced more swiftly than Holmes had dared hope, and Miss Colvin's attentions soon became entirely absorbed in the business aspects of the honey and candle operations.

Margaret assumed the care and feeding of the bedridden old man in the farmhouse, in addition to preparing our meals at the cottage. She had made her peace with Mycroft Holmes—following the discomforting revelations described above—upon his next visit to Went Hill, when he brought his statement for my records. It was during this visit that Mycroft took a room in the village to be closer to his brother, and workmen from London were soon spotted at the old telegraph house up the road, busily outfitting the structure with a telephone so that Mycroft could be in more intimate communication with the delegates at Versailles.

Thereafter, when he was not seated upon the settee consulting his books on the American Reconstruction or taking lunch or tea with his brother, Mycroft would put on his coat and disappear to the telegraph house for hours at a time.

Afternoons found Sherlock Holmes revisiting old cases with me, unless he was receiving visitors, for in the aftermath of his seizure he seemed to have shed his preference for solitude.

He especially enjoyed Vicar Evans, who came by several times a week now. The two would always insist upon being joined by Margaret, for her childhood in the land of the Buddha fascinated Holmes, while her memories of a year spent in the Holy Land as a young missionary were of constant interest to the vicar.

The three together often lost track of time during these sessions, although the vicar remained ever mindful that the exploration of the eternal mysteries must not ignore the well-being of souls upon Earth. Whenever Margaret and Sherlock had become too deeply immersed in the attributes of the Five Wisdom Buddhas, say, or the role of Melito of Sardis in the framing of the Paschal mystery, Vicar Evans would take his leave with this salutation: "So long as you remember that Mr. Smith's sheep must be sheared by St. Swithin's Day!"[79]

What of my relationship with Sherlock Holmes, you may ask?

Those April days were among the best I ever shared with him.

Our conversations moved easily from the dangers of beehive infestations to fond remembrances of old cases together, but Holmes came positively alive when the talk turned to his youthful days in America, which he could recall as if they had happened yesterday.

I, of course, was eager to hear him do so, but I had more on my mind about Holmes's young life than what he had written in his memoirs.

"How did you manage it, Holmes?" I asked one day after I had finished my morning duties and we sat drinking tea together, contemplatively watching the bees flying off on their routes.

"How did I manage what, Watson?"

"After your return from America, how did you make your way?"

A smile came to Holmes's face, as if the answer were self-evident.

"Work, my dear boy. Very hard work."

"Yes, but where did you live? *How* did you live? Where were you educated

---

79 *July 15th.*

and how did you begin your career as a consulting detective? How—how did you *become* Sherlock Holmes?"

My friend stirred beneath his blanket and reached for his pipe, but a sudden wracking cough caused him to take up the teacup instead, with a great crust of honeycomb.

When his throat had been soothed, he began to speak with the reflective air of a man reviewing his life.

"You can imagine how rather full of myself was I, Watson—a grand adventure behind me and all of life stretched out before my eyes. I was quite eager to seize that life, too, but I quickly learned that England was not quite so eager to provide it!" Holmes chuckled at the memory. "*Who is this untitled young man, of indeterminate lineage, with no university degree to his C.V.? How dare this bounder possess such aspirations!*"

He shook his head.

"The opportunities to make a mark in those days were not as they had been in America, Watson. I soon found myself back to where I had begun."

"But you had your brother, surely."

"Quite so, although Mycroft wisely let me flounder for some little time, until my pride gave way to my empty purse and I confessed my frustrations to him. He at once secured me a seat at the bench in Her Majesty's powder works at Wentworth, so that by day I crafted new forms of powder and by night I pursued the skills I had determined I would need for my chosen craft."

"That of criminal detection."

"Precisely so. I was tutored in Latin, of course, for that is the language of scientific knowledge, took University classes in botany and anatomy and sharpened my chemical abilities at Bart's. Above all, however, I made myself a familiar figure in the great reading room at the British Museum, where I embarked upon a systematic study of the history of crime."

"With an emphasis upon the most gruesome, of course!"

"Indeed. Mycroft later told me I had been closely watched by the docents there—they were alarmed at the rather sensational nature of the publications I was requesting! But I hardly saw any other way. Patterns repeat themselves—criminals repeat themselves. It is the fundamental premise of existence, Watson. Ask any chemist!"

Holmes nodded towards the hives.

"A comprehensive knowledge of the criminal's pattern of behaviour renders the solution to any given crime almost as intuitive as spotting the queen amongst a thousand worker bees. It is the most fundamental mistake of my imitators not to attempt to catalogue and store an exact knowledge of the history of crime."

"I met one of those imitators in Polegate the day of the murder, Holmes. That railway detective. A most unpleasant man."

"Ah, yes, Cummings. Poor fellow. I knew him, Watson. Undone by the *duhkha*, as lesser minds can be."

"The dooka—?"

"Forgive me, Watson. My conversations with Margaret and the good Vicar Evans rather persuaded me that we were all fluent in matters of a Buddhist turn. I suppose 'the human condition' might be the best way to put it." Holmes touched the tips of his fingers together and spoke in his most didactic fashion. "Here is a man who no doubt dreamt of unraveling the evil designs of the next Professor Moriarty, and instead finds himself investigating vandalism on the South Coast line. Bitterness and resentment follow—the *sumadaya*. Such fellows think what I do is easy. It is hard."

"But how did you know when you were ready to make a go of it?"

"The confidence of youth, Watson! At some point—it took a good ten years to get there, you understand—the connections among the various classes of science seemed to come together in my mind. And with an unparalleled inventory of criminal behaviour rattling around in my brain, I found my observations intuitively yielded deductions that nearly always resolved to the correct answer. And *that* is when I hung out my shingle, so to speak."

"When you were in your early thirties, as I now know from your manuscript," said I. "You know, I had pegged you for being a good five years younger, Holmes!"

"I never gave my true age, Watson. The less one knows about someone, the harder it is to ensnare that person. Besides," Holmes added with a thin smile, "I would not want some ruffian thinking he was dealing with an older, more infirm gentleman than he expected."

"Well played, Holmes. I take it your services were highly sought after, then?"

"On the contrary! It was my first comeuppance since leaving my brother's telegraph room—not a single inquiry crossed my threshold for six months! Even then, it was brought to me by my landlady and concerned a missing cat. Things only started to improve when Brother Mycroft began surreptitiously to send the police my way when a case had stumped them."

"Mycroft again! But who were your role models as a detective? Certainly not Allan Pinkerton!"

Holmes vigorously shook his head. "Not after my time in America, Watson."

"Melville of Scotland Yard, I suppose?"

"No, Watson, it was no one from the official police. My mind rather turned to the figures of the American Civil War, of whom I had made no little study, as you might imagine. Lincoln, of course—how could one not seek to emulate his clarity of mind and steady purpose? Grant, certainly, for his austerity of demeanor and his willingness to change his plans as circumstances arose, as he showed during the Vicksburg campaign most especially.

"And there was Stonewall Jackson, too—his method, certainly, if not the man. '*Always mystify, mislead and surprise.*'"

"Jackson? A Confederate, Holmes? Couldn't you find another Union man to emulate?"

Once more he shook his head.

"The Union generals were rather incompetent, you see. Most of them, anyway. Until Grant. You must remember, the Northern men weren't fighting for their homelands. Gettysburg and Antietam aside, all the fighting and dying took place south of the Potomac. And of course the Northern men could buy substitutes to fight in their place— and many did. Three hundred dollars was the going rate, as I recall.

"Certainly, many who *did* fight for the Northern cause—like those Topsfield recruits I met in the railway carriage—were good and true, but their generals were political men, in the main. They knew that whoever won the war for the North would become President, as with Washington and others after him. The stakes loomed large in their minds. It made them cautious, indecisive. I'm sorry to say, Watson, the more capable figures were often Southern men—and Jackson was the most capable of all."

Holmes's face lightened.

"He was also an orphan, and possessed of an older relative who had taken an interest in him and helped guide his young life. Does that not sound familiar to you, Watson? It certainly did to me. That affinity with my own background appealed to my young mind. I thought 'If he could become the most skilled of his profession, why not I?'"

"But Jackson was a slave owner, Holmes! He fought for the South—for *slavery*. Could you not have found a more...noble man to study?"

As in the old days, when in a reflective mood, Holmes reached for the old briar pipe, although he now refrained from charging it and instead gripped it in his hand.

"I have always found it a mistake to let one's self-righteousness interfere with one's capacity for rational thought, Watson."

"I think I am being quite rational, Holmes. Jackson was a slave owner, was he not?"

"Bravo, Watson! You have evidently been reading Mycroft's books again! But why, Doctor, would you hold Stonewall Jackson to a higher standard than your own line?"

"I beg your pardon?"

"Your ancestors in Liverpool and Bristol were fitting ships bound for the slave houses of Gorée long before Stonewall Jackson or Robert E. Lee were even born."

"You don't mean to say you've traced my line to shipwrights involved in the slave trade, Holmes?"

"I can assure you, my dear Watson, I know even less about your ancestry than you knew about mine before reading my manuscript."

"Then how is it you tie me to the slave ships of Liverpool?"

"For the very same reason you tie Stonewall Jackson to the institution of slavery in America. Slaves had been brought to Virginia two centuries before Jackson and his fellow Confederates were born. They grew up *within* that system—they did not create it. By the time they came to manhood, it was as natural to them as going to church on Sunday."

"I hardly think the subjugation of a peoples is equivalent to attending worship, Holmes."

"I never said it was equivalent, Watson. It most certainly is *not*. I am making a point. The system of slavery in America—and please remember that I saw it firsthand—existed from the moment those men first opened their eyes."

"But surely there were others born to the same system who nevertheless came to reject it, and even to fight for its abolition. General Thomas, as I recall?"

"You scintillate, Watson! Yes, Thomas— 'The Rock of Chickamauga.' A most noble Virginian who took up arms against the South. And surely there were many Englishmen who came to reject the enslavement of the Afghans, for which you fought at Maiwand—"

"I fought to enslave no Afghans!"

"But you served in that campaign, Watson. Quite enthusiastically, as I recall it in your telling."

"I was fighting for my Queen! Not for enslavement of the Afghans—"

"Quite right, Watson. And whatever Stonewall Jackson was fighting for, it was not for the institution of slavery. Both Jackson and Lee thought secession madness—but once sides were chosen, well, they chose for their homeland, Virginia. If Virginia had sided with the Union, they very likely would have ended up fighting *against* the Confederacy."

Holmes studied my face and read my skepticism.

"Tell me, Watson, did your extensive reading happen to mention that Jackson taught his slaves to read?"

"Well no, but what—"

"I thought not. Did you know it was *illegal* in the state of Virginia to teach slaves to read?"

"Why illegal?"

"To keep the Negro in chains, of course. An illiterate man would not likely happen upon the story of Exodus in his Bible, would he? Or Luke's message that Jesus had been sent to proclaim liberty to the captives? Illiteracy of the Negro was one more gear in the loathsome machinery of slavery, and Stonewall Jackson would have none of it."

"But he never renounced it," said I, finding at last what I thought was a chink in Holmes's reasoning.

"No, and I'll wager you never plan to renounce the Crown's rule in India?" He smiled when I found myself searching for a response. "You see how steep and thorny is that path to heaven, eh, Watson!"

"What, then, of Jefferson Davis?" I asked. "Would you defend his honour as well?"

"Not for one minute, Watson. Davis led the rebellion against his country, and slavery was the anvil upon which his blade was sharpened. There is no comparison with Lee or Jackson. Nathan Bedford Forrest, too, while an excellent general—more energetic and innovative than even Jackson or Lee—was a thoroughly despicable man. A slave trader before the war who presided over the massacre of Negro soldiers at Fort Pillow and became so-called Grand Wizard of the disgrace known as the Ku Klux Klan *after* the war."

"'Ku Klux Klan'! Why, they were responsible for the fate of poor John Openshaw!" I exclaimed, recalling one of our cases together.[80]

"Precisely so." Holmes turned towards me, his gaunt face serious, his voice solemn. "*Never* confuse such men with Jackson or Lee."

He erupted into a sudden coughing fit, and I replenished his tea with a copious amount of honey. When he had recovered, he seemed determined to complete his thoughts upon a man whose methods he claimed to emulate.

"It was the acquisition of knowledge which separated Jackson from his peers, Watson, and it was that trait to which I most greatly aspired. He employed his own cartographer! Carried an eight-foot long map of the Shenandoah Valley with him! Learned every hidden trail and footpath of that valley! Moved his men so quickly they were called 'Jackson's foot cavalry'!"

---

80 The Five Orange Pips.

Holmes turned a wry smile upon me.

"Knowledge was his most trusted weapon and he hoarded it like gold. Never divulged his plans to anyone. Not even to General Lee."

"Now I know where you got that trait, Holmes," I said dryly.

"Yes, I *was* rather a cold fish, wasn't I?" Sherlock Holmes gazed out at his orchard in a reflective manner. "I raised my capacities well beyond the common lot, it is true. But at the cost of being rather aloof and insensitive to those around me."

"If you were as aloof as you claim, Holmes, we never would have met. And I am forever grateful that we did," said I fervently.

"No more so than I, Watson."

As I glanced Holmes's way, I saw his eyes glistening in afternoon sunlight. I reached out for his hand—his skin was somewhat cold to the touch—and he took mine with a grip more feeble than last I had felt.

"Do you remember, Watson, I once said that I was often guided to the truth by your faulty deductions?"

I did, of course, remember, for it was a memory that had always rankled. But I shook my head.

"If you said it, Holmes, I don't remember."

"Thank you, Watson, but I know well—." A sudden chill caused him to withdraw his hand from mine, to grip the blanket tighter around him. When the chill had passed, he spoke in a quiet voice.

"I owe you a thousand apologies for ever suggesting you were anything but my most valuable companion."

"It is of no consequence now, Holmes—but why do you speak in the past tense?"

"Let us not be maudlin, Doctor. A time to plant, a time to sow, etc. etc."

"Holmes!"

"Come, come, Watson. How many of my youthful acquaintances in the slums of Wapping would have traded their lives for just one day of our adventures together? Or to see such a view as this?" He gestured at the apple trees now in full greening. "How can I be anything but grateful?"

It was a disconcerting turn of thought and I reached out to grasp

Holmes's wrist once more, stealthily setting my forefinger upon his radial artery and silently counting the pulse as he resumed his reflections.

"Like all those men, I set out to hone the qualities that would allow me to make a life for myself, and I tried never to stop learning. Even now, as I see it, the final education approaches. I anticipate it!"

"Surely not, Holmes!"

"The timing is in the hands of God, Watson, not in mine."

We sat for another moment in silence. Then Sherlock Holmes turned and met my eyes with a knowing look upon his sallow face.

"You will find my heart rate is somewhat elevated, Watson. One hundred twenty, or thereabouts, I should think."

Chapter Two

WHAT THE SUN NEVER
SAYS TO THE EARTH

Next morning, Sherlock Holmes's condition took a bad turn.

I detected no dangerous fever, but his face was drawn, his skin the colour of faded newspaper. Most concerning were the nails of his fingers, which were tinted blue, signifying a heart too weak to pump blood to the lungs.

And then there was the cough.

It seemed to lift him up out of his bed, every limb in contortion, eyes bulging, until he had succeeded in clearing his throat. Most alarmingly, the discharge now carried a disconcerting purplish hue. Margaret and I managed to get him dressed and seated in the basket chair outside, for it was a beautiful, warm day, and there was little to do but make him comfortable and see that he drank fluids.

I sent for Mycroft Holmes at the telegraph station, and he joined us for lunch. It was the first we had seen of him in a week, for the calls upon his time from the British delegation at Versailles had kept him occupied day and night. He appeared considerably alarmed at his brother's condition, and once more the Harley Street specialist was sent for and was soon on his way from London.

Meanwhile, the afternoon sun shone down brightly upon the flagstones, and the reflected heat gave off a radiating warmth reminiscent of the baths we had often frequented in our days at Baker Street. Holmes napped for some little time while Mycroft attended to the correspondence in his despatch box, and I monitored the deterioration of my friend's lungs with my stethoscope.

To my surprise, however, when he awoke from his sound sleep, he seemed refreshed and eager to talk, his mind sharp as ever.

"I have ceased to possess an outlet now that my writing days are behind me," he said. "I must seek my stimulation in conversation. Brother Mycroft, perhaps you would relate the state of the Versailles discussions for us?"

Mycroft Holmes set down his papers and muttered something about the intransigence of "the twins."

We had heard him speak of them before. They were a pair of His Majesty's delegates to Versailles[81] whose insistence upon harsh terms for Germany clashed with the advice of Maynard Keynes, the eminent economist whose argument for leniency ran very much along the line put forth by Sherlock Holmes when news of the armistice first reached us at Went Hill.

"We are at an impasse, Sherlock, and it is up me to break it. To do that, I must reconcile two irreconcilable sides!" Mycroft Holmes took a large pinch of snuff and studied his brother for some little time. "I wonder, Sherlock... how would Mr. Lincoln have handled them? What would he advise me?"

Sherlock Holmes looked off at some distant point, as he always did when his mind returned to 1865.

"Lincoln had one goal, Mycroft. It was Union above all. He kept that goal always in his mind. It made the choices clear."

"And therein lies our problem, Sherlock. There are four sovereigns drafting this treaty, each with a different objective. And, of course, my own delegation cannot even agree on a single point of view!"

"I dare say Lincoln would see this one clearly, Mycroft. 'Get the soldiers on both sides home to plant their fields and let the rebuilding begin.' Those were the instructions he gave to Stanton. 'Let them off easy, Edwin,' he would say when Mr. Stanton made his case for strict punishment. 'Let 'em off easy.'"

"But what of Jefferson Davis and the leaders of the insurrection?" I asked. "Surely they *deserved* punishment!"

---

81 *Lords Sumner and Cutliffe.*

"Mr. Lincoln rather hoped Jeff Davis would flee the country and spare the nation the spectacle of a trial such as Stanton was hatching. But it was not to be. Davis was caught before he could reach the Atlantic, and trouble was stored for all time."

"What made Mr. Lincoln so charitable towards Davis? Had they been friends in Congress?"

"Hardly, Watson. They stood on opposite sides of the slavery issue, and much else, even before Secession. But I do think they understood one another. Kentucky-born, log cabin men, both. Self-taught, self-made." Sherlock Holmes glanced at his brother. "Hard to imagine their kind becoming Prime Minister, eh Mycroft! No riffraff such as that inhabiting Downing Street, I dare say."

Mycroft Holmes grunted. "No bellicose slave masters such as Jefferson Davis, anyway."

"You scintillate, Mycroft. But Davis was not the monster he has been portrayed as. Like Lincoln, he was a hard-headed logician. I met him, you see."

"Jefferson Davis? Surely not!" I exclaimed.

"Why, yes, Watson, I did." Sherlock Holmes's face assumed an expression of intense recall, and there was a glint in his eyes and a flaring of the nostrils as he began a remarkable sketch of Jefferson Davis in flight from Richmond on a rickety, wood-burning railroad car carrying the Confederate treasury with him—and young Johnnie Holmes in hot pursuit.

Mycroft Holmes studied his brother with a puzzled expression, then gave me an almost imperceptible shake of the head and turned back to the papers in his lap as his brother rambled on.

Sherlock Holmes was continuing in this vein when Margaret arrived from the farmhouse, a look of shock upon her face. The old man who had been posed as Miss Colvin's uncle had finally succumbed. Miss Colvin was at the farmhouse attending to the arrangements with Vicar Evans.

It was at this moment that the surgeon from Harley Street arrived, and Margaret and I went inside the cottage to fix tea while he attended my friend. Upon our return, we found Holmes considerably agitated by the surgeon's presence, for the man insisted upon utter silence as he listened to

Holmes's lungs, and Holmes, meanwhile, had been intent upon finishing his story.

The surgeon finally packed away his stethoscope and took me and Mycroft aside. His only recommendation before returning to London, in addition to the care we had been providing, was to begin the administration of morphine. But as Holmes was able to sleep and did not appear to be in excessive pain, I could only promise to take it under advisement, and Mycroft concurred.

When the surgeon had departed, Sherlock Holmes quite recovered his spirits, and after a soothing cup of tea and honey, he continued his story until he lapsed into sleep with the warm sun upon his face. He slept soundly until the golds and lavenders of the sunset had lost their colour and Margaret called us inside for dinner.

Neither Mycroft nor I said a word about the fantastic story of the Confederate gold, nor did his brother mention it as he tasted the lamb curry soup Margaret had prepared. His eyes appeared alarmingly hollow now, almost protruding, and after only a few sips of the broth, he let his spoon fall into the bowl. Then, exhausted and limp, he asked if I would say good night to the bees for him.

Mycroft and I helped him to his room and placed him in his bed, and I noted with distress that the discharge unloosed by his wracking cough was now more black than purple.

It matched the cases I had seen at Summerdown.

Holmes slept fitfully that night, and Mycroft and I took turns alternately sitting at his bedside and napping upon the settee. When awakened by his own cough, Sherlock Holmes would return each time to America, in particular to that most remarkable meeting in the Stanton dining room, the morning of President Lincoln's reelection.

"Have I told you of our breakfast, Watson?" he would ask, shivering beneath his covers.

"Which breakfast, Holmes?" I would answer, feigning ignorance.

"With Lincoln!" Even in the dim moonlight I could see his eyes lighting up as his mind turned to that precious memory.

"Remind me of it, Holmes."

And off he would go, like a hound who hears the "view halloa."

"It is the morning after the great feast in the Island. Abraham and I are asleep in Franklin Square. We hear the rattle of a carriage outside our window..."

By dawn he had fallen into a deep sleep, and Margaret took my place by his side while Mycroft and I ate a quick breakfast. Then Mycroft Holmes excused himself for the telegraph station while I tended to the hives.

It was a responsibility I quite enjoyed now, for as my proficiency had improved, my fondness for the creatures had come almost to match Holmes's own. But on this morning, there was agitation in their movements, and I was stung several times, quite without provocation.

I think they knew.

In fact, I would swear to it.

By noon, Holmes had awakened and was feeling strong enough to take tea by the fireplace. Margaret took the opportunity to refresh his bedding, while I engaged him in his favourite topic.

"What was it to sit in his presence, Holmes?"

Sherlock Holmes turned his head toward me, his eyes lit from within. "The most penetrating gaze I have ever experienced, Watson. His eyes bored into one's soul. Prevarication found no place in his presence."

At that moment Mycroft Holmes entered the cottage, carrying his despatch box and muttering about the confounded *twins*. He chuckled as he removed his coat and took his seat.

"No prevarication, eh Sherlock? You'll not find such a man as that in all of Versailles! I'd like to watch Mr. Lincoln handle these dashed twins.... Thank you, madam," he said, accepting a cup of tea from Margaret.

"Oh, he could handle anyone, Mycroft." Sherlock Holmes smiled at a memory as he watched Margaret. "Mrs. Stanton's serving girl once spilled an entire cup of coffee in the President's lap, like this—" He held his palm out faceup, then turned it over. "— and Mr. Stanton began shouting at her to clean it up, which of course unnerved the poor thing, and she burst into tears. And all the while Mr. Lincoln is patting himself dry and comforting her. 'That's enough scolding, Edwin. She didn't pour it on my head, as the editors would prefer!'"

Sherlock Holmes chuckled softly.

"That was his way, Mycroft."

"Remarkable," said I. "To be so solicitous of a serving girl."

"Yes, isn't it," said Mycroft Holmes dryly. A hint of jealousy, I had noticed, underlay Mycroft's subdued responses to his brother's expressions of reverence for Abraham Lincoln.

"Oh, he was solicitous of everyone!" A fresh smile had come to Sherlock Holmes's face. "He often inquired of me whether the dinner had been cooked to my liking—"

"Dinner? At the President's table?" Mycroft raised an eyebrow. "Surely you exaggerate, Sherlock."

"Not a bit! I often dined with the family, to keep Tad company. His father was delighted to have an Englishman at the table. He enjoyed reciting Shakespeare for me—the words to Horatio spoken by Hamlet before his death evidently had great meaning for him. 'There's a divinity that shapes our ends, rough-hew them how we will,' most especially. And at other times he pestered me with questions."

"What sort of questions, Sherlock?" said his brother with a skeptical frown.

"Why, he had been very much pleased by the actions of the Manchester mill workers,[82] as you might imagine, but he desired to know if they were representative of the entire British citizenry towards the Northern cause."

"And you told him...?"

"I told him it mattered not one whit what a British citizen thought of the Northern cause! That the country was run by three old men in Whitehall and the widow of Windsor![83] This astounded him greatly."

"I suppose he thought he may as well rescue *us* once he had conquered the South?" Mycroft Holmes said with no little asperity.

---

82 *In 1862, mill workers in Manchester, England, voted in support of the Northern embargo on Southern cotton exports, despite the devastating effect it would have on the English textile industry.*
83 *Queen Victoria, who had retired from public view after the death of her husband, Albert in 1861.*

"Oh, there was no jingoism about him, Mycroft. He sought knowledge, not advantage."

"What else did you discuss at these dinners?" I asked, uncertain how much of this was my friend's imagination.

"The Queen, Watson. He was much intrigued by life under a monarch."

"I hope you did not disparage Her Majesty, Sherlock?"

"On the contrary, Mycroft. I told him we loved our Queen."

"And what did Mr. Lincoln say to that?" I asked.

"He laughed heartily, Watson. *'That's not an affection I'm familiar with! But I will wear them down in the end.'*

"And he did, Watson. He did!"

I have described this conversation without expressing the frequent coughing fits that made Sherlock Holmes's speech disjointed and difficult to follow. After dinner, when the intensity of the chills increased, we moved him to bed. Brother Mycroft slept upon the settee while I took the first watch by Holmes's bedside. His pulse was racing, the fever suddenly and dangerously high. The bed cover needed changing every hour, so drenched in sweat did it become.

Around midnight, Holmes was gripped by an intensity of recall that was as startling as it seemed fantastic.

"The battlefields, Watson!"

I turned up the lamp to find him sitting in his bed, his eyes fixed upon an object far away in his mind's eye.

"To the Wilderness and Spotsylvania, Vicksburg, Shiloh! Oh, how we rode, Abraham and I!"

"But surely Shiloh and Vicksburg were in the American West, Holmes, were they not?"

"We rode *everywhere*, Watson!"

"And when did you do this, Holmes? I don't recall it in your manuscript."

"No? Well...perhaps you are right, Watson." Sherlock Holmes sank back against the pillow. "It is becoming rather difficult to tell where my life ends, and my dreams begin." He reached out and gripped my arm with his skeletal fingers.

"Have a care by the cliffs, Watson. They crumble, you see. Inch by inch, foot by foot, the Seven Sisters this way come—like death's scythe, Watson! They will be here in time. Yes, all in good time. Are they at our threshold already? I feel the bed shake. The cottage trembles. The roof—see the lamp sways from its hook!"

His grip suddenly relaxed.

"No, Watson, of course, it is the breeze. You have opened the window."

I had not opened the window, but I said nothing about it.

A satisfied chuckle now came from the pillow.

"Anyway, the bees will be safe! They will fly away. So, should we all, Watson. I will fly away too, and soon. Do you join me, Watson? No, you have a wife to care for. A grandchild to bounce on your knee..."

He went on in this fashion while I fetched Mycroft Holmes.

Mycroft stayed with his brother the remainder of the evening and I returned to the farmhouse, for I needed to be my best self for whatever might come.

Shortly before daybreak, I made my way back to the cottage where I found Mycroft awake in the chair, reading correspondence as Sherlock Holmes slept soundly. I fixed coffee for Mycroft, whose presence was required at the telegraph station, and then took his seat by his brother's bed.

There I drank my coffee and glanced through the Bible upon the lamp table.

The familiar text was marked up in Holmes's precise hand—some of the passages quite heavily—and I had become engrossed in a passage when there came a knock to the door of the cottage.

The clock upon the mantel showed it was not even six o'clock.

"I perceive it is Death come to greet me, Watson," said a thin, rasping voice, and I could see Holmes trying to push himself up on one thin arm.

"Surely not, Holmes!"

"It is the simplest of deductions, Watson."

"No, Holmes," said I, rising from the chair. "It is the milkman, I expect."

"Your mind has always been less keen than my own, Watson." The words came weakly but with the precision so characteristic of my friend.

"You do not *observe*, much less reason. This is not the milkman's day. And it cannot be Brother Mycroft, for he would have tapped his welcome in the old telegraph code. The constable raps with his nightstick. The farmwife knocks with trepidation, for my reputation—though my body may be wasted—remains, I trust, formidable. Therefore, Watson, it must be my Krishna."

"We will soon settle the matter, Holmes." I left the room.

"Be gracious, Watson!" he called after me. "I am quite ready to leave this body!"

Holmes was wrong, of course. It was only the milkman. But the timing was propitious. I handed the fellow the empties and urged him to ask Vicar Evans to come around when he had a moment. Then I carried a fresh bottle of milk to the bedroom, knowing that even in his weakened state, Sherlock Holmes would demand proof of our visitor.

Sure enough, the eager look upon his face vanished when I showed him the bottle.

"Not the Krishna, then," said he, slumping back against the pillow.

"No, Holmes, not the Krishna—unless he comes disguised as the milkman!"

It was a joke, to bring levity to a rather gloomy situation, but Holmes fixed his gaze upon the bottle in childlike wonder, and it became evident he had taken me quite seriously.

"You scintillate, Watson! I deprecate your talents too quickly! Why *not* a milkman? The God of Abraham sent a carpenter to fulfill the prophecies of the Old Testament. And, of course, the Krishna tended cows as a boy. I dare say you are right, Watson!"

Holmes now feebly urged me to the door.

"Fetch him, man! Fetch him before he returns to Mathura!"

I took the milk bottles into the kitchen as Holmes continued in this rambling vein until he was overcome by a coughing fit, which quite exhausted him. When I returned with tea, he had fallen into a deep sleep from which he would not awaken until the vicar arrived mid-morning in the company of Margaret. They had been arranging the burial of the old man and now joined Holmes in the bedroom for tea while I napped upon the settee.

Sometime later I was awakened by Margaret. She had left the bedroom to fetch soup for Holmes, who had acquired something of an appetite, and there was concern in her eyes.

"What's this about a near-miss with the Almighty, John?"

I rubbed the sleep from my eyes. "It was only the milkman!"

"Well he is quite convinced it was the Krishna in disguise. He's got Vicar Evans half convinced as well! You know how masterful he can be, John."

"Shall I intercede?"

"Oh, no, they are having quite a time trading verses."

"Trading verses?"

"The Vicar from the Bible and Mr. Holmes from the Bhagavad Gita. Mr. Holmes references a verse—*'There is no purifier in this world like Knowledge'*—and Vicar Evans returns with *'A fool despises wisdom and instruction.'* I shall have to retrieve my nanny's old text from London if I am to keep up with Mr. Holmes."

Her voice faltered and she failed to meet my eyes.

"If there is time."

That evening, after taking dinner together in the kitchen, Margaret and I entered the bedroom to bring Holmes his tea and found him awake and seated against the pillow, his face knotted in thought.

"Are you uncomfortable, Mr. Holmes?"

He shook his head. "No, madam. It is that line from Hafiz," said he, in a voice little above a whisper, and between fits of coughing and long pauses. "I try to recall it..."

"How does it go?"

"Oh, it is most ancient and sublime! It concerns the earth and the sun— of course, all Hafiz concerns the earth and the sun!"

"How did you become familiar with it?" I interposed, for there was no such book upon Holmes's shelf. "Monsieur Vernet of DuPont, I imagine?"

"Really, Watson! Why, I learned from the great poet himself!"

"Indeed!" said I. "Where was this?"

"In Mecca, of course!"

"And that was, when, during your three years of sabbatical?"[84]

"When else? I practiced the ascetic technique of consciousness in the man's very presence, Watson. Forty days of hearing the hypnotic chants of an Arabian poet will put them in your head for all time, believe me!" Holmes smiled blissfully, his eyes tightly shut.

"And what is this verse of his you are attempting to recall?" Margaret asked.

"It runs in this way, madam—*Even after*—"

A pain jolted his body and Holmes gripped the coverlet tightly, then fell back with a bone-shaking cough. When it had passed, he turned his face upward to the ceiling, and, in the manner of one who is gathering all his strength in the effort to speak, he took a deep breath—or at least as deep as the coughing fits allowed—and exhaled these words:

"*Even after all this time, the sun never says...*" He stopped.

"What does the sun never say, Holmes?"

Sherlock Holmes's grey eyes looked at me, and then at Margaret. They were moistened by something other than the effects of his illness.

He shook his head.

He could not recall the line.

"Are you still with me, Watson?"

It was later that evening—when I know not—and Sherlock Holmes's voice came faintly from the pillow out of the gloom. The fire in the grate imparted a stuffy warmth to the bedroom, but Holmes lay shivering and convulsed, and he gripped the sheets with trembling fingers.

A solemn voice behind me answered him.

"Yes, Dr. Watson is here, as am I, Sherlock."

It was Mycroft Holmes, just returned from the telegraph house. Then, with all the authority of a figure of State and the stamina of a man half his age, Mycroft ordered me to the farmhouse with Margaret for rest, even

---

84 *Watson appears unaware that Hafiz lived from 1315 to 1390.*

though he had been up all evening on business.

"I wish time alone with Johnnie."

"Certainly. But you will send for me...?"

"Of course, Doctor."

"Thank you."

Reluctantly, I took my leave and found Margaret waiting in the kitchen. Together we walked to the farmhouse and fell immediately asleep.

Daylight was breaking over the Downs as we entered the cottage next morning. The atmosphere was rather foul, and Margaret put the kettle on while I opened the windows to admit fresh air.

In the bedroom I found Mycroft asleep in the chair beside his brother's bed, papers upon his lap and a sputtering lamp at his elbow. The room possessed the sour smell bred by illness, and I threw open the window. Mycroft Holmes stirred and shook himself awake while I took the pulse of the figure beneath the coverlet.

It was not good.

Margaret entered with tea, and Mycroft, his eyes fixed upon his sleeping brother, briefed us quietly.

"The evening was fitful. Flowery descriptions of improbable adventures in America and a brief period of lucidity in the quiet hour before dawn, when he quoted Jackson's last words.[85] And that's when Johnnie and I were finally together. As in the old days."

Margaret asked what it was they had discussed.

"We talked of nothing and yet of everything, madam," said Mycroft Holmes, with the tenderness of a brother. "I simply held his hand."

Outside the window the birds had finished celebrating the faint dawning of light in the east. Mycroft had removed himself to the telegraph house and Margaret was fixing breakfast. I was seated alone with Sherlock Holmes.

His breathing was halting and forced, and as the morning light filled the room, it revealed a gaunt, pale face staring blankly from the pillow.

---

85 *As he lay dying, accidentally shot by one of his own men, Stonewall Jackson imagined he was still directing his troops. His last words were, "Let us cross over the river and rest under the shade of the trees."*

"Are you with me, Watson?"

"Yes, I am here."

"The light dims, Watson. I no longer see the things of this world. The final education begins!"

A cold and overwhelming sensation gripped my soul. I could not speak.

"You must tell the bees, for me, Watson. Watson, do you hear me?"

"Yes, Holmes."

"*How* will you tell them?"

"Holmes—"

"*How*, Watson?"

"As you have instructed me, of course."

"Humour me, Watson. 'At dusk, when the bees...'"

"Yes, Holmes: 'When the bees have returned to their hives—'"

"At *dusk*!" Sherlock Holmes lifted himself from the pillow, and even in this weakened state his voice carried something of the sharpness of old.

"'At dusk, when the bees have returned to the hives, moving softly and speaking in a soft and soothing voice...'"

When I had finished to his evident satisfaction the instructions that I had memorized during our last few strolls among the hives, Sherlock Holmes fell back upon the pillow with a look of contentment upon his face, although his eyes remained closed to the morning light now illuminating his room.

"The Twenty-Second Psalm, Watson," came Holmes's voice. "'*My God, my God, why hast though forsaken me?*' it begins. Read it once more, please, if you will."

"Of course, Holmes."

As I had done many times since he had been confined to bed, I picked up the Bible—it was opened to that passage—and began to read this Psalm that was of great meaning to Sherlock Holmes ever since he had first heard its opening verse that morning on the shores of the Potomac River, in America.

He listened in silence, his eyes closed, a blissful smile forming upon his lips as I declaimed the final stanza, which he regarded as a message of great hope:

"*They shall come and shall declare his righteousness /Unto a people that shall be born, that he hath done this.*"

When I had finished, Holmes opened his eyes at the ceiling.

"Was Jesus not a scholar of the Old Testament, Watson? Did King David's words not presage His very ministry? Look to it, Watson. The Twenty-Second Psalm is as essential to Christianity as John Three-Sixteen."

Holmes turned to me, his eyes now shut tight.

"I once wrote a monograph upon that Psalm, you know..."

Then he drifted away into his own thoughts and soon fell asleep.

If Sherlock Holmes had written a monograph upon the Twenty-Second Psalm, I had never seen it.

Chapter Three

THE CLIFFS OF PROVIDENCE

In the end, it was not a small ivory box fitted with a tiny metal spring tipped in poison that killed Sherlock Holmes, nor a savage beating by hired thugs or an unwise experiment with a murderer's toxin known as the Devil's Foot. And it was most certainly not an impurity in the seven percent solution of cocaine which he had, in a previous time, injected into his veins with alarming regularity, that killed my friend.

What killed Sherlock Holmes was the influenza that had travelled from America with the troops of General Pershing, and swept the trenches of Verdun, and filled the hospital tents of Summerdown when there were no more beds in France to be had and made its way across the Birling Gap to Went Hill, where it had found its way into my friend, filling his weakened lungs with a foul, deadly mass that quite literally took his breath away early one morning as the sun began to warm the verdant slopes of the Downs and the bees were making their first forays of the morning from their hives.

Mycroft Holmes was asleep upon the settee and Margaret was in the kitchen cooking breakfast. I had opened the window by Holmes's bed, and the creeping vines that wreathed its frame now reflected in red the first promise of light from the eastern sky.

Suddenly a mockingbird began to announce the morning with a repertoire which sounded very much like squawking seagulls.

"Hist!" came the soft whisper of Sherlock Holmes. "Do I hear the gulls outside where the bees once toiled, Watson? Have the cliffs of Providence arrived?"

"No, Holmes. It is only the mockingbird."

Holmes cocked his ear to the high, shrill calling outside his window and shook his head.

"I'm sorry, Watson. I fear your skills in the field of observation remain as limited as ever. God wears so many faces, you see! But they all speak the same truth, do they not? *I will create new heavens and a new earth. The former things shan't be remembered or come to mind. But be glad and rejoice forever.*"

My practiced eye watched a new and more savage wave of pain suddenly course through my friend's body, the legs bending upward at the knees. When the contraction had passed, I judged it now prudent to administer a dosage of the morphia that had been left behind by the Harley Street surgeon.

It was the last Mr. Sherlock Holmes would ever take, and his arm twitched as the needle pinched the skin.

"You inject me, Watson? There's humour in that!"

"I will call for Mycroft."

"He will be found at the Diogenes Club." Holmes stirred. "*Mrs. Hudson!*" he cried out in a weak but commanding voice. "*Mrs. Hudson! Call a cab! The doctor and I make for the Diogenes Club! Brother Mycroft awaits!*"

The figure of Mycroft Holmes now appeared at the door. As he moved to his brother's side, I stepped to the end of the bed.

Mycroft Holmes bent close by his brother.

"I am here, Sherlock. We may ride together."

"Where is Watson, then? We *must* have Watson—the game is afoot!" Sherlock Holmes made one last effort to rise from his bed, but a violent contraction threw off the blanket and exposed his bare feet.

I reached out and gently massaged his foot to soothe him.

"I am here, Holmes, with Mycroft." I hoped my quavering voice would not disappoint my old companion.

Sherlock Holmes relaxed.

"Good old Watson. Did you bring your service revolver?"

"Why, Holmes? Do you think there is danger?"

The brow furrowed, the lips tightened. Then a thin smile came to the parched lips. It was the smile possessed of the radiance—as Mycroft later agreed—of an extra-worldly vision.

"No, Watson. I dare say we shan't need it. Not this time. Surely not this time."

Sherlock Holmes took one more shallow, laboured breath.

Then he took no more.

In the Parish of East Dean that year, the death of Sherlock Holmes was the second-to-last that would be recorded in which the cause of death was influenza.

The last to die of it was the greengrocer.

That garrulous fellow had picked up the deadly virus during his rounds at Summerdown, as Mycroft had suspected, and brought it to the cottage at Went Hill.

In all, thirteen residents of East Dean perished by that peculiarly deadly strain, all of them customers of the greengrocer.

It was one fewer than the number of village men who had died fighting in France.

How it chanced that no one else at the cottage at Went Hill had been struck down by that deadly virus shall remain forever a mystery, unsolvable even to Sherlock Holmes in his prime.

The greengrocer died three days after my friend.

Chapter Four

THE MANUSCRIPT
OF MR. SHERLOCK
HOLMES—CONCLUDED

It is two days after the tumultuous events described above.

I am seated at Holmes's old desk in the cottage at Went Hill, my pen poised above a fresh piece of foolscap as I gaze out the bow window upon the hives and the orchard, the meadows of Went Hill and the tiny figure of the Belle Tout lighthouse perched upon the edge of the Seven Sisters, where the rising sun slowly burns off the Channel mist beyond.

My mind is searching for the precise words to say at the service for Mr. Sherlock Holmes.

It is to be held tomorrow morning, and I have returned to this spot, hoping to find inspiration here, but time is running short.

Agents from Scotland Yard will soon arrive to remove from the cottage what Lestrade had described to me as "all items of interest to the official force"—which is to say almost everything in the cottage—and it will be necessary for me to relinquish my friend's chair while they go about their task.

The dustbin at my feet is already filled with discarded attempts to explain the man at whose side I spent almost half a lifetime, and yet I find myself no closer to fulfilling my task than when I started.

How to reconcile the otherworldly ambition that underlay my friend's cloak of modesty and reticence? The fitful spells of lethargic gloom that bracketed the energetic spasms of animation whenever a worthwhile case crossed his threshold? The self-centeredness that almost exactly mirrored the selflessness of my friend and companion?

I struggle to frame words that will reward the memory of a man who refused any reward—the Grand Cross, even! Whose preference, always, was to aid those in no position to reward him with anything other than their sincere thanks. Who gave away precious little of himself—except to his clients, to whom he gave all.

If there was a selfish aspect to Sherlock Holmes—and I try to think of one as I sit at his desk—I see it was reserved for his most valuable commodity, which is to say his *time*.

He certainly wasn't selfish about money.

On the contrary, Holmes never sought it, although it often sought *him*, and it was no surprise to me that his primary condition for the publication of my first brochure on our adventures together was that the proceeds from *A Study in Scarlet* would go to the poor, from whose circumstances he had risen. (The second stipulation being that the program be administered by Brother Mycroft, assuring our anonymity in the matter.)

"The needs are so great, Watson, and the means are so few," he had said.

And, of course, I had readily agreed.

But these qualities of his—almost superhuman, as I have described them—came at a very human cost, and it was a cost I had witnessed firsthand.

Almost from the moment he awoke each morning to the moment when he laid his head upon his pillow, Sherlock Holmes admitted to his consulting room clients bringing tales of the very worst behaviour humanity had to offer. And he could take no vacation from these unremitting degradations, for crime and injustice do not take weekends in the country or pause to celebrate a wedding or to mourn a death.

Being unmarried and childless, Sherlock Holmes could not even comfort himself in the arms of a spouse, or the love of a child.

Is it any wonder, then, that this constant dwelling in darkness contributed to my friend's need for otherworldly stimulation, even at the point of a needle?

All these things and more, I want to say, but I cannot shape them into a coherent form that will fit upon the paper before me. If I say just one of them, I feel I must say them all, and yet to say all there is to say about this man—truly all—seems impossible as I sit at his desk. I wrote some two thousand pages describing our adventures together over thirty-some years in a vain attempt to define Mr. Sherlock Holmes.

How can I hope to do it in just a few pages more?

The clock upon the mantel tells me the men from the Yard are expected at any moment, and I give up.

Putting down my pen, I study the cloth cover of the hulking typewriter before me. It is torn and discoloured from its flight out the window that strange evening, which now seems so long ago, although the damage to the machine was swiftly repaired by the same fellow who fixed the mantelpiece clock. I recall how Holmes had worked here each morning, until the coughing and discomfort sapped his ability to remain seated at the desk.

On an impulse, I remove the cover.

There, upon the rolls, rest two sheets of onionskin paper, identical to that upon which his manuscript had been typed. My heart leaps. I pick them up and notice one more still in the rolls. Removing this, I find the three pages are filled with the closely typed paragraphs favoured by Holmes. Also, that almost every line has been marked in some way by his precise hand.

As I study the pages, however, I realize these are not, as I had expected, his musings upon rational deduction. Rather, they were evidently meant for inclusion in the introduction to his manuscript.

I replace the cloth cover and, as the distant sound of an approaching motorcar reaches my ears, I begin to read to myself the last extract of the remarkable manuscript of Mr. Sherlock Holmes:

When I Met You, Watson

Charming as your tale of our first encounter at Bart's[86] may have been, my dear Watson, I fear the overall impression presented to your readers deserves to be corrected while I am still able to do so.

You give the thing a convincing air of serendipity—*we met; we discussed our habits; we agreed to terms; we proceeded to share lodging and something of a life together.* And while that may be your true memory of the circumstances, our first meeting was never so casual an affair.

That a mutual acquaintance brought us together in the chemical laboratory at Bart's is beyond dispute, but you were by no means the first candidate to whom I had been introduced. Indeed, before you walked into that dark, lofty chamber, I had already spent a considerable amount of time meeting with—and dismissing—a half-dozen other candidates brought my way.

You were merely the first to fit all my requirements.

Those requirements included—in addition to the obvious imperative of personal compatibility—three qualities which I deemed necessary to compliment my own unique skills as I embarked upon my career as a consulting detective.

First and foremost, I had decided my companion must be a medical man, for while I knew much about the dead and how to infer the means by which a body might have come to that poor station, I knew comparatively little about the living and their ailments. Reasoning that in my chosen line of work I would be exposed to a variety of individuals in various states of health and well-being, I concluded that a man trained in the medical arts would answer my purpose admirably.

Second was that he had spent time on the battlefield. This may strike you as odd, Watson—it struck Brother Mycroft that way—but I had learned something of the unpredictable nature of armed conflict during my youthful adventure in America, and it had convinced me that such experience provided invaluable training for the kind of work I had in mind, involving, as it would, a certain degree of ready travel, indifferent lodgings, unpredictable circumstances and bizarre injuries.

---

86 *A Study in Scarlet, 1887.*

The third was that he be self-employed—but not so successfully that his practice would prevent him from accompanying me at a moment's notice.

I wanted no "University Man," of course. I had encountered that type lounging in the hallways outside Brother Mycroft's telegraph room and had marked them as utterly ill-suited for the kind of improvisational experiences that would constitute my working days. But neither did I wish to be teamed with a budding detective whose talents might duplicate my own, for there could be no second-guessing my conclusions.

I was not without a healthy ego, as you know.

Until the moment you crossed that dim threshold at Bart's, Watson, no one had possessed even two of those three qualifications. Yet when you appeared, I perceived at once that the solution to my tripartite requirements was at hand.

It was evident you were not only a medical man but an army doctor, just back from Afghanistan, with an injury to your shoulder and a temperament that bespoke a colleague of independent mind—although one not inclined to boastful self-promotion—who would be unsatisfied merely to attain the trappings of wealth and respectability.

In brief, I saw that you would be the perfect companion for the adventurous occupation I anticipated.

I had no foreshadowing, of course, that you would find in my work the inspiration to turn some of our little adventures into memoirs that spread word of my small abilities to the Continent and beyond, bringing an entirely unanticipated clientele to my practice from all corners of the globe.

It is true that your emphasis upon the romantic and somewhat sensational aspects of my methods in those stories did little to advance the understanding of rational deduction in the minds of the public—a deficit I pointed out to you many times over the years, to your (admit it, Watson!) considerable annoyance—but the casework I received thanks to those effusive memoirs of yours was enriching to my mental health. And the publishing royalties...well, Doctor, the London poor is measurably smaller in number than it might have been, thanks to you.

I must point out, however—with the frankness I have always employed in our communications together—that I would almost certainly have become the premier consulting detective of Europe even had our paths never crossed. There are only two men in all the world to whom such credit might be due, one being my brother Mycroft, the other being a certain American, a giant—literally and figuratively—of whom more will be revealed later in this memoir.

But *never* would I have had the career I did without you, Watson—and not merely because you saved my life in at least two cases which, in your excessive modesty, you chose not to draft for the public memoirs. It is because the aura which attached itself to my reputation—thanks to your books and articles—was so convincing that everyone from the lowliest chamber maid to the highest minister of state felt they knew me—that I somehow *belonged* to them—and therefore, that I would help them.

And, in a sense, I did indeed belong to them all. For good and—quite frankly—for ill.

I suspect you already know what a double-edged sword such faith in my abilities proved to be. The responsibility I felt to honour that faith weighed greatly, as indeed it must weigh heavily upon any man possessed of a conscience. Is it any wonder, then, that when those anxious, needy faces from my consulting room began to inhabit my dreams, I fled to the Downs—to my bees—and cut off all communication except through Brother Mycroft?

But do not, I pray, feel guilt at this last, Watson.

The inconveniences placed upon me by unwanted, or at least unexpected, fame were modest indeed when weighed against—if I may say it without seeming immodest—the peace of mind my abilities brought to some number of the human race.

And I would have had it no other way.

This life is, after all, for living as best we can, and to nurse the mustard seed of talent planted within us by our God and to use that talent to help shade and nourish others in need.

In that regard—and once more in the utter frankness I believe this document demands—I will turn the tables on you, my old campaigner, and perhaps surprise you when I say that it was *you*, my dear Watson, who, I think, lived life best of all, for you shared yourself in ways I could not. And although I sometimes mocked your attachment to the fair sex, I did so only because I knew, deep down, that such an attachment was something I could never achieve on my own.

Perhaps the scars of childhood had hardened that muscle in my own heart, or perhaps the habits of a lifetime of observation and deduction allowed no room for the softer passions to make themselves felt—or perhaps it was both those circumstances—so let me say here that your shining example of the goodness of, yes, love, rather smoothed those rough edges off me over our years together, and I thank you for that.

And I thank you for sharing your life with mine.

By now, I expect you have found Mr. Lincoln's book—the Weems book. And you have discovered exactly how I got my name, and why young Moriarty was desperate to have that book.

And why Mycroft was anxious he not succeed.

But I hope you have discovered something else, Watson—something less tangible but far more important.

It is this. You were no mere scrivener or amanuensis, Doctor, as some among your readers might have had it. You were my complement—a balancing counterweight to my own highly developed faculties, enabling me to function with energy and vigour without running so hot that the machinery was torn to pieces. The Tao shaman might say you were the bright and energetic yin to my rather over-dark yang.

I would only say that, above all, Watson, you were my friend.

And as I watch you these days from my window, carefully tending the hives whose product nourishes us all, I think of those words of Hafiz:

"Even after all this time, the sun never says to the earth, 'You owe me'."

He was speaking of you, Watson, and of me.

Chapter Five

A DISTINGUISHED GUEST

The first day of May, 1919 dawned warm and bright, and the parish bell had begun to call mourners to the memorial service for Mr. Sherlock Holmes. It was set to begin sharp at ten o'clock, and Margaret and I left the farmhouse for the short walk to the old stone sanctuary of the church of the parish of East Dean.

Mycroft Holmes was being driven directly there from London, and Miss Colvin was already at the sanctuary assisting Vicar Evans in the preparations of what was to be a small and intimate affair in accordance with Holmes's wishes. He had often said the townsfolk with whom he had shared his remaining days on Went Hill should be allowed to honour his memory without suffering the inconvenience of a more public spectacle (which, as Mycroft pointed out, was quite beyond the capabilities of East Dean to accommodate in any case).

And the friendly newspapers had, of course, complied by suppressing any mention of the ceremony.

I nevertheless expected an ample turnout for the man the villagers called "Mr. Sherlock," even among those who worked the land, for the weather had been favourable that spring and the wheat and barley crops had all been planted. But as we passed the bake-house and turned the corner onto the village green, what I saw considerably astonished me.

It seemed the entire village was responding to the call.

Farmers and farmwives; ostlers and automobile mechanics; the butcher, the baker and the milkman; Tony the cab driver and Jack, the landlord of the Tiger; his barmaid and her son; all these and many others—those of means and those of modesty and those just making do—could be seen crossing the green (the zeppelin gun having finally been removed) for Lower Street, to the Parish Church of St. Simon and St. Jude.

And when there could be no more residents of East Dean to answer the calling of the bell, the omnibus from Eastbourne pulled up at the Tiger, depositing seven girls in white lab coats (Mr. Holmes's candlemakers, Miss Colvin later informed me), the Lord Mayor of Eastbourne and his family and a group of rather rougher-looking men of middle age whom I could not place—but whose bearing and swagger I thought somehow familiar.

Imagine my surprise and delight, then, when the leader of these last rushed to catch up to me and introduced himself as Wiggins, of Holmes's old Baker Street Irregulars! It was with no little emotion that I introduced Wiggins and the others to Margaret, and then, together with that ragtag group of mates who had survived their early lives in the streets of London thanks in no small part to the man whose memory we were prepared to honour, we made our way down the hill to the church.

Vicar Evans, in collar and black shirt, stood at the threshold greeting everyone with a familiar handshake or a polite bow. Margaret and I entered the cool, quiet sanctuary and made our way to the front pew, where we joined Miss Colvin, who was seated on the aisle.

Our old friend Lestrade now appeared, having arrived not with Mycroft Holmes, evidently, but by another, mysterious means. He took a seat away from us, near the end of the pew and close by the north transept, then proceeded to glance furtively at his watch as I studied the gathering congregants.

Among these I noticed a very elderly, very prosperous-looking man with something of the American about him, making his way to one of the chairs set up in the south transept—the pews having run out of room—and I guessed he was a representative of the American government or one of Holmes's old contacts in their detective circles.

By the time Vicar Evans took his chair by the pulpit and the strains of *Balm in Gilead* had begun to sound from the organ, every seat was occupied except for that of Mycroft Holmes, which was between mine and Lestrade's, and a space on the other side of Lestrade at the far end of the pew.

Mycroft now entered the sanctuary, and at a sign from the vicar he walked slowly down the aisle, carrying in his gloved hands a plain clay urn—the sight of which caused within me a sudden burst of emotional turmoil. Margaret was there to steady me, however, and by the time he reached the altar and carefully set down the urn upon a credence table garnished with flowers, I was myself again.

Mycroft then took his seat between me and Lestrade, but as the last chorus of *Gilead* was echoing throughout the sanctuary, Lestrade suddenly rose and ducked into the dark shadow of the north transept, where a brief rectangle of light revealed the opening and closing of a door. Murmurs were heard, and footfalls sounded, and Lestrade reappeared, his short and stout figure leading a tall, erect silhouette instantly familiar to all within the church.

A collective intake of breath was heard, and the congregation rose in one body for George Frederick Ernest Albert—His Majesty, King George V.

The King took his seat between Lestrade and a bowing Mycroft Holmes as the strong scent of tobacco, of which the King was known to be fond, overwhelmed the scent of the flowers from the altar. As we resumed our seats, I squeezed Mycroft's arm and bent to whisper my surprise, but he touched a gloved finger to his pursed lips.

Then he nodded to the vicar.

The service that followed was bare and simple—as simple and bare as Holmes's life had been, when stripped of the adventures and excitements of his unique profession.

Vicar Evans gave a plainspoken but eloquent homily, deeply informed by his long friendship with Holmes and their mutual affection for the honeybees, for the ancient archeological mysteries of the Downs and for the great mystery of faith.

A second hymn, *Wade in the Water*, was sung. It is a simple verse set to a delightful melody, and Holmes had first heard it at that baptism on the Potomac during his adventures in America—albeit in a rather more ecstatic fashion than was mustered in that English church!

And then it was my turn to speak.

But here I failed my friend.

I had thought to make a few brief remarks in an extemporaneous manner. It would simplify my task, I had decided, to let myself be moved by the occasion rather than to try to sum up the entirety of my friend's existence, as I had been unable to do in those drafts left behind in the dustbin of Sherlock Holmes's cottage.

And yet in that sanctuary, in front of my wife, my King and the best country stock England had to offer, I lost my nerve utterly. I half-stood, then sat down again.

Lestrade was beside himself. I heard his sharp voice hissing at me to *get up there for your King!*

But I could not move.

It was Margaret who once again came to my rescue.

She rose in my place and began telling, softly and beautifully, her own story.

It was the year 1892, she said, and a cable had reached her in India from a man whom she had only read stories about—a seemingly egotistical and eminently selfish man called Sherlock Holmes.

The cable suggested she leave the life of a young governess in Madras and return to England to aid her sister Mary, whose illness had reached a critical stage. Mary's husband—and by that, of course, Holmes had meant *me*—had been too consumed with grief to think clearly of such a thing, and so the author had acted on his own initiative. No consideration of the expense involved in such a voyage was necessary, the cable concluded, for arrangements were in place through the offices of the sender's brother, Mr. Mycroft Holmes of Whitehall.

That telegram, Margaret told the congregation, was only the first of many such kindnesses by which Sherlock Holmes would demonstrate to her the soft heart which underlay his austere demeanor and efface the somewhat churlish impression my stories had made upon her of the famous consulting detective.

But it was not until our move to Went Hill, she said, that she would discover a deeper bond with Sherlock Holmes, thanks to his breathtaking familiarity with the Bhagavad Gita, of which she had learned something from her devout Hindu nanny, and she described how Holmes had delighted in unraveling the common threads woven through the world's faiths during the many hours they had spent in conversation with Vicar Evans by the fireplace at Went Hill—or at Holmes's bedside during his final days.

Holding aloft Holmes's own copy of that sacred book, which she had thought to bring to the service for just such an exigency, Margaret displayed to the congregation a passage that had been so marked with lines, exclamation points and side notes that it appeared difficult to read.

The greatest consulting detective who ever lived had marked up the entire volume in the manner of his case notes, she explained, but the passage she chose to read in a firm, joyous voice was the most heavily annotated of all:

"'The soul is neither born, nor does it ever die; nor having once existed, does it ever cease to be. The soul is without birth, eternal, immortal, and ageless. It is not destroyed when the body is destroyed.'"

Then she closed the book, gazed at the high timbers of the lofty sanctuary and quoted a different book altogether.

"Let us be glad and rejoice."

She took her seat next to me as the final speaker rose.

Mycroft Holmes appeared stiff and uneasy. There was discomfort visible in his stooped figure—odd, perhaps, for a man whose audience might as easily have been the Prime Minister's cabinet as the King himself— but it was of course the emotions that gripped him as he turned to face us in that somber sanctuary, which caused some fumbling and hesitation until he found his gruff, familiar voice.

"I am not, I would be the first to admit, well up on these matters of the spirit," Mycroft began. "That was my brother's department. Johnnie—he may be 'Sherlock' to the world, but before he was given that name so famous to you now, he was Johnnie to me," he added, causing a surprised murmur to arise from the congregation. "Johnnie heard those voices—the voices by which we are called to act in communion with those around us—and whether they were of an Eastern or a Western cast, it made no difference to him."

He held up a slim, tattered copybook. "This was his first monograph. '*The Final Words of Jesus at Calvary.*' He wrote it when he was all of seventeen."

Mycroft put on his spectacles and glanced through the pages, which, I could see, had been written out in what was, even at that early age, Sherlock Holmes's precise hand.

"Johnnie had been puzzling over those final words of Christ on the cross, as recorded by Saint Matthew—'*My God, my God, why hast thou forsaken me?*'"

"Rather a despairing thing for the Son of God to say, don't you think? Anyway, Johnnie thought so. But as he was making his way through the Bible for the first time, he instantly saw that those words came from the Twenty-Second Psalm, which is said to have foretold the entire ministry of Christ.

"And that's when Johnnie made the deduction he writes about here: Jesus, being a rabbi, would have been reciting from the cross *the entire Twenty-Second Psalm,* not merely crying out words of distress.

"And once he made that deduction, why, the inference was clear: Saint Matthew had recorded only the first verse of the Psalm—'*My God, my God, why hast thou forsaken me?*'—on the assumption that anyone reading his words would grasp the reference entirely."

Mycroft Holmes peered over his spectacles at the congregation.

"I showed this to the Archbishop of Canterbury and asked him to look it over. He was so impressed he wanted to ordain my brother on the spot."

This brought chuckles from the congregation.

Then, slowly and with great care, Mycroft Holmes read from his brother's monograph King David's words in that psalm, from the first verse to this, the last:

"They shall come, and shall declare his righteousness unto a people that shall be born, that he hath done this."

He removed his spectacles and glanced at the urn.

"That was the greatest deduction Johnnie ever made, I think."

No notice was given—and no account ever appeared in print—of the visit of George Frederick Ernest Albert, His Majesty, King George V, by the Grace of God, of the United Kingdom of Great Britain and Ireland and of the British Dominions beyond the Seas, King, Defender of the Faith, Emperor of India, to the small parish church of East Dean on the first day of May of 1919.

But no more fitting conclusion to a commemoration of the earthly life of my friend and companion of half a century could have been imagined than the sound of His Majesty's husky, off-pitched voice rising in chorus with the Lord Mayor of Eastbourne and his wife, the seven candlemakers and the various grownup Baker Street boys, along with a hundred more friends and townsfolk for whom Sherlock Holmes had provided a last court of inquiry, as the final hymn—"Amazing Grace"—shook the rafters.

Jack led the procession to the Tiger.

Chapter Six

THE MAN IN THE WINDOW SEAT

The late afternoon rays of the sun were climbing the whitewashed walls of the Tiger Inn, while inside the pub the sentiment had moved, as these things do, from sad reflections and sober tributes to the raising of the glass and the telling of stories by the well-lubricated remainders.

As the stories, in this case, concerned Mr. Sherlock Holmes, they nearly always started, "There was the time he helped me..." and concluded with salty expressions of incredulity at the offhand manner in which Holmes had deduced the solution to a seemingly insoluble problem and dismissed the supplicant in his brisk, businesslike tone after refusing the proffered payment.

Lestrade and I were seated at the bar with Tony the cabman, talking with Jack the landlord who was working the taps. Mycroft Holmes had departed for the telegraph station some time before, as urgent messages from Versailles awaited his attention there, and Margaret had returned to the farmhouse at the same time, for the smoky atmosphere had proven too much for her lungs.

The tables now held a collection of regulars and, alone in a corner, the American I had seen at the church, who was nursing a ginger beer. The middle-aged men we once knew as the Baker Street Irregulars had taken over the dartboard and were engaged in a raucous match.

Holmes's window seat was vacant, draped in crepe, a glass of his favourite stout upon the table in his memory.

From the effects of the sherry Lestrade had stood for us, my mind had acquired a relaxed and mellow glow, and a thought came to me as I studied Holmes's table, where he and I had sat together not four weeks before, discussing his remarkable time in America.

"Now there's a mystery," said I to Jack, as Lestrade followed my gaze.

"What's that, then, guv'nor?"

"The window seat. How did you know that was Sherlock Holmes's customary seat?"

Jack chortled. "Mr. Sherlock *always* sat there!"

"But he was in disguise, surely!"

Jack shared a knowing smile with Tony, but said nothing as he wiped down the bar.

"Well, he *was* a master of disguise," said I.

"He weren't all *that* masterful, were he, Tony?"

The cabby shook his head and raised his glass. "No, Jack. No, he weren't."

The landlord, seeing my puzzled look, put down his rag. "You see, guv, me and some of the boys knew it was Mr. Sherlock from the first."

"But he thought no one recognized him!" I protested, as Lestrade let out a rather annoying chuckle.

"Now that's one over on the great Mr. Sherlock Holmes! Rest in peace, of course. Rest in peace."

Jack cast a sharp eye at Lestrade while a regular at one of the tables spoke up.

"A fellow'd have to be daft not to know something's off when a bloke you never saw at the sheep dip sits down there and spends half the night nursin' a pint, talkin' about his flock."

"Remember the blind fiddle player?"

"The bricklayer!"

"All right, boys, all right," said the landlord.

"Why did no one confront him?" Lestrade asked the landlord, with something of condescension in his voice.

"And why, sir, would we do that?"

"You might have had quite the laugh at Mr. Sherlock Holmes's expense!"

Jack seemed overcome and nodded at the cabby. "You tell him, Tone."

The cabby downed the last of his drink, set the glass firmly upon the bar and turned to Lestrade.

"There ain't a soul in the Tiger would've done a thing at Mr. Sherlock Holmes's expense. Pick one o' the boys—go ahead! Ask how Mr. Sherlock helped 'em! Here's Jack. Ask how he saved Jack when the French came over for their war games and confiscated the village fishpond!"

"Why didn't you call the police?" Lestrade asked, but his question was drowned by laughter from the regulars and his face turned red as the landlord set down his rag and met his eyes.

"And what were the police going to say to a French officer dressed in his Army getup with stars on his chest and wavin' a letter signed by our War Minister tellin' us to hand over the pond, eh?"

"Well then, what did Sherlock Holmes do about it?" asked Lestrade, somewhat chastened.

"Mr. Sherlock didn't do a thing—not here, anyway," said Tony. "He just sits there with his fiddle and his dark glasses like he can't see nothin'. But three days later that same fellow comes back here, tail between his legs, throws the letter in the fire grate, says no hard feelings he hopes, and oh they ain't needin' the fishpond anyways."

"Paid for all the drink they nicked, too," said the landlord.

"But how do you know Sherlock Holmes was involved?"

"Because Mr. Mycroft tells me, next time I pick him up at the station! Says his brother telegraphed him that very night, and Mr. Mycroft brought hell down on the War Minister next day."

"I never heard that story," said Lestrade, with some wonderment in his voice.

"Very like, sir, very like," said the cabby. "There's a lot of stories people could tell on Mr. Sherlock you maybe never heard." Tony fixed his eyes upon the window seat, and now the landlord spoke confidentially.

"Mr. Sherlock helped Tone here when some o' the officers at that Summerdown started making themselves familiar with a house in Eastbourne. For the women, you know. Couple of the girls were married, to boot—husbands off to war and they needed the money and what could they do? Well, Mr. Sherlock puts the girls to work with his candle making. Then he pays Tony what he lost by not driving those men to that house."

"Full fare!" said the cabby in wonderment.

"And my boy Jimmy was forever in trouble until Mr. Sherlock got him working with the vicar in that barrow of his," continued the landlord. "Straightened Jimmy right out. Went off to France to fight, and now he's back helping Miss Colvin with that honey business."

At this moment, the gentleman whom I had recognized from the church by his American appearance picked up his glass of ginger beer and approached me. He was very tall and forced to stoop beneath the low beams.

"Dr. Watson, is it?" His accent told me I had been right, and when I allowed that it was indeed I, he extended his hand with characteristic American straightforwardness. "Edwin L. Stanton. Mr. Holmes knew me as 'Eddie.'"

"Why, Eddie! Young Eddie!" I cried. "My dear chap!" I made the introductions all around. "It is so good of you to come!"

"It was the least I could do, sir. The very least," said he, waving away my expressions of thanks. "I was attached to the American delegation in Versailles when Mr. Mycroft Holmes telegraphed me the news. Well, I had to come." He turned to Lestrade and held his eyes for a moment, then spoke in a voice filled with emotion, and loud enough for all to hear. "He saved my life, you know."

"I should like to hear the story, sir," said Lestrade, nodding as he finished his drink. "I have a story or two of my own I could tell, but I should like to hear yours. Drinks all around, landlord. For my good friend, Mr. Sherlock Holmes."

And as Jack poured another ginger beer for "young Eddie"—now a prosperous and gracefully stooped, elderly man—the American began to tell the patrons of the Tiger Inn how the quick thinking of a preternaturally intelligent boy named Johnnie Holmes had rescued him from death by alcohol poisoning one bleak summer evening at the Navy Yard Bridge, in Washington City, in America.

The sky outside was showing the first colours of sunset, and the crowd inside the Tiger was changing over as the barmaid began to set the tables for dinner.

"Leave that one be, Claire," Jack called out before she could clear the pint at Holmes's window seat. "Mr. Sherlock would be settling up with me right about now," he said to Tony, who was drinking coffee, preparing to drive the American to the Eastbourne station for the London express. "Always had to get back to his bees when the sun went down. I can't turn that table yet, Tone."

"Too right, Jack. Too right."

At this, the American went over to the window seat and placed three five-pound notes under the glass.

"What's that then?" asked the landlord. "You're all paid up, sir."

"That's for anyone else who wants to drink a toast to 'Mr. Sherlock,'" the American said. "I don't drink myself, but you tell them to have one on 'young Eddie'."

The landlord bowed his head for a moment, then wiped his eyes with his cloth. When he lifted his head, his eyes met mine, and they were still moist.

"You know Mr. Sherlock could be a queer one at times, but he never failed us. And we loved him for it. That we did."

"Aye, Jack," said the cabman. "We did."

The landlord leaned into me. "You tell them that, Doctor. We hear you're writing books again. Well, you make sure you tell them we loved him."

I promised I would.

Then I followed Tony and 'young Eddie' out of the Tiger, for there was one more promise it was my duty to fulfill.

The sun had dropped below the headlands, the stars were visible in the darkening sky and the evening breeze was stirring together a rich mixture of the salt air from the Channel, the sour odour of cow and sheep and the sweet fragrance of grape and lavender as I walked along Went Hill Way to the cottage of Sherlock Holmes.

The thin break in the yew hedge, I saw, had been much enlarged by Lestrade's men when they conducted their inspection of Holmes's cottage, but as I pushed through it I found its blossoms were alive with foraging bees, and I thought how satisfied Holmes would be to know his small winged charges were making the most of such a day. Then, following the pathway Lestrade's men had trampled through the wayward thistle and cocklebur, I soon arrived at the familiar threshold, where I set down the clay urn, unlatched the door, and stepped inside.

Holmes's cottage appeared to have been stripped clean by thieves.

Where casebooks and encyclopedias of reference had once stood in row upon row, the shelves were now bare. The tin box was empty, too, and had been left rather carelessly in the middle of the floor with its lid thrown open. On the desk still stood the typewriter and its accoutrements, but its drawers, which once held obscure medical publications and other relics of his quest for knowledge, had been emptied. For reasons known only to Lestrade, the old chemical table in the corner had been entirely removed, and the meteorological instruments were gone. Even the chalkboard upon which Holmes had scribbled his observations of the weather and tides had been unscrewed from the wall, evidently packed up with everything else and shipped to Scotland Yard.

Taking it all in, I was disappointed, but not surprised.

Lestrade had warned me to be prepared for a strange sight. It had taken his men a full day to examine and remove every item that might relate to Holmes's work, he said, so vast was the amount of material accumulated by Sherlock Holmes over the decades, and so thorough was their search.

From the living room alone over three hundred casebooks containing the records of some two thousand cases had been taken and logged, along with several dozen scrapbooks chronicling the agony columns and other miscellany which had informed Holmes's monitoring of the criminal underworld during his active years, plus every edition of the British Register from 1872 onward.

Beneath Holmes's bed there were found several boxes of medals and decorations from Holmes's long career, dust covered and forgotten. These had gone to Brother Mycroft, of course, along with the mantelpiece clock, the bust of Lincoln, the diaries from Holmes's time in America and the Wilkes Booth newspapers. (The violin, being a Stradivarius of considerable value, had already been bequeathed to the Liverpool Philharmonic, where Holmes had established a chair in memory of a musician whose talents, though deprecated and dismissed during his lifetime, had given Sherlock Holmes his first taste of what would become a lifelong devotion.)

But it was the garret above the bedroom, Lestrade had said, which had taken the longest to sort out.

His men had removed fifty-seven thick diaries, each containing meticulous records of Holmes's daily expenditures on such things as rent, food, newspapers, train tickets, telegrams, dinners and the like, as well as thousands of old newspapers, some five hundred books of scientific and criminal interest, and hundreds of periodicals from publications ranging from the *Anthropological Journal* to *Scientific American*, along with a dozen boxes of printed monographs from Holmes's own pen on various topics of criminal interest, and one complete set of *Gray's Anatomy*.

He did not mention the Weems book.

And I had not dared to ask.

I snatched a candle from the mantelpiece and lit it against the gloom. Mycroft had assured me I could retrieve anything the police had left behind. Taking up the empty tin box, I set to work, moving swiftly, gathering the few items remaining while inspecting every inch of the room for a sign that the book had been secreted in some clever hiding place invisible to the untrained eye. I even inspected the wall behind the etching over the mantelpiece and lifted the cover off of the typewriter once more, but it was not there.

My eye now caught a publication that had been left behind in one of the desk drawers. Holding the candle to it, I recognized it at once. It was the *British Medical Journal*, dated 14 December, 1918, that had been given to me by Major Graeme Gibson during my visit to Summerdown, after Holmes's collapse at this very desk.

It was entirely devoted to the current strain of "Spanish Influenza" and contained Gibson's own monograph upon the topic. It had disappeared from my armchair one day, however, and I had entirely forgotten about it.

Evidently Lestrade's men had considered it too current to be of interest in their search, but upon opening it, I saw that the monograph by Gibson had been marked up in Holmes's neat, familiar hand.

My friend had known what ailed him all along.

And how dim was the prognosis.

I placed the magazine in the tin box with the pipe rack and other items from the mantelpiece, then crossed to Holmes's bedroom. This I found equally stripped of his belongings. Only the Bible next to his table lamp and a translation of the Quran upon the shelf remained. I placed them in the box and continued my search, for these keepsakes—though I was immensely relieved they had been left behind—were not what I was after.

What I was after, I suspected, was in the garret.

I set down the tin box and climbed the ladder, hoping against hope that somehow the men of the Yard had dismissed as a meaningless memento of Sherlock Holmes's early life the old, leather-bound book written by Parson Weems. Holding out the candle before me, however, I saw at once how vain was my expectation. The garret had been emptied of everything but Holmes's old wooden sea chest, its lid left open, a stack of penny dreadfuls from Holmes's youth exposed within.

I closed the sea chest and with some little effort hauled it down to the bedroom. Then I sat down upon it, gazing at the items in the tin box before me, a feeling of exhaustion and deep melancholy overtaking me. How long I sat there, I cannot say, but as I closed my eyes and breathed deeply in that gloomy space, I sought to relax my muscles and therefore my mind, as I had witnessed my friend do when he was at his most contemplative.

Suddenly I felt the familiar bony hand upon my shoulder, its grip strong, its voice bright and encouraging in my ear:

"Think, Watson! Think! Eliminate all the possibilities, and the one that remains—the one that remains..."

And in that moment, I realized that one possibility still remained.

I sprang to my feet and made for the kitchen, certain that Holmes had not, after all, changed the hiding place of the book.

My heart sank as I entered, however, for even by the dim light of the candle I could see at once that the kitchen had been as thoroughly searched as the rest of the house.

The cupboards were opened, their contents removed and stacked upon the table. The drawers to the sideboard had been emptied out in the same manner, and I was startled to see a heap of cold ashes scattered across the floor.

They had even searched the oven!

But the shelf high above the sideboard appeared undisturbed, and this gave me hope.

Pulling over a chair, I climbed up and held the candle stub to the greasy spines of the dusty volumes of Scottish recipes and *Modern Housecleaning Methods*, until the flickering flame illuminated a thick leather-bound volume with no lettering upon its spine.

And no dust upon the binding.

I pulled it out and found I was holding in my hand Mr. Lincoln's book —the Weems book.

There was no mistaking the aged leather cover that Sherlock Holmes had cradled as he sat in his armchair and pondered where to hide it that evening, after reading for Margaret and me the farewell address of George Washington.

It was the book that had been passed down from the most rightly famous American of his times to the best Englishman I had ever known.

Sherlock Holmes had made certain Margaret and I had seen him fingering it while glancing about the cottage—then he had simply replaced it in the very spot he had hidden it all those years.

With a fresh candle from the mantel, I carried the book to Holmes's desk, set it down and turned the cover. It opened directly to the title page, for the binding naturally creased there, and I immediately understood why.

Upon the page there was revealed an inscription, written in a neat hand, that read in this way:

To Mr. Sherlock Holmes (née Johnnie)

I recalled my friend's name and now bequeath it on you, if you'll take it. Remember to start with the Bible but don't forget your Shakespeare. There is indeed "a divinity that shapes our ends."

Yours Truly,
A. Lincoln

Mr. Lincoln had promised my friend a name, and, as the scripture writer said, "he hath done this."

Many minutes passed and the candle burned down almost to my fingers, but I continued rereading the inscription which had forever changed my friend's life—and the lives of so many others who would be helped by his unique powers of detection—until a strange tap-tapping upon the cottage door startled me out of my reverie.

I closed the book, blew out the candle and answered the door.

Standing in the light of the rising moon was Mycroft Holmes and, looming behind him, his driver. Mycroft gazed at me for some few moments through the piercing grey eyes that were so reminiscent of his brother's.

"I take it that is Mr. Lincoln's book you're holding behind your back, Doctor? Sherlock never told me where he had hidden it."

"He never told me either—until just now."

Mycroft started. "I beg your pardon?"

"Your brother came to me as I sat in his room."

Mycroft smiled with understanding. "'*Eliminate all other possibilities,*' eh? And where did you find it?"

"Among the cookbooks," said I, holding it tightly by my side.

"Of course." Mycroft Holmes chuckled softly. "Well done, Johnnie," he said to the urn at his feet. Then, to me, "Miss Colvin was half French and Margaret half Indian. My brother knew those Scottish cookbooks would never be disturbed."

"But why did he never show it to you?" I asked. "And why was young Moriarty so keen to have it?"

"I should think the answers are obvious, Doctor! A book signed by Lincoln, dedicated to my brother? Why, the price it would fetch could have financed any criminal's fondest ambitions! As for keeping it from *me*—well, how do you think it would have been taken by the insecure personalities of Downing Street and Buckingham Palace that England's national treasure had been granted his name by the greatest American President? Even *you* must realize how poorly that news would have been received. Johnnie knew that once he showed it to me, he would never see it again."

"Will I?"

Mycroft Holmes shrugged his shoulders. "That depends entirely upon what Mr. Churchill wants with it."

"Churchill!"

"Yes, Winston heard about it—don't ask me how—and wants a look. I could only say, 'Yes, Minister,' you understand."

"But see here, Mycroft. Your brother left this book behind, expecting that I would find it if your man didn't. He didn't. I did."

Mycroft Holmes gazed at me with a passive face. Then he gave a slight nod at the urn, and the driver stooped to pick it up.

"Now, the book, Doctor, if you please."

We left the cottage together, Mycroft with Mr. Lincoln's book, in a car bound for London, and I with the urn holding the ashes of Mr. Sherlock Holmes, making my way to the hives.

Chapter Seven

TELLING THE BEES

Although I am a native of that teeming city of London, and the rude noise and pungent reek of the metropolis once appealed more naturally to my senses than the melodious sounds and pleasing fragrances of the countryside, I had become well adapted to the ways of the Down in the months since Margaret and I moved to Went Hill, and the instructions of Sherlock Holmes played in my head as I walked comfortably among the white wooden boxes teeming with their venerable winged inhabitants while the last rays of the setting sun climbed the branches of the apple trees and disappeared into a darkening sky—a sky that was made slightly darker, to my practiced eye, by the swollen pollen sacs of a thousand still-returning bees.

No longer did I feel unease as these industrious workers buzzed and whirled about my head. And while I could not say I placed them on a level with mankind, as my friend did, I had come to see in their selfless act of instinct on that strange night in his cottage something very much like the sacrifice Sherlock Holmes had made in devoting *his* life to solving those "little mysteries" which collectively threatened his own species, even to the detriment of his health and well-being.

And so I moved calmly among them, speaking in the same soothing tones with which I had heard my friend speak as we walked together in the fading light of an evening.

But I was not saying "good night," as he would have done.

Rather, I was informing them of what had become of their friend.

One must, after all, tell the bees when their caretaker has died.

And this I did, all the while sifting slowly from the urn the ashes of my friend onto the thin soil of this corner of Went Hill, obeying in death—as I had always obeyed him in life—the last request of my friend, Mr. Sherlock Holmes.

"Ashes to ashes, Watson," he would say during our evening rambles among the hives, indicating with his stick where he wished his remains to be scattered as we walked. "I'll have no vainglory in my memory, thank you! Church vaults are stuffed with the mouldering bones of the dead whom nobody remembers, let alone cares for. The last full measure of my devotion lives on within the souls of those whom I served. Let it suffice that I gave my all in this life and saved nothing for the next."

Then he would pause, and with a cocked ear listen in evident satisfaction as his charges seemed to be making their appreciation known to him.

"You hear it, Watson?" he would ask. "You hear that sound? It is the sound of a happy hive."

Yet when I had honoured my promise to Sherlock Holmes that evening, and had spoken to the last winged insect of the last hive, and had offered the last wisps of dusts from the clay urn to the soil, and had paused to listen to the bees as Holmes would have done, it was evident to my ears that there was no sound to be heard.

The bees were silent.

And while some readers may attribute this to the lateness of the day or an impending change in the weather—or to the imagination of an overwrought and loyal companion—I will swear upon the Bible bequeathed to me by Sherlock Holmes that his winged charges had taken comfort in my utterances, and had been soothed by them, for it was then that I felt what the Psalmist called "the breath that passes and does not return" sweeping gently across the greening downs, rustling the leaves upon the ripening trees and infusing the hives and honeycombs with its warmth, cloaking in its comforting mantle all their inhabitants even as it lifted towards the heavens the soul and spirit of Mr. Sherlock Holmes—their caretaker and protector, and ever my friend.

THE EPILOGUE
OF DR. WATSON

Upon the peg by the door in the cottage at Went Hill, where Margaret
and I now live, there hangs a very old and stiff pea-jacket which, when the
weather turns damp, emits a hint of the sulphurous odour of rotten eggs
absorbed within its fibres whilst a certain young chemist wore it to and
from his workbench at a rather large and important gunpowder works in
the Brandywine valley in America many years ago.

And upon the shelf of the bookcase nearby there stands a row of very
old and very well-thumbed penny dreadfuls that had fired the imagination
of that young chemist to become something else—something no one had
ever envisioned—and which, after years of intense study and self-disci-
plined research, he had become.

Too, on the stone-flagged floor between the two armchairs there sits
an old wooden sea chest which now holds the newspapers and books I
am currently reading, but a careful eye will discern that the initials "J. H."
stenciled into its wood were long ago altered by hand—the "J" being turned
into an "S" by the use of charcoal—so that the lid bears the imprint "S.H."

Over the fireplace there hangs the etching of a very famous and very
deadly encounter at the Reichenbach Falls long ago, and beneath this, upon
the mantelpiece, stands a pipe rack bearing several old, well-used pipes—one

a long black clay, one a long cherrywood and the third, a short briar—each ready to be charged, depending upon the mood of the smoker, with the thick shag tobacco from the Persian slipper nearby.

And between the pipe rack and the slipper sits a harmless-looking black and white ivory box, about the size of a cigarette case, that was once fitted with a poison-tipped spring designed to kill its recipient in a most clever, most unexpected manner, and which, but for the unique powers of observation and deduction of that recipient, would have done just that.

Closer at hand, beside the old, covered typewriter upon the desk at which I sit and work—and, upon occasion, gaze out the bow window to the hives and the apple trees and the green headlands of the Sussex Downs towards the great English Channel that lies beyond—there rests a book. It is a very old, thick, leather-bound book which, like the other objects I have described, was a silent witness to many remarkable days in the life of one of the most remarkable men who ever lived.

The presence of these keepsakes gives me comfort as I think, and write. And remember.

John H. Watson, M.D. (retired)
Went Hill
East Sussex, England

ACKNOWLEDGEMENTS

Jamie Campbell, a friend and writer who possesses what Hemingway famously described as "a built-in s—t detector" and is never afraid to share it, is the person who, after reading the first 25 pages of a manuscript I was writing about Sherlock Holmes meeting Abraham Lincoln (a story I wasn't quite sure about at the time) said, "Yeah, you have to finish this."

And so I did.

In the years after Jamie spoke those words of encouragement, however, the manuscript would be profoundly altered by two developments I had never contemplated when I set out to bring the world's greatest detective together with our greatest President.

One was the realization that a surprisingly large portion of the public believes Holmes was a real person—a detective back in the 1800's whose life has been fictionalized in the many retellings of his story onscreen and in novels—so compelling is the persona introduced to the world by Sir Arthur Conan Doyle in 1887.

Once I understood this, I sensed a new direction for the book. If Holmes is thought to be an historical figure, I decided, I would not merely bring him together with Abraham Lincoln in a twist of historical fiction, but I would then place Sherlock Holmes in the manhunt for John Wilkes Booth after the assassination of Lincoln.

And I would tell the story as *history*.

That change in plot and narrative tone coincided with the second key development that would shape the book: a movement to purge Confederate statues from public lands without serious, informed debate or enlightened discussion beforehand.

A snarky tweet would do.

And when the revisionists set out to remove Abraham Lincoln's name from public buildings for perceived flaws that somehow overshadowed the difficult-to-overstate accomplishments of his presidency in the minds of the revisionists, it seemed only right and fitting to bring the calm and rational voice of Sherlock Holmes to the public square and raise the question of whether it might not be wiser to first *understand* our history before attempting to alter it or erase it.

That's when "One Must Tell the Bees" took the shape it now holds, but there was still much work to be done to get it into its final form.

Good friend Gus duPont—yes, of the family which figures so prominently in the book—read an early draft and provided insights only a sixth generation descendant of the founder of the Éleuthèrian Mills could offer. He also put me in touch with David Cole, Executive Director of the Hagley Museum, which oversees the site of the original DuPont gunpowder works outside Wilmington, Delaware; Jill MacKenzie, the Museum Director, who set up more than one excellent tour of the Hagley for me and my wife; and Hagley Historian Lucas Clawson, who patiently answered numerous and detailed questions about daily life at the mills during the 1800's.

For the British portion of Holmes's life I turned to Lloyd Brunt of the East Dean & Friston Local History Group, whose supply of booklets provided invaluable historical detail about East Dean, the village near the English Channel where Holmes settled in his retirement. Subsequently, my wife and I visited the area to walk the footpaths along the chalk cliffs overlooking the Channel and to inspect the small parish church where Holmes was eulogized. (Happily we found comfortable accommodations at The Tiger Inn, which readers will recognize as the pub favored by Holmes himself, and I can strongly recommend the English breakfast at the Tiger before setting out on the Downs.)

Once the manuscript was more or less complete, many friends read it and provided helpful criticisms and immeasurable encouragement, including Gussie and Pedro Wasmer, Terry Brewer, Bob and Sandy Santy, Pete Bewley, Tom and Kathy Smith, Tom and Ann Weiss, Jim Balakian, George Busse, John Gaetjens, Will Peters, Herb Greenberg, Barb Darrow, Vic Zimmermann, Wendy Davies and the crew otherwise known as Basket Eddy: Paul Hulleberg, "Duane" Almon, Dave Greenberg, Jonny Stone, Jed Drake, Patrick McGarey, Sr. Scott Cecil, Roger Tarika, Todd Becker, Laura Christophersen and Brad McLane.

And when the book was as polished as I could make it—this would have been the twenty-fifth or twenty-six draft—I finally showed it to my wife Nancy, whose judgement is unerring. I nervously hid in my office that day while she read it in the living room, but after a time I smelled smoke owing to a wind inversion in the living room fireplace, and when I raced downstairs to open the windows and saw that she was ignoring the smoke and continuing to read without looking up, I took it as a good sign.

Sure enough, Nancy gave me her unvarnished "yes," and when our daughters Sarah and Claire likewise expressed their approval I possessed all the confidence I needed to begin the just-as-hard work of getting it published.

The first step was to place the manuscript into the incomparable hands of Beth Stein, my editor. Beth's insights were quite literally invaluable and even more keenly perceptive than I had been led to believe by the man who introduced me to her.

That man is songwriter and dear friend Layng Martine, Jr. who had relied on Beth while crafting his remarkable memoir, "Permission to Fly." By recommending Beth (who subsequently found Michael Mann, the superlative proofreader who saved readers more aggravation than I care to admit) as well as the masterful book designer Glen Edelstein (who then hired a brilliant illustrator, Robert Hunt, to create the beautiful illustrations that grace the object you hold in your hands), Layng—like those many others I have already mentioned—gave "One Must Tell the Bees" its own permission to fly.

Having clearance from ground control is one thing, however, and leaving the ground is quite another, and the publicity folks at Books Forward in the form of Ellen Whitfield, Corrine Pritchett, Hannah Robertson, Stephanie Koehler and website wizard Jeizebel Espiritu have worked tirelessly in that regard to create the recognition that brought this book to your attention.

Sherlock Holmes may or may not have been fiction, but he very much lives on, as I hope you will find in this book. —J. L. Matthews

ABOUT THE AUTHOR

J. LAWRENCE MATTHEWS has contributed fiction to the New York Times and NPR and is the author of three non-fiction books as Jeff Matthews. "One Must Tell the Bees" is his first novel. Written at a time when American history is being scrutinized and recast in the light of 21st Century mores, this fast-paced account of young Sherlock Holmes's visit to America during the final year of the Civil War illuminates the profound impact of Abraham Lincoln and his Emancipation Proclamation on slavery, the war and America itself. Matthews is now researching the sequel, which takes place a bit further afield—in Florence, Mecca and Tibet—but readers may contact him at jlawrencematthews@gmail.com. Those interested in the history behind "One Must Tell the Bees" will find it at jlawrencematthews.com.

Printed in Great Britain
by Amazon

82804540R00322